NICHELLE CLARKE CRIME THRILLER, BOOKS 1-3

FRONT PAGE FATALITY / BURIED LEADS / SMALL TOWN SPIN

LYNDEE WALKER

Severn River
PUBLISHING

Published by Severn River Publishing.

ISBN: 978-1-64875-004-5 (Paperback)

ALSO BY LYNDEE WALKER

The Nichelle Clarke Series

Front Page Fatality

Buried Leads

Small Town Spin

Devil in the Deadline

Cover Shot

Lethal Lifestyles

Deadly Politics

Hidden Victims

The Faith McClellan Series

Fear No Truth

Leave No Stone

Never miss a new release! Sign up to receive exclusive
updates from author LynDee Walker.

LynDeeWalker.com/Newsletter

As a thank you for signing up, you'll receive a free copy of
Fatal Features: A Nichelle Clarke Crime Thriller Novella.

FRONT PAGE FATALITY

CHAPTER ONE

THINKING about blood spatters and ballistics reports before I'd even finished my coffee wasn't exactly how I wanted to start my weekend.

"More dead people? Really, guys?" I asked, as if the beat cops whose chatter blared out of the police scanner in my passenger seat could hear me. They, of course, kept right on talking. Apparently, this dead guy had lost a good bit of brains to a bullet, too.

I reached for my cell phone, keeping one hand on the steering wheel and my eyes on the morning traffic. A body before I'd even made it to the newsroom was usually a good thing—but not that Friday. If I'd had to pay by the corpse, my MasterCard would've been maxed out by Wednesday that week. Especially given the eBay charge for the new heels on my feet.

I glanced at the clock and stomped my sapphire Louboutin down on the gas pedal, thumbing the speed dial for police headquarters.

"Aaron, it's Nichelle," I said when I got the department spokesman's voicemail. "I hear y'all are having a party out on Southside this morning, and I seem to have misplaced my invitation. Give me a call when you get a minute."

Tossing my phone back into my bag, I turned into the parking garage of the *Richmond Telegraph*. Why couldn't I have an idiot crook who'd called in an order under his real address before robbing the pizza delivery guy, or a couple of stolen BMWs out in the Fan? Anything but another body.

If I had to go chase death again today, at least it should guarantee me the Metro lead for tomorrow. I flashed a half-smile at my editor as I strode into his office a few minutes later.

"I've got another dead drug dealer on Southside. They just found him this morning." My words dissolved his annoyed expression to one of interest, his perpetual aggravation with my last-minute arrivals for the morning staff meeting forgotten at the mention of a homicide.

"Another one, huh?" He leaned forward and rested his elbows on his massive mahogany desk. "Do we know if this one is related to the guy they found out there a couple of weeks ago?"

"Aside from the bit about him being a dealer I caught on the scanner, not really." I dropped into my usual seat. "I left a message for Aaron White on my way in. I should have something for you by this afternoon."

Bob nodded, appearing satisfied and moving on to the sports section. "What's going on in your world this morning, Parker? Anything worth having an opinion on, or am I paying you to make stuff up yet?"

Our sports columnist (and de facto sports editor since the real thing was still on leave with his wife and new baby) raised his voice over the round of laughter and began a rundown of the day's sporting events.

"And I'm writing my column on the women's basketball coach over at the University of Richmond," he finished. "She's in the middle of treatment for breast cancer, and she still led the team to the playoffs again this past season." He glanced at his notes. "This makes four years in a row."

"Nice," Bob said. "I love a human interest story on a woman in the sports section."

The international desk was following an uprising after yet another questionable election in the Middle East, and the government reporters were still covering the bickering between the senate candidates who were gearing up for the fall race.

Political jokes fired faster than a drunken celebutante's antics circle the blogosphere, and I chuckled at the warring punch lines as my eyes skipped between the faces of my colleagues—my family in Richmond, really. They had adopted me the second I'd stepped into the newsroom without a friend in a six-hundred-mile radius, the ink still wet on my degree from Syracuse.

"Bawb." The drawling soprano that belonged to our copy chief came from the doorway as if on cue, chasing away my warm fuzzies and twisting my smile into a reflexive grimace. Every family needs at least one annoying cousin, and Shelby was happy to fill that role for me. "Could you please make sure everyone has their copy in by deadline tonight? My staff would like to leave on time, since it is Friday and all."

It wouldn't be morning if Shelby wasn't trying to crash the news meeting. Maybe I could at least stay far enough under her radar to avoid the trademark backhanded compliments she was so fond of throwing my way, especially in front of Bob. Or not, I thought as she swung her phoniest smile on me. Here it comes. I left out a comma, or a hyphen, or there's an extra space somewhere.

"Nichelle, what a great job you did on the murder conviction!" Shelby put her hands on her tiny hips and stuck out her inversely-proportionate chest, straining the cotton of her simple cornflower t-shirt. "Though I'm pretty sure the prosecutor was approaching the *bench*, not the beach."

My temper flared, but before I opened my mouth to tell her that quickly pounding out the day's lead story was different than writing up the garden club meetings she covered before her big move to the copy desk, Bob cleared his throat.

"That one's on me, since I edited that story, Shelby," he said, before he dismissed her with a promise that deadlines would be adhered to by all.

"Sorry, chief." I shrugged at Bob as Shelby's spiky black hair disappeared into the maze of cubicles. "Bench, beach. Potato, tomato."

Bob chuckled before he turned to the features editor. I tuned out what they were talking about. For the most part, I preferred hard news writing to any other kind.

I had grabbed the police report on the first drug dealer murder from my file drawer on my way into the meeting, and I pulled it out and read it again. Noah Leon Smith, age twenty-six, had died the Friday before Memorial Day of a massive head injury inflicted by a .45 caliber bullet. He'd been found sprawled across his own sofa in a neighborhood that saw more than its fair share of violence. The easy assumption was that he'd been killed by another dealer, or maybe a desperate customer. But now did a second victim prove that easy assumption faulty?

My eyes scanned the detective's narrative with that in mind, and four simple lines jumped out at me like a pair of old sneakers at a Manolo collection debut.

Bathroom sink, lower cabinet: four kilograms beige powder, two large plastic bags dried, green leafy substance. Upper cabinet: fifteen large bags containing tablets, various sizes and colors. Lab results: powder: heroin. Green leafy: marijuana. Tablets: Oxycontin, Vicodin, Zoloft, Effexor, Ritalin. Kitchen, freezer compartment: three paper grocery sacks containing a total of $257,400 in large bills.

I'd dismissed it before. Sure, a business rival or a junkie would have stolen the drugs and the money—if they had time, knew where to find it, and weren't already flying on a sample of Noah Smith's pharmaceuticals. But another dealer with holes where he shouldn't have them made me wonder if the crime scenes were similar. If the new victim still had a house full of smack and cash, now that was a story.

My fingers wound around a lock of my hair, my thoughts hijacked by scenes from old Charles Bronson movies as I considered the possibility the shooter was more interested in payback than a payday. That could be a very sexy story.

Bob's endearingly cheesy dismissal snapped me out of my reverie. "All right, folks," he said every morning. "My office is not newsworthy, so get out and go find me something to print."

I paused outside Bob's door, where Grant Parker was chatting with the features editor about the baseball season. I couldn't remember ever having spoken more than a dozen words to Parker, an almost-professional pitcher who was regarded around Richmond as just slightly more mortal than Zeus' son, but the column he'd talked about in the meeting caught my attention.

I cleared my throat lightly and he turned his head, his bright green eyes widening a touch when they met mine. He was tall, but in my heels, I was almost nose-to-nose with him.

"What can I do for you, Miss Clarke?" He flashed the smile that made most women here channel their corset-bound ancestors and swoon—and sold a fair number of newspapers, too.

"I wanted to say thank you," I said, shifting my file folder to the other arm. "For the column you're doing today. My mom is a breast cancer survivor, and it's nice you're writing about it. The sports section isn't usually where you'd look for a breast cancer story. So thanks."

"You're so welcome." His eyes dropped to the square-toed perfection of the shiny blue stilettos I'd shoved my feet into between my early morning body combat class and my mad dash to the meeting, then raised back to mine. "Nice of you to say so. I didn't know you read my column."

"I don't." I smiled. "But I will tomorrow."

"I guess I'd better be on my A game, then." He ran a hand through his already-messy blond hair and grinned at me again.

"I guess you'd better." I took a step backward. "I'm told I can be tough to impress."

"I do love a challenge." He raised his eyebrows and twisted his mouth to one side.

"I bet you do." I shook my head, making a mental note to call my mother as I turned and headed for my ivory cubicle, Parker and his too-perfect smile forgotten. Charles Bronson. Dead guys. The nagging feeling there was something beyond the obvious on the murdered dealers got stronger the more I thought about the scattered details I'd heard on the scanner.

My hand was already on the phone to call Aaron again when I snatched up the pink slip on my desk, but the message was from my friend Jenna. She was probably looking for my input on which restaurants had sufficiently-stocked bars for our every-other-Friday girls' night, which I'd been looking forward to roughly since the opening gavel had banged on Monday morning.

Before I could pick up the phone to return her call, my favorite detective returned mine.

"Why didn't the shooter take the drugs and the money in Noah Smith's house? The dead dealer, from last month?" I asked, barely bothering to tell Aaron good morning. "And was the murder scene this morning the same?"

He sighed, and I felt my eyebrows go up. That would be a yes. I fumbled for a pen.

"It was," he said after a pause. "And we're not sure."

"You think it was the same shooter?"

"I don't know. Maybe."

I could almost hear the wheels turning in his head as he weighed what to tell me. The uncomfortably symbiotic relationship between police departments and the media was an odd line to walk: I needed him for stories, and he needed the stories for the key witnesses they sometimes brought in his door. I didn't have to file a Freedom of Information request for every routine report, but Aaron's job was to let out only the information the department wanted to release. Mine was to get my readers as much as I could. Most days, we struck a decent balance.

"We rushed the ballistics, but it still won't be back for another few hours at the earliest," he said. "Maybe not 'til Monday. I don't know how busy they are. You want to come by this afternoon?"

I asked for the first half-hour he had available. "Bob wants something on this for tomorrow, and it is Friday. I'd like to leave at a decent hour one night this week."

"I hear that." Aaron laughed. "We've been busy down here lately, too. Too many bad guys out there. I saw your piece on the conviction in the Barbie and Ken case this morning. Such a sad story."

I murmured agreement as the mention of the capital murder trial I'd spent the whole week chronicling called up unwanted impressions of the poster-sized, high-resolution crime scene photos the prosecutor left on display for the jury the entire day before.

It had been nearly two years since budget cuts (and a little finagling on my part—trial stories were bigger and often juicier than initial crime reports) had added the courthouse to my list of responsibilities as the crime reporter. It meant insane hours, but I didn't mind, considering almost a third of our news staff had been laid off and I still had a job.

I'd dreamed of being a journalist ever since I could remember. It paired my love of writing with the ability to do good in the world. I hadn't yet developed the intestinal fortitude covering the Richmond PD often required, though, and the trials were worse.

Aaron promised I'd have my interview with him in time to make the first Metro deadline.

Lacking anything pressing to do, I called Jenna back to see if she had her heart set on anything special for our dinner date. I was in the mood for Mexican food. And a margarita. That damned trial had made for a long week.

"Nicey!" Jenna practically shouted the nickname I'd reserved for those closest to me since preschool, when a playmate's speech impediment had dubbed me "nee-see" and my mom had turned it into an endearment.

"Anything good going on in the news today?" My friend's tone came down a few decibels.

"There's seldom anything good in the news I write," I said. "But I think I might have something interesting. And Grant Parker is working on a great story about the women's basketball coach at U of R."

"Oh, yeah? And how is Virginia's hottest sportswriter this morning?"

I laughed. "He seemed all right. And you're still, you know, married."

"Married. Not blind," She said. "Speaking of my darling husband, I told Chad not to wait up, so we have no curfew. Have I told you how glad I am the baby isn't nursing anymore?"

"Just now, or the other fifteen times I've heard that this week?"

"Only fifteen? And I thought I was excited about this."

"I believe the word you're looking for is 'thrilled,'" I said. "Possibly even 'euphoric.'"

She laughed again. "Euphoric. Yes. Has a nice, festive ring to it. Anyway, what do you feel like doing tonight?"

"Margaritas?" I knew Jenna was more interested in libations than food that particular day. "I want Mexican if that's okay with you."

It was. I returned the phone to its cradle after promising to meet her at six-thirty, and went to tell Bob to save me a little space for my drug dealer story. Even he hadn't escaped the cost-cutting, inheriting the metro editor's job duties when she'd quit the year before.

His door was open, as usual, but I tapped the doorframe before I walked in anyway.

"Hey, chief," I said, sticking my head around the corner. "Got a minute?"

"Just one." He turned from his monitor to face me, tucking a pen under the tuft of thinning salt-and-pepper hair that peeked over the top of his left ear. "Anything on your dead guy yet?"

I took the same high-backed orange armchair I'd occupied at the morning meeting. Bob's office décor was heavy on Virginia Tech's sacred maroon and orange, his walls cluttered with a hodgepodge of framed copies of his favorite *Telegraph* photos and our best front pages. I flipped my file open.

"I think I have something coming from the PD this afternoon." My roaming eyes lingered on Bob's Pulitzer, centered on the far wall in an impressive bronze frame, before I focused on him. "Or, I know I have something. I'm waiting to see how good it's going to be. I'm going to headquarters this afternoon to talk to the detective who's working on this morning's murder. Both murder scenes had hundreds of thou-sands of dollars in drugs and cash left behind."

He raised his thick white eyebrows. "They think there's a vigilante on Southside?"

"Maybe. That's kind of what I'm thinking, but Aaron hasn't said much. They're waiting for ballistics to come back on the second bullet before they assume it was the same shooter."

"Sounds like you have at least a promise of a decent story there."

"We'll see. A vigilante is definitely sexier than a broke addict looking for a fix. I might only have a short write-up on the murder tonight, depending on when they get the ballistics results, but we'll have it in there tomorrow. And I'll have more if anything comes of it."

"Sounds good, kid."

I would've bristled at the last word from anyone else, but I knew he meant it affectionately, and the feeling was mutual. I didn't make it all the way to my feet before he picked up the newspaper on his desk and spoke again.

"You know, you really have turned into quite a reporter since the first time you walked in here, hugging your little college portfolio, afraid I wouldn't give you a job," he said, his voice a little softer than I was used to hearing it. "I wasn't at all sure you could handle both cops and courts when you came in here begging, either—"

"Hey! I can be accused of doing a lot of things for a story, but I have never begged," I objected.

Bob grinned. "Beg, wheedle; 'bench, beach.' Call it what you will, I know wheedling when I hear it—I was married for almost thirty years. My point is, I made a good call. Both times." He thumped my final report on the Barbie and Ken double homicide case, which was destined to become an over-dramatized TV movie. "We sold more newspapers this week than we have in any single week since the end of the '08 election. And what's good for the bean counters is good for the news department nowadays. Good job."

Well, hot damn. To say Bob wasn't terribly forthcoming with compliments would be like saying John Edwards was a little unfaithful to his wife. The journalism equivalent of a decorated war hero, my editor expected excellence from his staff and rarely commented on anything that wasn't a shortfall. My week suddenly seemed less taxing.

Upside down pictures of the victims smiled at me from the newspaper on Bob's desk. It was the sort of story that wasn't a whole lot of fun to write, but everyone wanted to read—the essence of my love/hate relationship with covering crime. The cops and courts beat was among the best places to begin building a career, though, and I told myself that reporting on crime kept people aware of their safety, and what was going on around them, which was a good thing. It made the parts of the job I found less than fun easier to take, especially with stories like that one.

All the elements that drove producers (I was pretty sure I'd counted five at the courthouse the day before) to stalk heartbroken couples who'd just buried their children were there: a bloody crime of passion perpetrated against beautiful people, a lopsided college love triangle, and a conviction that left the last man standing facing Virginia's electric chair, probably before his thirtieth birthday.

The TV folks, ever fond of their graphics-friendly catchphrases, had dubbed the case "the Barbie and Ken murder" in homage to the victims' perfect, flaxen-haired good looks. I had twenty bucks in the courthouse pool those words would appear somewhere in the movie title.

The usual sandpapery scratch returned to Bob's voice as he dropped the paper and smiled at me. "Go get your dead dealer story. And then go have a good weekend. Treat yourself to a new one of those crazy puzzles of yours, or a pair of shoes. I believe you've earned it this week."

Still glowing with pride twenty minutes later, I fit my back against the trunk of an ancient oak tree at a tiny, hidden park on the banks of the James River. It was my preferred place to ponder a story, write, or just sit and think when I had the chance. The water whispering over the rocks and the postcard-perfect downtown skyline were still enough to make me wonder if being on the east coast would ever stop feeling like a vacation to me.

Vacation. The word roused unexpected images from my memory: the beauty of roadside seas of bluebonnets in the spring, succumbing in the summer to flat, oppressive heat that browned the landscape and shimmered off the streets in visible waves by noon. My last trip to Dallas had been more of a vacation than a visit home.

It's probably nice to know where home is, even if you can't go there again, I thought. I supposed my cute little stone craftsman in the Fan—the historic neighborhood named for the way its tree-lined streets fan out from downtown Richmond like the paper and lace creations that once aided Virginia ladies with everything from cooling to courting—was as good a place as any to feel like I didn't belong. But I wished there was someplace I did.

The rootless feeling was unsettling. I shook my head as though I could clear it like an etch-a-sketch and shifted my thoughts back to the comforting familiarity of the dead dealer and the detective I was interviewing in a couple of hours.

Home or not, I would've been on the first plane back to Texas if I had any idea what that particular dead guy was about to get me into. But that's the thing about dead people: they can't warn you to keep your nose out of things that are going to put your ass in danger.

CHAPTER TWO

"HAVE A SEAT." Aaron cleared a stack of paper off a black plastic chair in his cluttered closet of an office. An ever-changing collection of maps, photos, and notes made it impossible to guess the color of the walls, and the small metal desk was buried under piles of manila case file folders. Judging by the detectives' offices, Richmond was a downright dangerous place to live.

His gray upholstered chair rocked backward as he settled into it and looked at me expectantly, the genial manner that made him the department's king of confessions evident in the smile that lit his round face. Aaron's charm was his central talent. He had a real gift for getting people to talk to him, and was nearly as good at keeping his own hand close. Often, reporters left his office with little or nothing, and felt like they'd somehow been done a favor. Not me. Usually, anyway. Aaron and I had a nice little groove where he tried to bullshit me, I called him on it, and then we bantered until I talked him out of some actual information. It wasn't personal. It was the job. Personally, I liked Aaron, and the feeling seemed to be mutual.

"Who is our unfortunate friend who was shot in the head?" I asked.

Aaron flipped a page on a legal pad. "Darryl Anthony Wright, african-american male, age twenty-five. Formerly a resident of cell-block seven at Cold Springs."

I jotted that down and pulled the police report on the Noah Smith murder from my bag.

"Are you guys looking for some kind of Charles Bronson wannabe?"

He pinched the bridge of his nose between his thumb and fore-finger and chuckled. When he looked up, his hand slid down his face so his fingers rested over his lips and muffled the first part of his answer.

"Not pulling any punches today, I see. But I think so." His hand dropped to the desk and he shook his head. "I can't say anything for sure without ballistics."

"When is the report supposed to be back?" I smiled as I scrawled his words into my notes. That was easier than I thought.

It took about thirty-five seconds to figure out why.

Ignoring my question, Aaron cocked his head to one side and grinned. "This whole damned thing is about to turn into a giant pain in my ass, isn't it?"

I arched an eyebrow. His Detective Adorable routine was usually reserved for the TV crews. I waited, eyebrow up, for him to go on.

"In a lot of ways, a vigilante is going to be harder to prosecute than just another dealer or a junkie." He widened the baby blues just enough to smooth out the lines that were really the only evidence he was pushing fifty. "The public tends to sympathize with vigilantes. I don't suppose you want to keep that part out of the newspaper for me, do you?"

I felt my mouth drop open a little, and the other eyebrow shot up. "You've got to be kidding. I talked to my editor about this before I left the office. He'd fire me. Between what I have here," I brandished the report, "and what I heard on the scanner, our copyeditor-cum-aspir-ing-cops-reporter could figure this one out. I can't sit on it, Aaron. Not unless you're offering me something pretty damned amazing in return."

"What would it take?" He sounded like he meant it.

I sat back in my chair and studied him. Aaron's people skills had contributed to the soft edges on his average frame, making him the obvious choice for department spokesman and thereby trapping him behind a desk in a building with too many Krispy Kreme boxes for too many years. His face looked as puppy-doggish as it ever did, but there was something else in play here. Something I didn't see. Why on Earth would he care so much about keeping something that, in the grand scheme, was pretty insignificant to him, out of print?

"Are you serious?"

"Don't I look serious? When you get past the dashingly, heart-breakingly handsome, that is?"

I snorted and shook my head. "How could I have missed it?"

I felt my fingers wind into my hair as I focused on the roof of my house on the aerial map behind his head. A vigilante was a sexier story angle, but not having it didn't preclude me from writing about the murder today. And if it turned out the killer was on some sort of Death Wish trip, I'd get it at the trial anyway. Letting my hand fall back to my lap, I met Aaron's eyes and nodded.

"All right, detective. I don't know why you care, but I can keep the word 'vigilante' out for now. It's going to cost you, though. One all-access pass, to be used at my discretion, on the story of my choice. No arguments, no negotiations, nothing held back."

He rested his chin on his left fist and twisted his mouth to the side.

"That it?" Aaron was rarely sarcastic, and it sounded funny in his cheerful tenor.

"No."

His eyes widened. "I was kidding!"

He wanted this. And badly. And I didn't like not understanding why.

"I'm not. All access. Story of my choice. To be determined later. And someday, you're going to tell me why you made this deal with me."

"Done. Anything else you need today?"

"Just the report on this morning's murder. I'll leave out the vigilante hoopla, but I have to have something. Bob knows I'm here. Speaking of, how are you going to get around the TV guys?"

Aaron grinned. "Not worried about it. You and Charlie are the only ones who've even asked about the other guy so far. There's a new girl at Channel Ten. Green as a March inchworm. And Kessler over at RVA..." he rolled his eyes and I laughed.

"If the report wasn't on his makeup mirror, he didn't look at it for more than ten seconds," I said. "But what'd you tell Charlie?"

Charlotte Lewis at Channel Four was my biggest competition, usually one step ahead of or behind me on any given story. If she was going with the vigilante, Aaron would just have to get over it.

"Hey, if I can handle you, I can handle Charlie." He laughed. "She left about an hour ago. She didn't ask for nearly as much as you did, but she did make me swear on my grandmama's grave I'd call her if you were running it. So you just made my afternoon a bit more pleasant. Thanks."

"You're welcome. When can I have my report?"

"It's waiting on forensics, but I asked Jerry to bring it in with him. He won't be too much longer."

He didn't get the words out before the door flew open and a disarmingly handsome detective who looked like he was good at hiding from those Krispy Kreme boxes in the gym rushed in. His sheer mass made the small space feel crowded.

"Jerry," Aaron said, "this is Nichelle Clarke from the *Telegraph*. Nichelle, this is Jerry Davis, the detective working on this morning's shooting."

I smiled, extending my hand and shaking his firmly. "Nice to meet you, Jerry."

"Nichelle." Jerry nodded, offering Aaron a folder full of papers and photos. He shot a sidelong glance at me, then focused on Aaron, who was reading something he'd pulled from the file.

An eight-by-ten glossy from the scene lay on top of the stack in the open folder. Darryl Wright, lifeless eyes staring at nothing, was sprawled across his sofa in a relaxed pose that mimicked the first dead dealer. Part of Darryl's black leather baseball cap was gone; the shot had come from the front and blown the hat and its contents across the lamp on the table next to the sofa and the wall behind it. I swallowed a curse, averting my eyes.

"Ballistics worked fast today. Same gun." Aaron dropped the report over the photo and tapped it with his pen, raising his eyes to mine. "So, yes, Nichelle, we can't say for certain that it's the same shooter, but it's looking that way. Jerry can answer some questions for you."

Jerry folded his big frame into the other chair and rested his elbows on his knees, facing me.

"How does that change your investigation?" I asked, pen poised over my notepad. I prided myself on the fact that I'd never once been accused of misquoting anyone, especially since my inexplicable disdain for gadgets extended to tape recorders (and pretty much everything else with a battery that wasn't my laptop or my cell phone). I'd invented my own form of shorthand after I'd gotten frustrated trying to learn the real thing, but the accuracy of my notes would've made them admissible in court.

"Well, we can combine resources on the cases since we're likely not looking for two different killers," he said. "The more heads you've got looking at it, the better."

"And what are you looking for? You have any working theories?" I asked.

Jerry glanced at Aaron and Aaron shot me a warning glare I pretended to ignore.

"We're not ruling anything out yet. We have officers canvassing the neighborhood, and we're waiting for all the relevant information to come in before we construct likely scenarios."

Wow, that was a long way of saying a fat lot of nothing. I scribbled anyway. I was long-since fluent in cop doubletalk, and figured it would serve me well if I ever made it to covering politics.

"So you've stepped up police presence on Southside?"

"Yes. The number of uniformed officers on the streets of that particular neighborhood has been doubled and will stay that way until this is resolved. We don't want our residents living in fear."

I nodded. It wasn't much, but I had two dead guys killed with the same gun. Not exactly Son of Sam, but worthy of a little space.

"Anything else?" Jerry asked.

I finished my notes and asked for the report, looking for contact information for the victim's next of kin.

"Thanks for your time, guys," I said as I stood up. "Aaron, you'll call me if anything comes up?"

He nodded. "Always a pleasure, Nichelle. Have a good weekend."

Not even my favorite CD could get the dead drug dealers out of my head on the way back to the office. I wondered if the victims knew each other as I sat at a red light, my mind attempting to order the jumble of information by creating a puzzle. A lot of the pieces were blank, though. Two drug dealers, living in the same part of town. It wasn't such a stretch. I reached for my phone, but before I could hit the speed dial for the PD, the startling effect of the beeping horn behind me sent it clattering into the fissure between my seat and the console.

Gunning it through the green light I hadn't noticed, I managed to worm my hand through the narrow space to retrieve the phone just as I parked in the office garage, where there was never a signal. I rushed to my cubicle, drummed my fingers on the desk through the hold music, and blurted my question at Aaron as soon as he picked up.

He chuckled. "Nichelle, have you ever thought about a career in law enforcement? Jerry's on his way out there now to look for family members and neighbors, trying to figure out if they might have been friends—or enemies."

I laughed, and not just at the idea of the police uniform shoes. "I don't particularly care for people shooting at me, thanks."

He promised to call if Jerry managed to find anything interesting and reminded me about our deal.

"Oh, I won't forget," I said. "Just don't go getting amnesia when it's time for you to make good, okay?"

"I have a mind like a steel trap."

I killed the line momentarily, my laughter fading as I dialed the number on the report for Darryl's mother. I hated bothering people who just lost a loved one. It was the only thing about my job that felt like a burden. I let it ring a dozen times, sighing with equal parts relief and disappointment when I didn't even get a machine.

Turning to the computer, I started typing.

Richmond detectives are investigating the shooting death of a second convicted drug dealer in three weeks on the Southside, stepping up patrols in the area until an arrest is made.

"The number of uniformed officers on the streets of that particular neighborhood has been doubled and will stay that way until this is resolved," RPD Detective Jerry Davis said Friday. "We don't want our residents living in fear."

The latest victim, Darryl Lee Wright, Jr., was found early Friday morning in his home in the 2900 block of Decatur Street.

Wright, 25, was released from Cold Springs Penitentiary 18 months ago after being convicted of possession of a controlled substance with intent to distribute in 2009. Ballistics analysis found that Wright was shot with the same gun as Noah Leon Smith, who was found dead in his home last month.

I sketched out the few details I could and mentioned Wright's family wasn't immediately available for comment. Reading back through it twenty minutes later, I sighed. It would only amount to about an eighth of a page after they added a headline, but it was all I had. I pushed the key to send it to Bob for approval and went hunting for caffeine.

Wrinkling my nose, I strolled into the break room in the back corner of our floor. Proximity to the darkroom made the air in the narrow space perpetually reek of chemicals, even in the age of digital photography. Too many years of the smell seeping into the walls, I guessed. The old darkroom had become the photographers' cave, outfitted with computers and high-definition monitors for photo editing. They didn't seem to mind the smell.

I stared at the soda machine, debating between diet and not, then decided to save the sugar consumption for margarita mix. A third of the bottle was gone in one gulp. I was too thirsty to notice the artificial-sweetener aftertaste.

"Any more dead people pop up in your day?" Grant Parker's voice caught me by surprise and I inhaled part of my second mouthful of soda. Dropping the bottle on the orange laminate next to the sink, I grabbed the edge of the countertop for support while I tried to clear my lungs.

"Are you okay?" Parker stepped forward into my line of sight. "Sorry. I didn't mean to startle you."

I nodded as I coughed up the last of the soda, tears streaming down my face. I took a deep, hitching breath.

"I didn't assume you did," I croaked. "I just have the one corpse today. How about you? That column represent your A game, Mr. Baseball?"

"My A game, yes. That woman is amazing. I hope I did her justice. Your A game is probably in a whole different league, though. I've been reading your stuff on Barbie and Ken all week, and it was good. Really good. No matter what Shelby says. She's just bitter. She's been after the crime desk since the first time she set foot in this building." He shoved his hands in the pockets of his khakis and flashed me the million-dollar grin.

I wiped my cheeks one last time and faced him, vaguely remembering a couple of the sports guys bantering about Parker banging a brunette from copy a while back.

"Well, thank you. And I know. About Shelby, I mean. It took me forever to figure out what she had up her ass when I first came here, but I finally caught on. I've read some of her stuff in the archives. Her writing is solid. Given a chance, she might be good at this—if she could handle the crap and jump through the hoops. But I'd like for her to keep those skills at the copy desk for now." I tapped the bottle on the countertop and smiled. "Keeps me on my A game."

He nodded. "So, just the one dead guy? Is he an interesting dead guy, at least?"

"Yeah, there's something," I said, deciding to skirt the details of the deal I'd made with Aaron just in case Parker and Shelby still had a thing going. It didn't really sound like it, but better safe than sorry. "I'm not exactly sure how interesting it is, but I can do a little digging."

Parker's eyes narrowed as he listened to a synopsis of what I had on the presses that night, which anyone could have pulled off the server and read.

"So all the drugs and money were still in the house?" He laughed, but it wasn't the relaxed sound I'd heard in the meeting that morning. There was an edge to it I couldn't place. "That sounds kinda suspicious to me, but what do I know?"

"How many RBIs did Jeter have last season?" I grinned, pushing the subject away from my story. I wasn't in the habit of sharing the down-and-dirty of what I was working on before I finished an article. People talk, sometimes to the wrong person, even when they don't mean any harm.

He half-smiled, running a hand through his hair.

"Hey, speaking of Jeter, do you like baseball? The Yankees are in town tonight." Parker's once-pitching-hero status and blinding grin had landed him the cushy star sports columnist gig, and though it didn't require evening hours, he still loved baseball and chose to spend his summer nights at the stadium covering the city's big league team. Bob, not surprisingly, didn't object. "Want to hang out at the ballpark with me and a bunch of over-opinionated sports guys?"

"Tempting." I laughed, not sure if I was lying or not, but relieved to have a better excuse than sitting at home with the dog and one of my ridiculously monochromatic puzzles. "But I have plans. It's girls' night. Margaritas and Mexican food."

He nodded. "Some other time, then."

Not likely, I wanted to say, but I kept my mouth shut. Parker was the kind of guy who dated the kind of girls who starred in beer commercials. And I generally preferred men who spent less time on their hair than I did on mine.

I smiled instead and turned toward the door.

"I need to go see if my story's set before it gets too much later," I said. "Nice talking to you."

"Back at you. Have a good time tonight."

"You, too. I hope they win."

I hurried to Bob's office and tapped on the doorframe.

"Yeah?" He didn't turn from his computer monitor.

"Did you need me to make any changes to my piece before it goes?"

"No. Not a lot of bite, but it looked like you didn't have much to share. What happened to the vigilante?"

I kept my eyes on my shoes. "They didn't have it. Not yet, anyway. Maybe Monday," I said, making a mental note to come up with a plausible story to put him off again before then. "The cops are trying to figure out if these guys were connected. Hopefully they'll get lucky this weekend."

"Just as long as Charlie Lewis doesn't have it Sunday." Bob's eyes never left the screen—I'd bet he didn't even lose his place in the story he was editing. "Have a good weekend, kiddo. See you Monday."

Not even sticking around to chat with Melanie at the city desk as I normally would, I called a goodnight to anyone who happened to be listening as I unplugged my laptop and slid it into my bag. Striding to the elevators, I waved at our features editor, a grandmotherly woman whose home cooked treats could've come straight out of Aunt Bea's kitchen. She carted in batches of various baked and fried goodies at least once a week (twice, if she was stressed or there was an upcoming holiday) and was thereby solely responsible for any widening of my ass that might occasionally occur.

"Have a good one, darlin'." The "g" disappeared into Eunice's native Virginia drawl. "Enjoy your Friday night."

"Friday night, hell, I'm out of here until Monday," I stepped into the elevator with a grin. "See you then."

The promise of a whole weekend with nothing to do was thrilling all by itself. I parked my little red SUV in the Carytown shopping district and melted into the collection of people who made up the city I had come to love in the six years since a stinging rejection from my dream employer brought me south to look for a job.

There were impeccably-dressed mothers pushing babies in hip strollers along the sidewalks, teenagers still high on the excitement of school letting out the week before, and couples walking hand-in-hand looking in the shop windows. The eclectic storefronts beckoned passersby with everything from toys and Christmas decorations to maternity clothes and jewelry.

A cobblestone sidewalk led to the heavy oak door of Pages, so picturesque it could have been conjured from the narrative of a nineteenth-century novel. The shop was housed in an old stone cottage that had surely been someone's home in a previous life, the door flanked by mosaic stained glass windows half-hidden behind climbing roses and jasmine vines, growing thick in twin shoebox-sized gardens and making the summer air sweeter with their perfume.

I turned the brass knob and shoved the stubborn old door, instantly overtaken by a very different fragrance. The smell of ink and paper and aged leather inside the little shop bordered on intoxicating. There were no maps, no sections, no pretty directional signs. Just tall shelves stretching from wall to wall and floor to ceiling in the small space, cluttered and piled with a fantastic collection of great stories. Jenna was the store's buyer, and she spent hours each day hunting down rare volumes and first editions. Pages was no generic bookstore; it was a book lover's haven.

"Hey." My friend waved from behind a stack of books perched on the sales counter. "You're early! How'd you manage that?"

"There was annoyingly little to be written of the story I spent the whole day chasing. I'll tell you all about it at dinner."

Shoving her reddish-brown curls out of her face, Jenna turned back to the MacBook that was the only evidence of the twenty-first century in the room and scooted her square, blue-rimmed glasses down the bridge of her nose.

At least she'd remembered them. I was convinced Jenna was going to go blind or kill some random blotch that was actually a person with her car, she forgot her glasses so often.

"Dying to hear all about it," she said. "Just let me finish one thing and we'll go."

I nodded and surveyed the nearest shelf, picking up a fat brown hardcover. My eyes widened when I checked the copyright page: MacMillan Books, May 1, 1936. A first edition of *Gone With the Wind*.

"Scarlett O'Hara was not beautiful, but men seldom realized it when caught by her charm as the Tarleton twins were," I recited the first line under my breath as I flipped the book closed and trailed my fingers along the cover, noting the missing dust jacket. But still, an actual first edition. I couldn't believe Jenna didn't tell me she'd found it. *There were only ten thousand of these printed*, I thought as I made a mental note to check the asking price with her. I was no rare books expert, but I knew enough about the one in my hands to land a guess in the ballpark, and that park had expensive seats. Even a thousand dollars—which might be a lowball for this one—was usually way above my price range, given that it was more than my rent. But it was *Gone With the Wind*. Maybe I could survive on Ramen for a few weeks.

I laid it on a high shelf and picked up a thick leather-bound Dickens tome. Shopping at Pages was like perusing some great collector's personal library. Every visit was an experience.

"Almost done," Jenna called, clicking her mouse and twisting up the corners of her lips, which were seldom more than a twitch away from smiling.

I admired the flowing simplicity of the wine-colored linen dress she wore. Like most of her wardrobe, it well suited her true passion: Jenna was a great book-buyer, but she was a better artist. "The bookstore definitely pays better," she said whenever I asked if she thought she'd ever buy the store from its retired owner, "and I love the thrill of the hunt in my job. But I will always be an artist at heart."

I owed her friendship, and by extension my sanity, to the abstract of a mother and child I'd talked her into selling me right off the shop's wall on my second visit. The painting had given us a reason to start talking, and once we had, we'd never stopped. I loved not knowing what I'd find when I popped into the store, and as I built a collection of books rivaled in my heart only by my shoe closet, Jenna and I had gone from casual acquaintances to the best of friends.

By the time her little boy came along the previous spring, I was planning the baby shower and driving her to the hospital when her water broke at a Friday night karaoke experiment (our unscientific method determined that lack of intoxication made singing off-key in front of strangers a lot less fun, and also that drunk people were surprisingly eager to help when you went into labor in a bar, some more appropriately than others). She was my non-newspaper family.

"Ready?" Jenna appeared at my elbow with her straw bag on her shoulder and her keys in her hand.

"Starving," I said, laying the book back on the shelf.

We were quiet for a half-block or so, until we turned up the brick sidewalk to an old row house that had been painted bright purple and converted into the home of the city's best Mexican food.

"You ready to talk about your week yet?" Jenna asked. "You know I get all my thrills vicariously through you."

"My week started and ended with gross crime scene photos. I think that entitles me to at least one margarita, so I guess we'll just have to force ourselves to stay for a while."

"Ah, to not have to be home by the children's bedtime! Leave nothing out."

We followed the hostess up the narrow stairs to a square table covered in brightly-hued paint. The top was lavender and each leg was a different shade of the rainbow.

"Did you have time to actually read the paper today?" I asked, sinking into a ladderback chair that was just as colorful as the table.

She wiggled one hand back and forth as she popped a blue corn chip into her mouth with the other.

"I started your story, but I only got through the part on the front page before I got busy looking through the ads." Jenna found a lot of the bookstore's inventory at estate sales. She usually spent Fridays combing through the classifieds for the weekend and calling all the ones that mentioned books.

I filled her in on the gory details of the trial as we waited for our drinks. When I got to the part about the murderer confessing to his mom, the color drained from Jenna's face.

"So, this kid really just walked into his mother's kitchen splattered with other people's blood and sat down and told her what he did?" She gaped at me, her hand fluttering to her throat. "As a mother, you want your kids to trust you enough to tell you anything, but...Oh, my God. I can't even imagine."

"I know. That was the most dramatic part of the whole trial for me, when his mother testified. I felt so bad for that poor woman. Here her kid has done this horrible thing and she knows he did it and she kept looking at the victims' families and telling them she was sorry, but you know she still loves her kid and she's worried about what's going to happen to him, too."

"And she probably feels guilty," Jenna said. "I know I would. I'd never stop wondering what I did wrong. How my kid grew up to be the kind of person who could murder someone. It would drive me completely batshit insane."

The first round arrived and we nibbled chips and sipped margaritas (well, I sipped, Jenna gulped) as we studied our menus, the usual hum of other diners' conversations drowned out by the mariachi band that played on Friday nights.

We smiled thank-yous at the striking Hispanic waitress when she dropped off another margarita for Jenna and a glass of iced tea for me. She turned to the next table after she jotted down our order, and I raised my eyebrows at my friend.

"I wonder what it would be like to be one of those women people turn to look at when they walk by?" I asked, my eyes on the girl's bobbing ebony ponytail.

"You're pretty, Nicey." Jenna smiled. "I've never seen anyone with eyes like yours."

Neither had I, and I wasn't fishing for a compliment. I knew my striking violet eyes were my best feature. They always made people think I was lying when I said I wasn't wearing contacts. I also had long legs that were well-shaped by hours at the gym every week, and long, thick brown hair that didn't need much work in the mornings. I wasn't knocking my brand of unobtrusive, B-cup-and-brains beauty, just imagining how the chosen few lived. Maybe it was a reporter's curse. I often mused about what it would be like to be in other people's heads.

"So?" Jenna prodded as I watched the waitress sashay through a hot pink swinging door into the kitchen. She even had the pretty-girl walk. "What else is going on in the seedy criminal world in

Richmond?"

The chips and salsa dwindled to crumbs and chunks of onion as I related the story of Darryl Wright and Noah Smith for the third time.

"I think it might be a vigilante," I finished. "Though, the cops wanted that kept quiet badly enough to give me a hell of a favor in trade for not running it tonight."

"My friend, the investigative reporter." Jenna sighed. "My life is so boring."

"Exaggerate much?" I snorted. "Investigative reporters bring down corrupt politicians and bust slimy, thieving CEOs. That's what I want to do when I grow up. I'm afraid I've just been working with cops for so long I'm starting to think like one. I think Aaron was only half-kidding this afternoon when he asked if I had ever considered going into law enforcement."

"Seriously?" It was Jenna's turn to snort. "Cops don't make enough money to keep you in shoes."

"Warren Buffett barely makes enough money to keep me in shoes." I smiled, pausing to thank the waitress as she set a sizzling plate of fajitas on the table in front of me, before I finished my thought. "If I paid retail for my shoe collection, I'd have been in bankruptcy court before I got out of college. Thank God for eBay."

I stuck my foot out from under the table and Jenna smiled at my barely-scuffed latest treasure.

"Ooh, pretty," she said. "Manolo?"

I lifted my foot to show off the red sole.

"Ah. That's the other one. Louboutin? I have kids. I have little frame of reference for overpriced, wobbly shoes."

"Louboutin is right, supermom. Less than a hundred dollars, because of a couple of scuff marks and a tiny wine stain that I took off with a Tide stick. I can't believe the number of people who wear these once and get rid of them. This pair was twelve hundred last spring."

Jenna shook her head. "Twelve hundred dollars. For a pair of shoes. If I was going to pay that kind of money for heels, George Clooney had better be in the box with them to give me a pedicure and a long foot massage."

I laughed. "I think George's rates for massage therapy would definitely price me out of those. But I do love my secondhand steals."

"You really have a talent for that. Somewhere, I'm convinced there's a market for it that you're missing."

"Ace reporter, professional bargain hunter." I held my hands up in a pantomime of scales and furrowed my brow. "I think I'll stick with the gig I have for now.

"In other news," I sipped my tea as she flagged the waitress down and ordered another margarita. "It's entirely possible that, at least in the most technical sense of the phrase, Grant Parker asked me out this afternoon."

Jenna's eyes got so big I could see white all the way around the brown.

"What? Where are you going? When?"

"I'm not." I laughed at her horrified expression. "Don't look at me like that. First of all, he's a has-been baseball player, not young Elvis incarnate. I told him thanks for the column he's running tomorrow on the basketball coach who has breast cancer, and I think he was trying to be nice by asking me to go with him to the game tonight. That's work, so it's not an actual date, but it's the closest I've gotten in longer than I care to admit."

"Who gives a rat's patootie?" Jenna slammed her glass down on the table for emphasis. "Going out is going out. You could have a t-shirt that says 'I went out with Grant Parker.'"

"Don't you use your 'mom voice' on me, missy!" I giggled at her chastising tone. "Though, I think you just hit on a viable business idea. There have to be a fair number of women around here who could use such a t-shirt. You could sell them at Pages."

Jenna carried on about how many women would jump at the chance for a date with Parker, and I drifted into my own world. It had been a long time since I'd been on a date with anyone, a fact that listening to witness after witness detail "Barbie and Ken's" undying devotion had brought to the forefront of my thoughts that week.

Someone sexy and exciting, who could hold their own in a conversation and knock me off my feet with a kiss—that's how my internet dating "what are you looking for in a partner?" would read, if I were brave enough to fill one out. I didn't think that was too picky, though all recent evidence said it might just be.

I didn't regret any of the big choices I had made, but my eighteen-year-old self had been so sure of her "where do you see yourself in ten years?" list: finish college, embark on a fabulous career as a political reporter for the *Washington Post*, and fall madly in love. And even though I was content most of the time, twenty-nine was just around the bend, and I couldn't help feeling I had fallen short of what that girl wanted her life to be.

I stared at a bright red tile in the middle of the sun mosaic on the far wall. Almost like I was back there, I saw Kyle's soft smile as I leaned my head on his shoulder in the front seat of my old Mustang, heard the huskiness that always came into his voice when he told me he loved me.

For a split second, it seemed like yesterday that he was the most important thing in my life. I'd nearly lost myself to the point of giving up on Syracuse and my dreams of the *Post*, which had scared me into a convent-like college existence. He'd walked away when I'd refused to stay, and I still couldn't so much as bring myself to look him up on Facebook. Maybe some people only get to fall madly in love once.

Whether she was a tiny bit psychic or I was just easy to read, Jenna could almost always tell what I was thinking. She patted my hand, drawing me back to the bustle of the restaurant with a lopsided grin.

"Honey, you have yet to find the great love of your life. Kyle was a high school boy. You need to fall in love with a man."

I recognized her I-know-more-about-this-because-I'm-older-than-you voice and smiled. She thought being thirty-four made her positively wizened.

"I shudder to think what my life would be like if I had married the guy I was dating at eighteen," she said. "Last time I saw him he was standing on the side of I-64 wearing an orange vest and holding a 'stop ahead' sign. You're still looking for the right one. He's out there."

She spent two hours getting reacquainted with Jose Cuervo and helping me forget my lovelorn woes, her ability to make me laugh increasing in direct proportion to her level of intoxication.

"So, the light is green, but there's a big truck in front of us that's slow getting moving," Jenna said, her words already garbled by laughter as she started a new story. "I didn't say a word. I was listening to the radio, and all of a sudden from the backseat, I hear Gabby: 'It's the long vertical pedal on the right! What, are you waiting for the light to get greener? Some of us have places to go!' I thought I was going to wreck my car I was laughing so hard. Is that my kid, or what?"

I gasped for air and wiped at the tears streaming from my eyes. "Undeniably. And I'm going to pee my pants if you don't stop making me laugh."

Jenna giggled again. "I'm having a great time, hon. I love going out with you. You laugh at my stories, you love my kids, you drive me home—you rock!"

"I do, huh? Okay. I think you're sufficiently blitzed." I savored the last bite of a flaky white chocolate and caramel empanada. "I have done my job. We can't end the evening with a disappointed Chad."

I drained my tea glass for the sixth time and glanced around. The band had called it a night and the place was practically empty, the cartoon-colored walls not as bright in the soft yellow glow from the overhead bulbs. I pulled my phone out of my purse to check the time and frowned. It was coming up on midnight, and I'd missed two calls in the last hour.

I held up my index finger as I pressed the button to check my voicemail, skipping through a week's worth of messages, hunting for the most recent ones. I never listened to them unless I was looking for something specific, which had long-ago led Bob to order the receptionists to leave me notes.

"Someone tried to call me," I murmured as I finally got through the three from that afternoon. "Just a second."

Aaron White's voice froze me in my chair for an instant, and I listened to him make a crack about a free favor before I jumped to my feet, looking around for the waitress and reaching for my keys.

"What's going on?" Jenna lifted her glass again.

"I have to go back to work, and I guess you're coming with me." My words were clipped as I silently cursed the mariachis for drowning out the phone's musical tinkling, and myself for leaving my scanner in the car. "I have an accident to cover. Apparently there was a boat crash about an hour ago."

CHAPTER THREE

JENNA WAS STILL GIGGLING twenty minutes later when we climbed out of the car by the river side a few miles south of the city. She was positively giddy from being forced to accompany me to an accident scene. Well that, and tequila.

I tried to look severe as I ordered her to do her best to appear sober and avoid making me laugh when I was supposed to be working, but her twinkling eyes and eager grin reminded me of a little kid with a Toys "R" Us gift card, and it was damn near impossible to maintain decorum while I was looking at that.

"Yes, ma'am." she slurred, proving my point as she offered me a weak salute and then winced when I giggled. "Oops. Sorry. I'll try to be less funny. Damn you, Jack Daniels."

"You were drinking margaritas, honey. Wrong label." I chuckled as I tucked her arm into mine so at least she wouldn't fall. I knew I had no chance of getting her to stay in the car.

All the emergency vehicles had made it difficult to get the car within field-goal range of the crash site, and the flashing red and blue lights made the natural beauty of the riverbank unnaturally eerie. The shredded boats still burning on the black water in the distance didn't look promising for a happy ending.

I canvassed the fringe of the emergency personnel for Aaron, but it was hard to even distinguish the policemen from the firefighters in the strange half-darkness so far from the accident scene.

The blond head bobbing just above most of the crowd, however, I knew instantly.

"It can't be," I muttered, even as I recognized the butter-colored polo I'd seen twice that day already.

"There you are!" Parker said when I caught up to him. "This is a madhouse. How do you ever get any work done at one of these things?"

"Hey, Parker." I stared, still unable to come up with a single logical reason for his presence. "I've never been to anything like this before. Boats don't usually blow up on the James. But I'm about to find a cop and see what's going on. Forgive my manners, but what are you doing here?"

"I know a little about what happened." He grimaced. "The coach got a call during my interview after the Generals game. The little speedboat belonged to Nate DeLuca, one of our pitchers. I don't know the details, but it hit a Richmond PD boat. Like you said, there was an explosion. The fire department is searching the river and the banks on both sides, but they don't think anyone survived. After I called in my story, I came to see for myself what happened to DeLuca. I'm going to write a feature on him for Sunday. He should've been at the ballpark tonight, but he had friends in town, and since he wasn't pitching, the coach gave him the night off."

"Sweet cartwheeling Jesus. Let's go see what else we can find out," I said. "Kiss your Saturday goodbye, Mr. Columnist. You're going to be at the office tomorrow." And so was I. So much for my leisurely weekend.

I turned to dive back into the crowd in search of Aaron and mid-whirl, I noticed Jenna standing there, still and surprised. Her eyes were doing that white-all-around thing again.

"People died out there?" she squeaked.

I patted her hand. "You want to go back to the car?"

"No." She squared her small shoulders and gripped my arm a little tighter. "I want to go to work with you."

I turned back to Parker. "Grant Parker, this is my friend Jenna Rowe. This mess crashed our girls' night. She drank too much tequila, but she's very excited to see the glamorous world of journalism up close."

"The best way to do that is after too much tequila," he said. "Nice to meet you, Jenna."

The thin fingers around my arm dug in tighter, and I didn't think their owner was breathing. I elbowed her lightly in the ribs, rolling my eyes. Her forceful exhale sounded like a sigh as she gazed at Parker.

"I really love your column," she lied. Jenna hated sports in any incarnation. She was already bemoaning the start of Gabby's soccer season, and it was three months away.

"Thank you." He smiled.

We moved through the crowd as a unit until I saw a familiar face.

"Mike!" I waved at Sergeant Sorrel from the narcotics unit.

"Nichelle," he said, turning from the water to face me when I stopped next to him. "Where've you been? You missed the TV crews. They all left about twenty minutes ago."

Damn. Charlie no doubt drank her margaritas with her scanner in her lap.

"I was out and I missed the call, but got down here as quick as I could. I didn't even take my poor friend Jenna home first."

Mike smiled at Jenna and held out his hand. "I guess you never know how your Friday night is going to end up when you're friends with Nichelle, huh?"

I started to introduce Parker, but quickly learned women weren't alone in their rambling worship of him.

"Hey! You're Grant Parker!" Mike said before I got a word out. "I watched you play ball when you were in college here, man. You had some arm. Too bad about all that, I guess—but I read your column. I'm a big fan."

Parker smiled and shook Mike's hand. "Thanks. I appreciate that."

I stared at Mike, and then at Parker. Parker had fans? I was impressed. And a little jealous.

"I guess you heard a baseball player was driving the little boat, huh?" Mike asked Parker.

Parker nodded, but I jumped in before he could say anything, impatient to get to the bottom of at least one story that day.

"Aaron's here, so he's taking point on this, right?" I asked.

"I saw him down closer to the crash site a little while ago," Mike said. "Let me see where he went."

He called Aaron on the police radio attached to his shoulder, and we all heard Aaron say he was about fifty yards downstream from us.

With Jenna and Parker in tow, I headed down the bank. It was tricky, navigating over the slimy rocks in the middle of the night. We'd had a wet spring, and the river had swollen almost to flood level, leaving the rocks along the banks coated with a layer of slippery goo once the water began receding. It was still fuller than normal and moving fast, judging by the bubbly whooshing that underscored the sounds around us. I wished I'd worn more practical shoes.

Aaron looked up at me with a grim half-smile when I found him. "Nichelle. Nice night to be out on the river. I can't believe this. Such a fucking waste."

"What happened?" I asked.

"Probably be several days, and even then we won't have the whole story because there were no survivors." Aaron talked, I scribbled. "It looks like the ballplayer and his buddies were going too fast, and when they came around that bend, they didn't have time to avoid our boys.

"The little speedboat came apart around the hull of the PD vessel," he continued. "Their gas lines and tank also shredded, and the sparks set it off, so our guys ended up basically wrapped inside the explosion."

Jenna whimpered behind me and I closed my eyes, as if that could somehow banish the image he just put into my head.

"Good God, Aaron."

When I had my wits about me again I returned to my questions. "Who was it? On the police vessel, I mean?"

"Couple of rookies." He shook his head. "Both under twenty-five, not too long out of the academy. This kind of shit makes me sick. Senseless."

I had never seen Aaron so upset. Not often at a loss for words, I laid a hand on his arm. He stared at the flames as he spoke. "I know. It's all part of the job, right?"

"I don't like it, either," I said, remembering some of the stories that had made me feel as bad as he looked. "What were they doing way out here? Isn't that the big patrol boat? Did somebody drown?"

"Yes, it is," he said, his shaking head seeming to contradict the affirmative answer at first. "And no, no one drowned. At least, not that we got a call about. I'm not sure what they were doing, and we still haven't been able to get the commander of the river unit on the phone. He's going to have a very unpleasant day tomorrow."

I nodded, still writing. "I'm going to need the names and records of the officers who were killed, and contact info for the next of kin. I'm sure Parker here will have a piece on the baseball player."

Aaron looked over my shoulder.

"Hey! Grant Parker!" Aaron's dark mood appeared at least partially forgotten.

Stepping forward, Parker shook Aaron's hand. Aaron gushed about Parker's golden arm, just like Mike had.

I waited for a break in the Parker-adulation, and when Aaron started stumbling around the inevitable apology for the way Parker's pitching career had ended, I took the opportunity to steer the conversation back to the crash. "When can I have the accident report?"

"We should have something Monday," Aaron said. "Probably not any earlier, though."

I made a face. Monday didn't do me much good when I wanted the story for Sunday's early edition.

He walked away after I thanked him, both for the phone call and the interview, and I tried to stand taller in my ridiculously unsuitable shoes, scanning the rest of the crowd for another familiar face.

Jenna was still wobbly and still silently hanging on my arm, and my teetering attempt to see better was all it took to throw her off balance. She probably would have ended up with a broken ankle if Parker hadn't reached for us, his hand catching my elbow as I started to fall with her. Leaning on him, I grabbed Jenna's left arm with both hands and pulled. She weighed next to nothing, and my grip was enough to help her get her feet back under her.

"Nothing like nearly busting your ass on a big rock to kill a buzz," she said.

I twisted my other hand around and grabbed Parker's forearm, jerking my heel out of a crevice between two rocks and grimacing. I imagined the blue stilettos I'd so painstakingly cleaned wouldn't look quite as fabulous after hiking along the waterfront.

"Thanks." I smiled at Parker as I regained my balance and let go. "Turns out my shoes aren't suited for traipsing around slimy rocks in the dark."

"Shoes like that are only suited for one thing: making a woman's calves look good," he said, the grin that garnered thousands of readers three mornings a week making his eyes crinkle at the corners. "That's what my mom always says, anyway. Were you looking for someone? Before, I mean. I am a little taller than you. Maybe I can help."

"Oh, I…no one in particular. I was just checking to see if there was anyone else here I wanted to talk to."

He nodded, stepping up onto a bigger stone and surveying the riverbank himself. The rocky shoreline dissolved into overgrown grass, and the grass gave way to mammoth trees, their hulking outlines creeping right up to the water's edge a few hundred yards downstream.

"Hey." Parker stepped down and pointed through the crowd. "That's Katie DeLuca. She is—was—Nate's new wife. They got married in March."

I followed his gaze to a striking young blond woman standing near the crash site with two uniformed officers and an older man in a Richmond Generals baseball cap. She nodded at the officers as they talked and gestured toward the river, her face frozen in a mask of horror.

We picked our way toward her and as we got closer, I could see the tears streaming down her face. The patrolmen walked away, deep in conversation themselves, before we reached the little huddle.

"I hate this part of my job," I grumbled, my stomach lurching as my foot slipped a fraction of an inch on another rock. "I can get on a tight-lipped cop like a duck on a June bug, but just exactly what are we supposed to say to this woman who went from star pitcher's bride to twenty-something widow in the past hour?"

"Beats the hell out of me," Parker said. "This is your gig. I've met her a few times. You want me to try first?"

I started to say no, but a closer look at the young woman made me think twice. Maybe a familiar face would be a good thing, for her and me both.

Jenna bumped into me when I stopped short, motioning Parker ahead of me as we approached Katie. *She's probably not even as old as I am*, I thought. Parker nodded at the man who had his arm around Katie's waist and I thought I recognized him from the sports section as the Generals' head coach.

"Katie?" Parker's voice was low and smooth; soothing. "I'm Grant Parker. We met at the team's playoff celebration last fall. Do you remember me?"

Katie looked lost. She tilted her face up, gazing at Parker like he might tell her the way out of this nightmare.

"Aren't you from the newspaper?" she asked.

"Yes, I work at the *Telegraph*." Still that same melodic voice.

It put me in mind of the way you would talk to a frightened child, surprising coming out of Parker. Ultra-confident and a little smar-tassed is how I'd describe his normal conversational tone. I stepped forward so she could see me, and Parker continued seamlessly into an introduction.

"This is Nichelle Clarke. She works with me at the paper. We're handling the coverage of the accident tonight."

Katie furrowed her brow as if she didn't quite understand why he was telling her that. Her eyes were red and swollen from crying, and flicked from one group of people to another with almost manic speed, as if searching the riverfront for something, anything.

We watched for a long minute, but she gave no indication she wanted to talk.

"Can you get me a phone number where I can reach her tomorrow, Bill?" Parker asked finally, exchanging a sad look with the coach over Katie's head.

I might have protested under more ordinary circumstances, but it would've taken a meat cleaver to hack through the raw emotion cloaking Katie DeLuca. Maybe she'd be up to talking later, maybe not. That was more important for Parker's human interest piece than it was for my accident coverage, anyway.

Katie's eyes lit on the wreckage, and sorrow overran her silent stare. She pulled in ragged breaths that issued back anguished sobs I wouldn't soon forget.

"Nate!" she screamed, then crumpled to the ground, reaching toward the flames that still danced on the water.

Parker and Coach Bill tried to pull her to her feet, and I was sure the rocks were slicing into her bare knees, but she just sagged when they tried to lift her and they let go. My hand clapped over my mouth and I felt tears well up in my own eyes as a lump blocked off my throat. I had never seen anyone in such agony.

"No," she moaned between sobs, her head tossing back and forth hard enough to shake her whole torso. "Not Nate. No. We were going to spend our whole lives together. He's not dead. He's not."

All right, dammit. I couldn't lift her, but Parker's hours in the gym ought to be good for something besides making the interns giggle and blush.

Elbowing him none-too-gently in the ribs, I swallowed my tears and balanced—or tried to—on my tiptoes to get my lips close to his ear. "Do something. She's not in any shape for any of this. Get her out of here."

Parker nodded, concern plain on his face as he watched Katie drop her blond head to her knees. He knelt next to her and laid a hand on her back. "Katie? You can't do anything out here, honey, and you're hurting yourself on the rocks. Let me take you to your car and Bill will drive you home."

"Nate," she dissolved into a fresh round of sobs.

"I know. I'm so sorry." Parker scooped her into his arms and looked at Bill for direction.

I gasped when Parker stood up. The blood streaming down Katie's shins testified her legs had indeed been mangled. She didn't seem to notice.

The coach pointed in the general direction of the gravel road, and Parker walked that way, Nate DeLuca's widow cradled against his chest.

Jenna pulled on my arm and I turned. She looked like someone had backhanded her.

So much for Mr. Cuervo, I thought.

"That was horrible," she said.

I sighed. "She didn't ask to be newsworthy tonight. She'd much rather have her husband walking in their front door right now telling her about his boys' night. And no matter what kind of story we're doing about the victim, I can never quite get past feeling like an ass when I ask the family to talk to me."

"That's officially the uncool part of your job. I couldn't do it."

"You think you've seen enough now?" I slung my arm around her shoulders. "I'm not going to get much more tonight. I can take you home and call Aaron for an update in the morning when I get to the office."

She nodded, and we turned toward my car and ran into Parker. His face was pained. This was pretty far from the kind of story he usually worked on.

"Bill's taking her to her mother's house after the fire department finishes patching up her legs," he told us, gesturing behind him to a red BMW coupe where Katie was slumped in the passenger seat, a crouching paramedic tending to her wounds. "Thank God her parents live around here. I didn't really want to think about her going home alone tonight."

"You're a good man, Charlie Brown." I nodded sympathetically. "That was nice, what you did for her."

"What I am is out of my element. And I have to say I much prefer talking to my players and covering my games and writing my column to moving in your world. This shit is depressing."

I laughed. "I guess to most people it would seem that way. There are accidents and murders and people dying every day. Is it terrible that I'm pretty happy most of the time?"

"On the contrary, I'd say it's admirable," he said.

"I'm going to take Jenna home now. Her girls' night out has become a little more than she bargained for, I think."

"I think I'm gonna go home and try not to have nightmares," he said. "I want that column in on Sunday, though, so I guess I'll see you at the office tomorrow?"

"You'll like it," I said. "It's quiet on Saturday."

He moved off through the still-bustling crime scene with the unconscious grace of the professional athlete he should have been. I watched him go, impressed by the way he'd dealt with Katie and wondering for a second if it was sad for him, writing about people who did what he'd always dreamed of doing.

I helped Jenna into the car and then climbed in myself and started the engine.

"Sorry about all that," I said.

"Don't apologize. I got to go to work with you. And I got to meet Grant Parker. He's so gorgeous. And he seems nice. Do you think you should—"

"Don't start," I interrupted. "What would I even talk to Grant Parker about? I like baseball enough, but that will only take a relationship so far."

"But —"

"Jenna, seriously. I never said a dozen words to the man before today, and I'm sure I won't say a dozen words to him in the next five years, either. I'm glad you thought it was fun to meet him, but leave it alone. I'm not some twit who's going to go chasing off after biceps and a killer smile."

She opened her mouth and sat there for a split second, then closed it again. "Whatever."

I stayed quiet, running back through the interviews I'd gotten at the accident scene and focusing on the long list of phone calls I needed to make the next morning. The silence wasn't uncomfortable, lingering until I slowed the car to a stop in front of a lovely white colonial nestled in a wooded suburban neighborhood with great schools.

"We'll do it better next time," I said as she hopped out of the car.

"I had fun," she called over her shoulder as she walked a pretty straight line up her sidewalk. "At dinner, anyway. Really. Thanks for a great girls' night. Chad will be disappointed I'm not still blitzed, but he'll live."

"Next time," I repeated, inching the car away from the curb. "I promise to return you suitably intoxicated."

The porch light flickered on automatically when I pulled into my driveway. Drained, I dropped my keys on the counter and grabbed a tall glass from the overhead cabinet, pushing the door shut with enough force to make it stick even though several layers of paint made it difficult.

I gulped the lukewarm tap water and set the glass in the farmhouse sink. Yawning, I untied the bow on my hip and tugged my wrap shirt off as I walked through the house, pausing at the archway to the living room.

"Sorry, girl," I told my tiny Pomeranian, patting her head. "It looks like you're going to be a bachelorette again this weekend." Unless Jenna wanted a playmate for the little ones. I brightened at the possibility.

"You want to see Gabby?" Darcy hopped in a circle and barked. Jenna's daughter was a tireless fetch partner.

I shuffled to the bathroom and scrubbed my face, pulling on boxer shorts and a tank before I shut off the lights. The imposing cherry four-poster that dominated the floor space in my bedroom beckoned with mounds of down pillows wrapped in lilac silk and a sage green duvet so soft it could make a cloud jealous.

It was coming up on three, according to the glowing numbers on my alarm clock. Good Lord. I bet the White House Press Corps gets to go to bed at a decent hour.

I flipped onto my stomach and snuggled deeper into my pillows, the backs of my eyelids playing a montage of Darryl Wright's blown-out baseball cap, Katie's grief-stricken stare, and the burning river. It had been a long day, and I had a feeling there was a longer one coming. I slowed my breathing, dreading the nightmares that often came with covering tragedies. But I was so tired, I didn't even dream.

CHAPTER FOUR

By the time I made it to the office Saturday, I'd nearly mowed down an unfortunate cyclist who'd thought better of crossing the street just as I'd careened around a corner with my passenger side tires off the ground. Minutes later, I barreled through the half-open elevator doors to the newsroom and some surprisingly sharp reflexes were the only thing that saved Bob from getting better acquainted with the tacky seventies carpet.

I stopped so suddenly I dropped my bag, and he dodged to one side and waited until I had collected everything before he looked pointedly at the big silver and glass clock on the wall between the elevators.

"Good morning, sunshine," he said. "Sleep well?"

"Chief! I didn't think anything short of another Kennedy getting shot would get you in here on a Saturday." Shit. If memory served, I'd heard the last time my boss came to work on a Saturday was when the space shuttle Columbia came apart in the skies over Texas in 2003. "I'm sorry I'm late. I didn't set the alarm. I can't believe I overslept."

"You're behind on the biggest story of the year," he said, his eyes disappointed. "You've got five dead people, two cops and a ballplayer among them, and an explosion half the city heard or saw last night.

Charlie had four and a half minutes on the early show, and she's done two newsbreaks since. The last one said something about the FBI being out there this morning."

Damn, damn, damndamndamn. And after all the nice things he said to me the day before. Bob was undeniably the father figure in my little pseudo-family in Virginia—the closest thing I ever had to a father, period, when you got right down to it—and I didn't want to let him down.

"I really am sorry, chief. I'll get it. They can put it on the web as soon as I'm done, and I'll find you something she hasn't had for tomorrow. Everyone was gone by the time I got Aaron's message last night or I'd have sent something in from the scene. You'll have it by four, I swear."

"Really?" Shelby's drawl came from behind my left shoulder

And the hits just keep on coming.

"This is huge, from what I've been watching on Channel Four this morning. Charlie's got a good head start on us." Shelby kept her eyes on Bob as she talked. "Are you really going to have it ready in just a few hours? Maybe I could help you. I've been here since before eight, and today is my day off."

"I think I can handle it, but, wow, it's so nice of you to come by on your day off." I fixed my best attempt at a put-upon smile on Shelby and imitated her syrupy tone. "I would have been here early, too, but I was working until three o'clock this morning, covering an accident. Those unpredictable hours are the most inconvenient thing about reporting. Though I don't suppose the garden club ever had a midnight meeting."

Bob cleared his throat. "Don't go home, Shelby," he said, cutting a glance at me. "If Nichelle can't get it together in time, we may need you to pitch in. Nice of you to offer."

I stared at him. Over. My. Cold. Corpse.

Shelby assured Bob she'd be available and tossed a smirk at me before she sashayed off.

"Nothing personal, kid. Just the wrong day for you to sleep in," Bob said, following the glare that should've burned a hole right through the back of Shelby's flimsy camisole. "We have to have it nailed down. It's leading page one."

"A lesser reporter might feel pressured by that," I said. "I was just on my way to pester Aaron."

"Don't let me keep you," he said. "I'm looking forward to reading."

"You're staying all day?"

"This is a big story. Call me a micro-manager, but I'm going to see it before it goes. The TV has been all over it since early this morning, and I want to make sure that between your piece and Parker's piece, we have them outdone." Bob winked. "He has a good start on that. There have been reporters camped out at the pitcher's family's houses all day today, but no one's said a word to any of them. Somehow, he's on his way to interview both the guy's parents and his in-laws. I love it."

Scooped on a news story by Mr. Baseball? And Shelby Taylor on standby to help me get my story out? Oh, yeah. This was shaping up to be a helluva day.

"Find me something great, Nicey. Anything Charlie hasn't had," Bob patted my shoulder as he walked back toward his office. "You outdid yourself all week. But Ken and Barbie have gone out with the recycling."

"Twenty column inches of greatness, coming up." I spun on my heel and hurried to my desk, grabbing a pen and the phone before I even sat down.

Aaron's uncharacteristic grouchiness told me his day wasn't going any better than mine was.

"I'm tired of talking to reporters about the accident last night," he said when I asked how he was. "I wish I was out on my boat with a beer and a fishing pole. No offense."

"None taken. I don't exactly want to be here, either. Has the daylight given you guys anything new? I saw you told Charlie they sent a unit from Quantico." I did like the sound of that, even as irritating as it was to hear it secondhand.

"I told Charlie no such thing," Aaron said. "She saw them in their damned logo-emblazoned hats and windbreakers and probably frigging boxers, out there picking through every black rock lining the shore of the James."

Damn. She'd been back to the scene. The only thing keeping me from pulling my hair out was the knowledge that FBI agents are about as welcoming of TV cameras as a PETA convention would be of Michael Vick.

"Why are they here?"

"Something about the police vessel that was involved." He sounded huffy. "Like they think we did something wrong. Not that they've turned up anything. Their official report won't be ready for weeks, probably, but they're sticking with the scenario I gave you last night. Man, those guys are a pain in the ass, but don't you dare quote me on that!"

"I wouldn't." I laughed. "But why don't you tell me how you really feel, detective?"

"You have no idea."

"Do you have an official statement on the FBI involvement?"

"You'd have to call their field office to get that. All I can tell you is they have people working at the scene."

"Is there any chance the driver of DeLuca's boat was under the influence?"

"Unfortunately, we won't ever know that." Aaron's tone turned somber. "There wasn't enough left of any of the victims to check."

I swallowed hard, closing my eyes. "Oh," was all I said.

"Anything else?" he asked.

"I need the service records and background on the officers who were killed," I said. "I also need contact information for the next of kin, and I need to know who to call to find out what they were doing out there."

"If you check your fax machine, you will find you already have what I can give you from their personnel files and the families' contact information," he said. "You're welcome. And call Commander Owen Jones over at the river unit. When I talked to him this morning, he was pretty shaken up, but he should be able to give you what you need."

"Thanks, Aaron. What would I do without you?"

"Have a lot less fun at work? I hope you at least get tomorrow off."

"I may. You going fishing?"

"Absolutely. I've had as much of this place as I can stand for one week."

I grabbed the faxes and dialed Commander Jones as I stared at the grainy photos of the dead officers, Alex Roberts and Brian Freeman. Both so young. I wondered what they had been doing when the other boat hit them. Did they see it coming?

I introduced myself when Jones picked up. "Is this a good time to ask you about the accident on the river last night?"

"As good a time as any," he said. "I think I'm going to be busy with this mess for a while."

"Let's start with the obvious: what were they doing?"

"That's the first question I've gotten from everyone today, and it's one I don't have an answer for. I didn't give those orders, so I don't know."

"Oh." I hadn't seen that coming. "Where did their orders come from, then? Is there someone else I can talk to?"

"I'm not really sure, to tell you the truth. I can't find anything in the system about why they were out there. Orders for use of the aquatic fleet would go through me or someone above me. If it came from over my head, you need to talk to the big brass downtown, but I would be very surprised to find any of them in the office today, and I haven't even had time to turn around twice because of all the media calls this morning."

Nothing like another story with more holes than the back nine at Jefferson Country Club. Especially when Bob was hanging around just to read my stuff. Dammit. I scribbled down his comments, such that they were.

I asked Jones about date of the last fatality accident in his unit. He told me there hadn't ever been another one, and the only other accident of any kind involving a police boat had been in 1967.

"How long had Roberts and Freeman been with your unit?" I asked.

"They weren't part of my unit, strictly speaking. They both went through the training for this unit, but neither requested a transfer over here. I can't tell you how much wish I had more answers, Miss Clarke, but I'm figuring this out as I go."

Thanking him, I tried to piece it together in my head as I put the phone down. What the hell? I stared at the picture of Jenna's kids that sat on my desk without really seeing it. Did they take the boat for a joyride?

With a new picture of the rookie cops out fishing, maybe even drinking, I reached for the phone again. Charlie hadn't come anywhere close to that, but someone else—someone important—had to say it. How could I get ahold of the command staff on a Saturday?

I drummed my fingers on the handset, one of the little pink message slips that covered the surface of my banged-up desk catching my eye.

Yes!

I dug first through the pile closest to me, then two others, before I hit pay dirt. Three weeks before, I'd interviewed the deputy chief of police about the success of the anti-bullying program he started in the city's public schools. And he'd left me a message to call him. On his cell phone.

That'd teach Bob to pick on me for having a desk that looked like an episode of *Hoarders*. If I succeeded in doing anything but pissing Dave Lowe off by calling him on a Saturday, of course.

I turned back to the file Aaron had faxed me before I picked up the phone to call Lowe.

According to their service records, Roberts and Freeman had been exemplary officers. No reprimands, no poor reviews, no trouble. Was it possible these two guys stole a city-owned boat?

I grabbed a pen and settled the handset on my shoulder, determined to find out.

Lowe sounded mildly irritated when I identified myself, but he didn't hang up on me, so I plunged into my questions before he could think to. My sails depleted as quickly as they'd filled when he explained he wasn't sure how much help he could be if I'd already talked to Jones.

"Commander Jones said he hadn't ordered the officers to be out on the boat," I told him. "He also said any orders that didn't come from him would have to come from a member of the command staff. Do you know who sent them out there and what they were supposed to be doing?"

He was silent for so long, I wondered if he had hung up.

I waited.

Still nothing.

"Chief, are you there?" I asked finally.

"I'm here." There was something in his tone I couldn't read. "I'm not in Richmond at the moment, and I've mostly been following Channel Four's coverage on my cell phone, to tell you the truth."

My jaw clenched so abruptly my teeth clacked. The deputy chief of police was getting his news about dead officers from Charlie? Ouch.

Lowe paused again before he continued.

"I assumed the orders had been given by Commander Jones," he said slowly. "I can't fathom who or what put those boys on the river if they weren't doing something for Jones."

Scooping Charlie looked more improbable with each phone call, but the thought of Bob sending Shelby in as reinforcement was enough to make me nauseous, and I refused to let Parker best me on an accident story. I opened my mouth to thank Lowe and go back to the drawing board, but he spoke again before I could.

"You know, Miss Clarke, I've been meaning to call and tell you how much I appreciated the piece you did on my program," he said. "That project is very dear to my heart. I'll tell you what, I'm going to make a couple of calls and see if I can figure out what the hell's going on up there. If I hit on anything, I'll give you a call back. What's the best number to reach you?"

The heavens might as well have opened to a choir of angels.

I thanked him and cradled the phone in a daze. My weekend just kept getting more curious. First, it was matching drug dealer slayings that likely had nothing to do with fat stacks of drug money. Then, two dead cops on a boat they'd ostensibly had no reason to have out.

I threw my pen down and stomped in the direction of the break room, mulling over the scant facts I had.

"I thought you were out of here until Monday?" Eunice, our grandmotherly features editor, called from behind me.

I turned, waiting for her to catch up. A helicopter crash in Iraq during the first Bush administration had left our former war correspondent with a bad hip, a new job at the features desk, and plenty of time for cooking.

"I thought I was, too." My eyes flicked to the clock between the elevators, which practically chuckled at me that it was five after one.

"Unfortunately, tragedies don't care about weekends." I waved a hand toward the TV, where Charlie clucked about Nate DeLuca's boat and its maximum speed capability "I was late this morning, and it's already after one o'clock. I'm never going to make deadline. Especially without caffeine."

"You better grab some and get moving." Eunice patted my shoulder before she stepped into the elevator. "Good luck, sugar."

Walking back to my desk with a half-empty Coke bottle, I found renewed determination. There was someone, somewhere, who knew what the hell was going on. I just needed to find them. In the next two hours and ten minutes.

"Damn." My eyes fell on the pink message slip on top of my laptop. Of course, I'd missed the call from Lowe. Under it, I found a post-it from which I learned two things: the first was that Parker had God-awful handwriting, which I had to decipher to get to the second: he was back and would email me his story when it was done in case he had info I wanted.

Well, at least he hadn't screwed up. *The Telegraph* would have something on Sunday no one else did, and in the age of digital information, that was damned hard to do. But my ego was getting more bruised by the second.

I snatched a blue Bic out of my pen cup and dialed Lowe.

"I'm not sure how much good my gratitude is going to do you

today," he said. "I can't find anyone who knows diddly about Roberts and Freeman being on that boat last night. But I can tell you I ordered internal affairs to open a file. No one knows that but myself and the captain I spoke to."

An internal affairs investigation? I could work with that.

I scribbled. "What does that mean? Do you think they were joyriding?"

Lowe's voice made a low, rumbling sound through the phone, like a murmur or a fading cell signal, but then came through loud and clear again.

"We're looking at this case from every angle. The theory the officers took the boat without orders certainly is among the scenarios under review, but it's not the only one. We'll know more as the investigation progresses."

From doing me a favor to doubletalk in less than a minute. Welcome to covering cops.

After we hung up, I dialed the next number on my list. I read Charlie's stories on the Channel Four website and hummed along with two Aerosmith covers and a Rolling Stones song as I waited for the FBI agent assigned to avoid questions from the press. Experience told me this call was probably an exercise in futility. Special Agent Starnes said nothing to disprove my theory.

"What I can tell you is limited by the constraints of an ongoing investigation." Her words were clipped.

Charlie had footage of FBI agents, logo caps and all, squatting and peering at blackened bits of something on the riverbank, but no quotes from anyone at the FBI, including Starnes. Which meant I was more determined than usual to get something I could use.

"I understand that," I said. "I also understand this is the first police boating accident in Richmond in more than forty years. Does the FBI always investigate water accidents involving police vessels?"

"Not always."

"Then why this one?"

"Miss Clarke, I really can't discuss an ongoing investigation," she said. "It's bureau policy."

I sighed. Her wall was well-fortified against badgering, so hammering at it with quick questions was unlikely to produce the information doorway I needed.

"Agent Starnes, I appreciate that. I know you're just doing your job. I know the police detective who blew off the FBI's involvement this morning is just doing his." I didn't think I threw Aaron too far under the bus, and I hoped the idea of the locals dismissing the feds might annoy her. "But I have a job to do, too. I have readers who want to know why these men are dead. Clearly you're investigating for a reason. Give me something, anything. Why is the FBI involved?"

She paused. "We got a tip."

I added another line of chicken scratch to my notes, hoping she might elaborate but knowing she probably wouldn't.

She didn't.

"A tip that there might be foul play? That the boat was stolen?"

"That this might be...more than it seems."

"Have you found anything to support that?" I asked.

"I'm sorry," she said. "Ongoing investigation."

I wondered if there was a daily budget for frustrated sighs when another one escaped my chest as I laid the phone down, partly because her cryptic answers weren't hugely helpful, and partly because it was time to call the families. Last on my list..

Valerie Roberts sounded spent, her voice scratchy and hollow when she answered the phone. I stumbled over my words as I apologized for bothering her and asked if she felt like talking about her husband.

There was a heavy, hitching sigh on the other end of the line. "Maybe," she said. "I can try, I guess."

"Thank you. I won't keep you long. How long were you and—" I glanced at the file again. Nothing like saying the wrong name to win points with the family. "—Alex married?"

"Two years." Her voice broke. "We just started talking about trying to have a baby."

I bit my lip and forged ahead. "Your husband was with the police department a little under a year. Did he ever tell you why he wanted to be a police officer?"

"He talked about it all the time. We dated for three years before we got married, and the whole time we were in college, all he could talk about was being a cop. He got his degree in criminal justice and he went straight to the academy after graduation. He wanted to help people. And he thought the guns were cool." Her tone lightened as she told me about him.

"I was nervous about him wanting to do this for a living. I didn't know if I would be able to handle him putting himself in danger every time he went to work. He reassured me constantly, and he showed me all his safety gear. I was always afraid he was going to get shot. Something like this never even crossed my mind."

The tears returned then, making her voice thick again. She took a deep breath before she continued. "Alex was a good man. Caring and thoughtful and generous, and honest to a fault. He was my soul mate. I truly believe that. He would have been an amazing father."

She dissolved into sobs at the last, and I waited as she collected herself. I tried to think of something to say, but "I'm sorry" seemed woefully inadequate, so I stayed quiet.

I asked her if there was a phone number where his parents could be reached, and she told me they both died in an accident when Alex was young. He'd been raised by his grandparents, who also died in recent years.

"I see," I said. "Just one more question. Did Alex mention anything about why he went out on the river last night?"

"No. He said he had to go to work. Didn't the department tell you what he was doing?"

"They can't find anyone who ordered the boat out last night. They're investigating the possibility it was taken without orders."

She sucked in a sharp breath and when she spoke, her tone was a peculiar mix of incredulous and hurt. "Wait. They're saying Alex and Brian were what? Fishing? Partying on the department's boat?" There was a long pause, and I didn't even chance breathing too loud.

"Miss Clarke," she finally said, her words deliberate. "My husband was not the kind of man who did anything even remotely against the rules. Alex was the straightest of straight arrows. Eagle Scout, honor society, the cleanest record in the department. I may not know why he was out on that boat last night, but I sure as hell know him. He did not take it without orders. If someone suggested he did, they're lying. I'd stake my life on it."

CHAPTER FIVE

THERE'S nothing more frustrating for a reporter than a heap of unanswered questions. Facing a blank computer screen with only a sketchy idea of what killed five people, each of whom had been the center of someone else's universe, had me zipping past frustrated and aiming straight for pissed off. Talking to Brian Freeman's mother had only made me feel worse. She lost her husband in January, and Brian had been her only child.

I slammed my hands down on my desk and jumped to my feet. What the hell was so hard about "Why was the boat out there?" I paced behind my cubicle as my mind tried to force this puzzle into some logical order. There were way too many holes to see a clear picture. I finally asked myself what I'd tell Jenna first. Which, of course, was what Charlie hadn't already told the greater Richmond metro area. That worked, and I resumed my seat and quickly lost myself in the rhythm of the keystrokes.

After receiving information regarding Friday night's fatal boating crash on the James River, FBI agents joined Richmond police in combing the riverbank for clues Saturday.

"We got a tip," Special Agent Denise Starnes said Saturday, "that this might be more than it seems."

I quoted Lowe about the internal affairs investigation next, and wrote about the victims, including notes Parker emailed me about the pitcher, DeLuca, and his two friends. Describing the scene at the river, I used Aaron's estimation of how the accident happened. I put the accident history for the unit I'd gotten from Jones toward the end, and finished with Valerie Roberts' emotional assertion of her husband's innocence.

I added Parker's name to the bottom of the article as a contributor and copied him when I emailed my story to Bob.

While I waited for a reply from my boss, I skimmed through the twenty-seven emails in my inbox, saving three replies from defense attorneys about other cases I was following, and deleting the rest.

Bob's edits arrived as I finished reading the last junk press release. He asked me to clarify a couple of things and said he hadn't heard about the FBI's tip-off or the internal investigation. His equivalent of a thumbs-up, which was especially gratifying when a story had actually given me a headache. I fished two Advil out of my purse.

I was halfway through my second Coke of the afternoon when Parker found me loitering in the break room. Once it was time to leave, I'd discovered I didn't want to go home.

"Thanks for the stuff you sent me." I leaned back in my chair and smiled when he stopped in the doorway. "It was good. Nicely done, scoring an exclusive with the families."

"Thanks. And anytime." He walked into the room with his hands in the pockets of his navy blue slacks. "What are you going to do tonight?"

"I have no plans," I said. "After the day I've had, I should go home and go to bed. But I'm starving. So I need to eat first."

"That sounds suspiciously like a plan. I could eat. Mind if I join you?"

Really? I opened my mouth to make an excuse, and realized I didn't have a good one. I eyed him for a second. Oh, what the hell? I'd been to dinner with people from work before, and he'd certainly been a lot of help.

"Why not?" I stood up. "Let me grab my purse."

"Anyplace in particular you were planning to go?"

I grinned as my stomach growled. "Do you like barbecue?"

Pop-Tarts were never intended to provide an entire day's nutrition, and the hickory-and-meat smell in the air reminded me of that as I climbed out of my car in the restaurant's postage stamp of a parking lot a few minutes later.

Parker strapped a shiny red helmet to the seat of a still-dealer-tagged BMW motorcycle in the space next to me and I raised one eyebrow. It was a nice bike for a reporter's salary. Maybe he had family money or something.

I followed him through the picnic tables on the covered porch. He held the door as I stepped inside, the fantastic aromas coming from the kitchen momentarily overpowered by a clean, summery cologne when I ducked under his arm.

"I have an ulterior motive for inviting myself to dinner," he said as we joined about ten other people waiting in line in the cramped entryway. "Did you read my column today?" His eyes dropped to the floor and I laughed.

I wasn't sure what I'd expected to hear, but that wasn't it.

"I wasn't going to ask," he said. "But I can't stand it anymore. If it sucked, you can tell me."

"I have not," I said, wondering why he cared what I thought. "Though not because I don't want to. I will, I promise. And you know, I meant it when I said your stuff was good today. So I'm sure it doesn't suck."

"I hope not. Sometimes I wonder if people are just nice to me because I used to be a decent ballplayer, you know? But you've never seemed impressed by my slider." He cocked his head to one side, and I surmised he wasn't too used to people who didn't fall all over him. "You're the real deal. Syracuse, right? I hear their j-school is the best. How'd you end up here, Texas girl in Virginia by way of New York? There has to be a story there."

I stepped up to the counter and ordered a chopped barbecue sandwich and a double helping of sweet potato fries, glancing at Parker as

I signed my credit card slip. "There's a story. I'm not sure it's very interesting, but everyone has one, don't they?"

He ordered ribs and spoon bread and dropped a few bills from his change into the tip jar, stuffing a thick wallet back into his hip pocket and turning from the counter.

"Something tells me yours is more interesting than most."

We found a booth in the back of the tiny dining room, making small talk about how the place should really be bigger. It boasted what was easily the best barbecue I'd ever eaten, and given my Texas roots, that was saying something. With less than a dozen tables inside, standing room only was a common state of affairs.

I left Parker at the table with his bottle of Corona and went to fill my glass with the best sweet iced tea in town, glancing at the flat screens on the far wall as I waited in line. One offered a cooking show, the other a Red Sox game. His and hers entertainment. What ever happened to talking to each other over dinner?

Parker flashed me a grin when I sat down across from him again.

"So? What brings you to this neck of the woods, Miss Clarke?" He leaned forward on the wide walnut bench, resting his forearms on the scarred wooden table and looking genuinely interested.

"You really want to hear this?" I laughed.

"Shoot."

"Well, I did grow up in Dallas, and I did go to Syracuse," I said. "I thought I was hot stuff when I graduated, too. I was the editor of the *Daily Orange*. I was a University Scholar, which is a big deal award given to twelve people in the graduating class every year. I even got to go to a dinner at the Chancellor's house for that one. I carried a double major in print journalism and political science, and I just knew the *Washington Post* was going to fall down and beg me to come take their seat in the White House press corps."

"Ah. But they didn't so much commence with the begging?"

"They did not." I shook my head. "They all but dismissed me. The politics editor wouldn't even see me, and the metro editor said he didn't need the headache of training a green reporter. Told me to come back when I was seasoned."

"Ouch."

I nodded. The memory stung a little, even half a decade later.

"That's about it. Confidence shot to hell, I figured I wasn't going to get hired anywhere. My mom let me whine for a while and then told me to apply in a medium market close to DC and get to work making the guy sorry. Bob took a shot and gave me the police beat. I saw a way into the courthouse when they started slashing personnel two years ago, and I took it. I'm just waiting for the story that's going to make the *Post* notice me. I thought Ken and Barbie might get it, but so far...crickets. The FBI interest in this one makes it sexier than your average accident. Maybe if there's really something to this and I can stay ahead of Charlie this week, I might blip up on their radar."

He nodded. "See? Interesting. And good luck. Though it could be hard for Bob to fill those heels of yours if they stole you from us."

They called our order and he stood up before I could.

"You hold the table," he said. "They're a precious commodity in this place on a Saturday night."

He disappeared into the growing crowd.

A pulled pork sandwich, sitting tall in the plastic basket next to a huge pile of cinnamon-sugared sweet potato fries, appeared in front of me with a flourish.

"Dinner is served, ma'am." Parker's Virginia drawl didn't quite lend itself to the Texas accent he tried to affect.

"Why thank you, kind sir." I grinned, not even waiting for him to sit down before I popped a fry into my mouth. I devoured half the pile in the ensuing three minutes, ignoring the fresh-from-the-fryer temperature. I moved to get up as I gulped the last of the tea that was soothing my blistered tongue and Parker raised one hand.

"Iced tea?" he asked, already on his feet. "You eat. I've seen starving linebackers who couldn't plow through fries like that. Something tells me you're hungrier than I am."

I thanked him when he came back with my refill, and tried not to laugh when he dripped barbecue sauce down the front of his pumpkin-orange polo before he'd taken two bites of his food.

"Blot it, don't swipe at it," I said when he made the stain twice as big trying to get it off.

"Oops. Oh well. I see shirt shopping in my future."

"Spray some hairspray on it and let it sit," I said. "It's my mom's cure-all for stains and it's never failed me."

He raised a skeptical eyebrow, then shrugged.

"Who am I to argue with mom?" He washed the beef ribs down with a swig of Corona. "Speaking of your mom, you said yesterday she had breast cancer. Is she okay now?"

I nodded. "She's been in remission for almost four years. Five is the benchmark. She's pretty amazing."

The conversation drifted into a natural lull as we ate, and my thoughts strayed to my mother, and how proud I was of her. Not many women would have been able to do the things she'd done, leaving California the day after she graduated high school with her seven-month-old in the backseat of the car that held all her worldly possessions, and stopping in Texas because the bluebonnets were the prettiest thing she'd ever seen. She'd raised me by herself after my grandparents disowned her. Her pregnancy, and subsequent refusal to marry her boyfriend, embarrassed them at their Hollywood cocktail parties.

She fussed over me and I tried to make her proud. We had danced around our cozy living room like Publisher's Clearinghouse had arrived with a giant cardboard check the day my acceptance from Syracuse came.

I'd been determined to go, thousands of dollars in student loan debt be damned. Then the week before I'd turned eighteen, my absentee grandparents had dropped the bombshell of all bombshells. A courier arrived with a fat yellow envelope full of legal papers from a firm in Malibu telling me I had a college fund.

The smaller envelope that fell out of the paperwork had "Lila" written in intricate calligraphy, and my mom had tears in her eyes by the time she finished reading the letter.

Her mother wrote an apology, explaining there were no strings attached to the gift and they hoped I'd use it well. I'd read it so many times in the last ten years, I had to tape it back together when the paper gave from being folded and unfolded over and over. I'd often picked up the phone and started to dial the number in the letter, always hanging up before I pushed the last button. Ten years and a free education later, and I still wasn't sure if I could forgive them for not wanting me. Or for punishing my mother for so many years just because I existed.

"Did you find out anything more about what happened to your drug dealers from yesterday?" Parker's voice snapped me out of my reverie and I tore a paper towel from the roll on the table and wiped my mouth.

"I didn't even have time to ask," I said. "But the good news is, neither did anyone else. I'll check Monday, though."

"Your job is never dull, huh?" He spun his empty beer bottle back and forth between sure hands.

"Very rarely. Though it's usually not quite this insane, either. I miss my happy medium."

We chatted about nothing in particular for another half hour. As the sun sank in the western sky, I told him goodnight and slid behind the wheel of my car, flipping my scanner on and sighing in relief when I heard nothing but normal Saturday night traffic cop chatter. Thank God. I wanted nothing more than to sleep until Monday.

By the time I tended to my Pomeranian, Darcy, and crawled under the duvet, my thoughts were tangling again, my headache threatening to return. Charlie. Shelby. Dead people in a boat accident nobody could explain. Dead drug dealers nobody robbed. They all fell together in a hopeless jumble, making my brain hurt. I wondered, as I closed my eyes, if the odd cast of characters heaped together in my head would create weird dreams. If they did, I didn't remember them by morning.

My phone was ringing when I got to my desk on Monday. I stared at it for half a second, my innate inability to ignore a ringing telephone battling with the certainty that answering it would make me later for the meeting.

"Clarke," I sighed, picking it up. "Can I help you?"

"Nichelle?" The voice that came through the line was so hesitant I almost didn't recognize it as belonging to my narcotics sergeant.

"Mike? Is that you?" Maybe Sorrel had something on the dope dealers. I dug in my bag for a pen, flipping over a press release and scribbling Mike's name and the date across the top. "What can I do for you?"

"I, uh, I need to talk to you. There's some stuff I think, well, you might be interested in." He sighed. "Not might. Will. It's big. Can you meet me for coffee?"

"Sure." Curiosity made it difficult to keep my voice even. I knew Sorrel fairly well, and he didn't sound like himself. "Meet me at Thompson's in twenty minutes?"

"NO!" I moved the phone away from my head, but it was too late. His Greek heritage came with a booming voice that left my ear ringing. "I'd rather go someplace out of the way. Can you meet me at the Starbucks in Colonial Heights in forty-five minutes?"

Agreeing, I cradled the phone wondering what was all the way out in Colonial Heights.

I hitched my bag back onto my shoulder, the desire to avoid snapping a heel on my newish, strappy red Manolos the only thing keeping me from breaking into a sprint on the way to the garage.

CHAPTER SIX

I SIPPED my white chocolate mocha while I waited for Sorrel, recalling my first meeting with him. After I'd managed to get past my rookie jitters and through the interview about the biggest drug bust in department history, my first crack at covering cops had come out pretty good. Good enough, at least, to earn Sorrel's respect and trust. And leave my mind racing, a half-dozen years and hundreds of stories later, through possible explanations for his peculiar call.

Just as I was digging in my bag for my phone, I saw his unmarked cruiser turn into the lot. He pulled a briefcase out of the passenger seat and ambled toward the door. Mike was about as tall as I was, and twenty years of chasing bad guys kept him in good shape. He had broad shoulders, but a wiry build, and with his dark coloring and clean-shaven face, he cut a striking figure in his pressed chinos and camel-colored blazer.

I waved unobtrusively from my post in the corner. He picked up his coffee and sat down in the simple wooden chair across from me, pulling a file folder out of the handsome black leather case and pushing it across the shiny round table.

"We have missing evidence," he said.

"Missing evidence?" I echoed as I reached for the file. "From where?"

I scanned the page on top and gasped, casting a quick glance around and ducking my head even though no one was paying attention to us. I looked at Mike, my eyes wide.

"The drugs and the money? How the hell does that even happen?"

He shrugged. "I wish I could tell you."

I turned back to the file. Between my two murdered drug dealers, the police department had confiscated nearly four hundred thousand dollars in cash and a veritable truckload of various narcotics, the last of which had been cataloged on Friday afternoon. It should've stayed in the PD's evidence lock-up until after the killer's trial, when the drugs would have been incinerated in a sealed steel drum, and the cash given to the city to subsidize the cost of the narcotics unit. But that morning when Mike went down to look at one of the prescription bottles from the second murder scene, he'd discovered it was all gone.

"Did someone break into the evidence locker over the weekend?" I asked the obvious question first, but I knew I would've already heard about it if that were true.

Mike shook his head. "No. This thief had clearance. A cop, or someone from the CA's office, maybe."

In Virginia, prosecutors are known as commonwealth's attorneys instead of district attorneys, a quirk I'd finally gotten used to.

I nodded as I scribbled, and he continued.

"There was no sign of forced entry."

My mind colored some of those blank pieces in my drug dealer puzzle with stolen evidence and the possibility of crooked cops. Hot damn. Talk about a sexy news story.

"Are you sure, Mike?" I exploded in a loud whisper. "That's...wow."

He just nodded.

"How much can I have on the record?"

"That depends on how you feel about using unnamed sources. I don't want it attributed to me, at least not now. If it's someone in the department, it could get ugly."

I flipped through the file and nodded. "This corroborates what you said. I have no problem citing it as 'a police department source.'"

I paused and studied him for a minute, taking a longer drink of my cooling latte.

"This is huge. And it's not going to make the department look so good," I said. Mike was nothing if not loyal. "I'm grateful to be sitting here, but why bring me this? Why not keep it quiet?"

He exhaled slowly and toyed with his keys. "Because this is just flat-ass wrong, any way you look at it," he said finally. "You're my insurance it's not going to disappear. While I don't relish the idea of the department being dragged through the mud, I also know if I don't say something, this may never go anywhere. It happens. Shit like this goes on and it just gets swept under the rug. I love my job, Nichelle, but I hate how I've felt about it the past couple of hours. I've known some of the guys I work with for more than twenty years, and now I'm looking at everyone like they're a suspect."

"Maybe it wasn't a cop," I offered. "Didn't you say something about the CA's office?"

"If they can tie it to a lawyer, they will. Keeping the department's collective halo shiny is priority one." He tapped the file. "The only prosecutor who signed in this weekend came in yesterday afternoon. The major crimes unit is picking him up for questioning, but if someone's going to steal evidence, they probably wouldn't sign the log at the desk."

"Doesn't everyone have to do that?"

"I don't," Mike said. "Anyone my rank or better can go in and out at will. Since we go in the most, it simplifies the record keeping."

"Was there anything else missing?"

"I don't know. The inventory will take a while. A few days at least."

I nodded. "Did you talk to internal affairs?"

"Yeah, right before I called you. I've never done that before. I feel like I'm tattling to the teacher on the playground."

I jotted a note to call the captain of internal affairs, wondering if he'd tell me anything. A lock of hair escaped the clip at the nape of my neck, and I pushed it behind my ear as I looked back up at Mike and reached for the file folder. "Can I take this with me?"

"What the hell?" He pushed it toward me. "If I'm going to risk my badge to get a story in the newspaper, I might as well not half-ass it."

"What's the use in that?" I winked. "I'll keep it safe."

"Just make sure you keep you safe, too." Mike drummed his fingers on the table. "You read about this happening in other places, but you never think it will happen in your own backyard, you know? I see you're itching to get to your keyboard, Nichelle, and I want you guys to blast this all over the front page. I wouldn't be here if I didn't. It'll force the brass to figure out who did it and fire their sorry ass. But be careful. If this was a cop, they're into something very serious. Something they could go to prison for. And going to prison is pretty much every cop's worst nightmare."

The solemn look in his dark eyes sent such a chill through me, I actually shivered.

"I'm not trying to scare you. But you should know what you're getting into."

"I'll be careful," I promised, shoving the folder and my notebook into my bag and hooking it over my shoulder as I stood. "Thanks, Mike. I appreciate the call. I owe you one."

"I guess that depends on how you look at it," he said, picking up his briefcase and moving toward the door. "You get a headline, I get to sleep at night. Win-win. But remember this next time you're bugging me about something I don't want to tell you, huh?"

"I'm sure I won't," I said as I walked through the door he held open. "But you'll remind me."

The thought of an exclusive put a bounce in my step as I crossed the parking lot, already stringing my lead together in my head. Mike had his pick of reporters to meet with that morning, but he called me. Boy, was Charlie going to be pissed. The rush of warmth at the thought wasn't even iced over by the memory of his parting words.

Kicking the door of the car open before I'd even put it in park when I got back to work, I made a beeline for Bob's office, stopping short and grumbling when his door was closed. Bob's door was never closed, and this was a hell of an irritating time for it to be that way. I went to my desk to wait, figuring maybe I could get more information before I talked to him.

My only experience with Captain Simmons at internal affairs had been pleasant enough, but it had also been a relatively minor case of an officer being arrested for drunk driving, so I wasn't sure what kind of reception I'd get when I dialed police headquarters and asked for him.

Voicemail. I rattled off a quick message with my deadline time and a plea for him to return my call, which I wasn't at all sure he'd do. But I'd tried. If he didn't call back, I could stick a "didn't return a call seeking comment" into my story.

I blew a raspberry at nothing in particular as I put the phone down and picked up my pen, tapping it on the desk. So many questions. And answers had been hard to come by lately. I was beginning to miss the simplicity of Barbie and Ken and the gruesome homicide trial.

Popping halfway to my feet, I looked at Bob's door. Open. I grabbed my folders, half-running to his office.

"Chief? Did you get my message? Wait 'til you hear what I've got!"

"I didn't have time to check my messages this morning," he said, his bushy brows knit together in a glare that would've been scary any other day. "I had a meeting. That you didn't bother to show up for. The staff meeting is mandatory for the crime reporter, Nichelle. You know that."

"But I did call," I protested. "I had an interview, and you're going to be glad I went. I've got an honest-to-God exclusive. And it's fabulous." I took a deep breath and launched into the story. I may not have inhaled again before I finished.

Bob leaned forward in his seat. The more I talked, the faster he nodded, and though his brow furrowed when I got to the part where "my source" warned me to be careful, he certainly didn't look pissed anymore by the time I sat back in my chair and grinned.

"So, what do you think? It's great, right? And no one else will have it."

"Holy shit, kid. Nice work. But slow down. How much do you trust your source?"

"Implicitly. I have a copy of the file on the missing evidence right here, and I already called internal affairs. Maybe they'll give me confirmation."

"Don't bet on it," Bob said, opening the file as soon as I handed it to him. "But this looks pretty solid. And it's damned fabulous, all right. You're sure no one else has it?"

"No one," I said. "My source assured me I was the only reporter he talked to."

"Then we'll hold the web version for morning and release it when the papers hit the racks," he said, his face wrinkling up in a grin. "I need it by three. Legal will want to check it, I'm sure."

I nodded and started to get to my feet.

"One more thing," he said.

I stared at him blankly. What? I had solid information. It was a huge story. I eyed the Pulitzer on his wall again. Most of the time I wasn't terribly interested in contests or awards for my work.But that one was different.

"Nicey," Bob spoke slowly and his expression was serious. "You're a good reporter, but you're young. I know the only way for you to get experience is to go get the story, but watch yourself. If you're dealing with crooked cops, then everyone you talk to at the PD is a suspect. I want the story. It's a great story. But you just mind how you handle yourself."

"There's no reason for you to worry." I smiled my most reassuring smile. "Really. I think my guy was being a little dramatic."

"I'm not convinced of that." Bob gave me an age-begets-wisdom look. "There are dangerous people out there, kid. You might not want to think about the things they're capable of doing, but they can be pretty horrible."

I held his gaze for a moment. He wanted the exclusive, and I didn't want some misguided concern for me to trump that desire.

I looked back at the Pulitzer. I knew he had won enough awards in his career to fill a good-sized closet, which was where I suspected the rest of them lived.

"Why do you keep that on the wall in here?" I asked him, gesturing to the frame.

"The Pulitzer?" He looked confused. "Well, because it's the one I'm the most proud of. I think I actually did something special to earn it."

"Why?"

"Because that series was great," he said softly. "There were civil rights activists who said my stories helped heal wounds that festered here for more than a century. I'm still proud of that."

"Didn't you tell me the KKK threatened you while you worked on that series?"

Bob's mouth tightened into a thin line.

"Nicey." He sighed. "This is different."

"Why? Because you don't mind putting yourself in danger, or because I'm a woman?"

He flinched.

"That's not fair," he said. "It was a different situation. The crackpots I dealt with weren't armed public officials who stood to lose everything because of what I was writing."

"But they threatened your life," I pressed. "No one has done that to me, and besides, I've already called internal affairs, so it's not like my source is the only person at the PD who knows I know about this."

Bob was quiet for a long moment, bending his head and massaging both temples. He took a deep breath before he looked up.

"It is one hell of a sexy lead, isn't it? Go get it. Just be careful. And get it to me by three in case it needs shoring up."

I leaped out of my chair and managed to resist the impulse to pump my fist in the air. Grinning instead, I pushed Mike's warning to the back of my mind and locked it there.

"You'll have it," I said. "This is going to be huge, Bob. I can feel it."

"Three o'clock," he repeated.

"Not a second past," I promised over my shoulder, already on my way back to my desk to see if Captain Simmons returned my call.

Sprinting the last few steps, I grabbed the ringing phone, my breathlessness more from excitement than exertion.

"Hi, sweetie, I'm sorry to call you at work." My mom's voice deflated my enthusiasm. "You didn't call me this weekend. Is everything all right?"

"Mom?" I hastened to cover up the disappointment in my tone. "Hey! How are you?"

"I'm fine. Tired. But fine. You don't sound happy to hear from me. Are you very busy today?"

"I am, but I have a minute. I'm waiting for a call, though, so if I hang up on you, don't take it personally."

"Noted." She laughed. "What are you working on? There was something yesterday about a boating accident over the weekend? I didn't read it yet, but it looked like a sad story."

"It is. The guys who died were all my age or younger. Not a fun weekend. I'm sorry I didn't call you yesterday. I was at the accident scene until ridiculous-thirty on Friday night, and then back here all day Saturday, and I stayed home with Darcy and tried to relax yesterday."

"I see." Her tone brightened. "Speaking of relaxing, I went to the pool for the first time in years yesterday, and guess who I bumped into?"

"A handsome doctor who swept you off your flip flops?"

"Not quite." I could hear the smile in her voice. "But I did have a nice chat with Rhonda Miller."

"Aw, really?" It was entirely possible that I missed Kyle's family more than I actually missed him. His parents were among the sweetest people I'd ever met. "How is she?"

"She's doing really well. And so is Kyle. He's somewhere up there, actually. She said he followed his dad into law enforcement and he's in Virginia working on a case."

"I'll be damned," I said, tapping a pen on the desk and wondering how to steer the conversation away from my old boyfriend before she asked me to look him up. There were a variety of reasons why I had no interest in doing that, none of which I wanted to discuss right then. "Small world. Hey, Jenna says to tell you hello."

"Wow, that might be the worst segue ever," she said. "But all right. I won't push it. Just wanted you to know. Give Jenna my love. How is she?"

"She's great. Carson isn't nursing anymore, so she had her first margaritas in two years at girls' night Friday. Then she went with me to the accident scene at the river, which she was very excited about until we got there and she got an eyeful of why reporting isn't always as much fun as it looks in the movies."

"Ah." My mother fell silent for a minute. "I can sympathize with that. I'm happy you love your job, but I don't think I would care to see it for myself. I read your stories and I can't imagine how you stand dealing with that day after day and stay off medication…"

She trailed off and when she spoke again she sounded slightly alarmed.

"Nicey, you're not on medication, are you?" she asked.

"Not unless you count vitamins." I laughed. "Contrary to popular belief, my job does not generally depress me. It's usually pretty exciting. I have a story going out today I'm very excited about, in fact."

"About what?"

"All sorts of intrigue at the police department this morning," I said, refusing to elaborate any further. "You'll have to read it like everyone else."

"I gave you life, and you won't even tell me what you're working on," she lamented. She sounded so convincingly pitiful, I almost felt bad, but then she laughed and I could picture the mischief flashing in her blue eyes.

"I love you, mom," I said, my voice thickening slightly. Growing up the only child of an "I was an attachment parent before attachment parenting was cool" single mom definitely made for a different dynamic. I missed her. And I lived in constant fear of her cancer returning. "Are you okay? Why are you tired?"

"I love you, too, kid. I'm fine. You stop worrying about me. I'm a pretty tough chick. I've just been busy at the shop, that's all." She'd expanded her flower shop into a one-stop wedding boutique after she'd recovered from the mastectomy. She loved it, which I found hilarious given that my mother's opinion of marriage echoed the regard most women hold for sandals worn over socks: almost always good for a laugh and almost never a good idea. No wonder I had issues with my love life. "Have a better week. And call your mother more often."

"Yes, ma'am."

I hung up the phone and shoved the stray lock of hair behind my ear again before I unfastened the clip and twisted all of my hair back up into it, my thoughts still on my mom.

The ringing phone jerked me back to the present. I picked it up and tilted my head to brace the receiver against my shoulder as I reached for a pen and paper with both hands.

"Miss Clarke, this is Don Simmons at the Richmond PD." A smooth, deep voice came through the line and my pulse quickened.

"Captain! I won't take up too much of your time today," I said. "I'm working on a story about the missing evidence from the Southside dealer murders."

"So you said in your message," Simmons said. "Do you mind if I ask you how you know about that?"

"I do, actually." So that's why he'd returned my call. "I can't reveal my source on this story. But I am wondering if you have any comment on your investigation."

"The situation is being investigated by internal affairs for possible officer involvement, but we don't know anything definitive yet," he said a little stiffly.

Strike one.

"Captain, I know you're frustrated. I can imagine your job is pretty stressful, and I'm really not trying to make it worse." If the sympathy plea had worked on Agent Starnes, it could work on anyone. "I'm just trying to do mine, that's all."

Silence. I held my tongue, knowing this game well: he who speaks first loses.

Simmons hauled in a deep breath. "I can appreciate that, ma'am, but I need you to understand this is a very sensitive matter."

Strike two. I had one tactic left.

"Yes, but the taxpayers who pay your salary have a right to know what's going on. I'm not the only person in town who thinks so, or I wouldn't know about it in the first place."

More crickets. Another long breath.

"Look, lady," he said. "This has everybody upstairs convinced the four horsemen are on their way or some shit, pardon my French. I'm sorry—no comment."

A swing and a miss, and the two most dreaded words in the English language for the out. I thanked Simmons for his time and hung up, tapping the nail of my index finger on the handset. He confirmed the theft, but I wanted more than that. Though given his position, I supposed I should be thankful he'd even called back.

I glanced at the file Mike gave me. Gavin Neal. The attorney who'd been in the evidence room on Sunday. Assuming he wasn't busy stashing four hundred thousand dollars in drug money, maybe he'd talk to me. Lawyers were generally easier to pump for quotes than cops.

I dialed the CA's office and found Neal in the robot-voiced directory. And got his voicemail. Reeling off my name and phone number, I wondered if my aversion to checking messages stemmed from having to leave people so many of them.

I cradled the phone and stared at the log from the evidence locker. The longer I stared, the fuzzier the lines became, until something finally jumped out at me. Neal's signature was scribbled hastily. So hastily, someone went back and printed his name next to the scrawl. If I were planning to make off with half a million dollars, I'd be in a hurry, too.

I wondered if my friend DonnaJo, who was also a prosecutor, might be able to help me track down Neal before deadline. I called her cell and dispensed with the pleasantries quickly, asking if she knew him.

"He's one of our best attorneys, Nichelle," she said. "A great guy, and a damn smart lawyer. Very charismatic—juries love him. I just cannot believe this rumor that he's a crook. Anyone who knows this man knows he's not a thief."

My eyebrows went up.

"Jump to conclusions much, counselor?" Not that I hadn't, but she seemed pretty defensive. "I think they just wanted to question him."

"Which would be no big deal, if he were around to question. The grapevine has it the cops went to pick him up and his wife reported him missing. He never went home after he went to the PD yesterday. I hear she's pretty freaked. Their kid has some sort of medical condition, so Gavin never misses her calls."

My thoughts careened in several directions at once. Part of what I loved about covering crime were the puzzles embedded in the stories, but this one was getting more complicated than the three-dimensional Capitol Building my mom sent for my last birthday. It had frustrated me to the brink of throwing it out half-finished, and I'd never attempted another.

Now the lawyer was missing? Did a family man with a successful career really take off with hundreds of thousands of dollars in evidence and not even tell his wife? Or was the wife lying?

Medical condition meant medical bills. And prosecuting isn't where the big bucks are in the legal game. Sounded like a motive to me.

I cleared my throat.

"Hey, DonnaJo," I said, running a finger over the evidence locker sign-in. "Do you have any idea why Neal would have been at the PD on a Sunday?"

"I go up there sometimes, if there's evidence I want to look at again when I'm prepping for court," she said.

"How long would it take you to get me a list of the cases he's working on?" I asked. "The PD isn't talking, and I want this for my piece today."

"About an hour. I have a hearing."

"Can you also see if there's anyone he put in prison who's gotten out recently?"

"Sure. It might take a bit longer, but I'll send you both. If you're going to run them, they didn't come from me, though."

"No worries. The courthouse fairy brought them to me."

I thanked her and hung up.

Glancing toward Bob's door, I got up to go ask if he wanted a separate piece on the attorney by way of the soda machine. I decided as I ambled along, the condensation from my Coke bottle mingling with the sweat breaking out on my hands, that my best bet was to lay out the facts for him as lightly as I could, and ask him if he thought the attorney's disappearance warranted its own headline. Writing about a lawyer, I didn't want to get in hot water with legal for tying him to the missing evidence if there was a reason I shouldn't.

I kept my eyes on the mottled brown carpet as I walked through Bob's door, my nerves overriding my manners and making the knock more cursory than usual. Perching on the edge of my seat, I began listing the latest developments in my story before I looked at my editor, who was slumped over in his chair, barely breathing.

CHAPTER SEVEN

"Bob!" I knocked over the wastebasket and pushed a tape dispenser and a bottle of white-out off the desk dragging Bob's heft from the chair, which crashed into the wall when I kicked at the casters under it to get it out of the way.

Once he was on his back on the floor, I knelt and popped his cheek with my palm, rapid-fire style.

"Bob!" I shouted, my nose inches from his. My hand left a red mark on his otherwise bloodless skin.

He didn't move, his breathing still shallow.

"Help!" I turned my head in the general direction of the door I couldn't really see from behind the desk.

"HEY!" I bellowed in my best press conference voice. "In Bob's office. Someone help! We need an ambulance!" Damn. Mid-morning on a Monday was not the best time to find newsroom staff in the office.

"Nichelle?" Shelby's voice came from near the doorway.

"Shelby, thank God." I'd have been glad to see Adolf Hitler himself right then if he knew how to call the paramedics. "Over here, behind the desk.

"Call 9-1-1. Then go get someone who can help with CPR, just in case he stops breathing." I barked the orders automatically, having been through this more than once when my mom was weak from her chemo.

For the first time ever, Shelby didn't argue with me or offer a smartass retort. She gaped at Bob for a split second and then snatched up the phone, giving the operator the *Telegraph* building's address before she sprinted out into the newsroom.

She returned shortly, hauling Eunice behind her.

"Christ on a Cracker, what's going on in here?" Eunice's golden brown eyes widened as they studied Bob, and she laid a hand on my shoulder. "Shelby said you needed help with CPR, but he's breathing."

"I just want to make sure it stays that way," I said, stroking Bob's hand and meeting Eunice's gaze as she gripped the edge of Bob's desk and eased herself onto the floor next to his legs. "His pulse is thready. His breathing is getting worse. Shelby called an ambulance. This looks like a cardiac something-or-other. Or maybe a stroke."

I pinched my eyes shut, actually praying for the heart attack. People survived them every day. A stroke...well, what that might do to my quick-witted editor was too horrible to contemplate.

"Don't you worry, sugar. The Good Lord don't want Bob up there giving Him orders. It'll be just fine." Eunice reached out and patted my knee as I laid my fingers over Bob's carotid artery and stared at my Timex.

"Hang on, chief," I whispered. "The cavalry's on its way."

Just then, shouting from the newsroom heralded the paramedics' arrival. They brought a small gang of onlookers from our floor, comprised of section editors and copy desk folks. Most of the people in the building continued about their Monday with no idea that our resident journalistic legend needed medical attention, sprawled on carpet that still stank faintly of cigarettes from the days when chain-smoking and reporting went together like champagne and straw-berries.

I took two steps backward, willing away the pricking in the backs of my eyes that meant tears were coming.

"He'll be fine," I said, my nails digging into my palm. "He'll be just fine." A couple of deep breaths dispelled the waterworks.

Shelby whimpered, and I looked around to thank her for her help and found her burying her face in the managing editor's shirtfront, sniffling as he patted her back.

"Are you all right, sugar?" Eunice asked me, watching the medics lift our boss onto a gurney.

"He was slumped in the chair when I came in." I cleared my throat. "I got him onto the floor so his airway would be less constricted."

"Great land of plenty." She folded her arms over her soft chest and shook her head. "I just saw him at the meeting. He was fine."

"Obviously not," I said. "But he will be. He has to be."

The medics started for the door.

"What do you think?" I asked the one closest to me.

"Looks like a heart attack. I can't say anything for sure, though," she said, not looking up from her watch on Bob's heart rate and oxygen level. "We're taking him to St. Vincent's. Has anyone called his family?"

"He doesn't really have one," Eunice said. "His wife's been gone three years now, and he doesn't have any children."

Both medics nodded as they rolled Bob, still unconscious, through the onlookers.

I closed my eyes and took a deep breath. He did, too, have a family. Just like me, the *Telegraph* was his family. And I'd be damned if he was going to wake up in the hospital alone. I stepped toward the door and Eunice put a hand on my back.

"You going to watch after him, sugar?"

I turned slightly and smiled, blinking at the threatening tears again.

"We're his family." I said simply.

She wrapped my left hand in her arthritis-twisted fingers and nodded. "You're damned right we are. Give him our love when he comes to. And let me know if you need me to do anything."

I packed up my things and turned into the hospital parking lot less than ten minutes later.

I had grown up without a father or a grandfather, and I'd always thought I didn't need either in my life. Then I came to Richmond with no job and no friends, and Bob hired me. After his wife died, he found himself as orphaned and out of place as I sometimes still felt. That kinship, coupled with our fondness for each other, had forged a bond as strong as one shared by any blood relatives. Sure, he gave me hell about deadlines and scoops, but that was his job. I knew he liked me, and there wasn't much I wouldn't do for him.

I left the car at the curb, tow away zone signs be damned, and rushed through the sliding glass doors, accosting the first white coat I saw.

"You have to check in with the front desk before you can see him," the doctor said, raising an eyebrow in the direction of the fingers I'd curled around his arm. I ignored the look, but thanked him over my shoulder as I bolted for the desk.

I tried my best to be patient with the harried clerk, but it seemed to take hours for her to so much as glance in my direction, and when she finally did, she flashed a halfhearted smile that looked out of place on her perky face. "I'll be right with you."

I fidgeted as I waited, my thoughts running to the weeks I'd spent at Parkland Memorial with my mom. But she was fine now. Making bridal dreams come true every day. Bob would be back to glaring at my tardiness soon enough. I refused to entertain another option.

By the time the clerk began typing information into the computer for the fifth person who'd walked up after me, I was over polite waiting. Glancing around at a roomful of people who were caught up in their own problems and paying me absolutely no mind, I edged to the end of the long counter and slid a black clipboard off the edge of it, then turned toward the doors to the treatment area.

Bob shared a theory with me once that clipboards are the most commanding of office supplies, instantly lending an air of authority to anyone carrying them.

"I hope you're right, chief," I muttered, flattening myself against the wall outside the secured double doors.

When a tiny redheaded woman carrying a sleepy toddler came out,

I slipped inside. Straightening my shoulders and ramrodding my spine, I kept my eyes on the clipboard and walked to the back edge of the nurse's station. A dozen or so women and men in scrubs milled about, talking. Hanging near the corner, mostly out of sight, I scanned the whiteboard of patients' last names, doctors, and room numbers. Jeffers, no doctor name, room twelve.

White-knuckling the clipboard, I strode down the hallway, not making eye contact with anyone. And it worked. Either Bob was right about the power of the clipboard, or everyone was too busy to notice me, but I rounded the corner into his room without so much as an eyelash batted in my direction.

Once inside, I stopped so suddenly I teetered forward on my stilettos. Bob looked frail, half-reclined in the narrow bed, a myriad of tubes and wires tethering him to four different machines. So much like my mom had after her mastectomy, it knocked the wind out of me.

I pulled in a long breath and looked closer. The heart monitor's beeping was reassuringly steady, and Bob's chest rose and fell in a much deeper, more even pattern than it had before.

I stepped to the side of the bed, grasping his big hand in both of mine, and Bob opened his eyes.

"Nicey?" He blinked and looked around, the confusion obvious on his face. But that face was symmetrical, his words clear. "What the hell?"

"They think it was a heart attack," I pasted a smile on my face and tried my best to sound breezy, thanking God silently for the lack of stroke markers. "We tried to tell the paramedics that we give you those every day around deadline, but they insisted you come see a doctor."

Bob laughed and then winced.

"Shit. That hurts. No more wisecracks," he said.

"Yes, sir." I saluted and clicked my heels together and he smiled.

"A heart attack, huh?" Bob surveyed the equipment in the room. "Well, hell. You want to fill me in?"

"I went to tell you about my latest hot scoop and found you passed out in your office," I said. "I pulled you out of the chair, screamed for help, the paramedics came. And here we are."

"Thanks, kid." Bob half-smiled at me. "I owe you one."

"Eh. Just keep ignoring my tardiness so I can keep up with my workouts, and we'll call it even."

"Done." His color was coming back, at least a little. The monitor kept up its steady rhythm, and I smiled.

"Speaking of tardiness, my story's going to be late if I don't start typing soon," I said. "What time is it?"

Bob pointed to the clock on the wall before he read it to me. "When the big hand is on the six and the little one is just past the one like that, it's one-thirty. You find out anything from the internal affairs guy?"

I poked my tongue out at him.

"Smartass comments mean you must be feeling better." I planted myself in a chair in the corner where I could keep an eye on him before I reached for my laptop. "Internal affairs was less than forth-coming. Lucky for me, I have a girlfriend at the CA's office. Guess what? That prosecutor who signed in to the evidence locker yesterday didn't go home last night."

Bob grunted. When I looked at him, his brows were knitted together over his closed eyes.

"Really?" He sounded a little less tired. One of the machines next to the bed beeped, and I jumped.

"Don't go getting too excited about that, chief." I smiled. "I wouldn't want to have to cut you out of the loop."

Bob smiled, his eyes still closed. "I wouldn't know what to do with myself if I was ever out of the loop," he said. "I am the loop."

"Truer words may have never been spoken." I opened a blank document. "And we're glad to still have you around."

"I'm too stubborn to die," Bob said, and his tone was so genial that I burst out laughing.

"I stand corrected," I said. "I think that might be the truest thing ever said."

"Get back to work." He tried his hardest to sound gruff. "Your copy isn't going to write itself, is it?"

"No, but I'm going to write it from this lovely little beige room where I can keep an eye on you," I said. "I'm not leaving until I talk to a doctor."

"You don't have to stay here," Bob began, and I raised a palm in his direction.

"Don't even try it, chief. Have laptop and cell phone, will travel. Eunice and everyone else send their love."

He eyeballed me for a long minute and then seemed to give in, muttering about overreacting as he closed his eyes. I turned my attention back to the blinking cursor on my screen and decided for myself to mention the missing CA in my evidence piece, and try to get more information before I devoted a whole story to his whereabouts. If I watched the wording, I probably wouldn't get an ass-chewing from legal. As far as I knew, I was the only reporter in town who knew the evidence was gone, and I might be the only one who knew the lawyer was gone, too.

I grabbed my phone and checked my email. The courthouse fairy had landed, and though the recent parole rosters didn't show any of Neal's bad guys, he did have a murder case scheduled to open Wednesday. It was just a simple domestic dispute gone very wrong, but the weapon was probably in the evidence room, assuming they'd found it.

The question became, then, was the trial the reason for his presence at police headquarters on Sunday, or was it a good excuse?

"Hell if I know," I mumbled, thinking about what Mike said about the department's halo. "But I'm going to find out."

Bob began to snore softly as I started to type.

A search for suspects turned inward Monday for Richmond police after more than $600,000 in cash and street-valued narcotics disappeared from police headquarters over the weekend.

Documents show the last of the evidence in question was cataloged Friday afternoon. Monday morning, it was nowhere to be found, a confidential police department source said.

Also missing on Monday was Assistant Commonwealth Attorney Gavin Neal, who, with a murder trial scheduled to open Wednesday, was one of the last people to sign into the police evidence locker. An official who asked to remain unnamed said Neal was being sought for questioning about the theft.

I stopped there and picked up my phone again. As soon as I was outside, I dialed the PD and launched into a preemptive apology when I heard Aaron's voice. "I'm working on a story about the missing evidence in the drug dealer murders, and I have an unnamed source. It just occurred to me the internal affairs guys probably think it's you."

He chuckled. "Why yes, as a matter of fact they did. I'm not sure why they give two shits. The report is public information. I guess they figure they could have kept it out of the news if no one had tipped you off, since this wouldn't make the list of routine report subjects you people request. They're pissed about someone telling you. They checked the records on every phone line I have readily accessible, but they seemed satisfied when they saw I hadn't talked to you since Saturday."

I caught a movement out of the corner of my eye and was surprised to find a young, good-looking guy with cocoa skin and serious brown eyes staring at me from a bench on the other side of the sidewalk. He didn't look familiar. I smiled at him. He didn't return the smile, just kept staring.

I shifted my attention back to my phone call and repeated the apology.

"Good luck with that mess you're working on today," Aaron replied. "And don't worry about IAD. I can handle them, especially when I didn't actually tell you anything they don't want you to know. Though I'm dying to know who did. I have a list."

"Police department sources." I clicked my tongue. "I know you understand. That's why you're my favorite detective."

"And here I thought it was my boyish grin."

"Well, that goes without saying." I laughed. "Hey, speaking of 'us people,' has anyone else asked you about the missing prosecutor today? And what can you tell me about him?"

"How the hell do you know about that? I'm beginning to suspect

I'm not as great an information gateway as I thought." Aaron made a tsk-tsk noise, but he didn't sound even a little bothered. "They want to question him. His wife says he's disappeared. Missing persons is on it. That's all I got. And no, Charlie doesn't have it. Or at least, if she does, she didn't get it from me. But apparently you people have other ways into this place, so take it for what it's worth."

I looked back at the bench across from me as I thanked him and hung up, but the kid was gone. Shrugging off my curiosity, I dug my keys out of my pocket and walked down the short brick path to my car, which was still ticketless. Thank Heaven for small favors.

I parked it in the ER lot and hurried back inside, the sharp sound of my heels on the tile increasing in tempo when I saw Bob's door closed.

I had been booted from enough hospital rooms to know that meant the doctor had arrived, which meant my computer was captive for however long it took to examine my boss. I leaned against the wall and closed my eyes.

I didn't have to wait long.

"How is he?" I blurted, righting myself when the door swung open.

"He's going to be fine." The soft brown eyes behind the doctor's wire-rimmed glasses were just as kind as her smile. "I'm Doctor Schaefer. And you're...?"

"His daughter," I smiled, feeling no remorse about the lie. I knew she wouldn't talk to me if I wasn't family, and I was pretty sure I'd find myself tossed back out to the waiting room.

Dr. Schaefer didn't look much older than me, if she was older at all. About a head shorter and a little softer, she had a tidy chestnut bob and wore a pretty batik skirt and a violet top beneath her lab coat.

She flipped a page in Bob's chart. "I didn't see a mention of the family being here."

I kept the smile in place and offered a little shrug, holding her gaze until she returned the smile and let the page fall back into place. She shook my free hand and told me Bob had indeed had a heart attack, but a fairly mild one.

"He should make a full recovery," she said. "We're going to keep him here until tomorrow, or possibly Wednesday, but then he'll be able to go home and ease back into his regular routine. We have a few more tests yet to determine the exact cause of his episode and how to treat it best, but I'm confident he'll be fine."

"Is OD'ing on burgers and hot wings an actual diagnosis?" I grinned, her reassurance the happiest thing I'd heard in weeks. "I don't think he eats at home—well, pretty much ever, since his wife died."

"I see," she nodded. "So, your mother was the cook in the family?"

"My—" damn. I flinched. Not visibly, I hoped. "My stepmother. Yes, she was."

"Well, if you're in town, and you can, maybe you cook for him sometimes," she said. "If he keeps eating that much junk, he'll end up right back here, and we don't want that. He seems like a nice man, but I'd rather not see him again."

I thanked her and she flipped his chart closed and nodded. "I'm sure I'll see you around. Just have them page me if you have any questions."

I peeked into the room when she walked away and found it dark, my boss snoring again. Slipping my Manolos off, I tiptoed to the chair and picked up my laptop and my bag, then snuck back out. I'd just pulled the door closed and put my shoes back on when my stomach made one of the rudest noises I'd ever heard.

My nose wrinkled at the prospect of hospital cafeteria food, but I decided there had to be something prepackaged I could scarf down before I finished my story. I turned, intending to ask someone at the nurse's station how to get to the cafeteria, but my eyes locked on a still figure maybe twenty yards down the hallway.

Hunger forgotten, I stared at the same teenager I had seen outside. Because he was staring at me. Again.

Taking in the dingy jeans, over-washed wifebeater, and backwards Generals cap, I stood up straight and started walking, the click of my shoes on the tile echoing in the quiet corridor.

"Hi," I said when I reached Mr. Sullen Stare, extending my hand and smiling. "I'm Nichelle."

"You work at the newspaper." His voice was flat, his baby face made older by the somber expression and serious brown eyes.

I blanched, surprised he knew that. "I do. Have we met?"

"No, but I heard you give your name to someone when you were talking on the phone outside, and I remember it because you wrote that story about my brother," he said. "Darryl. Somebody shot him. And it wasn't a random gangbanger like the cops want folks to think. Darryl knew something he wasn't supposed to know."

CHAPTER EIGHT

DARRYL WRIGHT's little brother scuffed the toe of his worn sneaker over the marble floor in the waiting room, tracing the outline of the diamond-shaped inlay and staring past me at the coral-colored blooms on the azalea outside the picture window.

"Troy?" I leaned forward in my dusty blue armchair. "Do you want to tell me what you think happened to your brother?"

He nodded, and when he raised his head I saw tears in his eyes.

"His friend Noah was bad news. That's what happened to him. They worked for the same pusher. They knew something. Darryl said he had a big payday coming and Noah was helping him with it. And now they're both dead."

I inhaled sharply at the mention of the first victim, but I stayed quiet.

"I didn't pay any attention to him," Troy said, his voice dropping. "To be really honest, I was embarrassed I had a brother who was dealing, you know? I'm trying so hard to get a scholarship for college, and there's Darryl, looking for the easy way out of everything. Sitting on his butt waiting for the junkies to roll up. He liked to talk big, so when he started jawing about all this money he was getting because of some big secret he and Noah knew, I just blew it off. But it looks like he was telling the truth."

The borders on the puzzle in my head shifted to make room for the new pieces.

"You know he didn't even take drugs?"

"Isn't that unusual for a drug dealer?" I asked.

"Yeah." Troy sighed. "But that was Darryl. He didn't mind taking the money from the junkies, but he said the stuff did bad things to people. He saw it with the addicts he sold to. So he didn't ever get into it."

"And the other victim, Noah?" I asked. "How did Darryl know him?"

"I'm not sure. That guy moved up here from Florida about six or seven years ago, I guess. I don't remember how they met, I just remember him being around. I was in elementary school the first time I remember him being at our house.

"He was into drugs, and he thought it was really funny Darryl sold them when he didn't use them. He was always telling Darryl he sold more because he had more faith in his product. Then he got busted, and it was only a few weeks after that that Darryl got busted, too. They both ended up in the same prison, and then they got out within a few months of each other, too.

"It was like this guy Noah was Darryl's personal bad luck." His fingers flew to a gold cross that hung from a thick chain around his neck. "I won't ever know if my brother would have had a decent life if Noah hadn't been there. I'm not sorry he's dead."

Troy's chin dropped to his chest, and the tears made little wet spots on his jeans as they fell. They came faster for a few minutes, and I sat with him as he grieved. When he looked up, he drug the back of his hand across his face and took a deep, slow breath.

"Anyway, do you think there will be anything else in the paper about Darryl?"

"Yes, Troy, I do." I looked straight into his earnest eyes. "This story keeps getting curiouser, and I'm not about to let it go. I appreciate you talking to me. If I need to talk to you again, or if my guys at the police department have any questions for you, how do we get in touch with you?"

Troy jotted his phone number on the back of an old receipt he pulled out of his pocket and handed it to me. The vulnerability in his eyes when they met mine hadn't been there before, and it tugged at my heart.

"I miss him," he said. "I didn't know I would, but I really do."

I patted his hand.

"I'm not a cop, Troy, but it seems to me like there's a lot more to what happened to your brother than anyone's saying. Let me nose around and see what I can find out."

He nodded and excused himself to check on the friend he'd brought in with a broken ankle. I settled back in the chair and pulled out my laptop, my quest for food lost in the abyss of weirdness that had invaded my world since Friday.

The dealers had been friends. And not just any friends, but conspirator friends. I drew a blank when I tried to figure why their pusher would've left the drugs and money, though. A drug pusher would know the cops would confiscate that stuff.

Unless the pusher knew he'd get it back.

Oh, shit.

My little puzzle was suddenly a lot more interesting.

I dug out Mike's file on the missing evidence and scanned the sign-in sheet a fifth time.

Just cops. And Gavin Neal.

DonnaJo sounded pretty sure her friend Neal was innocent. Just like Mike sounded sure the cops he worked with couldn't be crooks. Everyone was a good guy, yet it looked more and more like someone was in bed with a drug pusher. Curiouser and curiouser indeed.

The clock caught my eye, and I grabbed for my notebook. I had a story to get out, and if Les Simpson was pinch hitting for Bob, I'd better not be late. Crooked cops and shady lawyers would just have to wait.

I flipped through my notes for the quotes I wanted as I added the rest of the information about the internal affairs investigation and the vanished prosecutor, throwing in Aaron's confirmation of Neal's disappearance.

I leaned my head back after I sent my story to Les, closing my eyes and letting my mind meander through everything that had happened since that morning. Bob, Mike, Parker, Aaron, and Troy whirled on the backs of my eyelids as if riding a souped-up carousel. I listened to the whisper of the doors sliding next to me as people came and went, punctuated by the occasional siren from the ambulance bay. It was nice to just sit still.

I jerked myself awake, disoriented as I rubbed my eyes with my fists and looked for a clock. Whoever decided twenty minutes of sleep was a "power nap" must've been recharging a pretty dim bulb, but it would have to do.

I found my phone and called Les to make sure he had my story.

"I wish you could've cited your source on the evidence thing. I haven't seen it anywhere else, and it'd be nice to have it from someone credible," he said. "And that bit about the lawyer was interesting, but kind of thin. I got a green light from legal, but I didn't see where you mentioned the family refused to comment. You did call his wife, didn't you?"

Wow. Les was usually hard to impress, but I figured the exclusive would make him happy since the paper's bottom line was his chief concern.

"First, my source is quite credible, I assure you. Second, I didn't see the point in calling his wife." I clenched the phone too hard and tried to keep the frustration out of my tone. I'm not sure I did a very good job. "If she knew where he was, wouldn't she have told the police?"

"If he's really the prime suspect in a robbery of the police department, do you think the police are going to be completely honest with you?"

I opened my mouth to fire back a reply and instead just sat there, realizing I didn't have a quippy answer for him. To tell the truth, I hadn't considered the possibility of anyone outright lying to me. I knew how to dig information out of the PD better than anyone in town, except sometimes Charlie, but Les was right. I assumed they told me the truth.

"I've worked with some of these guys for better than twenty years, and now I'm looking at everyone like they're a suspect," Mike had said.

What if he was right?

Shit, shit, shit.

"You know what, Les? I didn't think about it that way," I tugged at a strand of hair. Missing something on Bob's watch was bad enough, but at least Bob forgives the mistake so long as you learn from it. "You're right. This isn't exactly a typical burglary. Let me see if I can get ahold of her."

"You do that," he said. "For tomorrow."

"But— "

He cut the objection off before I even got going.

"But nothing. It's almost six o'clock, the front is already down in the pressroom, and I'm not spending tens of thousands of dollars we don't have because you fucked up, Clarke. Do it better tomorrow."

The clatter in my ear told me he was done talking to me.

"Well, you have yourself a nice evening, too, jackass." I muttered, dropping the phone back into my bag. Dammit.

I found no trace of Bob in the room where I'd left him, but a nurse with too-bright lipstick and a severe blond bun scrawled the number of his room in the cardiac unit on a purple post-it and pointed me to the elevators.

I heard the familiar arguing voices from CNN and scattered laughter from the hallway as I approached the open door to room three-two-three.

"I'm sorry, I thought I was in the cardiac ward," I teased as I peeked around the corner, "not the newsroom."

My grin widened when I saw Bob sitting up in the bed eating dinner, surrounded by half of our editorial staff. "You look like that nap did you a world of good."

He nodded, smiling back at me and looking much more like himself than I had seen him look all day.

"I think the drugs helped a little, too," he said, and my smile widened. Yep. He was going to be fine.

I leaned against the wall next to the door and sighed.

"I heard you found him." Parker separated himself from the crowd and gave me a worried once-over, running a hand through his hair. "I wish I'd been there. What happened?"

I recounted the story for the third time.

"Damn." He leaned a shoulder on the open door next to me, throwing an affectionate smile at Bob. "My dad had a heart attack three years ago. I'm glad you went in when you did. He looks great, all things considered, and this is the best cardiac unit in Virginia."

"The doctor said he should make a full recovery." I smiled. "Thank God. It scared the hell out of me. He's going to have to change his diet, but he can do that."

"If my dad can learn to like vegetables, anyone can." Parker grinned and stuck his hands in his pockets before his eyes went skipping between the people and the monitors. "What did you need to talk to him about it the middle of the morning, anyway? You didn't show for the staff meeting today."

"A story." I stepped to one side as the nurse poked her head in and shot the crowd of well-wishers the stink eye. "I had an interview that pre-empted the meeting. Though I wasn't aware you were keeping tabs on my attendance." I waved as people trickled out, leaving me, Parker, and Bob.

Smiling at Bob, I dropped into a chair and cast a glance around what resembled a fairly-tastefully-decorated bedroom, with soft blue walls accented with handsome navy and emerald borders. The bed was one of those hospital numbers I'd seen on TV shows. The kind with a headboard and footboard that tries to impersonate a real bed.

"You're really not going to tell me what you're working on?" Parker asked.

Bob opened his mouth and I shot him a look that clearly said "shut up."

"You can read all about it in the morning," I grinned at Parker. "And you don't even have to cough up the seventy-five cents."

Bob did the chuckle/wince thing again.

"I thought I said no more wisecracks."

"No wisecracks? Why don't you take away her shoes while you're at it, boss?" Parker shook his head, his eyes on me as he addressed Bob. "Good to have you talking to us again. You gave everyone a nice little jolt of adrenaline."

"Sorry." Bob grinned. "No game tonight?"

"Nope. I was at the ballpark trying to hunt up a story when all the excitement actually was in your office today. And you always say nothing newsworthy happens in there." Parker glanced at the heavy, stainless Tag Heuer on his wrist. "I have to run, though. Rest. Feel better. We'll miss you, but we'd like for you to, you know, not die."

Bob snorted. "Thanks."

Parker nodded as he backed out the door. "And holler if you need anything. I'm usually around somewhere, and I have certifiable experience. I made sure my mom got downtime when my dad was recovering."

Well, check you out, Captain Ego. I felt a grudging wave of respect for the second time since Friday as he disappeared with a wave. First he'd been gentle with Katie DeLuca down at the riverfront. Now Bob. I remembered the days after my mom's mastectomy all too well. Caring for an ailing parent was a damned sight harder than chasing crime stories or interviewing ballplayers.

Bob turned his attention to me. "I take it you got your story done?" he asked between bites of what appeared to be instant mashed potatoes.

"I did. Les wasn't happy with it, though. He's sort of a prick, you know that? Get better."

Bob chuckled. "He means well. I like to think, at least. He is completely unforgiving with the budget, though, and he doesn't miss much. What'd you do?"

"What'd I fail to do, actually. I didn't call the lawyer's wife."

"You trust your cops."

"And you think I shouldn't, either?" Damn. If they both thought I should've called her, then Charlie might have actually done it, if she knew Neal was missing. I reminded myself she hadn't called Aaron about it, and hoped she didn't have another source on the force. I'd seen nothing on the station's website at five-thirty, but there was always a chance they could be holding it for the eleven.

Bob shrugged. "Most of the time? I think you're okay. It's hard to cover a beat and not grow fond of the people, and I know you have your favorites down there. But on something like this, you have to question everything. No sense in losing sleep over it, but get it tomorrow."

"Consider it done."

"Anything new?" He sipped milk out of a carton so small I wondered if they'd swiped it from an elementary school cafeteria.

"Don't you need to be eating more than that?"

"This is what they brought." He shrugged. "What else did you find out?"

"Good stuff. Not on the lawyer, but on the drug dealer murders and the missing evidence. You'll never believe who I happened across this afternoon."

I talked while he finished what passed for dinner. He murmured or looked surprised occasionally, but didn't interrupt. When I sat back and sighed a few minutes later, he stared at me for a long moment and then cleared his throat.

"Damn, kiddo," he said. "This really is like chasing the white rabbit down the hole, isn't it? Things keep popping up, and one is more spectacular than the last. But listen to an old man and take some advice. You're getting into investigative territory, here. These are the stories that make careers, and the kind of thing that might get you noticed by the guys up at the *Post*."

My mouth popped into a little "o" at that and he smiled.

"I might be old, but I'm still pretty sharp. I know that's your brass ring, and I'm glad you want it. Makes you work harder. It's my job to talk you into passing it by if the time comes—and that could be sooner than later if you're really onto something here. But I'd feel like an asshole if I didn't warn you to watch yourself. Investigative reporting is a whole different beast. You'll be in as much real danger as a cop working a case would be. Drug pushers, crooked cops. These are not people you want to piss off."

"I am careful. I promise. But you wouldn't give that speech to one of the guys." I hated being treated like I wasn't as capable as a man, but it wasn't worth arguing with him about. I like it when guys open doors for me and kill bugs so I don't have to, and I figure the chivalrous impulse that makes them do those things also compels the good ones to be protective.

"I'm a big girl. And you know all those meetings you bitch about me being late for? I take body combat four days a week. So maybe it's them you should worry about."

"Judging from your stories, they have guns. And experience using them." He leaned back against the pillows and I noticed his coloring had faded a bit. "But remind me not to piss you off."

I changed the subject. He had no business being preoccupied with dangers lurking in my story.

"So, I was thinking today, after I met Troy," I began, trying to sound flippant. "And no matter what happens with this case, I might do a feature story on his family. A sort of 'growing up in the city' piece."

Bob didn't open his eyes as he shook his head. "A feature? Do you even remember how to write one?"

"Of course I do."

"I didn't say you couldn't. I am shocked you want to. That kid must've made quite an impression. I don't see why not, though you might not want to start until you finish this. You can only do so much at once."

I agreed and told him goodnight as the sun faded into half-light outside his window. "I'll check on you tomorrow. Have to make sure you don't, you know, die." I stretched my face into my best exaggeration of Parker's wide smile, and Bob did the chuckle/wince thing again.

"Dammit, Nichelle, that's three." His smile didn't fade. "Knock it off."

"Yes, sir."

"Go find your story," he said. "And don't get too crossways with Les, either. They say I'm on house arrest for a while, and I don't want you on his shit list when I get back. He never forgets anything, and he's a pain in my ass when there's someone in the newsroom he doesn't like."

"I'll do my best to fly under his radar."

"You'll have to fly under Shelby's, too," he said. "He's suddenly become her biggest fan the last few weeks, which makes me think I don't want to know exactly what's going on there."

"Are you fucking kidding me?" I rolled my eyes, thinking of her sniffling into Les' chest in Bob's office earlier. From Parker to a snappish, balding bean counter? There was no figuring Shelby out on any front. "No pun intended. And ick."

"It's none of my business, so long as it doesn't affect my newspaper. But just watch it. I know you two ladies don't get along, and I know why." His words began to slur sleepily. "She's not as good as you are, kid, but she could get there. She's a hell of a writer. She just lacks your personality and experience. But if she's got Les' ear, you might have a rough stretch coming. So don't screw up."

"You got it." I backed out of the room as he drifted off.

A bike with a red helmet was in the space next to my car, but it was a Honda, not a BMW like Parker's. I considered our resident jock for half a second, a little ashamed of myself for stereotyping him as a talentless, shallow ass. He seemed like a decent guy, really. The kind I wouldn't mind having as a friend. When I had time for friends again, anyway. I hadn't even spoken to Jenna since Friday.

I rolled the windows down and turned the music up as I tried to make sense of what might be going on at the PD. What if it was a cop? What if it was the lawyer, and he took off because he didn't want to share with the drug pusher? What if said drug pusher had someone on the inside?

I tried to ignore Bob's allusion to "investigative reporting," but the words pulsed through my head in time to the music. It was what I'd always wanted. And it might be right in front of me, if I could just figure out how to get to the answer first. And who I could trust to help me.

I grabbed my phone and dialed Aaron's cell number. Everyone might be a suspect to Mike, but Aaron couldn't be in on this. I'd heard enough of his war stories to know he'd been a damned fine detective, back when he'd worked in homicide.

"Nichelle?" he said when he picked up after the third ring. "What'd I miss now?"

"Don't get me started," I said. I gave him the short version of Bob's medical situation and continued into how I'd met Troy and what he'd told me about his brother and Noah.

"Look, Aaron, there's something really bizarre here. Something that could be huge. I want this story more than I've ever wanted anything, and I need to know what you know. On the record, off the record, whatever. No bullshit. I'm calling in my favor."

He let out a short, sharp breath.

"How do I get myself into this shit?" He paused, and I waited. Finally, he said, "off the record, you promise? You cannot put my name on this. Internal affairs hauled in everyone and their brother for questioning today. They've got this case locked down tighter than a nun's panties, and even I don't know everything. I can tell you where to look, but that's about it."

"What have you got?"

"Someone really wants the lawyer to go up for the stolen evidence," he said. "His wife reported him missing, and she and his buddies at the CA's office suspect foul play. But I'm getting a lot of pressure to put out a story listing him as our prime suspect in the robbery. They know you're going to have that in the morning anyway, so they're throwing this guy under the bus solely on the strength of a signature on the log, best I can tell."

"But you don't think he did it?"

"I don't know what I think. This is all really fucked up, if I'm being honest. And I don't like being asked to put my name on something that's trumped up. Especially when all accounts paint this guy as a decent one, as lawyers go."

"What if the kid was right, and the drug pusher is your murderer?"

"You're thinking he left his stuff at the scenes to throw us off because he was going to steal it back?" Aaron sounded doubtful. "Except this wasn't a breaking and entering situation. They've searched every inch of that locker. There's no sign of anything wrong. Except the shit that's gone, that is."

He paused.

"You think this kid will talk to me?" he asked.

"I told him you guys might have a few questions for him. He seemed fine with it."

"This might be the break we need. Jerry's gotten little or nothing out of anyone he's talked to. I suppose it's too much for me to hope the kid knows who his brother worked for?"

"If he did, he didn't tell me. But I didn't get the idea he knew." I fished the receipt out of my bag and read Troy's phone number aloud.

"Thanks. And off the record, remember?" Aaron said.

"All access, remember?" I countered. "If you come up with anything, you call me. You promised."

"I suppose I did," he said. "All for keeping a vigilante out of the paper. I think I'm getting screwed on this one. Just don't get me fired."

"I wouldn't have anyone to call for information if I did," I said, my mind already chasing Bob's rabbit down the next hole. "Hey, Aaron? Did you happen to hear if there was anything new on the boat crash today? I didn't get around to calling Jones."

"As far as I know, they're still trying to figure out what Freeman and Roberts were doing on the river, and they haven't had much luck. Your story was good. What'd you make of Roberts' wife? I saw that she told you her husband absolutely would not have been out there without orders. You think she's telling the truth?"

"I think she believes that, at the very least."

Aaron murmured something I didn't catch and then he was quiet for a minute. Whatever he wasn't sure he wanted to say arced electricity through the air.

"What?" I half-whispered.

"I don't know," Aaron said. "I have a hunch. I used to be good at following them. Let's see what I can manage to stir up if I poke this hornet's nest."

"Don't stir up more than you can handle. I recently got a lecture about these particular hornets being nasty business."

"Could be," he said. "I'll call you if there's anything here. If I'm right, I may need your help as much as you need mine."

"If you're right, you're going to need a week out on your boat when this is over. You going on vacation this summer?"

"I'm good." He laughed. "I'll have two kids in college come September. No vacations for a while. I'll take the extra paycheck for my time off. I can always go out to the boat on the weekends, when I don't have a media shitstorm at work."

Passing the *Telegraph* office as I hung up, I glanced at the trucks lined up to transport the papers coming off the presses in the basement, resisting the urge to hop out and grab an early copy to see what Les did to my story. But it'd be there waiting to stress me out in the morning. I wanted a hot bath, a decent meal, maybe a glass of wine—and my bed. And to not ever have another day like this one.

I shoved the kitchen door open and bent to greet Darcy out of habit, but she wasn't there. And she wasn't barking.

I turned and looked over the low wooden fence, but she wasn't in the backyard, either.

"Darcy?" I dropped my keys on the counter and walked through the kitchen into the living room. The last of the evening light was just enough to illuminate the shadowy shape that didn't belong. I froze, wondering if I should scream as my heart rate shot into the stratosphere.

"Is that her name?" the broad-shouldered man who was sitting on my sofa holding my shedding, long-haired dog with complete disregard for the Armani suit he wore asked in an Italian-by-way-of-Jersey accent. "Nice dog you got here, Miss Clarke."

CHAPTER NINE

"WHO THE HELL are you and what are you doing in my house?" I
started to step forward and thought better of it, trying to remember if
I had anything handy to use as a weapon. Save for a tennis racquet in
the back of my little SUV, I didn't think I did. Fuck. I made a mental
note to remedy that situation immediately.

I trained my eyes on the dog, swallowing a wave of nausea and
trying to control my breathing. Darcy wasn't barking. She wasn't even
whimpering. She was licking his hands. Darcy didn't lick anyone.
Ever. Either he had cheddar-flavored fingers, or he wasn't a terrible
threat—my dog was an excellent judge of character.

I raised my eyes slowly to his face.

Mr. Breaking and Entering smiled at me and held his hands up,
letting go of Darcy. She flopped over on his knee. I shot her a you-
little-traitor look. Throwing a sad glance back at her new friend, she
hopped down, scurried to my feet, and laid across the right one. Her
belly was smooth and warm on my toes, which peeked out of the
Manolos I hadn't had time to kick off.

"Please, sit down," Mystery Man said, gesturing to my tufted red
chaise as though I were the guest. "I'm not here to hurt you. I'm here
to help you, as a matter of fact."

"I'm good." I folded my arms over my chest, hoping I looked braver than I felt. "Easier to get back to the door from here."

Knowing my phone was in the car, I slid a hand into my pocket anyway. No dice. Damn. I scooted the foot Darcy hadn't occupied back into a punching stance slowly, trying to make it look like I was getting comfortable in the doorway.

"I'm not here to hurt you," he repeated.

Because large men break into the homes of single women with benign intentions so often. I was scared. In my own house. And that pissed me off.

"Then why don't we get to why you are here." My hands clenched at my sides and my breathing sped again, from anger instead of fear. "And why the hell are you sitting on my couch when the house was empty and the doors were locked?"

He stared for a long minute.

"You're not afraid of me." It was more a statement than a question. A statement that was a hundred and eighty degrees wrong, but maybe my bravado was working. A glint of what looked like appreciation shone in his amused brown eyes. "You got some guts, Miss Clarke. I respect that. And I like people I respect. That spirit of yours will come in handy."

I bit my tongue to keep from telling him it was about to come in handy kicking his ass out of my house, returning his silent stare instead. I wondered just how afraid I should be.

He met my gaze head-on, and I could read nothing menacing in his eyes or on his face. In another setting, I'd call that face attractive, all dark eyes and strong jaw, and the cut of the suit showed off a nice physique. But there was definitely something about him that put my asshole radar—perfected by years of regular exposure to murderers, rapists, and assorted other lowlifes—on a low hum. His body language was relaxed and open, though. He didn't appear to be an immediate threat. My pulse slowed to near-normal and I relaxed into the doorjamb.

He flashed a sardonic little grin. "We okay?"

"Look, I've had one hell of a day, so could we just get on with this,

Mr....?"

"Call me Joey." Again with the grin. He cleared his throat and continued. "I know something. A few things, really, that I think you'd like to know, but I need your help finding out more."

I cocked my head to one side. Come again, Captain Cryptic?

"Let me lay it out for you," he said. "You've had quite a weekend, even for someone in your line of work. First, a second drug dealer complicates an open-and-shut murder case, then a boat blows up and kills a handful of people, two of them cops. Now you have a conspicuous vacancy in the police department's evidence room and a missing attorney. What I came to tell you is that all of those things are related. The evidence was on the boat. And the lawyer is in on it, but I'm not sure which side."

Well, then. While I wasn't sure of much of anything right then, that was pretty far down the list of things I'd suspected Mr. Hair Gel might want with me. He leaned forward, resting his elbows on his knees, and waited for me to answer him.

"I guess it's possible," I said slowly. "The last time anyone knew the evidence was in the locker was Friday afternoon. So if someone took it after that, and before the boat went out..."

I trailed off, shaking my head. "I saw the logs from the evidence room. Roberts and Freeman were nowhere on the list. Patrolmen have to sign in. So they couldn't have taken it."

"Unless someone else loaded the boat and sent them out on it."

Well, hell. I opened my mouth to ask him another question when it dawned on me we were talking about the missing evidence. Shit.

"Wait, how do you know about the evidence and the lawyer? That's in *tomorrow's* newspaper." Suddenly way more interested in whether or not someone else had my story than in the man who'd broken into my house, I stood up straight. "Did one of the TV stations have that at six?" I had checked Charlie's stuff, but what if someone else had gotten wind of it somehow?

He shook his head and smiled. "Your scoop is safe, Miss Clarke.

And it's a good one, too. But I'm offering you a chance at something so much better. I have friends everywhere. They tell me things. I came here to ask you for a favor, in return for this information."

I raised one eyebrow and waited for him to get on with it.

"I know what's going on, or most of it, anyway. What I don't know is who's doing it. I'm working on finding out, but I've been following your stories closely, and you can help me. You have access to people I might not be comfortable talking with. Interested?"

"I'm interested in everything. It's an occupational hazard." Holy shit.

His gaze was level, his expression unguarded. I'd interviewed so many criminals I could spot a lie at twenty paces. And this guy was not lying. The puzzles in my head shifted and melded together as I studied my uninvited guest. Who the hell was he?

The suit was Italian. And expensive. I was pretty sure it was authentic Armani. The men's department at Saks was adjacent to women's shoes, where I tried on things I couldn't afford, making a list for eBay. He had big rings on three of the long fingers of each hand, and a chunky gold watch on his wrist. His nails were neat and shiny, probably recently manicured; his black hair slicked back from his oval face. The features and accent smacked of an Italian heritage. He wasn't much older than me, and exuded a throwback debonair quality that belonged in a black and white movie. Sort of like DeNiro's portrayal of Monroe Stahr from Fitzgerald's *The Last Tycoon*. But taller, with a better smile.

"Are you a cop?" He was too well dressed, really, but I wouldn't know most of the internal affairs or undercover guys if I tripped over them, and I couldn't figure out how he'd come by his information.

He shook his head and laughed, a deep, rich sound I found pleasant in spite of myself.

"I think that's the first time I've ever been asked that." He winked.

Bob's comments about Washington popped into my head and I tried to match his face with one from C-SPAN. I had a nagging feeling I'd seen him somewhere. "A politician?"

"Not the kind you mean."

"There's more than one kind?"

"Politics is making people think what you think," he leaned back and draped one arm over the sofa cushion. "It wouldn't be unreasonable to say that's one of the things I do."

"But you're not going to tell me who you are, or what it is you actually do?"

"It's not important."

The hell it wasn't.

"Why should I believe anything you say if you won't tell me how you know it?"

He sat up straight and adjusted his suit jacket, holding my gaze without blinking.

"Because I'm right," he said. "And when you have time to think about it, you'll know it. Tell me something, what happens to evidence after a trial ends?"

I shrugged. "They destroy most of it. Once they're pretty sure the case won't go to appeal."

He nodded. "Anything noteworthy they should have destroyed recently?"

Noteworthy? There was a ridiculous variety of stuff in the police evidence lock up on any given day. People could turn some crazy things into weapons when they were mad enough or drunk enough or any combination of the two.

Evidence was destroyed depending on the court calendar. The drugs and the money from the two dealer murders shouldn't have gone anywhere for at least a year. There hadn't even been an arrest made in the case.

So what had cleared the courtrooms by enough to be trashed lately? If he was right and everything was connected, Neal's cases made the most sense. I ran mentally through the list DonnaJo sent me, trying to tie the missing lawyer to whatever Joey was talking about.

"Oh, shit." I clapped a hand over my mouth. "The guns. That trucker from New York." I could picture it, Gavin Neal waving a gun over his head during his closing argument and dropping it back into a sizable trough of semi-automatic and automatic weapons seized off of a truck on its way from New York to North Carolina over a year before.

Neal got the truck driver convicted of transporting the stolen weapons across state lines with intent to sell. There had been a lot of guns in that box in the courtroom that day, and I'd watched the bailiffs carry them out to a police van after the verdict came back.

I shoved the pesky lock of hair that wouldn't stay in my clip behind my ear again. I didn't know a lot about guns, but I'd bet a whole shitload of them with unregistered serial numbers would be worth a pretty penny on the black market.

"The guns." Joey nodded. "Along with the drugs and cash from your murder cases, were on the boat. That baseball player and his buddies cost someone a lot of money Friday night."

"And you really don't know who? Or you just don't want to tell me?"

He smiled again. "I don't know. Truly. I do think this could work out well for us both if you handle it right, and I'll help you as much as I can, but I'm not what you would call a quotable source." He rose smoothly and walked toward me. "So you'll have to find some things out for yourself. See what you can dig up, and if I come across anything I think might help, I'll be in touch. I hear you're a very determined lady, and I have a hunch you'll get to the bottom of this. You'll have the story of the decade when you do, I promise you."

I held my ground and kept my eyes on his face. His movements were easy. His lips turned up slightly as he slid sideways through the door, brushing closer to me than he needed to. I caught my breath at the unwanted shiver that skated up my spine. He smelled good, too.

"What if you're wrong?" I turned and walked with him to the front door, noting it wasn't damaged. Just like the evidence lock up. "Why would anyone steal evidence from the police and put it on their own boat?"

"I suggest you think about that, because I am not wrong." He turned his head so that his face was inches from mine, then stepped out onto the porch before I could think too much about that. "I like you. You're smart. You're determined. I'm going to be your friend, Miss Clarke—and I'm a very good friend to have."

I waited while he walked to the end of the sidewalk, where a black Town Car idled at the curb. What a day. I couldn't even come home and go to bed like a normal person. No, I had to have James Bond's better-looking Italian cousin giving the dog Stockholm Syndrome. I closed the door and turned the deadbolt, slid the chain home, then tugged on the knob to make sure it was secure.

Moving through the house with Darcy on my heels, I checked every door and window and closet; even peering under my bed. When I was sure I was alone, and likely to stay that way for the rest of the night, I freshened the dog's water and filled her bowl with kibble before I went to the cafe-style kitchen table with a legal pad and a pen, recording every detail of what was very possibly the strangest conversation of my life. The mental puzzles I'd been juggling all weekend suddenly melted neatly together, a chunk of the picture clear, if I believed Joey. And I did.

Still mulling it over, I stirred the contents of a can of chicken noodle soup around in a pan on my aging GE stove and then took the pad with me to the couch. I pulled my legs up onto the cushion beneath me while I ate, picking my notes back up when I put the bowl down.

"What'd you think?" I asked Darcy, who had retreated to her pink bed in the corner after her own dinner, curled up so she resembled a furry russet pom-pom. "He's telling the truth, or at least, he thinks he is. But before I get too far into this, I need to find out who our visitor was and why he doesn't want me to know."

Remembering Joey's comment about not being a quotable source, I flipped back through my notes. An undercover cop couldn't be quoted or it would blow his case. But he'd thought it was funny when I'd asked about him being a cop.

He'd said he was like a politician, but "not the kind you mean."

"Oh, shit, Darcy," I whispered. "What if he's more Vito Corleone than Monroe Stahr?"

I flipped faster between the pages, my eyes lighting on certain words. "I have lots of friends. They tell me things… Politics is making people think what you think." He expected me to be afraid of him. He was dressed in an expensive suit, he'd left in a chauffeured sedan, the accent…"I'm a good friend to have."

Of course. The cherry on top of my crazy Monday sundae. The first sexy guy I'd met in months, and he was probably an honest-to-God mobster. Why the hell not?

I leaned my head back against the damask-covered sofa cushion. "Stolen evidence. Missing lawyers. And the fucking Mafia in my living room," I laughed, mostly because it was better than screaming. The dog whimpered. "Well, Tuesday, you have a heck of a lot to live up to. Monday set the bar high this week."

Darcy looked downright indignant when I ordered her through the runt-sized doggie door on my way to bed, but I didn't even want to unlock the door to let her go pee, nevermind step out for her customary game of fetch. She took less than a minute to do her business and bounce back in, turning her head away from me as she trotted to the bedroom. I double-checked the locks and turned off the lights, peering out the window into the still darkness, not even really sure what I was looking for.

As a peace offering, I lifted Darcy out of her bed and onto mine when I crawled under the covers. Drifting off to sleep with *Goodfellas* and *Donnie Brasco* playing in my head, I felt her snuggle behind the crook of my knees and knew I'd been forgiven.

By the time I got out of the shower the next morning, I had convinced myself the Mafia was the only logical explanation for "you can call me Joey," altogether dismissing the idea that the guy was a cop. I just knew, down in my bones, and going with my gut had never failed me. I also couldn't shake the feeling that I'd seen him somewhere before.

I brushed my teeth and tried to place Joey's angular features in a courtroom, focusing on the handful of times I had heard rumors of Mafia activity along the Atlantic coast and trying to remember things I'd once made a concerted effort to forget.

My initiation into the courthouse fraternity had been a formidable one, and among the first trials I'd covered was a particularly grisly murder case that sanity and sound sleep had demanded I repress in the nearly two years since. I tried to call up the details. The guy was an accountant, and he had been beheaded. His girlfriend found his head on his desk atop a stack of files that detailed a little side action. He'd been skimming cash from several local business owners who trusted him with their books, and he'd built an offshore nest egg that would've supported a family of four comfortably for at least a decade. The crime scene photos fueled my nightmares for weeks.

The prosecutor walked into the trial almost cocky. He had a gruesome murder that was pulling huge ratings for the TV news, and consequently getting him a lot of face time with the cameras, and he had a confession from the defendant. The accountant had stolen money from the guy's construction company. A slam dunk. The prosecutor didn't mind that he didn't have a murder weapon or DNA or any witnesses putting the accused at the scene of the crime. He had it sewn up, he'd told us at his self-organized ego-fest of a pretrial press conference on the courthouse steps. I hadn't seen that lawyer in court since, but it wouldn't occur to me to miss him.

Ultimately, the New York legal celebrity who'd argued for the defense got the charges dismissed. It had been quite a show. No fancy loopholes or backroom deals, just outright dismissal by the judge on the most ridiculous of technicalities. The defense attorney, in his shiny wingtips and Hugo Boss, reminded me of a hunter stalking his prey as he'd led the arresting cop into admitting on the stand that he hadn't read the guy his rights when he picked him up. Simple as that: no Miranda rights, no conviction. But thanks for playing.

Before that little revelation swept the courtroom into chaos, however, I'd been eavesdropping on two prosecutors who were sitting in the cheap seats with the rest of us between court appointments of their own.

"You don't tend to live long when the Mafia catches you skimming money off the top," one of them had said, chuckling. The other lawyer had agreed, and I'd rolled my eyes, tuning out their conversation and thinking they had seen too many movies.

Suddenly sure I'd been mistaken, I shook off the memory of Joey's eyes moving over me on his way out. It didn't matter if he liked what he'd seen, because I didn't find organized crime attractive, shivers or no. I gave myself a stern glare in the mirror to punctuate that thought.

"I'm going to be your friend, Miss Clarke, and I am a very good friend to have."

I spit out the toothpaste and grabbed my hair dryer.

So I just had to figure out if he was the kind of friend I wanted. I threw on a five-minute face and decided to skip body combat in favor of learning exactly what I was dealing with. Filling a travel mug with Green Mountain Colombian Fair Trade, I added a shot of white chocolate syrup and headed out.

Halfway to the office, I thought about Bob.

The worry of Monday afternoon eclipsed the evening's interview with the young Godfather, and I laughed at the absurdity of such a convergence of drama.

"Was there some kind of planetary alignment?" I asked out loud, raising my face to the heavens. "Have I angered somebody up there? How the hell does that much happen to one person on one day?"

Somehow, ranting—even if it was just at my sunroof—made me feel better. When I noticed I was parked in the garage at the office, I shut off the engine and crossed the space between the car and the elevator quickly, looking over my shoulder twice in no more than two dozen steps. I figured I'd be paranoid for life because of that one interview.

It was quiet in the newsroom in the early morning. I was used to the silence at night, but I was never at work before eight a.m. It was eerie for it to be so still with light outside the windows.

I reached for my headphones and turned on a pulsing dance

number before I opened my browser and clicked the Google tab on my favorites bar. I stared at the screen for a long moment before I typed "Mafia" into the box and hit the search button. I got more than forty-seven-million results.

Scrolling down, I chose a Wikipedia article that turned out to be a complete history of organized crime in Sicily. It was fascinating, even if it wasn't particularly relevant, and I read through half the page before I saw a link to something more promising. I waited for the article on the American Mafia to load and became engrossed in the information on the screen. It could've been lifted from any one of a hundred novels.

"Yeah, I never would have believed any of this yesterday morning," I said to the empty room, my eyes getting big as I read the long list of American cities with known Mafia families. Some of them were an easy day's drive from Richmond. And the fine print said the list was a partial one.

"Holy shit." I exhaled forcefully, sat back in the chair, and dropped the headphones to my desk. Looking at a chart of how Mafia families are organized, I surmised Joey must be up there. I didn't figure foot soldiers wore three-thousand-dollar suits and rode around in chauffeur-driven cars.

There was a whole section on initiation and how it usually involved murder. I remembered the sardonic smile that played around Joey's lips for most of the time I had talked to him, and shivered. Had someone, or more than one someone, taken their last breath looking at that smile?

"A good friend to have," he'd said.

I guess if my choice was limited by him being in my living room, I'd certainly rather he like me than not.

Bob was right. Missing lawyers, stolen evidence, and organized crime. It was a bona-fide investigative story. But I needed to know more about what I was dealing with. I clicked over to the *Telegraph* archives, searching old courthouse photos for Joey's face. I found it in a shot from the decapitated accountant trial. Joey was part of a crowd of onlookers, leaning on a column behind the bigheaded prosecutor. I couldn't zoom in too much without making the image fuzzy, but I'd recognize that little half-grin anywhere.

"What the hell am I getting myself into?" I wondered aloud. Even as I said the words, I had a feeling it was too late to back out. And I wasn't at all sure I wanted to.

CHAPTER TEN

"No telling, where you're concerned," Shelby's voice came from behind my shoulder and I jumped, whacking my knee on the underside of my desk. That would leave a mark. "Anything interesting?"

Seriously, universe? I searched the memories of my college religion class for the words to the Hail Mary. Not that I was Catholic. I was just trying to cover my penance bases as Shelby stared at me with her ping-pong-ball eyes, making a *tsk-tsk* sound with her tongue.

"Nothing you'd be up for," I stretched my lips into a tight smile and cocked my head to one side. "Though, you know, I've read your stuff. It's not bad."

She smiled, her eyes getting impossibly bigger. "I know."

I shrugged. "Like I said, not bad. But here's the thing: covering cops and covering garden parties are about as similar as the Oscars red carpet and a kid playing dress up. You wouldn't last a day in my shoes. Bob's not giving you my job, so give it up."

"Bob's not here, is he? Les wasn't happy with you last night. Not to kiss and tell, but I'd watch my step if I were you."

"Are you serious? Is there anyone in this building you haven't boinked trying to get a promotion? Do you have, like, any self-respect?"

"Sure. I respect my ability to find ways to get what I want," she smiled. "You're a good writer, Nichelle. And you're a good reporter. Bob thinks you're the next Helen Thomas, and it's totally obvious to everyone how much you love that. But I'm a good writer, too. I just got hired for a beat that was expendable. Cops is not, and once I get away from the copy desk, I have no intention of going back."

I narrowed my eyes and started to say something, but she kept talking.

"So do me a favor. Go get your story. I don't even have to know what it is right now. Les said you were into something big he didn't think you could handle. I, ever selfless, offered to help, which he thought was very sweet of me." She smirked. "And as long as we're talking about what everyone knows, we all know you've got your eye on the Post. And we all know if you were really good enough, you'd already be working there. Look, Nichelle, at the end of the day, it makes me no difference how you go. Ride off into the sunset to be a politics superstar, screw up and get yourself fired. All I care is that right now, Les is in charge, and I'm next in line for a byline as the crime reporter. So you have yourself a nice day. Just remember, I'll be around."

She shot me one last smug grin, turned on her heel, and started to walk off.

"Hey Shelby?" I called.

She turned back.

"If you were so great at what you do, Bob wouldn't have hired me in the first place. You were already here, remember? Too bad you're not his type. You may be leading Les around by his dick right now, but Bob still makes the staffing decisions. And just because you were a convenient threat on Saturday, doesn't mean you're next in line for jack shit." I sounded way more confident than I felt, and her smile faltered, which made mine widen. "So you have yourself a nice day at the copy desk, okay?"

Tuesday, mercifully, did not live up to Monday in terms of drama. I didn't see Shelby again, and my day passed in a blur of phone calls and faxes. I called Gavin Neal's wife (who had no comment, thank you, Les, but at least I had it in my day-two story), and looked through Neal's recent cases again. The case I had remembered while I was talking to Joey, with the stolen guns, was the only notable one. A search of public records revealed a bankruptcy filing, mostly for medical collections, that hadn't been granted, but I couldn't access more than the final judgment, which held that Neal's bills must be paid because of tougher standards in the bankruptcy code.

Money was always good motive.

But then Joey's words rang in my head, and no matter how I turned them over, I couldn't fit Neal into a scenario where the money blew up on the river. First, he went to evidence on Sunday, not Friday. Second, why would he put it on a PD boat if he was stealing it from the PD?

If Joey was right about the boat, then Neal wasn't the logical suspect in the evidence theft. Yet Charlie had blasted Neal's face, superimposed over images of the evidence room, all over Channel Four beginning with the early show. Aaron was right—the PD cast Neal as the bad guy. Charlie had nothing on his financial troubles, but I knew she would soon, and that only strengthened the case against him.

After a good deal of back-and-forth, my desire to not lose to Charlie beat out my doubts about Neal and I went with it, bankruptcy and all. I threw in comments from DonnaJo and other prosecutors who proclaimed Neal's innocence to balance my story, but it still didn't look too good.

If he didn't take it, who did? I wondered about Aaron and his hornet's nest, but I didn't hear anything from him and he didn't answer when I called.

I went to see Bob on my way home and found him holding court in a hospital room that looked like it had been attacked by a florist on speed. I nodded to the mayor, three guys in suits I didn't recognize, and the *Telegraph's* advertising director, who all rose to leave when the phone rang just after I walked in.

Bob talked to Les about the next day's newspaper for a few minutes, picking at a tray of overcooked chicken, limp broccoli, and orange Jell-o. He looked almost like himself. He was even wearing pajamas Parker dropped off that morning instead of the hospital gown.

Dr. Schaefer stopped in before I left, and she said she planned to send Bob home the next day. I grumbled about insurance companies and told Bob I'd be happy to help with whatever he needed. He said Parker had already volunteered for that job.

"It sounded like he has some experience." I smiled. "Something tells me he'll take good care of you."

Bob muttered something about a babysitter and I laughed, wishing him a good night.

Darcy streaked to the door in a little furry blur, barking her head off like always, when I got home. I scooped her up and kissed the top of her fuzzy head, scratching her chest while I inspected the house. After a third check of all the locks, I relaxed a little.

I spooned a can of beef and carrots Pedigree into Darcy's bowl and ate a sandwich at the counter while she snarfed it down, then took her out for the shortest game of fetch in history, checked the locks again, and fell into bed, comforted by the soft feel of the sheets on my skin and the heft of the duvet as I settled back into the pillows.

I dreamed of Joey.

We were in a long room, like a conference room minus the table, and he was at the other end trying to tell me something. I couldn't hear him for the god-awful buzzing noise, like honeybees in hyper-drive, and no matter how I waved or beckoned, I couldn't get him to come closer. He reached into his jacket pocket and produced a fat brass ring. He held it out to me, then pulled it away when I reached for it, holding it up and thumping the outside of it instead of tossing it over.

I woke up Wednesday with the covers twisted around my legs as if I'd been fighting them in my sleep, my hair damp with sweat in the air-conditioned room. I stretched, grumbling as I climbed out of bed, still craving sleep. The unsettling dream had kept me from resting.

I went to the gym anyway, and as I threw jabs, angled, and perfected my *ap'chagi* (I was fairly certain the instructor was butchering the Korean when he called for the front kick by shouting "ap shaggy," but no one seemed to mind), I thought about Joey. Freud probably wouldn't see anything deeply hidden in my dream. Bob had called the Post my brass ring. I was pretty sure Joey had the key to it, but he wouldn't give it to me. Fair enough. Except I couldn't get past the feeling I was missing something.

Jab, jab, bouncebouncebounce, uppercut. Brass. What else was brass?

Gallop, gallop, *ap'chagi*! Old chandeliers. Saddle fittings. Military officers.

Oh, shit.

I stopped suddenly, and the guy behind me *ap'chagi*-ed me in the ass. I think he apologized, but I was already halfway to the door.

The police command staff. Brass. Dammit, I hated feeling slow.

I tried Aaron again on my way into the newsroom, wondering if his hornet's nest was on the top floor of police headquarters.

When I got to my desk, I called Captain Jones and asked him if the destroyed patrol boat had been taken out recently, besides the night of the accident.

"I pulled that on Saturday, and there was only one other outing in the past month, a training." I heard him typing in the background. "Here it is. Looks like two weeks prior to the accident." More keystrokes. "Huh. I didn't check the notes on this the other day, the damned phone was ringing off the hook and I got sidetracked. This is a little odd, actually. It was a Saturday, and Deputy Chief Lowe ordered it out on a training exercise. I wonder what kind of training he was doing?"

"Lowe?" I asked. My breath sped. "I take it you didn't know anything about a scheduled training that day?"

"I don't do training on the weekends, and I know I wasn't here that Saturday, because it was my wife's birthday and we were at the beach."

"Was Lowe the only officer on the boat that day?" I asked.

"It doesn't say," Jones said.

I couldn't tell from his tone if he was talking to me, or to himself.

He sounded far away, as if thinking out loud. Then more clicking. I scribbled furiously.

"There's another notes screen. Says one of my sergeants went to the boathouse, found Chief Lowe there on the boat. At which time Sergeant Mayer reminded Lowe he had to log the boat out, even for training. Mayer was heading out to search for a missing swimmer and noticed that the patrol vessel hadn't been checked out."

I stopped writing, distracted as I ran through the memory of my conversation with Lowe the day after the accident. Had the odd inflection I'd heard in his voice and dismissed as sorrow been something else? Like guilt? "You would think the deputy chief would be familiar with standard operating procedures."

"I certainly would," Jones said.

I stared into space after I put the phone down. Lowe? Joey's hints would fit: someone with enough clearance to sign the boat out, and avoid signing into the evidence locker. Was the deputy-fucking-chief stealing evidence and selling drugs and guns right out of police headquarters? Joey's face was replaced in my head by Troy's as I considered that: if Darryl and Noah knew they were working for the deputy chief of police, then it gave them ready ammunition for blackmail. And made them expendable.

I grabbed the phone and drummed my fingers on the desk while I waited for Mike to pick up. Before I went wholesale with Joey's version of events, I wanted to know if anyone saw the evidence on Saturday.

"Narcotics, this is Stevens." A low, unfamiliar voice came through the handset.

"I'm sorry. I think I ended up at the wrong extension. I was looking for Mike Sorrel."

"Ah," Stevens said. "The sergeant isn't here today. Is there something I can help you with?"

"No, thanks, I'll try his cell phone," I said. "I need to talk to him today."

"He's not picking up his cell, miss," Stevens said, his tone a mixture of patient and concerned. "Can I ask who's calling?"

"This is Nichelle Clarke at the *Richmond Telegraph*. What do you mean 'he's not picking up his cell?' Is he sick?"

"I wish I knew, Miss. No one has heard from him for a couple of days now. His wife says he didn't go home from work Monday, and he wasn't here yesterday, either."

My stomach flip-flopped, my insides going cold. "He's...he's gone? Like, missing? I..." I couldn't finish that sentence.

"Every spare detective we have is searching," Stevens said. "We'll figure it out. Myself, I'm hoping he just needed to get away for a few days. Maybe a fight with his wife she doesn't want to tell us about. Wanted some distance from her. That's usually how these things end up."

"Sure," I said.

I closed my eyes and dropped my head into my hands when I cradled the receiver. Mike is missing. The words looped through my mind , speeding until they ran together. Mikeismissing. I pictured his grave expression as he cautioned me about the information he gave me Monday morning. And he didn't go home that night. For all I knew, I was the last person who saw him. But no one knew he'd talked to me.

Torn between keeping his confidence and worrying, I grabbed the phone and pushed redial, trying to keep the frantic note out of my voice as I asked for Aaron.

"Davis."

My stomach knotted again when Jerry Davis, the detective working the drug dealer case, answered Aaron's phone.

"Hello?" Jerry said, drawing the word out.

I struggled to make my lips work.

"Jerry? It's Nichelle Clarke at the *Telegraph*. Please tell me Aaron's in a meeting and you just happen to be hanging out waiting for him."

Jerry laughed. "You have some sort of hot scoop today?" he asked, misinterpreting the desperation clear in my tone. "Sorry, Nichelle, he's on vacation this week. He emailed yesterday morning that he was taking the boat out and he'd be out of cell range for a week or ten days, so I'm trying to cover for him. I gotta hand it to him. You people are pretty time-consuming. His job is harder than I thought."

"Vacation." I repeated, my voice hollow.

I heard Aaron in my head: "I'm going to have two kids in college, come September. No vacations around here for a while. I'll take the extra paycheck for my time off....Let's see what I can manage to stir up if I poke this hornet's nest."

What if Aaron stirred up more than he bargained for?

"You're sure the email was from Aaron?" My voice was too high.

"I didn't see him typing it, or anything, but it was sent from his RPD account. Hey, are you okay?"

"Yes. No. I don't know, Jerry. There's some weird stuff going on this morning."

"Anything I can help with?"

I bit my lip and tried to think of something. Was there anything he might not ask too many questions about?

"I don't think so," I said finally.

"Let me know if there's anything I can do for you while Aaron's gone."

"Thanks, Jerry. If you do happen to hear from Aaron, ask him to give me a call."

Twisting the top off a soda bottle in the break room a couple of minutes later, I remembered that Bob was supposed to be getting his walking papers from Dr. Schaefer.

I went back to my cube and called my boss' house. He picked up on the second ring, and if I hadn't seen him looking so frail two days before, I would never have believed the man had a heart condition.

"Hey, chief," I said. "How are you feeling?"

"Nicey," Bob said, more cheerful than I was used to. "I'm fantastic. I'm home! It's nice to be in my own clothes and watching my own TV. I have two news channels on, but Warden Parker here won't let me talk to Les for more than seven minutes an hour, which is driving me insane."

He didn't sound the least bit annoyed.

"You're not fooling anyone, chief. And he's trying to make sure you get well quickly," I said. "He's done this before. You just listen to him and you'll be back in here hollering at us in no time."

I could hear the smile in his voice. "Yes, ma'am."

"I'm glad to hear you sounding like yourself. I want to come by and see you."

"Sure," Bob said, his grouching about babysitters apparently forgotten, at least for the moment. "I think Parker said he has to run up there at three to get his column filed because he forgot his laptop."

"Tell him no rush," I said. "I'll come hang out with you while he gets his piece taken care of. Do you need me to pick up anything on my way?"

"I don't think so. He got groceries already." His voice dropped to an exaggerated conspiratorial whisper. "He's making some kind of soup. Do you figure whatever he comes up with will be edible?"

Parker's good-natured laugh rang in the background.

"I'm sure he's not going to kill you," I said. "It's good to have you back, Chief. Get some rest."

As far as actual printable copy was concerned, my day was pretty light. There were a couple of follow-ups on small trials I had been waiting for verdicts on, but nothing worthy of sitting at the court-house. One was a hit-and-run (minor injuries, acquitted), the other an animal cruelty case (puppy mill, convicted). I interviewed the prose-cutors and defense attorneys for both cases, pounded out the stories, and sent them to Les. Two hours early. That ought to shut Shelby up for a while.

Parker's bike was still in the driveway when I pulled up outside Bob's stately brick-front colonial that afternoon. I sat in my car, listening to the radio and rehearsing what I was planning to tell my editor. I needed to keep it light so I wouldn't give him another heart attack, but I also wanted to know what he really thought. I wondered if there was a punch line to a mob boss being in my living room. Knock, knock. Who's there? The Mafia. Except he didn't knock. Yeah, there's not much funny about that.

Parker left before I had a good plan, waving as he settled the helmet on his head. Damn. I stepped out of the car. Short of a sudden flash of brilliance, I could just watch my tone, lay it out straight, and hope for the best.

"Nicey?" Bob called when I opened the front door. "I'm in the living room."

I walked down the long entry hall, past the parlor and the dining room, and found Bob, looking normal save for the plaid pajamas and blanket, stretched out on his brown leather sofa watching CNN. MSNBC was running in a small box in the corner of the screen.

I grinned. "Glad to see you up and around, sir," I said.

"Not up and around," he scowled. Being at home evidently lost its novelty quickly. "If someone would let me up and around, I'd go to the office. Instead, I'm here with another babysitter, and Parker ordered me to stay on this couch unless I have to use the bathroom. I feel like I'm in first grade. I should have eaten a few more salads, I guess."

"It's not too late to remedy that, you know." I tried not to sound too reproachful. "We need to introduce you to the farmer's market."

"So I've been told," he said, gesturing to the big brown leather recliner. "Sit. Tell me what's going on with your story."

I took a deep breath, surprised it had taken him more than two minutes to ask.

Still lacking a better idea, I tried to keep my voice light as I told him about my uninvited guest. It didn't work.

"Jesus, kid." Bob blew out a slow, controlled breath. "I'm out for three days and this is what you come up with? The goddamned Mafia? Are you sure?"

"It's not like he gave me a business card that said 'Goodfellas, we deliver.' But the story fits. And I found him in that photo from the embezzler murder trial, too. I heard a couple of the ACAs down there talking about the guy stealing from the mob. What do you think? You're the first person I've told about this."

"As much as I don't want it to, I think you're right. I've heard rumors. Once you get involved with these people, you don't get uninvolved until they get what they want. But why? And why haven't you asked your guys at the PD about this Joey?"

"Because they're not there. Either of them." My voice caught a little on the last word. "Mike didn't go home Monday night and they're saying Aaron is on vacation. I guess that might be true, but he just told me he wasn't taking vacation this year."

"Did either of them take the money?"

"I don't want to think so." I sighed. I needed his opinion, and for him to give it to me, he needed to know what was going on. "Here's the thing: Mike's the one who brought me the story on the missing evidence. He went down there to check something out and it was gone, and he called IAD and then he called me. So, part of me wonders if Mike stole it, but why would he bring me the story if he was the one who did it?"

"To make it look like he's not?"

I dropped my head into one hand. And Mike had been at the river on Friday night, too. As much as I hated the idea, if Joey was right and the evidence was on the boat, what if Mike wasn't just being helpful?

"Yeah, that's kind of where I landed, too." I peeked through splayed fingers at Bob's furrowed brow before I raised my head. "Shit, Chief. I don't know. I don't know who to trust. I don't know what to think. I do have another theory, though. I think there's at least a decent chance it's the deputy police chief who is running this whole thing, no matter who's involved in it." I forged ahead, talking so fast I wasn't sure he could keep up.

"I think he stole the evidence and sent those rookies to take it somewhere," I said when I finally sat back in the chair. "But if that's it, what I don't know is whether or not Roberts and Freeman knew there was anything illegal on the boat. Or who else might be in on it."

"It's a hell of a sexy story, isn't it?" Bob asked. "I can't say I'm quite as excited about it as I was Monday, but...good God, you can't not go after it. I know you, and I remember what it's like. But you can't imagine how shitty I'm going to feel if you get yourself hurt chasing a headline."

"Well, no worries, because I have no intention of doing anything but cracking the case and saving the day. Step aside, Lois Lane."

I grinned, and he laughed in spite of the crease in his forehead.

"Work fast, huh, Lois? The sooner you're out from under this one, the better I'll feel. Plus, Charlie won't be far behind you. You don't want to end up second chair after all this mess." He smiled at me and changed the subject. "Let's talk about something a little less stressful before we both have a heart condition. Tell me everything else that's going on. I'm going through withdrawals."

Two hours later I had him fully back in the loop and we had moved on to politics when Parker walked in the front door.

"Just checking in before I head out for the night." He nodded a hello at me and focused on Bob. "You need anything, boss? That minestrone should be done by now, and I have a date. Did y'all know there's a new reporter at Channel Ten? She was at the DeLucas' house the other day. Said she likes my column."

He glanced at me. "Speaking of, at the risk of being a pain in the ass, did you ever read my piece from Saturday?"

I shook my head, unable to keep a rueful smile off my face.

"I'm going to, I swear," I said. "I've just been busy. Nothing personal."

"Sure it's not. What could possibly have you so busy you don't have time for a fifteen hundred word story?"

Bob's eyes flicked between us as I paused for half a beat too long.

"Mostly personal stuff," I said, not wanting my lead offered up as a way to get the new girl at Channel Ten into the sack. "Nothing that would interest you. But I really will get to it. I don't break promises, even when I have to delay them."

Parker pinched his lips together and studied me for a second before he flashed the trademark grin and told us goodnight.

We heard the door click as he let himself out.

I moved to follow suit and my boss shot me another warning glare.

"Quick and clean. Don't piss Les off, don't get us sued, and for fuck's sake, don't get yourself killed," he said.

"Yessir," I said.

My thoughts tangled up in my story as I drove home to the gravelly twang of Janis Joplin, and I pondered what Bob had said, wondering if Aaron and Mike really could be knee deep in this and unable to think of a single person who could tell me the answer to that.

But what if I could find out for myself?

Cranking up the music, I cut across two lanes and hung a sharp left on Thompson, heading for the freeway. The often-annoying ability to remember anything I read, which tended to leave my mind cluttered and hard to shut off at night, produced a perfect image of the map on Aaron's office wall—and the big black circle around the marina on the Appomattox River where he docked his boat.

CHAPTER ELEVEN

THE APPOMATTOX IS NEARLY an hour south of Richmond, and the sun was low in the sky by the time I got close enough to check my maps app for the exact location of the marina. There were two in the vicinity of Aaron's black circle, and I pulled into the nearly-deserted gravel parking lot at the first and hopped out, not sure if I was excited or nervous.

I wanted the boat to be gone—though I wouldn't know for sure until I'd checked both locations. But the wringing in my gut told me I would find something. True, he didn't answer to me, but it didn't seem like Aaron to tell me he wasn't going on vacation and then take off the very next day. Especially not in the middle of such a big case.

"Alyssa Lynne," I muttered, strolling down the dock trying to look like I belonged as I checked the names of the vessels tethered there. He'd told me once that the boat was his other baby, so he'd named it after his daughters.

I counted thirty-four boats on one side of the slip and turned to start up the other, still alone with the sun sinking fast in the distance. A breeze ruffled my hair and I closed my eyes and took a deep breath, unable to relax even in such a peaceful place.

Still no dice on the other side. Slightly buoyed by that, I went back to my car and sat with the windows down for a minute, listening to the water.

My phone binged the arrival of a text just as I started the engine and I glanced at it, only the top half of the message visible over the edge of the cup holder.

It was from Les.

"What now?" I sighed, talking to the message on my screen. "All my stuff was done early today, in case you didn't notice."

"Charlie has the missing lawyer's wife on camera," it read. "If you can't handle this, there are other people here who can."

Shit. I'd called the woman and she'd refused to comment. What did he want me to do, stalk her?

My mobile browser was lousy with streaming video, but I clicked onto Channel Four's site and tried anyway. Charlie's story was the second from the top, and a scan of the text didn't reveal anything Earth-shattering. I didn't even see the wife's name, which was Grace, according to the court papers I'd found the day before.

I tried the video, and after several minutes managed to put together enough patchy footage to see it was close to the same story they'd run the night before, save for the addition of the bankruptcy filing, some information on a few of Neal's old cases, and about five seconds of a puffy-eyed Grace Neal telling Charlie "no comment" and shutting the door in her face.

"I'm getting threats over a 'no comment?'" I tossed the phone back into the cup holder and banged my head against the back of the seat. "Is he kidding me?"

I slammed my foot down on the accelerator and spun the tires on the gravel, not wanting to lose the sunlight completely before I got to the other marina. What I did want to do was text my makeshift boss a very polite "please bite my ass," but I knew Bob would frown on that, so I focused on the road, taking the unfamiliar turns too fast, Janis wailing loud enough to rattle the windows.

Twilight had fallen by the time I parked at the second marina, which had roughly three times as many slips, though about half of them were empty.

I hurried down the closest dock, the bait shop closed and not another soul in sight, cursing my lack of a flashlight and scanning the names on the boats as I went.

I found nothing on either of the first two docks and was almost at the end of the third, ready to decide he'd changed his mind and I was losing mine to paranoia and conspiracy theories, when I saw it.

My stomach twisted as I stared at the RPD shield painted on the hull next to his daughters' names.

Damn.

So he wasn't on vacation. One question answered, but five new ones in its place.

Had he lied to Jerry? Had Jerry lied to me? Aaron knew all about boats and rivers. Was it really him the whole time? Had he taken off after the crash because he was afraid he'd get caught? Or had his hornet's nest been nastier than he'd anticipated?

I stepped closer to the boat, which was a nice one—with a small cabin and everything— especially for a guy with two kids and what I knew about cops' and teachers' salaries. Dammit. I hated feeling like everyone was a suspect, and I had no idea what to think.

If it was him, and he had taken off, why would he say he was going on the boat and then leave it here? And in that same vein, if they were moving the goods over the waterways, what if there was something on there?

I took another step toward the boat and stopped, biting my lip. It wasn't exactly a house, but still private property. And a cop's private property at that.

But what if it wasn't him? What if something was wrong, or something happened to him, and there was a clue on there somewhere?

I looked around, the first of the evening stars twinkling overhead. Nothing out here but me and the fish and the man in the moon. It wouldn't hurt to take a quick peek. If he was guilty, I wouldn't care if he minded, and if he wasn't, I was nearly sure he wouldn't mind.

I stepped onboard shakily, looking around the deck and wondering what my chances were of finding anything interesting.

There was a console near the captain's chair, which looked like as good a hiding place as any, but held only a box of fish hooks, a flash-light, and a package of batteries.

Maybe down in the belly, then. I crossed the deck to the galley door, jerked it open, and slipped inside before I could change my mind, telling myself I wanted as much to know what had happened to my friend as I wanted to know anything else about this case.

It was a tight space, with sleeping berths stacked up the walls on both sides, then a kitchen, bathroom, and booth-style table in the back. At first glance, there didn't look to be much in the way of stor-age, but when I lifted on the lowest bed, it came up easily to reveal a bin full of life jackets. I dug through them, but the only thing sharing the space with them was a dead spider that might have made me shriek under different circumstances—the thing was almost as big as my thumb not counting the legs.

"Jesus, they do grow things bigger out here." I shuddered and closed the lid, then crossed to the other bed and lifted it.

Empty. As were the kitchen drawers, the toilet tank, and the refrigerator.

So maybe he wasn't a bad guy. Or if he was, he kept it to police department boats. But he wasn't on vacation on this boat, that was for sure.

Where was he, then?

I sighed and kicked the door open a little too hard, looking for any other visible storage on Aaron's sportfisher, but there was none.

So much for my first attempt at trespassing.

I'd just turned back toward the dock when I heard footsteps.

I glanced around, but there wasn't much in the way of places to hide. I dove behind the end of a long bench seat and curled myself up as small as I could, listening for more steps and cursing the water, which was suddenly deafening as it slapped the hulls of the boats.

The steps grew louder, pausing just outside, from the sound of it, and I held my breath.

I heard a low voice, but I couldn't make out what it was saying, let alone who it belonged to or who it might be addressing, and I was afraid to look.

Then the voice stopped and the footsteps retreated as quickly as they'd come.

I stayed in my ball, in case whoever it was decided to come back. When it seemed reasonable I was alone again, I unrolled myself and crept back onto the dock, looking in every direction and listening hard for company. I only heard the water and cicadas.

I stared at the name on the hull for a long minute. Aaron's family was his whole world. His face always lit up like a frat boy on Friday night when he talked about his daughters. His youngest had just been accepted to Princeton—he'd about popped a button off his shirt relaying that news, and I'd passed it on to Eunice and the features team, where it begat a very flattering profile of his little girl in our "Senior Class" section.

But was money for college really enough motivation to risk the job that put food on the table and paid the mortgage? To risk prison?

I didn't think so. Especially not when that boat itself was probably worth about a hundred grand. Assuming dirty money hadn't paid for it in the first place, selling it would buy her four semesters, at least.

I picked my way carefully back to my car by the moonlight, not wanting to lose a heel off my slingback Jimmy Choos to the spaces between the boards on the dock. Climbing behind the wheel and starting the engine, I wasn't sure the trip had been worth it.

Pulling out of the lot, I turned the puzzle around in my head.

Someone was lying about Aaron being on vacation. The boat at the dock said that much. But whether it was Jerry, or someone lying to Jerry (Aaron or Lowe, maybe), I had no idea.

The road was narrow, with tight curves that looked much different by the light of my high beams than they had in the fading sunshine. I tried to push the story to one side of my brain so that the other could focus on not running the car into a tree, and thought I'd made good progress when a wide sedan roared up behind me, headlights either off or broken, careening to the left and attempting to pass me while straddling the center line.

I slammed the brake and turned the wheel hard, depositing my mini SUV into a ditch full of wild grasses and chiggers. Breathing like

I'd been to the gym, I turned my head in the direction of the road. I didn't even have time to honk.

"You can't take your half out of the middle, Bubba," I hollered at the stillness, my heart still pounding.

It took twenty minutes, every swearword I knew, and about a dozen chigger bites to push/maneuver the car back onto the road, and even by moonlight, I could see the dent in the fender. At least it was drivable.

It wasn't until I was back on northbound 95 that I realized the only place the sedan could have come from was the marina, because it was the only thing between me and the water. The idea that my adventure in the ditch had been anything but a random bit of bad luck courtesy of a drunk redneck verged on terrifying when I considered it for more than thirty seconds, so I turned my attention back to Aaron. Or tried to. But if someone had tried to send me careening into the woods in the boondocks at forty miles an hour over the little info I knew, how far might they have gone to shut Aaron up if he'd actually found something?

I needed more background on Deputy Chief Lowe. And there was still the pesky issue of not knowing who I could believe. Tuesday, I'd have called Jerry without hesitation. By Wednesday night, I wasn't sure I trusted another soul save for my mom, Jenna, and Bob, none of whom could be much help to me right then.

As if delivered by the muses, the police chief's all-American face popped into my head as I exited at Grove, and I resolved to call him for an interview early the next day before I'd even finished wondering if he was suspicious of Lowe. Or anyone else.

Someone had to have the answers I needed, and Donovan Nash seemed like an excellent place to start.

CHAPTER TWELVE

SWEATING my frustrations out at the gym took a backseat to getting ahold of Nash's assistant, and by the time I walked into Bob's office for the staff meeting Thursday, I had an appointment with the police chief the following morning.

"What are you looking so chipper about this morning, Clarke?" Les leaned his big frame back in Bob's chair, not bothering to veil his sarcasm. "Given that Charlie didn't have anything breaking this morning, I assume it has nothing to do with your job?"

I ignored the dig. I'd scooped Charlie three times that week by my count, and numbers were supposed to be his forte.

"As a matter of fact, I have an interview with the police chief tomorrow. And if I'm right, by next week, I'll have all of Richmond going 'Charlie who?' for at least a month."

I thought for a split second about keeping my suspicions to myself, but Bob had warned me against making Les mad, and I figured even he'd be impressed with the possibility of a drug ring running out of police headquarters. Since no one else had arrived for the meeting, I went ahead and told him.

He listened to the whole story and studied me in silence for a full minute before he spoke.

"Why would he rat out his deputy to a reporter?" he asked. "You're assuming you're right about Lowe, but are you also assuming Nash suspects his right hand of being a crook? If he does, he's not going to tell you anything. And if he doesn't, there's no point in asking. You can't seriously be thinking about telling him what you think. His loyalty will lie with his man, I promise you."

So much for impressed. "I know it will, and no, I'm not stupid enough to accuse the deputy chief of being a crook. I'm counting on the chief being unaware of Lowe's involvement. I'm working on a list of very specific, yet routine questions, like 'Is Lowe responsible for training the officers in the river unit?' I don't know that I can get everything I need out of him, but I'll be closer by the time I get through talking to him."

"That might actually work." He laced his fingers together and rested his chin on them, his elbows on Bob's desk. "Make sure you have questions about a lot of different things: the boats, his role in an investigation like this, the FBI. As long as you're not only asking about Lowe, you're okay. Maybe."

He sat back in the chair again and spun it toward the computer.

"You just make damned sure you have it dead to rights," he said. "Libeling the deputy chief of police will not be good for your career, no matter how much Bob likes you. We cannot afford a lawsuit."

"You got it." I pulled out a notepad, jotting random questions for Nash around the important ones I'd already listed. As the rest of the staff began filing in, I wondered if there was any way to get on Les' good side, or if I should just try to stay out of his way.

Chatter about politics and sports swirled around me, but it was difficult to keep my attention on the meeting. My eyes must have strayed to the clock forty times in as many minutes, and as soon as Les pushed the chair back to stand up, I jumped to my feet and bolted for the door.

"Where's the fire, Lois?"

Parker. And I still hadn't read his column from Saturday. I mildly regretted talking to him about it in the first place as I stopped outside the door and turned around, apologetic smile already in place.

"I have about eleventy billion things to do today, but I swear I'll read your breast cancer piece tonight. Really."

"You know, someone with less confidence might be bothered by the fact you haven't made time yet." He grinned. "I can take it, though. But hey, I wanted to talk to you about Bob when you have a minute. I'll be around."

He started to turn away and I sighed, leaning against a long row of filing cabinets.

"You have ninety seconds. Go."

He glanced at his watch, feigning alarm. "What'd you make of how he looked yesterday?"

"He seemed fine to me, but he's Bob. He doesn't tend to let on when he's not fine, obviously."

"That's what I thought. He actually tried to talk the doctor into clearing him to come in for today's morning meeting when they were discharging him last night."

I laughed. "Only Bob would have a heart attack Monday and try to come to work Thursday. She told him he was crazy, right?"

"She told him the first week he was permitted five minutes of walking, five times a day. She said he could progress to short trips out of the house next week as long as he feels up to it. He argues he feels fine and this place is going to implode without him."

"Well, if Les doesn't get off my ass, I may implode. But I think we'll be all right long enough for Bob to recover."

"Why is Les giving you a hard time?"

"You mean besides Shelby whispering in his ear about how happy it would make her to have my job when she's not blowing him?"

Parker's eyes widened and he pinched his lips together. Oops. Les wasn't anywhere near Parker on a physical scale of one to ten, but he did outrank him in terms of pull with the powers that be. Still, that had to sting a little.

"Sorry," I said hastily. "I figured if Bob knew that, everyone did. I'm usually the only person around here who pays so little attention to office gossip."

"It is a newsroom," he said. "But I must have missed that bulletin. She really is something else."

He shifted his feet and stuck his hands in his pockets.

"So, have you found out any more about the missing lawyer or those dead drug dealers?" He flashed the smelling-salts grin when I raised an eyebrow. "See? I read your stuff."

I wondered why he wanted to know. "Nothing definitive," I waved a hand. "It's there somewhere, though. I'll get it."

"Good luck. Let me know if you ever get around to reading my column."

"Today. I swear."

He gave me an exaggerated nod and disappeared into the maze of cubicles. My thoughts turned to Aaron and Mike, and I went to call Jerry for an update.

"Nothing new on the Sorrel case," he said.

Except that it was now a "case." Damn.

"Aaron hasn't called in to check for messages?" I asked, but finding the boat had somehow cemented Mike and Aaron together in my head. If one of them was still gone, the other wouldn't have turned up, either.

"No, but he didn't say he was going to. Are you sure I can't help you with whatever it is you want to talk to him about?"

"I don't think you can, Jerry," I said. "Thanks, though."

I started to hang up.

"Hey, Nichelle?" His voice dropped in pitch and volume. "You can tell me to go to hell if I'm overstepping, here, but what's wrong? We've had some strange shit around town this week, and now you're worrying so much about Aaron calling in from his trip. I'm a detective, and a pretty good one. If you think something's up, I could help. I could meet you after work, if you like. I don't have plans to do anything tonight but watch the Seminoles in the College World Series, and I can DVR the game."

I tapped a pen on my desk blotter, wishing I knew who to trust.

"Thanks, Jerry, but I have a lot going on right now. I appreciate the offer, though."

"Just let me know if you change your mind."

I hung up and turned to the day's police reports. The lone interesting one had me giggling as I dialed the complainant for an interview. The man sounded older, a junkyard owner who had called 9-1-1
the day before when he got to work and found the driveway blocked
by an abandoned casket.

"Turned out the damned thing was full of rusty hubcaps, of all
things, but I made the cops come open it." He spit audibly as he
spoke and I swallowed a laugh, picturing a beer-bellied Bubba,
complete with overalls, staring at a coffin someone dumped in his
driveway.

He filled me in on the details of his call for help, clearly still
annoyed at the amused response he'd gotten. "They asked me what
was in there. Can you believe that?" he said. "I told 'em I wasn't
opening the damned thing. I didn't want to be looking at rotted old
bones first thing in the morning. That's what my tax dollars pay them
for!"

No rotted old bones before coffee. I could go with him on that.

Why anyone'd had the thing in the first place was a mystery, but
Jerry said when I talked to him again there was no forensic evidence it
had ever been used for its intended purpose. I laughed as I typed. It
wasn't a front-page exclusive, but the "news of the weird" vibe made it
an interesting read—the kind of story likely to get a ton of Facebook
shares, which usually made bean counters like Les very happy. So
score one for the crime reporter.

After I filed the story, I opened my Neal folder and stared at the
documents inside, trying to wedge him into my scenario with Lowe as
the drug pusher. My brain warred between DonnaJo's praise of Neal
and the idea that a failed bankruptcy filing and his kid's mounting
medical bills might make it pretty hard to walk past several hundred
thousand dollars in cash.

No matter which way I turned my puzzle piece, I couldn't make
Neal fit with Lowe. But if he wasn't guilty, where the hell was he?

What if he's the victim? I listened to my instincts as I thought
again about Mike's parting words: *If this was a cop, they're into some-*

thing very serious, something they could go to prison for. And going to prison is pretty much every cop's worst nightmare."

An assistant CA could certainly help put a crooked cop in prison. What if Neal suspected something? Or someone, and they decided their secret was worth killing Neal?

The skin on my arm pricked up into goosebumps. From everything I'd seen, if there was a way to make the lawyer the villain, the police department was determined to take it. Which made me wonder who would prove Neal's innocence if he hadn't done it. My short list consisted of DonnaJo and myself. A story that kept an innocent man out of prison and locked up a dirty cop as a bonus? There was no way the *Post* could ignore that. The goosebumps didn't go anywhere.

You're so far ahead of yourself, you're going to lose sight of your own ass, I thought, trying to couch the excitement. *One thing at a time.*

I snatched up my phone and dialed DonnaJo's cell.

"I have about three minutes. I'm in recess," she said when she picked up.

I talked fast, not mentioning anyone specifically, but giving her a broad overview of what I suspected.

"I'm still in the middle of this," I said. "But I have a pretty good hunch the cops want to send Neal up for it if they can."

"What do you need?" There was no hint of reservation in her tone. "Those assholes at the PD aren't going to set Gavin up. No way. He didn't do it, Nichelle. I'd bet my license on that."

"Hopefully I won't need you to. But I do need to know about Neal. If he's made any enemies, maybe? Assuming he didn't take off with the evidence, our most viable option is foul play."

DonnaJo was quiet, the background chatter from the courthouse the only sign I hadn't lost her.

"Jesus, I guess it is, isn't it? Makes you think," she said finally. "I love my job, but I'm not willing to die for it. I really don't know what Gavin has going on, but something's had him in a foul mood for the past few weeks."

I'd bet it had. And I had a sudden idea for how I might find out what that something was.

"Can we grab a drink tonight?" I asked. "I'll come by there to get you about six?"

"Sounds good. I can meet you, if you'd rather."

"Nope. I'll come get you."

She was quiet for a long minute, and I held my breath. DonnaJo was smart.

"I don't think I want to know, so I'll just see you when you get here."

Very smart.

"See you then."

I hung up and flipped open my computer, typing Lowe's name into my Google toolbar.

Facebook and LinkedIn were the top two hits, but his accounts were locked down to exclude everyone but friends or connections. I went back to the search results and kept scrolling. A ton of stuff from the *Telegraph*, most of it written by me, and a good many city council meeting minutes and agendas. TV news stories. A magazine article.

I was on page seven by the time I saw it.

The current command staff at the PD had been in place when I'd come to Richmond, and I'd never done any backgrounding on any of them. So until Google provided me with an old team photo, I had no way of knowing that Dave Lowe had been a trainer for the 1998 UVA baseball team.

And grinning his perfect grin from the back row of the photo on my screen was Grant Parker.

"Fuck me," I whispered, sitting back in my chair, my eyes locked on the photo.

No way.

And yet, there it was. Full color. Undeniable.

"Could I be any dumber?" I said, muffled by the fingers that had flown up to my lips. Parker had hardly ever spoken to me before I'd mentioned the drug dealers in that staff meeting, yet in a week he'd managed to become something resembling a friend. At least, I was beginning to think he might.

I ran back through every conversation, ticking off questions about my story he'd tossed into each one. He'd even shown up at the river Friday night.

Covering cops for six years taught me true coincidences are few and far between.

Closing my eyes, I called up the crime scene shots of drug dealers Noah Smith and Darryl Wright from my memory, their eyes open, blood and gore splattering the walls behind them.

Jesus. What if our sports columnist had been responsible for that?

I dropped my forehead into one hand and pulled in a deep breath, my head swimming.

Think, Nichelle.

With an enshrined jersey number at UVA and a popular sports column, Grant Parker was a local hero, beloved by thousands of people. Apart from his occasional ego Tourette's, he seemed like a nice enough guy, too. Why would he be in on a massive murder and drug trafficking scheme?

I had only one answer, and I'd never wanted so badly to be wrong.

The fancy new motorcycle. The thick stack of fifties he'd pulled out at the restaurant. I'd seen a lot in my tenure at the crime desk, and money was second only to sex on the list of motives for murder.

I thought about Parker carrying Katie DeLuca to her car and wondered if the kindness was motivated by guilt. What if Parker knew about the boat all along? Hell, what if he'd set up some sort of rendezvous between the cops and the ballplayers, then shown up to check it out when it went bad? Suddenly nothing seemed too crazy to consider.

I bookmarked the team photo on my computer and sat back in my chair, unsure of what to do with that information. I couldn't tell Les, and I sure as hell couldn't tell Bob. They'd laugh me out of the building—possibly the city. I had no one I trusted at the police department, even assuming that Mike and Aaron weren't part of my growing conspiracy theory, and staring at a photo of Parker and Lowe, that no longer seemed a safe assumption.

I glanced back down at my desk and saw DonnaJo's email about Neal and his active cases.

His wife had refused to comment on Tuesday, but she was just going to have to get over that. She had to know something, even if she didn't know she knew it. And I needed to know it, too.

Scribbling down their address in Henrico, I stuffed the files into my bag and took a drive to the suburbs.

Grace Neal looked positively haggard when she opened her front door, her flat brown eyes not even registering surprise to see me standing there.

"Could you please just leave me alone?" she said, her voice raspy. "I know everyone thinks my husband is a felon, but I just want to take care of my little boy and have my husband back at home. I told Charlie Lewis yesterday when she came by poking a camera in my face: I'm not giving interviews. Go away."

She moved to shut the door. Desperate, I stuck my foot in the crack, wincing at the pressure. She was strong for a petite little thing.

"Are you serious?" Her eyes widened and she pushed harder.

I gritted my teeth and stood my ground.

"Mrs. Neal, I know you don't want to talk to me, and frankly, I don't blame you," I said. "I can't believe I'm actually doing this, but I sort of don't have a choice. There's something wrong at the police department, and I think your husband might know what it is. I thought he might be part of it, but now I'm not so sure. So I'm going to need you to open that door and let some blood back into my foot, and then I'm going to need your help to figure this out."

She stared a good thirty seconds, my foot still pinched in the heavy oak door, before she swung it wide and waved me inside.

"Just be quiet, please," she said. "It's so hard to get him to sleep sometimes."

I hobbled through the bright foyer into her family room, wide and sunny with butter-colored walls and cushy, overstuffed furniture. It looked like a spread from Better Homes and Gardens, save for an end table that held a small lamp and a very large piece of medical equipment with a mask attached to it.

"My son has Cystic Fibrosis," she said, following my gaze. "It means he has a buildup of thick mucus in a lot of his organs, including his lungs. That helps him breathe a little easier."

"I'm sorry to hear that." I was, but the words sounded lame. I didn't really know what else to say.

"It is what it is." She flashed a tired half-smile. "He's a wonderful little boy, and I wouldn't trade him for anything. But sometimes it's hard. I've never had to take care of him by myself for so long before."

"And you haven't heard from your husband at all?" I watched her carefully for signs of dishonesty.

"Not since he left here on Sunday." Grace Neal held my gaze as she spoke, not fidgeting or wavering. "I know he didn't steal that evidence, but why do you suddenly think my Gavin's innocent?"

"I have a theory, and I'm wondering if your husband may think the same thing."

"He's suspicious of something." She nodded. "He got his nose all out of joint a few months ago over the guns from that case he worked last year. The trucker from New York?"

I nodded as I reached into my bag and pulled out a notebook.

"Tell me why he was mad." I clicked out a pen.

"Gavin has a thing about guns," she said. "A sort of personal vendetta. He had a good friend when he was a little boy who was in the wrong place at the wrong time and caught a stray bullet from an unregistered gun. He became a prosecutor to keep them off the streets. I've never seen him work so hard on a case. He triple checked every detail, staying at the office until midnight for a week before his opening argument. He was ecstatic at the thought of so many guns being destroyed after he won, and he spent months after the trial counting the days until they were sent off to be scrapped."

I guessed where her story was going from what Joey had said about the guns being on the boat.

"About two months ago, he went down to the police department to ride along while the guns were taken out of the evidence lock-up over to be chomped—they put them in this big shredding machine and the city sells the scrap metal. Gavin thinks it's the greatest invention of the twentieth century." She half-smiled, then sighed.

"But then he got to the evidence room and they told him he wasn't allowed to go. They kept saying it was against regulations. He put up a fuss because he knows the rules inside and out, but they wouldn't budge. The guy in the evidence room said he had orders from the command staff."

"Of course he did," I muttered.

"Excuse me?" Grace paused and gave me a quizzical smile.

"Sorry. Thinking out loud. Please, go on."

She sighed again. "So Gavin called the command office, and someone gave him some bullshit about how they couldn't be liable for putting Gavin in a dangerous situation in case someone tried to hijack the truck or something. Gavin argued, but the guy refused to give in. I felt so bad for him. Not that I wanted him to be in danger, but he was so excited about this. They finally said they'd send the deputy chief. That's the second-in-command, right?"

I nodded.

"He said he'd go along and then call Gavin as soon as they got back from dropping the guns off at the shredder.

"And he did. Called Gavin a couple of hours later, said everything went smoothly. Gavin was so excited. He brought home champagne."

"But then something went wrong?"

She nodded.

"The next day, he called his friend at the plant to see how much scrap they got out of them, and the guy said the guns never arrived."

I sucked in a sharp breath even though I had suspected the words were coming.

"Yeah," she said. "Gavin was pissed. We've been married for twelve years and I've never seen him so mad. He drove straight to the police department and demanded to see this deputy guy, but of course, the cop didn't have time to talk. Gavin filed a complaint with the civil service commission. It got bogged down in red tape, but he kept after it.

"Finally, the commission told Gavin the guy at the scrap plant swore under oath he destroyed the guns. Apparently he was 'mistaken' when he told Gavin the guns never arrived. Gavin didn't believe any of it, swore to me something fishy was going on at the police department, and from that point on, he made weekly random checks of the evidence room. Then Sunday, he never made it home." Her voice faded on the last word.

Bingo. I nodded my head as I scribbled.

"Did he tell you what he suspected?" I asked.

"He did not." She brushed at her eye and shook her head. "He said I didn't need to be part of it, and I didn't press him, to be honest with you. There were things he had to see at work that I didn't care to know about. When he comes home after this nightmare, he'll join a private firm with a fat salary and a corner office and a lot of tax law or something equally boring, if I have anything to say about it. He turns down half a dozen offers every single year. My husband is a brilliant lawyer, and he has a good heart. But I'm through with the crusading if this is how it's going to end up."

"Can't say I blame you," I said.

"Why are you asking, anyway?" she asked. "Do you think something happened to him? Something bad?"

"You don't?" I didn't mean to blurt it quite so bluntly, but I couldn't believe she didn't think the worst after what she just told me.

Grace bit her lip, her effort to control her breathing not really working. "I don't want to," she said, a small sob escaping with the words. "I just want him to come home."

"I hope he does," I said. "Thank you for talking to me, Grace. This is a big help. Can I ask one last favor?"

She sniffled and drug the back of one hand across her face. "Sure."

"Does your husband have a home office, and may I check it out?"

She stood up and moved toward the back of the house.

"In here," she said. "He likes to work in the sunroom where he can see the trees."

I looked over the desk, but all of the files were labeled with one of two things: the names of medical companies and doctor's offices, or defendants. I rifled through two drawers and a cabinet, but came up empty-handed. Damn. I had just turned back to the doorway to thank Grace for her time when an ear-splitting trill split the silence in the house.

"Shit," the word slid between clenched teeth as Grace lunged for the cordless phone on the desk. "I keep the ringer up so I can hear it over Alex's breathing machine." She hit a button on the white handset and raised it to her ear.

"Neal residence."

I looked back at my notes, but a small, strangled sound from my hostess snapped my head back up.

"Thank you." The words were automatic, little more than a whisper, her eyes wide and staring at nothing. The phone clattered to the tile floor and I jumped to my feet, dumping the notebook under the desk.

"Grace?"

"He's gone." She said it so softly I almost didn't hear, tears falling fast. "My Gavin. He's dead. That...they...the police pulled him out of the river an hour ago. They said his body was dumped there. Weighted down."

Her face crumpled into a mask of grief and she would've fallen if I hadn't caught her, leading her back to the sofa in the buttery-bright family room and holding her while she sobbed.

There are times when being right really sucks.

CHAPTER THIRTEEN

BY THE TIME I found a phone number for Grace Neal's mother scrawled across the babysitter pad on their fridge and waited for her to arrive, my cell phone had rung itself into a nearly-dead battery.

"Where the fuck have you been?" Les screamed in my ear when I called him back as I pointed the car down West Broad toward the city. "Don't you own a goddamn scanner anymore? Your missing prosecutor just turned up in the river, dumped like something out of an old gangster movie, according to Channel Four. Of course, I have to get my information from Charlie Lewis, because my cops reporter is nowhere to be found when the biggest crime story of the year breaks. They're having a press conference at police headquarters at five-thirty."

I checked my clock. It was already five-fifteen, and I was all the way out in the west end. Damn.

"I know about the lawyer. I was interviewing his wife when the cops called. I stayed with her until her mother arrived."

"You what? Since when are we in the business of babysitting strangers?"

Since I'm a decent human being, you prick. I clenched my jaw. He totally would have left the poor woman sitting there in shock. Of course, Charlie probably would have, too.

I gulped a deep breath. Don't piss him off, Bob said. And I didn't want to give Shelby any more ammunition.

"I'm sorry," I said, fighting to keep my tone even. "I did talk to the widow, and she told me her husband was suspicious that something wasn't right in the police evidence room."

I paused, waiting for an "attagirl." He was quiet. I gave up.

"I have my laptop, and I'm on my way to the PD," I said. "They never start press conferences on time, anyway. Watch your email for my write-up and tell Ryan to be ready to get it on the web. Has Charlie been out at the recovery site? Did you send photo?"

"Yes, I sent photo. I know how to do my job. And of course Charlie's been out there. Even the new girl from Channel Ten has been out there. Everyone has kicked our ass on this, thanks to you. Don't bother going to the PD. Shelby's already there. We can take it from here."

I slammed my foot on the brake just in time to keep from rear-ending the corvette in front of me, no retort at the ready for that. And the beeping in my ear told me he'd hung up, anyway. I threw the phone across the car and it clattered against the passenger window before it bounced into the floor.

"Dammit!" I slammed my hands down on the steering wheel. "This is really what I get for not being a heartless bitch? Hey, karma, I think I'm getting screwed, here."

The light changed and I drove aimlessly, the urge to kick something (namely Les) pretty strong as I replayed the conversation in my head.

Coasting up Monument Avenue, I passed the stunning collection of larger-than-life statues that began near the old city limits with Robert E. Lee and ended a mile and a half later with tennis star Arthur Ashe. The street itself was gorgeous, with stately antebellum homes peeking from behind rustling leaves, the shadows cast by the spires at First English Lutheran Church growing long in the evening sunlight. I rolled down the windows and took deep, calming breaths.

Les would have to eat those words when I exposed the corruption at the police department. And I would very much enjoy watching him do that.

Feeling more sociable and remembering my date with DonnaJo, I followed Monument until it turned into Franklin, then turned on Ninth, passing city hall and the library before I stopped in front of the John Marshall Courts Building, which housed the CA's offices. I flipped the mirror down before I got out, dabbing on lipstick and straightening my hair.

"Let Shelby have her fun," I said aloud to my reflection. "It won't matter. Les is just a jackass on a power trip. Just beat Charlie to the punch here, and it won't matter one little bit."

Since I had no way of knowing what Charlie had or didn't have, I needed to work fast and make sure I got it right.

I took the elevator up to DonnaJo's practically deserted office and found her staring at her computer, which was streaming Charlie's coverage of the press conference, though it still hadn't started.

"I didn't expect to see you." DonnaJo's blue eyes widened when I tapped on her doorframe. Judging by the red rims on those eyes and her smeared makeup, my beauty-queen-turned-hardass-prosecutor friend had taken the news about her colleague badly. "Why are you not over at the press conference? You heard about Gavin?"

"I'm so sorry, honey." I shook my head. "I was at his house when they called his wife. I stayed with her after she got the call, so the asshole who's filling in for Bob sent a copy editor to the press conference instead."

"Ouch."

"It stings, I admit." I sat on the gray velour sofa near the door. "But it's not the end of the world. It's one press conference. Though, good of the paper be damned, I hope she chokes."

DonnaJo laughed. "May Charlie Lewis wipe the floor with her."

"Charlie will eat her for breakfast," I said. "But hey, she wanted to play with the big girls."

DonnaJo spun the screen so I could see it, too, and my stomach turned as I watched Deputy Police Chief Dave Lowe take the podium outside police headquarters.

Lowe cleared his throat and faced the cameras, squaring his narrow shoulders as he gripped the sides of the podium with both hands, his dark, curly hair shellacked so the wind whipping the flags behind him didn't budge it. He wasn't a big man, probably shorter than me with a slight build. Looking into his round brown eyes, even on TV, gave me chills.

He began by telling the small group of reporters that Assistant Commonwealth Attorney Gavin Neal was found dead, his body weighted down in the James River after an apparently fatal gunshot wound. Two guys out fishing found Neal's body after one of them dropped a wristwatch in the water.

I made a mental note to get their names from Jerry and waited for Lowe to get to something else I didn't already know.

"No official cause of death for Mr. Neal yet from the coroner. We will know more after he completes the autopsy," Lowe said. "The hearts and prayers of the Richmond Police Department are with the Neal family today and in the weeks to come."

He nodded to the new girl from Channel Ten, who started with the obvious question. "Do you have any suspects yet, chief?"

"We are pursuing a number of leads in this case, and we have been building a list of suspects for nearly a week now," Lowe said. "Mr. Neal worked within the criminal world for many years, and he may have recently gotten involved, through a case he tried, with a very dangerous part of that world. Our strongest lead, given the circumstances surrounding his death, includes ties to organized crime. That's all I'm going to say about that today."

My mouth fell open. Somewhere far away, I heard Shelby's unmistakable high-pitched drawl, asking if there was evidence of foul play.

"Aside from the gunshot wound and the weights holding him under the water?" Lowe kept a straight face as he spoke, but Charlie's mike picked up her own chuckle at the reply. "There was not."

"That's your girl?" DonnaJo asked.

"She used to cover the garden club, now she wants my beat." I felt a little sorry for Shelby. But only a little.

"Nice."

Charlie hit Lowe with a barrage of questions about the exact time and place of the discovery, and how long they thought the body had been there, but I only half-heard, my mind looping back through Lowe's first answer like a scratched record.

"What do you make of that, DonnaJo?" I asked her as Lowe thanked the reporters and disappeared. "What he said about the mob?"

She shrugged, a thoughtful gaze narrowing her swollen eyes.

"I don't know what to make of any of it," she said. "I mean, the Mafia is, well, full of bad guys. But this sounds like something out of a black and white movie. We put people away all the time. We don't generally end up dumped in the river, though. What the hell is going on here, Nichelle?"

It sounded absurd even in my head, the idea that the cops killed Neal and were trying to frame the mob, so I just returned the shrug and kept my mouth shut.

"I'm not sure," I said. "But we're smarter than your average bear. Why don't we have that drink and see if talking helps us figure it out?"

She got up and moved toward the door.

"I'm going to stop in the ladies' room," she said.

I followed, leaving my bag on the floor in front of the sofa.

"Where do you want to go?" she asked.

"Capital Ale?"

"Works for me," she said, pushing open the bathroom door.

Drying my hands a few minutes later, I snapped my fingers.

"Damn," I said. "I forgot my bag. You go on down and I'll catch up."

DonnaJo eyed me sideways and shook her head slightly. But she didn't object. "Where'd you park?"

"Right outside on the street. You can't miss it." I turned back toward her office as the elevator chimed. "Be right there."

When the doors closed, I sprinted back to her office and grabbed my bag, teetering on my eggplant Nicholas Kirkwoods when I turned toward the door with Neal's name on it. I took a deep breath and darted inside, no time for second thoughts.

I jerked open file drawers one after another, finding only folder upon folder of numbered cases. Damn, there was a lot of crime in this city.

Dropping to my knees, I flipped open the credenza doors, already afraid DonnaJo would come back looking for me if I didn't go downstairs shortly. In the back corner of the cabinet, almost hidden by two reams of paper, I saw the corner of a red file folder.

I wriggled it free and flipped it open. My article on the Darryl Wright murder lay on top of a small stack of papers, two paragraphs highlighted and a question mark in the margin.

Jackpot. I wanted to make photocopies, but I was seriously out of time. I stuffed the folder into my bag and ran back to the elevators, smoothing my ivory linen tank dress and taking a few deep breaths while I waited. Before that week, I'd never violated anything worse than a traffic law. In two days, I'd trespassed on a cop's boat and stolen a file from the prosecutor's office. If I hadn't been so focused on the story, I would've felt guilty.

DonnaJo arched an eyebrow at me when I walked outside.

"You get lost?" she asked.

"I had to pee again," I clicked the button to unlock the doors and stowed my bag in the back. "Too much water this afternoon, I guess."

"Uh-huh." She climbed into my passenger seat. "Glad to hear you're hydrating properly."

We politely shoved our way through the after work crowd at the bar and settled into a polished oak booth in the back of the long, narrow dining room. As tables of power-suited professionals dove into platters of gourmet hot wings and fancy hamburgers amid discussions of politics and the stock market, DonnaJo and I sipped Virginia chardonnay and talked about Neal and the police department and the Mafia for two hours. DonnaJo dissolved into tears twice during the conversation, and while I wanted to be invested, I was itching to go through the file I'd swiped from Neal's office.

As the stars became visible overhead, I stopped the car and told

DonnaJo goodnight in front of her office building, offering my condolences again as she stepped out of the car.

"Hey Nichelle? I know you're onto something, and I know you don't want to tell me what it is," she said, holding the door open. "I'm okay with that. But Gavin was a good friend and a damned fine lawyer. So don't screw this up, okay? I want to see the guilty bastards put away. And you let me know if I can help you."

"You already have, honey," I said, easing my foot off the brake. "Get some rest. I'll talk to you soon."

She shut the door and disappeared into the parking garage.

Snuggling Darcy and sipping another glass of wine, I settled on my sofa and slid my heels off before I opened Neal's file.

My story on Darryl was first. He'd highlighted the paragraphs about the similarity in the crime scenes, with drugs being left at both of them, and inked a big question mark in the margin.

I kept flipping, finding more articles about drug arrests, a copy of his civil service complaint, and several police and lab reports. The upper corner of one page caught my eye, and I pulled it to the top of the stack. I scanned the data at first, then read again with more care, my jaw dropping as a big chunk of my puzzle fell neatly into place.

"Holy shit, Darcy," I said, and the dog's ears perked up. "They've been getting away with this for...well, for God knows how long. How many hundreds of thousands—or millions—of dollars are we talking about here?"

Hours later, my brain refused to stop running questions in circles, and I gave up on sleep. I fiddled with the five-thousand-piece rendering of *The Scream* that I'd picked up at the Virginia Museum of Fine Arts' expressionist exhibit when I'd gone with Jenna in May, but couldn't concentrate enough to finish the border. I gave that up after ten minutes, flipping open my laptop instead.

I checked my email and then scrolled through shoe listings on eBay, bidding on a pair of aubergine Manolos with transparent silk flowers on the ankle straps and hoping no one else would notice them before the auction's end on Friday night. I couldn't afford to go much higher, and they were the cutest pair I'd seen in my size in months. My feet are anything but dainty—a European size forty, which is about a nine in U.S. sizing. Secondhand ones that big can be hard to find.

Nothing made sleep any easier, though. I ended up staring at my ceiling fan until dawn, mentally paging through Gavin Neal's secret file.

By a quarter to seven the next morning, I was dressed to kill for my interview with Chief Nash: black pencil skirt, powder blue silk tank and my favorite black patent Louboutins giving my strut a little extra oomph as I rang Bob's doorbell.

"Come to apologize for the earful I got from Les last night?" Bob said when he pulled the door open. He'd traded the pajamas for khakis and a golf shirt, which he favored year-round even though he hated the game.

"Yeah, yeah. I'm sorry I'm not the kind of person who abandons a distraught wife when she finds out her husband turned up dead in the river." I stepped inside and followed him to the kitchen. "But wait 'til you see what I have!"

"It better be damned good," he said, pouring me a cup of coffee and pushing the sugar bowl across the high granite bar. "Les is pushing to give Shelby full rein on this thing with the lawyer."

"It's fucking fantastic is what it is." I handed him a copy of the lab report I'd found in Neal's file. The originals were tucked under a loose floorboard in my coat closet, which made me feel both ridiculous and important at the same time.

He squinted at the places on the report where the ink was faded, thanks to my aging scanner, and then looked back at me.

"What the hell does a bag of pancake mix have to do with heroin?"

"Everything, when you're talking about cops running drugs out of the police evidence room. How's that for a sexy story?" I bounced on the balls of my feet. "This is what I've been looking for—well, it's a big part of it, anyway. Look at the dates on the tests. There was a bag of heroin entered into evidence last summer, and the results of the lab tests to confirm that it was heroin got lost at the courthouse.

"The ACA on that case asked for another test, and the lab said it was pancake mix. Pancake mix! Then the PD claimed there was a mistake by the lab and sent another sample to be tested, and that time it was drugs again."

I stopped to take a breath, the hope this nightmare of a story might have a happy ending—for me, anyway—sending adrenaline through my veins in waves.

"It wasn't a mistake," Bob's thick eyebrows shot up.

"No." I sipped my coffee. "They're replacing the drugs in the evidence locker with ordinary stuff, but only after the samples have been sent to the lab to confirm what they are for the trials. Heroin is kind of a beige powder, just like pancake mix. And no one would look too closely after it had been tested. It's brilliant. And foolproof, except when someone loses their paperwork. This—" I shook the paper. "This is their mistake."

I remembered the copy of my story Neal highlighted, sudden certainty about his reason for going to police headquarters the day he disappeared making me shudder.

"Neal knew it," I whispered. "He was down there to test the drugs from the dealer murders, to see if they were still drugs. He figured they were selling the drugs, and probably guessed that his guns were being sold, too. I'd bet my entire shoe collection I'm right."

"This is great stuff, kid," Bob smiled and pushed the paper back across the bar. "But where'd you get it?"

"Where?" I dropped my eyes to the counter, pretending to be fascinated by the random onyx and cream flecks in the stone.

"Where." He drew the word out.

"I found it at the CA's office."

"You found it? Or you stole it from the dead lawyer's files?"

"Does it matter? We've finally got something concrete. It doesn't link Lowe to the actual drugs disappearing, but it shows what they're doing with them."

"It's good," Bob said. "And you're definitely onto something, but there's two things: one, since I didn't think it was necessary to spell this out for you before, you can't steal evidence from the prosecutor's office. Especially not when the prosecutor in question has just turned up murdered. You could get in serious trouble for this. Two, this is good, but it's not concrete. It says right here that the third test showed a mistake by the lab on the second one.

"And your guy Lowe isn't mentioned on it anywhere. We can't accuse the deputy chief of police of being a drug lord on something this thin. You have to get more."

Nice how he could burst my bubble so effectively, yet be kind about doing it.

"Of course I do." My shoulders heaved with the sigh that rushed from my chest. "Dammit. That's why Neal was down there looking for more evidence."

Bob patted my hand.

"You're doing good work here, Nicey. I know it's frustrating, but you really are. Here's the thing: they've barely cleared me to leave the house, and I'm not supposed to drive yet. Les is determined to make you look as incompetent as he possibly can. And while Shelby didn't exactly earn herself a Pulitzer yesterday, her story was more than decent, and she was there, which is his big argument right now.

"I pushed back as much as I could and told him you were in a very unusual situation, but he's going to go over my head if you screw anything else up, and the suits like him better than they like me. I'm just a dinosaur who's won some awards. Good to trot out for the old folks on the board who remember when I covered Vietnam and civil rights, but that's about it.

"Charlie had ten minutes this morning with the fishermen who found the lawyer yesterday. Go find them, get something new out of them, and shut Les up for today. I'm begging you. When you've done that, get to the bottom of this, pronto."

I opened my mouth to protest and he put up a hand and shook his head.

"I know it takes time to get something like this right, but your clock is ticking and I can't do much to slow it down from here." He sighed. "We need this story, Nicey. Every bit as much as you need it for your portfolio. Nail it down. Just keep me in the loop, and don't fuck up again."

I didn't think I'd fucked up before, but since my opinion didn't seem to be the popular one, I nodded and promised to toe the line in a timely manner.

"I'm going to interview Chief Nash this morning, and then I'll find the fishermen," I said. "You do me a favor and get better. Les and his girlfriend are getting on my nerves."

He smiled. "I'm doing my best. And Parker brought me dinner last night. He asked about you. Apparently Shelby put on quite a show on her way out to the PD yesterday. I told him you were with the lawyer's wife, and he said to tell you to ask if you need help with anything. Might be nice for you to have a friend in the newsroom."

If the friend wasn't Dave Lowe's college buddy, sure it would. I half-smiled and nodded, spinning back toward the front door.

"Thanks, chief."

I left the copy of the lab report under my seat in the car when I went into police headquarters to interview Nash.

His office was cavernous, the walls decorated with certificates and medals. A tall bookcase held copies of the criminal justice code, the Virginia Constitution, a smattering of legal thrillers, several coffee mugs emblazoned with logos from different police departments, and a Gators pennant.

"Miss Clarke." Nash stood when the detective who worked as his assistant showed me in. He offered a Parker-worthy grin from behind a polished cherry desk, putting a hand out.

He was bigger than I remembered, taller than me with broad shoulders and a thick, solid chest under his trademark charcoal jacket. While most of my non-uniform cops favored a more business casual dress code, I had never seen Nash in anything but a suit.

Not that I saw much of him. The head of a big-city department rarely has reason to talk to the press unless they just like seeing their name in the news, and Nash wasn't a limelight hound.

"Forgive me, but I'm going to have to make this quick," he said. "You've caught me on a very interesting day."

"I won't take too much of your time, and I appreciate you seeing me." I shook his hand. "We'll just jump right in, if that's okay with you."

He nodded and settled back into his tufted red leather chair. I took a black armchair across from him and pulled out my notes, firing questions and scribbling his answers.

He seemed fond of Lowe. Nash said though it wasn't part of Lowe's responsibility to train officers for the river unit, he had an interest in the water patrols thanks to a Hampton Roads upbringing, and often went above and beyond.

"He's invaluable," Nash said. "Spends hours outside his regular duties mentoring promising young officers."

How generous of him.

"To come back from his youthful indiscretions and be the kind of officer he is shows extraordinary determination," Nash continued.

"Youthful indiscretions?" I echoed, furrowing my brow and looking up from my notes.

Nash smiled. "I assumed you knew. Dave doesn't make a big secret of the fact that he had a bit of a wild streak when he was young. A couple of brushes with the law: drugs, misdemeanor theft. When he was arrested, it served as a wakeup call. He's really turned his life around."

Hot damn. I slowed my scribbling, mostly as an excuse to keep my face hidden behind my hair as I bent over my notebook. It took supreme control to refrain from jumping up, shouting "eureka," and sprinting back to my office.

I switched gears, moving the topic to the boat crash.

Nash didn't have much to say about the FBI investigation, which I expected, and his comments about the accident itself were restricted to things I already knew, but I needed the conversation to have more than one focus. The discovery of Neal's body was the hot news of the day.

"Chief Lowe mentioned yesterday that the department thinks the murder of Gavin Neal could be the work of organized crime," I said, thinking of Joey's smile and hoping it wasn't in spite of myself. "Can you elaborate on why that is?"

"I've taken a personal interest in that investigation." Nash shook his head. "We're working several leads, but given Mr. Neal's instrumental role in the New York trucker trial last year, we'd be remiss to ignore the possibility that this was a Mafia payback."

I nodded. There should be a course on cop double-talk in every college journalism department.

On a whim, I asked him about Mike.

He frowned.

"That's troubling, to say the least," he said. "Sergeant Sorrel is one of our best officers. We hope to have an answer for his family very soon."

I nodded as I scribbled, wondering if Mike really could be in on whatever had gotten Gavin Neal killed—or if he was in the river somewhere, too. Either seemed possible, and I honestly wasn't sure which I preferred.

"It's been a pleasure meeting you, Miss Clarke," Nash said, standing when I closed my notebook and smiled at him. "I enjoy the work you do, even when it doesn't make us look like the smartest cops around. *The Telegraph* is lucky to have you."

I smiled. If I was the type, I might've blushed.

"Thank you for your time, chief," I said. "I appreciate your fitting me in. This was very helpful."

Nash hit a button on his desk phone and the assistant came to show me out.

I cranked up the stereo and ran through my suspects as I drove back to the office. Though I had more on Lowe, Nash hadn't offered anything that substantially changed my list. Nor had he given me any real answers.

I made my living asking other people questions, but I was so tired of them I didn't care if I never thought of another one.

A copy of the morning paper, Shelby's story on Neal blocked off in pink highlighter, lay on my desk with a big red "thank you" scrawled across the top of it. Nice. Stuffing it in the recycle bin, I looked up a phone number for one of the fishermen who'd discovered Neal's body and dialed.

They were both there, already drunk at noon and way too excited about having their angling interrupted by a corpse. It was macabre. But also sort of funny, and I needed some levity in my day.

Jake Holly and Tony Ross had decided to spend the day together after they'd been on the early show with Charlie, Jake's wife said, "and they've been sitting on my deck drinking beer and reliving their adventure."

She put Jake on the phone and a nanosecond later, Tony picked up an extension.

I asked them to get further away from each other to avoid feedback from the cordless handsets screaming in my ear. They reminded me of a couple of little boys who'd caught a big fish. Creepy, but in a "Scooby Doo Meets the Redneck Brigade" sort of way.

"Which one of you jumped in the water to get the watch?" I asked, interrupting their race to tell me loudest and fastest what had happened.

"I did," Jake said. "Tony was afraid he'd get caught in the current. I'm a better swimmer."

"You wish," Tony snorted.

"Why didn't you jump in there, then?" Jake hollered.

I could hear the effects of the Budweiser and didn't want the nice woman who'd answered my call to have to break up a brawl in her kitchen, so I moved to the next question.

"Then what happened, Jake?" I asked. "Were you looking around for the watch, or did you see the body right away?"

"My watch landed right next to it. Er, him," Jake said. "I thought at first it was some sorta joke. Like, somebody had dropped a dummy down there, you know? But I got closer and I could see the man's eyes, and I knew it was a real person."

"He came up outta the water screaming like a little girl," Tony chortled. "I thought he was pulling my chain, but he kept screaming at me to call the cops and get him the hell outta the water."

"And then the police came?" I asked.

"Yeah, they brought a boat and scuba gear and went down there and brought him up, and the coroner's office took him away. There were chains with weights around his feet and his middle and his neck. It was pretty gross," Jake sounded less than excited for the first time since he'd picked up the phone.

Charlie hadn't asked about the weights. True, Charlie wasn't quite as invested in the details of this story as I was, best I could tell, but I'd take whatever advantage over her reporting I could claim.

"Weights? What kind? Did you see?"

"The kind you use to exercise," Jake said. "They were pretty big ones, too. I didn't know they made those things that big."

I pictured the shiny rows of dumbbells in the weight room at the police department and wondered if I'd just gotten a break. Surely they'd replaced them by now. Still, it wouldn't hurt to check. Everyone made a mistake somewhere.

They asked me in stereo if their names were going to be on the next day's front page. I assured them they would, then clicked the phone off while they were still hooting at each other about that.

I thought about the lab report from Neal's file, which I had read enough times to commit to memory, and dialed the state forensics office. When the tech who'd analyzed the pancake mix picked up, I introduced myself and asked if he remembered the case, crossing my fingers under the desk.

He laughed. "Yeah, I do. We don't get a lot of stuff through here that's not what it looks like. I knew when I opened that bag that whatever was in it wasn't heroin. The smell wasn't right. I played around with it for a while, trying to see if maybe it was some kind of new street drug, but the compounds in it were all wrong. I was curious, and eventually, I started testing stuff out of my pantry against it. That's how I figured out it was baking mix."

"But then the next sample wasn't," I said, still scrawling the last of his comment on my yellow legal pad.

"I don't want to speculate on that, if you don't mind," he said. I kept my hand moving, not missing a word. "I didn't test the third sample, and I can't speak to what happened with it. All I can tell you for sure is that my analysis was pretty thorough. More thorough than it had to be, because I was curious. There's no way I was mistaken."

"Would that be easy? To fake the appearance of an illegal drug with something else?"

"It wouldn't be hard," he said. "Clumps of baking soda tinted with a little food coloring come close enough to looking like crack cocaine, and any white or off-white powder could pass for cocaine HCL. As I said, pancake mix outwardly resembles heroin. Even the prescription stuff would be doable, if you were doing it right. Lots of stuff, from baby aspirin to mints, comes in little tablets, in just about any color you could want. A dealer could make a killing as long as he didn't want repeat customers. People would be fooled pretty easily until they actually took the stuff."

Except I was pretty sure the fake stuff wasn't being sold. I thanked him for his help, smiling as I cradled the phone.

The smile faded when a voice from behind me interrupted my thoughts.

"Bob is convinced that you're going to redeem yourself today." Les sounded less than convinced. "What do you have, since you skipped out on the meeting this morning?"

I spun my chair around to face him. I'd been avoiding him all day, but Nash was an excellent excuse for missing the meeting.

"I wasn't in the meeting because I was interviewing the police chief. I told you about that yesterday, remember?" I flashed a Shelby-like fake smile.

"Did you get anything good out of him?"

I bit my tongue. I wanted to tell him I knew exactly why he was giving me such a hard time, and it was a shitty thing for him to do no matter how good Shelby was in bed. But I wanted to keep my job, so I swallowed the words.

"I did," I said instead. "Turns out Lowe has a record. I'm going to see what I can dig up on that, and I already talked to the fishermen, too."

"Woohoo. So has everyone else." He leaned against the edge of the cube and folded his arms over his chest.

He stared at me for a long minute. I didn't look away.

"I hope you got something new from someone," he said finally. "You still have a regular job to do around here, and I bet you haven't even looked through today's police reports yet. This big investigative reporter act you're pulling won't play much longer if you don't come up with something to show for it, just so you know." He turned and stalked off.

Dammit. I spun the chair back to the desk and cradled my head in my hands. Shelby made a newbie mistake at the press conference because she was nervous and desperate to ask a question, but her story was good, I had to admit. And with all the unanswered questions swirling around me, Les breathing down my neck waiting to hand her my beat if I missed an apostrophe was crazy-making.

I called Jerry to ask if the PD had released any new information on Neal, the boating crash, or Aaron and Mike. Not surprisingly, he had nothing. And I had less than that in the way of excuses to ask for tour of the gym at police headquarters, so I hung up.

I flipped my computer open and wrote up what I had on the fishermen, which wasn't fantastic enough to impress anyone but should be sufficient to keep me at the crime desk for another day.

Filing the story with Les, I paged through crime reports. Nothing interesting, and my thoughts kept straying to the weights Jake Holly described.

Someone would have to be strong to heft a grown man chained to huge dumbbells into the river. Lowe was about as likely as Jenna to be able to pull that off. There wasn't exactly a shortage of biceps at the PD, but Parker's Polos—tailored to show off the hours he spent in the gym—blipped up in my thoughts, and I wondered if he was the muscle that sank Gavin Neal to the bottom of the James.

"Bob said you had quite a day yesterday." Parker's voice came from behind me and I whacked my bruised knee on the underside of the desk again when I jumped. Did the mere thought of him conjure his presence out of the ether?

Turning the chair toward him, I fixed a big grin on my face.

"Just the man I wanted to talk to today," I said, and his eyes widened.

"Does this mean you read my column?"

Aw, hell. I really would have to get to that at some point.

"Not yet," I said. "Quite a day, remember? But I do have a question, and you're my best bet for a straight answer."

"Shoot."

I leveled my gaze at his face, watching for telltale signs that something was bothering him as I spoke. "Dumbbells."

He cocked his head slightly.

"Pardon?"

"Dumbbells," I repeated, studying him carefully. "The kind someone like you lifts at the gym. How big do they make them?"

Google could have told me that easily, but I wanted to see his reaction to the question.

"There is an actual question." He laughed. "I thought for a second I was being insulted. My gym has them up to 75 pounds."

"And would three of those hold a grown man under the water?"

"Your lawyer that turned up in the river." He narrowed his eyes and nodded. "I'm no physicist, but I would say yes."

I murmured a thank you, a sinking feeling in my gut. If anything else about him jumped out at me, I'd have to say something to someone. If for no other reason than so they'd know who to blame if I turned up chained to a fridge at the bottom of a lake.

"Thanks. I think I have an idea."

"I'll let you get after it, then." He stepped backward and smiled. "Glad to help."

I opened my computer and clicked into the browser, typing what I assumed was the web address for the area's most popular sporting goods store. I got a popup, courtesy of the paper's pornography filters (who decided to name a business after that particular unit of the male anatomy, anyway?), and hastily clicked back into the address bar, wondering if there was some sort of porn offender IT list I'd just ended up on.

All I needed was for Les to get the idea that I was looking for penis photos online at one o'clock in the afternoon. I didn't want to imagine the fun he'd have with that. Shaking my head, I added "sporting goods" to the URL, landed in the right place, and scrolled through product categories.

They carried large dumbbells. I had a sudden yen for a little shopping.

CHAPTER FOURTEEN

"Three seventy-five pound dumbbells? You sold them Monday?" It took work to keep my voice even, and I flashed the pimply kid behind the counter at Dick's a grin. Though he didn't look like he regularly lifted anything heavier than a video game controller, he did look like he was a fan of my smile. And my legs, from the way his eyes kept wandering to the lower half of the glass counter between us.

The two locations nearest police headquarters had been of no help. This one was further out, but that didn't necessarily mean it wasn't what I was looking for. I asked who he sold them to.

"We don't have a record of that," he said. "They paid with cash."

I shifted my stance, hiking my hemline up the tiniest bit, and smiled again.

"I know it's not the kind of question you get every day, but I really need to know." I frowned slightly. "There's no magic you can work on that computer that will help me?"

"I don't think so." He pulled his eyes away from my quads and looked at his screen again. "Wait, maybe." He touched a few keys.

I held my breath.

"Well, I don't have a name, but I have an address. There were only two of those in stock. We shipped the other one." He rolled out a blank strip of register tape and scribbled on it, then handed it to me. I glanced at the address. I didn't know where it was, but it was not police headquarters. Damn.

I smiled and tucked the slip of paper into my bag.

"You have no idea how much better you just made my day." I checked his nametag. "Jesse, I could just kiss you."

"I wouldn't stop you." He smiled and leaned across the counter. Gutsy, for a skinny kid with skin problems. I couldn't help admiring his moxie.

"Something tells me your mom might not approve," I winked. "But thanks for your help."

"Come back anytime," he called as I hurried to my car, silently lamenting my lack of a GPS.

My phone binged the arrival of a text as I unlocked the door, and I smiled when I saw my mom's picture on my screen. "Love you more, kid," the message said. It was a game we'd played when I was a little girl, resurrected for the digital age.

"Nope. I love you more," I texted back before starting the engine. "Call you later. Been crazy this week."

Before I made it back to the office, my scanner bleeped an all-call for a bad wreck on the Powhite. Jackknifed big rig and possible fatalities. Shit. I didn't have time for that, but damned if I'd give Les an excuse to send Shelby to something else. I made an illegal U in the median and headed south, leaving Les' voicemail a heads-up that we might have an accident story coming as I drove.

I had barely gotten out of my car at the scene when Charlie Lewis tapped me on the shoulder.

"There's my friend from the print side of the world." A tooth-bleaching commercial smile beamed through the thick layer of peach lipstick that matched her tailored Nicole Miller suit. "I was worried about you, Clarke. You didn't show for the lawyer yesterday."

"I was busy." I peered over Charlie's shoulder at the truck, which at first glance appeared to be peeing on the tollway. "What the hell?"

The smell from the amber rivulets running across the pavement wasn't right for gasoline, and the troopers would've long since cleared the scene if that much gas was running across the road. I took a deep breath and giggled. It was beer.

I wondered how long that would have the Powhite shut down and turned my attention from the truck to find Charlie staring at me, one perfectly-waxed eyebrow raised.

"Busy with what?" she purred.

"A little less obvious next time, Charlie," I laughed. "Not that I'm suddenly in the business of giving you leads, but that was halfhearted, at best. I'm insulted."

"Then we're even. I was insulted by that neophyte you sent to the press conference yesterday," she snapped. "What the hell kind of reporter asks if there's evidence of foul play in a murder? Don't you dare bail on me like that again. You keep me on my toes."

"The feeling is mutual," I patted her shoulder a little too hard, moving her out of my way as I spotted a state trooper I knew in passing. "Speaking of, I have work to do. Nice chatting with you, hon."

I made a beeline for the trooper before Charlie could get turned around and collect her cameraman.

No one died at the scene, Trooper Staunton said, but there were serious injuries, some of them to children. That warranted a story. I checked my watch. It was already three. Double shit.

The trucker swerved to avoid hitting a sofa that wasn't properly strapped into the back of a pickup. Out of control, the big rig turned over, began spewing beer, and got hit by a minivan and an SUV. All the occupants of those vehicles, three women and five children between them, had been loaded into ambulances and taken to St. Vincent's before I arrived.

"Can I talk to the driver of the pickup?" I asked Staunton. "Are you charging him with anything?" Reckless endangerment, probably, but he had to say it.

"The trucker said he took off when he saw the commotion in the rearview." Trooper Staunton shook his head. "The sofa he dropped is over there, and we're pulling camera feed from the tollbooths a half-mile back to see if we can get a look at his plate. It looks like reckless endangerment. Unless one of those little ones don't pull through.

Then it's manslaughter, and he just ruined his whole life because he was too lazy to hook a strap over that couch."

I scribbled his quote down and thanked him, texting Les as I walked back to my car. Charlie pounced on Staunton as I pulled away, and my phone popped up a one-word response from my pseudo-boss: Hurry.

"When do I ever get to do anything else?" I sighed and aimed the car toward the office, the hard-won mystery address waiting in my bag.

It was after five by the time I got the accident story ready to go and noticed an emailed shot of the crash scene, courtesy of Larry from photo, that made me giggle. He'd framed the lighter side of a heavy story perfectly: the slightly mauled but still recognizable brewery logo on the truck, the river of beer running over the concrete, and a small band of onlookers waving straws. I shot back a quick smiley face and sent my story to Les. It was on the website before Charlie went on at six, which saved me from another ass-chewing.

Channel Four led with the wreck and I watched Charlie's report, relieved that she didn't have anything I hadn't. She was right. She did keep me on my toes. And if the *Post* and the Mafia and doing the right thing weren't motivation enough, I had to admit the idea of the look on her face when my investigative piece hit the racks was smile-worthy.

I grabbed a turkey on rye from the deli across the street and settled back at my desk for the night.

Google maps told me the extra dumbbell was delivered to what appeared to be a warehouse near Shockoe Bottom, though whether it was still used for that was anyone's guess. Many of those had been refurbished in recent years, turned into everything from trendy apartments to hot yoga centers.

Maybe it was just a gym. Damn. I clicked over to the city's property tax records and typed in the address, renewed hope turning up the corners of my mouth.

A Brandon Smith was listed as the sole owner. Another quick

search told me the place didn't hold a business license of any kind. Hmmm.

A DMV records search revealed hundreds of Brandon Smiths in Virginia. I tried Google and came up with an insane number of hits. Gotta love common surnames. Refining the search to include the word "drugs," I clicked on the first link that popped up.

And found something. Even though I didn't quite know what it meant.

"Officer arrested in evidence case takes plea deal" read the headline of an old news story from Miami, with a subhead revealing that the evidence in question had never been found. I scrolled through it quickly. Eight years before, a cop in Miami had been fired and arrested after more than a million dollars in drugs and cash went missing from their evidence locker. The cop's name was Brandon Smith. The story quoted the DA as saying Smith had a brother who was a small-time dealer with a record. The brother's fingerprints were found in the lock-up after the theft.

"Hot damn." The pen I was tapping fell to the desktop.

Noah. The brother's name was Noah Smith. I flipped to the police report on the first dealer murder to be sure, but I knew I was right.

A cop who'd been arrested in a strikingly similar case in Miami now might very well own a warehouse in Shockoe Bottom. And his brother's murder was likely the catalyst for all this craziness.

That was way too much coincidence to actually be coincidence.

But who the hell was Smith, and where did he fit into my story?

I thunked my head onto the desk, a screaming crick in my neck from the hours of research. I wanted answers, not more questions. At that moment even one answer would've tickled me pink.

"Everything all right?" Parker's voice interrupted my thoughts.

I raised my head and looked around, noticing the silence for the first time. It was dark. And there was no one else around.

"Fine. Just tired," I said, my tone too bright. "These hours are murder."

"Your whole world is murder lately, isn't it?" he leaned on one side of the cube door and put a foot up on the other. I'd never been claus-trophobic, but evidently there is indeed a first time for everything.

"It stays that way a lot of the time," I said, my eyes on his hands. They rested easily on his knees, and I didn't see any Magnum-shaped bulges on his person. I took a deep breath, catching a whiff of the same clean-smelling cologne he'd been wearing Saturday. "This has just been a very long week."

"Seems like it, doesn't it?" he said. "I was just thinking I didn't even really know you last Friday, and here it is Friday again, and I feel like we're old friends."

I had thought on Tuesday I might like that, but by Friday night, not so much. He had some old friends I wanted to keep my distance from.

"This story has had its share of weird twists." I smiled, easing the chair backward. Dammit, our cubicles were tiny.

"Anything new?" The question sounded light, but Parker's eyes were serious.

I saw two possibilities: I could play dumb, which I was lousy at, or I could maybe get an answer to one of my big questions. Curiosity trumped nerves, and I scooted the chair as far from him as I could get it and stood.

"Why do you ask? I don't recall you ever being so interested in my work before." It came out sharper than I intended.

He furrowed his brow.

"I read your stuff all the time. You're good," he grinned and held up his hands in mock-surrender. "I thought you knew that. But if you don't want to share, that's all right. I just wondered if I could help."

Perplexed, I studied him as he stepped backward into the walkway. I knew my murder mysteries. The bad guy wasn't supposed to flash a grin and back off when you pushed back. I opened my mouth to reply and my phone bleeped a text notification.

"Got a date?" Parker asked.

I laughed in spite of myself and shook my head, figuring my mom wanted to know why I hadn't called yet. Parker was still close, and I didn't want to take my eyes off him. Until I glanced at my phone and completely forgot he existed.

"Or yes," I said, shoving my laptop, files, and phone into my bag. "Maybe a hot one. Gotta run, Parker."

He called a goodnight as I ran for the elevators, killing two birds by getting away from him and to whoever had sent that text.

"RPD officer with answers. Meet me at the beanery on Parham in 20 if you want them."

I wanted nothing more.

Who does this guy think he is, Deep Throat? Why is he parked back there in the trees? I wondered. Unease fluttered in the pit of my stomach as I turned the corner a second time and stopped in a spot near the shadow-shrouded police sedan, far from the light spilling out of the coffeehouse despite the relatively empty parking lot.

"Officer?" I called, taking a step toward the car.

The middle-aged, uniformed cop in the driver's seat opened the door and unfurled a hulking form that towered over even my height. Shit.

The butterflies in my stomach morphed into bats.

I stood up straight and called up my most confident smile before I looked up at his dark eyes and extended my hand. "Nichelle Clarke. Nice to meet you."

Officer McClendon (according to the shiny nameplate on his uniform) had hazel eyes, upon closer inspection, but they looked darker because they had curiously little depth. It added to the nagging in my gut that something was off, and I was glad he didn't hold my gaze long.

"Nice to meet you." He mumbled, ducking his head.

I took a big step backward and asked if he'd had a chance to eat dinner yet. My instincts about people were almost never wrong, and everything about him screamed at me to get to a place where we weren't alone in the dark.

I considered sprinting back to my car, but dismissed the thought almost as quickly as it occurred to me. I wanted the story worse than I'd ever wanted anything.

Eyes on McClendon, I planted my feet and curled both hands into loose fists. My right hook had sent my trainer staggering a few times, and he was a pretty big guy.

"Um, no," McClendon said, staring at his shoes.

I knew that voice from somewhere. The hesitancy and soft tone were unusual for a cop. I tried for a better look at his face, but he kept it pointed down.

Maybe hearing him talk some more would help.

"Let's go inside, then. Have you ever tried their blueberry scones?" I took another, shorter step backward.

He shook his head and fidgeted with his hands, and I wondered if I was getting paranoid. Parker had turned out to be less than threatening. Maybe the weird vibe stemmed from fear that he was about to tell me something someone wouldn't want him to.

"Are you okay?" I smiled again, trying to catch his eye. "Whatever you want to talk to me about, you don't have to be on the record. At least not at first."

"Thanks. I've never talked to a reporter before." He looked up and to one side, toward The Beanery's windows, and something clicked in my head.

He was the cop who'd forgotten to read the accused his rights in the beheaded accountant trial.

Shit. How did he still have a job? There was only one answer for that, and it meant I wasn't paranoid after all.

I spun on my stiletto and started to run. I didn't get two steps before something hit the back of my head, and everything went black.

CHAPTER FIFTEEN

NOT EVEN A WEEK as an investigative reporter and people were already trying to bash my head in? That had to be some kind of record.

Pitch black surrounded me like a cloak on all sides, but I was pretty sure I was in the trunk of McClendon's cruiser. And the car was moving. Trying hard not to panic, I focused first on deciphering why I was there. I wasn't certain I knew anything too incriminating, but someone sure thought I did.

First the mysterious Mr. Smith, now this guy. The only way for him to still be a cop after losing a murder case to such a stupid mistake was for him to be in on something—or with someone—pretty powerful. Like David Lowe?

But I didn't have anything on Lowe that I could prove. Did I? I pondered that for a minute.

My stomach lurched as we took another corner and I decided none of what I'd compiled would mean squat if I didn't figure out how to get away from McClendon. I had no experience with being cracked over the head and tossed in a car trunk, but his intentions couldn't be good.

I remembered a salesman showing me the release handle inside the trunk of my old car. But they were supposed to glow in the dark, and I saw nothing. I ran my hands along the side walls. The lining was rough, the metal and plastic beneath it hard. I felt a thick, textured metal cable roll under my fingers, but it didn't lead to anything. Damn.

In the absence of an escape hatch, I needed a weapon. Maybe surprising him when he opened the trunk lid would give me an advantage. I was unsure exactly how I'd manage to hold my own with the Jolly Green Giant's cousin out there, but I damn well had to try.

Mostly, I counted on the fact that Officer Felony didn't know I had such a hard head. Whether it was conditioned or just a God-given gift to offset my uncanny ability to get brained by any object flying through the air in my vicinity, my skull seemed more resistant to damage than the average.

Which was nifty, given that I needed my brain at full speed if I wanted to see Saturday's sunrise.

Think, Nichelle. I had a sudden flash of slipping my phone into the small pocket in my skirt as I jumped out of my car.

Please, be there.

My fingers grazed smooth plastic when I slid them into the slit at my hip, and my heart leapt as I sifted through everyone I knew, trying to think of anyone I might be able to call for help.

Not the police ("Hello, 911? I've been abducted by one of your officers and am in the trunk of his cruiser on my way to certain doom. Please come save me." I could practically hear the click of the operator hanging up on me). Not Jenna. Not Bob. Agent Starnes at the FBI came to mind. Did I have a cell number for her?

I touched a key and the screen lit up.

No bars. Not even a fraction of the little one.

Most coverage in the country, my ass. I stared, willing the icon to change. The flashing "no service" verged on mocking.

I pointed the LCD away from me like a flashlight.

The metal cable I had felt during my tactile exploration appeared from the ragged end to be what was left of the safety cord. Fantastic. McClendon was a planner.

I moved the phone slowly, looking for anything I might be able to inflict pain with. A short steel bar strapped to the sidewall over my head looked promising. Probably part of a small jack for changing a tire.

I jerked the bar loose, grimacing at the ripping noise it made as the Velcro holding it to the wall gave way.

I shoved the phone back into my pocket and gripped my makeshift club with both hands, waiting for the car to stop.

After several corners and some brain-rattling bumps, it did. I had no idea how long I'd been out, so I wasn't sure where we were. Apparently, somewhere that wasn't on Verizon's big red map.

I waited for McClendon to come for me.

The air felt thick.

Stress, or an actual shortage of oxygen making it harder to breathe? I couldn't tell.

Bob could've been in the trunk talking to me, I could hear his words so clearly: "You're crossing into the world of investigative reporting, here...That means you're going to be in every bit as much danger as any cop working a case would be."

I thought of the hundred or so times I'd watched *All The President's Men* and imagined investigative reporting to be glamorous. Right. I'd be young and beautiful in my casket. And I even knew where mom could get a good deal on a "gently used" one. A stray hubcap wouldn't bother me.

A door slammed.

Fear obliterated the greater good I'd always wanted to serve.

I wished I could turn the clock back a week and do it all differently. I'd never cared less about a scoop.

Charlie was probably on her third sangria of the night, and I was locked in a car trunk. I failed to see where that meant I was winning anything.

I wanted desperately to be curled up on my mother's sofa in Dallas, watching trashy TV and eating chocolate and laughing.

I hadn't even gotten around to calling her. What if I never saw her again? I'd been so scared of that when she was sick, can't-breathe-can't-eat-oh-my-God-I'm-going-to-vomit   dread washing over me every time a monitor beeped or she shifted in her bed.

In a thousand tearful prayers, I'd begged and bargained, offering God anything and everything in trade if he would please just not take my mommy away. And he hadn't.

And McClendon would not take me away from her. Not without a fight, anyway.

Squashing the terror, I shifted my knees toward the back of the trunk so I'd have a clear shot with the tire tool.

Footsteps on...gravel? I held my breath and listened. Maybe. That would explain the rough ride at the end. So I'd have to watch my footing in my characteristically impractical shoes. If I got a chance to get my feet under me at all.

I gulped a lungful of heavy air and choked up on my steel club, preparing to swing for whatever vulnerability I could see when the trunk lid popped.

The footsteps stopped.

Would he take me out of the car first? My stomach knotted. Surely they didn't want blood all over the trunk of the cruiser.

I heard the gravel crunch under his shoes as he turned.

Showtime.

I steeled myself.

The key scraped into the lock.

I said a very fast prayer.

The pop of the latch letting go was heart-stoppingly loud, and I gripped my weapon tighter to keep from dropping it.

Blinded by the security lamp on the back of a nearby building, I stuck the pole straight out of the trunk and swung skyward as hard as I could, praying I would hit something.

From the scream, I did better than I'd hoped.

I fluttered my eyelids, and when my pupils constricted significantly I saw McClendon, doubled over, groaning, and holding his crotch. Bullseye.

I reached behind my head and grabbed the edge of the trunk

opening for leverage, flexing my ankles and thrusting both heels at McClendon's face.

He screamed again. Blood spurted down his left cheek, but he moved too fast for me to guess its source.

Staggering backward, he groped for his sidearm. Shit. My stilettos were no match for a police special.

I shoved with my arms and twisted my hips, rolling out of the trunk and catching my balance blessedly quick, though pain shot through my skull when I came upright.

I blinked away the dizziness, matching the pounding in my head with the memory of the upbeat training music from body combat as I stepped forward. The moves were almost second nature, though the target was new.

Punch, punch. Two to McClendon's midsection. He took another step back.

I bounced forward, then delivered a swift *ap'chagi* to his chest, stumbling only slightly because of the shoes.

He tumbled over backward, but managed to unholster his gun.

I looked down for just long enough to see that the blood came from his left eye, which was pinched shut. Aiming with his right, he fired as I dodged sideways. The bullet went wide.

I spun and sprinted across the wide gravel parking lot, no idea where I was or where I was going.

I should've stayed at the office with Parker. At least if he'd turned out to be a psycho, my car was there.

I zigzagged in an attempt to avoid the half-blind shots McClendon was popping off, then rounded the corner of the closest building and found a narrow street. Possibly an alley. The sprawling, boxy buildings all looked to be warehouses.

I tried the nearest door, but of course it was locked. Why wouldn't it be?

I started for the next one, afraid to look over my shoulder and also afraid not to, imagining McClendon as my very own lumbering slasher-movie villain: limping behind the running girl, yet somehow catching her anyway.

Except I wasn't in a movie, and my stalker had a gun. He didn't have to catch me. All he had to do was make it around the corner and get off one good shot.

As if on cue, his shadow stretched across the mouth of the alley.

"There's nowhere to go, bitch," he called.

I ducked behind a dumpster, peering into the dark. I couldn't even tell if I'd run into a dead end.

McClendon shuffled closer.

I tried to squeeze between the dumpster and the wall and succeeded only in ripping my skirt and slicing my thigh open on a rough piece of metal. I bit blood out of my lip to keep from screaming. Fuck.

The chirping that meant I had an eBay alert might as well have been a bugler playing *Revelry*, it was so loud in the stillness. I whacked my elbow on the side of the dumpster, but managed to fumble my cell phone out of my pocket and shut the alert off, resisting the urge to fling it into the nearest warehouse wall.

Of course it had a signal now. And look, I was winning the Manolos I'd bid on the night before with only a few minutes to go. Fantastic. I could be buried in them.

"Such a pretty sound," McClendon called. "Where, oh where, has this little birdie gone?"

Another gunshot. This one sounded like it zinged off the dumpster. Double fuck.

"Come out, come out," he cackled.

My breath coming fast and loud, I could still hear the shuffling inching closer.

I closed my eyes and prayed.

I opened them to headlights flooding the far end of the alley, followed by tires squealing around a corner and the roar of an engine.

Way to be on top of your inbox, big guy.

Mouthing a thank you to the heavens, I stared at the Lincoln emblem racing toward me and straightened my spine, trying to flag down the driver without leaving my hiding place.

The passenger window lowered as the car slowed, and I jerked the door open and jumped in without waiting for an invitation. I figured the likelihood I was in one alley with two murderers was pretty low.

"Drive, please," I crouched in the passenger floorboard, my voice raspy from ragged breath. "Now. And keep your head down. I'll explain when you get me out of here, I swear."

"My, my, Miss Clarke," Joey clicked his tongue, giving McClendon a once-over and gunning the engine. "Remind me not to piss you off."

CHAPTER SIXTEEN

I HEARD one more shot as the sleek sedan leapt forward, the alley fading quickly behind us. Sinking into the cool leather seat, I stared at my mobster "friend," the familiar sardonic smile on his face and his dark eyes on the road.

"It's bad that I'm not even surprised to see you, isn't it?" I asked. "This week has completely robbed me of my ability to be shocked."

"Damn. And I wanted to save the day and sweep you off your feet." He chuckled. "Fucking D.C. traffic. Apparently, everyone and their cousin leaves that town on Friday night."

"I'm not easily swept. But you could take me by the ER if you want some brownie points," I poked gingerly at my still-bleeding thigh, and his eyes widened when they strayed to the gash there.

"Ouch." He held the wheel with one hand and pulled off his cornflower blue tie with the other, tossing it to me. "Tie that just above the cut. Pull it tight. You need stitches. I know my flesh wounds."

Of course he did. So much for two murderers not being in the same alley. But at least this one didn't want to kill me. I didn't think, anyway.

I hiked up my skirt and cinched the length of blue silk—Brioni, no less—around my thigh. The bleeding slowed. Turning back to Joey, I studied him as he drove us easily out of the maze of warehouses. His expression was the polar opposite of stressed.

"How did you know the day needed saving?" I asked when he turned onto a better-travelled road and I recognized the less-touristy, more-industrial area of Shockoe Bottom.

"I didn't." He chuckled. "Though I would like to have a go at that sometime. I was looking for you. Glad I found you when I did. But I gotta say, it looked like you handled that guy pretty well. And he was a big fella." He glanced at me and arched an eyebrow. "There's nothing sexier than a woman who can fend for herself."

"I feel about as sexy as a saddle shoe right now," I said, sucking a hissing breath between my teeth at the pain in my leg and fighting the urge to smile.

This was not good, Joey Soprano over there flirting with me. I didn't need encouragement on that front. I needed to stop thinking he was hot. Remembering the headless accountant helped.

"And nice sidestep, but how exactly did you know where to find me?" I narrowed my eyes, looking for any tell that he might be lying and wishing I knew who to trust.

First I'd ditched Parker for a trigger happy cop who'd turned out to be a nutcase, and now I had escaped from him into a speeding car with the Mafia. If I was going to have to bail out, I needed to know it.

I believed his theory about the boat crash, mostly because everything I'd learned since Monday pointed in that direction, and his presence indicated that he knew something, maybe even more than he'd already said. And I still didn't get the same run-now-and-run-fast vibe from him I had from McClendon.

"Again, I didn't." He cut his eyes toward me and shook his head, turning the car onto East Cary. "Not like you think, anyway. You weren't home, so I went to your office. I ran into a big blond guy in the garage, and he told me you got a text about a huge story you've been killing yourself on and took off.

"I was going to go back to your house and wait for you, but I wanted to have a look at something down here first. It's what I came to tell you about, actually. I heard gunfire and went to check it out. I sure as hell didn't expect to find you in the middle of it."

"What were you looking for?"

"Open the glove box," he said, the smile returning.

"There's not an accountant's head in there, is there?"

He shot me a look from the corner of his eye as he weaved the car through traffic, the normal people around us stalking nonexistent street parking for the restaurants and nightclubs that lined this part of the slip.

Wishing I was out there with them, I kept my eyes on Joey's face, daring him to deny it.

He just shook his head.

"Smart," he chuckled. "You are one very smart lady, Miss Clarke. I like that."

"That's great," I said. "Though it would be more great if I didn't have a rule against becoming involved with felons."

"Even never-once-convicted ones with impeccable timing?" He winked, and I ignored the flip my stomach did in response.

"Even then."

"Rules were made to be broken. It's sort of a personal philosophy of mine."

"Not this one." The words sounded a lot more convincing than they felt, but that was good.

I had a whopper of a mystery it suddenly seemed my life depended on solving, and for all I really knew Sexy McDarkEyes here could be a decoy dispatched by the bad guys. I still wasn't sure why he was helping me.

"There are no body parts in my car." He chuckled, and I really hoped it was a sign of sarcasm. "Getting the smell out can be a real bitch, you know. But you might want to have a look at what's in the yellow envelope in there."

I pulled the latch on the glove compartment, which appeared to hold mostly the usual: a pair of Ray Bans and a black leather owner's manual, plus a manila envelope. I plucked it from the pile and ripped it open with the flair of an Oscar presenter, then sighed when I saw the articles about Brandon Smith I'd found earlier in the evening.

"I know this already," I said. "There aren't many reporters who aren't on a first-name basis with Google. I call her Gigi."

Joey laughed and I glanced at him from beneath lowered lashes, hoping he had more than a handful of old news.

"Do you know what happened to this guy? It would seem that he should be around, since I'm fairly certain his kid brother was my first drug dealer victim."

"It would seem." Joey nodded, turning the car into the ER drive at St. Vincent's. "I don't know where Mr. Smith ended up, though. I was hoping you might. My friends in Miami tell me he disappeared suddenly several years back, but they weren't sorry to see him go."

He did have one thing I didn't, and I studied the grainy copy of a half-decade-old mug shot, unable to place the round, bearded face scowling back at me. The guy was vaguely familiar, but I saw a hell of a lot of people every week, and he might bear a resemblance to any dozen of them. Nothing jumped out, at any rate.

"He wasn't working with your...friends...in Florida?"

"Not even close. They had about the same situation we have here," the corners of Joey's mouth turned up in a wry half-smile. "The cops were taking product off the streets and this guy was swiping it and selling it. It's a bit frustrating, having someone else pocketing our money."

So that's why he was pissed.

"But you wouldn't have made money on it if it had stayed in the evidence room and gotten burned up," I said.

"Call it the principle of the thing." Joey parked the car and turned to face me. "Losing to the cops every once in a while is expected. A cost of doing this business, you might say. But this is unsportsmanlike. Let's put a stop to it."

"Why is it someone like you needs my help to do that?" I asked. "I may be forgetting my manners, but I've just very nearly been turned into fish food over this. Why can't you just find this guy and..." I threw up my hands, unable to think of phrasing that didn't sound like I was enlisting a hitman. "And, well, do what you do?"

He stared for a second and I fidgeted, not wanting to think too hard about the fact that he'd probably killed people. Maybe many people.

Without a word, he got out of the car. Okay. I opened my door and he stepped up to it, offering a hand. I latched onto his forearm, wincing when my leg—absent the stalked-by-a-killer adrenaline rush —protested the weight I put on it.

"What I do, contrary to popular characterization, is not run around 'whacking' people left, right, and center," he said quietly, walking slowly next to me as I hobbled to the door. "Taking some-one's life is not an easy thing to do. It's a mortal sin. Something that stays with a man long after he's done the requisite 'our fathers.'"

I stopped walking and looked at him, feeling a bit like a child who'd been reproached for an accidental slight. The whole Mafia thing notwithstanding, I did like him. And I hadn't meant to hurt his feelings.

"I'm, um, really sorry," I stammered.

"For what? Figuring out something about me and thinking bad things?" He smiled, his lips tight and his eyes locked on mine. "No need for apologies, Miss Clarke. I am who I am, even if sometimes I wish I weren't."

His eyes said everything he wasn't, and I looked away.

Not. Happening.

He cleared his throat.

"Just so you know, I didn't have anything to do with that accoun-tant. I know people who did, as you have already deduced. But that wasn't my handiwork, if that's what you were thinking.

"A lot too much, what they did to that guy. I'm trying to resolve this differently. Call it an ideology shift. A savvier organization that uses technology and information, and those who purvey that infor-mation," he winked, "to work more around the edges of the law than outside it."

When he put it that way it didn't sound so bad. But not so bad was still bad enough.

I turned back to the door and resumed limping toward medical care.

"So, you really don't know who Smith is?" I asked.

"You don't, either? Logic dictates that he's either a cop here, or he knows someone who is. At least, from what I've read this week. Nice work, by the way."

"Flattery will get you nowhere."

"Honesty is not flattery."

The doors slid open and the harsh fluorescent light revealed a left leg that looked worthy of a slasher movie. Blood had run clear down into my shoe, drying brownish-red on my skin. My favorite skirt was trashed.

Looking at the gash seemed to make it throb more, and I felt a little sick. The petite gray-haired desk attendant jumped to her feet and pushed a wheelchair over.

"Oh, honey, what has happened to you?" She clucked like an old mother hen and wheeled me straight through to the treatment rooms.

"It's just a cut," I said. "I think."

I looked up to see that Joey had followed. Mother hen lady disappeared and a nurse swept in, tossed me a hospital gown, and smiled at him.

"Help her into the gown and onto the bed," she said. "I'll be right back."

She shut the door behind her with a loud click and Joey grinned and stepped toward me.

"I've got it, thanks." I held one hand up. "Could you excuse me for a sec?"

"I'm happy to help."

"Thank you, but I've been dressing myself for quite a while. I can manage."

He made a big show of turning his back.

"And they wonder why chivalry is dead," he said. "What were we talking about?"

"Smith." I kept my eyes on the back of his head as I kicked off my shoes and managed to get clumsily back to my feet. "Who he is and why you want my help."

"Ah, yes," he said. "Well, Miss Clarke, I find that the court of public opinion is far more influential in the actual courts than it should be, most of the time. If you get to the bottom of this and write about it, I get a double bonus: I know who to blame for it, and they've been exposed in the press.

"A news story lives forever on the Internet. And if enough people are upset about it, it can't get swept under any proverbial rugs no matter who's behind it. *Capisce?*"

I grunted agreement as I wriggled out of the skirt, which was stiff with dried blood, and dropped it on the tile. My silk tank top came off with a little work, and I jerked the gown on and tied it, hobbling to the bed and pulling up the covers.

"All right. I'm decent."

"Damn." Joey turned, the grin back in place, and I rolled my eyes. More at myself than at him, though I didn't want him to know that.

Before I got a chance to reply, the door opened and Dr. Schaefer came in.

"Hello there," she said. "I didn't expect to see you again so soon. What did you do?"

"I stumbled into a rusty garden tool and got a nasty cut," I said, figuring the actual details of my evening would either get the cops called or me a first-class ticket to the psych ward, neither of which sounded like fun.

She eyed the bloody Louboutins and slashed linen skirt.

"Gardening?"

"No, garden tool." I stressed the last word, dismissing the golf-ball-sized lump on the back of my head, because it was hidden under my hair and I didn't have a fake explanation for it. "I was on my way out."

Joey nodded when she looked at him.

"I see." She pulled the blanket back and examined the cut. "This is going to need a few stitches. When was your last tetanus vaccine?"

Shit. I hated shots. And since I couldn't remember the last one, I was due.

She bustled off and returned with the nurse and a tray holding two hypodermics and several other pointy medical things.

I took a deep breath and clamped my fingers around the railing on the right side of the bed, studying the cream wallpaper and trying to think of anything but needles and murderers. I felt the doctor remove Joey's tie from my leg and gripped the rail tighter.

"You all right, Xena?" Joey's voice was closer and a quick glance revealed that he'd walked to the foot of the bed. He stepped up beside me and leaned his head down, so close I could feel his breath on my ear. "Guns, kidnapping, overgrown maniacs. That doesn't faze you and this is what gets to you?"

I clenched my teeth and glared at his smirk.

"Shut up," I said, without moving my jaw.

"No judgment," he grinned. "Just trying to figure you out."

"Because I'm such a mystery." The sarcasm I intended to inflect on the words was lost in a hissing intake of breath when the doctor stabbed my leg with one of the needles.

"Lidocaine," she said. "It'll burn a little for a second, but you won't feel the stitches go in. That hurts a lot worse."

Apparently "burn a little" meant "set your entire thigh aflame from hip to knee," but it did fade quickly. Feeling odd pressure where the cut should've been, I glanced over to see her prodding it, squirting it with first a clear solution and then a rust-colored one. I stared, because it looked disgusting, but it didn't hurt.

"How about that?" I muttered.

She asked about Bob as she scrubbed dried blood off my thigh, and I told her he was stubborn, but improving.

When my wound was decontaminated to her satisfaction, she picked up a pointy doohickey that could only mean she was about to start sewing me up, and I looked away again. Deadened nerves or not, I couldn't watch that.

Joey could, though. And did, giving me the color commentary as the doctor closed up the unsightly souvenir of my crazy night. Seven stitches. The scar would limit my skirt-length options, but it'd make a respectable war story for the whippersnappers someday.

Dr. Schafer dressed the freshly-sewn cut with loose gauze as the nurse stuck a little round band aid on my arm over the blood drop from the tetanus vaccine. She smiled at my grimace and began cleaning up.

"You should be healed in about ten to fourteen days." Dr. Schafer pulled her gloves off and tossed them into a bin in the corner, picking up my chart and laying a hand on the doorknob. "Keep it covered until day after tomorrow, then let it air out as much as you can. Clean it with antiseptic solution twice a day, and put some antibiotic ointment on it after you do that.

"Your general practitioner can remove the stitches for you. After it's healed, make sure you use sunblock every day for six months to minimize the scarring, and if it swells up or gets red or oozes anything, come back here."

I thanked her as she left, signing a stack of papers for the insurance company while the nurse finished picking up. I handed her the papers, eyeing my bloody skirt with distaste.

"Why don't I see if we have a pair of scrubs you can wear home?" She asked, following my gaze. She took the paperwork and the tray of pointy things with her and returned shortly with a clean outfit, such that it was. I thanked her.

"Be more careful around your garden tools." She patted my shoulder and smiled at Joey. "Take good care of her."

I opened my mouth to tell her I could take care of myself, as evidenced by Burly McGiant the one-eyed cop, then snapped it shut. That's why I don't lie. My big mouth tends to get me caught.

I shooed Joey into the hallway and pulled on the pea green PJs before I settled back into the wheelchair and let an orderly push me to the car.

Joey insisted on driving me home, and since asking for help picking up my car would give me a good excuse to catch up with Jenna the next morning, I didn't argue.

The short trip to my house was mostly silent, me scrutinizing

Smith's photo and trying to place him, and Joey drumming his fingers on the wheel in time to Kenny Chesney.

A Jersey mobster who liked country music. Of all the crazy things about my week, that one might be the most unbelievable.

I looked up as he turned onto my street, still just a nagging familiarity about Smith's face dancing in the back of my brain. Maybe sleep would float whatever it was to the surface.

"Get your head down," Joey said in a low voice, throwing an arm behind me and yanking my torso over into his lap.

"Have you lost your mind?" I struggled to sit up, but he was strong. My heart rate took off like Earnhardt roaring out of a pit stop. Dammit, was no one trustworthy?

I didn't want to die in a Lincoln with Kenny crooning about tequila and toxic love in the background. I shimmied my shoulders, trying to get an arm free to swing at Joey.

"I count three cars that weren't here earlier, all within walking distance of your place. And your lights are on," he said tightly. "I know this isn't terribly comfortable, but would you be still?"

I froze. They were in my house? I didn't feel so ridiculous about having hidden Neal's folder under the floorboard anymore.

"Darcy." I swallowed a sob.

"No reason to hurt the dog unless they're just real douchebags," Joey said, stomping on the accelerator once we passed the house and letting go of me a second later. "I'll handle that. She likes me. You have to get somewhere safe."

I told him to take me to a hotel and laughed when he reeled off the name of the poshest place in town.

"You might be able to afford The Jefferson, Captain Armani, but those of us who don't have unlimited offshore accounts tend more toward Holiday Inn."

"Fair enough. Where is one? Far from here, preferably, and no using a credit card for that or anything else. We'll get you some cash."

Off the grid. Fan-fucking-tastic Friday I was having. At this rate, I'd be hacking off my ponytail and bleaching my hair by Sunday. I glanced at my reflection in the dark window, hoping it didn't come to that. Brassy hair and washed out skin would make me a shudder-worthy blond.

I directed Joey to a bank and emptied my checking account, which netted me a pitifully small stack of twenties, then navigated to a suburban hotel in my price range, turning to tell him goodnight when he stopped outside the revolving glass door.

"Thanks for your help." I said. "How do I get in touch with you if I do figure out who this guy is, anyway?"

"I'll be around," he said. "And I'll look for your byline. Try to stay out of trouble."

"That seems to be difficult for me this week."

"All you can do is the best you can do." He smiled, staring at me for a long minute. Not liking where that could go, I kicked the car door open with my good leg and climbed out, watching the taillights until they were out of sight.

CHAPTER SEVENTEEN

MORNING DIDN'T BRING me any closer to a match on Brandon Smith, but staring at Google Maps gave me an idea of what might.

Though I didn't remember exact details—owing to the darkness and the running for my life—the satellite view of the warehouse Smith owned in Richmond looked disturbingly similar to where McClendon had taken me. Which would also give me a reason for Joey's never-fully-explained cameo in the alley.

What if I'd been a hundred and eighty degrees wrong and this was all a criminal ex-cop who'd hooked up with a crazy patrolman looking for some extra cash?

I ran mentally through Mike's evidence log, but I didn't remember McClendon's name. For the first time, I wondered if Mike had brought me the actual documents, or if the ones I had were doctored versions designed to finger Neal as the bad guy. My stomach wrung like an old dishrag, uncertainty swimming through my head.

I pulled out a notebook and made a list of everything I knew and everything I didn't. The latter was much longer. And Les' timer was running out.

"A week of busting my ass, and I still don't have the first clue." I said to no one.

As much as I wanted a sounding board, the only people I trusted were Jenna, Bob, and my mother, and wasn't about to worry any of them with my near-death experience.

I stared at the lists until the letters blurred, instead, then tossed the notebook to the foot of the bed and sighed. Loads of suspicion, but very little actual fact.

And Brandon Smith's warehouse was the only place I could think of to find a few facts, whatever they might be.

It was early, and I was willing to gamble cab fare on a hunch McClendon had been so preoccupied with his injuries he'd forgotten about my car. I called a taxi to the hotel and forked over two of my dwindling stash of twenties when we pulled up next to my sporty little SUV. It was still at the coffee shop, my bag resting in the back-seat. Hooray for tiny awesomes.

Thanks to the deserted Saturday morning streets, it took less than twenty minutes to get to the warehouse. I circled it three times. The steel double doors that served as the main entrance were on the side of the building that faced the big gravel parking lot.

When I was reasonably sure no one was there, I parked in the alley around back next to a hulking green dumpster. An inspection of its back corner revealed a piece of jagged metal decorated with dried blood and black linen.

Bingo.

In the daylight, without a maniac chasing me, I could see a large bank of windows high on the wall above the dumpster.

I looked around for a stepping stool and spotted a big plastic crate at the far end of the alley. Dragging it over, I slid the side door on the dumpster open and clambered up onto the lid. The four Advil I'd gotten from the hotel desk kept the pain in my leg to a dull ache, though I still leaned heavier on the uninjured one.

Reaching the other side of my perch, I gripped the bottom of the window frame and pressed my nose to the glass, taking a deep breath as the interior of the building came into focus.

Boxes. Hundreds, maybe thousands, of stacked plastic crates like the one I'd used to climb up, their contents not discernible from the outside.

I groaned under my breath as my eyes swept the room again. A whole lot of nothing. Just a massive expanse of concrete floor, white walls, white and gray steel ceiling beams, and boxes.

I stood there for a long minute, contemplating the door, but knowing there was only so far I should push it. There was investigating, and then there was just plain asking to be murdered. Going inside that building looked like an excellent way to jump from one to the other.

Just as I turned to get down, I heard the low purr of an engine.

I froze for a split second, then nearly gave myself whiplash searching for the source of the sound.

Shit.

I started for the edge of the dumpster, but couldn't help wondering if I'd be able to see what lurked in the mysterious boxes if someone went inside.

The engine shut off, the alley still empty.

I was still out of sight.

"All or nothing," I whispered, spinning back to the window. *That curiosity that killed the cat is about to help the crooked cops whack the nosy reporter*, the little voice in my head that sounded a lot like my mother warned. Guns. River. Sleep with the fishes. Anything unclear?

I held my breath as the door on the opposite wall swung outward, and a large man I didn't recognize walked into the room. It could've been Smith. It could've just as easily been the tooth fairy for all I could really tell from so far away. I tried to focus on his face, looking for the features from the grainy mug shot.

He had a scar on one cheek I could see across the considerable distance, and his dark features looked frozen in a perpetual scowl. He was probably as tall as Parker and maybe even more muscular, sporting an expensive-looking tailored leather jacket in the middle of summer.

He jerked the big metal door closed behind him and walked to a small office, emerging with an empty plastic crate much like the ones that were stacked halfway to the ceiling throughout most of the room.

He stopped in front of a tower about ten yards from the door and pulled the top box down. Taking a large plastic bag of white powder out, he added it to the box he was holding. I blew my breath out forcefully and thanked my lucky stars, every fiber of my being zeroed in on Mr. I'm-Too-GQ-For-This- Heat.

He chose another crate and peeked inside it before he lifted the lid and moved a smaller bag, this one full of little yellowish pebbles, into his box.

I wondered if my mystery man was getting ready to make a delivery, already contemplating whether I was stealthy enough to follow him without getting caught.

The next box was full of guns, and he pulled two out and added them to his cache.

"Jesus," I whispered to myself. "Welcome to Costco for criminals."

Replacing all the lids carefully and straightening the boxes, he turned to take the one under his arm outside and froze.

I clutched the window frame, forgetting to breathe. In all my excitement over a building full of proof that I was right, I hadn't heard another car, but a long shadow stretched across the concrete floor in the light from the high windows.

Someone else was there. A very large someone.

And I couldn't see them because they were standing behind a tower of plastic crates. Shit.

Mr. Box o' Drugs and Guns shook his head hard, setting his loot on the ground and backing up three steps.

I wished I could hear what they were saying, and I would've traded my shoe closet for a camera. From the side of the discussion I could see, it appeared that maybe someone was taking things that didn't belong to him. Which shouldn't surprise people who employed criminals, in my opinion.

Leather jacket man fell to his knees, and inspiration struck me seconds before a bullet struck him.

Clenching my eyes shut and flinching at the faint scream that was cut off by a muffled gunshot, I snatched my cell phone out of the hip pocket of my baggy scrubs and hit the camera button.

Raising it to eye level, I pushed the selector and then the save key over and over, capturing the death of a drug dealer and wondering again if this was Smith. Whoever he was, he'd just become the story of the year.

The body slumped to the left onto the concrete, blood ebbing outward in a nearly-black circle on the smooth silvery floor.

The shadow moved.

I held my breath, my thumb still clicking automatically.

The shooter stepped out from behind the crates, sunlight glinting off the gun in his hand.

My entire body went numb. Clinging to the window frame, I managed to keep clicking the camera and tried not to throw up.

Tucking the gun under his pinstriped navy suit coat, Donovan Nash surveyed the warehouse with a satisfied smile before his attention turned back to the hemorrhaging form at his feet.

The body shuddered once and fell still. Nash's lips curved up and he pulled one foot back and sank his shiny wingtip into the man's midsection before he disappeared into the office.

Oh. My. Fucking. God.

Not Lowe. At least, not just Lowe.

I stumbled backward and clapped one hand over my mouth, the metal under my feet strangely less than solid all of a sudden. But even my shaking knees and roiling stomach couldn't keep me from getting the hell out of there.

I whirled, scrambling on all fours as I stuffed the phone back into my pocket and half-jumped, half-fell back to the concrete, my leg protesting through the double dose of painkillers. Not that I really noticed.

Diving behind the wheel, I started the engine and steered stealthily out of the alley, then squealed the tires when I got past the next building.

Shaking, I gulped deep breaths, the adrenaline fading fast. My stomach lurched and I groaned, barely getting the car stopped and the door open before I vomited Friday night's turkey sandwich into the grass between the road and the river.

When my insides were empty I sat up, fumbling in the console for a napkin and a stick of gum. The image of the police chief kicking the dying thief would haunt my nightmares forever, no doubt. I'd been so focused on Lowe that I hadn't even considered the possibility that Nash was involved.

I dug my phone out of my pocket. *Please, God, just let the photos be recognizable*, I thought.

Before I could call up the pictures, my phone started ringing, Bob's office number flashing on the screen.

"Clarke," I sighed as I picked up. I wasn't obligated to work Saturdays, and I really wasn't in the mood for Les' bullshit.

"Charlie Lewis has a nice interview with the FBI about how they've ruled your boating crash an accident," Les barked. "But it's the damnedest thing—being the managing editor of a daily newspaper, I'm getting tired of getting my news from Channel Four. So haul your ass out of bed and get me a story I can put online before three."

I barely heard him, my eyes resting on the printed copy of the story from the Miami paper Joey had brought me the night before.

Nash's cold smile and something I'd seen in his office the day before zipped through my thoughts. I put Les on speaker and opened my Google app, tapping Nash's name in.

It took less than twenty seconds for the results on my screen to make me swear I'd background every cop I ever worked with for the rest of my career.

Nash had come to Richmond from a post as head of the narcotics unit at the Miami PD eight years earlier—about two months before the date on the article in my passenger seat. I'd seen a Gators pennant on his office bookshelf, but by the time I'd found the story about Smith, I'd forgotten all about it. Dammit.

"Clarke? Are you even listening to me? I can send Shelby over to interview the FBI if you'd like," Les' voice blared from the tiny speaker in my phone.

I contemplated telling him to fuck off. But I'd pissed him off enough for one week and, exclusive of the year or no, Bob was right about Les. At his core, he was bitter and spiteful, and he could hang onto a grudge like a bride with a hundred-dollar Vera Wang at a Filene's basement sale.

"I have something better," I said. And I needed to let the feds know there was a dead guy in that warehouse, anyway. "And I have to talk to the FBI about it, so I'll get your story while I'm at it."

"You have something better than the FBI concluding this crash that killed five people was just bad luck? What'd you do, witness a murder?" He chuckled.

"As a matter of fact, I did." My lips turned up slightly, picturing his face when the line went silent. "And I have art. Charlie will be chasing my byline for the foreseeable future."

I actually shut him up for so long I thought I'd lost my signal.

"Les?"

"You have what?" he asked finally.

"You heard me. Murder. Art. It'll be ready in two hours. Just watch for an email from Bob and don't say anything to anybody. Please."

"Don't tell me what to do," he snapped. "But I'll be waiting. It better be good."

"You won't believe it." I hung up on him and stood, physically unable to sit still despite the injured leg that burned with every step. Pacing the length of the car, I waited for my actual boss to answer his phone.

Something so monumental was not going on our presses without Bob seeing it first. Les could bite my ass. No way he was touching this story.

"Bob, oh my God," I began when he picked up, the story tumbling through my lips so fast I wasn't sure I got the words in the right order.

"Jesus, Nichelle," he whistled when I stopped for air. "That's... Wow. I'm not often at a loss for words, but I don't know what to say. When will you have it done?"

I turned back toward my car and opened my mouth to ask him if I could go to his house to write. Before I got the words out, a silver sedan shot out of a side street and lurched to a stop near my back bumper. Shit.

I let out a short scream and dropped the phone, my battered leg giving way when I tried to leap for my door. Sprawled in the grass, I threw a glance over my shoulder, but the glare from the sun obscured everything except the barrel of what looked like a rifle in a pair of very large hands.

I should have called Agent Starnes first.

Shoving hard with my good leg, I made it back to my feet and tried to spin toward the rifleman.

He was faster.

I heard a harsh huffing noise, like air being forced through a tube too fast.

Something stung my right hip.

I didn't even get my hand there to see what it was before I was lost in the darkness.

CHAPTER EIGHTEEN

MY HEAD WAS BIGGER and heavier than I remembered, and my eyes opened to a world painted in watercolor, blurred and fluid at the edges.

I tried to remember where I was and how I got there, but the closest I could get was an odd urge to run. Except I couldn't muster the energy to get up. Everything seemed floaty and far away. Was this what dying felt like?

Voices filtered through the fog. I strained to hear the conversation, but it was akin to trying to listen to a television with the volume too low. I could make out syllables here and there, but nothing that made sense. And I couldn't hear them well enough to tell who they belonged to.

One rose in pitch and volume, angry. The other remained flat.

Blinking too-fat eyelids, I looked around. White, industrial-looking walls, exposed metal ceiling beams, and a corrugated tin roof.

So I wasn't dead. While I'd never given much thought to what waited beyond the pearly gates, I was pretty sure the hereafter didn't resemble a warehouse.

A warehouse. There was something important about that.

Then I saw the boxes.

Fuck.

My heart took off at a gallop, adrenaline blazing a trail through the haze in my brain. Stacks and stacks of plastic boxes, in a warehouse where I'd just witnessed a murder.

I preferred the view from outside.

I tried unsuccessfully to lift my arms and legs. I was lying on hard, cold surface, but from the distance I perceived there to be between my body and the ceiling, it wasn't the floor. I tried to calm myself with a few deep breaths and caught a whiff of something that stung my nostrils.

The voices got louder.

"We certainly can't stay here," Donovan Nash's booming tenor wasn't a huge surprise, but that didn't make it any less terrifying.

"Why not?" The reply was barely audible.

I closed my eyes and focused. Nash's friend sounded familiar, but I couldn't place the voice.

"I caught her before she got more than a few blocks from here, didn't I?" the mystery man argued. "No way they have a story yet. We get rid of her, and we've contained the situation."

"Didn't you say she was on the phone when you caught up to her?" Nash boomed. "How stupid do you think this girl is? If she figured out enough to know to come here, don't you think she told someone where she was?"

I wished.

It hadn't occurred to me to mention my location as I spilled the murder story to Bob.

"So check her phone," Captain Mystery said. "See who she talked to and we'll take care of that."

"Yes, because disappearing in the wake of the murder of an assistant CA and half the city's newspaper staff is not at all suspicious," Nash snapped. "Not to mention, we still don't know where the hell the boy scout brigade got off to. What if Sorrel and White know more than I gave them credit for?"

I sighed, a small smile breaking through the insanity surrounding me. I knew my guys couldn't have been crooked. And if he didn't know where they were, then they probably weren't dead.

"The FBI said they were done for now," Nash continued. "I don't need them poking around anymore. We need to clear out of here and I need time to figure our next move. Make those biceps useful and haul boxes out to the truck. If we can get out of the state, we can buy a little time."

Biceps?

And the voice. Damn. Mr. Mystery didn't really sound like Parker, but I'd never heard Parker sound mad.

"Rise and shine, sleeping beauty," Nash clapped his hands, the sound echoing in the cavernous space.

I turned my head toward him and bit back a scream, full-on panic drawing acid to the back of my tongue.

I was tied up and surrounded by at least two very large, armed men who wanted to "get rid of me."

Objectively, I didn't like my odds.

"Nichelle. I didn't expect to see you again today." Nash took two more steps and stared down at me with the same cold smile I'd seen from the window. Up close it was a thousand times more frightening, and a hundred and eighty degrees different from the charming grins he'd flashed in his office the day before.

"I knew you were working on a story about this." Nash waved a hand at the surroundings. "But I was pretty sure you suspected Lowe."

"And I thought I was being so secretive."

"I'd give you a solid B," he said. "I was impressed with your round-about questions yesterday. I thought having McClendon arrange a meeting with you last night would keep you from tying anything back to me. It appears I was wrong, on a couple of counts. Notice the ropes. I won't be losing an eye to one of those pretty shoes."

I raised my head and peered at my ankles. Like my wrists, they were bound to a big metal table with medium gauge, white rope. Fantastic.

"I'm sure you're wondering why you're here," Nash said. I concen-

trated on keeping my breath even, trying to slow my pulse. I refused
to let him see that I was about to pee myself.

"That crossed my mind," I said. "Why not shoot me in the alley and
be done with it? The river was right there."

"I need to know how you put this together. I already had to deal
with an unpleasant situation this morning. You showing up here was
not something I expected."

Killing a man was an 'unpleasant situation'? I'd hate to see what
really got him upset.

"Who tipped you off?" he asked.

"Why should I tell you anything? You're going to kill me anyway." I
nearly choked on the words. Saying it aloud made it real.

"There are many ways to die, Nichelle," Nash smiled and wrapped
a hand in my hair, jerking my head to one side and removing a few
strands. "Some of them are less pleasant than others."

I stared, keeping my silence.

"I suspect you've been talking to Mike Sorrel." Nash said, his hand
still in my hair. "Since he's jumped ship, I can't ask him, so I need you
to share."

"I'm an only child. I suck at sharing." The words slipped out before
I could stop them.

"You have a knack for sarcasm." He wrenched my hair harder, and
I gasped as I felt a clump give and a warm trickle down the back of my
neck. "I don't particularly care for it. Who told you?"

"No one." It was the God's honest truth, unless Google had been
promoted to personhood. Too bad he didn't believe me.

He snapped his arm backward and white stars of pain exploded
behind my eyes. I screamed. Nash flung a bloody clump of my hair
onto the concrete behind him.

"Don't make me ask again," he said.

I closed my eyes and took slow breaths, trying to mimic the
Lamaze breathing Jenna had used when Carson was born. When I
could speak, I focused on Nash.

"There is no mysterious trenchcoat-clad source." I said, blinking
back tears brought on by the pain. "Only my computer. Tax records

are boring as hell, but they're often a reporter's best friend. So is Google."

Nash didn't appear to know about Joey, and I wasn't about to tell him. Too bad I didn't have some kind of mobster bat signal, though. Joey could probably get me out of the warehouse without scuffing a wingtip.

"Is that a fact?" Nash held my gaze and appeared to relax, his grin returning as he pulled out his cell phone. "Nice detective work. Have you ever considered going into law enforcement?"

"Ugly shoes." I tugged at the restraints on my wrists, which were snug, but not too tight. My double-jointed left thumb could probably help me slip a hand out of them if I could stretch them a bit.Trying to look relaxed, I kept pressure on the rope and my eyes on Nash.

"Aren't you supposed to uphold the law?" I asked.

"There's not as much money in being a good guy." He didn't look up from his phone. "And look where it got Gavin Neal."

"Do you know that guy had a sick little boy?" I asked, already sure he didn't care.

"And if he'd kept out of my business, the sick little boy would still have a father. If you'll excuse me, I have some calls to make." He smirked. "Don't go anywhere."

He disappeared into the dwindling stacks of boxes, and I stared at the ceiling, contemplating a way to save my ass while Nash tried to cover his. The back of my head burned with what would've been all-consuming pain in any other situation.

Flexing my forearms, I strained the ropes against the table. They cut off my circulation when I pulled, but I could've sworn they felt looser every time I relaxed. How the hell could I get out of the building without getting shot, though?

Bob must have heard the commotion when I'd dropped my phone. I didn't want him to come riding to the rescue, but I hoped he'd call someone. Jerry. Starnes. Spiderman. I wasn't picky, though it might help if the someone had a gun.

After a few minutes, I popped my thumb flat and tried to wriggle my hand free. I almost had it when Nash's voice came closer again. I shoved my wrist back into the rope.

"Good news," he said, sticking his phone back into his pocket. "Things are going my way again. And in a way, I owe you my thanks for forcing my hand."

"You're welcome. I'll take a ride home in lieu of a card, if you don't mind."

"I'm not that grateful." Nash's eyes skipped around the warehouse and he nodded, appearing satisfied with the progress.

Faint chatter and the sliding, slapping sound of the crates being moved were the only sounds. From what I'd seen earlier, there was no one in earshot who'd care if I screamed.

"Hey, if you didn't know I suspected you, how did you know I was here this morning?" I asked.

"A combination of luck and brilliance." What could only be described as a shit-eating grin crossed his face. "Your copy editor wants your job."

"You've got to be kidding me." I stared, waiting for him to go on. That back-stabbing bitch. She better hope Nash finished me off before I had a chance to practice my *ap'chagi* on her.

"She called police headquarters this morning, asking for information on a murder. Of course, that murder hasn't been reported to the proper authorities." Nash said. "But she insisted that a *Telegraph* reporter had witnessed it. Since we LoJacked your car, it was easy to see you were nearby."

"How very Orwellian villain of you. When did you do that?"

"McClendon said you left it at the coffee shop, so Brandon went by before dawn and put in a tracking device. It came in pretty handy." He grinned like a father whose son had just scored the winning touchdown.

"Brandon Smith?" If my minutes were numbered, I had to find out who that guy was. "Why would he LoJack my car for you after you killed his brother?"

"Noah got greedy. He and his friend were trying to blackmail me when I paid them very well for the effort I asked of them."

From his tone, he could've been talking about the weather or his golf score.

"I wasn't sure what to do, because I can't afford to lose Brandon," Nash continued. "But he was surprisingly reasonable."

"I even went to Noah's house and explained it all to him. Right before I shot him." The voice Nash had been arguing with earlier came from behind a stack of crates to my left.

Except closer, with a more conversational tone, I recognized it instantly.

Fuck, fuck, fuckityfuckfuckfuck.

I clenched my eyes shut. No way.

"Brandon," Nash boomed. "How are we doing out there?"

"Almost done."

I opened my eyes just as Jerry Davis' face came between my head and the ceiling.

Smith was in much better shape than he'd been in when he left Florida, with darker hair. His clean-shaven face looked younger, too. But Jerry Davis was the man from the mug shot, plus one extreme makeover.

"Brandon?" I whispered.

"Yes, Nichelle?" He leaned over me and batted his lashes, his laugh low and disturbing.

How many times had I talked to him that week, with him "filling in" for Aaron? Christ on a cracker, as Eunice would say.

"You didn't know." He grinned. "How about that?"

"You're quite the thespian," I said. "I suppose that helps when you're trying to get away with murder."

"I was sure you'd pegged me when I let it slip that I was watching the Seminoles in the college series," he said. "I knew you had to know where Noah was from. Isn't that why you turned me down when I offered to help you?"

Strike two. Nash's gators pennant and Jerry's college world series. Fat lot of good it did me to put it together now.

As long as they were giving answers, I figured I'd try for a few more. The way Nash's eyes flicked to his phone every four seconds, he was waiting for a call. And the boxes were disappearing fast. Maybe I could buy a few minutes if I could get them bragging about their cleverness. Not that I knew what I'd do with more time, but I wanted it anyway.

"Why put the drugs on a boat?" I blurted the first question I thought of. "Doesn't that limit where you can take it?"

"We used to use trucks," Nash said. "But for the last couple of years, some friction has made that difficult. This spring, the river level rose enough that the water allowed us access to the coast, and I didn't need to fight anyone over transportation. No one was the wiser until that baseball player lost control of his speedboat."

"Friction. With the mob." Gavin Neal's guns had come off a truck, so it followed that Joey's friends had been involved.

"We tried to work a deal with them," Nash said. "I even had McClendon perjure himself during a murder trial and say he hadn't read the defendant his Miranda rights so their guy would get off. But they're stingy bastards."

Greedy crooks. Imagine that.

"And the guys who died in the boat crash—Freeman and Roberts? Did they know what they were hauling?"

Nash shook his head, staring at his phone again.

"They weren't the type," he said. "Which is what made them the perfect cover."

The phone binged and Nash turned his back, studying the screen and muttering to himself.

I turned to Jerry/Brandon, the crime scene stills of Darryl and Noah flashing up from my memory, both of them relaxed in the face of death. Because they knew him.

"You knew I was here because you tracked my car." I said, talking to keep from panicking as Nash waved an arm in a wrap-it-up gesture at whoever was carting off boxes. "It was you with the rifle. A dart, right?"

He grinned.

"I tried to aim for your hip. They hurt a lot more when they hit you in the neck. I do what I can for the pretty girls." He leered, trailing one finger down my arm, and I clenched my jaw to keep from spitting in his face.

Brandon turned his attention to something I couldn't see, and I tried again to yank my left hand free.

Success!

And not a minute too soon, if I could just think of some way to capitalize on it.

Arm still at my side, I looked around, noticing a muted splashing had replaced the slapping of the crates moving. The sharp scent in the air was suddenly strong enough to make my eyes water. Shit.

"What's going to happen to this place?" I fought to keep my voice even, because I already knew the answer.

"You don't smell the gasoline?" Nash spun back toward me, cold smile in place. "Enough chit chat. You've had a fine last interview, and we have somewhere to be."

His phone rang and he raised it to his ear.

"Are we good?" he asked.

He shot Brandon a thumbs up.

"Excellent." Busy swallowing nausea and tears, I wasn't sure which of them said it.

Nash slid his phone into his pocket and pulled a gun out of his jacket.

"Bullets are much quicker than flames, Nichelle," he said. "What's it going to be?"

CHAPTER NINETEEN

I CLOSED my eyes as Nash prodded my shoulder with the gun when I didn't answer him. Before I opened them again all hell broke loose around me.

The door slammed open with a metallic ringing. Nash and Jerry/Brandon whirled in two different directions as a barrage of sharp cracks split the stillness outside.

I froze for the tiniest fraction of a second before I wrenched my right hand out of the rope, losing a good bit of skin in the process. Clawing at the binding around my left ankle, I got it loose, then used the heel on that shoe to lever the rope and jerked my right foot free.

Swiveling on my tailbone, I pulled my knees to my chest and slammed both feet into the small of Brandon's back. The stilettos on my battered black Louboutins sank into his kidneys, and he let out a strangled cry and pitched face-first onto the concrete. He didn't move to get back up.

I threw my legs over my head, flipping backward and managing to land upright on the far side of the table.

Though his attention was on the commotion outside, Nash still stood less than ten feet away. And between me and the door. Leg throbbing and head wound burning, I stumbled back two steps, looking around for another way out.

"Not so fast." Nash whirled on me, and I planted my Louboutins and shoved the table with all the strength I could muster.

It flew at him, the casters beneath it gliding across the concrete. The wind left his chest in a *whoosh* and he staggered backward when the steel edge hit him squarely in the sternum.

A gleeful cackle came from somewhere. Maybe from me. I wasn't sure of anything but the relief that washed over me as the building filled with bodies encased in black tactical gear.

Brandishing large guns, the cavalry took its orders from a tall man in a bulletproof vest whose face was mostly obscured by a two-way radio.

"Watch the woman," he ordered, striding to the middle of the nearly-empty room. "Donovan Nash, you are under arrest."

I took my eyes off Nash long enough to see that Captain Rescue had a gun in his other hand. He didn't move the radio, but the ice-blue eyes peering over the top of it widened when they met mine.

I didn't process that before Nash caught his breath and raised his gun, swinging between me and Officer Cool. He settled on the sure target.

"Give my regards to Gavin Neal, won't you, Nichelle?"

The room was empty. Nowhere to hide.

A shot fired.

I screamed.

But the pain didn't come.

Nash crumpled to the ground, a dark spot blooming across the middle of his tailored navy suitcoat. A pair of SWAT-clad officers pounced on him.

I locked eyes with Captain Rescue, who holstered his sidearm as the radio handset fell away from a face I could never forget.

Adding shock to the adrenaline and sedatives was too much. The room wavered, the floor seeming to buckle under me as I fell.

But I never hit the ground.

Kyle Miller sprinted across the dozen feet of concrete between us and caught me as I drifted back into the fog.

More voices.

I lifted my eyelids, but couldn't focus on the backlit figure next to me for a full minute.

"Bob," I mumbled. "My story."

"That's the Nichelle Clarke I remember. Bleeding. Nearly murdered. But always thinking about the story."

Not Bob.

"Kyle?" I blinked. His voice had a commanding edge to it I'd never heard. He leaned forward and laid a hand on the edge of my cot, no longer silhouetted by the summer sun flooding the ambulance. The white sheet over my lap reflected flashing blue and red from the emergency vehicles crowding the parking lot around Nash's warehouse.

I probed gingerly behind my ear, finding hamburger where a sizable chunk of my hair had been. It hurt. And was still bleeding.

If I was dreaming, I had to award points for realism.

"Don't take this the wrong way, but what the hell are you doing here?" I asked. "Am I dead? Because when I heard your life flashes before your eyes, this is not what I had in mind."

"No, Nicey, you're not." He chuckled, gentle hands smoothing the hair I still had off my forehead. "All things considered, I think you're all right. But I want someone to check you out."

"How? Where did you come from?" I stared, even reaching a hand up to touch his face lightly.

He was older, with a neat goatee the same auburn color as his hair. But I'd looked into those eyes a thousand times in another life.

"I work for the ATF." He smiled. "And I guess you work for the Richmond newspaper, huh? We got a tip from the FBI this morning that there was a reporter taken hostage by a group of crooked cops who have been moving guns and drugs all over the east coast. We've been trying to trace something back to Nash for a long time. I came up a month ago to help with the investigation."

When my mom said "law enforcement," I assumed Kyle had joined the Dallas PD with his dad, but the Bureau of Alcohol, Tobacco, and Firearms made more sense in the context of him being sent out of state, which didn't happen often in local police work.

"Small world," I said. "Lucky for me, I guess."

"I'm a pretty good shot." He handed me my cell phone. "Is this yours? My guys found your car, too. The bag that was in the backseat is right here." He pointed to the floor.

"Thanks." I smiled.

"Nicey!" Bob's it's-four-o'clock-where-the-hell-is-my-copy shout rattled the windows, and Kyle turned to the open ambulance bay doors.

"Bob?" he asked.

I nodded. "My boss."

He stood. "I guess that's my cue. I have two corpses out there and a shit-ton of paperwork to do, anyway."

"She's in here," he called, sticking his head out of the back of the ambulance and waving one arm before he disappeared.

"Goodbye to you, too," I said. "Thanks for saving my ass."

Bob climbed into the ambulance, the lines in his face deeper than I recalled.

"Are you all right?" he asked.

The medic shooed at him from her perch behind my head.

"Sir, I'm sorry, but we're going to have to go," she said. "You can meet us at St. Vincent's if you want to visit with the patient."

"No." I tried to look at her, but succeeded only in scraping my injured scalp on the sandpapery pillowcase.

"No, what?" Bob asked, ignoring the medic and laying a meaty hand over one of mine.

"No, I'm not going to the hospital. Not until my story is done. Get me a computer."

"Excuse me?" The medic leaned forward, her red hair brushing my face. "Ma'am, you've been drugged, you have a bleeding head wound, and you've been in the middle of a police firefight. You have to see a doctor."

"I will. As soon as my story is done." I looked at Bob as I spoke. "My laptop is in that bag. There'll be TV trucks out there from everywhere between here and Fredericksburg in half an hour, and I'm going to completely lose my shit if I almost got killed twice so Charlie Lewis could break this story."

Bob laughed, bending to retrieve the computer and laying it across my lap.

"That's my ace," he said. "Always worried about the scoop."

"Miss, we really can't—" the medic began, but Bob cut her off.

"You might as well let it be," he said. "She won't sign the treatment consent until she gets her way. Besides, it looks to me like she's earned it."

The paramedics huddled behind me, muttering. Apparently, people don't often demand to finish work before being ferried to the hospital. Not that I cared—I had already started typing.

"Just tell Ryan to be ready to get it on the website and Facebook and everywhere else he can throw it as soon as I'm done," I said. "Get the pictures off my phone over to photo. And then hush up and let me work some magic for you."

"Get after it, kiddo." Bob sat on the bench Kyle had vacated and picked up my phone. "This is going to be one hell of a story."

The keyboard and my thoughts drowned out his conversation.

Hands in the air, an unknown man with a scar on his left cheek dropped to his knees on the concrete floor of a warehouse in Richmond's river district Saturday, begging for his life. His pleas fell on deaf ears, surrender not altering Richmond Police Chief Donovan Nash's plan.

Nash fired a single shot, then stood over his victim, kicking him in the ribs as the man lay in a growing pool of his own blood on the concrete.

Nash, in his ninth year as head of the RPD, confessed the murder to a Telegraph reporter he and RPD Detective Jerry Davis drugged and took hostage Saturday.

The journalist became a threat when she uncovered a drug ring operating out of police headquarters.

Nash and Davis, formerly known as Officer Brandon Smith of the Miami PD narcotics unit, used the RPD river unit to move drugs and guns throughout the mid-Atlantic.

Assistant Commonwealth's Attorney Gavin Neal, whose body was found in the James this week, was suspicious of oddities in the RPD's evidence procedures, his widow said.

"Gavin...swore to me something fishy was going on at the police department," Grace Neal said Thursday. "From that point on, he made weekly random checks of the evidence room. Then Sunday, he never made it home."

Nash confessed to involvement in Neal's death, among other crimes, including trafficking drugs and weapons and accessory to perjury that set a confessed murderer free.

Nash was shot Saturday by Bureau of Alcohol, Tobacco, and Firearms Agent Kyle Miller while threatening Miller with a gun. Two people were killed in the firefight between criminals and ATF agents, but their names were not available at press time.

I continued into the conflicting lab reports on the heroin, Smith's conviction in the drug thefts in Miami, and Roberts and Freeman's innocence.

Since I was the only person who knew the story of my kidnapping, we could hold it for the next day, but I tossed another teaser into the end.

I flipped the screen around and Bob read it silently, touching the keys only twice before he looked up at me.

"You have outdone yourself." He smiled and handed the computer back. "Just don't jump ship when Washington comes calling. I gave you a shot when they wouldn't, and don't you forget it."

I smiled, the pricking in the backs of my eyes telling me tears were coming whether I wanted them or not.

I brushed them away, grinning as I read.

I'd really done it. We had the story of the year. Grace Neal would know why her husband died. So would Valerie Roberts.

Hot damn.

"You want to do the honors?" Bob asked.

I turned on my phone's Wi-Fi hotspot and opened an email to Les.

"Bite me, you asshat," I muttered as I clicked send. He'd no doubt find a reason to be unimpressed.

"What a colorful—and accurate—description." Bob laughed, nodding to the medic. "I think she'll behave now."

She put a blood pressure cuff on my arm and Bob's grin dissolved into a glare.

"You scared the shit out of me, kid," he said. "I heard you scream, and then a scuffle, and then nothing—well, let's just say those pills must be working, because I'm still sitting here.

"Why the hell would you go after this guy without any help?" He shook his head. "I told you Parker said to let him know if you needed anything. He's a big guy. And he would've come with you."

"Which would have been great, if I was sure he wasn't in on it."

"If you what?" Bob stared. "What are you talking about?"

Sighing, I waited for the medic to decide I wouldn't expire on the ride to the hospital. When she returned to her seat, I pulled a copy of the photo of Lowe and Parker out of my bag, waving it under Bob's nose as I explained a suspicion that suddenly sounded far-fetched. Especially given that Lowe wasn't actually the big bad.

"Oh, Good Lord," Bob chuckled. "You have to remove *The X-Files* from your Netflix immediately. Impressive conclusion you jumped to. Did that take a springboard?"

"I didn't jump to anything," I argued, ticking off points on my fingers. "The designer bike, the flashy cash. And then the photo. Plus, he-who-has-never-spoken-to-me has been all into my story this week. It's weird. A long step, or a hop, maybe, but no jumping."

"Did it ever occur to you that he might respect you?" Bob asked. "And I imagine he was asking about the drug dealers because he had a friend from college who blew out his knee catching for the Cardinals not long after Parker wrecked his shoulder. Except his buddy got addicted to Oxycontin, then to heroin. Hung himself. Sad story.

"Parker's got a real thing about it. He gives speeches to school kids on the evils of drugs. And he has more money than you because we pay him more."

"What? How much more?"

"Grant Parker is a bonafide local hero," Bob said. "According to Les' focus groups, his column generates nearly a third of our daily subs and almost that much of our ad revenue. And he saves me paying a baseball reporter. He's also a good writer, which you would know if you'd ever read that column he's been begging you to critique for him. We can't afford to lose him. He makes more money than I do."

My eyes dropped to my lap under his reproachful stare. Bob and my mother were the only two people in the world who could make me feel so effectively chastised.

"Oh," I said.

"Oh, indeed. You may owe him an apology."

"Well, why didn't he mention knowing Lowe?" I cringed at what Parker must have thought of my insane behavior the night before.

What if he really was a decent guy who just wanted to be my friend? Though he probably wouldn't once he heard I'd labeled him a murderer.

"The cop was the waterboy, right? Didn't you go to high school? How many star pitchers knew the waterboy's name?"

Everything he said made perfect sense, which irritated me.

"Forgive me for being a newbie at the 'everyone's trying to kill me' platinum edition," I huffed. "Maybe next time I'll get to the bonus levels."

"Let's not have a next time," Bob said as the ambulance rolled to a stop outside the emergency room. The medic ordered him to the registration desk, and he took my bag and eased himself out the back doors.

I snatched up my cell phone.

"Miss, you can't make a call right now," the medic sighed. "You really do need medical attention. Everything else can wait."

"I'm not calling anyone," I smiled, clicking the browser open and looking for Parker's name on the *Telegraph's* mobile site. "But while I'm stuck here, I have some reading to catch up on."

CHAPTER TWENTY

IT TURNED out Bob was right. Parker was a hell of a good writer, and while I'll admit to being emotional when I read it, his piece on the basketball coach brought tears to my eyes.

I emailed my mom a link with "Read this. But get tissues first" in the subject line, and copied Parker. Maybe that would begin to make up for suspecting him of murder.

The doctor who patched up my scalp assured me my hair would grow back eventually and admitted me for observation because of the sedatives. I watched Charlie's coverage of the day's events and learned that Nash was one of Kyle's corpses. I didn't know how to feel about that, but couldn't say I was sorry.

Since I knew my name and who was president, they let me go Saturday night.

Jenna came to pick me up, listening to the tale with wide eyes before she stopped in my driveway. Leaning across the console, she hugged me, mumbling something into my shoulder about boring being a good thing. I could go with that. I climbed out and waved as she drove off.

"The dog is glad to be home." The voice floated out of the darkness and I smiled.

"Nope. Still not surprised," I limped up the steps and seated myself next to Joey on the white wooden swing that was one of the best things about my house. "Maybe it's you, because my old beau showing up with the cavalry this morning shocked the hell out of me."

"I used it all up on that first night." He snapped his fingers. "Damn."

"That must be it. To what do I owe the honor of this visit? You could've left the dog here. I do it all the time."

"I wanted to thank you," he said.

"Shouldn't I be the one thanking you? You called the FBI and tipped them off, right?" I knew Bob hadn't, because he'd told me so while we waited for the ER doctor. Joey was the only other logical assumption. "Which saved my life. Again. But how did you know?"

"I went snooping around the warehouse." His teeth flashed white in the darkness. "I thought I'd be in the clear, going early on a Saturday. Instead I found them moving stuff out and hosing the place down with gasoline. I found your car a couple of blocks away and called the FBI. They showed up while I was debating the best tactic for a rescue mission."

"You were?" I didn't know why, but that made me smile.

"Of course I was. I drug you into this. At least part of it." His eyes held mine and my hospital-issue broiled cod flopped around in my stomach like it was still alive. "I never wanted you to get hurt. I had no idea it went all the way to the police chief. But I also didn't want a shootout with a truckload of cops. I was outnumbered, and wouldn't have come out of it well no matter how it went down. So I called it in. Working around the edges of the law, remember?"

The edges. It still didn't sound so bad. I stared at his lips and wondered if he was a good kisser. Something told me that was a given. And something else told me the answer was there for the having if I wanted it.

I took a deep breath and leaned back into the throw pillows, not sure enough to stay so close to him.

"Was it you the first time, too?" Focusing on business seemed like a good bet, and I had a flash of what seemed like a long-ago conversation with Agent Starnes that made me wonder. "The boating accident? You set the FBI on him then, too, didn't you?"

"Nothing gets by you, does it?"

"I wish some things did," I said, more to myself than to him, but he heard me anyway.

"Me, too." It was little more than a whisper.

"Thanks for taking the dog," I said, out of questions and beginning to fidget. "I should go say 'hi' to her."

"Seemed like the least I could do." He stood up. "Goodnight, Miss Clarke."

"Goodbye, Joey."

He nodded, staring at me with an unfamiliar sadness. "I can't say I blame you. But I can be persistent." His lips turned up slightly. "And I'm not sure I'm ready to give up."

"I'm stubborn." I couldn't help smiling back.

"So am I." He disappeared into the night.

I got out of bed on Sunday only for coffee or food. Monday, I walked into the staff meeting to white chocolate chip banana bread and a lecture about being more careful from Eunice. From Bob, who was back for half-days because he was just that stubborn, I got a bear hug.

I stayed put when everyone filed out. Eunice paused to hug me, squeezing so long I smelled like patchouli the rest of the day. When she was gone, too, I tucked a wayward lock of hair behind my ear and smiled at Bob and Parker.

"Nice to be missed," I said.

"We're just glad you're okay," Parker said. "I would have come to help you if you'd called, you know. I wouldn't have even asked for a byline."

Bob cleared his throat with way too much fanfare and shot me a pointed stare.

"Hey Parker, about that," I said. "I owe you an apology. I was up to my ears in crooked cops and dead people and I found this old picture of you online and I sort of thought you might be in on it. A little." I held my thumb and forefinger a half-inch apart.

"In on what? Murder and theft with your crooked cops?" He shook his head and laughed. "I'd love to know what the hell kind of photo you found that made you think that."

He snatched it out of my hand before I got it all the way out of my bag, and laughed harder as he explained that he didn't even know Lowe.

"Someone told me that." I shot a glance at Bob and smiled at Parker. "Sorry I thought you were a murderer."

He grinned. "Glad you didn't get yourself killed."

"And what a story!" Bob leaned back in his chair. "Ad revenue hasn't been so high since Clinton was in office, and our page count has gone up 25 percent. Les even shuffled in here with a half-assed apology this morning. And every TV personality from Charlie Lewis to Anderson Cooper is quoting your story five times a day. This is great."

And it was. The only part of the RPD scandal's aftermath I didn't care for was the instant celebrity. I'd arrived at work to messages from reporters as far away as Los Angeles requesting interviews.

In the middle of the media storm, Kyle called to offer me an exclusive with the ATF in exchange for some company at dinner.

"How could I turn down a real-life hero?" I asked. "I heard from a little birdie on the TV that you're some sort of supercop."

"I don't know about that." The years had done nothing to his laugh. "But I do all right."

I gave him my address and told him to be ready to spill everything at seven-thirty.

Aaron and Mike were back at the PD and said they had a long story for me when I had time for it. All was right with my world again.

Bob just nodded when I told him about my date with Kyle.

"Promising," he said. "And if anything breaks tonight, Shelby can cover for you."

I shot him a glare that would've scared anyone else. "Not amusing."

He laughed. "I thought it was."

"Yeah, Clarke," Parker chimed in from the doorway. "We're all one big helpful family around here: cheapskate uncles, backstabbing cousins, and all."

Funny for Parker to put into words how I'd always thought of the staff as my family.

"And friends?" I smiled.

"Friends." He winked. "I meant to tell you before, thanks for that email about my column. Not bad for a murdering drug pusher?"

"Not bad at all." I grinned. "For a jock."

Turning back toward my desk, I smiled at the bustle of the newsroom, not even a little sad that my call from the *Post* hadn't come.

I had a job. I had friends. And I had a home here. There might be mobsters in my living room or coffins in random driveways, but life was rarely boring. And every beep of my scanner promised a new adventure.

BURIED LEADS

CHAPTER ONE

DEAD PEOPLE CAN HAVE the worst timing.

After a ridiculously long day of deadlines, criminals, and cops who did not want to talk to me, I wanted a hot bath and my warm bed. Is that too much for a girl to ask? Apparently so, because there I was, traipsing around the woods looking for a half-eaten dead guy who got himself discovered at eleven o'clock. At night. The glamorous life of a journalist.

Since the body recovery came over my police scanner while the TV stations were all seconds from their last broadcast of the day, though, I knew going out there would likely get me an exclusive for morning. Which meant the bath and bed could wait.

Ducking under another branch, I grimaced as I jerked the heel of one aubergine Manolo out of the composted leaves and pillowy moss that blanketed the ground. Someday, I was going to remember to put rain boots in the back of my little SUV. I didn't often have to slog through the middle of nowhere chasing stories, but I wrecked a pair of shoes almost every time I did.

I picked my way closer to the investigators' voices, reaching to the waistband of my khaki capris and turning down the volume on my police scanner.

Finally finding the scene, I tucked my pink flashlight into my pocket and scanned the faces inside the bright yellow tape. I didn't see any cops or coroners I knew, so I flashed a smile at the uniformed Richmond police officer who stepped toward me, then handed him my press credentials.

"Nichelle Clarke, *Richmond Telegraph*. I spoke with Detective White on my way here," I said, hoping the public information officer's name would lend an air of authority. I left out the part where I hadn't told the detective I'was headed to the recovery site.

"Nothing I can tell you until the official report is complete." He handed my press badge back without looking at it, the lines in his face evidence of a perpetual scowl.

I smiled at him again and leaned forward a little. "I'm sure there's something you can tell me. Who discovered the body? Is there a reason to suspect foul play?"

His expression didn't change. "Report will be available in the morning." The radio handset clipped to his shoulder crackled to life. He stepped backward and turned away.

Thank you, Officer Charming.

I peered through the hundred-foot trees, wishing this part of the woods smelled more like woods and less like decay. I wasn't entirely used to the forest scent after more than half a decade in Virginia, but I still loved it. It smelled green—dank and loamy, with a hint of pine. Texas had nothing like it. At least, not the part of Texas where I grew up. Fresh-cut St. Augustine grass, hay fields, and skunks: that's what the great outdoors was supposed to smell like.

Skunk is preferable to rotting human, though. Mercifully, the remains had already been zipped into a rubber bag and loaded into the back of the coroner's van, but the lingering stench of decomposing flesh snatched the woodsy fragrance right out of the air. It wasn't the first time I'd smelled a dead body, but the faintly sweet, acrid smell didn't get less putrid with repeated exposure.

The scene was quiet for a body recovery, just as I'd hoped. Not another reporter in sight.

But maybe witnesses? Off to my left, I spotted a pair of teenagers.

A boy, in purposely-worn jeans and a navy shirt, sat on the trunk of a police cruiser, his arms around a petite girl in short-shorts and a lavender silk tank top.

They looked like they'd seen a ghost. Or a half-eaten corpse.

I hurried toward them, sure Officer Charming had called their parents. If I wanted to talk to them, it was now or never. I stood by the back end of the squad car for a long moment, but the kids could've been rehearsing for a living art show, they were so indifferent.

I tried clearing my throat in an obvious manner, and when that didn't work, I offered a greeting followed with an apology. Still nothing.

I touched the boy's shoulder, and he flinched away like it had shocked him.

"I'm sorry." I pulled my fingers back. "I'm Nichelle. What's your name?"

His eyes were brown, and looked clouded when he focused them on me.

"Jack," he said. "I'm Jack. And this is Tina. We were just looking for a place where we could sit under the trees and look at the stars."

Sure you were. The leaves eclipse the view of the stars out here, Romeo. Aloud, I said, "I'm sorry. Definitely a different kind of night."

"That was a person," Jack said, his muddy eyes fixed on something behind my right shoulder, his fidgeting fingers strumming imaginary chords across Tina's shoulders. "Wasn't it? It didn't look like there was a whole person there, but there was enough. I know I saw a hand. And a shoe. But part of it was buried. And ..." He pulled in a hitching breath and closed his eyes. "It looked like something ate the face."

The hairs on my forearm pricked up. People don't turn up half-buried in the woods when they die of natural causes. And scavenging animals help dump sites get discovered. An exclusive on a murder victim was definitely worth postponing my bedtime.

"Do you feel like telling me what happened?"

"We were just walking along through the trees," he said. The girl whimpered, and Jack stroked her hair absently as he talked, his eyes still far away. "There's not a path out here, and I was looking at the ground, trying to make sure we didn't trip over anything. First, there was the smell. I thought there was a dead animal around somewhere. I told Tina to cover her nose and tried to walk faster, but then I saw a shoe."

His Adam's apple bobbed with a hard swallow.

"What kind of shoe?" I asked.

"Armani. It was on the sole. There was a hand, and part of someone's face." The choked voice was high and came from Tina, muffled by Jack's t-shirt. "I saw a face. A person's face. But it wasn't all there—" a sob cut off her words and her fingers curled into fists around the cotton tee.

Armani. So the dead guy probably wasn't destitute.

"And you didn't move anything before the police got here?" I asked. I was pretty sure I knew the answer, but I'd been wrong before.

"Move anything?" Jack looked confused for a split second, then his expression twisted into one of horror. "Like, touch it? God, no."

I thanked them and turned back toward the crime scene tape, shoving my right hand into my pocket in search of the pink flashlight my closest girlfriend, Jenna, had given me as part of an "investigative reporter essentials" kit she'd made for my birthday. It had latex gloves, big sunglasses, and a little magnifying glass, too. This was the first night I'd had occasion to use any of it, and I made a mental note to tell her.

The little white flags poking out of the dirt told me the police had already swept the area for evidence and footprints. I wanted a first-hand look at the depth of the makeshift grave, so I ducked under the tape, glancing over one shoulder. Officer Charming was talking to the coroner, his back to me. Not that it mattered—there's no law preventing reporters (or anyone else) from entering a crime scene. It's not a great idea if the forensics crews are still working, though. I'd had fingerprints taken, DNA typed—I'd even lost a gorgeous pair of silver Louboutins because I'd once accidentally stepped in blood at a murder scene. Plus, doing it too much can get a reporter on the PD's "no calls" list, the professional equivalent of a time-out.

Though I could tell forensics had likely come and gone, I walked softly, watching for objects on the ground. I wasn't trying to cause trouble. I just wanted to get the story right.

The grave was about three feet wide. I guessed my leg would fit to about mid-shin, though I didn't actually put my foot down to see, because—well, ew. So about a foot and a half deep. Not a very careful hole. Which meant the person who dug it didn't give a damn about the deceased or was in a hurry. Or both.

I turned at the sound of tires on the leaves, wishing I'd known I could drive back here so I wasn't facing a hike back to my car in the dark. A late-model Jaguar stopped near the teenagers and a petite blonde flew out of the driver's seat and swooped both of them into her arms.

I ran the flashlight over the hole one last time, to see if I could guess the height of the deceased, and the beam glinted off something white, nearly buried about halfway up. A missed bone fragment? I turned toward Officer Charming, but he was deep in conversation with Ms. Jaguar. I knelt carefully next to the hole and poked at the soil with my pen, unearthing a small piece of odd paper.

Not regular office paper, and not cardboard, either. It was shiny, which was why the light had hit off it. I used the pen to brush the loosened soil away. The dirt had been sifted, but it looked like the paper had been turned just right to slip through and escape notice. I had no idea whether or not it had anything to do with the dead guy, but my curiosity was piqued.

It wasn't even an inch square, torn on two edges with a pair of tiny holes punched in the top, like a staple had been removed. Using the pen, I flipped it over and found ink along the torn edge on the backside. I fished my cell phone out of my pocket and took pictures, laying the pen next to it for size reference. Standing, I brushed my knees off and waved to Officer Charming.

"What the hell are you doing nosing around in my crime scene?" His face flushed, eyebrows drawing down.

I explained what I found, and he glared at me as he used tweezers to slide the scrap into a baggie. "If your prints are on this, I can charge you with interfering with an open investigation. Damned reporters."

"This 'damned reporter' is not stupid, officer." I handed over my pen. "Here. I dug it out of the soil with this. You're welcome."

I shoved my cell phone into my pocket and ducked under the tape, leaving him muttering as I strode away.

I passed the Jag on my way to my own car and the woman turned from tucking the still-silent kids into the backseat and waved at me.

"My son said you asked him questions for the newspaper," she said, her voice neutral, but guarded.

I introduced myself.

"Is there any reason you must use his name in the press?" She fiddled with a heavy gold charm bracelet, then dropped both hands back to her side. "I can't imagine him having to relive this for reporters until a better story comes along. I'm not looking forward to the therapy bills, just from what he told me."

"Not at all." My beat didn't often involve minors, but when it did, I didn't use their names without consent unless they were being tried as adults. Moreover, this was protecting a child's privacy—the poor kids huddled on the calfskin seats in the back of that Jag were victims of being in the wrong place at the wrong time.

She thanked me and slid behind the leather steering wheel, nodding in my direction before the engine purred to life.

I pulled in a few lungfuls of blissfully uncontaminated air when I got closer to my car, thankful for the relief. On the drive home, I ran through what I wanted to lead with, not even noticing the sleeping city that blurred past the windows.

By the time I turned into my driveway, I was torn between wanting to take a shower—my default response to eau de dead guy—and wanting to write my story.

Shower first, I decided. I could work when the olfactory evidence of a decidedly odd late night was swirling toward the water treatment plant. Grabbing my bag out of the backseat, I completely overlooked the sleek black Lincoln sitting in front of my neighbor's house.

I'd made it almost to the kitchen steps before the smooth, familiar voice stopped me.

"Nice night to be outside. I thought I might interest you in a walk. But that was a couple of hours ago."

Joey. I turned and stepped toward the front porch, ignoring the tiny flip my stomach did. My sexy Mafia friend enjoyed his air of mystery, stopping by whenever the whim struck him. Or whenever something important stirred in Richmond's criminal world.

He strolled into the light spilling from the kitchen porch lamp, and my insides positively cartwheeled. It had been several weeks since I'd seen him, and his olive skin, strong jaw, and straight nose looked even better than I remembered. The shoulders under his Armani suit coat were broad; his lean, strong frame obvious through his tailored clothes.

"I might have gone for that. But if you come much closer, you'll get a whiff of why I can't. I've been poking around a body dump in the woods out toward Goochland."

"Anyone interesting?" He didn't look surprised, a sardonic smile tipping up the corners of his full lips. That was an upshot to having a Mafia boss as a friend. I could talk to him about the more disgusting aspects of my job and not freak him out.

"No ID yet," I said. "But I was the only reporter out there, so I'm going to write it up anyway. We can get it on the web first thing in the morning. The coroner will probably know who it is by tomorrow."

"Bodies don't get dumped in the woods by good guys."

"Could be interesting." I nodded.

"You all right?" he asked. "How much did you see?"

It took a minute for me to figure out that he was asking if my mental state had been impaired by the sight of the half-eaten dead guy.

"Yeah. I'm jaded enough that I don't go catatonic or throw up anymore. I think I might understand a little bit of how doctors get to be clinical about telling people they have some horrible disease. After a while, it's just a bad day at work. Not that I don't love my job. I just love the dead guys less than the rest of it."

"I can appreciate that." He nodded, starting to step forward and appearing to think better of it. "I suppose I should let you get to work."

"I need a shower before I do anything. I feel like there should be a little Pigpen-esque cloud of funk around me." I grinned, stepping toward the kitchen door when my toy Pomeranian started yipping and scratching the other side of it. "But thanks for coming by. I'm sorry I wasn't here. It might work better if you called first, you know. My cell number is eight-oh—"

He held up a hand. "I know your phone number. I like surprises. Maybe we'll get to take that walk next time. I need to talk to you."

"Anything pressing?" I asked.

"It'll wait. Watch yourself on this one, okay?"

"Why?" My stomach flopped again, for a different reason. What if Joey knew something about the dead guy? That idea wasn't nearly as appealing as a moonlit walk.

"We'll talk," he said with a low smile before he offered a tiny nod, then turned and strode back to the car.

The taillights disappeared around the corner before I shook off the uneasy feeling and hurried inside.

* * *

Two teenagers looking for a peaceful view of the stars found a body in the woods near the Richmond City limits late Tuesday, sending police on a search for the identity of the man, estimated by coroners at the scene to be in his early thirties.

"There's not a path out here, and I was looking at the ground, trying to make sure we didn't trip over anything," one of the youths, whose name was withheld at parental request, said at the scene. "First, there was the smell. I thought there was a dead animal around somewhere, and I told [my companion] to cover her nose and tried to walk faster, but then it was right there, and I saw a shoe."

. . .

My editor was thrilled with the early story, especially since the mystery dead guy led the morning TV news. He was also ecstatic to have exclusive comments from the scene.

"Good move, getting all that on the record." Bob sat back in his big leather chair after he finished reading it before the morning staff meeting. "Very nice, kiddo."

I returned his smile and stifled a yawn. I'd gotten up a half-hour early to run in lieu of my usual body combat class. "Anything for the team," I said.

I clicked my pen in and out. "I found something out at the scene last night," I began, but Eunice Blakely interrupted. Our features editor came bearing a foil-covered pan of deliciousness, as she did at least once a week—in spite of Bob's restricted diet. He may have had a heart attack last summer, but he still longed for Eunice's southern culinary creations.

"What'd you bring me?" I grinned, my growling stomach taking precedence over the paper scrap.

"Armadillo eggs in honor of Texas clinching their division last night." She grinned and set the dish on the corner of Bob's desk closest to me. "I know how much you love them."

I lifted the foil and snatched up an oval lump of yummy wrapped in amazing before she could lower herself into the other orange armchair. They were still warm.

"Not as much as I love you," I told her, the words muffled by the food.

"Cheese-stuffed jalepenos coated in sausage and Bisquick? What's not to love?" Bob stared sadly at the tray, and I stopped mid-chew.

"I brought you something, too." Eunice pulled a Ziploc of brownies from her oversized pink tote. "Carob, black bean, and cocoa. Taste one before you turn your nose up. They're pretty damned good."

Bob took a tiny bite and grinned. "Eunice, you could put topsoil in that stand mixer and it would taste like heaven." He popped the rest of the square into his mouth.

Brownies that wouldn't widen my ass?

"Can you do that with white chocolate?" I asked, watching the rest of the armadillo eggs vanish as the other section editors filed in.

"I don't know, sugar, but I'll give it a shot." Eunice winked over the sports editor's head as he wolfed down an armadillo egg and asked her to marry him, which he did every time she brought food. Spence swore his wife wouldn't care, either, if Eunice would cook.

Bob started the rundown with sports.

"It's September." Spence tapped a pen on his notepad. "I got baseball winding down and college football gearing up, a Redskins injury report that ought to make the fantasy diehards cry into their Coors, and a great column from Parker on that foundation the Generals set up in Nate DeLuca's memory."

The meeting flew by. My feature on an inner-city family and part one of the baseball season wrap-up led as the big stories for the coming weekend. When the international desk chief started arguing ideology with our political reporter, Trudy Montgomery—who had more big D.C. names in her phone's favorites list than I could count on both of her perfectly-manicured hands—I pulled out my cell phone and checked my email.

"Politics is perception," Trudy's words faded into background noise as I clicked an email from Aaron White, the police department's public information officer. "This election isn't going to come down to the economy or the schools or the roads or any of the things people should give a damn about. It's going to come down to the guy who looks best on camera or the one who doesn't say something stupid in the next seven weeks."

She went on about the senate race, hotly-contested for the first time in almost two decades, and I tore my eyes from the "loading" icon on Aaron's email. Covering politics was my dream job, and Trudy was one of the best on the east coast.

"Trudy, polling shows voters are more concerned about the environment and foreign relations than ever," Edwin Caruthers, who'd been covering foreign affairs in Richmond since The Bay of Pigs, objected.

"People don't always tell pollsters what they really think," I said. "Sometimes they say what makes them sound smart."

Trudy winked at me. "Thank you, Nichelle. My point exactly. The polls are close because they both look good on TV and they're both suave. Add that to the uproar in DC, and of course it's tight. But Ted Grayson's smart. He's also got a well-oiled campaign and a gift of charisma I haven't seen since Clinton. He'll pull it out."

I nodded, and Bob thumped a paperweight onto his desk to recall order. He quizzed the business editor, and I returned to Aaron's email.

Hot damn. The coroner hit on the dental. My dead guy was Daniel Amesworth, twenty-nine, of Henrico. By the time Bob dismissed us, my fingers itched to hit the keyboard.

I detoured through the break room to refill my coffee mug, frowning at the light weight of my white mocha syrup bottle. My coffee habit was going to get expensive if I started pigging up a seven-dollar bottle of syrup a week.

Back at my desk, I searched Amesworth's name in Google. He was a lawyer. Private firm in Henrico, single, no police record. Not even an unpaid traffic ticket. I found a picture of his whole, smiling face on his Facebook profile. Poor guy.

"How did you end up bobcat chow, counselor?" I mused, sipping my coffee and staring at his blue eyes. He was good-looking, in his tan jacket and azure silk tie. And he had a mother somewhere who would miss him. People are the reason I do my job—finding the truth, bringing them closure. It makes the grisly parts bearable.

Grabbing the phone, I called Aaron for an update.

"I heard you poked around our scene last night," he said in lieu of hello. "I wish I'd known you were going out there."

"Did I forget to mention that?" I asked.

Aaron and I got along well after nearly seven years of working together, so I could tell he wasn't really upset. I could also tell he wasn't going to say much about the victim. Which meant there was something worth hearing.

"You did. But I forgive you. You get my email on the dead guy?"

"I did, thanks. It's kind of thin. Google tells me he's a lawyer. You know anything else about him?"

"Not really."

"Liar."

"Sorry, Nichelle. No one gets anything but the basics."

"Has his family been notified?" I clicked back to Amesworth's Facebook account. Nothing helpful in his public information, which wasn't terribly fleshed-out.

"They have," Aaron said.

"Then why so cryptic?"

"I'm sorry, Nichelle."

That was Aaron-ese for "no comment."

I thanked him for being no help at all and hung up, turning back to my computer. There was something about this guy, because Aaron wasn't that tight-lipped about anything unless he'd been ordered to be.

I went back to the search results, staring at the name of the law firm for a long minute.

"Where have I heard that?" I tapped a pen on my desk and waited for their corporate page to load.

Holy Manolos. The pen fell to the desk when the firm's logo came onto the screen. Trudy. I'd heard Trudy talk about this firm because they did corporate and tax law—and political lobbying.

The latter wasn't advertised on their website, of course, but a quick search of the firm name plus "lobbying" landed me a list of the most influential lobbies in Washington and how much cash they funnel to campaigns.

The victim's firm was number five. And their biggest client? The largest tobacco company in the world, headquartered less than twenty miles from where I sat.

A dead lawyer is one thing. A dead tobacco lobbyist is entirely another. Washington. Politics. Murder. Everything I'd ever dreamed of.

I sighed, slumping back in the chair. It could be a hell of a sexy story. It also might not be my sexy story.

I opened an email and typed Trudy's name in the address line, tapping out the victim's name and where he worked, because anything inside the beltway was her domain in the pared-down twenty-first century world of newspapers with too little space and too few reporters. Twenty years ago, it had taken a bureau of four people paid by the *Telegraph* and living in D.C. to do Trudy's job, and it had taken three to do mine.

Arrow hovering over the send key, I scanned the message again.

There was no evidence, really, that the guy's death had anything to do with politics. Except I knew Aaron White. What he didn't say this morning told me way more than what he did: Something was up.

I trashed the draft I'd started, telling myself I just wanted to poke around, see what was going on. Between the upcoming election and budget deadlock, Trudy was swamped. She didn't need me bothering her with a murder.

Maybe I shouldn't have bothered me, either.

CHAPTER TWO

TWELVE HOURS since Jack and Tina found Amesworth's body, and the coroner's office still hadn't released a cause of death. Someone had to know how he died. Fortunately, an agent at the Richmond FBI office owed me a favor. Maybe he'd talk.

"What can I do for you, Miss Clarke?" Craig Evans asked when he picked up the phone.

"To tell you the truth, I'm not a hundred percent sure," I said. "I have a hunch, and I was hoping you could answer a few questions."

"Yes. Yes, I can," he said with a chuckle.

Hooray for guilt trips. I tossed out a few roundabout inquiries concerning lobbying and impropriety, hoping maybe he knew something. He just said the FBI commonly did months of planning and undercover work when they suspected such things.

"Why?" Evans asked as I scribbled the last of his comments. "You uncovering more corruption?"

"Corruption seems to have fitted me with a LoJack," I said. "But I don't have anything definite on this yet. Can I call you back if I get something?"

"Please," he said. "We can't have you people stealing all our fun.

You want to share what you've got so far? If I can come up with anything on this end, I'll tell you what I find."

Come again? The FBI was notoriously tight-lipped with the press, and the public information officer in Richmond was a nice enough woman, but she'd rather have a root canal than willingly give up details on anything they were doing.

"I thought media contact with agents working on an investigation was against policy," I said, regurgitating the line Agent Starnes had burned into my brain.

"It is. But I'm not working on an investigation, now, am I?" There was a hint of mischief in his tone. I laughed.

"I guess you're not." I paused and decided to be candid. "There was a lawyer found in the woods near the city limits last night. I don't think he was an ordinary lawyer."

Evans fell silent for a minute.

"You think right," he said. Something in his tone twisted my stomach into a knot. "You sure you haven't ever thought about being a cop, Miss Clarke?"

"Couldn't handle the shoes." I tried to keep my tone light. "Can you tell me anything about cause of death on that case?"

I heard papers rustling. "Let me find it," Evans said.

"They said an animal got to him. They weren't sure if it was before or after–" my words came slowly. I clenched the phone in my suddenly-sweaty palm.

"It was after," Evans interrupted. "The prelims I got this morning say the guy was hit over the head with something and shot. Not sure which came first, but someone really wanted him dead."

Indeed. I scribbled that down and thanked Evans for his time. Then I clicked back to the Google results. There was nothing that would mark him as a target, except the lobbying job. I clicked over to the Channel Four website. Charlotte Lewis at Channel Four was my biggest competition in Richmond, usually just a step ahead of or behind me on any given story.

If Charlie knew this guy was a lobbyist, she hadn't run it yet. Her story was a basic report that identified Amesworth as a lawyer. She might be onto it, but I had time to figure out what happened to the guy, at least. And if I could beat Charlie to the answer, it'd be worth big brownie points with the suits upstairs.

I pulled a file folder out of my desk and flipped it inside-out, writing Amesworth's name on the tab and printing off copies of his Facebook page, the firm's homepage, and the list from the *Post*. I added my notes from Evans and tucked it into the back of my drawer before I turned to the day's police reports. Amesworth's murder wasn't the only crime in Richmond that day, and as the lone cops reporter, I had other cases to check on.

Only one needed my attention: another drive-by on Southside. That part of town had a whole city's share of troubles, currently serving as Richmond's own drug war demilitarized zone. Every small-time dealer and wannabe badass fought by the hour to win control of the cash that changed hands on every other street corner.

I also needed an update on a rash of break-ins in the Fan—the part of Richmond named for its geography, the way it splayed out from downtown like the hand-held works of art favored by ladies in the days before air-conditioning. It was also the part of town where I lived, not that I had anything worth stealing except footwear. The police attributed the outbreak to a talented cat burglar, but Aaron got less forthcoming with information every time the guy got away.

I called Aaron back.

"You're not tired of being blown off yet?" he asked when he picked up.

"I've moved on. I'm good at that," I said. "I need to talk to you about this shooting on Southside."

"Another day, another shooting. I'm surprised it wasn't a reporter who got shot, with every TV camera within fifty miles hanging out down there all day." He sighed. "One of these folks is going to get themselves killed trying to get better footage or asking the wrong person for a comment. You people and your scoops."

"Hey, you haven't seen me out there dodging bullets." I twisted the phone cord around my index finger. "I've had enough of that for one lifetime. Let Charlie at it. She might win an Emmy for some of what she's done lately. More power to her. I'll stay here, far away from the crack-high teenagers with automatic weapons."

Banter with Aaron aside, I did hope Charlie was watching herself. Covering cops is not the safest gig in journalism.

"You do that," Aaron said. "I'll give you all the details you want. The victim is young, again, with a record, again. I'll fax you everything."

"Thanks, Aaron. I need an update on the cat burglar, too. Any leads?"

"Not a one." He was annoyed, though he tried to keep his voice neutral. In a month, someone had managed to get in and out of some of the biggest homes in town (with some of the most influential residents) without leaving a fingerprint. The detectives were stumped, and cranky. "The good news? It's been nine days since the last report of anything stolen."

"So he found what he was looking for?"

"Or he's on his way to the islands with the money from fencing that stuff."

"Any indication this is a team effort?"

"Who knows? This whole thing is bizarre. How the guy knows which houses have the fancy security and which don't, and how he can find and crack any type of safe without making a sound is beyond me. Guys like this usually work alone if they can. The more people involved, the better chance we have of catching someone."

I scribbled that down and thanked him before I hung up, glancing at the clock. Lunchtime. I didn't have anything on my calendar until the interview for my feature story at five, so I called my friend Jenna and asked if she wanted to grab a bite at the cafe across the street from the rare bookstore where she worked. I hadn't seen her in nearly a week, and her birthday was coming up.

Ten minutes later I settled into a little metal chair, struggling to keep my mind off the dead lobbyist and on Jenna's crisis of the month, which involved her husband and a certain medical procedure.

"He's right. We always said thirty-five was the cut-off for kids for us," she said, plucking the wedge of French bread that had come with her soup into a pile of snowflakes. "But staring down the barrel of it when Carson's getting so big, so fast, is a lot different than talking about it ten years ago. What if I want another baby in a year?"

I knew she wanted me to say something, but I wasn't sure what "something" she wanted to hear. I shoveled salad into my mouth and studied her as I chewed. The bread was gone and she moved on to her napkin.

"I'm sorry, Jen," I said finally. "But, do you really think you might?"

She sighed as she dropped the last piece of the shredded napkin. "No. I'm nearly thirty-five. I have a girl, I have a boy. I'm done with three a.m. feedings and my boobs are my own again."

"So why are you so upset?"

"I don't know. Honestly? Maybe I have PMS. But he didn't even tell me first. He just comes home and says 'I'm doing away with our ability to procreate as of nine o'clock Friday morning.' No warning. No, 'Honey, what do you think about this?' Happy freaking birthday to me."

"You're pissed because he didn't talk to you about it before he made the appointment," I said. "That's when your tone went from 'I married such a great guy' to 'My husband is the world's biggest asshat and I may end up on that Oxygen show about the women who go batshit and bludgeon their men to death with a garlic press.'"

She peeked up at me and smiled. "A garlic press? Nah. I'm definitely a *Wives With Knives* sort of girl."

"Hey, that was a joke. A small one, but still. See? It's not all doom and gloom."

"No, but it still sucks. Isn't it fun to be my friend?"

I laughed. "That it is. I certainly learn a lot about the mechanics of marriage, at any rate. Not that I'll ever need to understand them. But knowledge is good, on the whole."

She grinned. "Nothing from your sexy Italian friend?"

"I don't know that he's actually Italian. But in fact, he did stop by last night. I really wish I could stop wondering if he's a murderer, though. There was a dead guy in the woods just before I saw him." I clung to the hope that forensics would determine Mr. Animal Food had been there for a while, but I didn't know yet whether it had been days or hours.

"More dead people?" She raised her eyebrows. "We're going to have a population shortage around here before long."

"This was a gross one, too." I paused and looked at her half-eaten lunch. I didn't want to ruin the rest of her meal, but I had the borders of a new puzzle in my head, and Jenna was a good sounding board.

"You don't need details." I smiled. "Suffice to say that the FBI said this morning that the guy was shot and hit over the head with something. The exact quote was 'someone really wanted him dead.' " I paused, thinking about Jenna's joke about Chad. Was the killer someone Amesworth knew?

"What the hell are you getting yourself into now?" Jenna's eyes widened and she shook her head. "You can't go getting killed chasing a story, Nicey. Who else will listen to me bitch about my fantastic life with such convincing sympathy?"

"Gee, thanks," I said wryly. "I have no intention of getting myself killed. I just want to beat Charlie to this story, and I have a hunch I'd like to run down before my interview tonight. Thanks for listening to me."

"Back at you."

I stood up and leaned in to hug her. "It really will be all right, Jen," I whispered into her reddish-brown curls. "These things work out the way they're supposed to. Talk to him."

She nodded. "I know. I will."

I cranked the stereo on my way back to the office and let the Red Hot Chili Peppers lead my mind back to college political science class. Lobbyists in democracy gave me a place to start. My first order of business after filing my copy for the day would be to see if I could find where the money was going.

Back at my desk, I pulled up my story on the body and rewrote the lead to include the victim's name (Daniel Amesworth) and profession (attorney, as far as anyone else needed to know).

I found Aaron's fax and wrote up the shooting, too. The nineteen-year-old female victim had three prior arrests, and had been patched up at St. Vincent's and sent home overnight. The cat burglar story was easy, essentially rehashing what I already had, plus Aaron's comment about the nine-day lapse in the robberies, the longest since they started.

Once I'd sent those to Bob, I was free to hunt for background information on Amesworth. Clubbed, shot, and left as dinner for the local wildlife. If he'd pissed someone off that badly, there had to be a record of it in cyberspace. I just had to find it. Preferably first.

I typed a few words into the Google box, drumming my fingers on the desk as I scrolled through the results. He was a lobbyist for the tobacco industry, and that was big business in Virginia, from farming, to manufacturing, to sale. And yet, Google had nothing for me in ten pages of results. If there was one thing I'd learned from better than six years at the crime desk, it was that the answer to almost anything could be found on the Internet. The trick was knowing where to look.

I clicked over to the image results and scrolled through a surprising number of photos. Amesworth appeared to be a fixture in Richmond society. I ran my cursor over the thumbnails, finding loads of charity event shots from the *Telegraph's* site. I jotted a list of places he'd been, wondering who else had been there, too. Lucky for me, I had the means to find out.

I got up and hurried back to the photo cave. A darkroom in its former life, it now held high-resolution monitors for photo editing. The smell of stop bath and fixer still hung in the air ten years into the digital age. Larry Murphy, our senior photographer, was the only one not out on assignment that afternoon.

"Hey Larry, how long do you keep images from big charity events and society stuff?" I leaned on the table next to the monitor he was studying.

He pushed his wire-rimmed glasses up the bridge of his nose and peered up at me, his gray hair sticking out from under his faded Richmond Generals baseball cap in a dozen different directions.

"Forever," he said. "It's a nice little side income for the paper, because those people order reprints all the time, so Les won't let us trash them." Les Simpson was our managing editor. He was also a pain in my ass, since the copy editor he was sleeping with wanted my job. I felt my nose wrinkle reflexively at the mention of his name. I'd had a pretty successful run of flying under his radar lately, and I hoped to keep it that way.

"I'm not used to Les being helpful." I handed Larry the list of events where I'd found Amesworth. "Do you have time to find and copy the shots from these events for me?"

"Sure. And don't worry, Les didn't mean to be helpful. I heard him bitching last week because you've been writing about too many murders on Southside. His focus groups don't like it."

I shook my head. "I'll be sure to let the trigger-happy dealers know they're boring our subscribers."

Larry plugged a little USB drive into his computer, clicked his mouse, and handed me the drive. "Have fun. There are about twenty-three-hundred photos there. What are you looking for?"

"Needle. Sounds like I have myself a haystack. I see another late night in my future. Thanks, Larry."

I tucked the drive in my pocket, went back to my desk, and unplugged my computer. Amesworth's social life would have to wait. Eunice was counting on my feature for Sunday, and I had an interview appointment.

CHAPTER THREE

GRAFFITI-COVERED STOREFRONTS HAWKING LIQUOR, cigarettes, and soul food lined one side of the street. On the other, narrow front porches cluttered with junk sagged from years of neglect. My little red SUV slowed to a crawl as I looked for address markers. Some houses had them, some didn't.

The row house where Joyce Wright raised both a drug dealer and an honor student had three out of five numbers over the front door.

I made the block and parallel parked the car on my first try. Not bad for a girl who'd learned to drive amid the sprawl of Dallas' plentiful parking lots.

Joyce's was the neatest of the block's porches, occupied only by a battered ten-speed and a couple of metal yard chairs that looked like their best days had come and gone back when Lucy was trying to finagle a way into Ricky's acts on Monday night TV.

I smoothed my beige linen slacks, eyes on my sapphire Louboutins, and pushed the doorbell.

It opened quickly, and I looked up to meet Troy Wright's deep brown eyes.

"Miss Clarke!" His face lit with an infectious smile.

"It's nice to see you again, Troy." I returned his grin. "How's school?"

"Good." He stared at me for a long minute. "School is good. Life is getting better." Troy dropped his eyes to his shoes and shuffled backward, holding the door. "I should thank you for that. I didn't expect you to listen to me when I told you what I thought about my brother and why he died. So thanks."

"You're welcome." I laid a hand on his arm and stepped into a cluttered living room. The furnishings matched the era and wear of the porch chairs. No air conditioning, but the warmth in the homey little room was more than temperature. Love oozed from every chip in the once-white paint on the walls.

"Thank you, too. For trusting me." I squeezed his outstretched hand and laughed when he pulled me into a hug.

He shoved his hands into pockets of faded jeans that were at least two sizes too big. "So, what brings you to my neighborhood? Mama said you wanted to talk to us. Are you doing another story about Darryl?"

"No. I want to write a story about you. What it was like to grow up in the city with a single mom. I'd also like to talk about your academic achievements. Have you started applying to colleges yet?" I looked around. "Is your mom here?"

"She's...sleeping." He dropped his gaze to the worn red carpet. "She does a lot of that when she's not at work since Darryl ... well. She said to get her when you got here. I'll be right back."

He disappeared through a narrow door into a dim hallway. I studied the photos that covered the wall. Troy at different ages. And another boy, a happier one than the Darryl Wright I'd seen in mugshots. They posed next to a Christmas tree with vastly different-sized, new-to-them bikes. In another picture they sprayed each other with super soakers on the tiny lawn I'd crossed on my way to front door.

I could tell Joyce Wright loved her sons. Both of them. My throat tightened at the thought of her holed up in her bedroom when she wasn't at work. No parent should have to bury a child. A voice breached my reverie with a soft "hello," and I spun around, arranging my features into a bright smile.

"It's so nice to meet you, ma'am," I said, extending my hand to the robust woman who shuffled into the room. She was two heads shorter than me, with a full figure and close-cropped hair. Her handshake was firm, but the smile on her face didn't reach her eyes. The same extraordinary espresso color as Troy's, Joyce's eyes betrayed anguish.

"Likewise, Miss Clarke," she said. "I want to thank you for what you did for my Darryl. Not many people would care much about a black boy with a record who got shot with a house full of dope."

"They should," I said. "And thanks to Troy, they do now. Thank you for taking time to see me today."

She gestured to the small sofa that ran the length of one wall, and I settled myself on the floral fabric and dug a pen and a notebook out of my bag. Joyce took the La-Z-Boy in the room's opposite corner, and Troy dropped his long frame to the floor in front of her, pulling his knees to his chest.

"You want to talk to us about Troy's schooling?" Joyce asked.

"Among other things." I smiled. "But why don't we start there? Troy, have you made any decisions about what you're going to study in college?"

"I want to be a sportscaster." His eyes lit up, excitement creeping into his voice. "You know, like on ESPN. Sometimes when there's a game on TV, I turn the sound off and call the plays myself."

"He's good." Joyce rested a hand on top of his head. Her voice brightened the tiniest bit. "I tell him all the time, I don't much care for watching sports on TV, but I love to watch the games with him when he does the commenting. He knows everything there is to know about it, it seems like. And he's funny, too."

"That's great." I smiled. "Just know it's not quite as glamorous as it looks on TV. But this business is never boring."

"My baby boy here's done so much to make his mama proud." Joyce's fingers closed around her younger son's shoulder. "This is just one more thing. My boy in the *Telegraph* for being a smart kid. This one's not going to spend his life cleaning up other people's messes. He's going to do better. My Troy is going to be the first person in this family to go to college."

I nodded and smiled. "Do you know which college will be lucky enough to have you, Troy?"

He plucked at a dingy shoelace, his eyes trained on something on the floor. "That depends on whether or not I get my scholarship, and I won't know that until after Christmas," he said. "I'm going to apply to UVA and Tech, and we're going to try for financial aid."

"And we'll get it," Joyce said, determined. "And we'll get loans. And I'll mortgage this damn house if I have to. It's paid for. You're going to college, baby."

I stared at her ragged nails, betraying the work she did with her hands every day to keep food on the table and buy a home for her children, as her fingers sank into Troy's shoulder. I had no trouble believing she'd mortgage her soul to see her son get his bachelor's. She reminded me so much of my own mother a lump formed in my throat.

"If it's my choice, I go," he said. "There were a few kids in my school last year who got picked to go to Blacksburg to the Tech campus overnight, and I was one of them."

"He won an essay contest," Joyce interrupted. "First place."

Troy rolled his eyes. "Thanks, mama. Anyway, I've never seen anything like that. All the buildings are so big and the campus is huge. We went in the spring and there were people just sitting under trees reading and guys playing catch in the middle of the grass, and the library...I didn't think there were that many books anywhere."

I smiled at his enthusiasm as I scribbled, remembering the first time I'd ever stepped foot into the library at Syracuse. I'd had that same thought, staring at the shelves that soared toward the heavens on every floor of the four-level building.

"Troy, your mom is right to be proud of you. You should be proud of yourself. And put that essay contest on your applications. College applications are no place for modesty. You have to toot your own horn loud enough to get noticed among the other kids who are blowing theirs."

"Yes, ma'am," he said, nodding. "My counselor at school is helping me, and I'm taking the first SAT in October so if I have to re-take it I can."

"You ain't gonna have to re-take no test," Joyce said. "You might get an award for the last one."

"The National Merit program is a big deal, Troy," I said. Our schools reporter had forwarded me the Richmond finalist list when Troy's name popped up on it, and Eunice had jumped at my pitch of a feature on a drug dealer's brother up for such an award.

"Damn right," Joyce said. The first real smile I'd seen on her face radiated pride at her son. "I didn't spend my whole life cleaning other people's toilets for nothing. I made sure my boys had plenty to read and took them places when I could, too. I think Troy's read every book in that library up the street, and he could be a tour guide for most of the historical stuff 'round these parts."

"Can you tell me a little about your work, ma'am?"

"I don't see how that's going to make interesting reading. I wasn't much older than Troy is now, when I found out I was expecting Darryl. I'd have starved right to death waiting for their lazy-ass daddy to get a job. I thought he was Richmond's own Billy Dee Williams, he was so charming." She kept her eyes on her hands. "I learned charming wasn't everything, but not 'til I had my boys to take care of. I'd do anything for my boys. Scrubbing toilets may not be the proudest work there is, but it kept food on our table."

"You don't need to defend anything to me," I said, something in my tone bringing Joyce's eyes back to mine. "My mother was seventeen when I was born. And she's been a single mom all my life. When I was little, she worked as a secretary all day and went to school at night until she got a business degree. She owns a flower shop now, but it took a lot of work to get there.

"Things happen," I told Joyce. "I believe it's what you do when things happen that defines your character. And I'm looking at a young man who scored better than ninety-five percent of high school kids in the United States on a test that's not exactly easy, as I remember. I don't see where you have much to defend to anyone."

She sat a little taller in the chair and her chin lifted slightly.

"I saw an ad in the newspaper," she said. "It said they needed people to clean houses. I figured I could mop a floor or scrub a toilet if it would buy diapers and formula for my baby. When Troy came along, I figured out I'd have more money if I wasn't supporting their daddy's lazy behind. So I threw him out, got a second job and paid a lady down the street to watch my boys for me in the evening. When Troy was two, they give me my own crew at the cleaning company, and I could afford to quit moonlighting.

"In almost fifteen years, I've only had one employee leave my crew. They say I'm fair. I got the best crew in the city. We work mostly over to the Fan. Clean houses for big executives. Even got a few doctors and a senator on my list."

I nodded, my hand moving like lightning to catch every word exactly as she spoke it. She told me about the weekend days she'd spent showing her boys around the Civil War battlegrounds scattered across the Mid-Atlantic, and taking them to experience the living colonial history that defined the Williamsburg corridor.

Troy beamed at his mother. "My mama was like the Energizer bunny. She'd come home after being on her feet for ten hours and clean our house, cook us supper, and help us with our homework. I definitely learned the value of hard work. I don't care if I have to start out bringing someone coffee or making copies. I'll make the best coffee and the cleanest copies they've ever seen, and I'll have my own mic in the press box one day, you wait and see. When I was just a kid in middle school, I wanted my own column in the newspaper like Grant Parker. But then I started watching SportsCenter, and they get to report on all the games that happen everywhere, not just the ones that are in their town. I like that."

I kept writing, but I had an idea. "Troy, I know you want to work in TV, but how would you like to spend a day hanging out with Parker?" I looked up from my notes and felt a smile tug at the corners of my lips as his mouth dropped open.

"Seriously? Do you really think he might let me tag around after him? I won't be a pest, I swear it! Do you know him? Can you ask him if that would be all right?" He sounded like a little boy who'd just been told he might go to Disney World.

Parker owed me a favor. He had been walking around in a megawatt-grin daze for weeks, since I'd decided to play cupid with him and Melanie from the city desk. "We're friends. I think I can go ahead and tell you it'll be fine." I matched Troy's grin with one of my own. "Do you think you could miss a day of school next week? Parker's not much for coming in on the weekends."

"I'm ahead in all my classes, anyway," he said. "I have a part-time job at the grocery store two blocks up, but I'm off on Mondays and Tuesdays."

"Parker's column runs Tuesday, Thursday..."

"And Saturday," Troy interrupted. "I read it every time it's in. This is the baddest thing ever, Miss Clarke."

I laughed. "I'm guessing you'll see more of what he does on Monday, but I'll double check that with him and call you later."

"Thank you," Joyce mouthed over her son's head. I nodded.

I asked a few more questions about Troy's classes, and thanked them both as I shoved my notebook back into my bag and capped my pen.

Troy stood up to get the front door, and Joyce rose when I did. She crossed the shoebox-sized room in three steps and took both my hands in hers. I felt calluses under my fingertips.

"I'm obliged to you for coming, Nichelle," she said, holding her back straight. Tears swam in her eyes again, but she didn't blink them back. "My boys are the world to me." A tear fell, followed closely by another. "This is something. I'm obliged."

"Thank you for sharing your story with me," I said, returning the pressure she was putting on my fingers. "I hope I can tell it right."

* * *

Larry's USB drive full of photos burning a hole in my pocket, I pulled back into the garage at the office at ten after seven, detouring past the break room's vintage soda machine on the way to my desk.

Sipping a Diet Coke and thinking about Troy's game-show-host grin, I checked the clock and went past Parker's office, hoping he'd stayed late. Dark and empty. Damn. There wasn't a game that night, so he was probably out with Mel. I'd have to catch up with him tomorrow.

I plugged the drive into the side of my computer and waited for the photos to load, opening a slideshow so I wouldn't miss anything important.

Three hours and over a thousand images later, my head was starting to hurt. I rifled through my desk drawer for a bottle of Advil and washed two down with the last of my soda before I clicked to the next photo.

And found something.

I checked the information in the sidebar. It was from a charity casino night in April. There was Amesworth, laughing and leaning one hand on the shoulder of a tall, dark-haired man in a sharp tux. They looked chummy, which was interesting, since the dark-haired man was Senator Ted Grayson.

A tobacco lobbyist and a U.S. Senator in the middle of a bone-crushingly tight reelection campaign laughing over drinks and cards might mean nothing, except that Grayson could deliver a good punchline. But it was a hell of a coincidence. I'd covered crime for long enough to know true coincidences are few and far between. Playing the odds here, I might have an exclusive. The photo hadn't been published, so no one else had access to it.

I copied the photo to the Amesworth folder on my hard drive and clicked over to Google.

A search for the good senator's name brought up all the usual suspects: his official Senate page, his campaign site, a long list of minutes for both the Senate and the Virginia House of Delegates, where he'd served for six years before winning his first federal campaign, and a slew of articles. Some of them were written by Trudy, some were from the *Washington Post*, and some were from various other websites and publications that covered national politics. I clicked on news articles covering political campaign speeches and appearances, scanning the stories and photo cutlines for mention of Amesworth or the tobacco industry. Four pages and seventy minutes of Ted Grayson 101 later, I had bupkis.

Grayson had a background that consisted almost exclusively of public relations and politics. He did a short stint at his father's PR firm and then ran for Richmond City Council, leapfrogging through just two terms in the House of Delegates into the national spotlight. Then he went on to the U.S. Senate, where he was running for a second term. Ted Grayson was a political wunderkind.

I stared at the photo of the dead lawyer and the senator for a long while before I packed my computer up for the night. The pose was too familiar for strangers at a party.

But with no other link between the two of them, Bob wouldn't touch it, and I knew it.

I'd have to keep looking.

CHAPTER FOUR

MY TOY Pomeranian was positively indignant when I walked into my house at nearly midnight for the second night in a row. I bent and scratched her head, then opened a can of Pro Plan and scraped it into her bowl, ignoring my own rumbling stomach for the moment. I kicked my sapphire Louboutins off and flipped the TV on, my mind still on Grayson.

I fiddled with the five-thousand-piece jigsaw on my coffee table, while mulling over the mental puzzle of the story. My cell phone erupted into "Second Star to the Right" and I jumped, dropping a piece under the table.

I glanced at the screen. Agent Evans.

It was midnight. What the hell was the FBI calling me for?

"Clarke." I braced the phone against my shoulder, bending forward at the waist to reach for the lost puzzle piece.

"I have a tip for you that won't go to anyone else for another twelve hours," Evans said in a warm tone I wasn't used to hearing from the FBI. "I think we're even after this."

I forgot the jigsaw piece. "I appreciate that, Agent Evans," I said, rifling through a nearby basket for pen and paper. "At the risk of sounding redundant, you don't owe me anything, but I'm not turning down an exclusive from the FBI."

"There was an arrest this evening in that murder case we discussed earlier."

I scribbled, holding my breath. "Who?"

"James Robert Billings, age fifty-six, of Henrico," Evans said, rustling papers in the background. "He's a senior vice president at Raymond Garfield."

The tobacco company. Hot damn.

"Did he confess?" I asked.

"This is an inter-agency operation with the ATF, and I wasn't there for the questioning, but I'll go with no. Bank records show he was paying the vic off the books, and the bullet was fired from a rifle that belongs to Billings."

"How do you know that?" I asked. "Private citizens don't have to register guns in Virginia." I listened to Aaron complain about that often, because it made it harder to build a case in a shooting.

"Good question." Evans rustled more papers. "I don't have an answer. This isn't my case, but the warrant lists the gun as the reason and a judge signed it."

"I see. Do they have the weapon, then?"

"I don't know. What I do know is this: a guy like Billings won't talk without a lawyer in the room, and the kind of lawyer he can afford isn't going to let him give up anything. I imagine his attorneys will call in as many favors as it takes to have him on the early docket."

"Who's the ACA handling this one?" In Virginia, prosecutors are known as Commonwealth's Attorneys instead of district attorneys, but after covering cops for six years, I'd finally gotten used to the quirk.

"This paperwork says Corry's going to take it himself," Evans said.

Wow. That in itself was newsworthy. At thirty-four, Richard Corry was the youngest head prosecutor in Virginia history. He rarely showed up in a courtroom or in front of a TV camera, preferring to stay out of the limelight. I'd heard he was a damned fine orator. That should make for great copy when the trial rolled around.

"Anyway, they're going to try to get him through without the press knowing what's going on," Evans said. "So I thought you'd appreciate a heads up. If you're at the courthouse by eight in the morning, you won't miss it."

I thanked him, adding a last bit of chicken scratch to my notes. An exclusive was always a good thing. Especially on something like this. The senator would have been a sexier angle, but this was good stuff.

I stared at my notes and then lifted Darcy onto the sofa when she bounced and scratched at my bare foot. Sifting my fingers through her silky russet fur, I couldn't help wondering again how well the dead lobbyist knew the senator.

I texted Bob to tell him I would miss the morning staff meeting and flicked the TV off. Grabbing a protein bar out of the pantry to stave off starvation, I took Darcy out for a quick round of fetch so I could get to bed. Maybe Billings's hearing would shed some light on what was fast becoming a tangled mess of a story.

* * *

Dressed in unobtrusive neutrals right down to my most practical square-toed cream heels, I stepped out the door at seven-oh-one for the eight-mile drive to the John Marshall Courts Building on the east side of downtown Richmond. Traffic here was nothing compared to trying to get the same distance on Dallas' clogged roads, but I wasn't taking chances.

I sipped coffee from a tumbler with a hot pink Texas emblazoned across the silver—a gift from my mom—as I watched a jogger cross in front of me at Monument and Malvern. I was excited about the prospect of Billings being the killer. A powerful executive engaging in corporate political hijinks now suspect in murder? It was a hell of a sexy news story. And all mine.

I pressed the gas pedal and the legendary statues of Arthur Ashe, Stonewall Jackson, and Robert E. Lee that sat in the middle of the road blurred past. I barely noticed them, a moral conundrum worrying around my head. The story would be even sexier if Grayson really was involved. And while the "sexier" factor was definitely there, I was having trouble convincing myself that my intentions were completely honorable. Did I want the story because it was rightfully mine, or because it might give me a taste of covering politics?

While getting ready that morning, I'd spent a good deal of time brainstorming a way to sell Bob on the idea that the murder should trump the senator's involvement, if he was involved.

It was a valid point, but one that made my skin tighten with self-directed anger because it reminded me too much of Shelby Taylor, the copy editor who was perpetually after my beat. Resolving to talk to Trudy if I needed to, I parked at a meter in front of the courts building, forty-five minutes early. I flipped the sun visor down to avoid the glare of the perfect September morning and texted Jenna, "Happy Birthday! Tell Chad feel better. You stocked with frozen peas?"

Finishing my coffee, I watched bailiffs and attorneys enter the thick glass doors. Getting into the courthouse was a bit of an ironman event, involving heavy lifting to open the door and quick reflexes to avoid losing the hide off an ankle.

I wished for an arrest report to read, but I wasn't even sure if the arrest had been made by the Richmond PD or the FBI or the ATF. For all I knew, Batman could be bringing Billings to the courthouse.

I reached for my cell phone and dialed Aaron's cell number.

"I thought you went to the gym in the mornings," he said when he answered. "Didn't you tell Anderson Cooper that's where you learned how to fight?"

"I usually do, but decided the courthouse would be more exciting than body combat today," I coughed off the throat closure that came when I thought too much about how close I'd come, in June, to dying. At least the nightmares had dialed back to weekly from nightly. "You have an arrest report to email me?"

"For something going on down there this early? Not that I know of," he said. "Whose arrest are you nosing around?"

"James Billings."

"Who?"

So not the PD. I hoped whoever picked Billings up had at least notified someone at the PD, or I was about to find myself smack in the middle of a jurisdictional pissing contest.

"He's a big fish over at Raymond Garfield. And about to go before a judge on a charge of murdering the lobbyist those kids found in the woods the other night."

"Oh, really?" Aaron tried for interested, but annoyance bled through in his tone. "And do I get to know where you heard that?"

"From the FBI," I said, scrunching my nose apologetically even though he couldn't see me. "But, you know, maybe they called someone else and you haven't gotten the memo yet."

"Not likely. Damned irritating, them waltzing in and arresting people without telling anyone what the hell they're doing. If *you're* down there, every other reporter in town will be looking for information on this before I finish my second cup of coffee. And you know who they're going to call? Not the goddamned FBI, that's who."

"Well, thank me for the heads up later then," I said. "You're welcome."

"I'm not counting that as a favor," he grumbled. "Have fun with your hearing. I'm gonna go find out what the hell's going on before my phone starts really ringing."

I clicked the end button and dropped my press credentials over my head, stepping out of the car as the parking lot across the street started to fill up. No TV trucks. Not yet, anyway. I wrestled the door open and scuttled into the lobby.

Laying my bag in a battered plastic bin on the conveyor belt, I waited my turn before shuffling through the metal detector, offering the bailiff a smile and a good morning as I grabbed my x-ray inspected tote.

"What're you looking for this early, Nichelle?" Hurley asked over his shoulder as he waved a pinstripe-suited gentleman with salt and pepper hair through the detectors. "I haven't seen Charlie this morning. And when she's late she always gives me a hard time about security. Is she fixin' to holler at me because she got stuck in traffic?"

"Not sure, Hurley," I said, already striding toward the courtrooms and realizing I had no idea whose docket Billings was on. "Sorry."

I was about to stick my head into the clerk's office and ask when an auburn head in the middle of a throng of suits outside number four caught my eye. I stared at the profile, fear of smudging my makeup the only thing keeping me from rubbing my eyes. Kyle Miller. My old flame had grown up to be some sort of Bureau of Alcohol, Tobacco, Firearms and Explosives supercop. But he was supposed to be in Texas. What the hell was he doing here? I didn't have time to find out, but I walked over to the edge of the huddle anyway.

I cleared my throat and touched Kyle's shoulder.

"Nicey!" He pulled me into an unexpected hug when he turned and I lost my balance, clinging to his broad shoulders such that we drew a couple of snickers from his entourage. He still wore Eternity. Same old Kyle. Except for the biceps. The arms I remembered were skinny. The ones crushing into my ribcage were not. I pushed away memories of some very nice evenings spent in those arms as I gathered my wits.

I kept one hand on his arm and straightened myself, then smoothed my flared navy skirt and smiled.

"Nice to see you, too," I said.

He turned to his colleagues, all of whom also sported gun-bulges under their jackets. "This is Nichelle Clarke. She's the cops and courts reporter at the *Telegraph*."

"We've heard." A barrel-chested man with cocoa skin and a voice that belonged on the radio offered his hand, his teeth flashing stark white when he grinned. "It's a pleasure, Miss Clarke."

I shook his hand firmly and turned back to Kyle, one eyebrow up. "Some reporter I am. I wasn't aware you were back in town."

He ducked his head. "Busted. I was going to call and ask you to dinner. I got a transfer to the Richmond office. Meet your newest local ATF special agent."

I stared in silence for a full minute, my brain in hyperdrive. Once I'd thought Kyle Miller was the love of my life. It had taken me a decade to stop thinking it, actually. And now he decides to move halfway across the country to my city? Fabulous.

"Well, welcome to Richmond," I said finally.

His eyes told me that wasn't the reaction he hoped for.

The other three men laughed and introduced themselves as members of Kyle's new team.

"What brings you to the courthouse this morning, Miss Clarke?" Agent Silky Voice asked.

"I'm covering a bond hearing. James Billings. I need to go find the courtroom before I miss it. It was good to see you, Kyle." I turned back to the clerk's door.

"The courtroom is right here," Kyle said. "Billings is my collar. How the hell did you find out about this hearing? His lawyer got him set for bond before the ink on the arrest report was dry."

Interesting. I glanced around at Kyle's team, and everyone had the same casually-curious expression. Something told me it was a face they practiced in front of the mirror. Possibly as a group.

"I'm just that good." I winked and brushed past them, opening the massive cherry-paneled door and nodding to the agents. "Gentlemen first."

Kyle brought up the rear, pausing on his way in. "No reporter is that good. Who tipped you off?" he asked in a low voice.

"If I wanted you to know that, I'd have told you." I returned the no-nonsense tone and flat stare syllable-for-syllable. "If you don't mind, this door isn't as lightweight as it looks."

He narrowed his ice-blue eyes and looked like he wanted to say something else, but turned on the heel of his Justin ostrich dress boot and took a seat in the front row instead.

I slipped into the back and pulled out a pen and notebook as the bailiff called the court to order and announced the Honorable Reginald S. Davidson's entrance. Sure enough, Corry was at the prosecution's table, dark blond head bent over a yellow legal pad. He wore a tan suit that fit his lanky frame well, his wire rimmed glasses pushed up on top of his head as he studied his notes.

A petite bailiff who didn't look strong enough to restrain a school-yard bully led Billings to the defense table. In his wrinkled Hugo Boss, with a silver-flecked shadow beard playing across the angular planes of a face that had aged well, he looked like a rumpled movie star. A haggard, terrified movie star who had not enjoyed the jailhouse experience.

Kyle thought this guy was a murderer?

I had seen stranger, I guessed. I pulled a notebook and pen from my bag.

Billings didn't fidget or drop his head as the judge read the charges being levied against him. His attorney, wearing enough Aramis that I could smell the musky cologne from my seat, launched immediately into a plea for the court to allow Billings to be released on his own recognizance pending trial.

Kyle erupted into a coughing fit.

"Your honor, Mr. Billings is a model citizen, a pillar of this community, and a major contributor to many charities." The lawyer threw a glance over his shoulder at Kyle, who was still shaking, though whether it was with laughter or coughing was hard to tell from behind. "He has no prior record. These charges are false, insulting, and defamatory, and we will more than prove that at the trial. In the meantime, my client would like to return to his family, his job, and his community service."

The judge scooted his glasses down the bridge of his nose and looked over them at Billings and Overused Aramis, Esq.

"I appreciate everything Mr. Billings does for the community," Judge Davidson said. "However, in light of the severity of the charges, I'm not prepared to let him out without bond."

Billings nodded and leaned toward his lawyer, whispering.

Corry stood. "Your honor, Richard Corry for the Commonwealth. If I may, I'd like to request that Mr. Billings be held without bond until his trial."

Oh, my. Totally worth skipping the gym. I scribbled, not taking my eyes off the key figures in what had just become an even more interesting hearing. Kyle's head bobbed like a fishing lure with a prize trout on the business end, and Billings' lawyer gaped as though Corry had just branded him the antichrist.

"Ob-Objection!" he stuttered. "Your honor! Again, my client has no prior record. I've never heard of the Commonwealth holding a defendant with no priors over for trial."

"I'll hear him out," the judge said, his eyes on Corry. "Mr. Corry, that is a highly irregular request. Care to tell me why you're asking?"

"Your honor, Mr. Billings is a flight risk," Corry said. "Most of the murder defendants our courtrooms see don't have his resources, or his connections. The commonwealth wants to ensure that he stays in Virginia until the trial."

The Honorable Reginald Davidson nodded, his eyes flicking from Billings to Corry for a full minute.

"The court concedes the commonwealth's point," he said, raising one hand when Captain Cologne knocked his chair over jumping to his feet. "However, Mr. Kressley has a point, too. The defendant has no record, and the Commonwealth of Virginia believes very strongly in the notion of innocent until proven guilty. At least in my courtroom it does. The defendant may choose to post bond of two million dollars, but will wear an electronic tracking device at all times between now and the end of his trial."

My pen moved so furiously my hand cramped, but I ignored it until I had every word in my notes.

The judge waved his bailiff over for a quick conference before facing the attorneys again.

"I'll hear opening arguments on February sixteenth." He adjusted the specs for the look-down-the-nose thing again. "Mr. Billings, it would behoove you to keep every toe in line between now and then. Court is adjourned."

CHAPTER FIVE

KYLE FILLED in Billings's attorney's full name, which sounded vaguely familiar, and the particulars of the arrest warrant, much of which I'd gotten from Evans the night before. But the story coming from the arresting officer sounded better. I thanked him and high-tailed it back toward my office, grateful my scanner was silent throughout the ride. Speeding back down Grace, I slowed as I neared police headquarters, wondering if Aaron might be irritated enough with the feds to tell me whatever he'd been keeping quiet the day before.

I zipped into a tight spot in front of a meter and hurried inside, punching the elevator button for the ninth floor impatiently and hoping Aaron was there. The detectives' offices were bustling, as usual. Crime pilfers on.

I looked around the maze of map-and-photo-covered cubicles for a familiar face, my ears pricked for interesting bits of conversation.

"Can I help you?" A pretty brunette in a uniform cradled the phone in her hand and looked at me expectantly.

"They called from downstairs when I came in. Nichelle Clarke, from the *Telegraph*? I'm here to see Detective White."

"Is he expecting you?"

I shook my head. "I was driving by and had a question for him. I can call him later if he's busy."

She smiled and gestured to the chairs between the elevators. "I'll let him know you're here."

I turned toward the olive green vinyl seating, but before I'd made it half a step, a frustrated man's voice stopped me cold.

"But, ma'am, this break-in has to be investigated with all the others. We have a procedure." My head snapped around to find a middle-aged, shirt-and-tie detective who was running one hand through his graying hair while he held a phone to his ear with the other. Cat burglar strikes again? That story got more interesting every time the crook managed to get away. "Yes, I understand that. People tend to get upset when their home is violated. Yes, we know there have been robberies in the Fan lately. We're working on it."

I scooted closer to the chest-high wall of his cubicle, attempting to feign disinterest by skipping my eyes around the drab gray decor.

He dropped his hand from his head to the desk blotter and picked up a pen, flicking the button on the end of it. "I assure you, we're doing everything we can to catch this guy. We have every detective we can spare working on this case. But we do need your cooperation."

"Can I help you, miss?" A ringing baritone from behind me made me jump.

I turned, confused smile already in place. "Please. I'm waiting for Detective White, but I was looking for a restroom," I said, straining to hear the detective's phone conversation over my unwanted Samaritan.

"We generally like visitors to this floor to be escorted." He was shorter than me, stocky, with sandy brown hair, wearing pressed chinos and a cerulean Polo. His friendly smile didn't cover the questioning look in his hazel eyes.

"I've been here before," I said, offering a hand for him to shake. "I'm Nichelle Clarke, from the *Richmond Telegraph*. First time I've needed y'all's restroom."

He shook my hand, his grip firm. "The restrooms are right back there." He pointed toward a long hall that extended off the end of the row of cubicles where my frustrated detective was still clicking his pen. I took three steps, but just past the door to the cubicle where the interesting phone call was going on, I purposely failed to lift my foot high enough and stumbled over my stilettos, leaning far forward and dumping my bag all over the floor. My little flashlight, peppermint lifesavers, Godiva white chocolate pearls, pens, change, and tampons rolled and bounced into a scattered formation worthy of a broken piñata. I dropped to my knees and glanced up at the detective who'd given me directions, willing him to either go away or shut up.

He leaned on the edge of the empty cube across from me and watched me crawl around the floor picking up my belongings, his thick arms folded across his chest. Not one for touching tampons, then.

I focused on Detective Frustrated's voice behind me, taking my time and trying to keep from looking up.

"No, I don't have any idea how someone could have circumvented the security system." He sighed heavily. "Yes, I really do understand that. But I still need statements from everyone who was in the house. Are you sure we've spoken to everyone?"

I crawled forward a bit and snagged a runaway nickel, reaching behind me to make sure my skirt was still covering my lavender undies. I'd never be able to go to a crime scene again if half the detectives in Richmond had seen my Victoria's Secrets.

I stuffed the last pen back into my bag and stood up carefully just as Detective Frustrated finished his call.

His shoulders heaved with another sigh. "Of course. Thank you." All that eavesdropping effort for no information. Damn.

He hung up the phone, and I smiled at Cerulean Shirt. "Oops." I waved a hand toward my shoes. "I love them, but they're not always the best for balance."

"They're very nice," he said, not glancing down. "Right this way." He started toward the hallway and I followed, my thoughts still back in the tiny cube with the graying detective.

Another robbery. Now I just needed to know if it was connected to the others, but Aaron grew less fond of talking every day the cat burglar story stretched on.

My new friend watched me go into the bathroom, but wasn't there when I came out, three minutes of silent mulling bringing me no closer to a way to ask Detective Frustrated for the address of the most recent robbery. Which meant digging through every police report from the last few days to find it.

I made my way back to the vinyl chairs just in time for the pretty brunette to come back without Aaron.

"Detective White is very busy this morning, but he said he'll call you as soon as he has a chance," she said. "Is that all we can do for you today?"

"I think it is, thanks." Smiling, I flipped my notebook closed and tucked it back into my bag as I stood. I had some reports to read, and I still wanted to talk to Aaron, but maybe it wasn't an entirely wasted side trip.

* * *

As an exclusive, the hearing story took precedence over everything else when I returned to the office. Except for coffee.

Pulling my syrup bottle from the cabinet, I shook my head as I tipped it over my cup. It was definitely lighter than it had been the day before. Was someone else using it? I pushed it to the very back of the shelf and took a couple of sips before I started for my desk with an over-full mug.

I tried to stay focused on Billings and his arrest as I typed, but my brain raced ahead, ready to file this story and move on to the robbery.

Agents from the Richmond office of the Bureau of Alcohol, Tobacco, Firearms and Explosives made an arrest Thursday in the murder of Daniel Amesworth, 29, the Henrico man whose body was found in the woods near Goochland earlier this week.

James Billings, 56, also of Henrico, was held overnight and released early Friday despite the objection of Commonwealth's Attorney Richard Corry, who made a rare courtroom appearance to argue for keeping the Raymond Garfield executive in custody until after his trial.

"Mr. Billings is a flight risk," Corry told Judge Reginald Davis. "Most of the murder defendants our courtrooms see don't have his resources, or his connections. The Commonwealth wants to ensure that he stays in Virginia until the trial."

Corry didn't outline the particulars of the Commonwealth's case, but the Telegraph *has learned that the firm where Amesworth worked does political lobbying for Raymond Garfield.*

I debated that sentence for a full three minutes, but left it in because I wanted to have it first. Once Billings's arrest was live, all it would take for Charlie to find out Amesworth was a lobbyist was a Google search for the relationship between Raymond Garfield and the dead lawyer. I clicked over to my browser and typed the name of Billings's attorney into my Google bar to see where he worked. Holy shit: the guy's name sounded familiar because he was a principal in Amesworth's firm.

I clicked back over to my story, shaking my head. "Defending the guy accused of killing one of his own employees," I said. "How does Captain Cologne sleep at night?"

By the time I finished pounding out the story and sent it to Bob, it was nearly lunchtime. Which meant my three o'clock deadline for filing my feature with Eunice was fast approaching, and I hadn't even written the lead yet.

The morning's police reports sounded so much sexier after my eavesdropping adventure, though. I stared at my notes for the feature, ignoring my noisy stomach and three emails from Eunice wanting to know where her story was. I clicked over to the PD reports database and scrolled, hunting for the one on the robbery. I found it just in time for my scanner to start squawking. I turned up the volume.

"Why the hell do they need a structural engineer for a car accident?" I wondered aloud, jotting down the address and typing it into Google maps. They were calling an awful lot of ambulances out there, too.

When the little red pin popped up, I scrambled to my feet and threw my bag over my shoulder.

"Where's the fire, sugar?" Eunice asked as I almost mowed her down on my way to the elevator.

"The west end," I called over my shoulder, not slowing down. "Someone ran a truck through a jewelry store. I promise I'll have your feature ready by the end of the day."

* * *

It took twenty minutes to get out there. I stopped and rolled down the window to flash my press pass at the RPD uniform guarding the parking lot entrance.

"Miss Clarke." It was the officer who'd been at the body dump. And I couldn't remember his name to save my shoe closet.

I squinted, but I couldn't see his nametag in the glare from the sun, so I stayed with the generic. "Hello again, officer."

"You here to trespass in another crime scene?"

"Nice to see you again, too, officer."

"You can park over there." He pointed to a stretch of concrete shaded by a line of Magnolia trees where the Channel Four van was already sitting. Damn. "A word of advice: don't try to go inside this time. They aren't sure they can even pull that thing out of there without the whole place falling down. I'd hate for you to get hurt." His smirk said that last part wasn't true, and I shook my head, having learned the hard way that some cops just despise reporters. Period.

I looked past him at the back end of the double-cab that was buried in the side of the building.

"That's why I love my job, officer. Never a dull day."

He grunted and stepped out of the way.

I parked next to Charlie's van, climbed out of the car, and crossed the parking lot, picking my way around the shattered glass that littered the pavement as I waited for Aaron to finish talking to Charlie's TV camera. He rolled his eyes when he turned to me, waving an arm at the truck.

"Can you believe this shit?"

"Hey, who needs stealthy?" I grinned. "Just plow through the wall in broad daylight and clean the joint out while people are still shaking from the adrenaline."

"That would at least be funny," he said. "This was just a stupid mistake, best I can tell. Fool's lucky he didn't kill anybody. We had to transport the driver and three other people to St. Vincent's by ambulance, but the medics said none of the injuries looked life-threatening."

I scribbled as he talked.

"How does one manage to run a truck into a jewelry store on accident?"

"From what he said while they were loading him into the ambulance, the guy came into town to buy a gift, and when he was leaving, he thought he had the truck in reverse. But it was in drive, and he plowed right through the side of the building. That thing has some horsepower. There was a sales clerk who got cut up pretty bad by the flying glass, and a couple looking at engagement rings who got hit. The guy tried to throw his girl out of the way, so he took the worst of it."

"The driver was alone in the truck?"

"Yeah. It's entertaining, but it doesn't look like there was anything sinister here. Just an accident. Glad it wasn't a tragic one."

"Non-tragic is always nice," I said.

"Hey, I got a message that you came in this morning," Aaron said. "What did you need?"

"I wanted to pick your brain about the hearing I covered this morning," I said. "The story's done, though, and I'm buried today." I did want to talk to Aaron about Billings, but he didn't have time for a sit-down in the middle of an accident scene, and I didn't want to ask him about the burglary until I had time to find out if it fit the cat burglar's profile.

"Don't have to tell me twice," he said. "I know the feeling, and if I can brush you off, I'm going to. No offense." His grin brought out the lines around his eyes, but his round face was eternally boyish. Aaron had two girls in college and didn't look a day over thirty-five, if you didn't notice the flecks of gray at his temples.

"None taken." I thanked him and let him go back to work while I looked around the parking lot. There was a young woman sitting alone on the curb, hands buried in her auburn curls. Her pale pink pantsuit was splattered with blood.

I cleared my throat when I stopped next to her. She squinted up at me.

"Can I help you?" she asked. The pale features under her smattering of freckles looked tired.

I introduced myself and asked if she felt like telling me what had happened. Over her shoulder I saw Charlie stop on her way back to the van, poking her cameraman and pointing at me. I waved discreetly before I turned back to the pretty redhead, determined to get something good.

"Sure." The redhead shrugged and gestured for me to have a seat beside her. "I'm Brittany."

When I'd settled on the sun-warmed concrete and taken down the correct spelling of her name, she launched into her story.

"I was helping this couple with the engagement rings," she said. "They were really nice, and she was so excited about picking out her ring. They had been here for a while—she didn't like anything we had in the case and wanted to look at settings and diamonds to see if we could do a semi-custom. I love the engagement rings. Everyone's always so excited when they come in to look at those."

I nodded. "I can imagine. This was the couple who were taken to the hospital?"

"Yeah. I would've been hit, too, but I had turned around to get a color grading guide for diamonds out of the file cabinet. I got sprayed with the glass from the case when he crashed into it. Anyway, there it was, out of nowhere. This guy had just left with some big expensive tennis bracelet for his wife. Or his girlfriend." She snorted. "He was a character. Big, loud dude in boots and a cowboy hat. Made a real fuss of wanting the biggest diamond bracelet we had in the place, and paid cash for it. Most of those are looking for make-up jewelry for the wife or suck-up diamonds for the girlfriend."

I jotted notes, trying not to laugh. I knew the type: Dallas has its fair share of big, loud cowboys. They can be colorful, for sure.

"I see. Was this one a regular customer?"

"No. He lives out in the sticks. I heard him say he owns one of those big farms out in Powhatan." Her green eyes rolled skyward. "Been in his family for generations, he said. And something about his regular jeweler not having anything big enough. He wouldn't talk to anyone but my manager."

"That explains the truck and the boots," I said.

"The truck, maybe. Those boots hadn't ever seen a field, though."

I nodded, jotting that down.

"Are those people going to be okay?" she asked. "They were so happy. Excited about getting married. And my friend Janie—she was in the way. The glass from the windows cut her up pretty bad."

I patted her hand. "The police spokesman said the paramedics expected everyone to be fine. Thanks for your help."

"No problem. I guess I can go home now. I think we're closed."

I turned back toward the building, intent on finding the structural engineer, and saw a blue SUV turn into the parking lot.

I shaded my eyes with my notebook and stared as Kyle stepped out of the driver's seat. He paused when he saw me, then raised one arm and waved.

"You're just underfoot today, aren't you? What's this got to do with the ATF, Mr. Special Agent?" I asked when I met him halfway across the lot.

"On the record? No comment." He grinned. His eyes said he was happy to see me, and I smiled back. I had missed Kyle. Not that he needed to know that.

"Really?" I arched an eyebrow at him. "All right, then. I'll figure it out for myself."

He pointed to a group of men who were surveying the damage. One had a tie and wire-rimmed glasses, and two of the others had hard hats and clipboards.

"Looks like someone really did a number on this place," Kyle said.

"Yeah. The cops said they're waiting for a structural engineer to tell them if they can even pull the truck out of there. I'd bet that's one or both of the hard hat crew over there. Store clerk said the guy who did it was a real piece of work. Flashing a lot of cash and buying big diamonds."

Kyle's eyebrows went up.

"Really? Who did you talk to?"

I turned back toward the sidewalk, but she was gone.

"Oh. She said she was going home," I told Kyle, scanning the parking lot for the auburn ringlets. "I guess she meant right now. I didn't get a phone number, but I do have a name."

"That's okay," he said. "I'm sure I can find someone else. And if not, I know where to find you."

"Sure," I said. "If you're going to keep secrets, I'm going to go see what I can find out from these guys and get back to the office before deadlines eat me alive. I now owe Bob three stories, and I still have a feature due today."

"No rest for the wicked." He shook his head. "Though that doesn't really suit the Nichelle I remember."

I smiled a goodbye and turned back to the building. The engineers spouted a lot of technical jargon about load-bearing walls and danger of spontaneous demolition, and I wrote it down carefully. Climbing back into my car, I waved to Kyle, who was taking notes while he talked to Aaron.

Driving back to the office, I cranked the stereo and turned my conversation with my ex over in my head. The ATF only handled accidents when they involved certain chemical spills, and as far as I knew diamonds were way outside their area of interest. And even if they weren't, something like that didn't need the attention of a bigshot.

I tapped the power button on my computer, still no closer to why Kyle had been at the accident scene. Dialing St. Vincent's media relations office for an update on the victims from the jewelry store, I skimmed my notes from the scene again as I waited for a hospital PR person to pick up the phone.

"Those boots hadn't ever seen a field," I said aloud as I read the clerk's words and pictured her rolling green eyes.

A tobacco field, maybe? Powhatan was full of them. I'd bet my favorite sapphire Louboutins I was right. Kyle didn't give a damn about diamonds. He was there because of the farmer.

CHAPTER SIX

I HAMMERED out the jewelry store report in record time and plunged straight from that into the feature, with Eunice's three o'clock deadline looming. One hour. I could write a feature in an hour. I thought, anyway.

Troy Wright and his older brother, Darryl, grew up in the same house, went to the same schools, and had the devotion of a mother who loves her sons more than life itself. In a part of Richmond that sees more than its fair share of violence, where schools are underfunded and drugs and crime a part of everyday life for many, Troy Wright is a contender for a prestigious academic award and an honor student at Kingston High School, with dreams of studying broadcast journalism at Virginia Tech or UVA.

Darryl was a convicted drug dealer, found shot in the head in his own home in June.

I lost myself in the rhythm of the keystrokes, the rest of the newsroom falling away until I closed with a quote from Joyce about how proud she was of her son and checked the clock. Three-thirty. Eunice wouldn't be too upset at a half-hour tardy after the day I'd had. Thank God it was her waiting for the piece and not Les.

Unable to ignore my stomach any longer, I sent Eunice the story and went to the break room in search of something edible and a caffeine fix. I hoped Eunice had been in the mood to cook the night before, and that the sports desk hadn't already demolished whatever she'd brought in. But the fridge held only a half-eaten Taco Bell burrito and a salad with a slimy green coating that didn't look like anything a person should eat.

"Gross," I said, swinging the door shut.

"Nothing good in there?" Parker asked from behind me.

I spun to face him. "I don't think I've ever been that hungry," I said. "I'll suck it up until I get home. I have one more story to do, which will make four for today. I'm going to sleep until Monday."

"Damn. And I thought my days were busy when I had a column and a game story," he said. "Anything good?"

"My feature came out great." I spun the bottle cap between my fingers and sipped my Coke, then smiled at him. "Speaking of my feature, I need a favor."

"Anything. I'll owe you 'til the end of time for convincing me to ask Mel out. She's..." He shrugged, flashing a grin with more lovesick than star power behind it. "She's turned my life upside-down. And I love it."

I grinned back. I'd spent years dismissing Parker—an almost-major-league pitcher who looked like an underwear model—as an egotistical jerk who'd gotten his cushy star-columnist job on account of his baseball fame. But he really was a good guy, and a damned fine writer. I didn't often dip a toe into matchmaking, but the better I got to know him, the more I saw that my friend Melanie at the city desk was the perfect balance to his personality. She was smart, serious, and pretty in a non-beer-commercial way. I'd pitched it to him as trying something different than his notch-on-the-bedpost approach to dating, and they'd been fairly inseparable since.

"The kid I did the story on, the one whose brother was the

murdered drug dealer from June?" I set the bottle on the counter. "Do you remember any of this?"

"The drug dealer you thought I killed?"

I nodded. "That's the one. His kid brother is a National Merit Finalist and wants to study broadcast sports journalism. And he thinks you're a celebrity. So I sort of told him that maybe you'd let him shadow you for a day. He's a really great kid."

"I am a celebrity." Parker flashed the grin that made the female population of the greater Richmond area call for smelling salts. "But I like you because you don't seem to realize that. When does he want to come in?"

"Monday?"

"Nothing like giving a guy a heads up, Clarke." He dropped three quarters into the soda machine. "But sure. I'll show him around. I can take him out to the park for practice, and to the game, too, if he wants. It's the second to last one of the year."

"Thanks, Parker."

"It's cool. I like kids." He stepped aside when I moved toward the door. "Just get me the address and tell him I'll be there to get him about ten."

"I will." I patted his arm as I passed him. "I have a ton of stuff to do, but I'll see you around. And really, thank you."

"You bet. Have a good weekend, Clarke."

"Thanks. You and Mel doing something fun?"

"Dinner. Movie. I think we might take a picnic out to the country tomorrow. We're getting boring. It's fantastic."

"The great Grant Parker has been domesticated." His happiness was positively infectious, and knowing I was responsible for it gave me warm-fuzzies. I scrolled through police reports until I found the one on the break-in I'd overheard Detective Frustrated talking about that morning. I clicked to another screen and typed the address into Google Maps.

"Holy square footage, Batman," I said, looking at the satellite view of a roof that was easily five times the size of mine. It sat right on

Monument, too. A house that big, in that part of town, meant one of two things: old money, or new power. I snatched up the phone and dialed the police department, waiting impatiently for Aaron to pick up.

Voicemail. Damn.

"Hey Aaron, it's Nichelle," I said after the beep. "I'm sorry to be a pain in your ass, but you know you love me anyway. I have a couple of questions about this break-in in the Fan last night, and I'm pushing deadline so hard it's about to push back. Pretty please, could you give me a call as soon as you have a second?"

I cradled the handset and turned back to the computer screen, searching the city tax records for the property address. Maybe I should have bugged Aaron about it at the jewelry store. But with nothing to ask specific questions about, I wouldn't have gotten much, anyway.

The tax record loaded.

"You've got to be shitting me," I breathed, sitting back in the chair. No wonder Detective Frustrated had been so apologetic, and Aaron was dodging my calls.

The latest house on the cat burglar's route belonged to one Theodore Grayson, United States Senator for the Commonwealth of Virginia.

"That is way too much of a coincidence to actually be a coincidence," I said aloud to no one in particular.

"What is?" Bob's voice came from behind me and I clicked the browser window shut and turned around. Technically, every story I'd written was rightfully mine. But digging for something more on Grayson was definitely a gray area. If I found anything else, I'd take it to Trudy. Really. But I didn't want him to tell me I had to yet.

"Not sure," I said. "I have one more story for you today, because people aren't going to be sick enough of my byline by noon tomorrow. There was another burglary in the Fan last night."

"I know," he said. "That's what I came to see you about. Charlie Lewis has a teaser for the early broadcast, and it's already on the web at Channel Four and Channel Ten. I'm not fond of hearing from the TV folks that the home of a United States senator was robbed less than two miles from this building. How the hell did you miss that, Nicey?"

"I didn't miss it," I protested, trying hard to keep the annoyance out of my voice. "I've been busting my ass since six o'clock this morning, running on caffeine and Pop Tarts. I've turned in three stories already and am waiting for Aaron to call back about my fourth. That's not missing anything."

"They had it first," he said. "But if you can get him to talk to you, you'll have it better."

"He didn't give Charlie anything?" I asked.

"No comment from police officials," Bob said. "But Charlie doesn't have your in at the PD. Work it."

"I'm beginning to wonder if I've worked it almost to death," I sighed. "But I'll give it everything I've got. That piece on the hearing I covered this morning has Charlie beat, right?"

"Seven hours ago," he said. "Look, I love having the print exclusive for tomorrow, but it doesn't change the fact that you slipped on this."

"I was writing my feature." I caught his eye and smiled. "It came out really nice. That kid is a National Merit Finalist. He's coming in to shadow Parker on Monday. Wants to be Rick Reilly when he grows up."

The tight line he'd stretched his mouth into softened slightly.

"I'm sure it is," he said. "I'll read it with my coffee on Sunday morning. But you're not a feature writer. Your job is to stay on top of cops and courts. And Les is still pushing Shelby at the guys upstairs. The piece on the hearing is good, but if you want to keep covering both, they all have to be good. The suits wouldn't dream of just handing Shelby your job after the year you've had, but with the recent uptick in readership and ad revenue, your friend the managing editor is pulling for them to split your beat and give half of it to his girl-friend. He says we can afford it now. So just watch it."

"He's trying to get them to steal half my beat because we can afford another reporter thanks to me almost getting killed?" I shook my head. "Only Les. Balls of steel, that guy. Big ones. It's a wonder he can walk upright."

Bob patted my shoulder. "I'd like to not have that picture in my head this close to dinnertime, thanks. Just get me something Charlie hasn't had on the robbery before you go home. Trudy's trying to get an interview with Grayson. He's not commenting, so far, but I swear she has a little black book on those guys. Grayson's campaign is hollering Watergate, and the other guys are denying any part of it. This is leading the front in the morning, and I need it. Right now."

"You got it, Chief."

I clicked the bookmark for the Channel Four website and pulled up Charlie's story.

Damn. She had clearly spent every minute she wasn't at the demolished jewelry store working this robbery, and she'd pretty much knocked it out of the park, for a crime story the police wouldn't comment on. There was footage of RPD uniforms checking every inch of the perimeter of Grayson's house. The story had comments from neighbors, a bit about the history of the house (which included a stint as Confederate spy headquarters during the Civil War), and a long background on other crimes the cat burglar may have committed. Charlie's promo showed the entire yard had been taped off as a crime scene, which was a little odd. I needed Aaron on the phone. It was after four, and I didn't have time to go to Grayson's house before deadline.

I dialed Aaron's cell. Voicemail there, too. So he was either busy, or avoiding me because he knew I was nearly out of time.

I drummed my fingers on the desk, staring at Charlie's story until the letters on my screen blurred. I didn't have time to do all that research, and I'd rather wear saddle shoes for all eternity than quote Charlie Lewis's work in my write-up.

Which left me with what? I flashed onto the detective I'd eavesdropped on that morning. Had he said anything useful?

He had said, "I don't know how they circumvented the security system."

I pulled the police report up again and saw that the Graysons used ADT.

"Except this guy has been careful to skip houses with alarms," I muttered under my breath, pulling a file folder out from under a pile of press releases and flipping through the other burglary reports. That was part of the oddity of the case: the culprit knew which houses had good stuff and no alarm.

I scrolled back through Charlie's report. She'd missed it. I would have, too, if I hadn't managed to overhear the detective talking on the phone.

"So, has the burglar changed his M.O., or was this someone other than the cat burglar?" I mused aloud, thinking about the campaign commercials that were getting nastier every day and Bob's comment about Watergate. I wondered idly if that might be worth a trip by Grayson's campaign office. If I could get the inside scoop on this break-in, it would help make up for losing to Charlie on the first story.

I dialed Trudy's extension to see if she'd gotten anything from Grayson, but she didn't pick up, either.

"It would be so nice if one person would answer the damned phone today," I mumbled, replacing the receiver.

Whatever. There was a difference between this report and all the others no one had pointed out yet, so I'd lead with that.

Richmond Police were quiet about a search for suspects in a seventh robbery in the city's historic Fan district early Friday, but the break-in, at the home of U.S. Sen. Ted Grayson, had one difference from the other six burglaries: the senator's house had a security system.

"Statistics show that a security system is a deterrent to thieves," RPD spokesman Aaron White told the Telegraph *last month, after the third burglary of a home that didn't have a system in place. "These robberies seem to be following a pattern that affirms that."*

Until the break-in at Grayson's home Friday, none of the burglar's targets had a security system. Police reports show that the Graysons have a monitored system through ADT, but the company told police they didn't receive an alert.

Grayson, who has represented Virginia in the U.S. Senate for five years, is in the thick of a hotly contested re-election campaign.

I pulled some details about the campaign from Trudy's coverage, mentioned that there was no list of missing items in the initial police report, and added Trudy's name to the bottom as a contributor, not even reading it over in my haste. Once it was floating through cyber-space to Bob's computer, I thumped my head down on my desk, my stomach gurgling loud enough to be embarrassing, had I been less exhausted or more inclined to care.

Twenty minutes later, I had an "attagirl" from Bob in my email.

My cell phone binged the arrival of a text and I clicked to the message from Jenna: "C has frozen peas. I have pizza and Kool-Aid for my bday dinner."

"Hope he's healed for us to have girls' night next Fri." I tapped back. "Enjoy your mommy celebration. One more stop, and I'm going to eat, and then straight to bed."

I had just packed up my computer when my desk phone rang.

"Crime desk, this is Clarke, can I help you?"

"Hey there," Kyle said.

"Hey yourself, *Agent* Miller," I said. "Are you liking Virginia so far?"

"Come on, Nicey, don't be that way. I wanted to surprise you."

"Mission accomplished." My lips turned up at the corners. "It was kind of fun to see you with your minions this morning, though. Like an episode of *Where are They Now?* from my actual life."

"Why let the fun stop there? Have dinner with me. I haven't been able to find any decent food in this town, and I know you have to know where it's hiding."

I tapped a pen on my desk. I was tired. But I did need to eat, and Kyle had arrested a high-profile guy for murder that morning. He might be more talkative outside the courthouse and away from his fellow agents.

"What time?" I asked.

"I need about an hour to wrap up here."

I could still run by Grayson's campaign office, then. "Perfect. Tell you what—I made chili the other night, and it's always better when it's been sitting for a while. I'm ready to go home and kick off my shoes, so why don't you meet me at my house at seven?"

"You're inviting me back to your place already?" he said, his tone mischievous.

"I said chili, Kyle. Not lingerie." I gave him my address and hung up, turning for the elevator. So much for my quiet Friday night. But maybe I could trade sleep for some answers.

CHAPTER SEVEN

THE PARKING LOT was nearly empty at Grayson's tiny storefront campaign office on the northern edge of town. I poked my head in the front door and stepped inside when a striking brunette smiled at me from a banged-up metal desk in the far corner. Posters with larger-than-life images of the senator stared from every wall. He was good-looking, but had that smarmy politician air about him, even in two dimensions.

"Can I help you?" the brunette asked in a bright voice laced with exhaustion.

I smiled. I hoped so. She was young—younger than me. Probably her first job in politics, which meant the important people who worked here likely didn't notice her. "I'm looking for some informa-tion on the senator." I kept the smile in place.

"We have brochures and pamphlets over there." She pointed to a folding table just inside the door. "There's a list of upcoming campaign events, too. If you'd like to volunteer to help out with canvassing, I can take your name and put you in the database."

Her hopeful expression told me I'd found a way in.

"I'd like to get to know a little more about Senator Grayson first, but I might be interested in that," I said.

She grinned. "Great! I'll be happy to help you any way I can."

I picked up one of each piece of campaign literature, mostly trying to think up a way to find out something useful without being too obvious. "Here's the thing: I got most of this from the Internet," I said. "I want to know what he's *really* like. I'd like to help him get re-elected. But I'm not sure what to think about most of Washington anymore. What do you think about him? Why do you work here?"

She laughed. "Because I want to work in politics, and I had a foot in the door here. But Senator Grayson is very charismatic. People like him. And he doesn't take any crap from anyone. He's not afraid of a little risk. But I think it's his ability to control most situations that I like best."

"Decisiveness is certainly a rarity in D.C. these days," I said. "That's a good quality for a legislator to have, I think."

She straightened a thick stack of papers and shoved them into a manila envelope. "He doesn't let anyone push him around. Even when people try. I think that kind of conviction is good."

I tipped my head to one side. Who was pushing a sitting senator around? Or trying?

"I agree." I leaned forward. "I imagine it would take guts to tell someone like Senator Grayson what to do. But I guess it took guts for someone to break into his house, too."

Her head snapped up, her blue eyes wide. "I know! Can you imagine knowing someone else was in your home? How violating it would feel?"

"I wonder why someone would do that?" I tried to sound casual.

Either it worked or she was only half-listening. "I wouldn't be surprised if it had something to do with this campaign. I never would have thought politics was so nasty. I was here late one night last week, and then I forgot my purse when I left. I came back to get it, and the senator was in the office." She waved a hand toward a postage-stamp-sized room near the door. Gray mini-blinds covered the window that faced out into the main lobby. "There were two other men in there with him, yelling about getting their money's worth out of him. I know he technically works for the taxpayers, but I thought that was uncalled for. He's already so stressed."

I managed to keep my jaw from dropping, but just barely. Getting their money's worth? She was too naive for national politics. No way that snippet had anything to do with tax money. The photo of Amesworth and Grayson spun through my thoughts. What if this whole thing was a backroom deal gone bad?

"The nerve of some people." I struggled to keep my voice even. "Did you see them?"

"No, I didn't," she said. "I got my bag and left, and they were in there with the door closed."

Damn.

She smiled. "He's a good man. Can you find a couple of nights to come in and work the phones for us?"

Double damn.

Unable to think of a good reason to turn her down, I reached for her sign-up sheet. "I think you've convinced me." I jotted my first name and my personal email address, since I'd left out my job title during our conversation.

"I'll be in touch." She stood when I did and stuck out her hand. "I'm Allison."

"I'll look forward to hearing from you, Allison." It wouldn't hurt to have a source in Grayson's office, even if I couldn't quote her because she didn't know she was talking to the press.

I turned the radio up and rolled the windows down as I drove home, turning what I'd learned over in my head. Last week, she'd said. Amesworth had been killed sometime in the past week, though no one had said when yet. But Kyle had someone in jail for killing Amesworth. I wondered if Billings could have been the third man Allison had overheard. How could I get Kyle to talk about Billings—or Grayson—over dinner?

The kitchen porch light flashed on when I pulled into my driveway, twilight earlier each day as the calendar rolled toward winter. The little red maples that would have been big trees in Texas were dwarfed by the hundred-foot pines, oaks, and Bradford pears in Virginia, and were always the first to change, shading crimson like they'd been painted with a fine-tipped brush.

I loved autumn in Virginia, with cooler air, apples fresh from the orchards in Charlottesville, and earlier evenings. But the six months of bare trees and bitter cold on the way? I didn't care for those.

My toy Pomeranian bounced at the back gate, working her tiny jaw around a battered stuffed squirrel, managing to get a soft squeak out of a long-punctured insert.

I bent to scratch her head, taking the squirrel and tossing it for her each time she retrieved it, my thoughts still swirling around Grayson. Darcy played until the reaches of the yard were dark, then returned without her toy and trotted past me, up the worn wooden steps to the back door.

I barely had time to kick my heels into the corner of the living room before Kyle rang the doorbell.

Darcy yapped and scratched at the door. Kyle knelt and put a hand out for her to sniff when I opened it.

"She's cute. What's her name? Scarlett?" Kyle stood and stepped into the foyer when I moved out of the doorway.

"Darcy," I said, as I smiled and shut the door. I returned his hug, the smell of his familiar cologne making me hold on a few seconds too long, before I spun toward the kitchen.

"That's my girl," he said. "Always with her nose in a book. Good to know some things never change."

I bit my tongue and busied myself reheating chili, making small talk about my house and the city until I carried the bowls to the table. I opened a Dr Pepper for myself and handed Kyle a Corona before I sat down across from him at my tiny kitchen table.

"So, what's new with you, Captain Surprise?" I asked as I picked up my spoon. "Your parents okay with you moving out here?"

"My parents were so thrilled to hear you live here that I'm not sure they noticed anything else. They still think you're the daughter they never had. I've only ever tried to take one other girl home to meet them, and my mother put pictures of you and me on every flat surface in their house before I got there. Granted, that was years ago, but I've been too afraid to try it again since." He smiled wryly.

I couldn't think of a suitable reply, so I scooped more chili into my mouth and hoped he'd keep talking. He watched me over the top of his bottle.

"I was thinking it might be good for more than my career," he said.

Shit. He smiled, and I shoveled another bite into my mouth while I thought out a response.

"There's someone else?" he asked when I opened my mouth to speak.

"N—yes," I said. "There's me. Kyle, I lost myself in you to the point that I almost gave up what I'd wanted most since I was little girl. I've even wondered since if I made the right choice. But I did. I chose me. And I've found a girl who can interview a serial killer and kick some bad guy ass and rock a pair of stilettos, too. I like her. And I don't want to lose her again."

"I'm not saying let's get married tomorrow," he said. "We're not the same people we were. But that doesn't mean we can't like the people we are now."

My stomach flipped a little at the unblinking electric blue gaze. Could we? I dropped my eyes to my bowl. "I don't know, Kyle."

"I'll take that over 'No.'"

I smiled. "The glass is still half full, huh? Let's think about getting to be friends. Slow."

"How slow?"

"As slow as we need," I said with a gentle smile. "That's the best I can do tonight. Let's talk about something else, shall we? Anything interesting going on at work?"

He arched an eyebrow. "Are we off the record, Woodward?"

"Do you see a pen? I'm not always a reporter, Kyle. I can be interested in your job as a friend, too." And I was. But if he happened to say something that might help with my story, so be it.

"Okay." He swirled his spoon in the air to gather stringing cheddar and took a bite, his face thoughtful as he chewed and swallowed. "The press has not been notified of the case I'm working on, but there are some enterprising folks making a pretty penny off the high cigarette taxes in New York."

My brow puckered. Kyle took another bite.

"I think your cooking has gotten even better, Nicey. This is great."

"Thanks. How do crooks make money off taxes?"

"By stealing them. Virginia and North Carolina have the smallest per-pack excise taxes on cigarettes in the country. And we're not that far from New York, where the taxes are high. So these guys buy truckloads of cigarettes wholesale down here, then put counterfeit New York tax stamps on them and sell them at full price up there. It's a major interstate organization. They do a pretty good business, and ninety percent of their customers have no idea they're doing anything illegal."

"Wait. You're saying Joe Smoker doesn't know it's shady to buy cigarettes off a truck instead of in the store? No one is that dense."

Kyle shook his head. "A small percentage of the activity is on the Internet or in back alleys, but most of the sales are being made through convenience stores. I'm pretty sure most of the ones I'm talking about are run by folks who aren't nominees for citizen of the year, so they're getting a cut of the money for providing the outlet. The end consumer thinks they ran to the quickie mart to get a pack, but they're really funding organized crime."

Organized crime? Was that why Joey wanted to talk to me? I brushed the thought aside.

"Wow. That's...crafty. How do people come up with this stuff? It would never occur to me to sell contraband cigarettes to people in New York and pocket the tax money." I dropped my spoon into my bowl and rested my chin on one fist, my hair falling over my left eye.

"I'm afraid you'll never be a criminal mastermind." Kyle's hand fluttered toward my face, like he was going to brush my hair out of it. I smiled at him and shoved the wayward strand behind my ear. He focused his blue lasers on the nearly-empty bowl before he continued. "Anyway, that's what's been occupying my days since I got here."

"Just be careful," I said. "Criminal masterminds have a tendency to hold pretty poor regard for life—especially cops' lives."

He thumped a fist against his chest in a show of bravado and flashed a row of orthodontist-perfect pearly whites. "That's what my friend Kevlar is for. We call him Kev."

Every story I'd ever done on a cop who'd been killed in the line of duty flashed through my mind like lightning. "Kev doesn't protect your head, Kyle."

His eyes softened. "I know that. I'm careful. I'm well-trained. I'm not stupid. I don't want you to worry about me."

"Too late. I have a lot of friends who are cops. I worry about all of you."

Something flared in his eyes, and I found myself unable to look away until the soft flapping of Darcy's dog door broke the spell. She barked once and pawed my bare ankle, demanding a treat. Kyle cleared his throat as he pushed his chair back.

"Let me help you with that," he said, reaching for his bowl.

I set them both in the sink and smiled. "Done. I only use enough dishes to run the dishwasher every few days."

I scratched Darcy's head and gave her a biscuit, sorting through my thoughts. Kyle Miller in my kitchen. After all these years. Would it be so bad to try again? Maybe not. But could I stand losing him again if it didn't work out? My heart hurt just contemplating it.

When Darcy scurried away, I led Kyle into the living room and parked myself strategically on the tufted red chaise lounge, gesturing to the navy sofa opposite my perch.

"Didn't they just pass a law that's going to raise the tax on cigarettes here?" I asked him, remembering a story I'd seen a few weeks before.

"Very good. I guess you're up on the latest news," Kyle said. "My thieves have got to be salivating over that. There are more smokers here in Virginia as a percentage of the population than anywhere else, and the average income isn't nearly what you see in Manhattan, so this tax hike is going to hit a lot of people hard. The crooks will keep buying in North Carolina, and as soon as they figure out how to fake the new Virginia stamps, which even I haven't seen yet, they'll be selling here, too. Not for long, though. We'll catch them."

I nodded, my fingers twisting my hair into knots as I studied the fluffy geometric-print rug under my coffee table. Grayson. Billings. The farmer from the jewelry store. The dead lobbyist. Tobacco seemed to be popping up in my days an awful lot.

"What's up?" Kyle asked.

"Hmm?" I kept my eyes on the red triangle in the carpet.

"Nicey. You're playing with your hair. What are you thinking about?"

When I looked up, Kyle was waving his arms like he was guiding a plane home. I laughed.

"A story. Just trying to figure out what pieces go where in this one."

"Oh, yeah? I'm a pretty smart guy, you know. And the hair tells me there's something you're trying to figure out."

I turned and caught a glimpse of the right side of my head in the dark, flat screen of the TV that hung above my fireplace. There were at least four loops where I'd been bothering my hair as I stared at the floor. I ran my fingers through it and they fell straight again.

"What do you know about Billings?" I asked. "You seemed pretty sure this morning that he was responsible for killing the lobbyist. Why do you think so?"

Kyle leaned forward, studying my face for a moment.

"Off the record, Miss Clarke," he said. "Because I trust you. And I don't think I have to say that if this shows up in the newspaper, I won't make that mistake again, right?"

"Noted."

"I think Billings is paying someone off," he said. "And I have a couple of ideas, though I haven't found enough for an arrest warrant yet. But something went bad. Either the lobbyist grew a conscience, or he threatened to tell, or he asked for a bigger cut. I have a lead on a weapon, and forensics is working on more."

"And who do you think Billings was buying off?"

"That, I can't even tell you as a friend."

I nodded, tugging at my hair again.

He stared, thumb and hooked index finger sliding over the auburn bristles around his mouth a few times. "You think you know the answer to that already, don't you?"

I grinned. "If you're not sharing, neither am I."

"But you're working another angle on this," he said. "Irrespective of what you saw at the courthouse this morning. You're on another trail."

"I can neither confirm nor deny that, agent," I said.

"I don't need you to confirm it. I know you." He sat back and draped one arm over the back of the sofa. "As your friend, let me give you a piece of advice. Watch your step."

"I'm really not investigating anything," I said, turning what he'd said about Billings over in my head and wondering if I was lying to him even as I spoke the words. "But your concern is duly noted. And appreciated."

"Let me know if there's anything I can help you with," he said. "Without actually losing my job, anyway."

"Yeah?" I said, grinning. "Half of getting any story is about who you know. I guess you're a good person to know."

I was kidding, but something I couldn't quite read flitted across his face.

"I like to think so," he smiled, dropping his eyelids halfway and leaning forward.

Oh, I knew that look. It hadn't changed in ten years. Time to go home, Special Agent Bedroom Eyes. No need to test my willpower so soon.

I made a show of eyeballing the clock and yawning, complaining about my long day. He shook his head the tiniest bit, but rose and turned toward the foyer.

"Thanks for dinner." He leaned against the front door and smiled. "I'll give you a call if I come across anything that says I really am a good person for you to know."

I shook my head. "I don't think your worth as a friend is solely dependent on your ability to get me classified ATF information."

"I'm really glad I found you again, Nicey."

"I'm glad you found me, too. My ashes would be scattered all over Shockoe Bottom right now if you hadn't." I feigned horror and he chuckled.

Smiling back, I pulled the door open. And found myself nose-to-nose with Joey.

CHAPTER EIGHT

"Hɪ." The word popped out automatically, and I took a step backward and pushed the door open farther, hiding Kyle behind it.

"I thought we might take that walk." Joey stepped into the entry-way, his honey-colored skin particularly attractive against a lavender oxford shirt, sleeves rolled up and tie loose. It was the most informal I'd ever seen him, and I couldn't help noticing how his shoulders pulled at the seams of the cotton. Not enough to classify the shirt as tight, just enough to make my pulse flutter. I felt the corners of my lips tip up in a smile, and his dark eyes lit, crinkling at the corners when he flashed a grin.

It faded when Kyle stepped out from behind the door.

"Thanks for dinner," he said again, laying a hand on my shoulder before he put one arm around me and pulled me into a half-hug.

Joey stared, and my eyes flicked between the two of them, watching them size each other up. Oh, boy.

"I didn't know you had company," Joey said, not moving to leave. "We could go another time."

"Such things happen when you refuse to call before you come by," I chided, ducking out from under Kyle's arm and cutting a warning look in his direction. "Kyle was just leaving. And I could use a walk.

It's beautiful outside tonight." Two visits in a week's time was unusual for Joey. He wanted to talk to me, and I wanted to know why.

"I'll call you," Kyle said, turning sideways to slide through the wide doorway. Joey didn't move to make it easier, stepping closer to me only after Kyle was on the porch.

"Thank you, Kyle. It was nice to catch up with an old friend." I hit the last word too hard, and Joey chuckled under his breath. Kyle's smile faltered. I felt a flicker of remorse, but we certainly hadn't been anything more than friends in a long time, and I really wanted him to go before the two of them got into enough of a pissing contest for him to start asking questions about Joey. How would I explain a moonlight walk with a Mafia boss to the ATF?

Not well, that's how.

Kyle nodded and muttered something that sounded like "We'll see about that," turning and jogging down the steps.

I shut the door and flashed a smile at Joey. "Your timing is off. Do you have a fever or something?" I reached up to touch his forehead, and he leaned forward just enough to enter the danger zone in my tiny foyer. I ran my fingers through my own hair instead and laughed shakily, spinning toward the living room.

"Let me get my shoes."

"Preferably some you'll make it farther than a few blocks in," he called after me.

I dug through the basket in the corner of the living room where my less-important footwear lived, unearthing a pair of black ballet flats with purple roses embroidered on the toes. Hurrying back to the door, I found Joey examining my collection of beach glass.

"This is beautiful," he said.

"I love the beach. My mom grew up in California. In Texas, we went to the Gulf coast every year when I was little, and then to Mexico and even the Bahamas when I got older." I pointed to a sapphire piece with violet streaks. "This one came from a place near a coral reef off Grand Bahama Island. I can't come home from a trip without the perfect piece of glass."

I took a deep breath and got more than a faint whiff of a woodsy, musky cologne. He was standing awfully close. And he smelled so good.

"What?" I took a step back and returned his smile.

"You get a look on your face every time you mention your mother," he said, opening the front door. "You must be very close."

"That would have been accurate five years ago. Then she got cancer and I thought I might lose her. The only reason I didn't move back home was that she threatened to disown me if I did. She didn't want me to quit my job."

"She's okay now?"

"She's been in remission for more than four years. I don't close my eyes at night without being thankful for that. So far, so good."

"Good to hear."

We walked in silence, an occasional car passing or pebble scraping under a shoe the only sounds for almost a block.

"So, about your friend back there," Joey said finally. "Is he anyone important?"

Subtle, Joey.

"He's my long-ago ex-boyfriend. Who also happens to be the Richmond ATF office's newest special agent."

"No shit?" He became very interested in the moon, hanging low and blood orange. "How convenient."

I kept my eyes on the stars, which seemed brighter next to the dark harvest moon. Joey and I had chatted a handful of times over the summer, on warm nights when I'd come home to find him on my porch swing holding the dog. But we'd been careful to keep it light, avoiding reference to what we might think of each other outside a bizarre friendship. My stomach flipped at the notion that he might want to be more than friends, but my head warned against the idea. No matter what Freud might say about the dreams I had to the contrary.

"What's up?" Time to talk business.

"Excuse me?" He turned his head to look at me.

"You've been here twice in a week. You want something. I seem to remember you talking about 'using people who purvey information to work around the edges of the law.' So, what is it?"

He slowed his gait.

"You're nosing around Ted Grayson," he said flatly. "I need you to back off. And I'm already sure you won't do it, but I have to ask you. Before somebody decides to tell you."

I spun on one heel to face him.

He met my gaze head-on, looking down slightly because of my flat shoes.

I studied his face for a full minute before I spoke. His mouth was drawn into a tight line, his eyes liquid and pleading. And he wasn't the pleading type. What was Grayson into?

"How the hell do you know that?" I asked finally.

"Men like Grayson have all kinds of connections," Joey said. "And information is currency. If the right person decides to keep you quiet, you might get hurt. I don't want that." He raised a hand and pushed my wayward lock of hair gently behind my ear, his fingers barely grazing my skin. The simple gesture sent sparks shooting clear to my fingertips. I wanted to lean my cheek into his palm, but instead I tilted my head away. His hand dropped.

"Someone could hurt me?" I asked.

"I don't have say-so over everybody with a gun. Far from it. And this has the potential to get very ugly, Miss Clarke. Let. It. Go. Politics isn't even your game."

"Crime is my game. I think the good senator is up to no good. And you pretty much just confirmed that. I don't do well with letting go."

"Learn," Joey said. "Consider it self-preservation."

"I know you're not threatening me." God, I hoped he wasn't, anyway. But maybe I thought he was sexy because he was more than a little bit dangerous. "To the casual observer it might sound that way, though. What is your boy Grayson into?"

"He's not my boy," Joey said. "And I'm not telling you a damned thing. The less you can find out, the more likely you are to drop it."

"Have you met me? I am nothing if not tenacious."

"If it weren't for that, I wouldn't be here," he said. "Your ability to dig up dirt is exactly what has me worried." He laid a hand on my arm. "Back off."

"I can't." I stepped past him and started back toward my house, warmth lingering on my skin where his hand had been. "This dead lobbyist could turn out to be the story I've dreamed of my whole life. What if Grayson is the missing piece? I just have to..."

I faltered. The lobbyist's half-eaten face flickered in my memory, right behind an image of Joey standing in my driveway after the discovery of the body, which according to the coroner had only been out there for a few days at the most.

"You were here." My chili threatened to come back up. "Oh, God. Tell me you didn't."

"This would be more fun if you'd stop assuming I killed every dead person in five states." He didn't look away. "I did not hurt anyone. But your dead guy was in over his head. And you're about to get in over yours."

"Kyle already arrested someone for killing the lobbyist," I said. "They had a bond hearing early this morning. I have a story in tomorrow's paper about it."

"Who was it?" Joey's eyes widened slightly, his voice flipping from pleading to tight.

"James Billings. He's a veep over at Raymond Garfield." Puzzle pieces rained into place as I talked, Allison and Kyle echoing in my head. "I think he's the one paying Grayson off, and I think the dead guy was the go-between. Kyle is sure Billings is his man. He got the CA to take on the case himself, and the judge didn't give them the no-bond they asked for, but he made Billings wear an ankle monitor. So they've got to have something compelling."

"I'll be damned." Joey matched his stride to mine, shaking his head slowly.

He kept his head down the rest of the way back to my house, not talking. From his wrinkling brow and twisting mouth, he was either deep in thought or having some kind of internal conflict.

When we turned up my sidewalk, I broke the silence.

"Thanks for coming by," I said. "I'd rather you avoid any more chest thumping competitions with Kyle for obvious reasons, but I really do appreciate your concern."

He stood under the unlit coach lamp next to my front door and leaned one shoulder against the wall.

"I don't want you to get hurt. Follow the Billings story. You'll be safe. And if that agent has a thing for you, you'll stay ahead of your friend at the TV station, too. An executive going up for murder because of dirty money is a hell of a lead."

"It's not bad, but why do I get the distinct feeling that there's something better here?"

"It's not better if you don't live to see it printed, is it? Make yourself ignore it. You told me once I saved your life. I can't stand the thought of anything happening to you." He snatched my cell phone from my hand and tapped the keys for a few seconds, then handed it back. "Call me if you need me. If your old 'friend' can keep you safe, then that's where I want you to be. Consider it payback: forget you ever heard Grayson's name."

I unlocked the door and opened it.

"I'll be careful," I said.

"Dammit, this isn't a game." He grabbed my arm and spun me around. "Nobody wins if you get yourself killed, and there are people in this up to their eyeballs who won't give a shit if I say to leave you alone once you piss them off. Leave it."

I couldn't concentrate on anything except the feel of his breath on my face and the smell of his cologne, which seemed slightly insane, given the urgency in his eyes. I leaned back against the doorframe. He moved his hand to the wood behind my head, leaning on the wall with his arm alongside my cheekbone. I stared into his eyes for half a second and stumbled backward into the house.

"I won't get hurt," I said. "I swear."

I closed the door before he could say anything else, and watched him go down the walk through the trio of little windows that ran along the top.

Darcy barked behind me and I jumped.

"Talk about playing with fire," I said. "Let's get you a snack and me a cold shower and a good night's sleep, huh, girl?"

Darcy's pawing at the bathroom door popped the broken latch loose before I even got the shower curtain closed. I turned on the water and made a mental note to call the landlord about the door-knob. Standing under the showerhead, I ran back through the conversation with Joey, way too relieved that he hadn't killed the lobbyist. It wasn't until I was halfway through rinsing my hair that I realized what Joey had said without saying it.

James Billings hadn't killed anybody, either.

* * *

Sleep eluded me for the better part of three hours. When I'd tossed and turned to the point that every pillow I owned was scattered on the floor around my cherry four-poster, I threw off the covers and went back to the living room.

Carrying a glass of Moscato to the sofa, I picked up a puzzle piece and turned it every which way, trying to finish the border. But it didn't fit. Closer inspection told that it was one of those they'd cut from the middle with an almost-flat edge, so it wasn't really a border piece.

"Where the hell is the other one?" I muttered, studying the two thousand or so that littered the coffee table, most of them close to the same color. I loved puzzles. The harder the better, so I bought lots of monochromatic ones.

While my eyes searched the pieces on the table, my brain tried to order the week's events into a mental jigsaw.

If Billings didn't kill the lobbyist, who did? Grayson? My gut had sensed the senator was shady for days, and Joey all but confirmed it.

But murder? I shook my head. Not impossible, but I'd put it in the unlikely column at least until I knew more about him. Bribes are one thing. Murder is in a whole different league. I'd met and spoken to more than anyone's fair share of killers, and they are almost always motivated by one of two things: insanity or passion. And Grayson didn't get where he was being ruled by his emotions.

But Joey wouldn't have looked so surprised—or been so damned noncommittal—when I told him about Billings's arrest if he thought the tobacco executive did it. And while I didn't want to think my way-too-sexy mob friend was involved, it was looking like he knew too much about the inner workings of this case.

Kyle's comment about the cigarette taxes floated through my head. Were there federal taxes on cigarettes, too?

I dropped the puzzle piece and reached for my laptop, typing "federal tobacco tax" into the Google bar. Pay dirt: forty-five cents a pack.

I deleted that and typed Grayson's name in again, scrolling past all the same stories I'd seen the first time, looking for a mention of taxes or tobacco.

Halfway down the fourth page, I found something.

In a *Washington Post* article dated the previous October, Grayson's name was mentioned in discussion of a bill that would raise the federal excise tax on cigarettes. The reporter called him a swing vote because he was a moderate who might vote for the higher tax, earmarked for education, a pet project of Grayson's.

I copied the bill number and clicked over to the Senate website, pasting it into the search box.

Oh, shit.

The bill had spent nearly a year bogged down in committee. Until last week, when a retiring senator who was one of the co-authors had forced it onto the voting calendar for a week from Monday.

But I was staring at my screen with a slightly loose jaw because Ted Grayson was the sole dissenting vote on sending the bill to the floor.

The *Post's* analysts had expected Grayson to lean on this bill. Tobacco companies were increasingly unpopular with the public, but they had deep pockets and old friends in D.C. They needed someone on their side, and Grayson was a popular guy on Capitol Hill.

He also represented a fair number of farmers, here in tobacco country. He was the perfect target. And the information in front of me was just enough to make a person curious about why education had suddenly taken a backseat to tobacco. And give me a bad feeling that I already knew.

Allison had said, "Asked what they were paying him for." I sat back in my chair, my eyes on Grayson's Colgate-commercial-perfect smile as my mind clicked puzzle pieces together.

Tobacco was Virginia's biggest agricultural product, and had been since Thomas Jefferson held state office in Richmond. Farmers depended on being able to sell their crops. And the company that turned those crops into marketable product was an industrial giant. I had no trouble believing that either would be willing to pay for votes to stop a new tax that could hurt their sales. But how did the lobbyist end up dead? He was part of Team Tobacco, too, right? Was I looking in the right place? My gut said yes, because Kyle had arrested Billings, who was a tobacco executive.

I clicked last fall's *Post* article back up on my screen, reading the rest of it but finding no mention of the victim, Amesworth, or Raymond Garfield, the tobacco company.

Back to Google.

On page fourteen of my results, Grayson's name popped up in an article about a bill that made it illegal to smoke in restaurants in Virginia—because he'd written the bill. The story on my screen was written by the *Telegraph's* retired opinions editor, praising Grayson's dogged pursuit of the change. Said the Senator's favorite uncle died of lung cancer in his forties, and quoted Grayson as calling Raymond Garfield "Virginia's moneygrubbing, murderous devil."

It made no sense. If he'd flipped on such a major issue, someone would have noticed. A search of the *Post's* editorial archives turned up nothing.

I went back to the senate site and searched for bills concerning tobacco farming, subsidies, taxes, or smoking.

There'd been seven introduced in the past three years. Four that actually made it to the floor for a vote. I held my breath as I clicked into the voting record and scanned for Grayson's name. I found him on the first list and blew the captive air out through my bottom lip, fanning a wayward strand of hair off my forehead. Damn. He didn't vote.

I found him on the second list. Not there that day, either. I clicked quickly to the third. Blank. So was the fourth.

"They're paying him to *not* vote against them?" I shook my head at the screen. Bob would never buy it. But I couldn't shake the feeling that money, tobacco, the dead lobbyist, and Grayson were thicker than Eunice's cream gravy.

"Why would this guy be in bed with the tobacco lobby?" I said under my breath, sitting back in my chair.

My gut said money. It was always money. Well, when it wasn't sex. I clicked back to a picture of Grayson's smiling family, arms raised after his first senate election, and stared.

Why did Ted Grayson need money badly enough to take it from the devil?

I wondered if Agent Evans might be able to find out anything I could use without causing too much of a stir at the Bureau. A crooked senator could have friends God-knows-where, and I didn't want to get Evans in trouble.

With no good answer for that, I slammed the computer shut, turning back to my actual puzzle.

"Dammit, where is the last edge piece?" I grumbled.

I dropped to my knees on the geometric-print rug that lay under my coffee table and poked my head underneath. The puzzle piece was lying next to the carved oak foot of my coffee table, on top of a red Bicycle playing card. I picked both up and clambered back onto the couch.

"King of spades," I mumbled, flipping the card over. "How appropriate."

I snapped the puzzle piece in place and tapped the edge of the card on the table, something tickling the back of my brain.

Of course.

I flipped my computer screen back up, drumming my fingers on the arm of the sofa for the whole three and a half seconds it took the machine to boot up.

Opening the photo file Larry had given me, I clicked onto the image of Amesworth and Grayson. At casino night. Scrolling through the other photos, I watched for the senator's face, finding three shots of him playing cards. Two of them showed a somber, focused Grayson, his brow crunched as he studied his cards like he could will them to change.

"Why so serious, senator?" I whispered, clicking over to Google and holding my breath.

"United States Senators earn a base salary of $174,000 annually. Plus various allowances, speaking honorariums, and other sources of income," I read aloud.

Amazon told me Grayson had written a bestselling book on clean energy policy.

So why does that guy need money—especially money that the Mafia has a hand in? "Cards," I said aloud.

What if Ted Grayson played cards somewhere else—for more than charity chips? What if he was a gambler on an unlucky streak? I couldn't tell if it was brilliant or insane, but it jived with what Allison said about risk, and following hunches had ended well for me in the past.

I made a list of everyone I might be able to wheedle information out of on that front, starting with Allison and ending with Joey. He wouldn't want to tell me, but if I could see his reaction when I asked, it might be all the confirmation I needed.

I gulped the rest of my wine and tried to slow my thoughts. If Ted Grayson was even remotely linked to a murder...that was the kind of story that could make a career.

I just had to make damned sure I was right. And beat Charlie to the headline.

I climbed back under my duvet a little after two, Joey's pleading eyes floating through my brain as I drifted off, swearing I could still smell that cologne.

CHAPTER NINE

My Saturday started before sunup, thanks to a vivid nightmare about being tied to a table and burned alive. I took Darcy outside for a game of fetch before I scrambled a couple of eggs, hoping a relaxing morning would slow the heart-pounding adrenaline rush that accompanied those dreams.

The sun still hadn't peeked over the eastern horizon when my scanner bleeped off an all-call on a missing person. Which, in and of itself, may not have required my presence. But when four patrol cars, the K-9 unit, and a deputy police chief were on their way to the most exclusive (and expensive) assisted living facility in Richmond at o'dark-thirty on a Saturday, there was bound to be a story.

Thankful I'd showered the night before, I twisted my hair up in a clip and jerked on khakis and a sweater, shoving my feet into eggplant Nicholas Kirkwoods that were almost the same shade as my top.

I stuffed my gym clothes into a bag just in case I made it away from the scene in time for body combat and tapped my fingers on the counter while my Colombian Fair Trade brewed into a mug Jenna's little girl had picked out for my birthday. I added a shot of white mocha syrup and ran out the door.

Skidding my tires on the turn into the nursing home parking lot, I scanned the cars for Aaron's unmarked police sedan.

It was near the doors, just in front of the Channel Four satellite truck. How Charlie could look camera-ready at six a.m. was beyond me, but she managed it on a consistent basis. I hung back and waited for her to finish talking to Aaron, admiring her Donna Karan suit and bright eyes. It was too early to be perky.

"Good morning." Aaron shook his head when he turned toward me.

"How are you, Detective Unavailable?" I asked.

"Come on, Nichelle," he said, raising both hands in mock surrender. "You know how this works. Do you have any idea what kind of shit I'll get into with the feds if I give you anything on this break-in at the Graysons? They're acting like we've got our own little Watergate over in the Fan."

"You could at least call me back and say 'no comment.'" I gave him a half smile, not wanting to fight with him.

"And give you a chance to badger me into saying something I shouldn't?" He laughed. "I'll take my lumps, thanks."

I thumped his shoulder lightly. "Consider yourself chastised. What the hell is going on here?"

"Alzheimer's patient wandered off," he said.

"Bullshit. You're here. I heard Mike say he was on his way. And while I was driving one of the dispatchers said Chief Lowe had called in for a status update." I gestured to the pillared marble entryway on the other side of the open doors, the double staircase straight out of Twelve Oaks. "An Alzheimer's patient who's pretty important has wandered off. And I didn't drag myself out this early and possibly skip my workout for you to give me the runaround. Spill it."

He rolled his baby blue eyes skyward.

"You people and your damned scanners. I have to be careful what I say, though you already know a good bit about it. Remember that hearing you called me about yesterday? James Billings's mother is a resident here. She saw your story when she got up this morning. Apparently a member of the early to bed and early to rise generation.

They don't know how she slipped past the staff, but they found the newspaper open on her coffee table and she's gone."

I sucked in a deep breath and looked around. We were just on the outskirts of the city, in a surprisingly rural area. And it was unseasonably cold. Shit. I pulled out a notebook and jotted down Aaron's comments, fighting the urge to join the search party.

"Anything yet?" I asked. "They let him go, you know. He's got an ankle monitor, but he's not in jail anymore. The CA was pretty pissed about that, actually. It was all in the story."

"I know. We'll find her. K-9 is searching the surrounding area. She didn't have more than a half-hour head start."

"Thanks, Aaron."

"They said you can wait inside if you don't want to stand out here in the cold."

I shook my head. "I'm okay."

He stared at me for a second and then patted my arm. "It's not your fault. And we will find her. The good thing about this place being out here is that we're not near a freeway or in a shitty neighborhood like a lot of nursing homes. That's part of the reason they specialize in the care of Alzheimer's patients. K-9 says the dog has a scent. It'll be okay."

I tried to smile as I nodded. Stories can have unforeseen consequences. It was a lousy byproduct of reporting. And Billings wasn't allowed to leave his neighborhood, so he couldn't even come help look for her. Given my suspicion that he hadn't actually killed anyone, that seemed particularly craptastic.

"So, what did you make of Billings?" Aaron asked.

"How come Grayson's security system didn't trip up the intruder?" I countered. "Possibly because it wasn't the cat burglar?"

"Off the record?"

I pretended to consider that for a few seconds. Normally, off the record on a breaking and entering case wouldn't help much. But he didn't need to know I wanted information on Grayson for another reason.

"Why not?" I said.

"Possibly," he said. "A couple of things were unusual about this particular break-in. But we don't know anything for sure yet, and I'll lose my ass for talking about it right now."

"We can't have that. You wouldn't do well sitting on your boat with no ass," I said, my brain spinning through the reasons I could imagine someone would break into Grayson's house. Billings came to mind first because of Joey's comments, but he'd been in jail that night.

What if it was Watergate? And did that make it Trudy's story or mine?

Aaron's radio beeped and he stepped away to talk to the officers in the field. My thoughts wandered back to Grayson. I pulled out my cell phone and tapped my browser open, searching for information on the new tax law I'd talked to Kyle about the night before. Between what he'd said and Joey's ominous warning, I wondered if Joey and his friends were the bad guys Kyle was looking for. I also wondered exactly what the new Virginia law was poised to do to tobacco sales.

"Bingo," I whispered when the results flashed up on my screen.

I was no marketing genius, but given the information in front of me, I'd say the tobacco companies had to be pretty desperate to keep the federal tax from going up. In five states (including this one with the new state tax), the proposed doubling of the federal rates—from forty-seven cents to a dollar a pack—would have people spending $3.50 a pack just on taxes. In this economy, that would price a lot of people out of smoking.

And Grayson was the chairman of the committee holding up the federal bill.

It wasn't a leap to think folks had paid him to stop the bill. It wasn't even a long jump. But I had no proof. And no real idea who killed Amesworth, either.

I looked back inside the grand foyer of the nursing home where Billings's mother spent her days. Marble floors gleamed under elaborate crystal chandeliers that were probably worth more than my car. Whoever said money was the root of all evil was pretty smart.

So, the million-dollar question was: what did Grayson need more money for? If I could find that, it might give me enough to take the story to Bob. I considered my gambling theory. How could I find out if Grayson was a lousy poker player?

A hand on my elbow broke my concentration.

"They found her," Aaron said. "Dressed in her Sunday best, complete with hat and gloves, plodding through the pasture. On her way to the courthouse, she said. But she's fine. All's well that ends well."

I smiled at him, relieved. When I turned for the doors to the building, a round little man with a bad comb-over and a navy suit was taking questions on the front steps. I joined a small huddle of reporters that included Charlie, the still-relatively-new girl from Channel Ten whose name I couldn't remember to save my life, and Erica from the local talk radio station.

I pocketed my cell phone and dug out my notebook and pen again, jotting down his answers to the standard questions about the facility's security, the age of the patient, and the frequency of such incidents.

"Does Mrs. Lansing have family in the area?" Charlie asked.

I looked up.

"Her son," facility administrator Harvey Butters said, pulling at his collar. "He couldn't be here this morning."

"But he was notified?" Charlie asked, perking up. I cringed slightly, knowing she'd picked up a scent. I'd hoped no one else would connect the dots, since Billings and his mother didn't share a last name.

"We called him, of course," Butters said. "He's very concerned, and was happy to hear his mother was safe."

Charlie let it go, but made a beeline for Butters when he was finished, asking, I was sure, for a way to get in touch with Mrs. Lansing's next of kin.

He waved his hands helplessly as he talked, gesturing to the newspaper on the front doormat. Charlie shot me a glance and picked up the paper after Butters hurried inside. I watched as Charlie read, a small smile playing around my lips. She looked up and offered a nod. I waved, calling a goodbye to Aaron and checking my watch. I still had time to get to the gym if I hurried. And then I had a story to write and some answers to find.

* * *

The early body combat class on Saturdays was more advanced than my weekday class, but since I'd missed two during the week, I figured a little extra burn was in order. Particularly after the two (okay, five) of Eunice's white chocolate macadamia cookies I'd smuggled out of the break room on Monday afternoon.

With faster music, quicker punches, more jumps, and a new hooked side kick the perky brunette instructor called a "cheerio chagi" in an unmistakable lowcountry drawl, I felt about as graceful as a grizzly in stilettos. The insecurity bred like bunnies on pheromones, until the footwork that had earned me a spot as one of the best in my regular class was a distant memory. I stumbled sideways into the mirror twice, threw the wrong kick, *ap-chagi*'ed the girl in front of me, and came close to falling too many times to count. I also worked up a sweat that would do a football player running August two-a-days in Texas proud. How much of that was exertion and how much was embarrassment was a tough call, though.

By the time I shoved my gym bag into the back of my little red SUV, Grayson and his reason for needing extra income had pulled my attention from my Three Stooges imitation.

I stopped at my house to shower and toss on a quick face. Then I pulled on some jeans and a turtleneck, jammed my not-so-dainty feet into a pair of pink Manolos, and grabbed a pack of strawberry Pop Tarts out of my tiny pantry on my way to the office.

I stepped out of the elevator, rolling my eyes when Shelby Taylor came out of the hallway that led to the managing editor's office. Her fling with Les had been nothing but a pain in my ass since it began.

"Nichelle!" She grinned and folded her arms over her ample chest, which did not go with her tiny everything else. Shelby reminded me of a pixie Barbie with black hair. But jealousy had no hand in why I disliked her. She gave me plenty of reasons that had nothing to do with her appearance. Like the Splenda that coated every word she spoke to me, for instance. Shelby didn't know how to make a comment that didn't have razor edges. "Trying to get a jump on Charlie by sneaking in on a Saturday? She thumped you pretty good on the burglary yesterday. Did your scanner break?"

"My scanner was working fine yesterday, and this morning, when it tipped me to a missing person call at five-thirty. You really ought to be careful what you wish for, Shelby. I don't think my hours would be good for your boinking the boss. But good morning to you, too. Nice to see you're as sweet and sincere as ever. Now if you'll excuse me, I have a story to write. You remember what that's like, don't you?" I imitated her fake smile.

"I remember doing it better than you have lately." Shelby sneered, turning toward the copy desk. "Keep losing to Charlie, and I won't even need Les."

She sashayed off before I could say anything else, and I hurried to my cube, fuming and more determined to find out what the hell was going on with Grayson.

Today's deadline first, though. I flipped my computer open, digging in my bag for my notes from the nursing home. The woman's identity was definitely the most important thing about the story, given that her son had been arrested for murder less than forty-eight hours before.

I checked my notes and started typing.

Richmond police found an Alzheimer's patient who wandered away from Jefferson Meadows Assisted Living before dawn Saturday in less than an hour, returning Elizabeth Lansing to her home without incident.

Lansing's son, James Billings, was arrested Friday in connection with the murder of Henrico attorney Daniel Amesworth, twenty-nine. Officials said when Mrs. Lansing learned of her son's situation, she was determined to see him, even if it meant going on foot.

"They don't know how she slipped past the staff," Det. Aaron White, RPD public information officer, said at the scene.

Harvey Butters, the chief administrator at Jefferson Meadows, said Mrs. Lansing was unharmed and resting in her room by sunup Saturday.

I read back through the story twice before I sent it to Les, sure he'd find something to complain about anyway. And if he didn't, Shelby would.

"Can't please everyone," I mumbled, trying to channel my mom's bubbly self-confidence as I clicked my web browser open.

I didn't even have time to figure out what I was looking for before Les emailed me back.

"It'd be nice if I hadn't seen every word of this on Channel Four twenty minutes ago. Charlie's up by two in two days. Don't worry about the typos. Shelby will catch them."

"At least he's consistent," I muttered, turning my thoughts back to Grayson.

Before I could type Grayson's name into Google again, I had an idea. I checked the files I'd saved on him already and dialed my prosecutor girlfriend's cell number.

"It's Saturday," DonnaJo said when she answered. "I have fuzzy pink flowered pajama pants, coffee, and a new mystery novel. Unless you want a coffee book club meeting, I'm not talking to you."

"I wish," I said. "I'm at the office. Your Saturday sounds much more relaxing. One quick question?"

"Go home, Nichelle. The bad guys will still be there Monday."

"I will. I just need to ask you something first." I said, clicking my pen and fanning my notebook to an empty page.

She sighed. "What?"

"Do you know anyone who knows Ted Grayson?"

"Not anyone who can get him to talk to you about that break-in at his house."

Perfect.

"Damn," I tried to sound convincingly disappointed. "What about someone who can get me some background on his political opposition?"

"Can't your D.C. reporter get you that?"

"She's not here today." It came out a little too quickly.

"Uh-huh." DonnaJo was quiet for a minute. "I have an old friend who served in the House of Delegates with Grayson. He used to be a prosecutor. I'll give you his number, but leave me out of this. Ted Grayson has a lot of friends, and if you're nosing around, I don't want to be caught in the fallout."

"Got it." I smiled as I jotted the guy's name and number down. "Thanks, doll. Enjoy your book."

I dialed the number I'd just written down. Leon Casey picked up on the second ring.

"I'm working on a story about Senator Ted Grayson," I said in my most earnest tone after I introduced myself. "I ran across your name in my research. You're a former colleague?"

"You could say that," Casey said, his voice so smooth I expected honey to drip from the receiver. "Ted and I go way back. But I'm not in the loop about this election, if that's what you're looking for."

"I'm just trying to find general background information," I said. "Do you have time to answer a couple of questions?"

"If I can," he said. "I'm not sure how much help I'll be."

I asked about how they knew each other (school, and then the state house) Casey's career (prosecutor, politician, now private attorney handling mostly family cases in a poor part of town) and Grayson's family (married, one son studying computer science at William and Mary) before I got to the restaurant smoking bill.

"That was some fancy footwork on Ted's part." Casey laughed. "Can you imagine? He announced he was going after tobacco in Virginia and I thought he'd just sunk his political career."

I nodded. "I'm sure you weren't alone."

"That's for sure. The whole capitol building was in an uproar. Ted even got death threats. They had to hire bodyguards," Casey said. "It was crazy. But he was determined, and he's a charmer. He talked people whose great-grandaddies used to farm tobacco into voting for that bill. You ever heard the saying 'he could sell ice to eskimos?' Ted Grayson could sell heroin to Nancy Reagan."

My hand flew across the page, not missing a word. Something I'd seen online tapped at the back of my brain.

"Thank you so much for your time, Mr. Casey," I said. "I have one last question: what's your favorite non-work memory of the Senator? Is there a house of delegates guys' night?"

The question was vague to avoid raising suspicion, but I crossed my fingers under the desk. Boys' night and poker games go together like coffee and cream.

"Oh, I don't know," Casey said. "We didn't know each other well in school, but we had some mutual friends. We did play cards occasionally. Just friendly games, but Ted was pretty good. He has that way about him. You can't even be mad at him when he's taking your money."

I wouldn't bet on that. Maybe Casey couldn't, but plenty of people could. Maybe mad enough to make the senator desperate. I thanked Casey for his time.

I pulled up the Internet research I'd done on Grayson and scrolled through the voting lists on the tobacco-related bills again. Opening a new window, I went back to the story about the committee trouble with the cigarette tax bill.

Three other senators were listed as swing votes in the *Post's* article on the tax. They were all on Grayson's committee. And they had all voted in favor of the tobacco industry on bills Grayson had skipped out on.

Charming and popular.

"He's very charismatic," Allison had said.

"Are they paying him to deliver votes?" I mused, tapping a pen on the desk. "He skips out to escape questions about why his record has flipped, and then he gets the other guys to vote the way he wants them to on the bill?"

I shook my head at the screen. Maybe, but I needed solid proof.

Before I could figure out how to go about getting that, the phone rang. Who knew I was here on Saturday morning? I was tempted to let it go, but I have a mental block that renders me unable to ignore a ringing phone. I raised it to my ear.

"Crime desk, this is Clarke," I said.

"Remember how you went poking around in our body dump site the other night?" Aaron.

"Yeah," I said. "You still haven't told me why Officer Charming felt the need to tattle on me."

"Officer Charming?"

"Oops. Was that out loud? Sorry," I said. "He was…less than thrilled to see me. Didn't even thank me for pointing out that paper scrap."

"Well, consider yourself thanked," Aaron said. "The report says the lab results were forwarded to the ATF, and it doesn't say what the paper is, except that it's not any ordinary kind of paper. I don't know how our recovery guys missed it, but if you hadn't seen it, it would still be out there in the dirt."

"I think this is the first time in history that a cop has called a reporter to thank them for being nosy," I said, scribbling his comment fast.

"Thought the heads up was the least I could do, since you found the thing. You scratch my back, and all that," Aaron said. "It's all been added to the report, so it'll be fair game first thing in the morning, but if you can do anything with a half-day lead, you got it."

"I'll give it my best shot."

"Have fun. I'm going fishing. Right now, before anything else can require my attention."

"Have a drink for me." I clicked off the call and dialed Kyle's cell number, hoping he wasn't still a fan of sleeping in on Saturday mornings.

"Miller," he said, not sounding like I'd woken him.

"So, what kind of paper was that I found at the Amesworth body recovery site?" I asked.

"Good morning to you, too, old friend," he stressed the last word. "Have a nice walk with your new friend last night?"

All right. I held my tongue to keep from firing back a smartass retort. I needed him to tell me something no one else at the ATF would be willing to share, so I couldn't afford to piss him off. I had a feeling a bruised ego and a touch of hurt feelings were behind the sarcasm I was hearing, so I tried to soften the blow.

"You were awfully territorial for a guy I haven't heard from in a decade," I said. "You know you'll always have a special place in my heart, Kyle. But we're different people than we were then. Slow, remember? Can't we be friends? See where it goes?"

"Who was that guy?" He sounded less tense.

"A friend." That I'm not telling you anything else about. "And I didn't mean to hurt your feelings." Every word true, even if there were a few I'd carefully omitted.

"What do you mean, 'paper you found?' " He sighed, a more conversational, if guarded, tone replacing the injured one.

"I mean, paper I found." I said. "I was poking around after the coroner's team left, and I saw something in the soil and waved over the RPD uniform in case it was important. A little birdie tells me that it might be. So what kind of special paper is it?"

"The kind that could be material to my investigation, and is not public information at this time," he said.

That was just a shade shy of "no comment." I sighed. I wanted to know what it was, but I didn't want to get Kyle in trouble at work. "You wouldn't have it if I hadn't found it," I said finally. "What if I promise that we're off the record?" If he'd tell me what it was, it might lead me to something else I could print.

"I'm sorry, Miss Clarke," he said, all business. "It's evidence in an open investigation."

"Didn't you already make an arrest?"

"The investigation doesn't have to stop when the arrest is made," Kyle said. "How long have you covered crime?"

He was right, though that didn't happen very often. Normal police involvement in a case almost always ends when an arrest is made. But in something like this, they spend the time between booking and trial shoring up the case for the prosecutors. Tagging a guy like Billings for murder would require Kyle to have all his proverbial ducks lined up laser-straight. Defense attorneys who make the right kind of money can unravel a case quicker than a kitten can tear through a closet full of cashmere.

"All right," I said. "I give up. Thanks for your time. And for dinner last night. It really was fun."

"It was." I could hear the smile in his voice. "We should do it again sometime. When your other friend is otherwise occupied."

"That could be nice," I said. "As long as we have an understanding about expectations."

"Such as?"

"Such as I'm not hopping into the sack with you because you buy me a steak and a nice bottle of merlot."

"How about good enchiladas and a couple of margaritas?"

"Hardy-har-har, Kyle. Not even empanadas and tequila shots." I leaned back in my chair. "But we could get to know each other again." I couldn't deny that I'd felt something the night before, at the dinner table. I wanted to know if it was first love nostalgia or leftover gratitude for saving my life or something else. Something that might be worthwhile. Kyle presented his own set of challenges, but they certainly weren't the same ones I faced with Joey.

My heart didn't race in close quarters with Kyle like it did around Joey. And technically, they had both killed people. Sweet cartwheeling Jesus. From the life of a nun with cuter shoes to raining sexy men in a matter of months.

I promised to call him later and cradled the phone.

Flipping through the stack of message slips on my desk, I found a number for Agent Evans at the FBI. If he'd known about Billings's arrest, maybe he knew something about the paper scrap. But it was only his office number, and he wasn't there. I left him a message and blew out a short breath, drumming my fingers on the keyboard and thinking of Grayson playing cards. Where could I find information on card games—ones with the sort of stakes that a guy like Grayson would be interested in? I'd covered a couple of floating poker games that the police department's major crimes unit had blown open, but I generally only knew about such things after they'd been broken up by the cops.

Aaron and the guys at the PD wouldn't give me anything on a gambling ring they hadn't busted. And while the Mafia was an obvious angle for information on illegal gambling, Joey had made it clear the night before that he wanted me to keep my nose out of whatever I was trying to stick it into.

It's funny how hard it is to follow good advice.

CHAPTER TEN

I WAS HAULING a case of canned Purina Pro Plan into my grocery cart when it hit me.

If I wanted information on gambling, I didn't need to talk to the cops. I needed to talk to a gambler.

I scrambled to keep hold of the dog food, so startled by my epiphany I nearly lost my grip on the 24-can value pack—and a toe to my furry princess's beloved beef and carrots.

I hefted Darcy's food into the cart and took off for the checkout, tossing in a couple of cans of soup on the way so I wouldn't starve. Groceries stowed in the back of the car, I sped toward the office and ran to my desk, where I pawed through my file drawer in search of information on a trial I'd covered back in March.

I wriggled the manila folder free and flipped it open, paging through the police reports on a gambling ring that had been operating in basements on the Richmond American University campus for years, aided by a former professor, a baseball coach, and a security guard.

I checked the dates and clicked my laptop on, searching the *Telegraph's* archives for my story. The security guard had only been taking cash to keep his mouth shut and look the other way. He'd been fired, but wasn't in jail. The professor and the coach were a different story. I scanned the text for something I thought I remembered.

"Bingo," I mumbled.

The coach, one Peter Esparza, age forty, had also been nailed for fixing games for local bookies. And bookies were the kind of folks who might have dirt on high-stakes card games.

A quick search of the department of corrections website told me he was in cellblock six at Cold Springs, which was a little more than an hour away. I nearly lost a heel off my shoe sprinting back to the elevator.

The September breeze and just-turning leaves made it a lovely day for a drive. Halfway to the prison, I was still wondering how I'd get Esparza to talk. Fishing my cell phone out of my bag, I dialed Parker's cell phone.

"What's up, Lois?" he said when he answered.

"What do you know about Peter Esparza?" I asked.

"That he got fired and he's in jail," he said. "Which I believe I learned from a story you wrote, didn't I?"

"C'mon, Parker," I said. "You know everyone involved with sports in this town. You have nothing to offer me on this guy?"

He laughed. "I appreciate the vote of confidence, but I'm not sure I know anything that's useful to the crime desk. Has there been a new development in that case? I thought Esparza was convicted and serving time."

"No, there hasn't been, and yes, he was," I said. "But I need to talk to him. Tell me what he's like. Is he a dick, or am I going to get anywhere with him?"

"What the hell do you need with a mediocre has-been baseball coach?" he asked.

"I have a hunch," I said. "I'll fill you in later if I'm right."

There was a pause so long I wondered if I'd passed through a dead zone.

"Parker?" I said finally.

"Yeah. Sorry," he said. "Esparza's all right. Not the guy I would have pegged for fixing games and helping kids get into gambling. He's pretty full of himself, but he's not an asshole."

"Anything that might make him inclined to talk to me? Other than the fact that he probably doesn't see many breasts these days?"

"That could be enough," Parker said.

"Thanks. Tell Mel I said hi." I clicked off the call.

I pulled up outside the gates of the prison and handed my identification to the guard in the little stone shack. I gave him Esparza's name and he directed me to the visitors' parking area.

By the time I made it through security, issued a placard that told me which hallway to take and told them where I was supposed to be going, visiting hours were growing short. I tried to subtly adjust my bra as I walked, Parker's words ringing in my ears. A bra can only work with what's there, though. Maybe Esparza was a leg man.

I passed the placard through a thick plastic window at the end of the hallway. The guard on the other side looked at it, plucked a phone handset from the wall, and said something I couldn't make out into the receiver. Two minutes later, a buzzer worthy of a game show set sounded in stereo and the heavy steel door to my left clicked and swung open. Silent Jim the prison guard waved me inside.

The gray hallway smelled so strongly of ammonia, my nostrils stung. I followed it to a tiny interview room where a series of three little desks mirrored each other on a wall of the same thick plexiglass the guard sat behind. A slight man with olive skin and bushy, graying hair sat at the desk in the middle. The other two were empty. When I walked into the room, he stood. That was new. I'd been to Cold Springs a few times, though usually I was down at cellblock nine interviewing a killer who was some flavor of crazy and about to be put to death by the good people of the commonwealth for his (or her, once) crime. The murderers usually didn't stand when I came into the room.

Esparza watched me walk to the desk on my side of the glass.

I lifted the telephone receiver, wishing I had a Clorox wipe. I don't generally worry about germs, but the handset was nothing short of slimy, a film over the black plastic consisting of God-only-knows-what making me reluctant to put it near my face. The thing was heavy and there was no way to hold it gingerly. Esparza picked up his handset and I tried to forget about the sticky, bacteria-laden plastic, pressing mine to my ear and pasting a smile on my face.

"Have we met?" he asked in a light Spanish accent before I could introduce myself.

"We have not," I said, betting that Parker knew the guy at least in passing and hoping a little name-dropping would help. "I'm a friend of Grant Parker's, actually—I work with him at the *Telegraph*. I'm working on a story I think you can help me with."

"Unless it's about the state of the showers in this joint, I can't imagine how." He flashed a bright white smile, but his brown eyes didn't light.

"Not exactly." I took a deep breath, cutting my eyes to the guard in the corner, playing a game on his phone. "I'm working on a story I think may involve gambling, and I was hoping you might help me out."

He stared through the plexiglass and I held his gaze without blinking.

"Why would I want to do something like that?" he asked. "If there's one thing this place has taught me, it's that doing other people favors is for suckers. You go off and splash a card game or a dogfight across the front page, the guys who run it end up in here, and I might end up on the wrong end of a shiv."

The tough guy act was so obviously put on, it was almost funny. But laughing wasn't going to help me get what I wanted. Nearly seven years of interviewing the best and worst of society had given me a decent asshole radar. This guy wasn't a hardened criminal. I just needed to convince him to help me.

"I have no intention of telling anyone where I got my information," I said, still looking him straight in the eye. "Not only that, but I don't really care about the operation itself. I care who's playing."

"Why?"

"Research," I said, shrugging and opting for honesty. "Right now, I don't have a story assignment. I think I've got a lead on a dirty politician, but finding anything concrete on this guy is harder than salsa dancing in stilettos."

He stared for a good thirty seconds, and I stared right back, not blinking. His dark eyes softened a touch and he turned his head slowly and checked the guard, who appeared invested in killing all the bad fruit, or whatever else required one to frantically wave a finger back and forth over an iPhone screen.

"A dirty politician," he said slowly. "Someone important enough to get me the hell out of here?"

"I don't know," I said. "Maybe. While I can't imagine that the Governor and my guy share too many political ideals, I'm not sure how well they know each other. Or if they like each other."

His shoulders dropped. "I see."

"I could lie and tell you absolutely," I said after a minute. "But the best I have is maybe. I really don't know."

The corners of his lips tipped up in a half-smile. "Maybe is better than no, right?"

I nodded, trying to keep my expression neutral.

"I don't know much," he said. "But there are some political types around here who like to play cards. A lot of the games float. What you're asking about is big business, but it's also a relatively small circle of people." He paused, shaking his head. "Look, I've done some things I'm not proud of. If you were to stop by the sports dorm at RAU, you might find a pitcher who's in over his pretty-boy head. But I doubt he'll talk to you."

Maybe not, but I knew someone he might talk to.

I smiled and thanked Esparza, wondering as I watched him hang up his phone how this man had taken a turn so wrong it had landed him in this place. He obviously didn't fit in with most of the prison population.

I checked out and climbed back into my car as the sun was sinking in the western sky.

I punched the talk button on my cell phone twice so it would redial, and laughed when Parker asked if Esparza had fallen victim to my feminine wiles.

"I wouldn't know a wile if it bit me in the ass, so I'm going with no," I said. "What are you up to tonight?"

"Being boring." He sighed. "I was supposed to have a date, but Mel bailed on me about a half-hour ago. Her sister went into labor. Why?"

Perfect. I made a mental note to send balloons.

"Esparza would say I'm on a lucky streak," I said. "I need to borrow your star power. Put on something that looks expensive and meet me at Capital Ale in half an hour. I'll fill you in when I get there."

"Am I going to get shot at?" he asked.

"God, I hope not." I laughed. "But you told me once I could ask you for help if I needed it. So this is me asking."

"You really more told me than asked me, but that's cool," he said. "Going to work with you isn't as boring as sitting here watching *Die Hard* alone."

"How could young Bruce Willis and terrorists be boring?" I asked.

"Careful, you might talk yourself out of a partner."

"Point taken. Strike that."

"Expensive like coat and tie, or expensive like tux?" he asked.

"We're not going to the Oscars. I just want you to look like a celebrity. But no old baseball uniforms," I said.

"You got it." He hung up.

About to pass my exit, I jerked the steering wheel and drove home, my brain jumping from Senator Grayson to Billings the tobacco executive and back again. There was a connection. There had to be. But the sticking point hadn't changed: how had the lobbyist I was almost positive had been their go-between ended up dead? If Amesworth was in cahoots with the bad guys, like Kyle thought, then why would they kill him?

Patting Darcy's head and filling her food bowl on my way through the kitchen, I thought about Joey. He was worried about me. But it wasn't like I was going off alone to chase a criminal. I was going to a well-populated place, and taking Parker with me.

Ten minutes later, I climbed carefully back into the car in my go-anywhere black sheath dress and a pair of blood red patent leather Manolos I'd had since college. They were the first pair I'd ever bought, after spending much of my teenage years slouching to hide the height that made me different from the other girls. My five-foot-three Syracuse roommate had wealthy parents and a love of stilettos that had rubbed off on me after years of watching her wear shoes that could double as works of art while I slogged around in boots and sneakers.

I beat Parker to the restaurant and ordered a Midori sour.

Waiting in a corner booth with a good view of the door, I stirred my drink and wondered if it was smart to pull Parker into this.

When he walked in, nearly every female head in the place turned to follow his progress toward me. I had to admit, he looked the part: his tall, athletic frame was the perfect showcase for the dark chinos, emerald shirt, and leather coat that made him look like he'd just stepped out of GQ.

I returned his smile and gestured to the seat across from me.

"Thanks for coming."

"Bob might fire me if I let you get shot at again." He flashed the million-dollar grin. "So, what's up? Am I playing Hardy Boys to your Nancy Drew?"

I put my glass on the table and leveled a serious gaze at him. "Indeed. I need some dirt on RAU baseball."

"You made me get dressed up to ask me about work?"

"Specifically, I need to know about the pitchers. And who might be into gambling."

"Esparza." He nodded slowly. "Care to share what he told you?"

"He didn't say much, except that there's a pitcher I need to talk to."

"But he didn't give you a name?"

"Nope. That's where you come in."

"You don't need star power for that," he said. "Reading the stat sheets could give you a bead on who you need to talk to. Someone's record tanked halfway through the season."

"Why haven't I seen this in your column?"

"I have a suspicion, Clarke. Nothing I can prove, and certainly nothing you can print. He's a good kid in a bad situation. Assuming I'm right, anyway."

"I'm not looking to print it. I need information, not to bust a kid who's been stupid." I said as I grinned. "And reading through a billion pages of numbers sounds way less fun than getting dressed up and hauling you to a party."

"Party?" He looked around. "You need to take a powder, Clarke. I can't keep up with you tonight."

"It's Saturday night. I like the odds of a party going on at the jock dorm." I downed the last of my drink and grabbed the little black clutch I'd stuffed a handful of essentials into, unsnapping it and tossing a few bills on the table. "And a drunk pitcher is more likely to spill his guts to a celebrity than a sober one is to talk to a reporter. Let's go, superstar."

* * *

Rothschild Hall on the RAU campus is the biggest, most state-of-the-art of the school's dorms, housing the student athletes. A back-to-campus party was in full swing.

Parker strode through the doors like the building was called "Grant Parker is the Shit Dormitory," smiling and nodding at the coeds brave enough to make eye contact with him and not even flinching when at least two of them pinched his ass as he moved through the crowd. I tried to stay behind him, but the size and enthusiasm of the group made that next to impossible.

Two different boys handed me two different kinds of beer within three minutes of when I walked through the front doors, and I nodded a polite thanks and tried to keep my eyes on Parker's perfectly-tousled blond head as he scanned the giggling coeds and desperate-to-get-laid jocks, looking for whoever his statistics told him was suspect.

Music blared into the hallway from several of the rooms, and students darted in and out of the suites with drinks and food in their hands. A group of girls with their hair in pigtails strutted down the hallway in a conga line, trying to add to their train as they went.

"Conga!" A freckled blonde with purple glitter eyeshadow

squealed, letting go of her friend's hip to grab my hand as she danced past. "Come on!"

Feeling suddenly more dated than a pair of battered Doc Martens, I smiled and shook my head, waiting for them to pass before I charged after Parker. By the time I caught up to him, he'd been surrounded by a knot of college kids who were hanging on his every word as he told a story about digging his team out of a ninth-inning, three-run deficit with three three-and-outs in a row followed by a grand slam.

I laid two fingers on his elbow and he slid his eyes to me. He didn't miss a beat in his tale as he nodded subtly to a tall, dark-haired kid across the circle from him.

They erupted into spontaneous applause when he recounted crossing home plate and he laughed.

"It was fun," he said. "I played because I loved the game. Stick with that, and you'll never be unhappy."

He kept his eyes on the dark-haired kid as he spoke, and the boy suddenly became very interested in his shoes.

Bingo.

Parker shook hands all around, easily dismissing everyone except the dark-haired kid. When it was just the three of us, Parker flashed his best sports columnist grin and threw an arm around the younger pitcher's broad shoulders.

"Willis Hunt, this is Nichelle Clarke," he said. "Nichelle, this is Willis. He's going to go pro in the next couple of years, if he can get his arm under control."

The boy smiled a beer-addled smile and shook my hand sloppily.

"Thanks, Mr. Parker. I don't know about that."

"Call me Grant," Parker said, steering Willis toward a hallway that wasn't stuffed with gyrating bodies. I followed, keeping quiet and hanging on every word.

"You had one hell of a season last year," Parker said, stopping in a little alcove and sitting on a wide bench, gesturing to the simple gold sofa across from him. Willis flopped onto it. I perched on the edge of the bench next to Parker and tried to look unobtrusive.

"I did alright, I guess," Willis said.

"You had the best record in the east for the first half," Parker said.

"Half doesn't make a season," Willis mumbled, staring at his hands. "My dad and the coach told me that enough times that I won't ever forget it."

"It's a lot of pressure." Parker leaned forward and rested his elbows on his knees. "And a lot of people who want to tell you what to do. I remember."

"You were great," Willis said. "You should be a three-time Cy Young winner on your way to the Hall of Fame, man. I loved watching you play when I was a kid. My dad is a UVA alum."

"Thanks," Parker said. "Sometimes things don't go the way we think they will, do they?"

Willis raised his eyes, his dark irises sober as a preacher on Sunday. "They don't."

"You have amazing control for a kid your age," Parker said softly, holding Willis' gaze. "It was really something to watch. Then all of a sudden you're throwing wild pitches and hitting batters left and right."

"I got the jitters, I guess." Willis didn't look away, and his expression screamed that he was desperate to spill his guts. I tried not to breathe too loudly.

"But only when the odds were astronomically in your favor going into the game?" Parker arched an eyebrow.

"Mr. Parker, they'll kick me out of school," Willis whispered, conflict plain on his face. "I won't ever play again."

"You can only throw the nervous rookie thing for so long before you won't be playing anymore, anyway." Parker's deep tenor verged on hypnotic. "What happened? You owe somebody money?'"

Willis sighed, staring past Parker at the beige wall. "After my freshman season, people started to notice me. Some guys I met at a club took me to a card game one night. There were girls, an open bar, the whole deal. Just like out of a movie. I won over a thousand dollars, and I couldn't believe it was really my life."

He continued. "I went back the next weekend and the one after that, and I just kept winning. They started calling me Lucky Sixteen, you know, for my jersey number. It was a great time."

"Until you stopped winning," Parker said.

"I thought I'd get it back. They said I could have credit with them so I could keep playing. I thought I could turn it around."

"And then you ran out of credit."

Willis hitched in a deep breath and drug the back of his hand across his face. "Yeah. They said I had to pay up, and my family doesn't have that kind of cash."

"How much are you in for?" Parker asked.

"Almost thirty grand."

Holy shit, kid. I bit my tongue to keep the words from slipping out, my eyes flashing from Parker to Willis and back. Parker closed his eyes and shook his head.

"So they said you could work it off by throwing games."

"Please, Mr. Parker." A tear rolled down Willis' cheek. "If you put this in the newspaper, my career will be over."

"I have no intention of doing that." Parker shook his head. "You've been had, kid."

"They'll rat me out if I don't do what they want," Willis said. "I don't know what to do."

"Ratting you out rats them out, too," Parker said. "But this is a hell of a corner you've backed yourself into."

Willis dropped his head into his hands. "I know." The words were muffled.

Poor kid. I felt bad for him. Parker did, too.

"Let me talk to them," Parker said.

Willis raised his head slowly. "What?"

"Let me talk to them. Where are the games?"

Willis stared for a long minute.

"Why?"

"Because you're a decent kid," Parker said. "I like you. You have a chance at a future I missed. Tell me where to find a game."

"They move around," Willis said. "But one of the bartenders at the Tuscany always knows. Short guy, bald head."

Parker stood, pulling a card from his wallet and handing it to Willis. "Call if you need to talk. I know the pressure. But play your A game, kid. Your career will be over if you don't, anyway. Play every game like you might never get to play again, and you won't have any regrets."

A hitch in his voice caught my attention. Was Grant Parker tearing up?

I jumped to my feet and scooted out of the way. Parker moved back toward the front door, leaving Willis Hunt on the gold couch nodding and mumbling about dreams under his breath. I hurried after Parker, throwing a sad look at Willis over my shoulder. He was young to be in that much hot water.

"Where are we going?" I asked, following Parker back into the chilly evening air. My stomach flipped with equal parts excitement and fear.

"To a card game." Parker jerked the driver's door of my car open and slid behind the wheel. "These assholes have screwed with the wrong sport."

CHAPTER ELEVEN

The Tuscany was across town from the university. On a Saturday night, we were in for at least a half-hour drive.

I studied Parker's jawline as he wove the car in and out of traffic. "Tell me about it," I said.

"'Bout what?" he asked as he slowed for a red light.

"About baseball. What do you miss? What did you love about it? What was your best game? Freud would have a field day with that bit you just gave Willis about regret."

"I haven't talked to anyone about me and baseball in a long time."

"Talk to me."

He sighed. "Baseball was all I ever wanted to do. My dad started me in little league when I was four, and I fell in love with the way the bat rang in my hands when it connected with the ball. When other kids were going swimming in the summer, I was at the batting cages. I always got to pitching practice early and stayed late. I was varsity all through high school and my pitching got better every year."

Aside from Parker not running over anything or anyone, I wouldn't have known he even saw the other cars in front of him. His eyes stared straight ahead.

"By the time I was a senior we had won two big school state titles

and the scouts were coming to every game," he continued. "I graduated with a full scholarship to UVA, and my freshman year, I made the
travel team, pitching against juniors and seniors. My sophomore year,
I was the star. We won every game I started and I struck out a
hundred and seventy-nine hitters that year.

"About halfway through that season, the pro scouts started
showing up. I spent the rest of that year focusing on baseball. I
breathed it, I dreamed it—I don't remember anything about those
four months but practices and games and trying to impress the scouts.
And I did. I went into the draft in June and the Angels picked me in
the fourth round. The *fourth round*. I was going to get to play baseball
for a living. My dreams were all coming true."

"You're left-handed," I said. "That's good when you're a pitcher,
right?"

He glanced at me and smiled. "Yep."

"How fast could you pitch?"

"My second year in the minors, I was throwing ninety-six mile-an-
hour fastballs."

I whistled. "Wow. That's fast."

"The faster I threw, the harder time I had hitting the strike zone. I
worked my ass off getting a handle on that in double-A. I started the
next season in Salt Lake City with the triple-A team, sure I'd get to the
show by the end of summer. I wanted to play for the Generals, and
getting called up was the first step to getting traded home. I never
went out after the games. I got my sleep; I ate as well as I could living
on the bus and in shittier motels than I remembered from my tourna-
ment days. I wanted it."

"But you got hurt," I said.

"In July, just after the fourth." His hand drifted to his left shoulder
as his face twisted at the memory. "We had a four-night rotation, and
my game two nights before was tough: I threw over a hundred
pitches. I shouldn't have played that night, but it was the last game of a
big series, and the bull pen was having a rough time. They just needed
me for one hitter. Of course I went in. I was twenty-one years old and
I was invincible." The hard laugh sounded alien coming from Parker.

"I can still remember the pain. It felt like my arm was being ripped right off. The ball hit the dirt. I fell. The crowd got so quiet. I laid there and stared up at the lights and cried, because I knew it was over.

"That's pretty much it," he said, rotating his left arm. "Four surgeries later, it doesn't hurt anymore, but baseball is still a part of my past."

"Wow, Parker..." I floundered for the words that would banish the hurt I saw on his face. I wasn't positive there were any. "That well and truly sucks."

He chuckled.

"It was ten years ago," he said, turning into the Tuscany's full parking lot. "I survived. I'm okay, most of the time. But a kid with Willis Hunt's talent doesn't deserve to have the same fate because of one dumbass mistake."

"Agreed." I opened my door. "Maybe we can help Willis out of a jam and find a hell of a headline, too."

The bald bartender parted with the location of the game about three and a half seconds after Parker flashed a wad of fifties.

"Enjoy your game, pal." He waved a dismissal at us and turned to a striking redhead who wanted a glass of Shiraz.

Parker glanced at his watch when we got back to the car. "It's not even ten yet. You ever played cards?"

"Nothing racier than Go Fish," I said. "How about you?"

"Twice a month with the guys from photo for four years running." He grinned. "Much smaller stakes, but I hold my own."

"You're just damned handy to have around today."

"I do my best."

A few minutes later, we stopped outside what looked like an abandoned strip mall.

"There's no one here," I said, surveying the parking lot. "You think we're the ones who've been had?"

"Oh, ye of little faith." Parker pulled around back, where the lot was awfully crowded for such a dark building.

"Nice," I said.

We walked along the sidewalk in silence, stopping when we reached the door near the far end of the building.

"Assuming the place isn't haunted, there's a party going on in there," I whispered. Parker raised a fist to rap on the door.

A lock squealed inside the door and it opened a crack.

"Looking for a card game," Parker said, cash in hand. He laid an easy arm across my shoulders and I stiffened, then attempted to feign boredom. The door opened wider and a squat, broad man with a hawk nose gave us the once over.

"Seven-fifty cover," he said.

Parker didn't bat an eye, pulling fifteen bills off the stack and handing them over. Well, there went the cash I was hoarding for Louboutin's spring collection.

The man moved aside and I stayed close to Parker, my stomach lurching slightly as the door slammed shut behind us. Now what?

The room looked like a gentleman's study out of an old movie: rich, wood-paneled walls, a long bar with shiny brass fittings, and thick, felt-topped tables scattered over the cherry floors. I scanned the faces at the tables, looking for Grayson and trying not to sigh when I didn't see him.

A tall, thin man with graying temples pointed Parker to an empty seat in the far corner, and I followed.

"Hey!" A debonair guy with a Sean Connery vibe looked up from his hand and laid his cigar in a marble ashtray. "You're Grant Parker!"

I sucked in a deep breath, waiting for Squatty the doorman to come throw us out on our asses. Parker flashed the million-dollar grin and offered a hand.

"Guilty. Mind if I sit in?"

"Hell, no." The man stuck the cigar back in the corner of his mouth and shook Parker's hand. "Not every day I get to play cards with a star pitcher."

"Isn't it?" Parker spoke so softly I wasn't sure I heard him, and I really hoped no one else did. He pulled out the empty chair, folding his long frame into it. I stood behind him, a disinterested half-smile fixed on my face. Captain Cigar glanced at me as he dealt Parker in.

"You don't want to play, sweetheart?" he asked.

"No thanks," I said, winking. "I've been told I have a lousy poker face."

I turned, looking around at the fifty or so faces hunched over cards and hoping to pick out Ted Grayson's features. Still no luck.

I made my way around the room, chatting up the doorman, catching dirty looks from a few of the players who shielded their cards when I walked by, and coming up with diddly squat.

Reaching the bar, I boosted myself onto a stool, and ordered a glass of Riesling. I studied my six female barmates. All pretty. All dressed well. All young. What were they doing hanging out here? I caught a snippet of the conversation two stools over, where a blonde was carrying on about the miracle of Botox.

"Nice shoes," a voice from my left shoulder said. "Kirkwood?"

"Manolo," I said with a grin. "And thanks. I've had these a long time."

My eyes met large, dark ones set perfectly in deep olive skin. The woman leaning on the bar next to me had flowing jet tresses that were thicker than mine, a straight nose, full lips, and eyelashes most women would trade a kidney for in a heartbeat.

"They're timeless," she said. "And you're new. Please tell me you don't give a shit about having someone shoot poison into your face."

I laughed.

"I'd rather spend my money on shoes."

"My kind of girl." Her teeth flashed white against her dark skin. "I'm Lakshmi."

"Nichelle," I said. "Nice to meet you."

"Likewise," she said. "Who'd you come with?"

I pointed to Parker.

"Nice," she said.

"What about you?" I asked.

She gestured to a goateed man with thin shoulders and dark hair.

"He's a brilliant doctor, but he sucks at cards," she said. "I'm still not sure why he likes for me to hang around and watch him play, but at least he's not the only one." She nodded and raised her glass when the man winked at her.

I eyeballed the women in the room and figured they were walking trophies for these guys, but returned her smile.

"Me, either," I lied. "A doctor, huh? What kind?"

"Neurosurgeon," she said. "He also teaches at RAU Medical School. I'm a grad student at the university."

"Studying what?" I asked.

"Statistics and Political Science," she said. "I'm going to be the next Nate Silver."

"Oh, yeah?" I grinned. I liked her. "What do you make of the Senate race?"

"Grayson by two, two and a half," she said, confidence radiating off her in waves. "He won't hang on by much, but he's not in any real danger. Numbers don't lie."

"Have you ever seen him here?" I hoped the question sounded more casual than it felt.

"Ted? Playing poker?" Lakshmi threw back her head and laughed. "No. There are too many people here. He wouldn't risk it getting out."

Damn. I took another swig of my drink. Now I owed Parker seven hundred and fifty dollars, and I'd struck out.

She stood and excused herself to go to the restroom as I set the glass back on the bar, turning toward Parker. He was grinning while Captain Cigar was sweating buckets across the table.

He nodded in my direction and I smiled. At least one of us was having fun.

The blonde with the Botox addiction let out a high, squealing laugh that smacked of too much wine, and I turned toward her. She was chatting with a petite redhead, who was grinning at Lakshmi's doctor friend. The blonde leaned her chin on her friend's shoulder and giggled. "I hope he's winning. You know he's spending a pretty penny to have her sit here and watch him play cards. Maybe he'll get his money's worth later. I will never understand why men pay for sex. Isn't it cheaper to buy a girl a piece of jewelry and a nice dinner every once in a while?"

Oh. My. God. I gulped my wine so I'd have a reason to keep my mouth from falling open. Maybe I hadn't wasted my evening, after all. That could be a hell of a story.

Lakshmi walked back into the room and I pasted a smile on my face. We talked for an hour, about her brilliant statistics professor, shoes, and everything else but politics. When she'd had a third glass of merlot, I steered the conversation to more personal things.

"Where're you from?" I asked.

"D.C." Her words were starting to slur. "I lived there the longest, anyway. My dad was military intelligence. He works for the state department, now."

"So you come by your interest in politics honestly?" I smiled.

"I guess so," she said. "It's hard to not be cynical about politics when you know politicians, though. They're mostly weasels."

I stared for a second, her laughter at the idea of Grayson playing poker popping up in my thoughts.

No way.

But she'd used his first name. Could she know him? Like, in the Biblical sense?

"Do you know very many politicians?" My voice was too high. I cleared my throat and took a deep breath. "How about Senator Grayson?"

"He's an asshole. Everyone thinks he's so charming, such an upstanding family man." Lakshmi put her glass on the table and shook her head, snapping her mouth shut like she'd thought better of what she was going to say.

I stayed quiet.

"Well." She flashed a crooked smile and it was easy to see why men would pay to be with her. She looked like she belonged in a painting. "If people only knew."

Christ on a cracker, as Eunice would say. Not cards. Call girls.

The photo of Grayson's family flashed up from my memory and I pictured his short, round wife with her mousy eighties mom hair standing next to Lakshmi.

My gut said I'd found where the money was going.

If I was right about it coming from Billings, I just needed the filler pieces of my puzzle. Was Amesworth their go-between? And how and why had he ended up in a shallow grave?

"I think I'm done with the wine," Lakshmi said, standing.

"It was nice to meet you," I said. "Good luck."

"I make my own luck," she said. "It gives me the best probability of getting what I want."

I watched Lakshmi stumble toward her doctor friend, who was saying his goodnights, and wondered: was Grayson being bribed and blackmailed at the same time? Hookers, no matter their looks or price, are never good for political careers. What if Grayson had killed Amesworth to keep his secret?

Why was it that every time I found an answer, three new questions popped up? It was like an exhausting game of mental whack-a-mole. I pulled out my cell phone and checked my email. Nothing interesting. And it was after midnight already.

I looked up, and Parker caught my eye. The other men were trickling out. I nodded slightly and he stood, sweeping a stack of bills off the tabletop.

He shook hands with the other men at his table, bending over Captain Cigar from earlier and looking toward the door. A tall, thin man with platinum hair and an expensive suit had joined our doorman to bid everyone goodnight.

Parker held a finger up at me and made his way to the door. I followed, lagging behind a few steps as he took the guy aside and moved quickly from pleasantries to serious conversation. The man shook his head, holding his hands up. Parker took half a step closer, his easy smile fading, and said something else. I had a pretty good feeling he'd found who Willis Hunt owed money to.

Pulling out a roll of bills, Parker peeled several off and pressed them into the other man's palm, an uncharacteristically serious gaze causing his green eyes to narrow. The other man pocketed the cash and nodded.

Parker turned and caught my elbow. "Ready?"

"Am I ever," I muttered. "Do I even have to ask what you just did?"

He steered me out the door, smiling a goodnight at people we passed and muttering out of the corner of his mouth. "Probably not, but give me a second and I'll tell you, anyway."

I took my keys from him and jumped into the driver's seat, starting the car before he even had his door closed.

"Where's the fire? It's after midnight, you know," he said, clicking his seatbelt into place.

"Time doesn't matter to the news," I said. "I just got the scoop of the century. Now I have to prove it."

"Sound like a good time was had by all." He grinned. "Willis is even. As long as he stays away. I promised to keep their game out of the paper and left my winnings there."

"About that. I'll pay you back if you'll just let me know how much," I said.

He pulled out the cash roll.

"Zero," he said. "I told you I was good. I won my seven-fifty plus another grand, which I left with our host."

"Nice," I said, thankful I didn't owe him my shoe money. "Thanks, Parker."

"Thank you. I've known Willis was in trouble for months, and you gave me a way to get him out. Besides, this was definitely better than watching a movie alone."

"Indeed," I said under my breath, turning the radio up and pressing the accelerator harder. With an even juicier possible reason for Grayson being on the take, I was doubly anxious to get some research in before I crashed after a very long day.

The silent ride back to Parker's motorcycle was short.

I waved goodnight and pointed my car toward the Fan. Four blocks from home, I decided to take a small detour past Grayson's house and see what I could see.

CHAPTER TWELVE

THE HOUSE WAS a gorgeous Georgian restoration with soaring ivory columns juxtaposed against deep red brick, the entire front lit by floodlights so bright that even at two ticks 'til one, it was noon in the Graysons' front yard. The Graysons had to be gone. Who could sleep through that?

I tapped my fingers on the steering wheel, debating for half a second before I climbed out and walked the length of the yard on the opposite side of the street. I wanted a closer look, but wasn't stupid enough to go traipsing around outside a home which had been recently burglarized.

I studied the front of the house as I walked, assuming I wouldn't see anything out of the ordinary.

Call girls. The guy had a wife, a kid, and a voter base that didn't look kindly on philandering. So to keep the wife from finding out he was cheating, he was taking bribes. Seemed reasonable enough.

Still didn't give me a why on a break-in or a dead guy.

Turning on my heel, I started back up the street, looking at a large window that faced a ten-foot wall of hedges on the south side of the house. A window that appeared to have a hastily-patched hole in it.

Shit. I stepped closer to the middle of the street, peering into the darkness. I still wasn't going over there, but by squinting I could see duct tape crisscrossing a full pane of that window.

That, plus the presence of a security system meant this was almost certainly not the work of the catburglar. That guy got in and out of houses without a trace. He was the Criss Angel of breaking and entering. No way he punched out a window.

And no way a broken window doesn't set off the alarm. Right?

I climbed back into my car, trying to remember what Aaron had said that morning and wondering for the millionth time if the robbery was a political ploy or the key to this whole damned thing.

My headlights hit off a shadow on my front porch when I turned into the driveway, and I squinted into the darkness again. I'd taken all the summer flowerpots down already, but it looked like there was something hanging from the ceiling.

I hopped out of the car and hurried toward the sidewalk, a small, puffy shape coming into focus as I got closer to the steps.

"No." I stopped, my hand flying to my mouth, stomach churning.

A small furry shape. Hanging from a thick cord. My legs felt rooted to the sidewalk. I needed to see and didn't want to know, both with such overwhelming urgency that I couldn't move. I tried to scream, and finally was able to form a word. "Darcy!"

An explosion of yipping came from behind the closed front door, followed by unmistakeable scratching on the wood.

"What the hell?" A sob escaped my throat at the familiar bark, safely inside the house.

I ran up to the porch, poking the macabre new decor. Stuffed. I snatched it down and examined it. It was a toy. A stuffed toy Pomeranian dog. A piece of paper poked out of the collar.

I glanced around, hugging the doll to my chest and unlocking the door as quickly as the pitch dark and my fumbling fingers would allow.

Safely inside with the deadbolt and chain fastened behind me, I slumped to the floor and scooped my very alive, very hyper dog into my arms, burying my face in her fur and sobbing until she started to wriggle and whine.

"I'm so very glad to see you, princess," I said, wiping my eyes with one hand and ruffling the fur behind her ears with the other. She yipped, then bounced out of my lap and down the hall toward the kitchen. I got up to follow, turning on lights as I walked, the skin-crawly feeling I'd had on the porch returning when I pulled the note from the fake dog's collar.

Dear Nosy Nichelle, Next time it won't be a prop. BACK OFF.

Darcy barked, and I found her in the kitchen, tapping her food bowl with her foot.

"It's not dinnertime, girl. You ate already," I said.

She tapped again, and I turned for the pantry. "I've never been so glad to have to feed you in the middle of the night, that's for damned sure," I said, my hands shaking as I opened the can.

She gobbled her food while I unknotted the bungee cord around the toy's neck and examined it in the light. Nothing special: blue with black flecks, available at a million hardware stores and every Wal-Mart.

I stared at it, knowing I'd likely wrecked any fingerprints anyone might be able to lift from it and wondering who would do something so heinous. And how they knew what kind of dog I had.

I shoved the toy dog, cord, and note deep into the kitchen garbage can, covering them with tossed-out food and used tissues and shuddering when I slammed the lid. Walking through the house, I checked locks and debated calling someone.

Jenna and my mom were my go-tos with problems, but this would only worry them. I finally had Joey's number, but he'd probably hire me a bodyguard if I told him about this, and I didn't even know for sure it had anything to do with Amesworth's murder. Fifty people had seen me at the card game just an hour ago: what if someone had recognized me? Or what if the cat burglar was tired of being in the news?

As hard as I tried, I couldn't shake the creeped-out feeling. I checked the locks twice more, looked in all the closets and behind the shower curtain, and flipped every light in the house on.

I picked up the phone to call Kyle three times, but the years apart and the late hour stopped me before I pushed send. Antsy, I flipped through TV channels until I found a *Friends* rerun and turned the volume up too loud. I paced. I ran back through my week, wondering if there was anything I'd missed.

"I hope Aaron doesn't have plans for Monday morning," I finally told Darcy. "Because I'll be waiting with a cup of Starbucks Pike Place and a long list of not so fun questions when he gets to work."

I was afraid to take her outside, but she seemed to enjoy indoor fetch just as much, and I tossed her worn out old squirrel for twice as long as usual.

By the time she was played out and curled into a russet pompom in her bed, I had a decent list of questions for my favorite detective. I couldn't bring myself to turn the lights off, and fell asleep wondering if I'd still be Aaron's favorite reporter by lunchtime Monday.

My mishmash nightmares were full of dangling dogs and burning warehouses.

* * *

Aaron was happy to see the coffee when he got to work Monday, but he didn't look thrilled to see me. He faked it pretty well, covering his startled expression with a grin and waving me into his office.

"You going to start making a habit of dropping by unannounced?" He flipped the light on and gestured to one of the worn black plastic office chairs. "Because I could get you a key."

"No thanks," I said, taking the seat and crossing my left knee over my right. "Just in case anything ever goes missing out of the lockup again, I'd rather not be on the suspect list."

"Let's hope we don't have to worry about that." He settled into his rolling chair, shooting me a look that very clearly said "cut the shit and tell me what you want."

"The robbery at the Grayson house," I said. "There are several things that don't add up."

"Nichelle, you know as well as I do that there are B-and-Es and then there are B-and-Es." he sighed. "If I tell you anything beyond what's in the report, Grayson will have my badge. That guy may have a perfect smile, but he's a mean bastard when you cross him. It's hard to get to that level in national politics without being a certain kind of prick."

"It wasn't the cat burglar," I said, putting a hand up when he opened his mouth just in case it was to argue. I really didn't want Aaron to lie to me. "I know it wasn't the cat burglar, because not only does the alarm system not fit, but there was a hole in one of the downstairs windows. That was conveniently left out of the report."

He closed his eyes. "I know."

I studied him for a second. "Remember that favor you promised me several months ago? I think I want to call it in. What the hell is going on here?"

He shook his head. "I'm not sure you want to do that. Because I really, honest-to-God don't know. Off the record?"

"Do I get comments any other way lately?"

"We left the window out of the report on purpose. Like I told you Saturday, the general consensus is that this crime was not related, but we want whoever did do it to assume we think it's the cat burglar. The Graysons swear nothing of value is missing, that their maids came in and turned off the alarm system, but whoever broke in was watching for that and went in after it was deactivated. The crew was cleaning upstairs and someone heard a noise and came down, and the would-be thief took off."

Something tickled the back of my brain.

"No one saw the intruder?"

Aaron flipped open a file folder and read something for a second.

"Maid insisted the sound she heard came from the back of the house, which is where the senator's private study is," Aaron said. "But Grayson was very particular about the officers not going in there to check for prints."

"I bet he was," I said, finally connecting the nagging feeling to my memory.

Troy Wright's mother was a maid.

And she'd said her crew cleaned a senator's house.

I bounced in my seat.

"We have no idea what might actually have been missing," Aaron continued. "The damned campaign people are hollering that it's political—which it may very well be—but when the victims in a case like this don't want to cooperate, we find ourselves in a very awkward situation. He's a high-profile guy, so it's big news. If you print what I'm allowed to give you on the record right now, we're going to look like the goddamned Keystone Cops."

"Good thing you don't have to run for office." I grinned.

"True enough. But if we're going to look like third-rate nincompoops, I'd rather it be because we actually screwed something up."

"Fair enough," I said. "What do you make of the Billings case?" I asked, changing the subject.

"The ATF is running that show," he said, leaning back in the chair and lacing his hands behind his head. "I heard a rumor that you have an old friend who has recently joined their ranks over there. I bet you know more about it than I do."

"I doubt that. I know Kyle's convinced he's got his man. I'm not so sure."

"Oh, yeah?" Aaron raised his eyebrows. "What makes you say that?"

"A hunch, mostly. I don't have anything concrete."

"Always go with the gut. Mine has rarely steered me wrong. But I'm not in much of a position to help you with that. Not unless I want a pissing contest with the new special agent at the ATF, which I really, really don't. Good luck, though. Don't get shot at any more."

I laughed. "Thanks, Aaron. Sorry I ambushed you."

"You brought coffee. We're good."

* * *

Sitting in my parked car in front of police headquarters, I dialed Joyce Wright, certain she wasn't home, but hoping I could leave her a message. She picked up on the second ring.

"Joyce!" I said, so startled at her soft "hello" I almost dropped the phone. "Good morning! I thought you'd be at work. It's Nichelle Clarke from the *Telegraph*. Do you have a few minutes to talk to me?"

"I got all day for you." Her voice caught. "That story that was in the newspaper yesterday about my boy—there's no way I can ever repay you for that."

A warm flush flowed from the pit of my stomach, putting a smile on my face. Eunice had done a beautiful job with the pages, starting the story on the front of the "Richmond Lives" section with a collage of the photos Joyce had loaned me and running several more with the jump copy. I didn't often write stories that touched people the way Joyce's voice told me this one had touched her.

"I'm so glad you liked it." I had obsessed over it to the point of irritating the hell out of Eunice, who assured me it was lovely and the woman wouldn't be able to help being happy with it. I was glad she was right.

"It's beautiful," she said. "That sports reporter came by here early and picked Troy up to take him to the baseball stadium. He was more excited than I've seen him since the Christmas he got his first bike. You're good people, Miss Clarke, as my grandmomma would have said."

"Nichelle," I corrected. "And thank you. I have a question for you: you said the other day that you work in the Fan. Do you work in Senator Grayson's home, by any chance?"

She chuckled. "I do," she said. "I read your story about that break-in. Did the police tell you that nonsense? Because it wasn't in the middle of the night. It was after seven in the morning, and I had just gotten there. They said me coming downstairs scared the damned thief away."

"So I have learned, though not on the record," I said, thinking that an exclusive with Joyce would be a coup, but might get her into trouble if Grayson didn't want the real story in the press. And with what Aaron had said about wanting to keep the fact that it wasn't the cat burglar under wraps, it could muck up the PD's investigation and get me on their shit list as a bonus. That wasn't a good place for the newspaper's crime reporter to be.

"Joyce, do you have time for a cup of coffee?" I asked, checking the clock. I'd already missed three-quarters of the morning news budget meeting by going to see Aaron, which meant I'd have some explaining to do when I got to the office if I didn't want to end up in trouble with Bob. But as long as I didn't tell him everything, the idea of an exclusive might keep me out of hot water, and just because she told me what happened didn't mean I had to run it. She might know something about Grayson that would help me figure out what he was up to.

"I have to have the decaf these days on account of my blood pressure," she said. "It's hell, getting old. But why not? I been suspended from work. They say I can't come back until they know for sure I didn't break that window at the Grayson house and call the police to cover it up."

I almost dropped my phone for the second time in five minutes.

"Are you serious?" My thoughts ran to the aging furniture in the tiny living room and the boy with the electric smile who wanted to go to college. It wasn't a good time for his single mom to be out of work. "What is this, 1955?"

She laughed.

"I guess things don't change as much as people like to think, Miss Clarke. I got family and some savings. As long as they don't take too long about figuring out who did do it, we'll get along."

I asked her to meet me at Thompson's on Cary Street in half an hour as I pulled into the office garage. I stepped off the elevator and headed straight to Bob's open door, mostly because I knew he'd only get more pissed off if I tried to avoid him.

He glared when I tapped on his door frame, rolling his chair away from his computer and waving me into his office. Thunder rumbled through a wall of low, gray clouds outside the window, mother nature chiming in with her annoyance. I dropped into my usual orange-velour-upholstered wing chair and met the glare head on. Crossing my legs, I bounced my dangling left foot so much that my pink sling-back Jimmy Choo slipped right off my heel and dropped to the floor.

"I wouldn't get too comfortable, Nicey," Bob practically growled. I grimaced. He didn't get mad at me very often. "You missed the news budget meeting for the second time in as many weeks, and this time I didn't even get the courtesy of a warning phone call. You're a good reporter, kid, and you know I've got a soft spot for you, but Les is angling to give Shelby half your job already. You really don't need to force me into his corner. What the hell is going on with you lately?"

"I'm working on a story," I began then halted, still not sure how to tell him enough to get me out of this jam, but not tell him so much as to get me into another one. There were two people on our reporting staff Bob held in higher regard than me: Grant Parker and Trudy Montgomery. And I was desperate to avoid the appearance of pulling a Shelby with Trudy's beat. I really didn't think that was what I was doing, but I was terrified Bob would see it that way. I took a deep breath. Just the facts, Nichelle.

"I went by Ted Grayson's house the other night, and the break-in there was not the work of the cat burglar," I said. "The PD is keeping that all hush-hush because they don't want to piss off the senator—at least not while he still is the senator—but there's something fishy going on there, Bob. I can feel it. I just need a little time to figure out what it is."

He sat back in the chair and heaved a heavy sigh.

"Ted Grayson, huh? Have you talked to Trudy?"

"No," I said, and his eyebrows went up. "So far, what I'm dealing with is clearly a crime story. I didn't see the need to bother her during election season. She's already up to her neck in deadlines."

Bob studied me carefully for a long minute, then finally shook his head at me.

"What else have you got? You were unusually productive last week, but I need copy from you for today. Since you missed the meeting, I have no idea what you have coming in."

"I may have something on this robbery, actually," I said. "Aaron couldn't give me anything on the record, but the Graysons' maid was the one who called the cops, and she's meeting me for coffee in a little while."

"Nice." He nodded. "Not to turn you away from a good lead, but I know you, Nicey. It hasn't occurred to you that the maid could get fired for talking to you?"

"I don't have to print what I get from her," I said. "Besides, they already suspended her. They say she can't come back to work until the break-in is solved. It's ridiculous. If someone doesn't figure this out soon, she'll be looking for a new job anyway, and that's unfair. She might be able to point me to something I can get on the record, though."

"I see. So you have to find out who broke into the senator's house so she can go back to work?"

"Something like that. The more noble the cause, the more determined I am."

"Why do I have a bad feeling about this?" Bob leaned forward, resting his elbows on his knees. "Oh, wait; because the last time you decided to play Woodward and Bernstein, you almost got yourself killed."

"I remember. But I'm not investigating anything this time." I hoped the lie was convincing as it slid through my teeth. "I'm taking a source on a robbery story for coffee because she's a nice woman and I like her. That's all. If I can make more of a story than a day two out of it without getting her in trouble, I will."

"You're a lousy liar and you know it," he said. "But I trust you enough to let you go with it. I also need a follow on the thing with the jewelry store today. Les tells me that story went viral on Facebook—thirty thousand shares in one day—so the number crunchers want you to stay on top of it."

"I suppose it's not every day there's a pickup buried in the side of a building. I'm glad I had one that shut him up for a day."

"You didn't shut him up," he said. "Les is like a dog with a bone when he wants something. And he thinks putting Shelby on the courthouse would be the best thing to happen to journalism since moveable type. All your Facebook popularity did was strengthen his case that you're the best cops reporter in town and we should let you focus on the PD."

He looked up. "You want to think about it?" Bob's voice softened. "It would give you more free time and it would get Les off your ass."

"No. I wouldn't know what to do with free time if I had it, anyway." I didn't want to give up the courthouse because the trial stories were often juicier and wider-read than the initial crime reports. Which was exactly why Shelby wanted it. "And before you ask, no, I'm not handing the PD over to Shelby, either. I have sources there who skate dangerously close to being friends, and I don't want to give that up."

"I respect the hell out of your ambition, kid. Just take some advice from an old man: don't put one shiny heel out of line," Bob said. "Also, don't piss Ted Grayson off. I know he has some friends upstairs, and I know they would not hesitate to can you if he asked them to."

Great.

"Yes, sir." I stood and smoothed my skirt. "Anything else?"

"Other than don't get yourself killed, which should be obvious, but in your case seems to bear repeating?" Bob asked with a wry smile. "Just one thing: if your gut tells you to ask Trudy about the Grayson thing, do it. I don't need you ladies in some sort of standoff because she thinks you're bigfooting her territory. And don't miss the meeting tomorrow."

"You got it, chief," I said, flashing a grin and turning for the door.

* * *

I just barely beat Joyce to the coffee shop, and when I'd ordered myself a skinny white mocha and her a decaf caramel macchiato, we settled into overstuffed armchairs in the corner.

"It took me fifteen minutes to get over here," she said, staring at the line of brake lights on West Cary. "Silly little storm pops up and folks around here drive like they ain't never seen a raindrop."

I grinned. "That they do. But I'm guilty of holing up in my house like the zombie apocalypse is coming when there are more than three flakes of snow on the ground, so I can't say too much. Except that in my defense, I'm from Texas. Everything shuts down when it snows."

I studied Joyce's kind face and soft, honest eyes. Hardworking. Forthright. Her canary yellow shoulder-padded suit looked like it had walked out of a 1989 Sears catalog, but it was clean and pressed. I couldn't believe she'd done anything wrong.

If I was right about this, was I right about Billings, too? Kyle clearly thought he had his man, and while Billings might not be a stand-up guy, there was a difference between being a greedy asshole in business and being a murderer. Like, a life prison sentence.

"Joyce, did you see anyone at the Graysons' house on Friday morning?" I asked.

She met my eyes straight on and shook her head slowly.

"I was upstairs cleaning the bathroom, and I heard a noise downstairs. I thought it was Mrs. Grayson, coming in early from her trip. She goes to New York to shop all the time now, and I wanted to ask her if she was ready for me to change out the linens to the winter sets, so I went down the back stairs, calling to her. I heard footsteps, and when I got down there, the door was standing open. I peeked into the senator's office and saw the broken window, but I didn't go in there because he's very particular about no one being in that room but him. I closed the door, called the police and Mrs. Grayson, and then waited for someone to show up."

"What kind of footsteps did you hear?" I asked.

She furrowed her brow. "I'm not sure I follow you."

"Were they light, sharp, loud?" I asked. "If you think about what different kinds of shoes sound like on wood flooring, what do you think the person was wearing, and do you see them as large or small?"

She tipped her head to one side and twisted her mouth, considering that for a second before her lips popped into a perfect O.

"I know who it was," she whispered, her left hand flying to her mouth. "Oh, Jesus, Miss Clarke, I think I know who it was."

"Who?" I leaned forward in my seat.

"I don't know the man's name, but I've seen him," Joyce said. "He's come to talk to the senator a handful of times here lately. He dresses like a western movie and drives a big pickup truck, and those boots he wears clomp on that floor in the back hall something terrible. That's why I heard him from the other corner of the house. But why would he break in? He'd been invited over plenty of times."

She lost me at "big pickup truck" and "boots." I stared at her, my brain reeling quickly through different pieces of my week. I dug in my bag for my cell phone and pulled up the *Telegraph's* mobile site, searching for my story on the jewelry store.

"This pickup truck?" I said, flipping the screen around.

She studied the photo on the screen for what seemed like a long time. "I think so, yes, though I can't see the front of this one, and I never paid attention to his plates," she said, handing the phone back. "Did he hurt himself?"

"No." I laid the phone on the table and stared at the photo. "He hurt some other people, though. How sure are you that his boots are what you heard?"

"As sure as I can be, given that I didn't see him."

"Did you tell the police about this man?"

"I didn't even think to," she said. "It hadn't occurred to me, about how the shoes sounded, until you asked me that question. They didn't ask me that. Do you know who drives this pickup, Miss Clarke? Maybe I can go back to work soon, after all.'"

"I sure hope so, Joyce," I said, locking the phone and tucking it back into my bag. "I would love to visit with you more, but I have to get back to the office and see what I can find out about this. Thank you so much for your time."

"Of course. Miss Clarke?"

I stopped mid-stride and turned back to her.

"The detective I spoke to gave me a card. Should I tell him about this? What you asked me about the shoes?"

I nodded. I wasn't sure they'd run down a lead based on faraway footfalls, but it couldn't hurt for her to call and tell them.

I darted to the car without bothering to open my umbrella, my brain rushing a hundred miles an hour through what I knew about this story. It got sexier—and more convoluted—by the minute.

Driving back to my office as fast as traffic would allow, I shivered a little in the chill that had come with the storm and cranked up the heat, wishing I'd thought to check the weather and grab a jacket on my way out to accost Aaron. I ticked off what I knew in time to the swishing of the windshield wipers as I waited for the light to turn green.

The girl at the jewelry store said the guy who ran into the building was a tobacco farmer. Kyle was probably looking for this farmer. James Billings, the VP at Raymond Garfield, and Amesworth, the dead lobbyist, were funneling money to Senator Grayson through the tobacco lobby to pay for his secret sexual escapades. And Joyce seemed pretty sure the farmer had broken into Grayson's private study. Which meant there was something in there he wanted, and if she spooked him, he might not have gotten it.

Parking in the garage, I glimpsed Trudy Montgomery's shiny convertible a few slots down. The nagging feeling I needed to talk to her was too strong to ignore.

I glanced at the clock. Just past noon. I had four hours to get Bob his stories. Plenty of time to have a heart-to-heart with the *Telegraph's* resident political insider.

CHAPTER THIRTEEN

"I'VE ALWAYS ADMIRED your knowledge of the inner workings of D.C."
I smiled at Trudy from her office doorway, sipping plain coffee
because the last of my white chocolate syrup had disappeared. "Bob is
right. You know more about the players up there than anyone this
side of the beltway."

Trudy cocked her head to one side, turning her chair toward me.
"Thank you. I think. Why do I feel a 'but' coming on here, Nichelle?"

I took a deep breath. I liked Trudy. I respected her work. I needed
her to tell me what she knew about Grayson, but more than that, I
really hoped she didn't know what I knew. It's easy to get close to
sources when you work a beat for a long time, and I didn't want to
think Trudy might be looking past Senator Grayson's transgressions
because she liked him. But it wasn't impossible.

"Not a 'but.' A 'so.'" I said. "So—how is it that you don't know Ted
Grayson is taking bribes?"

"What in the pea-picking hell are you talking about? Ted Grayson's
one of the straightest arrows on Capitol Hill. He wouldn't take a bribe
if his life depended on it."

"Only if his sex life depended on it," I muttered.

"Pardon?" She arched an eyebrow.

"Nothing." I waved a hand. "You really don't know anything about this? No one in the opposing campaign has anything on it?"

"I don't have the first clue what you're talking about," she said, never breaking eye contact. "Why don't you step in here and have a seat and let's figure it out, shall we?"

I obliged, shutting the door behind me and settling into the chair opposite her.

"I went by the campaign office Friday night, looking for information on the robbery at the Grayson house," I said.

"There some reason you didn't just ask me?" She leaned back in her chair.

"You didn't answer your phone."

"What did you find in your visit to the campaign office that makes you think Grayson is on the take? Was there a confession letter taped to the front door?"

"I talked to a girl who works there. She said she overheard him arguing with two other men who asked him what they were paying him for. I've been running my ass off chasing this murder story on the lobbyist, and Grayson's name just keeps coming up. If he's the straightest arrow on the hill, we're in serious trouble."

"Do you have anyone to corroborate this story? Or any other proof?"

"Grayson is taking bribe money from Raymond Garfield tobacco and who knows who else. Trust me. You want my notes?"

"I think I can do my own research, doll. And I will. In November." Trudy ignored me when I opened my mouth to protest. "Do you have any idea the lengths a campaign can go to plant information? The Internet is a powerful tool. If you have the right people doing it, you can make anyone look guilty of anything. This has been the single nastiest race I've ever covered, and it's not even October yet. Unless you've got a photo of Grayson standing over the corpse with a weapon and blood on his hands, you have nothing I'm interested in. And even then, I want the negative."

"Trudy, I've covered cops for a long time—" I began.

"I know, and you could be on to something. Or you could be

looking too hard for something that's not there in an effort to get catch the eye of a certain section editor at the *Washington Post*. That's immaterial to me, really. If Grayson's dirty, which I would have a hard time believing, then he'll be dirty when the election's over, too. And I'll trust your information a lot more the second week of November."

Her computer beeped and she turned her attention to the screen.

"The new *Post* poll has Grayson by two." She glanced at me.

"I can't let this go," I said. "I have a dead guy and a man in prison I'm almost positive shouldn't be. And I'm not sure that's even all of it."

She stared at me. "I believe you. At least, I believe you believe what you're saying. But you really ought to drop it. I am not risking my reputation based on your gut. You're a big girl. If you must chase it, go on. What do I care? If you dig something up on him, you're that much more valuable at cops and courts. Or maybe someone in D.C. will notice you. If you don't, it's your job on the line, not mine. Just watch it. If you're dealing with Calhoun's campaign, he'll come at you harder after this poll. You'll have a helluva time knowing who to trust."

I nodded, pushing myself out of the chair and turning for the door. "Thanks, Trudy." I paused and looked back at her. "You don't know anyone else in the newsroom who likes white mochas, do you?"

"I'm a hot tea girl, myself," she said. "Why?"

"No reason." I let myself out, thinking about my deadlines and Joyce and wondering if I could pump Aaron on the farmer without him knowing what I was up to.

* * *

I dialed Aaron's cell phone, tapping a pen on my desk blotter.

Why didn't Trudy want a story this big? Bob was right—she knew everything about everyone inside the beltway. I replayed her nonchalant dismissal in my head. She couldn't possibly want me walking such a close line with a big story on her beat. Did she know something she wasn't letting on? It hadn't seemed like she was lying, but she was obviously tight with Grayson. Could she be trying to throw me off to cover for him?

"What now?" Aaron barked when he picked up.

"Did you guys hold that farmer who ran into the jewelry store over for a hearing?" I asked, unfazed by his annoyance. I was fairly sure a guy flashing wads of cash around the jewelry store would have easily made bail, but it didn't hurt to ask.

"He was out in two hours," Aaron said. "Hearing is tomorrow morning. Why?"

"Bob wants a follow on the story today." I twisted my fingers into my hair. It wasn't a lie, because Bob had asked me for a story, but it still felt a little smarmy. "I can tease the hearing. I'll pop in and write it up for Wednesday, too." An evidence hearing wouldn't get thirty thousand Facebook shares in a hundred years, but it would make Bob happy. And at least remove one of Les' reasons for bitching.

I thanked Aaron and hung up, drumming my fingers on the handset and staring at the cream wall of my cubicle before I flipped my computer open and searched for the police report on the accident at the jewelry store. I copied down the farmer's address and grabbed my bag, hurrying back to the elevator. While calling would certainly be faster, I'd get a better read on whether the guy was lying to me if we were face to face. I wasn't sure if or where he fit into my larger story, but the possibility of getting Joyce back to work was enough to make the drive out to Powhatan worth it.

Virginia's early-autumn splashes of warm reds and bright yellows blurred with the green that still clung to most of the trees as I laid on the accelerator outside the city, my thoughts racing through everything I'd seen and heard at the jewelry store. Lots of cash. Big, loud guy. Looking for obnoxious diamonds. A showoff with a heavy foot, too, if he'd intended to peel his big red bubba truck out backward as fast as he must have been going to plow into the store as he had. Which all added up to this: he probably wasn't going to want to talk to me. Playing the bimbo and using flattery would be my two surest ways to get his jaw flapping. I detested both and wasn't good at either.

I slowed the car and turned onto a narrow gravel road, then took a left into a driveway flanked by stone lions guarding an open wrought-iron gate. The drive wound through a grove of manicured magnolias that were just losing their blooms to the early fall chill, the soft slope of the hills in the surrounding fields golden brown with tobacco plants. I flipped the radio off and rolled the windows down, the *whir-chug* of a combine coming from somewhere I couldn't see.

A majestic, whitewashed house with black shutters appeared, the closest thing to Tara I'd ever seen in real life, making me catch my breath.

"Jesus," I whispered as I stopped the car, staring at soaring white columns that lined a portico built for hoopskirts and mint juleps. "Welcome to Dixie." The house was so far from the suburban tract home where I'd grown up it was positively intimidating.

Squaring my shoulders and trying to shake the feeling that I didn't belong, I hitched my bag over one shoulder and climbed out of the car. There was a stable-sized garage to my right, but no other vehicles in sight.

In place of a regular, push-button doorbell, there was a heavy, braided cord with a tassel on the end. I shook my head slightly and yanked, bells chiming over my head like Saint Luke's on Sunday morning. An honest-to-God plantation. And from the looks of the fields and the sound of the combine, the folks who owned it had fared just fine with paid labor.

One of the eight-foot, black double doors swung inward, and a petite woman with a sweet smile and skin as pale as her uniform smiled at me. The flush in her cheeks just made her look that much paler.

"Can I help you, darlin'?" she asked in an accent that spoke more of the Appalachian mountains of West Virginia than it did of Richmond.

I flashed my widest smile.

"I'm here to see William Eckersly. My name is Nichelle Clarke, and I'm a reporter at the *Richmond Telegraph*. I was wondering if he might be able to help me with an article I'm working on?"

She shook her head.

"Mister Will isn't here this morning," she said. "He had business to attend to in town. But if you'd like to leave a calling card, I can make sure he gets it when he comes home."

"Who is it, Doreen?" A voice that was impossibly wispy and gravelly at the same time came from deeper in the house, and even before the slip of a woman it belonged to rolled her wheelchair into my line of sight, I had a mental picture of a little old grandma who was once the formidable lady of this enormous house.

"Miss Lucinda! You're supposed to be resting." The maid shot a chastising glare. "This here is a reporter who wants to talk to Mister Will."

"I'll have time enough to rest when I'm dead," Lucinda Eckersly took a long draw on a mask attached to a green metal oxygen tank that rode alongside her chair in a little rack. "Lord only knows what my son has done to drag our name through the mud now. Because losing his family to that whore of his wasn't enough. What can we do for you, young lady?"

She leveled a gaze at me that could have terrified a professional linebacker into doing exactly as she said, and waved me into the foyer.

"Doreen, show Miss?" Lucinda arched an eyebrow at me.

"Clarke," I said. "Nichelle Clarke."

"Are you kin to the Prince William County Clarkes?" Lucinda's head snapped up, a gleam in her watery blue eyes. I smiled. Plantations, feuds, uniformed servants and pull chain doorbells. I began to wonder if I'd driven through a space-time vortex on my way out to the country.

"No, ma'am. I grew up in Texas, and my family's from California."

"Well then," she said, giving me a critical once-over. "Follow Doreen to the sitting room, and I'll be with you directly. I need a new tank."

I followed Doreen, trying not to let my jaw drop at the massive works of art that lined the foyer walls, interspersed with swords, framed papers, and dark, heavy, very antique-looking furniture. Jenna would bust something to get a look at some of this stuff. A painting I was pretty sure (from having an artist like Jenna as a friend) was an actual Chegal hung just inside the front door. A wardrobe that would have taken up half my living room sat along the wall opposite the polished staircase that rose to the second floor. My shoes clicked on the hardwood, the sound echoing through the cavernous hallway.

"Nice shoes," Lucinda called behind me. "I used to be a high heels girl myself, before I got too old to walk in them anymore."

"Indeed she was," Doreen said, stopping in front of a set of rich, golden wood double doors. "Miss Lucinda was a beauty in her day. Belle of the county. Richest husband, biggest house. To look at her now, you wouldn't know it, but she was quite a lady."

"I believe it," I said, stepping through the doors into a dim, silent room with an oversized rectangular piano in one corner and a pair of sculpted wood and silk sofas flanking a fireplace in the other. The musty smell said it wasn't used too often anymore. Doreen pulled heavy drapes back from the floor-to-ceiling windows and tied them with thick cord, flooding the space with sunlight. Dust motes, no doubt from the drapes, danced in the beams. I perched on the high-backed settee facing the window, crossing my legs.

My eyes fell on a framed photo on a wooden side table: A burly man in camouflage and a neon-orange vest with one foot on the ribcage of a humongous buck. Twisting the deer's head up by an antler with one hand, he brandished an ornate, old-fashioned looking rifle with the other. William?

"How long have you worked here?" I asked Doreen as she fussed with the drapery cords and straightened the music books on the piano.

"Forty-one years in November," she said, not looking up from her work. "I was the first person Miss Lucinda hired when she married Mister Harold, God rest his soul. My momma kicked me out when I was sixteen and I came east looking for a better life than coal mines and dirt floor shacks. I found it here. Miss Lucinda has been through a lot. But she's a good woman. A real blessing to me and my family."

She raised her eyes to meet mine at last, and something serious in her stare sent a chill through me, sunshine be damned. I smiled and nodded, but before I could ask any more questions, the door creaked open and Lucinda wheeled herself into the room, preceded by the distinct odor of a burning cigarette.

"Sorry to keep you waiting, Miss Clarke," Mrs.Eckersly said, a Virginia Slim dangling from her lower lip. She rolled herself to an opening in the furniture arrangement opposite me and cut a defiant glance at Doreen, who shook her head as she shut the door behind her, but didn't say a word.

I tried to keep my features arranged in a neutral expression, but my eyes locked on Lucinda's oxygen tank, which was full, according to what she'd said, then flitted to the lit cigarette. I was pretty sure I was suddenly in mortal danger, sitting and chatting with a little old lady in the middle of the afternoon.

On one hand, I wanted her to talk to me about her son, and I was pretty sure she wanted to talk, too. On the other, I was fond of remaining in one piece, and she was going to blow herself right the hell up, sitting there smoking with an oxygen tank strapped to her. I couldn't tell if she got points for stubbornness, or lost them for stupidity.

"Would you like a smoke?" she asked in her gravelly half-whisper as if on cue, fishing the pack and a pink Bic lighter out of her flowing blue satin housedress.

I sucked in such a sharp breath that I dissolved into a coughing fit, trying to smile. I desperately wished I'd paid more attention in science class. How far would an explosion from a liter or two of oxygen be lethal? If we combusted, would I walk away in blackened Louboutins, or maybe just lose a hand?

"No, thank you," I said.

"I know." She flashed a tight grin, her wrinkled lips parting over nicotine-yellow teeth. "You youngsters think tobacco is bad for people. I'm seventy-nine, and I've smoked since I was fourteen. I like it and it makes my family a good living, so I'm not quitting. There's lots of folks like me who won't quit, either. No matter how much they want to charge in taxes. But you didn't come here to listen to me prattle about that. What has my Billy done now?"

I tilted my head to one side and studied her before I answered, assessing quickly that this momma was no fool, and "her Billy" prob-ably thought he got away with more than he actually did.

"I think you know way more about that than I do, Mrs. Eckersly." I folded my hands in my lap, trying not to flinch as she flicked burning ashes directly over the oxygen tank. "More than William thinks you do, too, don't you?"

"He doesn't pay any more attention to me than he does those paintings out there," she chuckled, and it sounded like rocks rattling in a box. "Too wrapped up in following his libido, not paying near enough attention to the things he should. This place has been Eckersly land since Jefferson's day. But times are changing. The economy is different. And my son likes beautiful women who like him to buy them expensive things."

"Does your son have a girlfriend?" I asked.

She took a long drag off her cigarette, staring at me as she blew the smoke out slowly. I stifled a cough.

"My son has a whore," she said. "Not the kind that hangs out at bars looking for a good time, but an honest-to-God member of the oldest profession. She likes diamonds, and furs, and shoes like those ones you're wearing. She's young. She's pretty. She's got Billy acting like a fool. I'm glad you came by today, Miss Clarke, because I'm tired of talking at my son. I'll be damned if he's going to run this farm into the ground over a good piece of ass. So, how can I help you?"

I studied her determined gaze, wondering why she wanted to help me at all. I wasn't asking, because she might think better of talking to me. I considered her words. Money. Prostitution. Lakshmi. Grayson. What if the farmer and the senator shared a call girl?

"You said William's girlfriend is pretty," I said, trying to keep the raw excitement out of my voice. "What does she look like?"

"Dark hair. Pretty face. Prettier than my daughter-in-law, sure, and Lord knows men aren't always faithful, but this has become more than a little boyish fun. My grandsons will have their legacy." She lost the last word in a coughing fit. Holding up one finger, she fumbled for her mask, taking several deep pulls on it before she put it down.

The steely determination in her rheumy eyes was jarring, and I found myself wondering for a second if I suspected the wrong Eckersly. But studying the frail frame that was swallowed in the dressing gown and watching her cough at the slightest excitement dismissed the thought. This woman didn't overpower a twenty-something attorney who played ball three nights a week and just finished a triathlon.

But her son—depending on how dire his financial situation was— certainly might have. If Joyce was right and Eckersly had broken into Grayson's place, what if he'd shot Amesworth like the deer in the photo? Joyce could go back to work and I would have the second story of the year. Third, too, counting Grayson's call girl.

Charlie would have a hard time covering jealousy green with makeup.

Lucinda stared past me, at something I couldn't see. "I love my son. I don't want my family name dragged through the mud. But I cannot let him lose this farm. He won't turn it over to me or hire an overseer no matter how much I beg him. He's into some things he shouldn't be. Besides the girl. I'm not sure about what or how, but he whispers a lot, on the phone. Maybe you can help me, too. If Billy's done enough wrong to go to jail, I've got a power of attorney that turns the farm over to me."

I studied her face, sadness and disappointment plain in every line.

"Is there anything else you can think of that might help me?" I asked. "Is your son active in politics?"

She laughed. "Billy's not the public service type."

"Does he know a James Billings? He's—"

"A bigwig at Raymond Garfield," Lucinda finished my sentence. "Of course we know him. This industry is a pretty small one."

Hmmm. So maybe a small lead, but still nothing I could print. I sighed. I needed more details, and it was obvious she didn't have them.

She pulled another cigarette from the pack.

"Thank you, ma'am." I jumped to my feet before Lucinda could light up again. "It was so nice to meet you, Mrs. Eckersly, but I have to scoot back to my office."

She nodded in dismissal, dropping the cigarette pack in her lap.

I hurried from the room, the sound of the Bic clicking making my steps faster. Letting myself out without bidding Doreen goodbye, I hoped her employer didn't blow them both to kingdom come.

Back at my desk, I fired off a follow-up to the jewelry store story, quoting Aaron about the bail and the hearing and recapping the details of the accident. A quick phone call to the store's manager got me a comment about the structural damage, which was irreparable. They were waiting for the insurance check to clear and hiring a contractor to raze the premises and build a new store.

"This one will have kevlar in the walls if they do such a thing." She laughed.

"I understand the customer who was driving the truck had just bought a rather expensive piece," I said, trying to remember if Lakshmi had been wearing a bracelet and failing. "Had you seen him in the store before?"

"Not that I remember," she said.

"Was there anything unusual about the bracelet he bought?" I asked.

"It was big. And pretty. Why do you ask?"

"Just curious," I said. "It goes with the job."

"Is there anything else I can help you with?"

"Not that I can think of." I thanked her and hung up.

I sent the story to Bob just before four and wandered to the break room, hunting for a Diet Coke.

Halfway there, I heard a round of hearty laughter pouring from Parker's office.

Sticking my head around the doorframe, I felt my face stretch into a grin when I saw Troy, spinning Parker's seat back and forth and holding court with half the sports desk. He looked so happy it was positively infectious.

"So, what do you lead your story with?" Parker asked, gesturing to the computer and pushing a notebook across the desk at Troy. "You interviewed the coach. There's one game left in the season. Give me your lead."

I shot Parker a smile and mouthed a "thank you" when he glanced at me. He nodded and focused on Troy, who was studying his notes with a furrowed brow.

"I guess I'd say to start with the comment he made about focusing on pitching in the draft this year?"

"Yes and no." Parker grinned. "Nice job picking out the most important thing. But you write the lead. You don't start with his comment."

Troy tilted his head to one side, and I could almost see the sponge soaking up every detail. "Why?"

"Clarke?" Parker turned toward me and I stepped through the door and waved at Troy. "Care to explain the whys and wherefores?"

"Your lead is supposed to catch your reader's attention and summarize your most important point, and very rarely does someone say something that captures the most important part of a story more succinctly than you can write it," I said. "My favorite prof in college had a saying in a frame over his desk: every journalist gets to lead a story with a quote twice in their career. Once when they're too green to know any better, and again when the Pope says 'fuck.' "

"Hear, hear! I'm totally framing that and putting it over my desk," Spence said from the black metal chair in the corner. "And I'm giving Bob one for Christmas."

"I always thought that'd be such a great story to write," I said, leaning on the edge of the desk and cutting a glance at Troy. He probably heard worse before first period, if I remembered high school right. "Can you see it? 'Vatican City, AP: 'Fuck,' the Pope said Friday. 'Just fuck it all.' Bishops were stunned speechless when his holiness erupted in a string of swearwords during morning mass. The Associated Press has learned the Pope was frustrated with level 15 of Angry Birds. In a statement released this afternoon, the Vatican apologized. 'It was not intended to be said aloud,' the press release reads."

"Damn, Clarke, you missed your calling." Parker grinned. "You ought to be writing for the Onion."

"I'll take that as praise." I turned to Troy. "Have you had a good day?"

"The best!" He bounced in his seat. "Mr. Parker took me to the ballpark and then over to RAU to watch football practice. He even listened to me practice calling plays and gave me pointers, and he let me interview the baseball coach and took me to eat barbecue for lunch, and he said I could help with his column." The words spilled out so fast I could hardly keep up, and that was saying something. Taking Troy's notes, I flipped through at least twenty pages.

"Jeez, kid, you don't need shorthand lessons," I said. "These are pretty detailed."

"I want to make sure I don't forget anything," Troy said. "Thank you so much, Miss Clarke."

"Did they win you over to the print side of the world?"

"I still want to be on TV," he said. "But I never knew newspapers were so much fun. It wouldn't be a bad place to start."

"A backup plan is a good thing to have," I said with a smile.

"All right, y'all," Parker boomed, shooing everyone toward the door. "If Spence wants my column today, Troy and I have some work to do."

"Have fun," I told Troy, smiling when he gushed another thank you.

"Thanks again," I told Parker as I slipped out the door. "I owe you one."

"Nah. Setting me up with Mel is worth a few favors. Her sister had a girl. Cute little thing," he said. "What were we looking for the other night, anyhow? You find anything on your lead?"

I shrugged. "I'm still working on it." The fewer people who knew about my suspicions until they were more than suspicions, the better. Especially given what I'd just heard from Trudy.

He cocked his head, leaning on the doorjamb. "You're really not going to tell me? You don't think I killed somebody else, do you?"

I laughed. "You're never going to let that go, are you? I'm not entirely sure what it is that I'm into, and I don't want to talk about it until I am."

"Into? You playing Lois Lane again?"

"No." I took a step backward.

"Liar." Parker shook his head. "Does Bob know what you're doing, at least?"

"Part of it. Really, I'm playing it safe." I shoved the toy dog and Joey's warning to a vault in the back of my brain.

"Uh-huh. I'm buying you a handgun for Christmas."

"My shoes seem to work pretty well, thanks."

"I have to get to work or I'm going to miss deadline." He moved to close the door. "Stay out of trouble."

I rounded the corner into the break room, and the empty syrup bottle in the garbage can inside the door caught my eye. I scowled. What I really wanted was more coffee, though the Coke had fewer calories. And in the grand scheme of things, the mystery of the disappearing syrup was less important than a dead man and a crooked politician.

I jammed quarters into the Coke machine a little too hard and gulped half the bottle on my way back to my desk.

My cell phone binged the arrival of a text as I plopped into my chair.

"Miss you, baby girl."

My mom. I snatched up the phone and dialed her number, checking my email as it rang. Nothing from Bob yet.

"Hey, sweetheart," she said when she picked up. "Are you busy?"

"I can squeeze you in," I said. "I miss you. What's going on there?"

"Have you ever seen that TV show *Bridezillas?*" She sighed. "Those broads have nothing on this woman I'm working for. My God, Nicey. It's all I can do to refrain from slapping her about. Nothing and no one is ever right or good enough, and she's such a little snot; she insisted that I meet her for coffee on Thursday, and hand to God, she snapped her fingers at that poor server no less than ten times in half an hour. She's like that with everyone. The biggest part of the hours I've spent on this wedding so far have been running interference with other businesses for the bride, because she's so hateful people don't want to work for her."

"Then why are you working for her?"

"Because her grandfather's last name is on a few buildings downtown. Big ones. And I thought she was nice the first time she came in. I was wrong. It's like peeling an onion. The closer it gets to her wedding, the more layers of nasty there are to her. But her stuff is almost done, and I'll be rid of her soon. Thank God."

I laughed. "If anyone can get a Bridezilla safely down the aisle, it's you," I said. "What kind of flowers will she have?"

My mom's love of plants had led her to start a tiny flower shop when I was a kid, and it had grown into a thriving wedding-planning boutique. That was irony for you: my mother, who held the deepest disdain for marriage of anyone I'd ever met, made a living helping people do, in her estimation, something foolish.

"I used lilies, white roses, and orchids when I made the test bouquet last week," she said. "It came out lovely. It's a waterfall style with a lace handkerchief that belonged to her grandmother around the base. At least, she said it was her grandmother's. I'm beginning to think she escaped from some hell dimension."

I laughed. "It sounds lovely. Hang in there. When's the big day?"

"Next Friday," she said. "Twelve more days, and one more box of antacids. I think I can, I think I can."

I shook my head, waking the computer and smiling when I saw a thumbs up from Bob in my email. He also okay'd my request to cut out of the staff meeting early the next morning, so I could make it to the courthouse for the Eckersly hearing.

I glossed over my week, telling my mom about the jewelry store and relating the tale of Lucinda Eckersly, former grande dame of Powhatan County and current explosive hazard.

"It makes me smile to hear you so happy," my mom said. "I sure do love you, kiddo. Any chance you'll head this way anytime soon?"

"I love you, too," I said, shutting my computer down and closing the lid. "I'll be there for Christmas, which will be here before you know it. How many holiday weddings are there this year?"

"Three. And if you're really coming, I won't book any more." Her voice brightened considerably.

"Put it on the calendar." I smiled back. "I'll be there with bells on my Manolos."

I hung up and shoved my computer and charger into my bag, my gurgling stomach reminding me that I hadn't had time for lunch once again.

I ducked into the deli across the street. I ordered a turkey and smoked cheddar panini with tomato mustard on sourdough and carried it to a corner table when it was ready, crunching homemade potato chips that were perfectly seasoned with salt, pepper, garlic, and something else I could never place.

I watched Anderson Cooper as I ate, surprised to see a Virginia map flash up on the wall behind him a few minutes into his show.

It took the captions a minute to catch up.

"The new state tax, combined with a federal tax hike that has strong support in the house, would make the capital of the nation's tobacco industry the most expensive place in America to buy cigarettes."

I froze with a chip halfway to my mouth.

"They'll reverse their operation in Virginia." Kyle.

"No matter what they do with taxes." Lucinda Eckersly.

"Fake the tax stamps." Kyle.

"There are people in this who won't give a damn if I say to leave you alone." Joey.

What if Grayson wasn't just selling his vote (or, his friends' votes, as the case may be)? Could the dead lobbyist have been expendable because the senator had known the vote wasn't going to go his way, seen his hooker money slipping away, and decided to sell something else? Like stamp designs?

I looked out the window.

It was getting dark outside.

Suddenly focused on something much more important, I wolfed down my sandwich and ran out the door, wondering how many years I could spend in prison for breaking into Ted Grayson's house.

CHAPTER FOURTEEN

I SPENT the entire ten-minute drive home making a mental list of the reasons my plan was a) insane, b) unlikely to work, and c) very likely to get me arrested. The fact that Charlie would have a tickertape parade and crack a bottle of champagne with that story was my most compelling reason for going home and sinking into a hot bath, but my gut was convinced Eckersly had, in fact, broken into Grayson's study. Whatever he'd been looking for was likely still there, according to Joyce.

And according to the police and the campaign, the family had been in D.C. since the break-in.

My transmission squealed a protest when I threw the car into park in my driveway before it had stopped moving forward. I snagged the first-aid kit from under my seat, grabbed the latex gloves, and jumped out, unsure what to do next. Darcy yapped from the other side of the kitchen door, scratching at the wood when I didn't go inside right away. I'd blocked the doggie door and left her inside with puppy mats on the floor, which she disliked, because I was afraid to have her outside without me after the warning I'd gotten.

The nice thing about the Fan was that tiny cottages like mine sat side-by-side with million-dollar antebellum homes like Grayson's. It wasn't a terribly long walk, and I'd skipped the gym that morning. I glanced down at my pink Jimmy Choos, the peep toes cute, but impractical.

Scurrying into the house, I let Darcy out for just long enough to do her business and caught a glare when I called her inside.

"Sorry, girl. We'll play later," I said, stooping to scratch her ears.

I changed into black yoga pants and a black tee, slipping my feet into soft-soled leather flats and hurrying back outside before I could chicken out. Stuffing the gloves into my pocket, I turned toward the cracked old sidewalk and started walking.

The sun had officially disappeared, the chill that settled over the bricks of Monument Avenue with the late September evening air making me wish I'd grabbed a sweater. I shoved my hands into my pockets and ducked my head against the breeze, walking faster.

By the time I reached the drive alley that ran behind the Grayson home, I'd worked out a plan. Since the house faced a busy street, and the police had the front yard lit up like Rockefeller Center, I turned up the drive. Katherine Grayson seemed like the kind of detail-focused woman who'd have one of those stone plates with the family crest on it at the entrance to her driveway, even though it was behind the house.

I dug out my tiny pink flashlight, pointing it at each fence opening as I passed, and was beginning to wonder if I'd guessed wrong when the beam bounced off a polished marble plaque bearing the house number and the senator's name. Bingo.

I knew as sure as I knew my shoe size (nine US, forty European) there was no one inside, but I was nervous. I stood there, warring with myself over the insanity of this idea. Breaking into the private home of a United States senator was very different than anything else I'd ever done in the name of research—even the things that had bent the law. I shushed the little voice that detailed what could happen to me if I got caught.

Just when I'd resolved to go in, a crash came from my left and I jumped nearly out of my skin. Claws on pavement, then aluminum. A raccoon, probably. I gulped a steadying breath and stepped toward the house.

"Don't do that, Miss Clarke." The smooth voice was in front of me, and in the still darkness of the alley it carried easily. I scanned the fence line around Grayson's house, but Joey was better than me at keeping hidden. To be fair, he'd had more practice.

He stepped out of the shadows at the foot of the drive, debonair as ever in a charcoal suit and wingtips that glinted even in the moonlight.

"Go home. Stay out of this. This guy is so much bigger than you know."

I strode across the alley, arching an eyebrow when he laid a restraining hand on my arm.

"What the hell are you doing here?" I asked. "And cut the bullshit about trying to protect me, because I don't buy it. You're either protecting yourself, or your buddy Grayson, or the both of you."

"I was in town and came by to check on you. Hoping you'd taken my advice. I had a bad feeling when you took off on foot, and I was right. Tell me something: when have I ever steered you wrong?" He let go of my arm, the place where his fingers had rested tingling in the cool air, and I stared into his brown eyes. He didn't look like he was lying. His gaze was so intense I had to drop it after a minute when my stomach flipped like I'd gotten a side of jumping beans with my panini. Damn him and his gorgeous jawline. Why did he have to be a crook?

"It's not that easy," I began.

"Sure it is," he said, his voice soft and deep at the same time. "I can't recall ever having given you a personal reason to distrust me. I care about you. Maybe more than I'd like. Certainly more than is convenient with the sky falling around your boy here, and you refusing to listen to reason."

His eyelids dropped a fraction of an inch and he reached for my arm again. I stepped backward.

"I can't," I whispered. "Kyle's got an innocent man going up on a murder charge, and you know it as well as I do. I'm going to find out what the hell's going on here. Grayson's up to his Hermes necktie in hookers and bribes, and he may not have killed that lobbyist, but there's something in that house that's going to get me closer to figuring out who did. Someone else wanted it badly enough to break in, but I don't think they got it. I'm going to find it. So unless you want to share what you know, get out of my way."

He stared silently for a long minute. I drew myself up to my full height, nearly six feet even without stilettos, and stuck out my chin for good measure.

"Do you even know how to pick a lock?" He sighed.

"I'll figure it out," I said.

"You'll set off the alarm and get yourself arrested. Come on."

He crossed the backyard in a dozen strides, keeping to the shadows seemingly by second nature, and stopped in front of a door I wouldn't have even noticed on the far right corner of the house.

I managed to keep up without my heels to unsteady me on the emerald turf. Joey pulled a thin scrap of metal from his wallet and what looked like a tiny screwdriver with a funny curved end on it from inside his jacket.

He cut his dark eyes at me as he worked the tool around, first in the deadbolt and then in the button lock on the handle. When the second one clicked loose I gave an involuntary gasp of awe.

"My undesirable skill set suddenly isn't so undesirable, is it?" He flashed a tight grin.

I didn't answer, trying not to breathe too deep, every fiber of my being acutely aware that he was very close, and he smelled unbelievably good. Cologne, yes, but something else, too. Not aftershave, or hair gel, I didn't think. I couldn't place it, but it was downright magical, and making it damned near impossible to concentrate on anything else. There was nothing undesirable about Joey, no matter how hard I tried to remind myself there should be.

A tiny click pulled my focus away from the hollow alongside his

Adam's apple. Whatever he'd been doing now allowed him to open the door enough for us to slip through.

"No siren?" I asked.

"Magnets," he said. "Most of the security systems in these places were installed in the eighties, and not many of them have been updated. There's a magnet in the doorframe that tells the alarm system the door is closed. As long as the connection isn't broken, ADT will never know we're here."

The little piece of metal was stuck to the inside of the doorframe about halfway between the lock and the top.

"I'll be damned," I whispered, filing that away as very useful information I hoped I'd never need again.

I slid through the doorway and felt him tense when I brushed against him, fighting to keep a smile off my lips. At least it wasn't just me.

"Where are we?" I asked.

"What used to be the maid's quarters," he said. "Behind the kitchen, usually."

I flicked my little flashlight back on and crept down the hallway into the house, cracking a big set of double doors on my left.

"Laundry room," I said, the smell of Tide giving it away before I could make out the outline of the huge, front-loading washer and dryer alongside the sink on the opposite wall. White breadboard cabinets lined the perimeter of the room, three drying racks folded into the wall above the sink. "Damn. Martha Stewart's laundry room."

Two feet further and across the hall, I hit pay dirt.

"Study," I whispered, peeking through the French doors. The heavy scent of good cigars and better scotch was probably as much a part of these walls as chemicals were a part of the photo cave at my office.

Joey waved a "ladies first" gesture and I ducked inside, completely unsure why I was whispering and tiptoeing, but doing it just the same.

"I'll take the desk," I said, reaching into my pocket for the latex gloves and offering him one. "Put this on and look in the cabinets."

He pulled a pair of black leather driving gloves from inside his jacket and grinned. "Thanks, but I've done this before. What am I looking for?"

"You don't know?" I raised an eyebrow.

"I'll rephrase. What are you looking for?"

"Something that proves Grayson is dirty. I'll know it when I see it," I said.

"Good plan." Joey chuckled and turned to the cabinet.

I opened drawers and flipped through files, closing them when I didn't see anything promising.

In the very back of the second drawer, I spied a familiar name.

"Billings," I breathed. I wriggled the folder loose and opened it.

Spreadsheets full of six-digit numbers. Dollar amounts? I turned and laid them on the copier that was enclosed in the handsome cherry secretary behind the matching desk. A slip of thick paper fluttered from between the sheets and landed face down on the deep red and beige Oriental rug.

"What are you talking to yourself about over here?" Joey asked from directly behind my shoulder.

"A file on Billings," I said, picking up the slip, which was printed with a pattern of little curlicue doodles and numbers. Was that what a tax stamp looked like? Not being a smoker myself, I had zero frame of reference, but it looked promising. "What is this?"

Joey yanked the chain on the desk lamp and studied the paper before he sighed and thrust it back at me.

"What you came here for," he said. "Let's go."

I opened my mouth to object, pointing to the stack of documents. I froze when the floor started to vibrate.

"Garage door," Joey said. "Do you trust me?"

He held my gaze for a very long second.

"More than a rational person would," I said.

"Then move."

I did, crossing to the door silently.

Through the open door I heard a woman giggling and a deep voice I couldn't make out enough to recognize.

"He's supposed to be in D.C.," I whispered involuntarily. "Cheating weasel."

"Who says he's not in D.C.? He's not the only one cheating," Joey breathed in my ear, putting one hand on the small of my back and steering me through the dark hallway to the open door. He flipped the metal piece loose as he followed me out, since Mrs. Grayson and her friend had disarmed the alarm system. Turning the knob, Joey pulled the door shut silently, scanning the yard before he nodded an all clear and waved me off the patio.

I stuffed the gloves into my pocket and hurried toward the driveway, anxious to get home with the slip of paper and check Google for cigarette tax stamp pictures. Two steps into the lawn, my foot clipped a buried sprinkler head and my ankle turned under me. I bit my lip hard, but managed to avoid yelping. Joey's arm shot around my waist before I could fall, and I gripped his shoulder and leaned into him, hobbling silently to the alley. I blinked away tears and cleared my throat, my searing ankle feeling twice as big as usual.

"Are you alright?"

"I don't even have my good shoes on," I said. "What kind of shit is that? I can run in stilettos, but in flats, not so much."

"Look at it this way," Joey said with a barely-suppressed chuckle. "You might have broken it in the heels. Hobble this way, and I'll drive you home."

After a few steps I made out the outline of his Lincoln, parked under a willow three houses down.

He helped me into the passenger seat and rounded the front of the car, sliding behind the wheel.

I bent forward and probed my ankle gingerly, sucking in a sharp breath. It was swollen, and very tender.

"Do you need to go to the ER again?" Joey asked, concern clear in his tone.

"I don't think so," I said. "I will tomorrow if it gets worse, but I think some ice will be okay for tonight."

"What are you going to do with those stamps?" he asked tightly, laying an arm along the top of my seat as he turned to back the car up.

"Stamps?" I asked, playing dumb.

"The tax stamps you found in the file," he said.

Pay dirt. I reached into my pocket and patted the slip, sure it meant Grayson was going down, but unsure exactly why that was.

"What's Grayson doing with them?" I blurted the question, but after I said it I wondered if he was distracted or annoyed enough to fire an answer back.

Joey kept silent, studying the road as he turned up Monument toward my house. Fine. I could figure that out for myself. I stared at his jawline, trying not to imagine what the faint stubble there would feel like under my fingers as hard as I was trying not to care if he was caught up in whatever dirty dealings Grayson was doing. His arm had felt so natural around my waist, warmth lingering there even with the cool leather of the seat against my back.

But the truth was my goal, no matter what. Right?

He stopped in my driveway and shut off the engine, turning to face me.

"You're not going to let this go, are you?" he asked.

"I can't," I said.

"Billings is no angel."

"But he's not a murderer, is he?" Resting an elbow on the console, I twisted in the seat, trying to configure my throbbing ankle into a more comfortable position.

"No. But these are not nice people, Miss Clarke."

"Nichelle, for the eleventy thousandth time. And I've held my own so far." I didn't move my eyes from his, though I'd always been hesitant to hold his gaze for long in close quarters.

"You're flirting with danger." He leaned closer, his eyelids simmering.

"I'm well aware of that." My breath stopped. My sexy mobster friend was about to kiss me.

At least, I hoped he was. Because I was sure as hell going to kiss him, criminal status be damned.

It was fast and slow all at the same time. I wasn't sure who kissed who, only that suddenly his lips were on mine, and what he did or didn't do outside of that didn't matter one little bit.

I wouldn't even admit to Jenna how many times I'd fantasized about this moment, and the reality was so much better: sweet, rich, and forbidden. Like eating an entire box of Godiva white raspberry truffles when you're supposed to be on a diet. And surprising—Joey was an intimidating, do-as-I-say guy, but his mouth was soft against mine. Hesitant. His palm cradled my cheek the way a collector might hold a Fabergé egg.

I curled my fingers into his thick, dark hair and pulled him closer, parting my lips and pressing them harder against his.

He swept the tip of his tongue along the line of my lower lip and I gasped, dropping my hands to clutch his shoulders, certain I was about to melt into a puddle on the black leather seat.

Oh. My. God.

He tightened his arm, his hand between my shoulder blades pulling me to him, but kept the kiss gentle. My ribs protested melding with the console, but I didn't care. Electricity skated up my spine with every thump of my heart and flick of his tongue.

When I pulled away, his fingertips lingered on my jaw, his thumb streaking sparks across my cheekbone as he stroked it with the lightest touch.

It took everything in me to refrain from inviting him in. I leaned away instead, opening the car door.

"Goodnight, Joey," I whispered. "Please, please, if you're involved in whatever Grayson's doing, disappear before I find out."

"I have no intention of going anywhere, Nichelle," he said. I wanted to believe it was an answer, not an argument. "Sweet dreams."

I eased out of the car, gripping the top edge of the door as I tested my ankle. It hurt, but the kiss was working like morphine. I could feel the pain, but I truly did not give one damn.

I watched as he backed out of the drive, then turned for the door when he flickered the high beams at me.

I took Darcy out back and leaned on the wall as I threw her squirrel, then checked her food bowl, tucking the stamps into my utensil drawer as I limped through the kitchen. Dropping clothes on my way into the bathroom, I pulled a clean t-shirt from the dryer on my way out. I needed to ice my ankle, but I was too drained. It would still be swollen in the morning.

What kind of worms am I going to find in this can? I wondered, trying to think about anything but Joey's toe-curling sweet kiss. As if that were even possible. Folding the cloud-soft duvet back, I climbed into my big cherry four-poster, Joey's jawline waiting on the backs of my eyelids.

CHAPTER FIFTEEN

SLEEP WAS FITFUL, thanks to my ankle and a drawn-out dream that would've made a porn star blush. By the time first light peeped through my shades, I was ready to hobble to the kitchen for some coffee and an ice pack.

A little rummaging in the far reaches of my linen closet produced an ace bandage I'd used on a sprained knee that had ended my brief Venus Williams phase. I wrapped my ankle tightly, dropping a few ice cubes in a Ziploc and propping my foot on a stack of throw pillows while I sipped a homemade white mocha.

I picked up the stamps by the edges and studied them in the lamplight. The paper was an odd, linen-type adhesive variety, and the strip was scored for easy tearing. The mark itself was a curlicue design with an alphanumeric code printed underneath, and *Commonwealth of Virginia* printed across the top in bitsy letters.

Grayson was definitely dirty. Joey's cryptic non-information and the paper in my hand proved that much.

"Are they fakes?" I wondered aloud, trying to remember exactly what Kyle had told me about the huge case he was working on. "Why would Grayson have fake state tax stamps if he's taking bribes to keep the federal taxes lower?"

Darcy yipped from her bed in the corner, and I looked over at her.

"What do you think, girl? How did the senator get ahold of these?"

I laid them on the table and picked up my coffee, still thinking about Grayson. All the work he'd done at the state level for tighter regulations and banning smoking in public places didn't jive with any of this. And how did the dead guy fit in?

Hold on. The dead guy.

I snatched the stamps off the table and peered at the edge. Not paper, exactly, but like paper. With an odd sheen because of the adhesive.

"Ten to one the scrap I found near the body is this same kind of paper, Darcy," I said, knocking the ice to the floor in my haste to get to my feet. I grabbed my cell phone and pulled up the photos I'd taken at the scene, but I couldn't tell anything definitive from them. It looked promising, though. "I wonder what Kyle's up to this morning."

I limped to the bathroom, the ice, the bandage, and a double dose of Advil keeping the throbbing to a minimum.

Scrubbing my face with a wet cloth, I smiled at the determined flash in the violet eyes that stared back at me from the mirror. If the paper had come from the stamps, Kyle would have to at least acknowledge the possibility that he was wrong. I brushed my teeth and twisted my hair up into a messy bun, finger-combing a few strands around my face. A touch of makeup, and I debated which shoes would accommodate my bandaged foot.

I settled on a pair of Tory Burch pumps I'd picked up at a Salvation Army sale in July because I couldn't pass up the price even if they were a half-size too big. Stuffing Kleenex in the toe of the right one, I slipped it on my uninjured foot and paired the turquoise suede shoes with cream slacks and a canary wrap sweater. Professional, but cute enough to hold Kyle's attention.

I walked gingerly until I got the hang of slightly limping in heels, then climbed in the car and flipped on my scanner.

"Female, approximately twenty-two years old. Forensics is picking through the dumpster now."

A body.

Between the math building and the student union at RAU.

Having just covered a horrific murder case involving students there over the spring and summer, my stomach turned at the idea of another dead coed. Writing about murder is hard enough without tragically young victims.

I started the engine, fishing for my cell phone to call Bob.

"I'm really not trying to piss you off, Chief," I said when he picked up. "But I'm going to be late. There's a dead girl in a dumpster at RAU this morning."

"Really?" He was the only person in the world who could sound perky in response that statement and not come off as a creep. "Shot? Stabbed?"

"Don't know. They're not saying much on the scanner and I'm still in the car. But I'm on my way over there to see what I can see."

"Stay with it as long as you have to," he said. "Good thing I'm not the only person you're standing up."

"I'd never—" I began, but stopped when I remembered that I was supposed to go to the courthouse at eight-thirty. "Shit. The jewelry store hearing."

"Ding ding ding! It was in your copy last night. Early hearing. Any big reason you need to be there?" He meant was there any reason for him to send someone else; in this case "someone else" would likely be Shelby Taylor.

"Not really. I just wanted to get a look at the guy," I lied. I wanted much more than a look at William Eckersly. "It's just a bond hearing."

"I can send photo," he said. "It won't hurt to have a shot of that guy in a courtroom on file. Let me see if we've got anyone available."

"Thanks, Chief." I clicked off the call, thinking he had no clue just how handy that picture might be.

I turned onto the campus, a half-dozen RPD cars, an ambulance, and forensics, coroner's, and TV vans making it even more difficult than usual to find a parking place.

Finally double-parking next to the Channel Four van, I hurried around the student union to a sidewalk looking out on a picturesque courtyard. Students stood clustered in groups, whispering and staring toward a large blue dumpster. A thirty-foot radius was blocked off by crime scene tape, the grass between the sidewalk and the dumpster hidden beneath the feet of better than fifty reporters, cops, medical examiners, and suit-and-tie university administrators.

I found Aaron at the center of a circle of microphones, giving the first media briefing of the day.

"...pending notification of next of kin," he was saying when I walked up, and I dug for a notebook and pen. "The remains were discovered when a university employee came outside to dump the garbage early this morning."

I scribbled, looking around for a traumatized janitor while Aaron talked about the forensics team's deconstruction of the dumpster's contents.

When he offered a thank you and turned back toward the crime scene tape, I spotted a woman who was sitting by herself on the back steps of the union building, her arms wrapped tightly around her knees, her RAU-gold apron barely visible the way she was hunched over.

"Late to the party this morning, Clarke," Charlie Lewis purred from behind my left shoulder, and I shifted my attention to a group of students standing on the opposite side of the sidewalk for her benefit, not wanting to clue her in to the possibility that the woman who'd found the dead girl might be available for an interview.

"Some of us need our beauty sleep," I grinned, turning to face her. "We don't all fall out of bed HD-ready like you do, Charlie."

She rolled her green eyes and shook her head, her perfectly-coiffed bob not swaying. "Flattery will get you nowhere," she said. "I have a lead on this girl you won't believe. And you can see it at noon with everyone else."

"Fabulous. That gives me plenty of time to run down something better before press time," I said, watching Aaron over her shoulder. He cut the tape and motioned for the crowd to stay put. They were moving the body.

"Speaking of," I said, stepping around her. "Excuse me for a second."

I hobbled quickly to the back end of the coroner's van, craning my neck for a glimpse of the stretcher. Peering at corpses wasn't my favorite thing about my job, but was sometimes a necessary evil. Without a name to attach to the story, I needed to be able to describe the victim.

I saw dark hair, matted and strewn with something that looked like shredded lettuce.

Then the medical examiners lifted the gurney and the early-morning sunlight flashed off a large bracelet on her wrist. Who kills a coed and doesn't steal her oversized bling?

Wait—a big flashy bracelet. Like the one Eckersly bought his girlfriend?

I elbowed past the cameraman from Channel Ten, not caring about catching a glare and a muttered curse in reply. I managed to get a good look at the victim's face.

Holy shit.

Allison. The girl from the campaign office.

"No." The word popped out before I could stop it and I bit my tongue, staring at the paramedic who'd stepped up to the back of the ambulance and obstructed my view like his midsection might suddenly sprout a window.

I closed my eyes, trying to erase the image of the girl's expression-less face from the backs of my eyelids. I'd only met her the one time. Maybe I was wrong. But my gut said I wasn't. Why was a Grayson campaign intern dead in a RAU dumpster?

I spun on my heel and winced when my ankle protested, steadying myself for a second and starting back toward the steps where I'd seen the woman I suspected had found the body.

When she wasn't there, I sighed, but then saw her white and gold baseball cap disappearing through a door further down the side of the building. I hobbled faster, trying to catch up.

Checking over my shoulder, I could see Charlie with her mic in a medical examiner's face. Channel Ten was talking to the kids gathered on the quad. I pulled the door open and ducked inside, finding myself in a large room with a fireplace on one wall and several groupings of overstuffed furniture that had probably survived the Reagan era. I saw the woman huddled in a ball in the corner of a sofa next to the fireplace.

I slowed my steps as I approached her, experience telling me she might startle easily after such a traumatic experience.

"Hi," I said, my press credentials in my hand, but dangling at my side. "I'm Nichelle. That was a pretty terrible thing to see. Did you find her?"

Upon closer inspection, I put her age closer to the girl in the dumpster's than my own. Jesus. She was probably a student, too, doing work-study at the union.

She didn't answer me at first, hugging her knees with her legs crossed at the ankle, whimpering so softly I wasn't sure if I imagined it.

"I just opened the door to put the bags in," she said. "I can't reach the lid. And her hand fell out. Her hand. I touched it and she was so cold. I screamed and screamed, and someone came to call the police. She was so pale. They pulled her out. Her neck had a funny bruise. Just a purple line. She wasn't even wearing a coat. Just her tank top and jeans and that tacky bracelet. And it was cold this morning. So cold." She stopped and let her head drop to her knees. "I wish I could reach the lid."

"The bracelet was a little on the gaudy side," I said, wondering if she'd gotten a good look at it and making a note to ask Aaron about the bruising around the victim's neck.

"The bracelet didn't go," she mumbled. "Why would a girl that classy wear fake diamonds?"

"Fake?" I eased myself down onto the edge of the sofa. My ankle wasn't complaining much, but it needed a rest.

"As a Rolex hanging in a trenchcoat," she looked up.

"You're sure?"

"My father has worked for the Rothschild family for almost thirty years. That bracelet was fake. What does it matter? Her arm fell out of the dumpster! Right in my face. Someone killed her. Maybe right here on campus."

She resumed rocking and whimpering, and I pondered that. Eckersly hadn't given her a fake bracelet, so scratch that. But why would a girl like Allison have a gaudy fake tennis bracelet on? Did someone kill her for the bracelet and leave it when they got a better look at it? I shoved the thought aside. I was more likely to get a personal one-of-a-kind masterpiece from Christian Louboutin himself than that was to be true. Way too coincidental.

I asked for the girl's name and jotted it down, not sure I'd need it. She'd been through enough for one day. Most of what she'd told me I'd have to confirm elsewhere. It had been chilly that morning, which meant a scantily-clad corpse would be cold no matter if it had been in the dumpster thirty minutes or twelve hours. I'd have to wait for the autopsy report to get time of death.

I thanked her and headed back outside, nearly walking into Charlie when I opened the door.

"There you are!" she practically shouted. "Would you mind moving your heap out of my way? Some of us have actual work to do today."

Oops. I'd figured she'd hang around for a while getting extra footage.

"Sorry, Charlie." I hobbled toward my car. Her camera guy was in the van's driver's seat, and he looked irritated, too.

"What were you doing in there?" She kept pace with me, arching an eyebrow at my limp, but not asking about it.

"Bathroom," I said.

"Bullshit." She laughed. "You are a lousy liar, Clarke. But keep all the secrets you want. You've got nothing on me today. Just don't miss the noon broadcast."

"We'll see." I knew Allison worked for the Grayson campaign already, but I wasn't telling her that. And I had bigger things to worry about if Charlie was onto the senator. Shit.

I peeled out of the parking space. I'd have to be in the office in front of a TV at noon. Just in case.

Checking the clock, I knew I had better than three hours to get the body discovery ready to go on the website. What else could I find out in the meantime? The dead girl was connected to Grayson, and Grayson was connected to Kyle's case. I was sure of it.

I rummaged in my bag for my cell phone and called Kyle, really grateful for the first time to have my ex in Richmond. No way I'd have an ATF agent's cell number under any other circumstance.

"What's up?" he said when he picked up.

"You have time for coffee?" I asked, thinking about the stamp thingies I'd hidden under the loose floorboard in my coat closet that morning. I was glad I'd never gotten around to reporting that to my landlord. It was damned handy for keeping things hidden. Better than a safe.

"Actually, yes. IT is working a bug out of our computer system this morning, so I'm staring at papers and twiddling my thumbs," he said. "You hear any more from your walking buddy?"

"Give it a rest, Kyle," I said. "It's unattractive, this territorial thing. Who I walk or do anything else with is just big fat none of your business. But I need to talk to you. You're sure Billings is your guy on the Amesworth murder?"

"You heard Corry ask for them to no-bond him, right? How often does that happen?"

"Almost never." But even if Senator Grayson didn't kill the lobbyist, he was into something he shouldn't be. Possibly more so than the rest of his cohorts on Capitol Hill, though who could really tell about that? Maybe he was just dumb enough to get caught. My gut was surer every hour that all this had something to do with Kyle's big contraband cigarette investigation, though.

But how was I supposed to convince Kyle of that without confessing to a federal agent that I'd broken into a senator's house?

"Just come meet me at Thompson's—it's a little coffee shop on West Cary," I said. "Ten minutes?" I'd figure something out.

"Twenty."

I hung up and shoved the phone back into my bag.

What did I know? Nothing I could prove.

What was I pretty sure of? That Allison, a volunteer on Senator Grayson's campaign, was not dead in a dumpster because of a failed robbery or a random coed slaying. I'd bet my favorite Manolos on that. But why was she dead, and who killed her? I had a feeling that was the key to this whole mess. And I had no idea what Charlie was so excited about, so I needed to find the answer quickly.

I flipped through mental notecards on the case, beginning with Amesworth, the lobbyist. On the surface, suspecting that he was killed by someone involved in bribing Grayson didn't make sense, because all the players should have been on the same team. So something went wrong. That was plausible. Maybe Grayson wanted out. Maybe Amesworth was shaking James Billings, the tobacco company executive, down for more money to support the lifestyle the *Telegraph's* photo library told me Amesworth enjoyed. Except Joey didn't think Billings was the killer, and neither did I, really. Plus, he was on house arrest. If he'd killed the girl, Kyle would be able to place him at the scene.

Then there was Eckersly, the tobacco farmer who shared a proclivity for expensive call girls with the senator.

I parked in the coffee shop lot fifteen minutes early, blowing out a frustrated sigh. I knew just enough to know there was something there, but I needed the middle piece of my puzzle that would pull it all together.

Hopefully Kyle had it, and I could convince him to share.

* * *

Kyle looked good. My stomach gave an involuntary flip when his ice blue eyes met mine across the coffee shop. I tried not to notice the biceps ringed by the sleeves of his fitted blue Polo, or the way his torso tapered at the waist like a cartoon superhero's, and I squelched the little voice singsonging a reminder that he seemed more than a little interested in picking up where we'd left off. I didn't date cops. And Joey was a way better kisser than I remembered Kyle being. Though one kiss wasn't exactly picking out china; not to mention his occupation not being exactly desirable.

Kyle ordered his coffee and I watched, not liking the way his eyes lit when he spun from the counter and saw that I'd been staring at his tight ass in his khakis.

"Enjoying the view?"

"Knock it off. Old habits die hard."

"Sure they do. Especially when old habits have a bitch of a fitness test for work every three months and spend hours in the gym every day." He sat down in the chair across from me and not-so-subtly flexed a bicep as he sipped his latte. "Is ogling all you wanted me for, or can I do something else for you?"

"Your head has definitely gotten bigger," I said.

"It's not the only thing."

"Oh my God, Kyle," I thumped my cup down on the table and laughed in spite of myself. "Are you twelve? Shut up. No, don't shut up; tell me about Billings."

He sat back in the chair and laced his hands together behind his head.

"I'm afraid I can't go on the record with the press about an open investigation, Miss Clarke." He winked.

His ability to push my buttons had not changed.

"Dammit, Kyle," I said. "I have a ton of work to do, two different bosses breathing down my neck, and a story that has more rabbit trails than Mr. MacGregor's garden. I don't need it on the record today. I just need to know why you're so sure it's him."

He stared for a long minute, not saying a word.

"He's part of the other thing you were telling me about, too, isn't he?" I asked. "The contraband stuff and the stamps. That's why you picked him up so fast." He twisted his mouth to one side, and I knew I was onto something.

"Just tell me!" I didn't really mean to shout that. People turned to look and I ducked my head. "I heard you had a weapon. Do you have positive ballistics? Any other evidence? I need to know whether or not to believe you before I have a stroke."

"Same old Nicey." He laughed. "Off the record?"

"Sure." I made a show of tucking my pen and my cell phone back into my bag.

"The bullet that killed Amesworth was fired from a very special gun. A Sharps eighteen-fifty-nine Confederate Carbine rifle. It's a piece that was used by Civil War sharpshooters. Very expensive to manufacture back then, and consequently very rare. Like, there were only about two thousand of them made a hundred and fifty years ago."

"And Billings has one of these rifles?"

"He does, but it's missing from the rack in his office where he keeps it. He says he loaned it out, but won't say to whom. He hasn't filed an insurance claim on it, either."

Hmmm. Rare gun. Suddenly missing.

"That's pretty damning," I said. "But why the hell would anyone use a gun like that to murder someone?"

"This guy is a real bastard," Kyle leaned his elbows on the table. "I've been working this contraband case since before I left Dallas. It's one of the reasons they transferred me here."

"He's the vice president of a company that makes money off of a product that kills people," I said. "He's not supposed to be a stand-up guy. That doesn't mean he murdered someone."

"You have a better explanation for his gun vanishing just after someone was shot with one just like it?"

I considered that for a second.

"No. But how did you know he had one, anyway?" I asked. "Guns don't have to be registered in Virginia."

"I got a lucky break. The new family smoking prevention law says the FDA has oversight of tobacco manufacturing. I sat down with the inspector who'd been over to Raymond Garfield a few days before Amesworth was killed, and we got to talking about guns. His father was a collector. He was telling me about this beauty in Billings's office, and then this guy turns up, shot with the very same antique gun. After years of work, I finally have Billings on something."

"That's a lucky break." It sure sounded like he had Billings on the weapon. But Grayson had those stamps. I sipped my coffee, mulling that over.

What if Billings was telling the truth? If the gun really had been loaned to someone, why wouldn't he just cough up their name to save his ass? Because the someone was Senator Grayson and it might make the ATF wonder why they were so buddy-buddy?

"What do you know about Ted Grayson?" I asked.

He raised his eyebrows.

"United States Senator for the Commonwealth of Virginia, fairly middle of the road politically, historically not a fan of guns or cigarettes."

"Thank you, Wikipedia," I said. "But I've been poking around in his backroom dealings, and there's something fishy."

"What do you have on him?"

"Nothing concrete," I said, unable to come up with a single possible way that I should know he had those stamps. "I think he's taking bribe money. I've been wondering if it's from Billings. But everything about this is so convoluted, I'm not sure of anything. My gut says there's something more here, though. I don't think Billings is your murderer." I sipped my coffee.

"Well, I'm very glad all your years of training in criminal investigation have led you to that conclusion." He didn't even have the decency to sound annoyed. He sounded amused.

"I'm sorry, have we forgotten my ability to channel Nancy Drew?" I asked.

"Beginner's luck." He waved a hand.

Asshole. I folded my arms over my chest and glared.

"You're pretty sure of yourself for a guy with no murder weapon," I said. "Don't you even think it's worth looking into anything else?"

"I'm looking into plenty else," he said. "My guys are checking the tire tracks from the body dump against Billings's cars as we speak. I'm almost certain Billings had a couple of folks from the House of Delegates on his payroll, and I think that's why Amesworth is dead. But come on, Nicey. How am I going to go back to the office and open a file on a sitting U.S. senator—one who's in a smackdown of a reelection campaign at the moment, let's not forget—because my ex-girlfriend told me she has a hunch? You're going to get me laughed right out to the podunk sheriff's department."

"I'm not asking you to open a file. I just think you should consider the possibility that you've got the wrong guy. He might be an asshole, and he might well be a criminal. I don't know what you've got on him with the cigarette case, but think about it, Kyle: what does contraband tobacco carry? Five years? If he's not a murderer, he doesn't deserve to be called one."

"I've been doing this for a while now, Nicey," he said, softening his voice. "If he wasn't a murderer, he'd give us the gun."

"I think you're wrong." I sounded petulant, and I wasn't proud of it, but I couldn't really tell him why, either. I wasn't sure I knew myself. "But I'm not going to convince you of that, am I?"

"Not based on your gut, you're not," he said.

"Thanks for coming to meet me." I stood.

"Have dinner with me tomorrow night," he said, getting to his feet and gesturing for me to walk ahead of him to the door.

"I have work to do," I said.

"Come on, Nicey, don't be that way. I'll buy. Anywhere you want to go. I still need you to show me where they have good food around here."

He pushed the door open and I walked through it, sighing as I looked back at him. He was a good friend to have. And he did fill out those khakis nicely.

"Bring me what you have on Billings," I said.

"Do what?"

"I'll have dinner with you, but I want copies of your file," I said. "I won't run it, and no one will know I have it. I'll even give them back. I can't shake this feeling, though. So prove me wrong. Let me see what you've got."

He stood on the sidewalk in front of the coffee shop, shading his eyes and staring at me for a long minute.

"It's been a long time," he said. "How can I be sure you won't throw away my career for a scoop?"

"You can't," I said. "But you want me to believe you. Believe me."

He shook his head. "I'll pick you up at six-thirty."

"I'll be ready for some after-dinner reading."

I unlocked the car, annoyed that I'd spent a half hour and had nothing on my new murder victim to show for it.

I climbed behind the wheel and dug my cell phone out. I had four texts and three missed calls from Bob.

I clicked the messages open.

"Your dead girl was a prostitute. Channel Four just blew the top off a college call girl ring. Where the hell are you?"

Double shit. Charlie had dropped the noon time slot into conversation twice. I should have known she was lying. And Bob hated nothing worse than losing to the TV folks on a big story.

CHAPTER SIXTEEN

"Tell me one more time why you were busy with the ATF and a murder case the CA himself is calling a slam dunk while Charlie Lewis was digging up a call girl ring that makes sorority row look like the goddamned Chicken Ranch?" Bob's face was nearly purple, and despite cringing because his anger was almost never directed at me, I worried about his blood pressure and his heart.

"I'm sorry," I said, wondering how Charlie had known that and whether she was closer on my heels than I wanted to think. I dismissed the thought quicker than I usually would, largely because Charlie was the least of my problems. "I didn't know."

"Except that we pay you to know," Bob practically roared. "Dammit, Nichelle! Do you have any idea how stupid it makes me look when I spend months—*months*—going to bat for you with the suits upstairs and you turn right around and drop a ball the size of Mercury? Les was practically glowing when Andrews gave him the go-ahead to send Shelby over to the campus to knock on doors. They even made Parker go with her because he knows so many people on the faculty over there."

I closed my eyes for a long minute, inhaling for a ten count.

"Bob, I'm working on something," I said, holding my voice in check and hoping it would calm him down. "When have I ever let you down?"

"Today." He sat back in the chair and sighed. "This morning, you let me down. If Charlie knows it, you could know it, too. Nobody in this town is better at covering cops than you are, kiddo. But you're only as good as what you're getting for me next, and you know it. You're not the only one Les is gunning for."

I nodded. The *Telegraph* was Bob's entire reason for getting up the morning, but he lived under constant threat of being forced out by Les, who was as smarmy and backstabbing as they come. I couldn't imagine the newsroom without Bob, and it wouldn't be a place I wanted to work.

"I'll apologize to Andrews myself," I said. "But you have to believe me. Grayson is crooked. And I am *thisclose*," I said, holding up my thumb and index finger, barely touching them together, "to finding something that pulls all this together. The girl, too, possibly."

"No." Bob shook his head and leveled a don't-fuck-with-me-on-this glare at me. "Ted Grayson is a politician. Rick Andrews, who happens to be the publisher of this newspaper, is one of his biggest campaign contributors, which you would know if you'd asked our actual politics reporter for information about him. You will back off of Grayson this minute. You will throw yourself into the call girl scandal and find me something that will redeem us both for today. You will work with Shelby for the duration of the story, since she's already been assigned to it. And you will not put another toe out of line, or Shelby Taylor will be my new courts reporter. Are we clear?"

I returned the stare, biting my lip to stave off the pricking in the backs of my eyes that meant tears were threatening.

"Yes, sir."

"Get to work." He turned to his computer screen and flipped it on, dismissing me.

I walked out of his office and saw the back of Les' balding head bobbing through the cubicles toward the break room, but managed to keep myself from chasing him down and delivering a swift *ap-chagi* to his ass. I couldn't even tell if I was madder that he was still trying to help Shelby get my job or that he was after Bob's. I could probably go somewhere else, but Bob...If Les managed to convince Andrews that Bob wasn't still at the top of his game, he'd be pushed into retirement. I didn't think Bob would last long without the newspaper.

I limped to my desk, determined to dig up something on the call girl ring. Shelby could run around RAU banging on doors with Parker all day long, and she could sleep her way into my byline, but she didn't have my connections. I snatched up the phone, feeling stupid for not figuring it out sooner. Lakshmi had told me she was a grad student there, for Christ's sake. Apparently, so was Allison. She also worked for Grayson's campaign, which tied him to it at least marginally. But was her earnest admiration of the senator professional, or had she fallen for her client?

I called Aaron first, and left him a message begging for any five minutes he had that day.

Next, I dialed the head of security at the campus, who, not surprisingly, was in a meeting. But he'd always seemed to like me well enough, and he was an old-school guy who preferred print to TV.

I called Evans at the FBI next. He answered.

"Are you the only law enforcement agency in town who isn't working on the call girl thing?" I asked.

"Not federal jurisdiction, as far as I can see, but it is quite a story," he said. "What can I do for you today, Miss Clarke?"

"Why did you call to tip me off about Billings's arrest?" I asked.

"I thought you'd be interested in it," he said. "You called me asking for information about the dead lobbyist and bribery investigations."

"You know about the bribes, right?" I asked, tired of skirting the issue and in desperate need of an answer. Though I wasn't sure what I'd do with it if I got it. Bob and I had a special bond, but he didn't love anything more than he loved the paper. He would absolutely hand Shelby my job if something I did put his in jeopardy.

"What do you know?" Evans asked.

"I don't have time for this," I said. "You're on Grayson, Kyle Miller at the ATF is on Billings. Got it. But there's something here that ties the two of them together, and it has to do with these two corpses."

"Which two corpses? The lobbyist and the call girl? What's the girl got to do with anything?"

"I was hoping you could tell me that." I sighed. "Look, I don't have a positive I.D., but I'm nearly a hundred percent sure that she's an intern on the Grayson campaign, and she tipped me off about the bribes, though she didn't realize she was doing it. I also hear there's a good chance Grayson's name might be in the call girls' little black book. And he's in the middle of a fight for his career. That's entirely too coincidental, don't you think?"

"Where'd you get that?" Evans asked, his voice suddenly tight. "About Grayson and the call girl?"

"I pieced it together from a couple of interviews."

I didn't know if Grayson was sleeping with Allison or Lakshmi or both, and I wasn't sure I could trust anything, given that my earnest-campaign-worker source had turned out to be a prostitute. And was now dead. The only person I knew hadn't done it was Lucinda Eckersly, because if she strangled a young, athletic girl, I'd deliver my beat to Shelby on a platter and probably never get out of bed again.

Evans was silent for a long minute.

"Let me see what I can find," he said. "I won't talk to another reporter before I talk to you, but this could take a while."

Thanking him for his time, I hung up. Fabulous. Except I didn't have a while.

"Dammit." I grabbed my bag and hurried to the elevator, ignoring my ankle and trying to remember if I had any Advil stashed in the car.

"Where are you off to?" Eunice asked as I stepped onto the elevator. "I thought Bob was going to bust something when he couldn't find you this morning."

"I've got to save my job from Shelby Taylor," I said. "And somewhere around here, there's a murderer who needs catching."

"You leave the murderers to the police, huh, sugar?" she called as the doors closed and saved me from having to reply.

"They think they've got him already," I muttered, pulling my cell phone out of my pocket and tapping out a text to Parker. I paused to send it as I pulled the car out of the garage and got my signal back.

"Keep Shelby away from the math building."

There was a call girl in the statistics department I wanted to get some answers from. My phone binged.

"Chasing her up and down Greek row," his reply read. "This is bullshit. She's waving her press badge under their noses. No one's talking."

"Let her go," I tapped back. "Sorry you're wasting your day. I'll fill you in later."

"Better be a hell of a story. You can buy drinks."

"Capital Ale @ 7. Bring Mel."

If I didn't find something by the time Charlie went on the air again at six, I'd be toasting my new job at the copy desk—or my outright unemployment.

* * *

I scanned the office directory in the math building for the professor Lakshmi had mentioned, hoping he'd know where I could find her. Three-oh-six. Stairs. Yay.

My ankle protested the whole way up, but I found the office, door ajar.

I tapped lightly.

"Come in," a gruff man's voice called.

I poked my head around the doorframe, smiling at the gray-haired, tweed-clad man I assumed was Professor Gaskins.

"Can I help you?" he asked.

"I'm looking for a student of yours, actually, and I could swear she told me she works in your office," I fibbed. "Lakshmi?"

He smiled. "She's my teaching assistant. One of the most brilliant grad students I've ever taught."

"Do you know where I might be able to find her?" I asked. "It's kind of important that I talk to her."

"She usually teaches a freshman course for me this time of day," he said. "Something tells me it might not be packed today, though. It's downstairs in the auditorium."

"Thanks."

I limped back down and opened the lecture hall door, Lakshmi's sweet-as-bells voice ringing clear in the empty hallway. She smiled confused recognition as I slipped into a seat in the back row. There were three students down front, all boys, hanging on her every word.

"Well," she said. "I think that's enough for today, guys. I'll see you Thursday."

"Do you remember me?" I asked once we were alone and face to face.

"From the card game, right?" she asked. "I didn't know you were a student here."

"I'm not." I held her gaze. "I'm a reporter at the *Telegraph*, and I'm working on a story about the call girl who was found in the dumpster outside this morning. I think you might be able to tell me something about that."

Her expression faltered for a split second before she stretched her lips into a thin line and started gathering up her books. "I have no idea what you're talking about."

"I think you do," I said. "I heard your friend the other night making some rather snide comments about your companion and how much he was paying you. I think other people are paying you, too. And I think some of the same people might have been involved with the victim of last night's murder. How do you know you're not next?" Nothing like a healthy dose of terror to make people spill their guts. "I won't use your name. But if the cops get to whoever's behind this, you might live to get your Master's. Talk to me."

Lakshmi shoved the books into a canvas bag and sighed, her eyes on the desk. When she looked up at me, they were full of tears.

"My dad left the government to work in experimental energy. His company went under two years ago," she said. "I would have gotten kicked out of school because we couldn't pay the tuition. He made too much the year before for me to qualify for any aid, and they didn't care that he'd lost everything. Allison offered me a way to stay on campus. She made it sound like fun, and the money was amazing."

"She was in charge?"

"I don't think so, really. She was president of the Delta Kappas when we were undergrads. I took her the money at the end of the night. But I got the idea she was fronting for someone."

I pulled out a notebook and jotted that down.

"Was Senator Grayson a client?"

Lakshmi nodded. "My client, for a while. Allison thought it was funny, because of my major."

"So you were the only girl Grayson saw?"

"A lot of the clients had certain girls they liked, and they liked the girls to be 'theirs,' too, so we had to be careful about what we said. Some of the guys are real bigshots. But either they were old and bald and wanted a young, pretty girl on their arm for some function, or they had wives who weren't into the same things they were in the bedroom. Mostly, I got those guys."

"Ted Grayson?" I guessed.

"He likes his women bound, gagged, and in a little bit of pain, for the most part."

My eyebrows went up.

"Pain?"

"Not torture, or even really heavy masochism," she said. "But he likes to pull hair, hit you, push you around. Pretty tame stuff, on the whole, but still nothing he wanted anyone to know. He pays a pretty penny to have that secret kept."

"How much?"

"Five thousand a night," she said. "I kept three, took two to Allison. I don't know where any of it went after that."

I nodded and kept scribbling. Two thousand dollars a night and multiple girls, it sounded like. So what the hell was with the fake diamonds?

"How often did you see Grayson?" I asked.

"Once a week or so," she said. "Until he got tired of me. I don't miss him. He was creepy. Treated me like I was his property. About the only thing he ever did talk to me about was how beautiful a prize I was, and how I had to stay 'unspoiled' for him."

I jotted her words down, but the other half of my brain was spinning through the numbers. Twenty thousand dollars a month wouldn't exactly be easy to hide. So Grayson sold his vote to the devil to feed his sexual fantasies. And Allison knew this, yet still worked in his campaign office. Blackmail? Was that why she was dead?

"You don't happen to know who got Grayson as a client after you, do you?" I asked.

"I think Allison did." Lakshmi shook her head. "You don't think Ted has anything to do with her death, do you?"

"She was strangled," I said, another thought popping through my head. "Did he go for the bedroom asphyxiation bit?"

"Not with me," Lakshmi said. "But I wouldn't say it's impossible."

I scribbled. Holy shit.

"What am I going to do?" Lakshmi dropped her head into her hands and sobbed, and I wasn't sure she was even talking to me. "I was getting out. My parents are back on their feet and I don't need the cash anymore, and I was going to cut ties with the whole thing after Christmas. Now my whole life is ruined."

"As far as I'm concerned, you're a confidential source," I said. "I'm not the only reporter in town who knows Allison was a prostitute, but if I were you? I'd get suddenly ill, take the rest of the semester off, and hope no one turns your name in. Allison's dead, right? Lay low for a while. It might have the bonus effect of keeping you alive."

She nodded. "What's one semester?"

"Not much compared to a lifetime," I said. "Thanks, Lakshmi. I wasn't kidding when I said I liked you. Good luck."

"You won't print my name?"

"You have my word."

"Consider me gone." She grabbed the bag and headed out the door.

Grayson was taking bribes from Billings. Evans had all but confirmed it. And I knew why. But there were still so many questions.

I was running out of time to find the answers.

Trudy's words about Calhoun came to mind, and I wondered if his local campaign office was open. And who I might find there.

CHAPTER SEVENTEEN

I STRUCK out at the Calhoun campaign office and trudged back to the newsroom, racking my brain for anything about Allison or Grayson I might have missed. I wondered for a second if I wanted the truth, or if I wanted the story I'd been chasing. Which could turn out to be two different things, if Trudy and Kyle were right.

I pulled out the notes from my conversation with Lakshmi and flipped open my computer. At least I'd managed to pull something out on the call girl thing. Bob would have to love an exclusive with one of the girls. Parker hadn't been in his office when I passed, so Shelby was probably still dragging him all over the campus, which meant she didn't have anything.

An arm falling from a dumpster at Richmond American University Thursday morning led Richmond police to a call girl ring operating out of the campus. A former member of the group spoke to the Richmond Telegraph *on condition of anonymity, weaving a tale of powerful men and large stacks of cash.*

"Some of the guys are real bigshots. But either they were old and bald and wanted a young, pretty girl on their arm for some function, or they had wives

who weren't into the same things they were in the bedroom," the source said. "I made five thousand [dollars] a night. I kept three, and gave two to [the victim]."

The source identified the victim as a leader in the prostitution operation, but said she was unsure who else might have been involved.

I finished with some scattered information about Allison and her murder, withholding her involvement with Grayson until I knew if anyone else had it yet. I smiled as I sent it to Bob. The smile faded when I clicked into my browser to check Charlie's coverage.

"Son of a bitch."

I had a call girl as an anonymous source and a link to the sorority house.

Charlie had the madam. On camera. Being led out of an ivy-covered building in handcuffs, Aaron standing at the foot of the steps to ward off the gaggle of reporters.

I watched the footage with a building wave of nausea.

The goddamned dean was running the whole thing, huge white letters across the bottom of my screen screamed, right under "Channel Four exclusive investigation." Charlie had officially kicked my ass. The camera panned to the left and I groaned out loud.

Shelby was talking to a uniformed RAU security officer, scribbling as fast as she could and grinning like a Kardashian in front of a paparazzi.

Why the hell hadn't I heard they were making an arrest?

I fumbled for my scanner. No static. I fiddled with the switch and shook it.

Dead battery.

"Dammit!" It was louder than I intended, and Melanie popped her head over the wall between our cubes.

"You miss a fire sale at Saks or something, doll?" she asked.

"I wish," I said. "I missed the story of the...well, of the day. Maybe the month. But really, when you're only as good as what you have today, what the hell does it matter?"

I dropped my head onto my desk with a dull thunk. I hate losing. And I'm not good at it.

"Oh, shit. Is that the dean of the college of fine arts?" Melanie asked from behind me. I had forgotten she was an RAU alum.

"Yup."

"Running a call girl ring? Daaaamn." She drug out the word and wolf-whistled for good measure. "That's one sexy story. No pun intended."

"Yup."

I got up and turned toward Bob's office, figuring it better to throw myself on the sword than to wait for him to come hunting for me.

"What have you got to say for yourself?" he asked, not turning his eyes from the monitor— which I knew without looking was streaming Charlie's feed—when I tapped on the open door.

"I screwed up." I dropped into my chair. "I could say my scanner died and I was busy trying to get the exclusive interview I just sent you, but you don't care, and it doesn't really matter. Charlie beat me. And it's making me sick to my stomach how badly she beat me."

"She's got you whipped today," he said, leaning on one hand and massaging his temples. "Andrews called me ten minutes ago. Shelby's leading page one with your story going as a companion piece. And she's on the courthouse for a trial period effective Monday. I'm sorry, kid."

I closed my eyes.

"This thing with Grayson—"

Bob's head snapped up. "I told you to back off. Nichelle, I couldn't love you more if I'd raised you, and you know it. But I swear to God, if you tell me you blew this story and made me look like a fool in front of the wunderkind upstairs chasing politics after I told you to drop it, I'll put you on leave. I might even fire you."

"I wasn't chasing Grayson today," I said. "I was interviewing the hooker. I tried to give Grayson to Trudy after I talked to you about it last week, but she doesn't want it. She said she didn't believe it and wouldn't take it 'til after the election. But there's something there, Bob."

"You have enough to do keeping the part of your job you have left," he said. "You don't need to try to do someone else's, too. Trudy knows D.C. better that most of the guys who work up there. Let it go. Pull something out on this and I'll put you on it with her after the election, if you want."

But...

The word didn't make it out of my mouth. Bob had never been so mad at me. More than that, he was disappointed. And that sucked.

"Yes, sir."

I went back to my desk, checking my watch.

I wasn't due to meet Parker for two hours, but I wanted to be in the newsroom for Shelby to gloat over when they got back about as much as I wanted to trade my Louboutins for Birkenstocks.

I stuffed my laptop and charger into my bag and told Melanie goodnight.

"We all have shit days," she said, laying a sympathetic hand on my arm. "You'll get her tomorrow. It will be okay."

I nodded, thinking about Shelby covering the courthouse and wanting to kick something.

"I have to get out of here," I choked out.

"Wine. Sleep. Kick ass," she called after me.

Halfway to the garage, I had a flash of the bracelet on Allison's wrist.

Lucinda Eckersly said her son's whore liked diamonds. But the girl who'd found the body said the bracelet on Allison's wrist was fake. It didn't make sense, unless she'd sold the real one, maybe? What if Grayson was still possessive? Or Eckersly was offering to take Allison away from the mess she'd gotten herself into? Bob's purple face followed close on the heels of that.

But Eckersly wasn't Grayson. I desperately needed a way to redeem myself. Answers about the dead girl would do it. Maybe I could find them in the huge white house.

* * *

I squealed to a stop in front of the Eckersly home, ignoring my sore ankle as I sprinted up the steps.

I yanked the doorbell pull and after about a minute, I reached for the cord again, but Doreen swung the door inward before I could pull it.

"Miss Clarke! How nice of you to call again." She beamed, the picture of old southern hospitality. In this part of the world, people weren't expected to call for an appointment or schedule a meeting. Dropping by was not only acceptable, but welcome. "Miss Lucinda doesn't get much company nowadays, and she liked you."

"I'm glad." I smiled. "She's a firecracker. I liked her, too. Is she up for visitors this evening?"

"She's in the great room watching TV. Did you hear about the poor little girl they found in the dumpster this morning? Such a tragedy."

"Indeed." I stepped through the door.

"I'll just tell Miss Lucinda you're here," Doreen said, scuttling off into the reaches of the enormous house.

I browsed the art and artifacts decking the walls, my eyes coming to rest on a gun rack over the doors that led to the dining room. There were three long-barrel rifles in it. They all looked old, and two of them had ornate carvings on the stocks. Like the one William Eckersly held in the photo in the study.

"Nichelle!" The raspy, wispy voice came from behind me, and I turned with a smile, filing the gun in the back of my mind and grinning wider when I saw that she didn't have a lit cigarette. Maybe I could talk to her for a bit and not risk getting blown up.

"Mrs. Eckersly." I reached down and squeezed her outstretched hand. "How are you?"

She gave me a shrewd once over.

"I think you know how I am, or you wouldn't be here, sugar."

I nodded. "I suspected as much."

"Come on in." She took a drag off her oxygen mask and wheeled herself into the front parlor. She stopped her chair opposite a sofa that would comfortably seat seven and gestured for me to sit down.

"Your son knew Allison?" I asked, reaching into my bag for a notebook and pen.

"Was that her name?" Lucinda chuckled. "Fits her. Perky little thing. That's Billy's whore. Wouldn't say I was sorry, either, but I'm a Christian woman and she was somebody's little girl. Sad situation. Billy tore out of here when the news first came on this morning, and I haven't heard from him since."

I pictured the man from the photos I'd seen on my last visit, wondering about the marks on Allison's neck for a moment. Eckersly was a big guy, and a farmer. Which meant he probably had strong hands. That comment about the men liking to think the girls were "theirs" could go both ways. What if Eckersly found out Allison was seeing Grayson?

"Do you know if Billy knew that Allison saw other men?" I asked.

"I don't know why she'd need to. Billy spent fifteen thousand dollars last month on her 'fees' and dinners and gifts. What twenty-two-year-old girl needs more than that?"

"So he didn't think she had other clients?"

She snorted softly. "He didn't think he was her client. Damned fool thinks he was in love with her. Told me the other night he wasn't paying her to screw him, he was helping put her through school. 'The William Eckersly scholarship program,' he said."

"That's a hell of an application process," I muttered.

"You can say that again," she answered.

"I'm sorry," I said. "I didn't mean for you to hear that."

"Never apologize to anyone for telling the truth, child," she said. "If there's one thing I've learned in near-eighty years walking this Earth, it's that."

"You are very direct," I stopped writing and smiled at her.

"It's a privilege of old age. I get to say what I think and not give a damn whether anybody likes it or not."

"Mrs. Eckersly, did your son kill Allison?"

She cackled. "There you go, sugar. Just honesty. No, I don't believe he did. Thought she was the love of his life. I'm pretty sure the reason he bought her that big diamond bracelet was that he was eyeballing the wedding rings."

"Do you know where he was between midnight and six this morning?"

"I'm sure he was in bed."

"But you don't know that for a fact? You didn't see him come in?" I tried to keep the excitement out of my voice. It would undoubtedly be weeks before the police would be able to get a list of clients out of the madam, because she'd have top-notch attorneys who would keep her from giving them anything incriminating, so they'd have to get warrants and find it. Which meant they wouldn't be looking at Eckersly for a good while. Maybe there was a way to get back on Andrews' good side sitting right in front of me. Sex was a powerful motive for murder. What if he'd found out she was sleeping with other men and just gone apeshit and throttled her? Strangling was almost always a crime of passion.

"I didn't see him come in, but he often stays in the fields or in the city until after I go to bed." Lucinda looked wary.

"Would Doreen have heard him come in?"

"Possibly." Lucinda didn't snap, but I could see the wheels turning. She was pissed at her son, but family is family, especially in the country. Power of attorney be damned, she didn't want him charged with murder.

"You're not going to tell me anything else, are you?" I closed my notebook.

She stared at the fireplace, focusing on the Eckersly family crest above the mantle. "Jesus. Do you really think my boy could have killed that girl?"

"I don't know, Mrs. Eckersly."

"Could you tell Doreen I need my pills?" She gripped the arm of the wheelchair, her voice wispier than usual.

Shit.

"Doreen!" I jumped to my feet and strode quickly to the door, ignoring the twinge in my ankle. "Mrs. Eckersly needs her medicine!"

Doreen bustled in with a silver tray holding a highball glass full of water and a saucer full of pills.

"Miss Lucinda," she fretted as she handed over the pills one at a time and held the water glass steadily against Mrs. Eckersly's lips. "You know better than to get yourself so worked up." She cut a glance at me. "I think you'd better go."

"Is she going to be all right?"

Doreen laid a protective hand on Lucinda's shoulder as Lucinda groped for her oxygen again.

"She needs to rest. I take good care of Mrs. Eckersly, Miss." She nodded to the door and fixed me with a positively shiver-worthy glare.

CHAPTER EIGHTEEN

I WAS ALMOST to the bar where I was supposed to meet Parker and Mel—early but craving a very large glass of Moscato—when my phone rang.

I fished it out of my bag with one hand, keeping my eyes on the increasingly heavy traffic in front of me as parking garages throughout the city began to empty.

"Clarke," I said, pressing it to my shoulder with one cheek.

"What is it your gut is telling you, again?" Kyle's words were clipped.

"What? Why? I thought you had your man."

"I thought I did, too, but the goddamn tire tracks don't match any vehicle Billings owns," he said. "So either you're right and he didn't do it, or I need to figure a way around this before the judge gets wind of this report. I'm searching rental car records for five states and pulling everything else I can think of, but so far I haven't found a damned thing. I've been at it for hours and everything's blurring together. The defense attorneys have the report and are requesting a meeting with the judge tomorrow morning. Can you come up here and talk me through this?"

So much for my glass of wine. "I'll be there in twenty minutes."

I stopped at a light and sent Parker a text.

"Change of plans. Rain check?"

I was to the next light when my cell phone binged his reply.

"No wound-licking. Shelby got lucky. Practically tripped over the cops leading the dean out."

"Changes nothing," I tapped back. "But thanks."

I pulled the car easily into a street space in front of the federal building a few minutes later. Most of the worker bees had gone home for the evening. Inside, I handed my I.D. to the guard at the desk and waited for Kyle to come escort me inside.

"Thanks." He flashed a tight grin as he opened the door for me.

"Don't mention it. It's not every day I get invited into the middle of a federal investigation, Mr. Special Agent. How much of this do I get on the record?"

"Can I answer that after I figure out what the hell's going on here?" He led me down a long, sterile hallway to a conference room and flipped on the lights, waving me toward a table stacked with file folders and boxes of records that looked like months—or years—worth of work.

"Holy shit, Kyle." I whistled. "What is Billings into?"

"Are we on the record?" He flattened his palms on the table and leaned toward me, his eyes probing.

I held his gaze for a long second.

Something worth promising him we weren't was in those folders. I could find a way to confirm what he gave me later.

"Not if you don't want to be."

"He's up to his ass in dirty money and shady deals." Kyle flipped open a folder and pushed it across the table. "He's even got connections in the goddamned Mafia. But he's a slippery sonofabitch. I've never been able to get anything to stick."

I inhaled sharply at his mention of the Mafia, flipping through eight-by-ten glossies of Billings in various places and with various people, scanning the images for Joey and hating that I felt a little sick at the idea. But it would explain how he knew what was going on.

"So you had him on the gun and you thought you'd gotten your big break," I said, thinking about the guns I'd seen in Eckersly's foyer. Kyle had said the one that killed Amesworth was rare, so I wasn't sure how likely it was that there was another one in the Richmond area, but it was worth bringing up. "That's why you went so hard at it with the prosecutor."

"If he gets off, he'll disappear," Kyle said. "Or insulate himself so well I'll never get at him again, and all this work will have been for nothing. So what have you got?"

I tapped my index finger on the black laminate table, still staring at the last photo. Billings was sitting at an outdoor cafe table with a man in a dark suit, and a young woman in large sunglasses whose face was partially hidden behind her hair. No Joey. Thank God. I wasn't supposed to care, but I did anyway.

I shook my head slowly as I raised my eyes to Kyle's. I knew that look. It was the same one that had gotten me to give up my virginity in a secluded spot along the banks of Lake Ray Hubbard.

Kyle was begging.

"I want an exclusive on the whole thing," I said. "Not just whatever we get on the murder, but all of this," I waved a hand at the records on the table. "The ATF talks to no one until the *Telegraph* runs the story. Print, not just online."

"I don't have any control over what the media relations people do," he said, but I could see his thought pattern clearly. He was figuring a way around it the same way he'd figured a way around my bra that long-ago July evening.

"You'll find a way." I flashed a grin and arched one eyebrow.

"I suppose I'll have to." He grinned back.

"All right," I leaned back in the chair. "I don't think Billings is your boy. Not on the murder."

"So you said. But why?"

"Well, for one, he's on house arrest. Was he at RAU in the wee hours this morning?"

"No, he was at home all night. I pull the reports every morning. Why?"

"Then he didn't kill Allison."

"Who?"

"Do you own a TV? The call girl at RAU. It's been all over since early this morning." I grimaced.

"All over the TV? But not the newspaper?" He tilted his head to one side.

"It's been a shit day."

He leaned his elbows on the table and dropped his eyelids halfway, smiling a slow smile that used to make my pulse flutter. I didn't want to admit it still did. "I could help with that."

"Slow down, Captain Hormones," I said, clearing my throat and dropping my eyes back to the photos. "I want my job back."

"You lost your job?" His mouth dropped open. "What the hell happened to you today?"

"Not all of it. Just half." I shook my head and tapped the pictures, pushing them back to the middle of the table. "I really don't want to talk about it. Who are these people?"

"New York Mafia, mostly," he said. "I told you, there's a contraband cigarette trafficking ring running the east coast that steals enough in tax money every year to run a medium-sized country. Well, Billings provides their product at a good rate for a cut of the action."

"How can he do that and still keep his job?"

"They have about thirty fronts set up, some of them as cigarette wholesalers," he said. "And they run an above-board operation in three different states. So on paper, Billings isn't doing anything he shouldn't. But some of the trucks are overweight." He dug through a box and produced a file folder full of weigh station reports. "Only the ones going from the Raymond Garfield factory to certain wholesalers. And only in South Carolina and New York, where the state taxes are some of the highest in the country."

"So there are more cartons in there than they're reporting," I said, flipping through the logs and comparing the weights. "How many cigarettes are there in three hundred pounds?"

"About a hundred and thirty-five thousand." Kyle said.

"And this isn't enough for a warrant?" I asked.

"Not with the kind of defense lawyers Billings can afford," Kyle sighed. "I know he's doing it, but they'll say the trucks were carry-ing...I don't know. Bananas. Luggage. Without an inspection of the contents, I can't prove they're not. And without knowing which trucks are carrying too much, I can't get a warrant to check them. I petitioned for one to cover the whole Raymond Garfield fleet for a month about a year ago, and the judge said there weren't grounds. Trucks turn up overweight every once in a while. These guys are good."

"And the Mafia is running this contraband tobacco thing?"

"There's a shit ton of money in it, and it takes massive organiza-tion," he said. "No one else could handle one this big. I've busted little one-off operations where people fake the tax stamps or just buy packs here, where the taxes are low, and resell them out of alleys in New York, where they're high. People buy a sixty-dollar carton of Marl-boros in an alley for fifty dollars, and the thief still has fifteen in profit per carton because the taxes are so high there. But these guys...They wouldn't have this operation up and running if Billings wasn't supplying their product. There's no other way they could do this volume without it looking suspicious."

I nodded, flipping through the labels on the folders in the box, which were mostly numeric codes I didn't understand.

"And if you get him, you might get them," I said.

"Bingo. Organized crime is a tough nut to crack. They have a lot of practice covering their asses. But if Billings turns on them to save his own ass—" Kyle smiled slightly. "Well. That's the kind of bust that could make a guy's career."

"And the kind of story that could shut Les Simpson up once and for all," I muttered, pulling a folder free from the box.

Kyle leaned forward. "So, what do you say, Nicey?"

"Do I get my exclusive?" I asked.

"I will do everything in my power," he said. "You have my word."

"Show me what's what," I said, waving my hands over the table. "I don't get your numbering system. Where's your file on the murder?"

He pushed a fat folder toward me and flipped it open. A smiling, work I.D. photo of the deceased lay over a glossy of the gnawed-on remains.

"Jesus," I whispered, turning to the forensics report.

"So someone killed him and dumped him almost right away?" I said. "Blunt force head trauma and gunshot wound. Which was the cause of death?"

"The shot."

I nodded.

"Did you get the DNA back on the samples they took?"

"Still waiting. The lab is backed up."

I looked at the report again.

"But the hair was blond. Billings isn't blond."

"No, but the victim was. And the hair doesn't always come from the killer."

I rolled my eyes upward to look at him from under my lashes. "Especially when the investigating officers don't want it to?" I asked, but my brain was considering Grayson and his silver-at-the-temples chestnut coif. Blond hair didn't come from the senator, either.

What if we were both wrong?

If the murders were connected, then it had to be someone who knew Allison, too.

A photo I'd seen in Lucinda Eckersly's parlor flashed through my brain.

Eckersly was hunting, with that old rifle. And he had blond hair peeking out from under his flannel hunting cap.

"Kyle, tell me about the gun," I said, picturing the carvings on the stock of the old rifle hanging over the dining room doorway in the Eckersly's foyer.

He shoved a printout of a picture across the table and I caught a sharp breath. I wished I had a picture of Eckersly's gun to make sure I was right about this one being almost identical.

"Did Billings say where he got this gun?"

"He bought it at an auction."

"And you're sure the bullet came from that gun?"

"No."

My head snapped up.

"I thought you said you had him on the gun."

"I'm sure the bullet came from that kind of gun," he said. "He won't produce the weapon, so I can't be certain if it came from his gun. Convenient time for a priceless rifle to go missing."

"What if it didn't come from his gun?" I tapped my pen on the table, my puzzle starting to fall into place. "Bill Eckersly was a client of the dead call girl. He's also involved somehow with Senator Grayson, and maybe Billings, too. I saw a funny looking old fashioned gun in the foyer at his house today. One with a carved stock like this one. And you know something, because you wouldn't have been there when he drove his truck into the jewelry store the other day if you didn't. What do you make of him?"

"He's supplying Billings with tobacco off the books," he said. "He doesn't strike me as the murdering type. Also, what would he have against a lawyer who's half his age and lives forty miles from him?"

I bit my lip. He was right. I had no motive on Amesworth I could pin to Eckersly, which was why I hadn't seriously suspected him before. But the gun matched the one in Kyle's printout. I was more sure of it the longer I stared at it.

"His mother was worried about him losing the farm," I said. "Maybe he wanted more of the money?"

"Then why kill the lobbyist?" Kyle said. "That guy didn't have any control over who gets what percentage of anything."

The jewelry store clerk's comment about the wad of cash he flashed around the store danced through my head. That didn't fit, either. Especially not with the fake bracelet Allison had been wearing.

Allison.

"The girl?" I asked. "Eckersly's mother said he was in love with her, and she was a prostitute. If it's not money, it's usually sex when someone gets killed."

"So you think Eckersly killed Amesworth over the call girl, and then killed her last night because...?"

"She didn't love him? She was going to tell?"

Wait.

I reached for the forensics report.

"There was slight remodeling on the head wound," I said.

"Yeah. He was hit before he was killed," Kyle said.

"Like, hours before he was killed," I sat up straighter, warming to the scenario in my head. "What if the attorney wanted a little pretty college girl company, so he calls up the dean at his alma mater and they send over Allison—"

"And the lawyer is into something she doesn't want to do?" Kyle grinned.

"Exactly." I nodded. "So she cracks him over the head and panics, calls her best client for help—"

"And Eckersly shows up, says he'll take care of it."

"He loads the body in his truck and takes off, but then he shoots the guy and dumps him instead of taking him home. Allison flips her shit, and says she's going to tell someone."

"So now she's dead, too." Kyle closed the folder. "How did she die?"

"Strangled. Eckersly is a big man."

Kyle stared at the wall behind me, and I could see him putting it together in his head.

"You saw the rifle in his house earlier today?" he asked finally.

"And he has blond hair. What kind of tires are you looking for?"

"Big ones."

"The kind that go on a double-dually pickup, maybe?" I pictured the red monstrosity buried in the side of the jewelry shop.

"Yep." Kyle shook his head. "It wasn't Billings, was it?"

"Nope. Is that truck still impounded somewhere?"

He flipped open his laptop and punched a few keys.

"The Richmond PD has it," he said. "Looks like I'm going to check out tire treads."

"Looks like I have a story to write," I stood. "Call me when you have the warrant?"

"You got it, Lois." He opened the door and pulled me into a tight hug as I tried to slip past him. "Thanks for your help. We always did make a pretty good team." He loosened his hold, but didn't let go.

My breath caught as his eyelids lowered again. My eyes fell shut and I leaned toward him.

Stop. Bad idea, kissing a cop. And bad for him, kissing a reporter in a building that didn't have a dust bunny the security cameras couldn't see.

I ducked under Kyle's arm and stepped into the hall.

"We have work to do," I said from a couple of paces away.

Kyle nodded, his smile not quite reaching his eyes.

"I'll call you when we pick him up."

CHAPTER NINETEEN

I STAYED in the tub until the water turned chilly and my fingers were pruned, then drank nearly half a bottle of pinot noir, but still couldn't sit down for more than five minutes. I finally dug out a duster and started attacking my house room by room, thinking about Senator Grayson. And Allison, the dead call girl/campaign volunteer. And Billings, Lakshmi, and Lucinda.

Darcy gave up following me around after an hour and retreated to her bed in the corner of the living room while I dusted the bookshelves, muttering to myself.

"Grayson is dirty, too." I thought about the stamps that were hidden in my closet. Part of one of them had likely been on the murder victim. How did he get that if it was Eckersly?

And what if Kyle let Billings go and never caught up with him again? I'd seen photographic evidence that Billings was a creep. Somehow, making a fortune stealing tax money from schools and social programs while peddling a product that killed people didn't seem any better to me than shooting someone.

"Jeez, Darcy!" I threw the duster into the corner, whirling on my still-sore ankle and putting my hands on my hips. "What the hell is going on here?"

Darcy raised her head, considered me for a few seconds, sniffed the air for signs of food, then plopped her chin back onto her front paws and sighed.

"Me, too, girl." I said, checking my cell phone for a text or missed call from Kyle.

Nothing.

"I'm missing something," I mumbled, retrieving the duster and returning it to the kitchen cabinet.

But the story Kyle and I had come up with made sense. Maybe I was just operating on adrenaline overload.

"Maybe," I said, eyeing my reflection sternly as I reached for my toothbrush and a tube of Colgate, "you just want the senator to be in this so you weren't chasing the wrong guy the whole time."

Then why did he have the stamps?

I didn't have an answer for that, so I pushed it aside. I shut off the bathroom light and returned to the sofa, where I picked up a puzzle piece and started filling in the bottom corner of my meadow, laying my phone on the cushion next to me where I'd be sure to hear it.

I'd finished the bottom half of the jigsaw by the time Kyle's text came at one-thirty.

"Tires match. Picked him up at a motor lodge outside Ashland with a stripper and a nearly-empty fifth of Jack. Guilty?"

"Maybe." I typed back. "Call me when you're free."

* * *

Agents from the Richmond office of the Bureau of Alcohol, Tobacco, Firearms, and Explosives arrested a local farmer early Friday in connection with the murder of Daniel Amesworth, 29, a west end attorney whose remains were found near the city limits last week. William Eckersly, 37, whose family owns the largest tobacco farm in Powhatan county, is also a suspect in the death of RAU student Allison Brantley, whose body was found on the campus Thursday.

"I'm limited by agency policy," ATF Special Agent Kyle Miller said early

Friday. "But I can confirm that Mr. Eckersly is a person of interest in two open murder investigations."

I had the story ready for Bob when he arrived at seven, and his eyebrows raised higher by degrees as he read through it. By the time he turned the chair to face me, they were almost on top of his head.

"I haven't heard a word about this," he said. "Where the hell did you get it?"

"I'm just that good, I guess," I said. "Consider it a peace offering. I'm sorry I pissed you off yesterday."

"This is quite an amends," he said. "How long do we have before Charlie gets wind of it?"

"He promised me an exclusive until we'd printed it."

Bob shook his head. "Not sure I want to know what you had to do for that."

"Not what you're thinking," I said. "I'm me, not Shelby. Even if I have been acting a little like her lately. I don't want Trudy's job, Bob. Today, I don't even want the *Post.* I just want my beat back the way it was."

"I'm not sure I can promise you that," he said. "This is good, but Les is pretty determined. "

I nodded. "I'm prepared to impress Andrews on a daily basis for as long as it takes."

"Something tells me you'll win him over eventually." Bob grinned. "This will help. I'm going to have Ryan put it on the web now. Twenty-four hours is a long time for something like this to stay quiet in a town like Powhatan. The ATF talking is the least of my worries."

I stood. Bob's voice stopped me in the doorway. "Hey, kid? Nice work."

* * *

I had to be at the courthouse for the dean's arraignment at eleven. I checked the docket for the prosecutor's name at ten-fifteen and grinned when I saw it. DonnaJo. It'd been a while since I'd seen my friend in action, and she was a good lawyer who had a flair for firing off intensely quotable snippets in her arguments. She was also a former beauty queen who usually won points with the jury for her blonde good looks and southern belle charm. Tough break for the dean. I reached for the phone.

"I can't tell you shit until I get into the courtroom, honey," DonnaJo said in place of a hello when she answered.

"Aw, come on, DonnaJo," I said. "I'll buy you a glass of wine after work."

"Not today, doll," she said. "Boss's orders. There are reporters camped out in every corner of this building, and Corry threatened to put me on parking detail if I breathed a word to anyone. Everybody from the Mayor to Ted Grayson has been in his office since yesterday afternoon, and I think he's worried about his own ass. Folks are afraid this mess is going to be the end of the university, and the school is important to the city."

Yeah, and the local politicians are in the dean's little black book.

"Plus, that big murder case he took on himself is about to walk, because the ATF picked someone else up last night," she said. "Come to the hearing; I've got some good stuff."

"I'll see you in a bit."

I typed a couple of things into my notes before I turned my computer off and headed for the elevators.The doors had just started to close when a small hand with a perfect scarlet manicure shot around the edge of the frame.

"Going somewhere, Nichelle?" Shelby stepped into the elevator, her big eyes bigger than usual and a smirk firmly in place on her lips. She pushed the basement button.

"I have a hearing to cover this morning." I smiled and swallowed the "you backstabbing bitch" part of that comment. "It's not Monday yet."

"You should say goodbye to your friends down there." She grinned as the doors closed, but it was the kind of grin I'd expect from a cartoon cat with yellow feathers poking through its teeth as the little old lady searches for her pet canary.

"Don't get too comfortable, Shelby," I said, stepping out of the elevator. "I'm not going anywhere for long."

"We'll see, Nichelle. Enjoy your last day at the courthouse."

The doors closed and I turned and strode to my car. Shelby could gloat all she wanted. I wasn't much for giving up.

I sped toward the courthouse and managed to wedge my car between two of the TV trucks out front by blocking one's door, turning sideways and flattening myself against the car to get out. I hurried through security and into courtroom number six, where DonnaJo was opening her briefcase at the prosecution table. I chose a seat caddy-cornered from her so I could see her face, and watched the gallery fill with reporters and curious lawyers. By the time the judge came in, it was standing room only.

The dean sat, still in the clothes she'd worn to work the day before, her mascara running and her head down to shield her face from the cameras, silent for the duration of the hearing except when she was ordered to stand and offer a plea.

"Not guilty." It was barely above a whisper.

DonnaJo produced bank statements and a witness list that even made the judge raise an eyebrow at the defendant. I held my breath waiting for Grayson's name, but didn't hear it. Two city councilmen and a couple of high-profile state officials, though. And more names would come.

The judge banged his gavel after an hour, holding the dean over for the grand jury with no bond. Wow. A no-bond was rare, even in murder cases. This lady was in deep shit.

On my way out, I saw Kyle standing outside the front door shouting into his iPhone. I paused, looking toward the TV reporters who were scrambling to get the dean's hearing ready for the noon broadcasts, which were already half over. I turned back to Kyle, wondering what he was mad about.

"On what planet does it take six days to get a fucking rush ballistics analysis?" He spat. "I dropped that weapon off at six a.m. I don't give two shits if you're doing work for the President himself, I want my report by tomorrow morning."

He clicked off the call and shook his head, then looked up at me.

"Ever feel like you're surrounded by lazy assholes?"

"I've been there. You found Eckersly's rifle?"

"Right where you said it was. His mother is a spitfire, isn't she? She squawked about it being a family heirloom and threatened to sue if we so much as breathed on the damned thing. It's a beauty," he said. "But seriously. All the hell I'm asking them to do is fire it into a bucket of sand and compare the casing with the one they pulled out of Amesworth. How long does that fucking take? If I could do it myself, I would. But the difference in the striations from two such similar guns might be pretty subtle, and I could miss it. I don't want to make another mistake."

"I do know that feeling," I said. "And well. Speaking of, I'd better get back to work."

"Want to grab a drink later?" he asked.

"I've been up for essentially twenty-seven hours right now," I said. "But I'll call you tomorrow, if you want."

I wasn't sure I would, but seeing the way his blue eyes lit when I offered, I wasn't sure I wouldn't, either.

"See you. Thanks for talking me through it last night."

"Thanks for giving me the exclusive. I'm off my editor's shit list. Now I just have to impress the publisher."

"I have utter faith in you." He grinned.

"Have fun with your interrogation."

"Always." He winked and disappeared into the courthouse.

CHAPTER TWENTY

CHARLIE HAD Eckersly's arrest at noon and six, but Kyle didn't talk to her, which had to be frustrating the hell out of her. The ATF's public information people were every bit as forthcoming as the FBI's—which is to say they weren't forthcoming at all. But the dean's hearing and the aftermath of the bust at the university was the big story of the day, and by the time I finished my piece on the hearing, got it to Bob, and made the corrections he wanted, nearly everyone else had gone home.

I was exhausted, and had pushed through the afternoon with a lot of help from the coffeemaker. But there were a couple of police reports I wanted to read before I went home.

I went back to the break room in search of more caffeine, reading a printout of a new burglary report as I waited for a fresh pot to brew. I filled my mug and reached for the upper cabinet to get my syrup bottle, momentarily forgetting it wasn't there. People suck sometimes. I made a mental note to fill an empty one with soap and leave it for the bandit at some point.

I added three packets of Splenda to my cup and grabbed the robbery report, which looked much more in line with the cat burglar than Grayson's house had. Turning to go back to my desk, I wondered what the chances were that Aaron was still at work.

I tried his office and his cell and left messages in both places, setting the printout on top of my inbox and turning to my laptop. Eckersly had the right tires on his pickup, and he might have motive. Billings, a tobacco executive, was running contraband cigarettes he was making from tobacco he was getting from Eckersly. And the two of them were bribing Senator Grayson, who was into call girls and kink.

Something still didn't fit. Grayson was the wacky-jigsawed odd piece of this puzzle, but I couldn't put my finger on why.

"Did Grayson want out?" I wondered aloud.

I typed his name into my Google bar.

Same stories, same homepages, and social accounts I'd seen before.

I clicked to the images. There was a new shot from a campaign rally two days before. Grayson's son had grown up since the last campaign, though he was mostly hidden behind the woman holding the senator's hand. But she wasn't the same woman from the family photo I'd seen before. That woman was a brunette who needed to lose about sixty pounds and looked uncomfortable in her own skin. This woman was a petite blonde with a winning smile.

I clicked to the image source and scrolled to the caption. Senator Ted Grayson, his wife, Katharine, and son, Jack, at a campaign rally in Williamsburg.

I typed Katherine Grayson into the search bar and clicked the images.

The very first one was a side by side, part of a story in *Washington Monthly* about Mrs. Grayson's transformation. According to the article, she'd grown up very poor, gone to Princeton on a scholarship, married well, but gained weight with her pregnancy and lost her self-esteem for a number of years. Then she lost sixty-five pounds, colored her hair, and adopted a new life philosophy of envisioning everything she wanted, all thanks to a yoga retreat in the Blue Ridge Mountains.

"Would she murder someone to get her vision?" I wondered aloud, staring at her perfect, Estee Lauder rose smile.

"Sex. And money." I closed my eyes for a second, then stared at the photos for another long minute. Katherine Grayson had a very nice life. And her husband's extracurricular activities could erase it. Her status and income depended on his. Damn damn damn.

I snatched up the phone and called Kyle.

Voicemail.

I clicked open an email and typed out a message.

"Bad news. I think we got it wrong again. Have those hairs from Amesworth's jacket checked for bleach. Call me when you get this."

I stared at the photos for another minute, a familiar nagging in the back of my brain telling me I knew her from somewhere.

"She's a senator's wife," I said aloud, stifling a yawn as I closed my laptop and shoved it into my bag. "It's not like her picture hasn't ever been in the news."

I turned Grayson, his wife, and Allison over and around in my mind on the short drive home. There was something there, but I was too tired to see it. Maybe a good night's sleep would shake whatever it was loose.

I unlocked the kitchen door and stepped into the house.

Something exploded on the far side of the room, flashing orange in the dark. A millisecond later, my shoulder caught fire. I staggered backward, the small of my back hitting the sharp edge of the tile countertop. I didn't really feel it, though. I couldn't concentrate on anything but my shoulder, which felt warm and sticky when I grabbed it. I slid down the front of the cabinet to sit on the floor, the coppery tang of blood in my nostrils making me nauseous.

I was pretty sure I'd just been shot.

* * *

Joey's warning floated through my head, followed closely by all the articles I'd read about the Mafia and every warning I'd blown off in the past couple of weeks. Was I about to become a Mafia statistic? Or was Mrs. Grayson still trigger happy?

Footfalls on the tile floor brought my attacker closer, and my whole body flinched when someone kicked my foot. Between the darkness and the blinding pain, I couldn't see.

"Who—who are you?" I stammered.

"I'm nobody." Male. Young. He stepped into the light spilling through the open kitchen door. "But my father is somebody. And he's going to stay that way."

"Jack." My mouth fell open. He was even wearing the same t-shirt he'd been wearing at the body dump site. Which was where I'd seen Katherine Grayson's blonde bob. She just hadn't been smiling that night. "Jack Grayson. Oh, kid, what have you done?"

"What I had to," he said. "My parents can't go down for this."

The pain in my shoulder and sheer exhaustion were taking their toll, because he wasn't making any sense. The parents couldn't go to jail, but the kid was going to kill me. What is this, *Clue*? "I'm not following you. Did everybody do it?"

"Technically, my mom killed that asshole Amesworth," Jack leaned a hip against the table, keeping the gun trained on me.

"How do you technically kill someone?"

"She begged him to stop bringing my dad money. She was terrified Calhoun's staff would get wind of it, and it would cost my dad the election. Amesworth laughed and told her he didn't have any say so over who Billings was bribing or for how long, and then told her if she was better in the sack her husband wouldn't need money for whores. She hauled off and slapped him. He got rough with her. I was coming in from a late class, and I heard the whole thing. I grabbed the closest heavy thing and swung as hard as I could. What else could I do?"

He was getting chatty in his defensiveness. Okay, tell me all about it, kid. "You fractured his skull," I said.

"It made a weird noise," he said. "He fell on my mom. And he bled. A lot. I pulled him onto the floor, and I lost it. I thought he was dead. He didn't look like he was breathing. I wasn't trying to kill him. My mom said I'd saved her and maybe saved our family, but we couldn't just claim it was self-defense. It would be a complete scandal for my dad's campaign. We did what we had to and rolled him up in a shower curtain and threw him in the back of that hillbilly pickup that my dad borrowed for his hunting trip. We drove to the woods. But when we pulled him out of the truck, he started moaning and moving. There was a rifle in the gun rack, and my mom grabbed it and shot him in the head. She said no one would ever believe us and he'd ruin our whole lives."

"But you couldn't stay away," I said.

"I had nightmares. I went back out there to make sure he was still buried, and something had dug him up. Tina was with me. She flipped out. I had to call the cops and report it."

The pain in my shoulder had dulled to a throb, but the wet warmth on my blouse was spreading, and I was getting lightheaded. Think, Nichelle.

What was in the cabinet behind me?

"So you haven't done anything, really," I said, reaching my good hand behind me and trying to open the cabinet. My weight was keeping it shut, and I couldn't move without him noticing. "You didn't kill him, and the cops don't have any idea you had anything to do with it. So why don't you go home, before you do something that really will ruin your life. I'll get some stitches and go to bed, and everyone's happy."

He stared for a second, then threw back his head and laughed. It was loud and hollow, telling me I was running out of stalling time. I scooted forward a few inches and flipped the cabinet open as discreetly as possible with the dark as my cover.

"Lady, I'm at William and Mary on scholarship. I'm eighteen and I'm a junior in college. I'm not stupid. How many college kids can hack into the ATF's email system? I got the message you sent your agent friend earlier. He will not. And my mother isn't going to prison because my father can't keep his dick in his pants."

Shit. That meant Kyle was probably drinking beer with his team, celebrating Eckersly's arrest while I was here with Captain Sociopath. No one was coming to save me. I felt around in the cabinet, trying not to move my arm enough for him to notice. My fingers closed around the handle of a heavy iron skillet. I'd have to get close enough to whack him with it before he could shoot me. How? I squeezed the handle so hard the iron bit into my palm and leveled a stare at Jack.

"If Kyle doesn't know, then your secret is safe, right? I'm not telling anyone."

"You're a reporter. It's your job to tell people shit that's none of their business."

"Not when I'd like to avoid getting shot again."

He chuckled.

"You're nice. I looked you up—pictures of your dog, shoes, and fluffy-bunny quotes was all I found. You were nice to us that night in the woods, too. I was really hoping you wouldn't figure this out. Your agent friend is way off the mark. I've been watching his emails for weeks." I remembered Kyle saying something about a bug in the ATF computer system. And Grayson's kid on a computer scholarship. Nice time to catch up, Nichelle.

"Jack, you don't want to do this," I said. "You had nightmares about Amesworth, right? And you didn't kill him. How do you know that won't happen again?"

"The whore isn't haunting me."

I grimaced. "Oh, kid."

"It wasn't as hard as I was afraid it would be," he said. "I just waited for her to come out of the building and got behind her with a guitar string and pulled. She didn't even fight, really. A couple of scratches, a kick, and that was it."

"Why?"

"This was all her fault."

Nice logic there, smart guy.

"How?"

"She was the reason my dad needed the money, wasn't she? Then she emailed him last week. Said she figured out where he was getting the money to pay her and she'd go to Calhoun's campaign with the whole story if he didn't make her a local campaign manager. But if he does that, everyone thinks he's screwing the pretty young intern, anyway, right? No way to win."

"Okay." I tried to force my brain to find the words that would keep me alive. "So she's dead. Who else knows? If Billings was going to talk, he'd have done it already, right? He's been on house arrest and charged with murder for a week. He has other friends that he really doesn't want to piss off by cutting deals with the ATF. Prison could be the least of that guy's worries."

He straightened up.

"You're a fast talker, Miss Clarke, but I'm afraid I don't believe you." He leveled the gun. "I even tried to scare you off. You should have taken the hint."

"Darcy!" I panicked.

I heard muffled yapping and claws on wood.

"She's in the bathroom," Jack said. "You don't think I'd actually hurt a dog, do you? I'm not a monster."

"Jack?" I tugged the pan to the edge of the shelf, done talking to the sociopath.

"Yeah?" He cocked his head to one side.

"Look out."

He turned to look over his shoulder reflexively, and the cookie sheets inside the cabinet crashed when I wrenched the skillet free. Darcy's scratching popped the broken door unlatched and she raced in, barking. Jack stumbled toward me, waving the gun the other way and firing a shot at the refrigerator.

"Darcy!"

She kept barking. I whipped the pan around to my front, used my injured arm to steady it, and swung with my good one.

The reverberation when the skillet connected with his knees sent a shockwave into my bleeding shoulder that made me scream, but he screamed louder, tumbling sideways onto the floor. The gun skittered across the linoleum into the dark.

"You bitch!" Jack howled.

"You should have taken me up on that offer, Jack." I tried to get to my feet and failed, my sore ankle giving at the worst possible time and causing me to lose my balance. He scrambled for the gun, and I willed myself to stand, fighting wooziness when I managed to pull it off.

My foot protested the two steps toward him as his fingers closed around the gun. Shit.

I raised the pan and brought it down on his hip, and he yelped and froze for an instant, but didn't let go of the gun. I lifted one foot and stomped my pump down on his empty hand with all the force I could muster, leaning all my weight on that leg. There was no doubt I was doing further damage to my sprain, but I knew from the crunch under my heel I wasn't the only one feeling it.

He screamed again, finally letting go of the gun. I dove for it, snatching it up by the barrel and flipping it around. I didn't have the first damned clue how to shoot it, but I figured I had decent odds of hitting something at that range.

"Don't move." My voice shook.

I wasn't sure if he replied, because my heart pounding in my ears was the only thing I could hear for a good thirty seconds. When it faded, he was still howling.

"My hand! You broke my fucking hand!"

The indignation would have been funny, if I'd had the capacity to laugh.

"Maybe you shouldn't have tried to kill me."

I backed carefully toward the door, my only thought that I needed to get to the car and get the hell out of there, when I heard footfalls on the steps. I held my breath.

"Nichelle?" The door flew into the wall and light flooded the room. "What the hell is going on in here?"

"Thank God." I handed Joey the gun and sagged into a chair. "Joey, meet Jack Grayson. He shot me."

"She hit me with a fucking frying pan and then crushed my hand," Jack howled.

"Shut up, kid. And be still." Joey shoved the gun into the back of his waistband and knelt in front of me, probing my shoulder with his fingers. "Always too late to save the day." He brushed my hair out of my face and smiled.

"Can you take me to St. Vincent's?" I asked. "I don't feel so good."

"You have a plan for dealing with the kid?"

"Kyle. My phone's over there somewhere." I waved a hand toward the door and collapsed across the tabletop.

CHAPTER TWENTY-ONE

I OPENED my eyes to find Joey pressing a dish towel over my wound and Kyle barking orders at a handful of agents who were cordoning off my kitchen as a crime scene. Jack was gone.

"Can I get medical attention now?" I asked when Kyle stopped and put a hand over mine, shaking his head.

"Of all the calls to miss," he said. " I'm so sorry. I wouldn't have seen this coming in a million years."

"S'ok. I was calling to tell you to go arrest that little psychopath's mother, but then I emailed you, and he intercepted the email. You might want to get your tech guys on that. He said he's been reading your emails for weeks. He was here when I got home." I laid my head back on the table and Joey's hands tightened on my shoulder.

"I need to get her to a doctor." Joey said. "What the hell is taking that ambulance so long?"

"What was your role in all of this?" Kyle asked. "I still don't think I caught your name."

"I didn't offer it," Joey said. "All I did was stop in to see a friend and walk in on the tail end of the attack. She had disarmed him already. I can't tell you anything."

The two of them eyed each other warily.

"Bleeding. Hospital." I smiled wanly, trying to get their attention off each other.

"I could've walked there by now," Joey said, scooping me into his arms.

"I'll be by in a while." Kyle glared as Joey turned for the door. I didn't have the energy to care. I laid my head on Joey's shoulder and mumbled an apology for getting blood on his suit.

"Not like it's never happened before." His lips grazed my ear as he whispered, walking down the steps and settling me into the passenger seat of his Lincoln. "Though I'd rather not wear any more of your blood, if you don't mind."

I smiled and leaned back against the seat. "I'd like that."

Joey laughed when I pulled out my cell phone and started typing. I shushed him, firing off an email to Bob with a short, hit-the-high-lights story on Jack Grayson. My shoulder throbbed, but damned if I was going to lose this headline to Charlie—or worse, Shelby—while I was getting stitched up. I called Bob to give him a heads-up since it was so late, and he roared "what?" so loud my ear rang when I told him I'd been shot. Assuring him I was fine, I rushed him off the phone when Joey pulled into the ER lot at St. Vincent's. I didn't like upsetting Bob, but I needed him to get the story up before Charlie caught wind of it.

A pair of stout nurses who clearly thought Joey shot me banished him to the waiting room and gave me the domestic violence inquisition, but after repeated assurance that he'd had nothing to do with it, they let him come in while a doctor tended to my shoulder.

The shortest nurse continued to give Joey the stink eye, even with me hiding my face in his shoulder and him stroking my hair as the doctor stitched up the wounds—which were on both sides, since the bullet went clean through.

"She should've been a nun." Joey laughed as the woman shot him another glare on her way to get a second unit of blood for me. "I feel like I'm back in Sister Mary Paul's classroom in ninth grade. She didn't like me so much, either."

"How could anyone dislike you?" I blurted, thinking I shouldn't say that out loud, but unable to fight off the haze from the pain medication enough to censor it.

"Plenty of people dislike me." He cradled my jaw in one hand, running a thumb lightly along my cheekbone. "I'm glad you're not one of them. But can you do me a favor? The next time I tell you to stay the hell out of something, will you listen?"

"Very possibly," I slurred sleepily. "I didn't believe you. And I never suspected Jack. Did you know it was him?"

"No. I was pretty sure it was his father, just like you." He dropped his hand to my lap and grabbed the one of mine that didn't have an IV in it. "Grayson's been talking to a few of my associates about their interest in keeping the taxes on cigarettes as high as they can go. He figured out Billings was double-dipping. He's been taking money from us for product under the table, and then doing the company's dirty work paying off politicians. Grayson decided he could eat his cake and have it, too. Vote his conscience on the tax hikes, but still have the money coming in for his girl.

"It was just coming in from my side instead of big tobacco. I thought he had it out with the lobbyist and shot him. But I knew poking around him would lead you back to some," he paused, "associates of mine. I worried about you pissing them off. Then I saw your story this morning and thought the farmer did it. But for a kid to be able to murder two people—almost three—in cold blood? Damn."

"I'm glad it wasn't you," I said, squeezing his hand.

"I would love it if you'd stop thinking I killed every dead guy who turns up in your day."

"I'm getting there."

My cell phone binged, but it sounded impossibly far away. I didn't have the energy to look around for it.

"That's my cue." Joey flipped the phone into my lap and crossed to the door. "Your federal agent friend is in the parking lot. Wants to know what room we're in."

"Hurry back," I said.

He turned from the doorway and smiled. "I don't think you're getting rid of me this time."

Kyle shoved the door open and strode to the side of the bed less than three minutes later, grasping my free hand and knitting his eyebrows together as he hovered.

"Goddammit, I feel like a first-class moron. Some supercop I turned out to be. I am so, so sorry, Nicey. I was so far from thinking it was that kid, I'd have suspected Lex Luthor first."

"The mother. I found pictures of her online tonight and recognized her, but I didn't place her at the body recovery until after I got home. Jack cracked Amesworth over the head because mom's begging him to leave her hubby alone turned ugly. They thought he was dead, but then they got him out to the woods and he woke up. She shot him with the rifle Grayson borrowed from Eckersly. So they both did it?"

"There's more, apparently–Billings and Eckersly had cooked up their own cigarette trafficking operation when the higher tax rates passed here."

"I see," I said, fighting to keep my eyes open.

He perched on the edge of my cot, eyeing the units of blood hanging from the IV stand. "They didn't need Grayson on their payroll anymore. So he stole a set of Virginia tax stamps from Amesworth's office and tried to blackmail Billings. Threatened to rat him out to the mob for bigfooting their territory while he's still selling them product. Billings and Eckersly were buying the stamps through a front at that jewelry store, paying real money for fake diamonds and taking the stamps with the receipts. Billings sent his boy Eckersly to talk the senator down because the two of them are tight. Eckersly is a big contributor to political campaigns. When that didn't work, Billings sent Eckersly to steal the stamps."

"Damn," I said. "Covering politics is not as much fun as I thought."

"You okay?" He laid a hand on my arm.

"I'm so tired," I sighed. "Sleep deprivation, adrenaline, blood loss. I want to sleep until next week."

"There's about a dozen reporters on your lawn driving your dog batshit, and a couple of your friends from the PD are in the waiting room."

"Aw, hell. Seriously?"

"Sorry. I issued an all call to your house when your friend called me. Where'd he go, by the way?"

"Coffee. He'll be back. I think."

"Who is that guy, Nichelle? There's something about him I don't like."

"Besides the fact that there's something about him I do?" I needed to deflect that question for as long as I could. "You promised me an exclusive. No talking to the TV guys," I slurred, my eyelids dropping shut.

As I drifted off, I felt Kyle's lips against my forehead and heard his voice from the other end of a tunnel. "I don't want to talk to anyone but you."

* * *

Kyle had a crew clean up the blood in my kitchen before Joey took me home the next evening. He walked me inside and checked the whole house to make me feel safe before he left me with a brief kiss and a promise to call the next day.

"So I get to talk to you on the phone now?" I asked, leaning against the doorframe and smiling. "I'm moving up in the world."

"I still say I'm more charming in person," he said.

I locked the door behind him and fed Darcy before I climbed into bed with my laptop. It took more than an hour to piece together everything I knew about Grayson for Sunday's front page, and by the time I finished typing and emailed the file to Bob, my shoulder was burning again. I took a Vicodin and managed to find a comfortable position with the help of several strategically-placed pillows, dozing the evening away.

Convincing my mom to stay in Texas was no easy feat, but her bridezilla client's wedding was in less than a week, and I begged her not to throw the account away because of me, tossing in a tiny fib about Kyle taking care of me to make her feel better. Kyle did call on Sunday. So did Joey. I snuggled back into my pillows after each conversation wondering what I was going to do about the two of them.

* * *

Whether it was the blood transfusions or the narcotic-induced full weekend of sleep, I felt like a new woman by Monday morning. My arm was in a sling, and would stay that way for three weeks. Instead of skipping the gym altogether, I settled for walking on the treadmill, watching a recap of Charlie's weekend coverage of the Ted Grayson scandal on the flatscreens that lined the wall. He'd resigned when my story about Jack went live, bribery and solicitation charges notwithstanding. I already knew that, but she had a tidbit on a possible challenger for Calhoun in the swiftly-coming election that I hadn't seen.

"Knock yourself out, Trudy," I said. "I can't wait to read it."

I walked into Bob's office at five 'til eight, sporting a pair of sapphire Louboutins that almost matched the color of my hospital-issue sling.

"Miss Clarke." Rick Andrews, our publisher, was in my usual chair. He rose when I walked in, putting a hand out and smiling. "Welcome back."

"You have no idea how glad I am to be here, sir," I said, shaking his hand with my uninjured one.

"We're very glad to have you. Your piece yesterday was outstanding, and the fallout from all this is just beginning, so I'm told." He smiled stiffly, and I thought about what Bob had said about Grayson being his friend. But not that good a friend, apparently.

"I'm on top of it," I said.

"So you've shown. I came down this morning to congratulate you, and extend the gratitude of this newspaper. But I also owe you an apology. Bob tells me you were working on this investigation last week, and I had no idea. The courthouse is yours again, if you want it back."

"I would love that." I smiled.

"Good." He stepped aside, and I lowered myself gently into my chair. Andrews and Bob exchanged nods.

"I'll leave you to running your newsroom, Bob," Andrews said from the doorway.

"I appreciate that, Rick."

Bob swiveled his chair toward me and I flashed a grin.

"Not bad in terms of making up for getting my ass kicked, huh?"

He narrowed his eyes at the sling.

"Are you ever going to learn?"

"I hope so." I moved my shoulder gingerly. "This is way less glamorous than it looks on TV."

"But you're still rocking the shoes," Parker said, shaking his head and sitting down across from me. "I'm going to appoint myself your full time bodyguard. Mel says someone has to do it."

"That could work," I said. "Will you drive me around, too?"

He rolled his eyes and looked at Bob. "Can you give her something less dangerous to cover? Like, I don't know, a war?"

Bob laughed. "Her escapades are always good for sales," he said. "Besides, this one got the other half of her beat away from Shelby."

"She's going to be pissed." I smiled at the thought.

"She threatened to quit," Bob said. "Les talked her out of it."

"Damn." I shook my head.

"Hey, before I forget; I left your coffee syrup on your desk, Clarke," Parker said. "Sorry it took me a couple of days to get it back to you. I had to go to three different stores to find the sugar-free one. It really is good, though. And better for me than sugar and half-and-half. Thanks."

Parker. I smiled, not even able to muster a little of the annoyance I'd felt as the syrup disappeared by degrees. "We'll take turns buying?"

"Works for me, Lois," he said.

Everyone filed in for the staff meeting, which Trudy finished off with a call for applause.

"I'm a big girl, and I can admit when I'm wrong. It's rare," she said, grinning at me, "but it happens. Nichelle, honey, you have my congratulations and thanks, and best wishes for a speedy recovery. I also owe you an apology. I should have listened to you last week. I thought I knew my people better than anyone else could. I won't make that mistake again. So, you know, anytime you feel like tipping me to the story of the year, bring it on. I promise to listen."

"Thanks, Trudy." I returned the smile. "No hard feelings?"

"Are you kidding? I'm going to be up for a Pulitzer by the time I get through with Grayson. I owe you a bottle of wine. Or a pair of new shoes."

"Size nine." I chirped. Everyone laughed.

Back at my desk, I scanned through police reports. Nothing except another robbery. This one looked to be the work of the cat burglar, too—which sounded nice and safe.

I opened my email, finger on the delete key for the usual Monday morning blitzkreig of "Miracle Weight Loss!" and "Penis Enlargement Now!" spam.

At the top of my inbox, sent less than five minutes ago from a washintonpost.com address, was a subject line: brava. My heart in my throat, I clicked it open. It was from the politics editor.

"Nicely done. I'll have an eye out for your byline."

"Holy headlines, Lois." I sat back in the chair and smiled.

SMALL TOWN SPIN

CHAPTER ONE

THE NEWS DOESN'T TAKE sick days.

Generally, the number of blocks on a calendar that I don't work are rarer than comfortable shoes at a runway show. But four hours into a double shot of Claritin and DayQuil on a sunny April afternoon, I still felt like I'd been hit by a truck, and had only managed to finish one story.

"I think pollen season has won the afternoon, kiddo," my editor said, eyeballing me from the doorway of my cubicle. I tried to lift my head to reply, but dropped it back to my desk with a dull *thunk*.

"I'm fine," I said into the blotter.

"Go home, Nichelle." Bob patted my shoulder.

Happy to oblige.

* * *

Settled on my overstuffed navy sofa with my toy Pomeranian snuggled in my lap and the TV remote in hand, I managed three sips of my honey-lemon tea before my cell phone erupted into *Second Star to the Right*.

The dog sat up and growled. I patted her and dropped the remote, reaching for the phone. Parker.

"I really am sick," I said by way of hello when I picked up. Just in case he couldn't tell—a shoebox full of clothespins clamped on my nose wouldn't have lent my voice any more of a ridiculous twang.

"You'll thank me in a minute," he said. "I have a story for you. An exclusive, if you can drag yourself back out of bed."

"Drugs or gambling?" I asked, tilting my head to hold the phone against my shoulder while I reached for a notebook and pen. Parker was the star sports columnist at the *Richmond Telegraph*, and I figured if he was tipping the crime reporter (that'd be me) to a story, it meant an athlete had been busted for one of those things.

"Suicide," he said.

"Aw, hell." I blew out a short breath and dissolved into a coughing fit. "Sorry. Stupid pollen. I hate writing about suicides. Of all the depressing stories I do, those are the ones that get to me the most."

"I need you to do this," he said. "Personal favor. It—" His voice broke, and he paused. "It won't stay quiet forever."

His pleading note left no room for excuses—or allergies. Parker was a good friend. I could suck it up to help him out. Plus, sad subject aside, I couldn't hang up without getting the scoop. Story of my life.

I sighed, pen poised. "Spill it."

"Tony Okerson," he said.

"The football player?" Holy Manolos. "How do you figure that's going to stay quiet for three seconds? That guy is a living legend."

"Tony Okerson, Junior," Parker said, and I pinched my eyes shut. A kid. Shit, shit, shit. I noted the name and listened as he went on.

"So far, they've kept a lid on it, but it's only been a few hours," he continued. "The local paper will run a spread tomorrow and it'll be open season. Tony is one of my best friends, Clarke. They're devastated."

"I can't imagine," I said, my heart dropping into my stomach at the depth of pain in his voice. "I'm sorry, Parker. But what is it you want me to do with this?"

"Tony's convinced he can control the media spin. I told him he has a better shot if he talks to you and lets us break the story. You know cops and crime better than anyone. Can you be in Tidewater by four o'clock?"

"Tidewater? Not D. C.?"

"When Tony retired last year, they moved into their beach house. It's on a little island out there. Tony wanted his kids to have normal childhoods. Thought moving to a real-life Mayberry was the best way to keep them grounded and safe." Anger bubbled just under the sorrow in Parker's voice. "He said he'd talk to you tonight. I told him he could trust you. But this whole thing is making me antsy. I'm just waiting for someone to tweet him a well-meaning 'My condolences.' It'll be all over the Internet in an hour as soon as that happens."

"Jesus. What a mess."

"Yeah. I just...I'm not asking you to print anything that's not true, but I figure if you soften it, maybe the TV folks won't smell blood in the water, you know?"

I shook my head, staying quiet. The suicide of a three-time Super Bowl champion quarterback's son wouldn't go unnoticed for long. The size of the town where it happened was likely the only reason it wasn't already all over ESPN. And the sleepy little burg was in for a rude awakening when the cameras descended.

"What happened?" I asked finally.

"I don't know," he said. "They found him out by the shore early this morning."

"Cause of death?"

"I didn't ask. Tony sounded—" He paused. "Broken."

I knew the tone. Too well. But I didn't want to think about that, so I shoved the memory to the back of my mind and locked it away. Parker. His friend. Big story, handle with care. Focus, Nichelle.

"No note?" I asked.

"No."

"History of problems?"

"Not that I know of." The words choked off and I heard a couple of deep breaths before he cleared his throat. "I'm not really clear on the details. But they'll fill you in. Take care of this for me, huh, Clarke? I taught that kid to throw a baseball. Bounced him on my knee.

Cheered at his games. He was a good boy. Smart. Talented. If we can keep it from turning into a media circus, let's do it."

"I'm on it," I said, ignoring Darcy's yip of protest when I moved her onto the floor and sat up. "I'll be there as soon as I can. Text me the address?"

"I'll send it right after I hang up. And thanks."

"Parker?"

"Yeah?"

"I really am sorry." The words felt lame, but I knew from too much experience they were the only ones that fit.

"Me, too, Clarke." He sighed. "Me, too."

* * *

Antihistamines and vitamin D on board, I changed back into a soft cotton pencil skirt and a powder blue cashmere sweater, sliding my feet into copper Jimmy Choo slingbacks I'd picked up at a thrift store the week before. Spring always puts me in the mood for new shoes. To be fair, so do summer, fall, and Wednesday.

I poured the rest of my tea into a travel mug and scratched Darcy's ears before I climbed back into my little red SUV.

Parker had sent me the address, and my maps app told me it would take ninety minutes to get there, which meant I needed to hurry if I wanted to make it by four. I pointed the car toward I-64 and cranked up the Elvis radio station, thinking about teenage angst and what might have caused this nightmare I was about to walk into.

Once outside the city, I set the cruise and sang along with Elvis, admiring the bits of green peeping from the tips of the tree branches. In a week, those baby leaves would shade the entire freeway. There aren't many trees in the part of Texas where I grew up, and the ones there are don't get as mammoth as Virginia trees. Though I'm not a fan of Mid-Atlantic winters, I loved that it wasn't already a hundred degrees outside in early April. Save for the pollen, I'd have driven to Mathews County with my windows down. But I was miserable enough already.

I pulled off the interstate at West Point and scrunched my nose at the stench from the paper mill while crossing the bridge. I bet that's horrible when a person can actually breathe.

The wide road narrowed to two lanes through rolling acres of farmland, corn and hay just sprouting in the fields lining the street. Houses, farms, and churches—in almost equal numbers—were the only things I passed for miles. I turned again by a 7-Eleven and slowed through a green stoplight before I crossed a short drawbridge and pulled onto the island where Tony Okerson had moved to protect his children.

Parker was right: Gwynn's Island was tiny, with a small handful of stop signs and only a few more streets. I passed a long-closed gas station and a vacant building that might have once been a supermarket. If it hadn't been for the manicured lawns and the children darting across roads that looked more like gravel driveways, I'd have wondered if Parker'd sent me to a ghost town.

My map led me to a small iron gate at the head of what appeared to be a private drive. There was no name, only the house number on small blocks the colors of the sand and sky, set into the stone of one post. Perfect for a celebrity looking for a hideaway.

I buzzed and gave my name to the man who answered. His deep voice sounded spent: exhausted and raw. I steeled myself for what was sure to be a tearjerker of an appointment. I try to hold myself together in front of the families, but it's not always easy. My gut said this one would be harder than most.

The gate swung inward, and I idled up the drive. Waves crashed nearby, though I couldn't see the bay yet. Scanning the property line, I caught a glimpse of the water just as a surprisingly modest stone and clapboard beach cottage loomed around the last curve.

I climbed the steps of the wide front porch. It wrapped down both sides of the house, bedecked with Adirondack chairs, palm-blade fans, and three different swings. A red plastic bucket in the corner brimmed with toys. Damn. It hadn't occurred to me to ask Parker how old the kid was. What was I getting into, here?

The front door stood open behind a wood-framed screen, and soft chimes rang through the house when I pushed the doorbell.

A petite woman whose honey-gold skin and sun-streaked hair said she spent a good deal of time outside appeared in the entry. She tried to smile, but it didn't come off.

"Nichelle Clarke, from the *Richmond Telegraph?*" My words sounded more like a question than an introduction because her face portrayed a level of pain I wasn't sure I wanted to tackle, no matter how big the story was. I didn't want to let Parker down, though. "Grant Parker sent me."

She nodded, snagging a friendly-faced Golden Retriever by his thick red collar as she pushed the door open. "I'm Ashton Okerson. Please, come in."

I stepped into a perfect oasis, my heels clicking on travertine just the right shade of blue-gray to match the panoramic views of the Bay I could see through each of three doorways.

"I'm so sorry for your loss," I said, shaking her hand. She didn't look much older than me.

"Thank you for coming to help us. Tony says Grant swears this interview will make it easier. I don't see how anything could." She closed her eyes for a long blink. They shone bright with tears when she opened them. "But thank you. Make yourself at home in the living room." She pointed to the doorway straight ahead. "I'll get my husband."

The wall to the right of the dining room held an artful collage that showed off a gorgeous family. I studied the center photo. Tony Okerson's blond, all-American good looks were framed by a flawless sky, his arm slung around Ashton, the surf in the background. An equally-handsome teenager knelt in the sand in front of them, a football tucked under one flowy-white-beach-shirted arm. Twin little girls with pigtails the color of sunshine leaned from behind Ashton and Tony, grinning.

I stared at the boy. He was the reason I was there, because he was the only male child in the picture. What could bring such tragedy to this peaceful place?

Looking around, I didn't see or hear any sign of Ashton or Tony. Maybe he'd gone for a walk. I would. If I lived in that house, I wouldn't even need shoes, and I could eat as much white chocolate and southern fried everything as I wanted, because I'd walk a million miles up and down that beach every day.

I strode to the open glass wall that ran the length of the living room, searching the shoreline before a soft sob pulled my attention from the water.

One of the little girls from the picture. Hugging a football and crying. I froze. I didn't want to scare her, and I was a stranger. My throat closed and tears burned my eyes. Before I could get my mouth open—though I wasn't sure if it was to speak to the child or call for her mother—I felt a hand on my shoulder.

I turned to find myself face-to-face with one of the most famous athletes in the western hemisphere. The anguish in his green eyes screamed that he'd give back every trophy and Super Bowl ring to have his son safe upstairs.

Oh, boy.

I closed my eyes and hauled in a deep breath, pasting on a smile and putting my hand out.

"I'm so sorry to have to meet you under these circumstances, Mr. Okerson," I said, clearing my throat between the words and brushing at my eyes. "My allergies are giving me the hardest time today."

He nodded, offering a small half-smile. "I understand," he said, and his gentle handshake told me he did. "Please, call me Tony. Come, have a seat."

"Um." I gestured to the little girl.

He peeked around the corner, his broad shoulders slumping. "She won't talk to anyone."

I followed him to a sprawling azure sectional. Ashton came in from the hallway and bustled around the kitchen, disappearing out onto the deck with a plate of cookies.

I shot Tony a look and started to get back to my feet. "Can I help her with something? I feel like she should be, um, not doing housework."

He shook his head. "She's been like this since the sheriff left. Keeping herself busy with mundane things. Almost like she can fix it." He watched his wife fill a pitcher with iced tea and put glasses on a tray, sighing and lowering his voice so only I could hear him. "Like part of her thinks if she goes about a normal Thursday, TJ will come home and this will be a bad dream. God, I wish she was right."

I nodded, trying to smile when Ashton brought the tray in and set it on the coffee table. She filled the glasses and handed me one, then offered one to Tony, who waved it away. Ashton sank into the couch next to her husband, laying her left hand on his knee.

"I'm not sure ...?" She let the question trail off, her turquoise eyes begging me for guidance.

"What to tell me? I understand that." I leaned forward and put the glass on the table, studying them.

Sorrow seeped from every pore. Clearly, I shouldn't vault into asking them about TJ's death. "I want to write a story more about who your son was than how he died, though I'm afraid I need to know that, too," I said. "What kind of music did he like? What was his favorite color, food, time of the year?"

Ashton opened her mouth and her face crumpled. One hand flew to her lips and a muffled sob escaped. "I can't. I can't talk about my beautiful boy in the past tense. My God, he's really gone, isn't he?" She buried her face in Tony's orange polo. "How did this happen to us?"

"I'm so sorry," I said, her muffled sobs tugging at my heart.

Tony nodded over the top of his wife's head. "Thank you. I know you didn't mean any harm. We asked you to come here. Grant said he dragged you out of a rare day off. This is just...surreal. We're still trying to process it."

"I'm sure that's a difficult thing to do," I said, my thoughts running back to the little girl on the deck. It would be especially hard for her to understand. I knew.

They sat for a moment, him staring at nothing, smoothing her hair as she cried. I tried to blend into the sofa. Some days my job felt more voyeuristic than I'd like. When Ashton sat up, I turned my attention back to them.

"TJ's a good kid," Tony said. "Good grades, lots of friends. No trouble. He's an old soul in a young man's body. Didn't ever seem like he wanted to be anything but grown up and responsible. He loves his little sisters, is really active in the church."

I scribbled as he talked, my Benadryl-fogged brain trying to pick through that to a place where this boy had killed himself. Nothing about that said "suicide."

"Girlfriend?" I asked.

"All the girls chased TJ," Ashton said, sniffling. "But Sydney was the only one he ever wanted."

Maybe unrequited teenage love?

"Did she want him, too?" I asked.

"Oh, yes. They've been dating seriously for over a year. Talking about growing up and getting married, like we did. They're in love." She glanced at her husband and he squeezed her hand. "We're not stupid. We told them they had to wait until they were through with school. Do it in the right order. We had TJ when we were still in college. We managed, but it was hard."

I nodded, jotting that down.

"Had the two of them had a fight?"

"No. She's studying in Paris this semester. She wants to be an artist. They Facetimed and talked on the phone every day. She's coming home next week, and he's so excited to see her," Ashton closed her eyes and tightened her grip on Tony's hand. "I guess she's coming home tonight, isn't she?"

Maybe he missed the girl? I put a star by that.

"Forgive me, but I have to ask: is there any history of depression in your family? Had TJ ever shown signs of it?" I bit my lip. Past stories had taught me that teen suicides almost always fall into one of two camps: kids who are outcasts or bullied, or kids who are struggling with the onset of mental illness.

"No," Ashton said, her face serious. "I've been over every minute of the last three weeks in my head today, wondering if I missed something. I have a psych degree gathering dust in the attic. I know the signs. For TJ to spiral that far, that fast, we'd have noticed. I'm a full-time mom and Tony's retired. We have nothing to do but helicopter our kids."

Hmmm.

"How many sports does TJ play?" I asked. They were obviously more comfortable with the present tense.

"Football and baseball." Tony tried to smile. "Quarterback and pitcher. Grant says he's better at baseball. I disagree."

I nodded, another lump forming in my throat at the reminder of the hurt I'd heard in my friend's voice on the phone. Parker had been a breath from being a major league pitcher when a blown rotator cuff ended his baseball career.

"He said y'all were old friends?" I knew Tony Okerson was a UVA alum, like Parker. "From college?"

Tony nodded. "The summer before my senior year, they assigned me a freshman buddy from the athletic program. I had fun showing Grant around the campus. He was serious. Laser-focused. I knew he had the stuff to make it in professional sports five minutes after I met him. He's a good friend."

"That he is," I said. Or, he had been since he'd forgiven me for suspecting him of murder. I'd played matchmaker as a peace offering, setting him up with our city hall reporter at the end of summer. They were getting serious.

I looked out the window at the surf, then back at Tony and Ashton. They didn't want to be there. Didn't want me there. Didn't want to deal with any of this. Their son's death was a circus trainload of elephants in the room, but I couldn't flat-out ask them to describe it. So I chose the roundabout road.

"Tell me about TJ," I said, raising my pen.

And they did. They told stories and laughed and cried for an hour. I wrote down everything from Ashton going into labor at a UVA football game (Tony made it through the third quarter before the offensive line coach whisked him off to the hospital just in time to see his son come into the world) to TJ's first day of kindergarten, to his belief that wearing the same socks and underwear for all of January helped his dad win the Super Bowl (ick, but an endearing sort of gross). When the story came around to that morning, Ashton dissolved into sobs again.

"He wasn't in his room," Tony said, clearing his throat. "I went to get him up because we always run in the mornings, and he wasn't there. I thought maybe he was already outside. It's spring break, but he's been up early every day. He went to a party last night, though, and we told him he could stay out late."

Party? My ears keened on the word. I stayed quiet and let Tony talk.

He stared past me at the dark flatscreen TV on the wall over the fireplace.

"I ran, probably a mile and a half down the beach. The shore gets rockier the further you go around the island. I saw the remnants of a campfire, and I know the kids build them this time of year when they're out on the water late. Then I saw TJ's jacket. I picked my way down to the water. He was slumped on a rock. It looked like he was sleeping."

I frowned. What about that screamed "suicide?" I hadn't heard anything to make me think this kid had killed himself, yet his parents told Parker he had. How was I going to ask them that without making Ashton cry harder?

I tilted my head and caught Tony's eye.

"I'm afraid I don't follow..." I said.

He nodded, his eyes gleaming with unshed tears. "There was a bottle of Vicodin in his pocket. It was empty."

Ah.

"He'd just picked it up yesterday," Tony continued. "His knee has been bothering him since he took that bad fall in the state championship game in December, and he twisted it in baseball practice last week." He bent his head and buried his face in Ashton's hair, tightening his arms around her. I ducked my head, jotting notes and trying to sort through their story.

A whole bottle of narcotics would do it. But why?

I looked around. The mirror image of the little girl I'd seen outside, but wearing a Mathews High football jersey that swallowed her tiny frame, waved at me from the kitchen doorway. There was a ring of chocolate around her mouth and a light missing from her blue-green eyes. The combination broke my heart.

I wiggled my fingers at her. She stepped into the living room.

"Mommy?" She paused at the end of the couch, and Ashton and Tony broke apart, wiping their eyes.

"What is it, angel?" Ashton flashed a half-smile and opened her arms. The little girl ran to her and climbed into her lap.

"I want TJ to come home," the child said, her whisper muffled by Ashton's shirt.

Dear God.

Tony Okerson looked at me over his daughter's head, pain and pleading twisting his famously-handsome face. "Please, Miss Clarke. Don't let the press turn my family's loss into a sales pitch."

I wasn't sure what I could do to stop it, but I offered a shaky smile as I stood, promising him I would, anyway. There was nothing else to say.

"Thank you for coming," he said, tears falling faster than he could brush them away.

"Of course. Thank you for sharing your memories with me."

I scratched the dog behind his soft, floppy ears as I let myself out the front door, tugging it to make sure he couldn't escape. I climbed back into my car, the effects of the medicine washing away with the adrenaline and emotion of the afternoon.

The image of the Okersons clinging to their wounded little girl burned the backs of my eyelids as I dropped my head and let the tears fall for a few minutes. By the time I rubbed my hands over my face and started the car, it was after six, the sun low in the sky. I wondered where the drugstore was. Another dose of Benadryl was definitely in my future. And since I was poking around town, I might as well meet the local law enforcement.

I glanced at the Okerson house one more time in the rearview as I started up the driveway. Something wasn't right. The details didn't add up. And I was already too invested in these people and their story to walk away without trying to find out why.

CHAPTER TWO

A DAZZLING pink sun sank into the Chesapeake Bay, rings of orange, violet, and gold flowing across the horizon and into the water. I slowed the car and watched from the rock-lined road that ran along the north side of the island, letting the beauty erase some of the turmoil I'd lugged from the Okerson house.

A dull honking behind me broke my reverie, reminding me I'd stopped in the middle of the street. I checked the rearview to find a John Deere occupied by an older man in starched jeans and a white straw hat. I waved an apology and gunned the engine.

I hadn't passed anything but churches and a couple of seafood places on the island itself, so I drove back across the little bridge, wondering as I breezed through the only stoplight in town if it ever turned red.

I stopped at the 7-Eleven on the corner that led back to the real world and shuffled inside, hoping they had cold medicine of some variety to get me through a couple more hours and then get me home. Leave it to me to take a sick day and wind up working 'til ten o'clock. The news doesn't wait for pollen. Or anything else, in the age of Twitter.

I found a packet of Sudafed and a small vat of diet Coke. Sipping the soda, I moved to the register.

"You're not from around here," the words were flat—a statement, not a question—from the wiry redhead behind the counter.

"Just passing through," I replied, trying to smile through my sinus pain.

"There ain't nothing out here but fields and water and the people who work them," she said, pulling my change from the till with a raised eyebrow that said she wanted to know why I was there. "You come here, you leave, but you don't pass through."

"Seems like a nice place." I turned for the door.

I hauled myself back into the car, shivering in the breeze and thinking I probably needed a couple of Advil, too. I laid a hand across my forehead. Fever. Hooray. After swallowing the Sudafed, I dug a vial of Advil out of my bag and took two, leaning my head back to rest for a second.

I tried to search for the sheriff's office address on my cell phone. No signal. Great. There weren't but so many places for the sheriff to be in a map dot this tiny. I turned the opposite of the way I'd come into town. I could find the office.

* * *

Or not find it. I tried following the arrows through the halls of the big red courthouse with the sign out front that said "sheriff's office." It was locked, paint buckets outside and drop cloths covering everything I could see through the window.

Twenty minutes later, I'd circled town three times and wondered if the police had closed up on account of remodeling. I stopped in the parking lot of an ancient service station that had been reborn as an antique store. The old-fashioned gravity-fed gas pumps out front were topped with blue and white globes emblazoned with "Esso extra" and flanked by vintage Standard Oil signs. The front walk displayed a charming array of merchandise.

If I wasn't crunched for time and feeling like absolute hell, I'd have browsed for an hour. As it was, I dragged myself to the door and asked the gray-haired gentleman behind the counter where I could find the sheriff.

"At the courthouse," he said, bustling around the end of the high, polished wood counter. His brow wrinkled deeper with concern when he stopped in front of me. "Why don't you come in and have a seat, sugar? You don't look so good."

"Allergies," I said. And decongestants for dinner.

"What business d'you got with Zeke?

Zeke? Sheriff Zeke. All right. "Just a few questions."

"You look like death on toast." He settled on a stool behind the counter. "Sit down."

"I appreciate the hospitality, but I need to go talk to the sheriff," I said with an effort at smiling. From the look I got in response, I probably managed a wince. "I tried the courthouse, and the office looks like it's being painted."

He nodded. "They moved out of the new office for the painters and back to the old office. At the courthouse. Go to the stop sign up yonder and turn right, then go behind the shops on Main."

"I'm afraid my cold medicine is fogging my brain. The courthouse is a block down on the right," I said.

"But the place where the courthouse used to be in the middle of town is where you want to go," he explained with a patient smile.

"I see." I didn't, really, but I'd go wherever he said if it meant I was closer to getting home.

The little Okerson girl's haunted turquoise eyes flashed through my thoughts and I stood up straighter, thanking him and trying to stride back to the car. Mind over matter, my mom always said.

I found the sheriff's office right where he said it would be and parked next to a pickup from the same era as the gas station/antique store. After blowing my nose, I climbed out of my car and started down the sidewalk. The hastily-stenciled "Sheriff" sign hung over a door next to what had to be the coolest vintage fire station in Virginia, a soaring two-story red brick building with twin open garage bays and an honest-to-goodness fireman's pole. The sheriff's temporary front door stood open to the April breeze, voices carrying to the sidewalk.

"Dammit, Zeke, you got to do something about this," a deep baritone boomed. "Those old bats are gonna skyrocket the divorce rate 'round here, and we don't have the manpower at the courthouse to handle the uptick in paperwork."

"It's not my jurisdiction, Amos." A tired sigh followed the words. "And they're not doing anything that's against the law."

"Neither are we," the baritone protested.

"Didn't say you were," the sheriff replied. "All I'm saying is I can't help you."

A tall, barrel-chested man in a sport coat, slacks, and polished black boots stormed through the door, nodding at me as he passed. The pickup's door groaned a protest when he jerked it open.

I peeked around the doorframe. The cavernous room held a handful of mismatched office furniture. A twenty-something woman with spiky hair the color of the fire engine next door sat behind a dispatch unit in one corner, flipping through a magazine. A man in a chocolate-and-tan uniform slumped in a wooden swivel chair in the center of the desk tangle.

"Excuse me," I said, wincing at my nasal twang. The Sudafed hadn't even made a dent.

They looked up—his sun-bronzed face softened into an interested smile, while she raised a brow. I smiled, focusing on the sheriff. He didn't look old enough to have a name like Zeke. I'd put him mid-forties, with dark hair, curious eyes, and a medium build that spoke more to leanness than muscle, but was fit all the same.

"What can we do for you, miss?" he asked.

"I'm Nichelle Clarke, from the *Richmond Telegraph*," I said. "I came out to talk to Tony and Ashton Okerson, and I want to ask you a few questions about TJ."

The dispatcher returned to her magazine when the sheriff nodded.

"Not much I can tell you that his folks couldn't, but come on in." He waved to a chair across his desk. "I'm Zeke Waters."

"Nice to meet you, sheriff," I said, falling into the chair he offered.

It took effort to lean forward and scrounge a pad and pen out of my bag. "I don't suppose you have a tox report back on TJ yet, do you?"

I knew the answer to that was almost surely "no," since it hadn't even been a day, but it was a small town. Maybe there wasn't that much for the coroner to do.

"We probably won't have it for several weeks," he said. "We don't have a crime lab or a coroner, so everything goes to Richmond for autopsy and testing. From the looks of the scene, they'll find a combination of narcotics and alcohol. Most kids who try to kill themselves don't actually pull it off, either because they don't really want to die or because they do it wrong. I can't tell you how much I wish TJ was in that group. The whole damned town is already in an uproar, and it's only going to get worse when word gets outside our little corner of the world."

"And y'all assume it was a suicide because?" I raised one eyebrow. I couldn't figure why it was the first place everyone went.

"Because smart kids don't chase a whole bottle of narcotic pain meds with booze if they don't want to die?" Sheriff Zeke leaned back in his chair and folded his arms across his chest. "TJ Okerson was a smart kid."

"But his parents say he wasn't troubled. Good grades, steady girl-friend, popular ... I've written about teen suicides before. This doesn't fit. Are you opening an investigation into his death?"

"Of course we are," he said. "I examined the scene and talked to the other kids who were out there with him last night. A couple of the boys said he was talking about missing his girl, and worried about his baseball season because of his knee."

I scribbled. "So he was a little upset. There's a difference between bummed and suicidal."

"You trying to tell me how to do my job, Miss Clarke?" Sheriff Zeke's tone flipped from conversational to stiff. "Because this is not my first rodeo. I know everything you're saying."

"Then why are his parents convinced he killed himself?" I asked.

Losing a loved one to suicide is hard, because the guilt that stays with the survivors can eat a person alive. I'd only been at the Okerson's house for a couple of hours, but I liked them. I didn't want them living with the "what if." And my gut said something was off. Even if the sheriff was looking at me like I was a moron.

"Because right now it's the most plausible answer. He was upset. Alcohol is a depressant. And I don't see a scenario where anyone made a kid as strong and fast as TJ Okerson swallow a fistful of narcotics."

"But you don't even know that's what killed him," I protested. "You don't have the tox screen back."

"It's the most likely possibility." He sighed. "Look, it's not like I assumed this all by myself. His parents said he got the pills yesterday. They're gone, he's dead, no evidence of trauma. How does two and two add up in Richmond? Because out here, it's usually four. This is a small town. I hate like hell the idea that a kid with everything in the world to live for decided he didn't want to anymore. But it happens."

I studied him. His whole posture was one of resignation and exhaustion. He didn't want this case any more than I did.

"I'm sorry. I didn't mean to sound like I was questioning your investigative skills. They just seem like such nice people," I said. Maybe he was right, maybe he wasn't. But arguing with him wasn't going to get me anywhere but frozen out of the loop. "Was there anything else unusual about the crime scene?"

His face and voice softened again. "Beach party. Bonfire. Beer bottles. Just kids blowing off steam on vacation," he said. "I was out there for over three hours this morning combing the shoreline. It's a sad situation. Got everyone on edge. But I've been at this for more years than I want to admit. The simplest answer is usually the right one."

I nodded, adding that to my notes.

"Thank you for taking the time to talk to me," I said, fishing a business card from my bag and handing it to him. "It was nice to meet you. When you hear about the tox screen, will you give me a call?"

"I'm about to get buried by the media, huh?" he asked, tucking the card into the top drawer of his desk.

"Very likely. But if it helps, national folks don't ever hang around long."

"Our local paper and some of the TV stations and the paper in Newport News are about the only reporters we ever get in here," he said. "This will be different."

I smiled. "I'm sure it's nothing you can't handle."

"I'd rather not have to."

I smiled understanding and turned for the door.

Back in my car, I contemplated napping for a full two minutes before I started the engine and turned out of the square, aiming the headlights toward home.

For most of the drive I tried to convince myself that Sheriff Zeke was right, but my gut said he wasn't looking hard enough. Honestly, I wanted him to be wrong. Murder was a sexier story all the way around, both because it would be easier on the people who loved TJ in many ways, and because murder sells papers. Plus, something about the sheriff's words nagged the back of my brain. I just couldn't grasp what through the germs and exhaustion.

After arriving home, I filled Darcy's food and water on my way to bed, thankful for her doggie door. Perching on the edge of my cherry four-poster, I kicked off my heels, too beat to even put them back on their shelf. I figured out what bugged me about the sheriff's story as I snuggled into my pillows.

Why would TJ Okerson be worried about his upcoming baseball season if he planned to swallow a fistful of Vicodin?

CHAPTER THREE

My head was no less stuffy the next morning, but I had work to do. I trudged into the newsroom at seven-thirty to write my story on TJ before the morning news budget meeting, texting Parker on my way. I wanted him to check the article before I turned it in. I was paranoid that my allergy meds had made my head so foggy I'd get something wrong.

TJ Okerson's favorite color was green. He loved football, the beach, and his twin little sisters. As a junior, he led the Mathews Eagles to a state championship last season, appearing set to follow in the footsteps of his famous father, retired Super Bowl champion quarterback Tony Okerson.

"He had the best smile," his mother, Ashton Okerson, said. "I know the saying is that someone's smile lights up a room, but TJ's smile lit up the world. My world, anyway. He made it a better place."

Ashton and Tony talked to the Telegraph *exclusively about their son Thursday evening, after Tony found TJ's body on the beach near their home on Gwynn's Island that morning. Local law enforcement officials said the death appeared to be a*

. . .

I paused, staring at the blinking cursor. I didn't want to type the word "suicide," because my gut said there was something else there. On the other hand, the Okersons believed sheriff Zeke. I didn't want to upset grieving parents and friends, either.

I blew out a short breath and sipped my coffee, scrunching my nose when my beloved white mocha syrup tasted more like tomato sauce thanks to my stuffy head.

"How's it coming?" Parker asked from behind my left shoulder. I smiled and turned to face him, waving a hello to his girlfriend as she dropped her bag to the floor in the cube next to mine.

"Slowly," I said, studying his face. The dark craters under his emerald eyes were unusual, and told me I should probably keep my mouth shut about why it was coming slowly. Parker loved this kid, and I didn't want to make my friend sadder. "These stories are always hard. And his parents were so nice," I finished simply.

He shook his head. "Of all the kids I've ever met, TJ was the least likely to do something like this."

I laid a hand on his arm and caught Mel's eye. She looked tired, too. She just shook her head, a pained look on her face.

"I'm so sorry," I told Parker.

"What did the cops say?" he asked.

"That they're looking into it, but they think it was a suicide."

"Why?" He stepped back and shook his head.

"Why what?"

"TJ loves his baby sisters. He loves his family. I just saw him two weeks ago. He was happy. Why would he do this?" Parker sat heavily on the edge of my desk and dropped his tousled blond head into his hands. Mel massaged his shoulder and offered me a helpless shrug.

I tried to pull in a deep breath, but the stuffy nose netted me a small gasp.

"His parents don't know. The cops don't know," I said. "It doesn't sound to me like a typical suicide, if there even is such a thing."

Parker raised his head and leveled his green eyes at me.

"Are you saying what I think you're saying?" he asked.

"I'm not sure what I'm saying," I replied hurriedly. "I just ... my gut says there's something off, Parker." So much for keeping my mouth shut.

"Are the cops out there really looking into it, or are they placating Tony and Ashton?"

"I can't tell. The sheriff seemed like a nice guy, but I don't know him or anyone else in the department. I'm flying a little blind, here. He said he's waiting for tox results, but they don't have their own lab, so that could take a while."

"How long a while?"

"A couple of weeks. Maybe three," I said. "It's not as complicated as a DNA analysis. Just testing his blood for hydrocodone levels and alcohol. It depends on what's in the queue."

"Painkillers?" Parker raised an eyebrow.

"There was an empty bottle in his pocket. His folks said he just got the prescription refilled."

"And alcohol? TJ wasn't stupid," Parker said. "He knows better than to drink and take painkillers."

"I think that's their evidence that he did it on purpose," I said gently. "It's the why that doesn't fit for me."

"Yeah." He shook his head again as he stood. "I should let you finish your story."

"Bob wants it early. Thanks for the scoop. I hope I do it justice."

"You will," he said, turning for the hallway that led to his office. "Keep me in the loop, huh?"

"Absolutely. I'm not sure how far I can get a foot in the door down there. It is a small town. Like, one stoplight, the-7-Eleven-clerk-gave-me-the-stinkeye-because-I-don't-belong small. But I'll keep after it."

"Thanks."

* * *

I finished typing my story, alternately giggling at funny anecdotes the Okersons had shared and swallowing tears at the memory of the little girls who missed their brother. Reading through it, I hoped it was good enough to make Ashton Okerson's day a teensy bit easier.

I copied Parker when I emailed the article to Bob, just in time to sprint to the staff meeting. Well, it felt like sprinting, but was probably more like dragging ass thanks to what I suspected was a full-blown sinus infection.

I stopped short when I rounded the corner into my editor's office and found Shelby Taylor parked in my usual seat.

Standing just inside the door, I shot Bob a clear WTF look and got an apologetic shrug in reply.

"Good morning, Nichelle," Shelby purred, folding her arms over her ample chest and grinning up at me. "You look as fresh as ever."

I didn't even have the energy to glare. Shelby was our copy chief, but made no bones about the fact that she wanted to be our crime reporter. And she'd tried everything from sleeping with the managing editor to ratting me out to the criminal underworld to get it, too.

I leaned toward her and coughed. She wrinkled her nose and shrank back into the orange velour of Bob's Virginia Tech chic armchair.

"You should consider things like the freedom to take a sick day when you're trying to steal someone's beat," I said.

"I don't get sick," she snapped. "Seems like you should take more vitamins."

I turned to Bob. "What the hell is she doing in here, and can you make her leave?"

"Now, ladies," he said. "Nichelle, Shelby's filling in for Les for the next week."

"She's what? A whole week?" I tried to groan, but it sounded more like a snort. "Why? What happened to Les?"

Our managing editor had never been one of my favorite people, seeing as how he was a brown-nosing weasel who wanted Bob's job as badly as Shelby wanted mine but, given the choice between my rival and her boyfriend, I'd take Les twice over.

"He's recovering from surgery," Shelby chirped. "Andrews asked me himself if I'd step in."

Right. Rick Andrews was the *Telegraph's* publisher, and didn't care about much of anything but the paper's bottom line and image. Les was generally so far up Andrews's backside the big boss didn't have time to notice any of the rest of us. I had a hard time believing he knew Shelby existed.

"How is it that we work in a newsroom and I hadn't heard Les was having surgery?" I asked. "Is he going to be okay?"

"It's a minor procedure," Shelby said, fiddling with the file folder in her lap.

"A minor procedure he needs a week to recover from?" I perched on a plastic office chair. "I'm practically dying, and here I sit."

"Are y'all talking about Les's hair plugs again?" Eunice Blakely, our features editor, asked as she ambled into the room and lowered herself slowly into the orange velour armchair opposite Shelby's. Eunice's war correspondent days had ended when a helicopter crash in Iraq earned her a half-dozen screws in her right hip. In the years since, she'd made our features section a consistent award-winner, and made herself our resident mistress of southern cooking and wry observation.

I sucked in my cheeks to keep from smiling.

"I think it will look good when it's healed," Shelby argued.

"But isn't the point for people to notice he looks different? Why hide? Also—why are you here?" I asked Shelby. "Les doesn't usually come to the news meetings."

"I want to know what I need to be on top of today," Shelby said with a grin. "Just trying to learn as much as I can from this opportunity."

Bob rolled his eyes, but she didn't notice, and I coughed again to cover a laugh. He knew as well as I did Shelby was there because she wouldn't miss an excuse to crash the meeting.

The rest of the section editors filed in and Bob flash-fired through the rundown, not turning to me until the end.

"We have an exclusive on a sad story today," he said, his gaze flicking to Spencer Jacobs, our sports editor. "We're going live with it on the web as I speak, because the police report will be in the local paper in Mathews County this morning."

He paused and sat back in the chair, eyes on me. Whispers flitted through the rest of the room.

"What's Nichelle got?" Eunice finally asked Spence. "And what's it got to do with you?"

"Tony Okerson's teenage son is dead," I said quietly when Bob nodded an okay.

"What?" Spence sat up straight, fumbling for a pen. "How? And why don't I have this at the sports desk?"

"Parker asked me to handle it," I said. "The Okersons are his friends. And your guys don't have much experience working with cops."

"It's her story, Spence, and you get her whatever she needs to do a good job of it," Bob said. "Listen up, folks. We have the only interview the Okersons are giving. When this breaks nationwide, it's going to be huge, and this poor little town isn't going to know what hit it. Everyone and their Poodle will want into this story, and no one here is sharing anything. Not a word. Are we clear? If you get a call from a member of another media organization, you forward it to Nichelle or to me. Nothing goes out without approval."

I nodded. Parker and Bob were close, and I could tell from the forceful note in Bob's voice that Parker had given him the same speech I'd gotten on the phone the day before.

"What's the *Telegraph*'s official statement?" Shelby asked.

I snuck a glance between her and Bob. He looked irritated, and she was too busy staring daggers at me to notice.

"Just send all inquiries to me," Bob said, impressive control in his tone. "I don't see a reason for you to get any questions. But if you do, I'll field them."

"What if you're not here?" Shelby asked. "If I'm putting in long hours and find myself needing to answer someone?"

"Take. A. Message," Bob said through clenched teeth, and I snorted. I didn't mean to. It just slipped out.

Shelby shot me another glare as she strode from the office.

I smiled, keeping my seat as the section editors ran for their computers, looking for my story. Curiosity is part of the gig when you work in a newsroom.

"Don't be so quick to gloat," Bob cautioned, leaning his elbows on his desk. "She's going to be as far into everything as she can get until Les comes back to work, and you are going to be up to your neck in this Okerson thing. I'll do what I can, but she has Andrews's ear, and his memory is about as long as Les's hair."

"That's so wrong." I didn't even try to suppress a giggle.

Bob grinned. "I think you sympathize with my ill will toward Les."

"I do at that," I said. "And I am going to nail this Okerson story. Something's not right, chief. I have a bad feeling about this whole thing. That interview was one of the hardest things I've ever done in the name of a story. And that's counting getting shot. It just rips your heart right out to talk to these people. They're so nice."

"I got the feeling from the story that you were hedging the cause of death." He sat back and laced his fingers behind his head. "What gives?"

"It doesn't fit. He was cute. Popular. Family has money. He had a girl. A looming career playing ball, for chrissakes. Why?"

Bob chewed on that for a five slow taps of my foot before he answered with a question of his own.

"What'd you make of the sheriff?"

"Eh. He seems nice. He's not stupid. He's also not excited about the media shitstorm. I think I can get on his good side. I just don't know how far he's going to dig."

"Well, kiddo, your gut has a good track record. Poke around if you must. But I know I don't have to remind you that you need to stay on top of your regular beat. And we cannot screw this thing with Okerson up."

I nodded, fishing a Kleenex out of the pocket on my soft lavender cardigan and swiping at my nose.

"March yourself to Care First and get an antibiotic." Bob drew his brows together in a parental glare, and I smiled.

"Yes, sir."

"And then get some juice and get to work. Find out when the funeral is and if you can go."

"To the funeral?" Aw, man. I didn't think I could handle that.

"There will be cameras on every inch of lawn at that church," Bob said. "I want you inside."

"You got it, chief." I grabbed my bag and turned for the door. The elevators seemed a Himalayan trek away, and the room seesawed a half dozen times when I stood up.

"Feel better," Bob said, turning to his computer. I saw my story flash on the screen, a photo of TJ Okerson from the state championship football game under the header.

I did not have time to be sick.

CHAPTER FOUR

A SINUSITIS DIAGNOSIS and two Amoxicillin capsules later, I was back at my desk with a steaming mug of honey-lemon tea, a sweating bottle of orange-pineapple juice, and a big question mark hanging over TJ Okerson's death. I dialed Richmond police headquarters and asked for Aaron White, the public information officer and generally one of my favorite sources.

I trusted Aaron's opinion more than Sheriff Zeke's.

"I'd ask if you have twenty minutes for me to come by, but I think I have the plague, and I don't want to stand up unless it's absolutely necessary," I said when he picked up. "So, I need to ask you a couple of questions. Got a minute?"

"For you? Usually. What's up? We don't have much for you this morning, unless kids ripping off car stereos is news."

"This isn't about a case. At least, not your case. But we'll come back to the kids later." Lots of car stereos could be worth a few inches of space. We could run a warning to residents in the area.

"Why are you asking me about a case that's not mine? How sick are you?"

"Sick. But the news doesn't write itself. Did you see my story this morning about the Okerson kid?"

"Ah." He fell quiet. I twisted the phone cord around my index finger. Aaron had two daughters, neither of them much older than TJ.

"Aaron?"

"I saw it. Those poor people."

"Indeed. So, the thing is, I'm not entirely sure it was a suicide."

"What? Why not? What does local law enforcement say?"

"The sheriff thinks he killed himself," I said, tapping a pen on the calendar blotter that covered the top of my paper-strewn desk. "But it doesn't track. I get the empty pill bottle and the booze at the party. That's damning evidence. But this kid, according to his parents, anyway, had none of the markers of being suicidal. Not one."

"How well do most teenagers' parents know them?" Aaron asked.

"I have no frame of reference. Only child of a single mom. We've always been tight. But I suspect you're looking for 'not well?'"

"As much as I hate to say it, that's usually the case."

I pictured Ashton Okerson's crumpling face, heard her "helicopter our kids" comment ring in my thoughts.

"These folks didn't seem to think so," I said.

"Not that they told you," Aaron said. "I mean no disrespect. Tony Okerson is a damned fine ballplayer and I hear he's a good man. But he's spent a lifetime working the media. If they didn't know what was up with their kid, they're not admitting it to you. Not now."

I sighed. Tony said they went for runs every day. Ashton knew all about his plans to marry his girlfriend. That more mirrored my life than your typical primetime teen angst my-parents-are-morons drama, but he had a point.

"So I should dig more." I said. "Thanks, Aaron."

"Anytime. Holler if you find something else you want to bounce off me. Such a sad story."

"Your girls home for break yet?"

"They came in Friday, bearing a small mountain of laundry." His tone told me he didn't mind a bit. It was the first year both of his daughters were away at college, and he was over the moon to have them home.

"Hope you have enough detergent," I said.

"Me, too. Though if I were the sort to do it, I could borrow some from the evidence locker. That might be an interesting one for you: narcotics seized three hundred gallons of Tide in a bust yesterday," he said.

"How did I miss that?" I asked. "And what the hell are drug dealers doing with detergent? Do I want to know? I can't imagine shooting up Tide is going to end well for anyone."

Aaron laughed. "No, I don't suppose so. But this isn't for shooting up. It's currency," he said. "They've been having this issue in New York for over a year. Looks like it's trickled down here. Tide is expensive, right? And it's something that's not usually stolen, so no one locks it up. People make a run for it with a shopping cart full, then they trade it to the dealers for drugs. The dealers take it back to another store and get a full refund, plus the sales tax. Nifty little scheme, huh?"

I flipped my notebook to a clean page and scribbled that down. "I swear to God, if these criminals directed their creative energies to good things, we'd have a cure for cancer. How the hell do people come up with this stuff?"

"It's job security," he said. "As long as there are creative crooks in the world, we've got jobs."

"I can always count on you for the bright side," I said. "Thanks for your help."

I asked him to email me what he had on the car stereo thefts and the detergent bust before I hung up.

Maybe it was mind over matter, but I felt a bit more human, and the room only rocked once when I stood. I grabbed my bag, tea, and juice, hoping I'd continue to improve on the drive to Gwynn's Island. The answer to the nagging feeling in my gut wouldn't come looking for me in Richmond.

* * *

I dropped my cell phone in the cup holder for easy access when I climbed into my car, dialing my friend Emily's office in Dallas when I got to the freeway. A perky-voiced receptionist answered and I asked to speak with Emily.

"Doctor Sansom is very busy this morning," she said, her tone sweet but guarded. "May I tell her who's calling?"

Once I had given her my name, Em was on the phone in four seconds.

"It's been ages, girl," she said, her earring clicking against the receiver. "What is going on with you? I thought you wanted to be Lois Lane, not Nancy Drew. Then I see you on Anderson Cooper talking about all kinds of crazy stuff. And, I hear Kyle moved to Richmond. Do tell."

"You're not charging by the hour, right, Dr. Sansom? Just so we're clear?" I tried to sniffle quietly, hoping I sounded a little farther from death's door than I felt.

Emily had the best laugh. Her head-thrown-back, full-blown chortle had been one of my favorite things about her since she loaned me her Strawberry Shortcake eraser in third grade and became one of my best friends.

It rang in my ear for a good ten seconds. "Shut up, Nicey," she said. "I've been meaning to call and bug you about Kyle since Christmas. My days keep getting away from me. What's going on? Do I need to clear my June weekends?"

"There are no wedding bells in my future," I said. "Kyle is...complicated. We're getting to know each other again. It's been ten years, and we're such different people than we were then."

"Last time I saw Kyle he was way hotter people than he was then, that's for damned sure."

"There is that." I grinned. "And he's very sweet. But I don't know."

"I'm guessing there's another guy," she said.

"Did they teach you to be psychic at shrink school?"

"Something like that. What's he like? Must be something else to keep you away from Kyle."

"He's something else, all right. Sexy, mysterious. But I didn't call to talk about my love life." I also didn't want to spill details on Joey. Talk about complicated.

"What did you call to talk about?" She stopped. "Shit. Have you been crying? Is your mom okay?"

"Mom is great, thank God. Five years remission this summer. I just have a sinus infection. None of that's why I called, either. Tony Okerson's son died Wednesday night."

"Tony Okerson, the football player?"

"The very same."

"Um. Not that I don't love hearing from you, but I'm confused."

"The local sheriff says the kid killed himself. I'm not convinced."

"I see." She paused, her voice softening. "You sure you're not projecting? It wouldn't be abnormal, with everything you and your mom went through."

"That, friend, is the million-dollar question." I sighed. "But I've covered other suicides, and this is different, Em. That's part of why I called you. I want your take on this kid."

"You know I can't analyze someone I've never met based on third-hand information. Certainly not in the space of a phone call."

"I know you can't give me expert opinion I can quote," I said. "I'm not asking you for an interview. I just want to know what you think."

No answer. I waited.

"Because I love you, tell me about him," Em said finally.

"Back at you."

I gave her the rundown. The only noise as she listened was the sound of her earring hitting the receiver when she nodded. "It just doesn't add up," I finished. "No matter how I try to force it, the puzzle doesn't fit. Or am I crazy?"

"You are not crazy," Em said. "Whether you're right or not, I don't know, but I hereby pronounce you as sane as anyone else. I'll go with your theory, though. There are statistical anomalies in everything, but if what you're telling me is true, this would be so far outside the curve we'd need binoculars to make it out."

"Why?"

"Well first, teenage boys who are suicidal are more successful at their first attempt, because they tend to do more permanent things. Taking pills is an iffy option. Maybe it works, maybe someone finds you and you get your stomach pumped. Or you change your mind and stop after two and have a bad hangover. Intentional overdose is more common among women. We tend to be more unsure of what we want."

Her voice dropped and I knew she wasn't just talking about pills.

"Yeah, yeah, I have commitment issues. We can discuss that later. Keep talking. What do guys do instead of taking pills?"

"Shooting, hanging, jumping off bridges," she said. "Things that have more permanent results."

I filed that away. "Okay. What else? You said 'first.'"

"I did. The rest is pure conjecture, because I haven't met anyone involved. But unless there's something you didn't tell me, or something they're not telling you, I can't find a reason. If the kid didn't have a psychotic break in the space of a few hours, you didn't give me anything that indicated he would consider suicide. There are warning signs."

I nodded. "That's what I thought."

"I'm not saying run a story crying conspiracy," Em said. "But if you think something's off, check it out. This will be hard on his family. The closure would help them. I don't suppose I have to tell you that."

Nope. "Thanks, Em," I said.

"Anytime. Now, about this mystery man," she said.

My phone beeped. I pulled it away from my head and checked the caller ID.

"Speak of the devil," I told Emily. "Let me call you later?"

"Sure, honey. Good luck."

I thanked her again and clicked over.

"Hello?"

"Nichelle?" Joey's deep tenor, with his slight Italian-by-way-of-Jersey accent, always made my stomach flip.

"Hey there. What's going on with you?" I put one foot on the brake as I took the West Point exit.

"What's going on with you? Have you been crying?"

"I wish. Tears are easier to get rid of than germs."

"You're sick? Are you at home?"

"That'd be fabulous," I said. "But no. I'm chasing a story to Tidewater."

"You should rest."

"Nice theory. I'll try it out later. I hope. What's up?"

"Just calling to say 'hi,'" he said.

"That's a new one."

"I was thinking about you."

My stomach flipped again. "That's nice to hear."

"I'm glad. Get done out there and get home. Feel better."

"Thanks."

I clicked off the call, a smile tugging at my lips. He was thinking about me. Kyle's face flashed quick on the heels of that and I sighed, considering Em's words. But I had time to figure Joey and Kyle out.

The clock was ticking on TJ Okerson's story.

* * *

The light was green again when I crossed the bridge to the island. I drove every street, which took all of twenty minutes at Sunday-stroll speed. It was quiet, the children I'd seen the day before tucked safely behind locked doors in the wake of the tragedy. I wasn't looking for an interview—just to get a feel for the place TJ had called home. It was Mayberry-like, in the most charming sense of the label. And it was an island. But for the ninety-minute drive from my office and my favorite coffeehouse, I'd consider moving.

I slowed as I approached the Okerson house, then slammed the brake and turned around when I saw Charlie Lewis's satellite truck from Channel Four parked along the side of the road. She was likely camped outside Tony and Ashton's gate, and I didn't want to lead her to my actual destination if she hadn't thought of it yet.

I crossed the bridge again and turned toward Mathews, parking in a visitor space at the high school. The building was TV-show-high-school-set perfect, red brick with bright white columns.

I walked into the front office and a plump blonde woman with a turquoise sweater set and shimmery pink lip gloss smiled and asked if she could help me.

The question was, *would* she help me? I introduced myself, and her smile faded. I didn't like my odds.

"We saw your article this morning." She gestured to the computer monitor on her desktop. "Lyle Foxhead at our local newspaper is my sister's boyfriend. He was tore up over the Okersons talking to you and not him. He rang their phone off the wall all yesterday and half the day today. How come they talked to you? You ain't from here. Of course, they're come-heres, too."

"Come heres?"

"People who aren't from the county. They come here to live. But they're not part of us. Not part of the area like the rest of us."

"I see." I wasn't sure I did. She made it sound like a club there was no way to pledge. "Well, as a journalist, I can certainly understand Lyle's frustration." I smiled. "The Okersons and I have a mutual friend who recommended they talk to me. So this is not a case of 'they just didn't trust him.' And I'm sure y'all know it's been a very trying couple of days for them."

She gave me a critical once-over. "A mutual friend?" She appeared to soften a bit.

"Grant Parker and I work together."

"Is that a fact?" She grinned the way women do when Parker walks into a room, and I knew I'd found my in.

"We're close." I smiled. "He went on and on about how hospitable the folks around here are."

"Did he, now?"

I nodded.

"I do pride myself on my manners," she said, fluffing her already-pouffy hair. "I'm Norma. Welcome to Mathews."

"Thanks. I'm wondering if some of TJ's teachers might talk to me."

"I don't know," she still looked guarded, but she reached for the phone on her scarred wooden desk and dialed a number.

She dialed three different people, the layers of pity in the smiles she flashed me between calls getting thicker each time. "This is just such an emotional subject for our faculty." She shook her head as she cradled the phone.

"I understand," I said, sure it didn't help that I was an outsider. I offered a last smile and moved toward the door, sniffling. She cracked.

"Wait!" She brandished a tissue box, picking up her phone again. "I know who you can talk to."

I took a tissue and wiped my nose as she murmured into the handset. She turned back to me, grinning.

"If you'll just go down this hallway to the back doors, follow that stairwell outside then down, and take a left at the foot of the stairs, you'll find the gym. Coach Morris will talk to you. He's used to reporters. And he and Lyle don't get along."

"Disagreement over a story?" I asked, wondering if the coach distrusted the press.

"No. Coach Morris used to be my sister's husband." She shook her head. "I don't know what's wrong with her sometimes."

No drama there. "Thanks for your help."

The school was eerily quiet for the middle of the day. It took me minute to remember what the Okersons had said about it being spring break.

I found the gym easily, but Coach Morris proved more difficult. After lapping the basketball court and checking the equipment room twice, I flagged down a couple of lanky boys with bat bags slung over their shoulders.

"I'm looking for Coach Morris?" I leaned on the wall as a sudden wave of dizziness hit, making me wish I was closer to the bleachers.

"He's probably in his office." One boy gestured to a side hallway. "It's in the locker room. We can get him, if you like." He poked the second boy, who trotted off that way.

I smiled a thank you before I ambled to the bleachers and sat. The boy tugged at the bottom of the basketball net, watching me with a curious expression. Looking toward the hallway where the other boy had gone and finding it empty, I studied the kid in front of me. Straight teeth, clear skin, good hair. And a baseball player.

"Did you know TJ Okerson?" I asked, knowing the answer from looking at him.

"Everyone knew TJ." He plucked at the white strings.

"So I hear. How well did you know him? He was a pitcher, right?"

The boy nodded. "A great pitcher. I pitch, too, but no one could touch TJ. His dad's arm is legend. Some days, I wished he'd stayed in D.C."

"I bet it's hard to compete with a guy like that."

He met my eyes for the first time since I'd mentioned TJ's name, his tone flat. "There's no way to compete with a guy like that. Can't be done. There's only standing in his shadow and waiting for him to get hurt."

Holy shit. I held the boy's gaze until my eyes went blurry. He didn't blink.

"I'm sorry to keep you waiting," a deep voice from the far end of the bleachers broke the tension and I turned. "I'm Terry Morris."

"Nichelle Clarke," I said, smiling and putting out a hand.

"You can go on home, Luke," the coach nodded a dismissal at the kid and he shrugged and wandered toward the outside door, glancing back at me once.

I focused on the man who probably knew TJ as well as anyone, wishing I felt better and trying to put Luke's steely gaze out of my thoughts for the moment.

"Thanks for talking to me," I said. "I don't think I'm the most popular girl in town today."

"Norma tells me you're the gal who wrote the story about TJ in the Richmond paper. Any enemy of Lyle's is a friend of mine." Morris smiled. He was good-looking, probably in his early forties with light brown hair, a warm tan, strong jaw, and nice smile. His physique suggested he took advantage of his job as a gym teacher to keep in shape.

I didn't mention that I didn't want to be the enemy of the local press. If Lyle was any good at his job, he knew the people I needed to talk to and could be a great source for me.

"I'm going to jump right in here," I said, reaching for a notebook and clicking out my pen. "Was TJ troubled? Did anything seem to be bothering him lately?"

"Besides his knee? Nope." Morris shook his head hard enough to muss his hair. "TJ was a happy kid. Smart. Gifted on the field. Nice. I don't think anything much ever bothered him. He led a charmed life."

I considered the scenarios on my list of reasons for a kid like TJ to commit suicide. Aaron's comment about the Okersons floated to the top.

"What about his parents?" I asked. "His dad is a big deal. Did they put a lot of pressure on him?"

"Not that I ever saw, really." Morris held my gaze. "I mean, TJ was a perfectionist, and sure, he worried about what his dad thought. But Tony wasn't one of those dads who came to every practice and bitched at the kid all the way through. He offered pointers. You'd almost think he was a bad parent if he didn't, wouldn't you? But full-on pressure? No. Luke there, the boy who was here a minute ago—he gets more of that. His daddy won a state baseball trophy for us twenty years ago, and it was the greatest thing he ever did. He rides the kid pretty hard."

I scribbled every word. Damn. I hate cases involving kids on either side, but on both? My head developed a dull ache at the thought. I put a star in the margin by that comment.

"Tell me about TJ's knee," I said, remembering the night Parker had told me about his career-ending shoulder injury. It had messed him up. Maybe TJ was just young enough that a serious injury had pushed him a tiny bit too far?

"He pulled the ligaments in the last football game of the season."

"Ligaments, plural?" I asked.

"Yeah. I joked with him that he didn't know how to do anything halfway. He wanted to play the rest of the game. I coach the offensive line. I didn't know how bad he was hurt. That kid had a tolerance for pain like nothing I've ever seen. The docs said it was a miracle he could walk by the time the game was over."

"No kidding?" I kept writing.

Morris nodded. "They had a physical therapist at their house three days a week for the whole winter, and he was ready to start when baseball got going this spring, but then he came off the mound funny last Thursday and twisted it. He was limping and babying it pretty good all day Friday. They've been on vacation this week. I told him to rest it. Hadn't heard anything from them about what the doctors said."

And TJ's dad hadn't given me those details. Could Parker find out more for me?

"What about his girlfriend? Any trouble in paradise?"

Morris shook his head. "Not that I could tell, no. She's been out of pocket for a while, but he still had a picture in his locker. Talked about her all the time."

Locker.

"Has anyone been by to clean out TJ's locker?" I asked.

Morris shook his head.

"May I see it?" I asked.

"Sure, I guess. As long as you don't take anything." He shrugged. "Let me make sure the boys are gone."

He disappeared and I cradled my head in my hands and took a few deep breaths. I dug in my purse for the Advil and choked two down dry before Morris returned.

"All clear." He grinned.

The locker room stank of sweat, mildew, and spray deodorant in heavy enough doses that even I could smell it with my stuffed up nose.

"Right down here," Morris said, pointing to the third row of lockers. "Number nineteen."

I perched on the bench in the center of the aisle, smiling at the small-town feel of the lack of locks in the locker room. Closing my eyes for a moment, I pulled TJ's open.

When I opened my eyes, a beautiful girl with long brown hair and a Mona Lisa smile stared at me from the inside of the door, her photo outlined by a magnetic frame decorated with hearts. Girlfriend. Check.

I picked through the rest of the contents, not finding much of anything but normal teenage athlete stuff. Deodorant, three baseball gloves, socks, jockstrap (I didn't pick that up). A bag hung from the hook in the back and I started to open it before something in my peripheral vision pulled my eyes up. Toward the back of the shelf in the top of the locker lay a piece of lime green paper. I pulled it down. It was curved, crumpled on one edge, with huge block letters printed on one side.

Wednesday night, Cherry Point beach, get your party on before the season starts. Go Eagles!

A flyer for the party TJ had gone to. Who invited him? I turned the paper over looking for a name. There wasn't one.

"It doesn't look like there's much here to see." I put the flyer back where I'd found it, peeking into the bag. Dirty socks, a pair of cleats, and a set of knee pads. Strike three.

"He was a good kid," Morris said. "I sure am going to miss him. He won games, yeah. But he was just nice to have around. Why in God's name would he do something like this? Could it have been an accident?"

I shook my head. "The police don't think so, I think because of the number of pills that were missing. No one takes a whole bottle of Vicodin unless they're trying to hurt themselves." Quoting Sheriff Zeke felt put on, but I could see the pain on Morris's face, and I didn't want to add my suspicions to it without more reason.

"I just don't understand." He slumped against the bank of lockers. "It's so sad."

"It is," I said. "Everyone keeps telling me he was such a wonderful kid. I'm so sorry for your loss, coach. Thanks for talking to me."

"Anytime," he said. "I'm always available for a reporter who's not sleeping with my wife."

So not touching that.

I made my way back through the silent building to the parking lot and drove the two minutes to the police station, finding the old pickup in the parking lot again. Letting myself in, I sat perched on the edge of a bench in the front entry. The spiky-haired dispatcher was probably at lunch, the office quiet except for an animated discussion between the sheriff and the same agitated man I'd seen there the day before.

"How is it possible that you can't put a stop to this foolishness?" he asked, tugging at his red suspenders.

"Amos, they are not breaking the law." Zeke spaced his words out for effect.

"Trespassing."

"It's a parking lot."

"Invasion of privacy."

"In plain sight?"

I cleared my throat and they both turned to me. The sheriff actually looked happy to see me.

"I have other business to attend to with Miss Clarke here, if you'll excuse me," Sheriff Zeke said. "She's from the newspaper. In Richmond."

Amos blanched, but recovered so quickly I wondered if I'd imagined it, offering a hand before hustling out the door.

"You have excellent timing," Zeke said.

"I try. He seems upset."

The sheriff rolled his eyes, but didn't offer a comment. Since Amos wasn't what I was there to talk about, I left it.

"I went by the high school and had a chat with the baseball coach," I said. "I just thought I'd stop by since I was out here and see if you'd had any new developments in your investigation."

"I'm still waiting to hear from the lab," he said. "But my statement for today is that according to the story I can piece together from witnesses, we have no suspicion of foul play. No matter how much you might want me to."

"I don't want this child to have been murdered. I'm just looking at every angle of the story."

"Or maybe trying to spin the story into something more sensational than it already is?"

Zeke sighed when my eyebrows went up.

"That's probably unfair," he said hastily. "But I've had twenty-seven phone calls from media outlets today. Every TV personality in the east is on their way here, and I expect they'll be arriving in time for dinner. I'm sorry for the Okersons. But right now, I have to find a way to keep this from becoming an epidemic. A kid like TJ Okerson committing suicide gets blasted all over the TV and the Internet, and there's liable to be a whole wave of kids who hurt themselves trying to be cool."

"I had the same thought this morning," I said. "Which is part of the reason it makes sense to look for other causes of death, right?"

"I can't waste taxpayer money running an investigation into an open and shut case," he said. "I'll pay for that next election season."

"You're that sure after two days with no lab results?" It sounded sharper than I intended, and the sheriff bristled. I raised one hand. "I mean no disrespect. I just think—there was a boy at the school today. Luke something. A baseball player. He seemed very jealous of TJ. Was he at this party?"

The sheriff shook his head. "You don't give up, do you?"

"Not easily."

"I don't believe there's an official list of who was at the party. I haven't heard the Bosley kid's name."

I stared, waiting for him to say something else. Like, "I'll look into that."

He returned my somber gaze without so much as a twitch of his lips.

Looked like I'd be the one checking out young Luke. A mustachioed deputy in a uniform that matched Zeke's and a wide-brimmed hat came through a side door, pausing and giving me an interested once-over. I tucked my pad and pen back into my bag.

"Thanks for your time, sheriff," I said as I stood, not wanting to leave on a sour note. "Again. Good luck tonight."

"You're not staying for the show?" Zeke asked.

"I've seen it."

The farther I was from Mathews when the satellite trucks invaded, the happier Bob would be. I was sure I had messages stacking up at the office, and my cell phone had been binging email arrivals all afternoon. Professional courtesy forbade me from outright ignoring them, but being sick and trekking around Mathews all afternoon were excellent excuses for putting them off.

CHAPTER FIVE

AFTER A FIVE-MINUTE CHAT with the elderly receptionist at the local newspaper office (Lyle wasn't there), I left a message and took a copy of that day's final edition home. I wanted to know what else was news in Mathews County.

I got Aaron's email about the car stereo thefts and the detergent and sent Bob a four-inch blurb about each for Metro from my cell phone before I aimed the car toward Richmond.

Dead tired, I turned into my driveway an hour and a half after I left the *Mathews Leader*'s office. I examined the flowerbed next to the mailbox, noticing that my hyacinths were pinking up, before I saw the black Lincoln parked under the low-hanging tree in the neighbor's front yard. I smiled.

"Joey?" I coughed over the last half of the word as I let myself in through the kitchen door. The first time I'd ever laid eyes on Joey, I'd come home from a long day to find him in my living room, waiting with a story tip. Apparently, the Mafia doesn't consider an invitation necessary. After that first scared-shitless encounter, he'd saved my life once and shown up to talk increasingly often. We'd developed a slow-growing relationship of sorts. He wasn't exactly a "good guy," but I'd been unable to find evidence that he was a bonafide bad guy, either.

The only thing I'd nailed down was that he was good to me. Years of up-close-and-personal with the worst of society had blessed me with a good creep radar, and Joey didn't set it off. Since he liked to stop in without calling (and clearly, I had shoddy locks), I'd given him a key shortly after Christmas.

"Straight to bed." I heard the low, warm voice from the hallway before I saw him, and my stomach flopped. Since we'd never been to bed together, I figured he was worried about my illness. I hoped, anyway. It's impossible to feel sexy with a nose full of yuck.

"Is that an order?" I asked.

"Absolutely." He stepped into the kitchen, his olive skin dark with scruff along his jaw, his full lips parting over a smile. I really was sick, because my pulse didn't even flutter. "You sounded horrible on the phone. And no offense, but you don't look two steps out of a funeral home."

Great. I smoothed my hair back and then gave up, too sapped to be self-conscious. Darcy yipped and pawed my ankle and I scratched behind her ears, dizziness washing over me when I bent down.

"Whoa." I grabbed the back of one of my little bistro chairs and hauled myself into it. "Hang on, Darce."

"Bed. You need rest. I can't believe you drove your car." Joey shook his head, a line creasing his brow. "I already took Darcy outside, and I fed her, too."

I smiled a thank you, staring after he turned away.

Damn, he looked good. His suit jacket was slung over the back of the other kitchen chair. He stepped to the stove in a perfectly-tailored charcoal vest and pants, his cornflower blue shirt making his skin glow warmer in the soft light. I marveled at the fact that this man was in my house. Cooking.

"This story is the kind you don't skip out on," I said.

"I saw it. Sad stuff." He lifted the lid off a pot and stirred and I caught a whiff of something delicious through the sinus fog.

"What is that?"

"My mother's minestrone will cure anything," he said, settling the lid back in place and turning to me. "It's full of vitamins, and it tastes good, too. It'll be ready in about half an hour."

"I have less than no appetite." I folded my arms on the table and dropped my head onto them, muffling the words. "I just feel...gross. Stupid germs."

"Which is why you need to eat. And rest." He looped one arm around my waist and fit the other under my knees, scooping me out of the chair and walking toward the bedroom.

"In all the times I've imagined you carrying me to bed, this is not what I had in mind," I said, laying my head on his shoulder.

"You imagined what?" His voice dropped. "Let's hear that story."

"I probably shouldn't have said that," I said. "My brain isn't firing on all cylinders. Disregard."

"Not on your life." He settled me on the edge of the wide cherry four-poster that dominated the floor space in my tiny bedroom. "But we'll table it for when you feel better." His dark eyes sparkled and my stomach cartwheeled.

"You really are an interesting guy, you know that? I never would've expected you to play nursemaid."

He chuckled. "Thank you. I think."

"Shutting up now," I said. "All the cold medicine I've taken this week is affecting my filter."

I kicked my eggplant Jimmy Choo slingbacks onto the floor and splayed my toes. "Everything hurts."

"Pajamas, medicine, and under the covers," he ordered.

I saluted. "Yes, sir."

He crossed his arms over his chest and leaned on the doorframe. "Well?"

"If I had the energy, I'd throw a pillow at you. Get out."

He raised both hands. "You said something about your filter being off. Can't blame a guy for trying." He stepped into the hall and shut the door.

I dug for cute pajamas and finally came up with a matching set. Wriggling them on, I climbed under the covers and called an all clear.

"So, what's the deal with this kid? Looks like he had it all and he just killed himself? Why?" Joey perched on the edge of the bed.

"That's what I said." I forced myself to focus on the story, so I wouldn't go all giggly at the sight of Joey on my bed. "I'm trying to figure it out, but honestly? The more I poke around, the more I think he didn't kill himself."

"Oh yeah?" He raised his eyebrows. "How come?"

"Well, because of what you said. It just doesn't add up. None of the suicide markers I've written about before are here. I mean, there were four kids who jumped off the Lee bridge three summers ago. I talked to more suicide prevention specialists and counselors and shrinks that summer than I did cops. This doesn't fit what any of them told me. Plus, my friend Emily is a big shot psychologist in Dallas. She can't talk to me on the record, but she says it doesn't fit, either, unless there's some big secret. And I can't see anybody in that town breaking wind without everyone knowing. Yet for some reason, the sheriff out there seems determined to mark it a suicide and close the file."

"Maybe you should think about why he's so eager to be done with it," Joey said, adjusting the covers so he could massage my foot. "Is he covering for someone?"

"Oh, Jesus, I hope not," I sighed. "That feels really good."

He smiled.

"I guess that's something to check out, though," I mused. "There was this kid I met at the school today. Luke ... I can't remember, but the sheriff said his last name, so he knows him. Or his family. Kid was pretty blunt about being jealous of TJ. And I didn't care for the vibe I got from him. I've been around more murderers than anyone ever should, and there's something about that kid. He might not have killed TJ, but it's not because he's not capable of it."

He switched to the other foot and I leaned my head back and let my thoughts roam.

"There's something else going on out there, too," I said, eyes still shut. "I've been to the sheriff's office twice in two days, and both times, there was a guy hanging out there badgering him about something that the sheriff swears isn't illegal. I sort of asked today, but he didn't take the bait. Could be an interesting aside if I can catch up to the other guy, though."

I sat up, thinking about the paper I'd brought home. Maybe there was a clue in there.

"I don't suppose you feel like bringing me the newspaper that's in the front seat of my car?" I smiled at Joey. "Not that I'm not loving the pampering, but I grabbed a paper in Mathews today. I'd like to get a better feel for the town and the people."

"I need to check the soup, anyway." He patted my foot and replaced the covers as he stood. "I'll be right back."

"Thanks." I grinned at the warmth in his eyes, pushing aside the where-could-this-possibly-go thoughts that came often when I was with Joey. He was sexy and exciting (and sweet, too, which was a cool bonus). We were having fun.

I grabbed the remote off the night table and clicked the TV on, CNN flashing up by default. Anderson Cooper was in California covering an earthquake. I wondered who they'd sent to Mathews. I flipped to ESPN, and found a young reporter in a polo shirt and blazer standing on the football field at Mathews High, talking about TJ.

"Okerson seemed on the verge of following in his father's footsteps, leading the Mathews Eagles to the state title last year. But he took a hard fall in the fourth quarter of the championship game, resulting in a knee injury that might have ended someone else's playing days. Tony Okerson talked to ESPN about his son's recovery last month."

They cut to a clip of that interview, and I watched Tony's relaxed smile, his eyes not the haunted ones I'd seen in his living room the day before.

"I'm very fortunate to have access to some of the best sports medicine folks in the country," he said. "Because of that, we were able to get TJ the treatment he needed soon enough after the injury to save his playing career, if that's what he chooses to make a career of."

The screen flashed a diagram of the ligaments in the knee, and a doctor from Johns Hopkins came on, talking about the type of injury

TJ had, and why it was so unusual for him to recover. I fumbled a notebook and pen out of the nightstand drawer and jotted down the name of the injury, pondering that.

"He had a better tolerance for pain than any kid I'd ever seen," Coach Morris had said.

What if he hadn't recovered as fully as everyone thought?

I flipped back to CNN, where a young female reporter I didn't recognize was "Live from Mathews County, Virginia," standing on the front steps of the high school. She didn't have anything I didn't know, and everyone had been gone by the time she got there. Maybe no one else had talked to the coach. I'd have to watch Charlie's broadcast at 11 and check the Newport News media websites to be sure of that, though.

I flopped back into the pillows and sighed. I probably ought to get my story written, but I didn't want to do anything except sleep. Maybe I'd feel more like working after I ate something.

Joey strolled back in with the paper and my bag and handed both to me, glancing at the TV. "Media circus, huh?"

"I knew it would be. It'll be a miracle if they get through the funeral without someone getting nasty. I'm waiting for the commentary about his famous father pushing him too hard."

"Was he?"

"Not that I've been able to find. Grant Parker at my office is an old friend of the family, and he would have told me if that was the case. I think. Maybe I'll ask. But I did ask the baseball coach today, and he said he never saw any evidence of that."

Joey nodded.

I glanced back at the TV, which showed a shot of the Okersons' front gate with a voice over about the idyllic little town being rocked by the popular athlete's suicide.

"Dammit, I can't afford to be sick right now," I grumbled. "Going up against Charlie is bad enough, but I'm trying to beat out everyone in the country, here." I shook an antibiotic from the bottle I dug out of my bag and swallowed it. "Pharmaceutical industry, do your thing."

"You need to get well so you can do your thing. The soup should be ready." Joey walked out of the room.

I spread the *Mathews Leader* open over my lap. The front led with a short write up on TJ, most of the page dominated by a photo of him hoisting the trophy after the championship football game. Lyle had quoted the sheriff and the football coach, who was reached by phone in the Outer Banks. That was the kind of connection I didn't have out there, and I was glad to see it. I knew how it felt when the networks descended on one of my bigger trials.

The second story on the front was also Lyle's, and made me giggle because it was such a one-eighty from the Okerson story. A giant snapping turtle had wandered up from the water and chased a preschool class down Main Street. The photos of the ensuing melee, showing Sheriff Zeke and a deputy facing off with the turtle—which was roughly the size of a child's picnic table and looked mean, with its hooked upper lip—were fantastic. It was the perfect portrayal of why I loved my job, wrapped up in one printed page. I never knew what each day would bring. And that was often truer for reporters in little towns, who covered a bit of everything instead of one dedicated beat.

Since I was pretty sure the turtle population wasn't what had Amos's suspenders in a twist, I kept flipping. I made it through all sixteen pages without finding anything suspect, but I did learn the names of the mayor (Jeff Ellington), plus the high school principal (Bill McManus) and PTA President (Lily Bosley). I found TJ's obit, too —it took up all but a business-card-size ad slot on page five.

Joey came in carrying a tray just as I set the paper aside.

"That really does smell good," I said. "And I can't smell much of anything. Thank you."

"Anytime." The way his lips edged up made me drop my eyes back to the newspaper.

He set the tray next to me and chuckled. "Find anything in the paper?"

"Not really. Some names I might need, but not what I was looking for."

"Maybe some rest will help you figure something out."

"I have a story to write. And then we'll see about that." I set the paper aside and laid the tray across my lap, lifting the spoon. "I didn't know you could cook."

"You didn't ask." He took a seat in the small chair in the corner.

"And me with the whole 'questions are my livelihood' thing, too." I took a bite. The soup was blistering hot, but amazing.

"This is fantastic. Thank you."

"I'm glad you like it."

I continued to mull over the story aloud between bites. By the time I put the empty bowl on the night table, I could've sworn I felt a little better. "Is there magic in that stuff? Or liquor?" I asked.

Joey shook his head. "Just vegetables."

"It was nice of you." I said, reaching for my laptop. "Truly."

"Someone has to make sure you take care of yourself. But I get the feeling you want me to go."

I frowned. "I don't want you to go. And I'm certainly not trying to be rude. But I have work to do, and sleep to get, so I'm afraid I'm not going to be great company. I'm shocked my cell phone isn't already buzzing with Bob wanting a story. I really should have done it when I got home."

"No offense taken." He stopped in the doorway. "Feel better. Maybe I'll see you next Friday?"

"Girls' night with Jenna," I said, scrunching my face apologetically. "Saturday?"

"You're on. I better be back to a hundred percent by then."

"Keep eating the soup. I put the rest in your fridge. It works, I'm telling you."

"I'm a believer." I smiled.

"I'll call you tomorrow. Sleep well." He stared at me for a moment, then crossed to the bed and dropped a kiss on my head. "Be careful."

"You know something I should know?" I tried to keep focused on his words, when all I wanted was to melt into a puddle on the bed.

"Nope." He raised both hands in mock-surrender and backed toward the door when I arched one eyebrow at that. "I swear it. I'd never heard of Mathews, Virginia until I read your story this morning. Probably why Okerson moved out there in the first place, right?"

"You know anyone who might know something?" I asked.

"About this kid? I can't imagine why."

"Or his dad." I felt an idea looming. "Tony Okerson was a big deal football player. Who knows who he might have come into contact with? I've never heard or seen anything about him being into gambling or anything ..." I let that trail off, almost feeling traitorous for wondering such a thing.

Joey nodded thoughtfully. "But that doesn't mean he's not. You'd be surprised at some of the athletes and celebrities who are. Hurting the kid to get at dad is low, but not unheard of."

"Yeah?" I didn't care for this idea, except that it'd be an exclusive. I didn't know any other reporters with an in at the Mafia.

He sighed and shoved his hands into his pockets. "Why do I have a feeling I'll regret this conversation someday soon?"

I opened my mouth to object and he shook his head.

"Tell you what," he said. "I'll see if I can find out anything for you if you swear that you won't go poking into this alone and you promise to watch yourself and call someone for help if it looks like it might be more dangerous than playing fetch with Darcy."

The dog popped out of her bed and yipped when he said her name.

"Who am I going to call for help?" I asked. I didn't want to make him a promise I couldn't deliver on.

"Your friends at the Richmond PD?" He dropped his eyes to the floor. "Your friend at the ATF?"

I nodded slowly, catching the resentful note in his voice, but unsure what to do about it. My long-ago ex-boyfriend was a Bureau of Alcohol, Tobacco, Firearms, and Explosives supercop. He was also interested in no longer being my ex-boyfriend. Joey didn't like Kyle. Kyle didn't like Joey (what he knew about him, anyhow, which wasn't much). I liked them both. Em was right. It was a mess.

"I promise," I said.

"I'll see what I can find." He backed out the door with a wave. "Get well."

I heard the kitchen door click shut and sank into the pillows for a second, closing my eyes and breathing deep. Kyle. Joey. Equally gorgeous. Equally exciting. Almost equally problematic.

Pushing the covers back, I sighed. "Since I'm not deciphering my love life anytime soon, what say we figure out what happened to this kid, Darcy?" I asked the dog, slipping out of bed. She pricked up her ears and bit her favorite old stuffed squirrel.

After washing my face and making some tea, I climbed back in bed and opened my computer. My fingers hovered over the keys, but I didn't get a single word into the lead before my cell phone lit up.

I glanced at the screen and frowned at the unfamiliar number. Not Bob.

"Clarke," I said, pressing it to my ear.

"Zeke Waters in Mathews County," came the reply. "Remember that epidemic we talked about? It's been thirty-six hours. And I have another dead kid."

CHAPTER SIX

"YOU AND THE local paper are the only media being notified tonight, and I only called you because TJ's parents brought you into this," Waters said tightly, letting me through the yellow crime-scene tape blocking access to the area under the drawbridge. Deputies combed the rocks with flashlights, and I tried not to slip as I tagged after the sheriff.

I'd had the sense to leave my Jimmy Choos at home in favor of a pair of Tory Burch ballet flats when I'd dragged myself out of bed and back to the coast, but I wasn't expecting rocky shore terrain. The flats were slick, and my balance was already off from being sick. I hadn't come this far to wait by the road for an interview, though.

Sheriff Zeke swept the area with a wide orange beam, and I swallowed hard at the memory of the summer I'd had the four jumpers in Richmond, scanning the rocks for blood. I turned to the sheriff when I didn't see any.

"Is this bridge high enough—or the water shallow enough—for a jump to be lethal if they didn't hit the rocks?" I stared at the far bank, which I couldn't really see, but the deputies were all on this side.

"No," he furrowed his brow at the question, looking up at the underside of the bridge. "This wasn't a jump. The kids have parties here a lot."

"Another party?" I clicked out a pen, glancing at the stout man with the dark beard and glasses who appeared next to me, holding a tape recorder. Lyle, probably. "Same kids?"

"Some, yeah," Zeke said.

"Cause of death?" I asked.

"Not immediately apparent," he said. "I'm sure the tox screen will reveal it."

"Then why did you tell me on the phone you suspected it was a copycat suicide?"

"There's a note," he said. "Maybe another overdose, or intentional alcohol poisoning."

"Are you releasing the name of the victim?" Lyle asked.

"Sydney Cobb," Zeke said, one hand flying up to rake over his face. "It's Sydney Cobb."

Something rang familiar, but I was too beat to get it on the first try.

A look flashed between Sheriff Zeke and Lyle.

"What am I missing, guys?" I asked.

"She was TJ Okerson's girlfriend," Lyle muttered. "Those of us who work here all the time know that."

I sucked in a sharp breath. Of course. "Sydney was the only one he ever wanted," Ashton had said. The picture in TJ's locker floated to the front of my thoughts.

"She left a note?" I asked.

Zeke nodded. "'It hurts.' That's all it said."

I closed my eyes for a second, then scribbled that down.

"Listen, folks," Zeke said, "every hotel in Gloucester and Hampton is full of news crews, and what happens here has the potential to happen in other places because of that. This is new territory for me, this national stage thing. But I want to do everything I can to keep any more children from dying."

I nodded, catching every word. I was pretty sure I still had the suicide prevention stuff in my files from the other cases. "I have some public service announcement stuff on this topic I can use in my copy," I said. "But once we run it, it's going to go all over, just like TJ's story did. We can't control what the other media outlets do."

Sheriff Zeke sighed. "I know." He dropped his head. "Dammit! If TJ Okerson was standing here right now, I'd take a swing at him, hand to God. The Cobbs ...I've never heard a human being make a sound like the one that came out of Tiffany Cobb when I showed up at her house tonight. Sydney stopped answering her phone a little after seven, she said."

"They were having a party that early?" I looked up from my notes.

"It was dark. They're upset."

Huh. I glanced between Zeke and Lyle again, but they didn't look like that was out of the ordinary. Damn. So now this girl had killed herself because of what had happened to her boyfriend, who may or may not have killed himself? It was a shitty story all the way around.

"How old was Sydney?" I asked.

The sheriff reeled off all the vital statistics and I took them down while Lyle stood by with his tape recorder. When Zeke excused himself to check something for a young deputy, I turned to Lyle. "I went by your office today," I said. "I wanted to introduce myself. I'm Nichelle."

"I know who you are." He shoved the tape recorder into his pocket and looked up at the underside of the bridge.

"Listen, the Okersons have a friend who works with me," I said. "It wasn't personal."

He nodded. "Hard to take it any other way when you've covered every jaywalking ticket in a town like this for ten years. Then something like this happens and I don't get the call."

"I can certainly understand that. Y'all had great photos of the snapping turtle rodeo, by the way. And your story on TJ was good. The football coach didn't talk to me."

"Coach B will talk to anything in a skirt, but not seriously. We had a female photographer on our staff for exactly half of one football game. He told her women weren't allowed on the sidelines, and she clocked him. She got fired."

"And arrested?" I asked.

"Nope. Zeke said he deserved it, and coach didn't want to admit it hurt bad enough for him to press charges."

"See? I didn't know to call him, and I might have punched him, too, so thanks for the heads up."

He grunted a reply, eyes roaming around the scene.

I followed suit, standing in silence and hoping to overhear something useful.

"What a week," Lyle finally said.

"Jesus, you can say that again," I said. "I've spent more time in your town than in mine."

"I've worked out here for a long time, ma'am." Lyle leveled a gaze at me. "I've never seen anything like this. This is a great town. Good people. God fearing. Hard working. Two dead kids in two days? And these kids? TJ and Sydney were the goddamn homecoming king and queen, for chrissakes. This is going to hit these people hard. And Zeke is right: it could spread like brush fire. I wish y'all would all go home and just let it die with Sydney."

I took a deep breath. "I can understand, and even sympathize. But you know as well as I do that that's not going to happen. So what can we do to help, Lyle?"

He stared at the ambulance on the other side of the bridge embankment, sucking on the inside of his cheeks and pursing his lips. "I don't know."

I dug a card out of my bag and jotted my cell number on the back. "If you think of something, call me."

He stuck it in his pocket, only half paying attention to me.

I pulled out my cell phone to text Bob an update and sighed when I saw that it was almost ten. "I'm never going to get well," I muttered, picking my way back toward my car.

Once out from under the shadows of the bridge, I spotted Zeke talking to his deputies up near the edge of the road. Passing a patrol car, I glanced into the open trunk and saw a box of bagged objects. Rocks, beer and Coke bottles, a crumpled piece of neon green paper, and assorted other teen party scene stuff. A mason jar crowned the pile. I paused, glancing toward the sheriff, who had his back turned. None of them were paying the least bit of attention to me.

Stepping closer to the trunk, I ran the beam of my little pink flashlight over the jar. The label looked like it had come off an inkjet printer, the three x's across it all faded in the middle.

In my years covering crime I'd seen dead people and drugs, interviewed murderers and prostitutes, and snuck into illegal gambling halls: but I'd never seen a jar of moonshine. Not the unregulated, not-sold-in-stores kind, anyway. Yet I was pretty sure I was looking at an empty one.

I fished my cell phone out and snapped a quick photo of it, then stuffed the phone back into my bag.

"Find something interesting?" Zeke asked, waiting behind me with crossed arms when I turned. My face must have betrayed me, because he put up one hand before I could get a word out. "Wait. Do I want to know?"

"Is that a moonshine jar, sheriff?"

"It is." He closed the trunk of the patrol car.

"You're pretty cavalier about that for a cop."

"Miss Clarke, moonshiners are Alcoholic Beverage Commission police business, not mine, first of all. Second of all, I have my hands full right now. I couldn't hunt for a still if I wanted to."

"Was there moonshine at the party the night TJ died?"

"There was. The kids drink it because it's easy for them to get. Teenagers are the perfect target market for moonshiners, because they're the ones who want booze and can't buy it, which has always sort of been the whole point of moonshine, right?"

I shook my head. "And you're really not doing anything about this?"

"I do when I catch them. The kids, that is. Underage drinking is against the law. But chasing moonshiners isn't my jurisdiction."

"Was Sydney drinking that tonight?"

"Very possibly," he said. "That jar was found near her. I'll run prints to be sure."

"Where do they get it? Is it a local operation? I mean, I cover a lot of shit in Richmond, and I've never run across bonafide illegal moonshine."

"I know of three stills on the island. When anyone drops by to check them out, they're family heirlooms gathering dust. But I'm sure that's not always the case."

I nodded, seeing a phone call to the ABC police in my future.

"Thanks again, sheriff." I pushed the button to unlock my car door and waved a good night. "I'm sure I'll see you soon."

* * *

Back home, I brewed a cup of coffee just after eleven, thanking my lucky stars I hadn't passed a bored state trooper as I lead-footed it home from Tidewater. Bob had called me twice and I had a story to write before I could sleep. Two, actually. And no promise of rest for my Saturday, either.

Settled on my couch with my laptop and a cup of Colombian Fair Trade, I stared at the screen.

"Two dead kids. Jealous baseball player guy. Moonshine. This is jacked up, Darcy."

I had no pointed reason to suspect that Sydney's death was anything other than exactly what it looked like.

But something nagged. I was too tired to get it, so I started typing.

For the second time in as many days, a well-known teenager in tiny Mathews County on the Virginia coast is dead.

Sydney Cobb was surrounded by friends Friday night, students toasting the short life of Mathews High quarterback TJ Okerson. Sydney was TJ's longtime girlfriend, his mother told the Telegraph *in an exclusive interview Thursday.*

"She left a note," Mathews County Sheriff Zeke Waters said as deputies around him scoured the rocky shoreline for evidence. Waters said Cobb's note read "It hurts."

. . .

I pulled from my story on TJ to finish the piece, and sent it to Bob with a promise that the day two on TJ was coming. After some thought, I'd left out the moonshine jar. I didn't want anyone else nosing around that until I had time to check it out.

Pondering it, I clicked over to my Google tab and typed "moonshine." The number of hits was staggering. I gathered from a scan of the pages that the Internet could teach me how to distill my own booze, and decided to look over that in the morning.

I dug out my notes from Coach Morris and wrote a day two on what a great kid TJ was, and how his parents didn't pressure him, which I was more sure about after seeing Tony on ESPN earlier. He'd even said something about TJ being healed enough to salvage his career if that's what he wanted to do. Which didn't sound like a psycho-pushy-dad thing to say. Maybe I could head off some hateful commentaries by highlighting that.

By the time I emailed Bob the second story, my coffee was cold and I was past ready to crawl into bed. I hustled Darcy outside, trying to focus on something more pleasant than dead teenagers and grieving parents in the last few minutes before my head touched the pillows. A few hours before, I'd been looking forward to the dreams I might have after Joey's surprise visit. By bedtime, I just hoped to keep them more Joshilyn Jackson than Stephen King.

CHAPTER SEVEN

INTERESTING QUIRK of Virginia law number three forty seven: all liquor stores are owned and operated by the state. Number three forty eight: the Alcoholic Beverage Commission has its own police department. With sworn peace officers and everything.

They're about as chatty as most other cops with reporters they don't know, too.

After the second guy in a row said "no comment" and hung up on me, I slammed my phone back into its cradle and jerked my tea cup off the desk with such force that it sloshed out all over a pile of press releases. Fabulous. I rooted through two drawers before I found a napkin, muttering every swearword I knew as I blotted my desktop.

"Tough day?" Parker's voice came from behind me, and I jumped and whacked my knee on the underside of my desk.

"What in God's name are you doing here on a Saturday?" I asked, spinning my chair to face him.

"I can't just sit around my house," he said. "Mel's at some kind of city council workshop, and I was going stir crazy, watching all the shit about TJ and his girl on every station. So I thought I'd come see if I could help you. I dragged you into this, and you've been sick and all. What can I do?"

His green eyes looked pained.

I sighed. "I wish I had an assignment for you. Have you talked to the Okersons? How are they?"

"How you'd think. Ashton wouldn't be functioning at all if she didn't have the service to plan and the twins to take care of. Tony is going over every minute of the last week in his head a hundred times a day, trying to find what he missed. And now they're upset about the girl, too. They adored her. Tony plays golf with her dad."

I nodded. "It's a suck situation, Parker. I'm sorry."

"What the hell, Nichelle? I mean, really. I read your piece this morning. You talked to the coach. Did he say anything else?"

"Not really."

He shook his head. "I just don't get it."

"That makes two of us. Hey—has Tony ever mentioned TJ having a drinking problem? Not normal teenage crap, but like an addiction? Hangovers? Excess? Moonshine?"

"Moonshine?" Parker laughed, but the smile faded when he caught the serious look on my face. "No. Why?"

"Look, I left this out of the story this morning because I want to look into it before it goes all over the TV, but there was an empty moonshine jar at the scene where the girl was found last night. I did some reading when I got here this morning, and it turns out alcohol isn't the only kind of poisoning you can get from drinking it. There's no way to know for sure what killed TJ or Sydney until the tox screen comes back, but I know good and well Sheriff Waters out there is assuming his case is closed while he waits for that report. I want to know where the kids are getting this stuff. I'm just not sure how to find out. I don't have a contact at the ABC police."

"Your guys at the PD must have one."

"It's Saturday. Aaron wasn't in yet when I tried, but I'll call him again in a bit and see if he's willing to share one with me. I have a drug bust and a car-on-pedestrian crash to talk to him about, anyway. Keeping up with my regular job and covering crime in Mathews on top of being sick is even too much fun for me. This kind of blows, to be honest."

"I imagine. How you feeling?"

"Better, I think. I'm on day two of antibiotics, and I had some magic soup for dinner last night. But I need some rest. Like, even just going home on time and getting in bed would be nice."

"You're dedicated. It's part of what makes you good."

"I might settle for mediocre and healthy this week." I grinned. "No, I wouldn't. I love it. And I want to help your friends."

"Good luck. I'll go hang out in my office and pretend to work, but if you come up with something I can do, holler. I'll be around. Even if you want me to go on a coffee run."

"Grant Parker is offering to run my errands? Cue the *Twilight Zone* theme." I widened my eyes and glanced around.

He flashed a ghost of the famous grin that made women in twelve counties call for smelling salts. "Just trying to make it easy for you to do your thing."

"I appreciate that, and I'm not one to look a gift coffee in the mouth, but listen: you did me a favor, too, Parker. This is a huge story with national exposure, and you insisted Bob give it to me."

"I wish I hadn't been in a position to do that."

"I do, too." I waved a stack of pink message slips. "I also wish I didn't have thirty reporters to talk around this with. I should probably get to it."

"Call me if you need me." He disappeared in the direction of his office.

I sipped my tea and surveyed my desk. I picked up the first message slip. CNN.

"Here we go," I said as I dialed the phone.

I made it through half the stack in an hour, politely saying as little as I could get away with, mostly describing the emotion in the Okerson house for them. After a particularly dogged woman from NBC sent me into a coughing fit (which was an excellent excuse to hang up), I took a break from giving interviews so I could conduct one.

"It's Saturday. And you said you were sick," Aaron barked when he picked up.

"I'm aware of that, and I am sick. Though more human today, I think. So far, anyhow." I clicked out a pen. "I'm behind. This Okerson thing put together with the sinus infection is killing me. But I have a regular job to do, too."

"Aw, nice of you to take a break from the glamour for me."

"You know I love you best."

He chuckled. "Which one do you want first?"

"The man versus car. What happened?"

"Guy was walking along the side of Patterson at close to eleven last night. Kid driving the car was sending a text. He mowed the pedestrian down and hit a tree. Knocked himself out. Phone was still in his hand when our guys got on the scene."

"Holy shit, Aaron." I blew out a breath. "Is everyone OK?"

"Driver was at St. Vincent's overnight, but they expect him to make a full recovery."

Thank God. "And the victim?"

"He wasn't so lucky. Doctors said he bled out about an hour into surgery."

I closed my eyes for a second before I scribbled that down. "Just walking down the street. And this kid did a stupid thing and gets to go the rest of his life knowing he killed someone. Jesus."

"Right? If I were smart enough, I'd make a device that disabled the text feature on any cellphone inside a moving car. These are the most senseless things we see."

"Amen to that." If there was one habit my job had made me positively phobic about, it was texting while driving. It caused several tragedies a month. I'd been known to snap at friends I was riding with when they reached for their phones.

"You want the drug bust, too?"

"You know me too well. That's the other one that caught my eye. Is Stevens around today, or are you giving up that info, too?"

"I saw him this morning," Aaron said. "He's got a lot of paperwork to go through. They've been working undercover in that club for eighteen months. I'll put you through to him."

I wished Aaron a happy weekend before he transferred me. The new narcotics sergeant relayed the details of a huge marijuana growing and trafficking ring operating out of a bar downtown. Almost a thousand plants, plus a literal truckload of ready-to-move product.

I thanked Stevens and hung up before I realized I'd forgotten to ask Aaron about the ABC police. I hit redial.

"He wasn't there?" He asked by way of a hello when he picked up.

"No, he was. But I forgot that I meant to ask you something else. I need some information from the ABC police, and so far this morning I've been stonewalled twice, just calling random officers. Do you have any friends over there who might talk to me?"

"A couple, but I doubt they're in today," he said and then reeled off names and phone numbers. "Anything interesting you need them for?"

"Maybe. There's something nagging the hell out of me about these dead kids in Mathews."

"It's because they're kids," he said. "I saw your piece this morning, and I've worked with you long enough to read between the lines. I know I don't have to tell you how common copycat suicides are."

"See, I thought so, too. And maybe you're right. But since no one else seems to be looking at anything other than the obvious answer, I'm going to make damned sure of it before I let this go. Those children have parents who deserve to know what happened."

"It's a small town and this will be a sore subject for a long time," he cautioned. "Just watch yourself. You can't go accusing people of murder willy-nilly."

"When have you ever known me to do anything willy-nilly?"

He was quiet.

"Yeah, don't answer that. But I'm not pointing fingers. I'm just poking around. If you're right and there's nothing to it, I'm totally safe, right?"

"Depends entirely on what you're poking around in. Why do you want the ABC police?"

"Out in the sticks? Why do you think?"

"That's what I was afraid of." He sighed. "I swear, you need a vest. And a gun. Folks who run illegal booze like their firearms, Nichelle."

"Noted."

I hung up and dialed the numbers he'd given me, but got voicemail both times. I didn't leave messages. I'd try again Monday when I could put them on the spot.

Turning to my computer, I wrote up the two stories I had for metro. I finished the second and opened my email program before I realized who I was sending my copy to for approval.

"Aw, hell." I attached the files to an email to Shelby. That was just what I needed. "I ought to add the *Twilight Zone* theme to my iTunes," I said as I hit send. "First Parker's offering to be my gofer, and now I miss Les."

"Your piece on the Okerson kid this morning wasn't your best work." It took me a second to realize that the voice came from behind me and was male, not Shelby prattling inside my head.

I turned the chair slowly.

Spence leaned against the wall behind my little ivory cubicle, arms folded over his chest and a studiously disdainful look on his face.

I'd never had reason to be crossways with our sports editor, who was generally full of witty commentary and whatever baked goods Eunice had brought in, though you couldn't tell it by looking at his lanky frame.

"Good morning to you, too, Spence," I said. "You have any constructive criticism to offer, or did you come in on Saturday just to be insulting?"

"TJ Okerson was left-handed, which made him a more formidable pitcher," he said. "That's worth mentioning in a story where you interviewed the baseball coach."

"No one told me that," I said.

"A sports reporter would know it."

"And the sports editor would, too." I leaned back in my chair. "I'm tired. I'm still sick. And it's been one hell of a long week, here, Spence. If you've got something to say, just say it. You want my story?"

"It's not your story. Or, it shouldn't be your story."

"Dead people are kind of my thing." I paused. "Uh. You know what I mean."

"Sports are my thing. It's my whole life outside my wife and kid. This is the biggest sports story to come out of Virginia in half a decade, and it gets assigned to the crime desk? What kind of bullshit is that?"

"The kind of bullshit you'll have to take up with Bob." I closed my laptop and put it in my bag. "I didn't ask for this assignment."

"I know. Your good friend Parker asked you to take it. As a favor. If he worked for me, I'd have canned him. But our big shot star columnist reports to Bob." He sneered.

I stared, dumbfounded. I had never heard Spencer Jacobs sound the least bit annoyed with...anything. And I'd worked with him for almost eight years.

"If it's that big a deal to you, seriously, talk to Bob."

"I was told pretty explicitly yesterday that I was to get you what you need to do a good job," Spence said, pushing off the wall. "So here's what you need: a background in sports journalism and some better interview skills."

"I'm sorry, have we left the newsroom and gone back to seventh grade? I'd feel sorry for you, except you're being an asshat. So go be one somewhere else. If you want to help, I'm happy to take suggestions and tips, and more than happy to share credit for the story. But if you're going to hurl insults and be petty because they picked me and not you? You can bite me. And you should go hang out with Shelby. Y'all have something in common."

I stepped around him and hauled my bag onto my shoulder, striding to the elevator. Technically, I should have waited for Shelby to okay my stories, but I was beat, and Spence had shaken me way more than I wanted him to see.

Parker poked his head into the elevator as I turned to the buttons. "You have a lead?"

"Yes. A hot one. On a nap. Also, steer clear of Spence. Someone pissed in his Wheaties, and he seems to think it was us." I punched the button for the garage.

"Nice." He stepped back as the doors started to close. "Feel better. Call me if you need any help."

"You have yourself a side job, sir."

The doors whispered shut and I sagged against the wall. Some days, an eight-to-five desk job sounded better than others.

CHAPTER EIGHT

JOEY'S MINESTRONE was even better the second day. I laid the bowl in the dishwasher after lunch, and settled myself on the couch for a nap. But sleep eluded me with all the nonsense running around my head.

I could sort of go with the sheriff on Sydney's death. I remembered being a teenager. Overly emotional the-world-has-ended came from way simpler stuff than your boyfriend dying.

But why would TJ do it? That was a puzzle with a billion jagged pieces, only half of which I had to work with. I kept going back to Parker's words from that morning, but I couldn't pin down why it was bugging me so much.

Was Aaron right? Was I making something out of nothing because the case involved young people?

Or was Emily right? Was I projecting personal memories into a mysterious suicide? I tried to be honest with myself about both, but kept returning to the summer of the jumpers. I hadn't prowled around Richmond thinking those kids had been pushed. There was something different about this story. I just needed to figure out what.

The moonshine was different. It had been at both scenes. Sheriff Zeke seemed pretty sure both of the dead kids had been drinking it. Was it a bad batch? Possibly. But no one else was sick, or dead.

Wait.

What if there was something in it? I mean, who could taste anything mixed with thousand-proof rotgut?

Possible. Especially if Luke "Waiting for TJ to Get Hurt" Pitcher had been at the party.

I kicked my blanket into the floor, sat up, and grabbed the phone.

"What's up?" Parker asked when he picked up.

"I can't rest, so we might as well work," I said. "This thing out in Tidewater is making me slightly nuts."

"You can say that again."

I'd been tiptoeing around this with Parker for days, but I needed an answer.

"Parker, you knew this kid. You know his family. Level with me. Does your gut say he overdosed on Vicodin?"

He didn't answer right away.

"It does not," he said finally. "But that sounds crazy, doesn't it? The bottle was empty. The cops say it's open and shut. Tony said they told him they're just waiting for the toxicology results so they can close the file."

"I don't think it's crazy," I said. "I've covered teen suicides before. This doesn't fit. The cops are telling me it's open and shut, too, but I can't let it go."

His voice perked up. "What else is there to do?"

"Play Nancy Drew."

"Want a Hardy Boy?"

I laughed. "I think I might."

"What can I do?"

"See if you can get anything else out of Tony and Ashton," I said. "I could go talk to them, but they'll speak freely to you. I want to know if TJ had any enemies. I know he was a popular kid. The guy from the local paper said he was the homecoming king. But someone always hates those kids, you know? I want to know who. If you can find out anything from them about a kid named Luke from the baseball team, that would be damned handy."

"I can do that."

Bob's orders from the staff meeting popped into my thoughts. "I also need an invite to the funeral. I like Tony and Ashton and I want to pay my respects, plus Bob is set on having an exclusive with the networks crawling all over the island."

"No problem. Come with me—Mel is doing something else Monday."

Something else besides going to his friend's kid's funeral with him? Really? I kept quiet about that. "Okay, sure. Thanks."

"Listen, Clarke, I know you have this whole sort of Lois Lane thing working with these big exclusives," he said. "If I'm being honest, that's why I called you with this in the first place. I knew it would get me on Spence's shit list. I'm not stupid. But, I also knew if there was anything amiss, you were the person who'd find it. I want Tony to know what happened to his son. Whatever that turns out to be."

"Me, too. Though I wish you would've warned me about Spence. He was well and truly pissed. Caught me totally blindside."

"Don't worry about Spence. I'll handle him."

"Hard to ignore him when he sneaks up behind me hurling insults. I have a feeling Shelby's got a new best friend."

"She won't look twice at him. He's got a wife and a kid and he can't get her promoted."

"I was hoping having to fill in for Les would get her off my ass. Why can't she decide she wants to be a feature reporter? Or, I don't know, cover the schools? She's not a bad writer. I'd just like for it to be someone else's turn in her crosshairs for a while. Especially if Spence is going to be all butthurt over this story assignment."

"I understand that." There was a commotion in the background and Parker muffled the handset for a minute.

My mind wandered back to moonshiners. Who could I talk to about that? If I could find out who was making the stuff, maybe I could find out who bought it and took it to the parties.

Lyle seemed to know the town he covered well, but I didn't want to tip my hand to another reporter, and I certainly didn't want the TV folks getting wind of what I was working on. The old man at the antique store with his adorable accent and fantastic treasures floated through my thoughts. I bet he knew everything that went on in Mathews. And he liked to talk.

"Sorry about that. FedEx," Parker said. "Anything else you want me to find out? I'm heading to Tidewater."

"I'm going to drive back out there myself. I just thought of someone who might be able to help me with an angle I'm working."

"Care to share?"

"Not yet. Let me see if it goes anywhere first."

"I'll let you know what I find out at Tony's."

"Thanks, Parker."

"Thank you. Go get 'em, Lois."

I dialed Joey's number on my cell phone after I got on the Interstate. I considered calling Kyle Miller, former love of my life and current Mr. Possibly as well as ATF supercop, but decided to wait until I had something more to tell him. Kyle had an irritating habit of blowing off my suspicions, and I wasn't in the mood for a fight.

"You feeling any better?"

Good Lord. Just Joey's voice on the phone made my toes tingle. Part of me was afraid of his questionable occupation. Another part was just downright chicken of falling so hard for a guy it could never work with. Yet I couldn't stay away from him. Oy.

"That soup is totally magical. Your mom should sell it at health food stores." It was kind of funny to think about Joey's mom. I hadn't ever considered Captain Mystery in a family setting. "I'm probably seventy-five percent today, and I'm on my way back to Mathews."

"Something new? Besides the other dead kid I saw in your story this morning? TV hasn't shut up about that all day."

I knew that, and I was hoping that going between broadcast times would keep me clear of most of the cameras. Though I was slightly worried they'd find the adorable little antique store and its owner as interesting as I did.

"Sort of. I left something out of the story and I'm wondering if you might be able to find me a lead on it."

"Me? What is it?"

"You know anything about moonshine?"

He chuckled. "Like, corn whiskey, moonshine? Only that it tastes God-awful."

I huffed out a short breath, noticing I could breathe through one nostril for the first time in days. "Seriously? The Internet says some of this is major interstate money. Especially around here where there are still so many places you can't buy booze on Sundays. You have to know something. Or someone who does."

"Why are you poking around moonshiners?" He switched gears without answering, which didn't escape my notice.

"Because the dead kids were drinking moonshine. Or, the girl was. TJ might have been. I'm working on that. Aside from the possibility that someone could have spiked their booze with poison, I read that if the stills aren't properly cleaned or any one of a billion things goes wrong with the process, moonshine can kill people. I found a crap ton of stories from the twenties and thirties about people going blind and dropping dead in speakeasies."

"I guess that's a hazard of drinking it. Why would a bunch of kids mess with that stuff? It has a nasty kick."

"My first guess is because they want to drink and they're underage. Which stores care about, but moonshiners don't. The ABC police have been cracking down on underage sales all over the state lately. There's only so much beer they can swipe from their folks before they get in trouble. So they get the moonshine because it's cheap and readily available. Especially if it's being made right there on the island."

"You could be onto something. Do me a favor?"

"If I can."

"Watch it. If the wrong person gets word that you're trying to prove their rotgut killed these kids, you could wind up in very real danger."

"I would blow you off, but that hasn't ended well for me, historically. So I'll be careful."

"Thanks. I'd tell you to drop it, but that doesn't ever work. So, you know, call me if you need me. Try not to get shot."

"Thanks. I'll do what I can. Call me if you find anything?"

His voice dropped. "I'll take any excuse."

My pulse fluttered as I hung up, pulling the car off the freeway at West Point. The drive seemed to go quicker every time.

* * *

By the time I turned into the antique store parking lot, I had a pretty good mental list of questions—hopefully enough roundabout ones to avoid suspicion.

I counted three other cars, but no news trucks. I stepped in the front door and smiled at the man with thick bifocals behind the ornate old cash register. It was the kind with big round buttons on individual levers and a pull handle that totaled sales and opened the drawer. And it worked—he rang up a glass perfume bottle as I walked into the shop.

He turned to another customer, explaining the history of a gorgeous footstool (it once graced the foot of the bed in the biggest suite at the island's only hotel, which had burned down years before) to a fifty-something woman in designer jeans and a Louis Vuitton belt that matched the dark honey color of her gold-tipped Chanel flats. She forked over cash and left with the stool, and he turned to me.

"You don't look two breaths from the grave anymore, Missy," he said. "You found Zeke, I take it?"

"I did. Thank you for your help."

"You didn't tell me you were a reporter." He pursed his lips. I smiled. News about strangers probably zipped through Mathews faster than Speedy Gonzalez on uppers. "Been reporters crawling all over since."

I twisted my mouth to one side. "I'm sorry. I didn't see where my job was pertinent to our conversation."

"Oh, don't apologize to me." He chuckled. "There's lots of folks complaining about it, but me? I've done more business the last three days than I have all month. People go crazy over famous folks. Everyone in three states who ever watched a Skins game is looking for a genuine article from the town where Tony Okerson lives."

I smiled. "Well, I'm glad it was good for something." I put out a hand. "I'm Nichelle."

He nodded. "Elmer. Elmer Daughtry. I don't suppose you came looking for a chair or a chat about the weather." He turned to the secretary behind the register, deep mahogany with detail work that looked like it might have been carved by Thomas Jefferson himself, and poured two glasses of iced tea. He handed me one as he settled on a tall chair, gesturing to a backless barstool between the door and my side of the counter. "What do you want to know today?"

I perched on the stool and sipped my tea, sizing Elmer up. He was sweet, and he wasn't mad about the press being in town, which was helpful. But he was shrewd, too. Maybe my roundabout questions weren't the best approach.

"Honestly? I'm looking for information on moonshine, Elmer. And I figure you probably know everything there is to know about the county. So I thought this might be a good place to start." I pulled a pen and notebook out of my bag.

"How do you know I'm not a moonshiner?" His face was so serious my stomach wrung.

"You don't seem like the type?" I said, my voice going up at the end and turning it into a question.

He laughed. "You have a good gauge for that type, do you, city gal?"

I sighed. "No."

"Well, you're right that it's not me. I drank my share of it when I was a younger man, but this is about as hard as my drinking gets these days." He brandished the tea glass. "I might know where to get some, though."

"I'm not interested in buying any." Or, I wasn't until he said that. "I want to know who's making it. I hear there are a few stills on the island."

"You hear right. There's families around these parts been into moonshine since prohibition."

"That's fascinating. How do they keep from getting caught?"

"They hide. Some have so many generations of kids spread all over the county, if there's a whisper of the law coming by to check a still, it gets empty quick."

"Surely the police must be able to tell if it's been used recently?" I raised an eyebrow.

"I expect they can. Don't do them no good if they don't catch you in the act. Or catch you with a truckload of shine." He paused and gave me a once-over. "You work in Richmond. I seen some other stuff you wrote about in the paper. You got friends in law enforcement. They can't tell you this?"

"Not like you can," I said simply.

"Want the local color, huh?"

"Exactly." I grinned. "So how do people making this stuff not get caught with big batches of it?"

"Used to be they outran the law," he said. "You know that's where NASCAR came from, don't you?"

"Where ... I'm not sure I follow."

"That's always a good one for the tourists." He nodded sagely. "Years ago, moonshiners used to soup-up their cars so they outran the cop cars. Had to have good shocks to carry big loads of shine, too. Eventually, the boys started racing their cars. And there you have the birth of NASCAR."

I stopped writing as he talked, leaning one elbow on the counter, totally engrossed in his story.

"No shit?" It popped out before I could stop it.

"God's truth." He winked.

"So, where could a girl find a jar?"

"Why you want to know?"

I paused. I liked him, but I wasn't telling anyone why I was asking about this yet.

"I'm trying to get a feel for how things work out here. It's a little different than Richmond." Every word true.

"I imagine it is. The Sidells, the Parsons, and the Lemows are the three families you'd want to ask about."

I scribbled the names. "And they still make it?"

"Hard to say about this generation, but their daddies and grand-daddies did. Only ones I can tell you for fact still do are the Parsons, because they run a still on the other side of these woods every once in a while, and I can smell it."

"What does it smell like?" I had a vision of driving around the island at night with my windows open, but Joey and Aaron's stern faces flashed right behind that. Maybe I'd bring backup if I was going to hunt moonshiners.

"Mash. Like spoiled corn," he said. "They use commercial hog feed, mostly. It's distinctive, that's for sure."

I wrinkled my nose at the thought, adding that to my notes.

"Thanks for your help, Elmer." I drained my tea glass and stood up, dropping the pad and pen back into my bag.

"Thanks for the bump in business," he said. "Holler if there's anything else I can do for you. Not much of anyone to listen to my stories anymore."

"They're missing out," I said. "It was nice to see you again."

He nodded a goodbye.

I opened the door and almost walked into Charlie Lewis. Damn. I felt my face fall, but recovered before she noticed. I hoped.

"I thought that was your car, Clarke," Charlie purred, looking around the shop, cameraman in tow. "What are you up to in here?"

"Shopping," I said with a grin. "Isn't it a cute little place?"

"Darling." She stared pointedly at my hands. "You don't have a bag. Nothing in here caught your fancy?"

"It's all out of my price range, honestly. I'd rather spend my money on shoes. But you might find something, with your big TV bucks."

"Uh-huh." She surveyed the store and seemed to buy my story, turning and following me back to the parking lot. Thank God.

"Listen, I'm stuck out here covering this mess with these dead kids because your boss gave you this story. My sports anchor is pissed at me, and I'd rather spend my days doing something besides chasing your tail around the sticks."

"Your sports guy, too, huh?"

"Too?" she arched one perfectly-waxed eyebrow.

"Spencer Jacobs could have grown another head before I'd have expected him to jump my shit about a story like he did this morning," I said.

Charlie stared for a minute, then dropped her head back and laughed.

"What's funny?" I asked.

"Who'd have ever thought we'd have a common enemy?" she asked. "For years, my motivation has been to kick your ass. And the past few days, all I've wanted was for the sports guy to have to admit he couldn't have done a better job on this."

"That sounds exceedingly familiar." I nodded, a reluctant grin spreading across my face.

"What say we show them a couple of girls can do every bit as well with this as they can?"

"Sounds good to me," I said. "I know a fair amount about sports."

"I don't know much about anything but soccer, because it's what I played in school."

"Maybe we could help each other out?" I asked. "With the sports stuff."

She grinned. "Of course. I still want to kick your ass."

"Not this week, Charlie."

"We'll see. But we'll show the sports section?"

"We will. I was told this morning that TJ Okerson being left handed was a big deal."

"Left-handed. Got it." She glanced at her cameraman and he nodded. She turned back toward her truck. "I have a live feed to set up for down at the bridge. Nice work this morning. How'd you catch that? My scanner won't pull from this far."

"Lucky break." I winked.

"Fair enough."

I waved as they drove off, glad she hadn't come in five seconds earlier and heard me talking to Elmer.

I pulled out of the parking lot, checking the clock on the dash: four-thirty. I wanted to explore a little after the story Elmer had told me, so I turned away from town on the main road, passing the fork that led to the freeway.

If I were going to make moonshine, I'd do it out here in the woods.

CHAPTER NINE

I WAS ALMOST TO GLOUCESTER, according to the road signs, when a cluster of flailing arms and screeching loud enough for me to hear over the closed windows and radio drew me into the parking lot in front of a squatty building with a dancer silhouetted on the front door. I stopped the car and looked up at the sign in the parking lot. Girls, Dance, Girls. A strip club? Here?

"Why not? There are men out here, too, right?" I muttered, turning to the source of the commotion.

The man in front of me was large, and bellowing at a pair of ladies in floral-print dresses and wide straw hats.

I climbed out of my car, my jaw dropping when I recognized Temper Tantrum: it was Mr. Suspenders from the sheriff's office. Amos, wasn't that his name?

"This is a public place and we have every right to be here!" A gray-haired woman with cracked lipstick the exact shade of the coral flowers blooming across her flared skirt drew herself up, inches from pressing her nose against bellowing Amos's.

"You old bats are going to wreck half the marriages in Tidewater!" Amos stomped a booted foot in the gravel. "What in hell's that got to do with family values?"

"I'll thank you to keep your insults to yourself, Amos McGinn. Your momma would wash your mouth out with soap, God rest her soul. She's probably tunneled halfway to Richmond rolling in her grave at your sinning."

I leaned against the back of my car, taking in the scene. It didn't seem, after watching for a minute, that anyone was in danger. But this had to be what Amos was hassling the sheriff about. And it might make a fun story for Monday. They were so busy hollering at each other, no one had noticed me.

"You and I clearly have two different ideas of what constitutes a sin, Miss Dorothy."

They argued more, and I turned my attention to the woman standing next to Dorothy. She was quiet, outfitted from head to toe in lavender church gear. She was younger than Dorothy, but looked older than Amos. And she had a camera in her hand.

Holy pasties, Batman. I pursed my lips and smothered a laugh, the comments I'd overheard in the sheriff's office flitting through my head as I pieced this puzzle together.

The church ladies were taking pictures at the girly bar and notifying the wives of the married men hanging out there. That's one way to get rid of a business a gal doesn't like, I guess. And from what I could hear and see, Sheriff Zeke was right: not only was it not his jurisdiction, it wasn't against the law.

What it was was a great story. The kind that would bounce all over Facebook and Twitter if I got the tone right, which made the bottom-line folks at the *Telegraph* happy. I whirled for the car door, digging for a pad and pen.

"Don't you point that thing at me!" Amos glowered at Dorothy's companion, who ducked her head and took a step back. I settled in for the show.

Dorothy swatted his shoulder. "Don't you threaten us! We have as much right to be here as you do. More, even, because we are doing the Lord's work and you are sinning."

"Stop saying that! It's not like anybody in there's nekkid or there's anything but dancing going on. It's... art. Like the ballet."

"With boobies." Dorothy shook her head. "I can't believe you just compared this to legitimate culture."

"You wouldn't know culture if it popped out of your Sunday bulletin in a bright red G-string—" Amos's words cut off, and I looked up from jotting that down to find him staring at me.

He looked pissed.

Uh-oh.

"Now see what you did?" He stomped past Dorothy, his boots kicking up little clouds of dust. "That's a damned reporter from Richmond. We'll be the laughingstock of the state by morning."

"A reporter?" Dorothy turned and straightened her hat, putting a restraining hand on Amos' arm as she skirted him. "I've seen TV cameras all over town this week."

I smiled and put out a hand. "Nichelle Clarke, from the *Richmond Telegraph*. I think I have a good hold on what's going on here, but would you care to explain the details, ma'am?"

She shook my hand. "Happy to. I think you are Heaven sent, young lady."

"Dorothy, have you gone completely off your nut?" Amos shouted. "Being in the paper isn't gonna make you famous. It's going to let the world in on how backward and crazy y'all are. And those of us who aren't will be lumped in with you." He turned to me. "This is not news."

"I think it's my job to decide that."

Dorothy thumped Amos on the back of his head with her tidy lime green pocketbook. "There is nothing backward or crazy about wanting my home rid of this filth." She turned back to me. "I'm Dorothy Scott, head of the First Baptist Ladies' Auxiliary. We managed to keep this place out of Mathews proper, but then they came right across the line and opened up here. We don't want our men's minds poisoned."

"For the love of God, Miss Dorothy, shut up," Amos groaned.

"Don't you take the Lord's name in vain with me, Amos!"

"What exactly is your mission here, ma'am?" I asked.

"For the past week, Emmy Sue here and I have been making sure these men's wives know where their grocery money is going."

Amos threw his hands up. "I hear the laughter from Richmond already."

I suppressed a chuckle. No sense in making him madder.

"Why do you object to this business?" I asked Dorothy.

"It's a house of ill repute! Young girls in there gyrating while these heathens watch them." She fanned herself.

"I can't even get a lap dance in there!" Amos bellowed.

That was a state law. I knew, because a club in south Richmond had been busted for violation of it in their back room. More than a few of my cops had groused about the law being stupid as they helped the handcuffed strippers into patrol cars.

Dorothy sighed, her voice rising to the condescending tone people often use with children. "Lust is a sin, Amos."

"Appreciating an art form and the beauty of the human body is not."

I kept scribbling as they continued to bicker, while the lavender-swathed Emmy Sue snapped photos of a couple dozen license plates.

"Is this a church-sponsored activity?" I asked.

Dorothy sniffed. "Not strictly speaking, though the board of the auxiliary voted unanimously to support my efforts."

I took down the correct spelling of everyone's name, except Amos's, because he wouldn't give it to me and said he'd sue the paper if I quoted him.

"I think your wife is going to find out you were here, anyway," I said. "But have it your way. I don't mind unnamed sources."

Dorothy pumped my hand and thanked me, but stiffened when I stepped past her toward the door of the club.

"Where are you going?" she asked.

"Inside," I said. "Part of my job is to have every side of a story before I start to write."

Her jaw loosened, but she recovered quickly, pursing her lips. "I suppose if it's part of your job."

I waved at Amos. "Thank you both for your time." I walked to the door as he berated her for talking to me and she shooed him off, turning to her station wagon with Emmy Sue in tow.

It took my eyes a minute to adjust to the dim room when I opened the heavy wood front door. The interior looked like I expected, with matted red carpet, leather-paneled walls, and about fifty tables and booths scattered through the room. The stage was front and center, with a catwalk that ran halfway to the back door and sported a pole at the end. The bar ran the length of the left wall, a mirrored backdrop half-covered by liquor bottles behind it.

The smell was the thing I didn't anticipate. My stomach rumbled at the distinct scent of very good barbecue. I looked around and sure enough, about half the sixty or so guys in the place were watching the dancer (who, in Amos's defense, was not naked. She wore what would amount to a skimpy bikini on any nearby beach), the other half stuffing their faces with brisket and ribs.

"Excuse me." Amos's voice came from behind me and I scooted out from in front of the door. He shot me a go-directly-to-Hell-do-not-pass-go-do-not-collect-two-hundred-dollars look and joined two other men at a table near the pole. A hot-pants-and-crop-top-clad waitress put a beer in front of him before he even asked.

I scanned the room for Boss Hogg, but didn't see anyone who stood out as the establishment's proprietor.

"Can I help you, honey?" A voice drawled at my elbow. I turned to find a pretty waitress in the same uniform looking at me with a raised eyebrow. "You just sit anywhere, we don't have hostesses."

I smiled. "I'm not here for the show." I offered a hand and introduced myself. "I'm a reporter from the *Richmond Telegraph*. I was hoping the owner was around and would have time to chat for a minute."

"Let me see," she said as she turned toward the bar. Another waitress walked past and mine grabbed her elbow. "Hey, is Bobby around anywhere?"

"I think so. Want me to go look?"

"That's all right." She turned back to me. "Make yourself at home. I'll be right back."

She sashayed toward the swinging door at the far end of the bar and I pulled out a chair at the nearest table, looking around at the clientele.

Mostly blue collar guys, though there were a few suits in the mix. On the whole, it was pretty tame. In college, I did a story on a strip club near campus that boasted fully nude women and fall-down-drunk frat guys who hooted and hollered demeaning phrases by the truckload as they flung money onto the stage.

The music here was way louder than the men, and a pickle jar sat on the far end of the catwalk, customers dropping a few bills into it every couple of minutes. It was a much more civilized girly bar than I'd ever heard of. More like an old-school roadhouse.

"You looking for me, honey?"

I turned to find the waitress I'd talked to, smiling next to a petite woman in jeans, a pale yellow cashmere sweater, and gorgeous stilettos in the same color. Even in the shoes, she was probably a foot shorter than me.

I glanced at the waitress, who nodded before scooting off to a nearby table where a man in a checkered button-down was waving for a beer refill.

The other woman pulled out the chair opposite mine and offered a firm handshake. "I'm Bobbi Jo Ramsley, and this is my club. Sasha said you're a reporter. What can I do for you?"

I pulled my notebook from my bag and clicked out a pen. Introducing myself, I smiled at Bobbi Jo. "I hear you've caused some controversy with the local ladies' auxiliary."

She rolled her green eyes skyward, pushing a wayward lock of blonde hair behind her ear. "None of those old biddies would know pornography if it bit them in their spandex-girdled asses," she said.

I jotted that down, giving her a once-over. She was pretty, her pale face devoid of makeup. And either the light was extremely forgiving, or Bobbi Jo wasn't over thirty.

She grinned. "I know. I'm young. I'm female. Why do I run a bar like this?"

"To be perfectly fair, I don't know that I've ever been in a place quite like this," I said. "The food smells divine."

"Thanks. My grandmomma was one of the best cooks on the island. I use her barbecue sauce and side dish recipes, and Sam's got a way with a smoker. I think it's magic, or something."

I nodded, my stomach gurgling again. Three days of tea and soup wasn't enough, apparently. Bobbi Jo flagged a waitress down. "Bring us a C-cup and two setups, an iced tea and a..." She looked at me. "What would you like to drink?"

"Is it sweet iced tea?"

Bobbi nodded.

"Iced tea, please."

The waitress nodded and moved toward the kitchen.

"A c-cup?" I asked.

"Barbecued chicken breast. Good size. I can't eat a whole one by myself."

I swallowed a giggle and made a note.

"I do have to admit, I am dying of curiosity here, Bobbi Jo," I said. "How did you come to run a barbecue joint with a sexy floor show when you don't look like you're any older than me? And if you are, I won't leave 'til you tell me what kind of moisturizer you use."

She laughed. "I'm twenty-nine. For the first time, anyway. And the short answer to your question is, the economy sucks. It sucks everywhere, but out here, it sucks worse."

I nodded, keeping quiet and waiting for her to elaborate. She obliged.

"So many places in the county have gone out of business in the past few years." Bobbi Jo leaned her elbows on the table, fiddling with a sugar packet from the bowl in the middle. "The mill cut a lot of jobs. When my grandaddy died two years ago, he left me his farm and a nice chunk of cash. There was a drought the first summer and the crops withered in the fields. I decided that wasn't a reliable way to make a living. And my friends —I bet ten girls I graduated high school with moved away in the last year. When there's only a hundred people in the class, that's a lot, you know?

"I started reading about how economic systems can collapse, and we had some of the warning signs. I love Mathews. I love the people and the town and the island, and I didn't want to see that happen here, but you can drive over the bridge and see for yourself how close we came to being a ghost town. So I read up on recession-proof businesses. Guess what's number one on that list?"

I looked up from my scribbling. "That makes total sense."

"Doesn't it?" She thumped a fist on the table. "And there wasn't a club around here. I thought I'd found the key to saving the whole damned town, and Dorothy Scott and her old band of bats decided they wouldn't have it. Look around. I'm a woman. I'm not in this to demean women, and I'm not 'peddling smut,' either. The girls don't look any different on stage than most of them do when they go to the beach, and the waitresses are dressed in Hooters uniform knockoffs. Though, Dorothy'd probably pitch a fit if Hooters wanted to come to Mathews, too."

I looked at the stage, where a new dancer in a neon pink bikini and fabulous black patent Louboutins (I had that pair at home) strutted toward the pole. She jumped and grabbed it, flipping upside down and curling her legs around before she arched her back and reached her arms over her head.

"Damn. That looks like something out of Cirque D'Solieil." I said.

"Exactly!" Bobbi Jo nodded. "There are so many women around here with so much talent. Becca there studied dance at RAU for four years. But when nobody's going to the ballet, the ballet can't pay new dancers, right? She came home and moved in with her momma. She was working at the 7-Eleven, for Pete's sake. Now, she's doing what she loves and she makes enough to have bought her own house last month."

"And some killer shoes," I mumbled, scribbling. This story was fast becoming more about what Bobbi Jo was trying to do for the town and how her club was different than about the showdown in her parking lot.

"So, it looks like you're definitely helping the economy, but you're not in Mathews," I said.

She sat back in her chair, frustration plain on her face. "Unfortunately, thanks to Miss Dorothy and her friends, I am not. We must have had ten town hall meetings last summer, and no matter how much I tried to explain or what I argued, she convinced damn near every woman in the county that their husbands were going to run off with my dancers if they allowed the club. First off, more than half the dancers are married. Second, I have a way stricter contact policy than the state. They can't even grab the girls' hands or give them money. That's what the pickle jar is for."

"Have any of the other women in the county actually been here?"

"You are the first female non-employee to darken my door since I opened. I wish I could get them to come see that I'm not threatening their marriages, but fear-mongering is a powerful tool."

"Indeed it is."

Sasha stopped at my elbow and laid a huge platter of barbecue chicken in the middle of the table, then a basket brimming with baked beans, coleslaw, pickles, and cornbread in front of each of us. My stomach roared.

Bobbi Jo giggled. "Don't be shy. Dig in."

Sasha handed me a fork and I scooped beans into my mouth. They tasted like they'd been smoked, with just the right hint of sweet in the sauce.

"Oh, my," I said, smiling at Bobbi Jo.

"It's good, right?"

"Indeed."

It was all good. The cornbread was the kind of crisp on the outside and moist on the inside that can only be achieved with the right recipe and a cast iron skillet, and the chicken really was magical. The pickles weren't standard-issue, either. Sweet and hot, they were addictive. I emptied my cup of them in half a minute and Bobbi Jo offered me hers.

"My grandmomma's recipe," she said. "Dill, sugar, and jalepenos."

Stuffed, I pushed my plate away and turned back to my notes.

"So, what kind of money are you making here? And how much has the county benefitted from it?"

"We clear about a thousand a night on the weekends after everyone's paid, and probably two-thirds of that during the week," she said. "That's twice what we made when we opened, and it goes up every month. I paid five grand in taxes last month."

"Seems a shame you can't have that money going to your hometown."

"I buy everything I can from Mathews. All the vegetables we serve in the summer come from the county. The baskets are from a local weaver. I'm trying."

I jotted that down.

"It was nice to meet you, Bobbi," I said, putting my notebook away. "I have to pitch this to my editor, but I'm sure it will fly. Do you have a card, just in case I have more questions when I start writing?"

She stood with me and pulled a business card out of her hip pocket. "Thank you."

"Thanks for talking to me. And feeding me. I'll be in touch."

She turned toward the kitchen with a wave and I watched her go, impressed with her business savvy and her dedication to the town.

It didn't occur to me to ask her about moonshine until I was halfway back to Mathews.

CHAPTER TEN

THE LAST OF the daylight faded as I reached the turn to the freeway, the budding trees disappearing into the night. My cell phone buzzed as I flicked my turn signal on, and I stopped in the turn lane to fish it out of my bag. Parker.

"Hey, are you still in Tidewater?" he asked.

"Just now heading home," I said. "What's up?"

"I'm at Tony's, and Ashton asked me to call you. She wants to talk to you. Can you turn around and come by here?"

Hot damn. Maybe I'd built up good karma, working while I was sick.

"On my way," I said, swinging the car back onto the main road.

I hurried across the bridge, my chat with Bobbi Jo coloring the island in a new light. Five grand a month in tax revenue. And all those guys going into the club every night. It seemed like the perfect save for a place that could use some recession-proof income. Shame it didn't work.

Stopping outside the crowded gate to the Okerson house, I cringed when three mics appeared in my face as soon as I rolled my window down. The press corps fired questions so fast and loud no one in the house could hear me on the intercom. I knew the look on the reporters' faces too well: they had been stonewalled by both families all weekend and were getting desperate. From the questions I got, they thought I was Sydney's mother. Did I look old enough to have a teenage daughter? I decided to brush that off with the darkness as an excuse.

I grabbed my cell phone out of the cup holder and called Parker back.

"I'm trapped at the gate, and the wolves out here are hungry," I said.

"On it," he said. "Try not to let anyone in with you."

As the gate inched open, I glanced around the media throng. "A person would need titanium cojones to sneak onto Tony Okerson's property. Especially today. But I've seen stranger," I said. When the gap was wide enough to slide my car through, I gunned the engine, watching the rearview mirror as the gate closed behind me. "I don't think anyone hitchhiked."

"Good," Parker said.

I stopped in front of the house and clicked off the call. Parker stepped out the front door.

"Thanks for coming."

"Are you kidding? Thanks for calling. What's going on now?"

He swiped a hand down over his face, his fingers muffling the first part of his reply. "Ashton is...not well. She...well, I'll let her tell you. They loved your first write-up. They trust you, and not just because I said so. You earned it." He stepped aside and waved me toward the door. "Go on in. She's in the living room."

"You're not staying?"

"I have to go pick Mel up for dinner. If I leave right now I'll only be really late, not unforgivably late."

I nodded. "Thanks, Parker. Y'all have fun."

I turned for the door, but his voice stopped me. "Hey, Clarke? I'm not sure how you can help them, but they could sure use it if there's a way."

"I'll do my best."

He waved and walked toward his BMW motorcycle, strapping his red helmet in place and disappearing down the drive.

I opened the storm door, using a knee to keep the dog inside and grabbing his collar as I stepped around him. He pawed my shin and licked my free hand.

"Hey, boy." I ruffled the fur behind his ears. He whined and craned his neck to look out the door.

"He misses TJ." The comment choked off at the end, and I spun to find Tony coming out of the study. He shut the door behind him, but I caught a glimpse of the far wall, dotted with trophy shelves and framed news stories.

"I'm sure he's not alone," I said.

"He is not." Tony cleared his throat and blinked a few times. "I owe you my gratitude for the story you did. A couple of the skeezier TV outfits have tried to make something out of nothing here, but everyone else seems to be following your lead, and I appreciate your help making this easier for my family to handle. Grant was right. Spin is everything."

I smiled, glad he thought I had helped.

"You spent your entire career building a practically untarnishable image, Tony. I'm ..." I sighed. "I'm just so damned sorry. And I hate that the press is camped outside your driveway while you grieve."

He shrugged his broad shoulders. "Goes with the territory. The NFL was awfully good to my family."

"Parker said Ashton wanted to talk to me?"

He waved toward the back of the house. "She's in there. Thanks for coming out."

"Anytime."

He turned toward the front door, pulling a leash off the hook next to it and clipping it onto the dog's collar. "We're going to get out of here for a while."

I paused to glance over the photos in the hallway: the girls, in matching dresses on first bikes, ponies, and the Dumbo ride at Disney World. TJ in various football uniforms, posing with the ball up like so many photos I'd seen of his father. His smile was always just a twitch away from a laugh, his eyes happy. I fished a notebook and pen from my bag and jotted that down.

I found Ashton on the sofa. At least, I was pretty sure it was Ashton. In the space of two days, she seemed to have dropped fifteen pounds, and she didn't have them to lose in the first place. She looked haunted.

The woman next to her had long, dark hair and hollows under her eyes that almost matched Ashton's. This had to be Sydney Cobb's mother.

The sliding doors on both ends of the living room's glass wall stood open, letting the sound and smell of the water inside. It was downright tranquil, save for the heavy sadness in the room.

I took a deep breath. "Mrs. Okerson?"

Ashton turned. "Nichelle!" She bounced off the couch with energy that so mismatched her haggard look it was creepy. Crossing the room in five long strides, she pulled me into a hug. "Thank you so much for the stories you did about my boy," she said, her words muffled by my shoulder and her sobs. "They're beautiful."

I patted her back and murmured thanks for talking to me, my eyes on the tears spilling down the other woman's cheeks.

Ashton let go of me and turned to her companion. "Nichelle, this is Tiffany."

"Sydney's mother," I said, stepping toward the couch and offering a hand.

"I was. I am," Tiffany's face crumpled. "Am I?"

I swallowed against a lump in my throat. The anguish on her face would haunt my dreams for weeks, I was certain.

"Sit down," Ashton said. "Can I get you anything?"

Sinking into the cushions opposite them, I smiled and shook my head. "I'm still full from dinner, but thank you."

A piece of driftwood on the end table caught my eye. "Heaven is a little closer in a house by the sea" it read, the letters burned across it in script.

I closed my eyes for a long blink, clicking out my pen. "Parker said y'all wanted to talk to me about something?"

They exchanged a look that radiated subtext. Uh-oh.

"You can't be mad at Grant," Ashton began.

"Mad?"

"He explained that you have a theory."

He what?

"Oh? Why should that make me mad?" I was impressed with my ability to keep my voice even. Grant Parker was a dead man. He did not come tell the parents I thought these kids hadn't killed themselves. I didn't have any more proof of that than the sheriff had that they did. What the hell did he think that would do, except cause pain?

"Now, we told him our theory first." Ashton put up both hands.

"Your theory?" Hang on. "Does it not match the sheriff's theory?"

"That's why we asked you to come. Our babies did not do this."

I hauled in a deep breath.

"What makes you say that?" I poised my pen.

"TJ was a happy kid," Ashton said.

Well, yeah. That's what I thought, but Sheriff Zeke didn't agree.

"Sydney was left-handed," Tiffany muttered, almost too quiet for me to hear.

My eyes snapped to her.

"Come again, ma'am?"

"She was left-handed. The note wasn't her handwriting. It was a good copy of it. Almost too good. But it wasn't her."

Hot damn. I scribbled down the new information. That was something I could work with.

"Did you tell Sheriff Waters that, Mrs. Cobb?"

"Of course I did. He smiled and said he'd take it under advisement." She looked up, her dark eyes windows to the gaping wound on her heart. "Look, Miss, we don't mean any disrespect. Zeke Waters is a good man, and he's a good sheriff. Fair. Sensible. But he thinks we're crazy. Maybe we are. But my Sydney did not write that note. And Ashton's baseball player friend said you didn't think the sheriff was right, either."

I sighed, keeping my eyes on my notes.

Parker hadn't told them anything that wasn't true. I knew he shared my suspicion about TJ, and now the girl's mother was sitting here saying her daughter hadn't written the suicide note the sheriff was using as his proof that her death was open and shut.

But what could I do about it? Either there was a bonafide serial killer in bitty little Mathews, and more lives were at risk, or someone had a vendetta against TJ and Sydney, and they were going to get away with murder.

I raised my eyes to meet Ashton's.

"Grant told me you've done investigative work on stories before," she said.

Seriously. He was at least looking at a swift kick in the ass. I did not want this woman thinking I could save the day when Zeke didn't want to talk about this and I wasn't at all sure I could get to the bottom of it.

"I have, but..." I searched for the right words. "Mrs. Okerson, this is a small town. It's an entirely different world than what I'm used to covering. I don't know anyone here."

"I understand that. I don't, either, really. Tony and I keep to ourselves. TJ was the one who had all the friends." Her voice broke and she curled her arms around her shoulders, like she could physically hold herself together. "Why would someone do this to my baby?"

Ashton buried her head in her knees and sobbed, and I pinched my lips together, studying them. I couldn't say no. These women were grieving the loss of their children, and had no one else to take their suspicions to. Monster exclusive notwithstanding, I had a personal reason for wanting to help, no matter how hard I tried to ignore it. Having the parents involved and on the record would help me get it right.

"I will do everything I can." I leaned forward, resting my elbows on my knees. "I'm going to need you to be completely honest with me."

They both nodded.

"I mean it," I said. "This won't be an easy conversation. You can't fudge facts to make the kids look good. Nobody's perfect, and if we're really trying to find a killer, you're going to have to start by telling me who had a reason to hate your children."

They exchanged a glance. Tiffany spoke first.

"There were probably lots of little girls who were jealous of Syd," she said. "She was a good girl, and a sweet kid, but everyone has their bitchy side, I guess. She wasn't best friends with everyone, you know?"

I jotted that down, catching Tiffany's gaze.

"Who was the girl they picked on?" I asked.

"I'm not sure I follow."

"There's one in every high school class in America," I said. "The pretty girls always have a girl they make fun of. Someone who wants to be part of their group, but doesn't fit in."

Tiffany appeared to consider that.

"Evelyn," Ashton finally said. "Evelyn Sue Miney."

I wrote the name down. "Tell me about her. Typical outcast?"

Tiffany shook her head. "Evelyn was Sydney's friend."

Ashton poked her gently in the ribs. "Tiff, she said we had to be honest. Evelyn and Syd hadn't been friends in a long while. And she had such a crush on TJ."

I kept my eyes on Tiffany as I put a star by the girl's name. A crush on the boy, a rivalry with the girl. Sounded promising.

"Evelyn and Syd were best friends when they were little girls," Tiffany said, dropping her head into her hands and sighing. "They did everything together. Evelyn spent as much time at my house as she did at her own. She couldn't have done this."

"Why weren't they friends anymore?"

"They just grew apart," Tiffany said.

The look Ashton shot her told me there was no "just" to it.

"When?"

"Last year. The summer before. I didn't notice at first, Syd was always so busy with cheerleading and her friends. But I started to notice I hadn't seen Evelyn in a long time."

"She's not a cheerleader?" I asked.

"No, she is. It's not that the girls are mean to her because she's not pretty. She's always been one of Syd's group."

"Until she started coming onto TJ," Ashton said.

Ah ha. I scribbled faster, underlining as I went. This sounded better the longer they talked.

"But TJ wasn't interested in her?"

"TJ was never interested in anyone but Syd," Ashton said.

I studied Tiffany, her face half-hidden behind unwashed hair.

"And Sydney didn't like her friend being interested in her boyfriend." It wasn't a question, because the answer was obvious.

"Who would?" Tiffany said. "She came home from a party last fall, and I'd never seen her like that before. She was sobbing and screaming at the same time. Evelyn kissed TJ. It crushed Sydney."

I turned to Ashton. "TJ didn't kiss her back?"

"He told us he pushed her down. He felt bad because he made her cry. He said they were talking while Syd went to get drinks and then Evelyn kissed him."

"So what happened to Evelyn?" Having been to high school, I had a good guess, but I needed them to say it.

"They froze her out of their group."

I nodded. Popular girl to social pariah overnight. It was worse, in some ways, than having never been popular at all.

"She emailed and texted TJ for months," Ashton said, and Tiffany and I both looked at her.

"Why?"

"It varied. Sometimes she was professing her love for him and telling him Syd would never be good enough for him." Ashton shot an apologetic look at Tiffany. "Other times, she said she was sorry and she didn't mean to kiss him and would he just talk to Sydney and help her explain? TJ finally came to me with it because he didn't know what else to do. He kept telling her he loved Sydney, that there was nothing he could do, and if she wanted to talk to Syd they needed to work it out."

"You said the other day that you studied psychology." I let the words hang in the air.

Ashton shook her head. "It's so hard to tell without talking to the person. But some of the messages I saw? She could be imbalanced."

Imbalanced enough to kill them? I didn't say it, but the looks on their faces said they were thinking it, anyway.

The boy I'd talked to in the gym flashed through my thoughts.

"What about Luke?" I asked.

"Luke?" Ashton furrowed her brow.

"There's a boy on the baseball team, another pitcher. I'm pretty sure the coach called him Luke," I said. "I talked to him when I went by the school the other day, and it was a weird conversation. Seemed like he didn't like TJ too much."

"Oh, the Bosley boy?" Ashton shrugged. "I don't really know him, and TJ never talked too much about him."

"He was the kid Sydney told me was mouthing off about TJ getting hurt last fall. How he would finally get his shot at baseball," Tiffany said.

I nodded at her. "The coach told me his dad was a baseball player in high school and does some major vicarious living through the kid. Puts a lot of pressure on him." I paused, a puzzle piece dancing on the edge of my brain. "Ashton, how did TJ hurt his knee?"

She tossed her hands up helplessly. "He fell. It happens. The grass was wet. He said his cleat slid right out from under him and he twisted his knee. Tore it all to hell."

"Do cleats slip?" It was an honest question. That was one kind of shoe I'd never had occasion to wear. "I thought the whole point of cleats was to give you traction."

"Tony said TJ's were too worn," she said. "That we should have bought him new ones. I didn't know."

I jotted that down. "Anyone or anything else that's stood out to you?" I asked.

"Not really. They were so happy. Sydney's been gone all semester. She should have stayed in Paris." Tiffany's face crumpled again, sobs shaking her shoulders.

"I think this gives me something to go on," I said, standing as Ashton moved to comfort her friend. "If only I could figure out how to get these kids to talk to me."

"Come to the street dance," Ashton said.

"The what?"

"Next Friday night, right in the middle of town. It's the welcome for the growing season. One of the biggest things the town does every year. Everyone talks to everyone. Dress in western wear and you'll fit right in. It's dark."

I smiled and patted her shoulder. "Perfect. Thank you."

She reached up and squeezed my hand. "No, thank you."

I let myself out quietly and inched back through the gang of reporters at the gate without literally steamrolling any of the competition. My thoughts raced for where I could find some help with the promise I'd just made.

It was time to suck it up and call Kyle.

CHAPTER ELEVEN

I MADE it back to the freeway before I dialed Kyle's number. We'd been to dinner several times over the winter, and it was fun, getting to know him again. But I had blissfully not had to talk to him about work in months. And I didn't want to start again.

"Hey, you," he said when he picked up.

"Hey, yourself," I said. "You have a few minutes?"

"For you? Sure I do."

I checked the clock on the dash. Almost nine, and it would be another hour before I got back to Richmond. But I'd rather talk in person. I had a way better chance of convincing Kyle I might be onto something if I could look him in the face.

"Are you going to be up for a while? I'd kind of like to come by."

"Oh, yeah?" His voice dropped a full octave. "From dinner and drinks to booty calls? I mean, not that I'm complaining."

"For the love of God, Kyle. Way to jump to conclusions. Because a booty call is so me. I need to talk to you."

"I know I'm irresistible. Waiting for you to catch up." He paused. "Nothing? Okay. Talk about what?"

"I'll tell you when I get there."

"I'll open a bottle of wine."

"You're impossible."

I clicked off the call and spent the rest of the drive to Kyle's apartment mentally rehearsing five different ways to keep him from blowing me off. I stopped in front of his building still unsure any of them would work.

Tapping my foot through the ride up the rattly old elevator to Kyle's loft, I took a couple of deep breaths and tried to calm my jangled nerves. At least I didn't still sound like death.

He opened his front door before I knocked, a smile playing around his lips.

"I saw you park the car." He slid one hand into the back pocket of his well-worn jeans, flexing his impressive upper arm as he did so. My eyes widened at the way his red t-shirt hugged every line.

"You sure you just want to talk?" he asked, watching my expression.

I cleared my throat and tore my eyes from his shoulders. "I'm sure." My voice hitched between the words.

"No, you're not." He grinned. "But come on in."

He waved me toward the big olive sectional that dominated the living room space, disappearing into the kitchen and returning with two glasses of white wine.

"Kyle." I tried my best to sound like I was giving him a warning, but wasn't sure it worked. Dammit, he looked good.

"No means no. Got it." He handed me one glass and retreated to the corner of the sofa with the other. I put three cushions between us, just in case, and sat down, kicking my copper Manolo peep-toes to the polished wood floor.

"What are you into now?" Kyle's smile went from sexy to intrigued as he studied me over the rim of his wine glass.

"Why do I have to be into anything?"

"Because you're sitting way over there. Which means you didn't call and invite yourself over at ten o'clock on a Saturday night because you're lonely. So you're working. I know you."

I laughed. "I guess you do." I took a deep breath. "I've been following this story out in Tidewater," I began.

"I've been reading it. Teen suicides."

"Well..." I drew the word out. "I'm not so sure about that."

"Oh, yeah?" He sipped his wine nonchalantly, but his ice-blue eyes were interested. "Why not?"

"The whole thing has seemed off to me since the first time I went out there," I said. "Why does a kid like TJ Okerson kill himself?"

"It happens more often than you'd think," Kyle said. "Especially with kids involved in sports at that level. It's a lot of pressure."

Just like Aaron. And Sheriff Zeke. Was all of law enforcement so jaded?

"I thought about that. But I don't think the Okersons were putting crazy pressure on TJ. His baseball coach doesn't, either. And Grant Parker from our sports desk is good friends with Tony Okerson. He says no, too."

"Girl trouble?"

"The girl is the second victim."

"I saw. I'm saying, maybe it was guilt? They fought, he killed himself, she couldn't live with it?"

I sighed. Kyle was a great devil's advocate. "The parents say no. That's actually my strongest argument. I just came from talking to both moms. They say they don't buy it. The girl's mother says the note the sheriff is pinning his 'suicide' label on wasn't in her daughter's handwriting."

He set his glass on the table and leaned back into the deep cushions. The expressions playing across his face said he was trying to figure out how to convince me I was wrong.

I raised one hand when he opened his mouth. "I get it. You think I'm nuts. But can we consider, just for a second, that I might not be?"

He raised one eyebrow. "I'm reluctant to encourage you. You have a history of getting yourself hurt."

"Only when I'm right," I said. "Which, can I just point out, I was last time. And you didn't believe me then, either."

"Nicey, I'm not sure what you want me to do about this even if you are right. Which I'm not conceding. This is so far from my jurisdiction your dead kids might as well be in Constantinople."

"I'll get to that in a second." I needed to ask him about the moon-shine, but I was pretty sure he was going to palm that off on the ABC police, and I'd gotten nowhere there. If he believed me about the kids, he'd want to help me with the moonshiners. "For now, can I just bounce this off you? You're Captain Supercop. I need to know if I'm missing something."

"It sounds to me like you're seeing something that's not there, not missing anything. Of course the mothers don't want to believe their children took their own lives. I don't have kids and I get that."

"Stop judging and just listen for a minute," I snapped. The words were sharper than I intended, but he was making me regret calling him in the first place. The mental tug-of-war between that irritation and my apparent inability to ignore the sliver of his toned abdomen I could see where his shirt had ridden up was making me testy. I gulped my wine and tried to steady my voice. "Sorry."

"You have the floor." He spread his hands, staring at me with a casually curious look.

"Thank you. So, the mothers say there was a girl. Another girl. Who was creepy-stalkering TJ and hated Sydney."

He tipped his head to one side. "You know anything else about her?"

"She's a cheerleader at the high school. Used to move in the same social circle, but she got blackballed last year when she kissed TJ at a party."

Kyle's hand moved to his chin, raking over the bristles of his barely-there auburn goatee. "Being demoted to social outcast is a powerful motivator for a high school girl. But it takes a certain kind of person to be capable of murder."

"I know. And I want to talk to this girl, but she's not exactly going to sit for an interview with me, especially if she did do something. Which is where you come in." I widened my eyes and smiled earnestly.

Kyle blanched. "I can't go out to Tidewater flashing my badge and haul a teenage girl in for questioning. Are you kidding? I'll end up in a manure truckload of shit over that. I don't care how cute you are." He smiled, shaking his head. "Stop looking at me like that."

I sucked my cheeks in and batted my lashes, and Kyle laughed.

"I'm not asking you to question her," I said seriously. "Not officially. But there's a big town street dance next weekend. I want you to come with me. Help me chat up the locals. In that kind of a setting, people will talk, right?"

"Like, on a date?" He leaned forward, putting himself in arm's reach, and let his eyelids drop halfway.

I sipped my wine. Oh, why the hell not? I wasn't committed to anyone. Joey was hot in a different way than Kyle, and I liked him a lot, but there were no promises on the table. Besides, I had never once in my twenty-nine years played the field. Maybe I should ask Parker for pointers.

"Sure."

"Yeah?" He grinned. "All right. I don't know how close we'll be able to get to teenagers without looking fairly creepy ourselves, but I'm game."

"We're younger than most of the people who play teenagers on TV," I said.

He chuckled. "I don't feel old. You ever wonder how the hell we got to be almost thirty?"

"Dude, a reporter mistook me for Sydney Cobb's mother tonight," I said. "I've wondered about nothing since."

"You don't look a day over twenty-one." His eyes locked on mine, a sexy smile tugging at the corners of his lips.

I leaned toward him, my hair falling into my face. Kyle reached up and brushed it away, his fingers trailing electricity across my cheekbone. His touch was thrilling and familiar at the same time. Like coming home to fireworks. I leaned my cheek into his palm, and he drew the pad of his thumb across my lips. My breath stopped.

"Nicey." He slid toward me.

I let my eyelids fall. "Kyle," I whispered.

The couch cushions shifted as he leaned in. Just as my cell phone erupted into the theme from *Peter Pan*.

My eyes snapped open. Kyle slumped into the sofa and let his head fall back, his breath coming like he'd been for a run. I knew the feeling.

"What?" I grouched at the phone, yanking it from the side pocket on my bag. "Oh, shit."

"What?" Kyle's head popped up.

"Hey." I put the phone to my ear.

"You sound better," Joey said.

"I feel better." And a little like a jerk. I shot a guilty look at Kyle.

"I think I might have a friend who knows a guy who knows something about your moonshiners. But you're not going to talk to him alone. When are you free? I'll set it up and come along for the ride."

"Really?" I grinned. Kyle's eyebrows shot up, and I tried to calm myself. Talking about going to a meeting with the Mafia in front of the ATF. I had some titanium cojones, too.

"Who is that?" Kyle mouthed.

I shook my head. Good Lord, what a can of worms. I turned my attention from the hunky guy on the couch to the one on the phone.

"I'll make time on Monday or Tuesday. I'm going with Parker to TJ's funeral, but that's all I have in stone right now. Er. You know what I mean."

"I'll call you tomorrow?"

"I'd like that."

"Sweet dreams."

He hung up and I turned back to Kyle, the spell broken. "Tell me what you know about moonshine."

He laid one arm along the back of the sofa and sighed.

"Why?"

"That's my other theory. I think TJ was drinking it the night he died. I'm pretty sure Sydney was, because I saw the jar in the stuff the cops retrieved from the scene. They said it was near her. I did some reading, and it seems improperly made moonshine can kill people."

"It can. That's one of the reasons it's illegal to sell it unregulated. People think the government just wants their cut of the money. But the laws are there to keep people safe, too."

"So how is it that people still get away with making and selling it in the twenty-first century?"

"Funnily enough, the same kind of crafty evasion that has been in place for a hundred years. That, and there are aspects of the law that protect them. Or that they hide behind. For example: agents can go right up on a still, but if it's not running, there's nothing we can do. Moonshiners know that."

"But why not stake them out?"

He shook his head. "First, that's expensive, and a lot of resources going into cracking what's usually a small operation. We have a budget just like everyone else. Second, it's harder than it sounds. Most of that stuff is made out in the country. You can't scratch your ass without everyone in three counties knowing. An unmarked sedan full of strangers with crew cuts? They'll keep everything shut down until it rusts before they'll run a still if we send a team out there. The best way to work moonshiners is to get undercover. But that takes for-bloody-ever. It's hard to get those folks to trust new people."

"But what if that's how these children died? What if more people die if you don't do something? Is it worth the money then?"

"Possibly. But slow your roll, Lois. There's also the whole business of placing an agent undercover. You're talking more money, time away from the guy's family. An operation like that can take months—hell, years—to infiltrate. And, it's not my jurisdiction unless it's crossing state lines. It's an ABC police matter unless I can prove that. "

"Of course it is. That's like, the one police agency in town where I don't know anyone. I don't suppose you have a friend over there who might talk to me?"

"I haven't been here long enough to make any good friends over there, but I know a couple of guys. I can vouch for you and see if they'll give you a few minutes. Does it have to be on the record?"

I bit my lip, considering that. It would help. Especially with new cops I didn't have a history with. Not everyone is a solid source. Ashton Okerson's gaunt face flashed through my thoughts. I wanted the information more than I wanted an attributable quote.

"I'd prefer it, but if the only way you can get them to talk to me is to tell them it's not, go for it."

He nodded. "Are you even considering the possibility that you're wrong about this?"

"About there being moonshiners in Mathews? Nope."

"Nicey." His voice had a warning edge.

I sighed. "Yes. But what if, Kyle? What if there's a moonshine outfit poisoning kids? What if one of these jealous little creeps spiked their drinks with something? The open-and-shut doesn't feel right. And no one else is listening to these people. Hell, even Aaron White at the PD told me it was probably nothing more than what it looks like. They deserve to know why they're burying their children. So what if I'm wrong? I'm out a few evenings and a couple of Saturdays. But if I'm right—if *they're* right—how could I ever close my eyes again if I don't try to help?"

His face softened. "You have a good heart. It's one of the things I've always loved about you. But you know you can't get emotionally invested in every case. You'll burn yourself out."

"I don't. But this is different." My voice broke, memories I'd held at bay for two days crashing through my defenses.

"I know, honey." He reached across the sofa and grabbed my hand. "Have you even talked to your mom?"

"No." I bit my lip, telltale pricking in the backs of my eyes a warning that tears were coming. I closed my eyes against the flood, but they fell anyway. I pulled in a hitching breath. "I keep hoping she won't read it. It's April. Weddings are dropping from the sky. She barely has time to eat."

"Probably a good thing." He stroked the back of my hand with his thumb, and I fell across the cushions, burying my face in his shirt and sobbing until the tears were gone. Kyle stroked my hair and made soothing noises at intervals, but mostly he just held me and let me cry.

When I finally sat up and dragged the back of one hand across my face, he was ready with a tissue box and a smile.

"I figured this would get to you," he said.

"Then stop giving me shit and help me." I wiped my eyes and blew my nose. "Parker asked me to help. Their parents asked me to help. I can't let it go, Kyle."

He nodded, a long sigh escaping his chest. "I guess I knew that when you called."

"So you're in?"

"However I can be, but I'm not sure how much that is unless you can prove the moonshine is leaving Virginia." He held my gaze, his mouth pressed into a tight line. "Just because the parents don't see what the cops see doesn't mean this is the same story, Nicey."

"Maybe. But my mom was—is—" I threw my hands up. "What if it is? No one would help her. Well, except for your dad. I will always love him for trying. But what if we can help the Okersons?"

He squeezed my hand. "Whatever you need."

I smiled and returned the pressure on his fingers, wincing at the damp circle on his shirt. "Sorry about that." I waved my other hand toward the spot.

"Eh. It'll wash." The look in his eyes was so sincere I almost lost it again.

"Thanks, Kyle. I've tried so hard to not remember. To make this be just a story."

"We all have cases that get to us, honey. But you have to watch yourself. You're not helping the Okersons if you get yourself shot by a pissed-off redneck who doesn't want to lose his moonshine money."

"Noted." I stood and turned for the door and he followed, leaning on the frame as I stepped into the hallway. I said goodnight, then spun back and pulled him into a hug, landing a soft kiss on his stubbly cheek.

"It's nice to have you around," I whispered as his arms tightened around me.

"It's nice to be here," he said into my hair.

I stepped away and opened the gate on the elevator. He was still watching when I disappeared toward the lobby.

CHAPTER TWELVE

SUNDAY PASSED in a blur of cold medicine, minestrone, and *Friends* reruns, punctuated by phone calls. Parker was first up, confirming plans to go to the funeral and thanking me profusely for "What you did for Ashton." I resisted the urge to jump his shit for telling them I suspected anything in the first place. He'd had a lousy enough week without me yelling at him.

I called Bob around lunchtime to pitch him the story on Bobbi Jo's roadhouse, which I had decided was a much more fitting term for a place boasting degreed dancers in sequined bikinis than "smut joint." He laughed for five minutes and gave me a green light. I dozed off and on all afternoon, and by the time Joey called at ten to seven I felt almost energetic.

"You have a handle on your schedule yet?" he asked.

"I'm free anytime except tomorrow afternoon," I said, trying to ignore the memory of how Kyle's arms had felt around me—and the double-edged sword I was walking. The only way Kyle could bust the moonshiners was if they were exporting their product. And the most likely way Joey would have a friend who knew the moonshiners was if the guy we were going to meet was providing the transportation. It seemed unfair to get them to talk to me and then set the ATF on them.

And selfishly, I wanted Joey and Kyle as far apart as I could keep them, for a multitude of reasons.

"How about Tuesday evening?" he asked. "We might even grab dinner, if you feel like it. I want to talk about those fantasies you mentioned the other night."

My stomach flipped. "I have no recollection of that." I cleared my throat. "But dinner sounds nice. And thanks. This story is a big deal to me."

"I recall enough for both of us. And no problem—this could be a big boost to your career if you're right. There's certainly enough of a spotlight here."

"It's not just the spotlight," I said softly. "I really appreciate your help, Joey."

"Getting you a source is easy. Keeping you out of trouble, I worry about."

"It's not like I go looking for it."

"You do sometimes."

"Not on purpose."

"Uh-huh."

A smile playing around my lips, I thanked him again and hung up, reaching for my laptop. Writing something non-tragic held a special appeal after the hollowed eyes that had haunted my dreams all week.

With menu items including a C-cup barbecue chicken breast and only "full racks" of ribs available, a roadhouse in Gloucester County is pulling in customers as much for the food as the show—and drawing the ire of a nearby church ladies' auxiliary.

"We managed to keep this place out of Mathews proper, but then they came right across the line and opened up here," Dorothy Scott, head of the First Baptist Church of Mathews Ladies' Auxiliary, said. "And we don't want our men's minds poisoned."

Scott and a friend have been frequenting the roadhouse's parking lot, snapping photos of license plates and using online sources to make sure the wives of the club's customers know where their husbands are spending their free time.

One of those customers tried unsuccessfully to run the women off Saturday, then defended the establishment when that didn't work.

"It's not like anyone's naked in there," he said, refusing to go on the record. "It's art. Like the ballet."

While there are dancers in the club, owner Bobbi Jo Ramsley said she opened it with an inheritance from her grandfather because the local economy needed a boost, and pointed out the sequined bikinis her dancers wear and the pickle jar she keeps on one end of the stage for tips as evidence of the strict hands-off policy she enforces.

I sent the story to Bob Sunday night. He loved it (he told me twice on Monday morning) proclaiming Bobbi Jo's menu item names brilliant and talking up a field trip for some of the single guys on the staff.

Still grinning, I went back to my desk to grab a file I needed for the staff meeting and found a copy of the morning's front page spread open across my desk. My advance on TJ's funeral in the bottom corner of the page was marked up in red pen. My smile faded.

"Here's what you need to learn," I read from the margin before I stuffed the paper in the recycle bin.

I avoided Spence's glare through the staff meeting, pretending I hadn't seen his little love note. Shelby watched him stare daggers at me with interest, bouncing her knee impatiently. I was sure she couldn't wait to corner him and commiserate.

Bob dismissed everyone but me and Parker, watching the rest of the staff file out before he asked Parker to shut the door. I steeled myself for a lecture about rising above office politics, figuring Spence had been bitching to him, too.

"You two square on the Okerson funeral today?" he asked.

Phew. I nodded, glad I was wrong. I might not have asked for this story, but I wasn't letting it go now. Spence could get over himself.

Parker nodded.

"I want this as an exclusive until it hits the racks in the morning," Bob said. "Everyone and their brother will be calling looking for a comment about it, but they get nothing 'til our story is in print." He glanced at me. "You feeling better?"

"Finally, thank God. I just have to finish the antibiotics they gave me," I said.

"Good. You've been on top of your game so far, and I want it to stay that way."

I exchanged a look with Parker.

"Bob, there's more to this story than you know," I began.

Bob leaned his elbows on his desk, shooting a glance between me and Parker.

I looked at Parker and sighed, opening my mouth and cringing in anticipation of the fallout. Bob waffled between loving the results and hating the process when I played detective.

"I don't think TJ killed himself," Parker blurted before I could.

Bob's eyes widened. "Now, Grant, I know this was your friend's son—" he began.

"I don't think he did, either," I interrupted.

My editor sat back in his chair, steepling his fingers under his chin.

"This has always been a hard thing for you to write about, Nichelle. I remember when that kid last year was bullied on the Internet, you were depressed for weeks while you worked on that."

"But I didn't ever question what the cops were telling me, did I?" I pulled in a shaky breath. "I'm trying to keep personal feelings from clouding my judgment here, Bob. Harder than you can imagine. And this doesn't feel right to me. It's too easy, and it makes too little sense."

"She's right, chief. I thought the same thing before she ever said a word to me. I've known TJ since he was a baby. His parents are like family to me."

Bob looked at me. "And the cops say what?"

"The sheriff is waiting for the tox screen to come back showing painkillers and alcohol so he can close the file. He's more worried about copycat suicides than he is about whether or not the obvious answer here is the right one."

"Given that there's already been one of those, I'd say he's got good reason for that," Bob said.

"Parker got me an exclusive with the mothers Saturday night. Both of them." I picked at a piece of lint on the arm of the chair, peeking at Bob through my lashes.

He put a hand up. "Don't tell me. It's a conspiracy. The girl was murdered, too, right?"

I swallowed a laugh at the skeptical look on his face.

"I'm poking around."

"Dancers. I like the dancers. Write more about them." He sighed, burying his head in his hands.

"I think there's a moonshine operation out there that might be poisoning people," I said. "Or people poisoning the moonshine, maybe. Either way. Illegal booze, dead kids—it's an impressive headline."

Parker coughed over a laugh and Bob peered at me from between splayed fingers. "Moonshine? Are you serious?"

"As a naturalizer nurse's shoe."

"Your friend at the ATF is helping you with this, I assume? The one who has a gun?"

I rolled my eyes. "Getting shot wasn't fun. I don't intend to repeat that experience."

"I want you to chant that at the mirror every morning while you do your makeup. Mantras bring about positive self-change. I heard it on Oprah once."

"Oprah is never wrong." I nodded, and Bob rolled his eyes.

"Hey, who am I to argue? If you're right, it'll be a hell of a story. But digging for something in a town that tiny won't be easy with all the TV cameras hanging around."

"The networks will clear out this evening," I said. "They're not interested in anything beyond TJ's funeral."

"Most of them, probably. But Charlie's been out there, too, and where you go, she'll go."

"I'm not advertising what I'm working on, and the families aren't talking to anyone else."

"Just be careful," he said. "And if you're looking for a murderer where the cops aren't, you better have it dead to rights before you bring it to me. You can't accuse someone of murder in the newspaper when there's no police report."

I nodded understanding. "Not planning on it. In a perfect world, the cops will come on board when I find something compelling enough."

"I know you'll make sure we have it first if you take it to them," Bob said.

"Of course."

"And the funeral is priority one today."

Parker checked his watch. "Speaking of priorities, if I'm going to file my column before we leave, I should get to work on it."

"And I need to call Aaron about a couple of police reports," I said. "The trials I'm missing to go to Mathews might have to wait 'til tomorrow, but I'll do my best to track down the lawyers and get an update in tonight. It might be late."

"We can hold Metro 'til nine-thirty before the guys downstairs get pissy. The drivers make overtime if we're any later than that, and Les will pop his hair plugs right out when he comes back if we let that happen, so if they're not in by then, they don't go."

"Yes, sir." I stood and saluted, clicking the heels of my classic black Louboutins together.

"Get to work." His voice was gruff, but he smiled.

Back at my desk, I flipped my laptop screen up and logged into the PD's online reports database. Armed robbery at a fast food joint on Southside. No fatalities, at least. I snatched up the phone and called Aaron, thankful for an easy story to get out of the way.

"You find any moonshine?" he asked when he picked up.

"Empty jars, so far," I said. "But I see the folks at Burger King on Hull found a guy with a gun last night."

"Two guys. One white, one black, ski masks, gun. Went in after midnight, ordered the staff to the floor, emptied the registers, and left."

I jotted that down. "Anyone get you a good description? See a car?"

"The manager said the guys weren't big. Five-eight to five-ten, a hundred and fifty or so pounds. No hair or eye color noted. They jumped in the back of a nineties sedan. Gray or white, possibly a Honda or Nissan."

"You have a sketch?" I asked as I wrote.

"Nope. Not enough to go on."

"We'll put it in Metro. Maybe someone saw something. Is Crimestoppers offering a reward?"

"The standard one."

"Thank you. This is an easy write-up, and I needed it today."

He chuckled. "I had very little to do with that, but you're welcome."

"Just try to keep things quiet around here this week, huh? This thing in Tidewater is getting more tangled by the day."

"You sound like you're feeling better, anyway," he said.

"Thank God for small favors."

I wished him a good week and hung up, rifling through the tea-stained papers on my desktop for the one I'd scrawled the ABC police officer's phone number on.

I crossed my fingers as I dialed, and smiled when the guy picked up on the first ring. I introduced myself and his voice went from congenial to guarded.

"Aaron White at the Richmond PD will vouch for my trustworthiness if you want to call him," I said. "I got your number from him, actually."

"Aaron's a good guy," he said. "But it's his job to talk to reporters. It's not mine."

"What if we're off the record? At least at first?" It wasn't my preference when dealing with a brand-new source, but I needed an in at the ABC police and he didn't have any more reason to trust me than I did to trust him.

"About what?"

"I'm working on a story that has ties to moonshiners," I said. "I would really love to know a little more about how the ABC polices that part of the illegal trade."

"Very carefully," he said.

I picked up a pen, not because I wanted to quote him, but because I didn't want to forget anything.

"Meaning?" I asked.

"Meaning moonshiners are a tricky business. It's practically a culture unto itself."

"Are there any active investigations into the manufacture and sale of illegal moonshine?"

"About fifteen, spread from the mountains to the beach and everywhere in between. We busted a group of bachelor businessmen with a still in their basement in Alexandria last year. Trial is coming up on that one, actually."

"So it's not just a country thing anymore?"

"Hardly. There are people who make the stuff all over the state. Though there are only a few operations with wide enough distribution for it to warrant our time and money."

"Any of those pushing their product across state lines?" I asked.

"I'm afraid I can't comment on that."

I tapped the pen on my notebook.

"Can you tell me if there's an open investigation in a little map dot called Mathews out on the bay?" I asked.

He paused. "I'm sorry," he said. "No comment."

Which was as good as yes. I put a star by that. I didn't know if Kyle had a way to find out what they were investigating, but it was worth asking.

After thanking the officer for his time, I hung up.

I fired through the armed robbery story and sent an email to our photo editor requesting a shot of the Burger King to go with it. Parker appeared at my elbow just as I finished proofing the article and got it ready to send to Bob.

"You ready?" he asked. "I want to get there a little early if we can."

I clicked send and closed my laptop, smoothing my black tank dress as I stood. "Since I don't fancy riding to Mathews on the back of your bike in this dress, I assume I'm driving?" I asked.

"I figured," he said.

I fished my keys out of my bag and turned toward the elevator, almost plowing into Spence.

"Teach her a little about writing sports on your way, Parker," he said.

"Lay off, Spence." Parker shook his head, putting a hand on the small of my back and trying to steer me around Spencer.

"Who plays infield between second and third bases, Clarke?" The words dripped so much sarcasm I was tempted to ask if he needed a napkin for his chin when I turned back.

Parker opened his mouth, but I laid a hand on his arm. "The short-stop," I said. "For the Generals, it's Mo Jensen, who hit two-ninety with thirty-five RBIs and only one error last year. Anything else, Mr. Jacobs?"

Spence rolled his eyes and stalked in the direction of Les's office. I sighed and strode to the elevator, Parker on my heels.

"I guess it might do Shelby some good to have a friend. Maybe she'll soften," I said, grinning at him as the doors closed.

He smiled. "I was all set to defend you and instead you shut him up," he said. "How'd you know that?"

"It was in your baseball preview last month. Things I read get stuck in my brain."

"Nice."

* * *

I drove to I-64 while Parker fiddled with the radio, a heavy sadness settling in the car.

"I'm sorry, Parker," I said. "This can't be easy for you."

"You can say that again. I'm sad. I'm worried about Tony and Ashton. And I'm pissed off, too," he said, running a hand over his face.

"At?"

"The cops. The kids. Just in general."

I paused, stealing glances at his profile. "So, when you went out there the other day," I said finally. "You were there for a while before you called me. And I know Ashton and Tiffany talked to me, but I'm wondering what they told you." And if it matched what they told me, but I kept quiet about that.

"I asked them what you told me to," he said. "About if there were kids who didn't like TJ."

"And?"

"Ashton said not really, at first, and then she told me a story about a cheerleader who had a crush on him. Said the girl texted him at all hours and some of the messages were 'I love you so much' and others were 'you prick, why don't you love me?'"

"They told me about her, too," I said. "That's definitely interesting."

Parker nodded. "You think a teenage girl could do this, though?"

"Have you ever watched a Lifetime movie?" I glanced at his puzzled expression and laughed. "Probably not. I don't know about this particular teenage girl, but is it theoretically possible? Abso-freaking-lutely."

"How do we find that out?"

"Well, I'm going to start by hoping the girl is at this big social event they're having Friday night and trying to chat her up."

"You always have a plan. Need help?" he asked, then snapped his fingers. "Oh. Wait. I think we're going to a play Friday night."

"Got it covered. Kyle's coming with me. But thanks, Joe Hardy."

The more I thought about it, the more I leaned toward the girl, just because the empty pill bottle and liquor pointed to someone conniving, someone who knew enough about TJ's every move to know he had a fresh bottle of pills in his pocket. Of course, that assumed there was foul play. I needed the tox screen to have a better idea of what I was dealing with. I couldn't see a cheerleader force-feeding a boy as strong as TJ a whole bottle of pills. But according to the sheriff, there were no obvious signs of trauma, so the blood test results had to hold the key.

I tapped my fingers on the steering wheel, my thoughts tangling up again. This whole thing was so damned convoluted. Every time I thought I had a new puzzle piece, it was just irregular enough that I couldn't find a place to make it fit.

"Was there anyone else Ashton talked about?"

"Not really." Parker shrugged. "She said she was sure he wasn't universally loved, but the girl was the only one who was weird."

I nodded. "Nothing about the boy from the baseball team? Luke?"

"I talked to Tony about him. He said that kid was jealous as hell, but he didn't mark him as a killer. Said the family is nice. Mom is the PTA president, Dad's super involved with the booster club."

Hmmm. "I don't know, Parker. I'm a total stranger, and he leapt right to 'I get to pitch now' with me like, the day after TJ died. That's a little narcissistic." But the M.O. didn't really fit with a jealous boy, in my opinion. I'd be more likely to go there with some kind of blunt force trauma, or even a bullet, being the cause of death. On the other hand, it would be harder to make those look like suicide.

"Tony said TJ told him Luke was really nice when he offered to take over for the second half of the football game after TJ got hurt. But TJ said he could still play, and the coach let him go back in. They talked some over the winter. Neither of them played basketball."

"Huh. Were they friends, then?" I couldn't shake the peculiar look on the boy's face out of my head, even as I asked the question.

"Eh. They hung out with the same kids, but in a town this size, almost everyone hangs out with the same kids, don't they?"

"They still have cliques. It's a high school. They're just smaller cliques."

I pulled off the freeway and turned toward West Point. Parker cranked up the stereo as I lost myself in this crazy, blurry puzzle. The tox results would really help. But Sheriff Zeke had no lab of his own and zero pull with the one in Richmond, so it could take weeks—hell, months—to get them back.

Kyle could maybe light a fire under someone on that front. I wanted to call him, anyway, and that was a better excuse than any I'd come up with. The pull I'd felt toward him Saturday night had knocked me for a loop, especially when I was so attracted to Joey.

I glanced at Parker when I turned toward the island, my throat tightening when I saw him staring out the window, tears flowing over his bronze cheekbones.

"I'm sorry," I said, patting his hand.

"It just..." His words choked off before he could finish the sentence, and I squeezed his fingers.

"Well and truly sucks. I know."

Yesterday, I'd talked to my mother for about five minutes. I rushed her off the phone before she could ask what I was working on.

* * *

I turned into the parking lot at the church, tall stained glass windows crafted with the kind of artistry you don't see anymore marking the century-old sanctuary.

A small handful of cars dotted the parking lot, but I recognized Tony's Land Rover.

I followed Parker through a side door and stopped by the back pew, studying the windows—there were twelve, depicting different scenes from Jesus's life—as Parker walked to the front and pulled Ashton into a hug. She fell into him, clutching his shoulder like a lifeline.

I walked back out to the welcome center and looked over the display Ashton had obviously spent days piecing together. There was a table full of TJ's favorite things, from his first little league trophy to his iPad and a handful of XBox game cases. His football and baseball jerseys hung from a makeshift clothesline. Another table was covered with photos. Baby pictures of him coming home from the hospital, grinning with his first tooth, sitting on Tony's Redskins helmet holding a football. Every birthday, up to him holding a set of keys and grinning from the driver's seat of a Mustang convertible.

"Sweet cartwheeling Jesus," I muttered, tears blinding me as I turned for the door. I'd seen so much tragedy in my career I'd be in therapy eight hours a day if I took it all to heart. But these people were Parker's friends. They were burying their baby, and didn't know why. I ran out into the sunshine and gulped air, silent sobs shaking my shoulders.

I closed my eyes for a ten count and took a slow, deep breath, wiping my cheeks before I spun on my heel to go back inside. I had one hand on the doorknob when three satellite trucks pulled into the parking lot behind me. The doors opened in unison and network-made-up Johnny Goodhairs in three-piece suits disembarked, carrying mics and racing for the best place on the lawn.

I slipped quietly into the church and strode past the photos and mementos, making a beeline for Parker when I spotted him sitting with Tony and an older couple in a hallway off the sanctuary.

I dragged Parker a few feet away. "Houston, we may have a problem," I said, pasting on a smile and hoping my waterproof mascara hadn't let me down.

A worried line creased his brow. "What's that?"

"The press is here," I said, the irony of me sounding that warning not lost on me. "Three network guys, already fighting for space on the lawn. All in dark suits. Want to bet on which one tries to slip inside the church first?"

He nodded and walked back to Tony, leaning over and murmuring to his friend. I hung back a few steps.

"Damned vultures!" an older man, who had that debonair look handsome men get when they age that always struck me as so unfair, exclaimed.

"Dad, they're just doing their jobs," Tony said, throwing me an apologetic look.

"This is a funeral, not a media circus," Mr. Okerson, senior, practically spat.

I shifted my weight, trying to blend into the floor. While Parker had asked me to be there, Bob had, too. And I was writing a story about the service. I didn't want to upset the family even more.

"Thanks for the heads-up, Nichelle." Tony stood and put an arm around me. "And thank you for coming, and for everything you've done for us. Ashton filled me in. I can't tell you..." His green eyes filled with tears and he paused. "If there's ever anything I can do for you, don't hesitate."

I nodded, trying to focus on the moment and the words and not the fact that Tony Okerson was hugging me. He wasn't a celebrity. Not today. He was a guy who was grieving a terrible loss, and I wanted to help.

"Y'all want me to go watch the door?" I asked.

Parker and Tony exchanged a look.

"Body combat or no, I think someone a little more intimidating might be better." Parker patted my arm.

Tony pulled out his cell phone. "Lucky for me, the same thing that makes them want to be here," he held up his hand, one Super Bowl ring glinting in the light, "gives me friends who are handy for intimidation. Excuse me for a second."

He walked back toward the sanctuary, holding the phone to his ear. Parker smiled and introduced me to Tony's parents.

"That article you did about our baby was just beautiful," Verna Okerson said, sniffling and squeezing one of my hands in both of hers.

"I'm so glad you liked it." My voice caught and she squeezed tighter.

We chatted, Parker checking the heavy stainless Tag Heuer on his wrist every two minutes, until Tony returned.

"Thank God, traffic was light." He glanced toward the Heavens. "There'll be two linebackers on the front door and one suitably-scary teammate on the other entrances in twenty minutes."

Parker and I watched as Tony showed his parents the display in the welcome center. Verna nearly collapsed looking at the photo table, and I turned away.

"I don't think I've ever been to a funeral with bouncers," I said.

Parker raised his head and grinned. "Welcome to professional sports."

"Sad, that they should have to worry about this today."

"It goes with the territory. Tony understands that. You want to be famous and have media coverage of the stuff you want them to cover, you have to manage them trying to get a piece of things you don't want them in."

I nodded.

People started to file in not long after Tony's friends showed up. I watched the back of the sanctuary carefully, but didn't see anyone who looked to be overtly recording anything. Most of the pews were packed with teenagers, their faces every variety of red and tear-streaked imaginable. I recognized a lot of folks from the school's faculty and staff, too.

Parker looked around. "I bet the whole high school is here," he whispered as the pastor closed the opening prayer.

I bet it was more like the whole town. Even Elmer was in a far right pew, looking somber in his starched gray shirt and shined shoes.

I scanned the crowd as the football coach took the podium and launched into a eulogy about what a hard worker and determined kid TJ was. He was followed by the baseball coach, the high school principal, and two teachers. I hung in there pretty okay until the pastor called Tony's name.

Parker's head snapped up as his friend made his way from the front pew to the red-carpeted stage. "How is he going to do this?"

"You're asking the wrong person."

Tony leaned his big hands on the sides of the podium and took a deep breath. "I came up here today to talk to you folks about who my son was. But now that I'm standing here looking at the faces of the people who miss him so much, I'm glad I made notes. My wife, Ashton, myself, and our parents would like to thank you all for being here." He picked up a few sheets of printer paper and held them up.

"This is what I had planned to say. And I apologize for putting him on the spot, but I wonder if I might ask my friend Grant Parker to come say it for me."

"Shit. I'm going to cry," Parker said.

"You'll be great."

Parker stood and made his way to the front of the room, swiveling heads following his progress up the aisle. I reached for the tissue box. As I turned toward it, my eyes lit on a young blond girl, lithe and pretty, shrinking into the end of the pew across and one behind from where I sat. She was wearing a black sundress, her slight shoulders caved over as she sobbed. By the time Parker started talking, her whole body was shaking.

Was this Evelyn the stalker? The description fit. Not that she was the only blonde in the place, but she was tall and pretty like Ashton said, and she was certainly more upset than the rest of the girls I could see.

Watching her saved me from losing what little control I had during Parker's impromptu eulogy, which started off with teaching TJ to throw a baseball and moved on to Tony's comments. The speech focused on the fact that TJ was a happy, helpful boy with a big heart who just happened to have a good arm. That's how Tony and Ashton wanted their son remembered.

"For the way he lived, not the way he died," Parker said. "We love you, Teej. We'll miss you every day."

Suspected-Evelyn sobbed hardest when Parker said the last words, and I dabbed my eyes with a Kleenex, keeping them on her.

I passed Parker the tissue box when he took his seat, then stood and sang along with *Amazing Grace* and *How Great Thou Art*. Bowing my head for the closing prayer, I couldn't resist stealing glances at the girl as the pastor's soft tenor carried through the church.

She was a hot mess by the time she stood to file out to the reception, which was through an annex in the community room. We lost her in the crowd, but I had a hunch I knew where to look.

"I'll catch up," I whispered to Parker, squeezing his hand. "I think I might have spotted stalker girl."

He raised an eyebrow. "She's here? That's brave, if she killed him, don't you think?" His voice was quiet, but loud enough to turn the heads of the people immediately around us.

"Parker!" I shushed him.

"Sorry," he whispered.

I ducked into the ladies room. There was a line of three women who moved through and did their business quickly, anxious to get to the smells wafting from the community hall. Nothing like a funeral to bring out the inner Aunt Bea in folks.

I leaned on the wall and watched the door that didn't open for three cycles through the stalls. When the room was empty, except for me, the blonde girl came out, her makeup smeared and face swollen.

She stepped to the sink, but spotted me and flinched before she managed to get cold water on her face. "I thought I was alone," she said, her voice hoarse.

"I didn't mean to startle you. I just need to wash my hands." I stepped to the sink. "I'm sorry for your loss. It seems like TJ was a great guy."

"He was the best. At everything." She sniffled, turning the water on.

"You were friends?"

"I—" she splashed water on her face, tiny droplets clinging to her lashes when she looked up at me. "Yes. He was special."

I dried my hands and put one out. "I'm Nichelle."

She shook my hand. "Evelyn. Nice to meet you." Bingo.

"It's very nice to meet you, too."

I followed her to the community hall, trying to make small talk about school and getting nowhere. When the doors opened, she slipped inside with her head down, muttered a goodbye in my direction, and scurried to a corner like a mouse in a roomful of emaciated lions.

"Nothing going on there," I muttered, watching her grab a glass of iced tea and sip it as she played with her hair.

"Where?" Parker asked from behind me.

I turned and found him holding a Dixie plate piled high with fried chicken, ribs, half a dozen kinds of casserole, and three biscuits.

My stomach growled. "Do you have a hollow leg, or something?" I asked as he shoveled cheesy hash browns into his face.

"Good metabolism, I guess." He shrugged. "What'd you find in the bathroom?"

I nodded toward Evelyn. "It's her. The girl Ashton was telling me about the other night. She's torn up. You should've seen her when you were talking. Nicely done, by the way. Not a dry eye in the place."

"Thanks. I guess. So, you think she's upset because she thought she was in love with him, or because she feels guilty?"

"No way to tell. I tried to talk to her, but I struck out." I watched from behind Parker or the corner of my eye, trying not to be too obvious. Evelyn stayed by the drink table, toying with a napkin, her eyes darting around the room. I followed them and found that they lit often on two groups of kids who stood in circles, whispering and shaking heads, or laughing.

"Jesus, they might as well point," I said.

"Who?" Parker asked around half a biscuit.

"The kids who are milling around talking about that girl."

"It's high school. You expect something different?" He swallowed.

"I guess I've tried to block it out." I turned for the buffet, wanting to snag a piece of chicken and some banana pudding before Tony's former teammates demolished everything.

I picked up a plate and had just grabbed a chicken leg when an indignant cry came from my elbow. "You!"

I flung the chicken in the air when I jumped, watching it fly end-over-end toward a group of large men in dark suits. It seemed to defy the laws of physics, taking forever to cross the room. Just when I cringed and started to cover my face as it flipped toward a huge expanse of bald head, one of the guys grinned, snatching it out of midair. He took a bite and waved at me.

"Nice hands, Petey," someone behind me called.

Something to be said for tossing chicken in a room full of professional athletes, I guess.

"Can't let that secret recipe go to waste," Petey replied, taking another bite.

I spun toward whoever was so annoyed at my presence and found myself staring at a broad white hat. I looked under it and discovered Miss Dorothy from the roadhouse parking lot showdown. Oops.

"Hello, Miss Dorothy." I smiled my best I-have-no-idea-why-you're-mad smile.

She did not bite. "I cannot believe you wrote that..." She sputtered. "That...you defended that..." She pinched her lips together and balled up her fists, taking a deep breath. "How dare you call that house of smut anything but what it is," she shouted.

The chatter around us fell silent. I kept my eyes on Dorothy, but felt every other cornea in the place on me.

"My job is to tell both sides of the story, which is exactly what I did," I said calmly, keeping the smile in place. "If you disagree, you're welcome to submit a letter to the editor. The email address is on our website."

"And we all know how handy Miss Dorothy is with the Internet, don't we, boys?" The booming voice came from my left and I bit the inside of my cheek to hold in a giggle, turning toward Amos. He nodded in my direction.

"Nice. I even reposted it on my Facebook. So my wife would see it." He shot Dorothy a pointed look. "I suggest every man in the county do the same," he bellowed.

I smiled a thank you. "I appreciate that, but I don't think this is the best place for this conversation."

"I'm sorry I didn't let you quote me, now." He winked.

"Well I'm sorry I did," Dorothy stomped a foot. "You were right, Amos, you tried to tell me she'd make me look a fool, and I should have listened."

I glanced around for reinforcements, my eyes lighting on Tony, who looked on with as much interest as he could muster.

A navy-pinstripe-suited arm appeared around Dorothy's shoulders. "Is it at all possible, Miss Dorothy, that you made yourself look a fool?" the pastor asked. "We had this discussion a month ago, and I believe this is just about what I told you would happen. Well, minus the Richmond media attention."

I had to cough to cover that laugh, and wouldn't have won any Oscars for the performance. Bob had texted me earlier to tell me the story was at seventeen hundred Facebook shares and climbing. And he'd had people tweeting it at intervals all day, so it was up to six thousand retweets by eleven a.m. The purple shade under Miss Dorothy's makeup told me it wasn't the right moment to mention that.

Dorothy squared her shoulders and shot me a withering look. "You tricked me."

"I don't think I misrepresented anything. I told you I was writing a news story, and I told you I was going to get the other side of it, and that's exactly what I did," I said gently. I didn't want the whole town making fun of her. "Miss Dorothy, have you ever been inside the club?"

"I would never." Her mouth gaped open, unable to finish the sentence, the color draining from her face.

"Is it murder if you give someone a stroke?" Parker whispered from behind me. I shot a heel back into his shin. "Ow." He hissed.

"I just think if you were to go inside the club, you might see it's not what you think. I found the ladies to be very nice. You might find the same."

"And some damned fine barbecue," someone hollered. A round of laughter and murmured agreement followed.

"Abigail did make the best sauce in the county," the pastor said, squeezing Dorothy's shoulder.

She snapped her mouth shut and shook her head. "I'd rather die."

"Better not say that around this bunch," Parker whispered. I kicked him again, turning my head. "Stop trying to make me laugh," I whispered sternly. "She really will have a stroke and it'll be your fault."

Dorothy tossed the general population of Mathews a final glare and stalked out of the room. A handful of other women scurried after her, and everyone else turned back to their food and conversations, drama forgotten.

I followed Parker to where Tony and Ashton sat, him alternately talking to people and trying to get her to eat, her staring at the wide expanse of white wall.

Parker laid a protective hand on Ashton's shoulder, but she didn't move to acknowledge it. The service was done, Tony's parents were watching the twins—those things had been her wind for days, and without them, her sails hung loose. She looked lost. And broken. It both wrung my heart and pissed me off, two emotions I wasn't sure I'd ever felt simultaneously.

My cell phone beeped a reminder, and I fished the prescription bottle out of my bag and shook an antibiotic capsule out, excusing myself to grab a glass of tea and swallow the pill. Tucking the bottle back into my clutch, I scanned the crowd for Evelyn, but didn't see her. Damn. She must have left while Dorothy was scolding me for telling the truth about Bobbi's club.

Stopping next to Parker, I spied Luke Bosley in the middle of a group of kids on the far wall.

"Lucky break," I murmured.

"What?" Parker asked.

I nodded toward Luke. "I need to borrow your baseball star power again, Parker."

"A football star isn't helpful?" Tony looked up at us.

"Not for this, I don't think," I said. "I'm so sorry. Excuse us for a second."

I grabbed Parker's arm and hauled him away.

"That's him," I said.

"Who?"

"The boy. Mr. I-get-to-play-now."

He nodded understanding, turning on the megawatt grin that made women who didn't know a slider from a swan dive read our sports page—and star-struck pitchers feel chatty.

Parker didn't even have to wave. He simply made eye contact. Luke pushed through a pair of girls who were giggling at his every word to pump Parker's hand as though Texas crude might spurt from his fingertips.

The girls frowned, and I rolled my eyes, hanging back a couple of steps so Parker could work his spell. In less than a minute, he had one arm around Luke's shoulders, leading him to the side door and a quiet courtyard. I followed.

"I was just a little kid when you played for the Cavs, Mr. Parker, but watching you pitch, and hearing my dad talk about your arm, was what made me want to be pitcher."

The way I'd heard it from the coach, a whole lot of nagging from his father was responsible for that, but okay.

Parker smiled a thank you. "I hear you're the one to watch for the Eagles now, Luke."

"You did?" Luke's eyes showed white all around the hazel. "For real? From who?"

"I have some friends out here."

Luke became very interested in his black loafers. "Mr. Okerson is your friend, huh? Your speech was nice."

"TJ was a good kid. I taught him to throw a ball when he was just a little guy."

"You said. I'm sorry for your loss, Mr. Parker."

"Call me Grant."

Luke's head snapped up and he smiled. "No, sir. My momma will pitch a fit."

Parker chuckled. "Lose the 'mister' at least. I'm getting an old man complex."

"Yes, sir."

"I thought you might like some pointers, if you're leading the team. The season is just starting. It's a lot of pressure."

Luke nodded. "I can take it." His eyes flitted back to his shoes, then to a statue of an angel behind Parker. "I wish it didn't have to be like this. Why did TJ have to be so good, you know? When he got hurt, I thought my chance was coming, but then he got better. Why—" He dropped his head back, staring toward the Heavens.

I held my breath, and it looked like Parker was holding more than that. Something resembling rage simmered beneath his understanding nod.

Was Luke about to confess? I'd seen stranger. And kids are often guilty of running off at the mouth. I stared, willing him to go on. He kept his eyes on the clouds.

The door that led back into the church opened, and a stout woman in a navy suit that had last been fashionable in nineteen ninety-seven stepped outside.

"Lucas Cameron, there you are." She shook her head and tapped her watch. "It's past time for your medicine. And you eating all this junk, too."

"Coming, Momma." Luke said. His eyes shot from her to Parker to me, and he blinked like he hadn't noticed me before and offered Parker a hand. "It was nice to meet you. Thanks for taking the time to talk to me."

"My pleasure," Parker said, doing an admirable job of holding his tone even. If I didn't know him so well, I wouldn't have been able to tell anything was bothering him. As it was, Luke was lucky to pull back unbroken fingers.

Luke moved toward the door and Parker stopped him halfway. "Hey, kid?"

"Yes, sir?" Luke turned back, squinting into the April sunshine and shading his eyes with one hand.

"You go to the party? On Wednesday night?"

"No, sir. I'm behind in history." He tossed a glance at his mother, who nodded a what-am-I-going-to-do-with-this-kid and waved him inside.

Parker turned to me when the door clicked shut. "Was it just me, or—?" He let the unspoken words hang in the air.

I shook my head. "It was not just you. Hell, my heart is still racing. I thought you had him. Nice, asking him about the party off guard like that."

"You buy it?"

"Nope. He answered too fast. My guess is mom told him he couldn't go, and since she was standing right there, he blurted the no. But is there another reason he doesn't want us to think he was there? Maybe. Sure seemed like he almost said something interesting before his mom came outside."

"That's not enough though, is it?"

"It's a hell of a start. He just passed Evelyn on my suspect list."

CHAPTER THIRTEEN

THE LAVENDER SKY deepened to indigo outside the church windows as we chatted and cleaned up. By the time we got to the car, I was glad I'd already filed my "have-to" court copy for the day.

"I need to send Bob an update," I said, tossing Parker my car keys. "Can you drive?"

After climbing into my seat, I opened my email, hoping I had something from Kyle. Or Aaron. Anyone who could be any help with the moonshine angle.

I'd gathered empty cups and picked-over plates for an hour, turning Luke's dazed monologue over in my head. Was he feeling guilty about hurting TJ, or just glad his rival was out of the way? It was impossible to tell, backtracking through what he'd said. Evelyn had vanished during the great chicken brouhaha of Mathews County, and I figured she was glad Dorothy had made a scene because it got everyone's attention and gave her a chance to slip out. Having spoken to both of the kids, I was no closer to knowing if one of them was actually the killer. If there was a killer.

So my brain went back to trying to find cause of death. For the seventy billionth time in my career, I wished forensics labs weren't so overworked. Having tox screen results would be ever so helpful.

"How likely do you think it is that TJ got hold of a bad batch of moonshine?" I asked Parker, looking up from my email. I had fifty-seven new messages, but none interesting enough to read right then.

"He was training, but it was vacation." He trailed off and appeared to consider that. "I don't know. The pain meds make me think he wouldn't have had too much of anything."

"Well, we're assuming he took any of the pills. I mean, if he didn't take them all, like the sheriff thinks, what if he didn't take any of them?"

"Where'd they go?"

"Into the bay? Down the toilet? On the Internet for sale?" I paused, considering that. "Do pharmacies track lot numbers on prescriptions?" Maybe I could figure out where the pills went, if they weren't in TJ's stomach.

I opened my web browser and turned to my trusty friend Google for the answer to that. They did not. Damn.

Parker was quiet, lost in thought from the look on his face. We were halfway to Gloucester before either of us realized we'd missed the turn to the freeway.

"Sorry," Parker muttered a curse under his breath and jerked the car into the turn lane. I looked up from an email I was sending Bob—slowly, thanks to the spotty signal—and spied the sign for Bobbi Jo's club less than a football field up on the right.

"You want to go check out the roadhouse?" I asked, wanting to show him I'd been right about the place, and jonesing for a glass of Grandma Abigail's sweet tea. Calories, schmalories. That stuff was worth every ap-chagi it took to work it off. Plus, maybe I could get someone to answer a few questions.

He raised an eyebrow at me. "I don't need domestic drama."

"You're in my car, so they can't trace your plate. Anyhow, you're not married. And Mel would love this place. They have the best iced tea in Virginia, hand to God."

"Why not?" he asked. "I bet I'm the only guy with a date."

"I bet I'm the only customer with better shoes than the dancers."

The parking lot was fairly full, for a club on a Monday evening. I followed Parker inside to find it just as packed as I'd seen it on Saturday. Miss Cirque du Soleil was hanging upside down on the pole and Parker's eyes widened. I scrutinized her attire, making sure my story hadn't been skewed by the fact that I liked Bobbi.

"See?" I spun to Parker with a triumphant grin. "Not only is she wearing a bikini top, it's taped in place! Otherwise, her boobs would be falling out of it every three seconds with all that flipping. Does anything about that sound indecent to you?"

"There's not much indecent about her." He tore his eyes from the stage and shook a dazed look off his face. "One word to Mel and I'll never talk to you again, Lois."

"Whatever. Have your secret." I rolled my eyes.

"Nichelle!" Bobbi's voice came from behind me and I turned, then stumbled back into Parker when she tackle-hugged me, crushing my ribs. She was strong for a teeny little thing.

"Hey there," I said when I could breathe.

"Your story rocked," she stepped back and grinned. "Look around. It's Monday. Monday! There are guys I've never seen in here, both from the county and not. Some of them even said they'll bring their wives for dinner. You are my very own personal Annie Sullivan."

"Not sure how much of a miracle worker I am, but I'm glad someone liked the story. Miss Dorothy nearly caused a food fight at a funeral today with her disapproval."

Bobbi waved Parker and I into a round booth on the far wall and called for a waitress. "Bring them whatever they want," she said. "On me. Nichelle, honey, hold that thought. I have a couple things to do on the floor here, and I'll be right back to join you."

I ordered a pitcher of tea and a C-cup, and Parker asked for a beer and a double-D (a half rack of ribs, plus the chicken). That was some metabolism, all right.

The waitress sashayed off, but was flagged down by another table before she made it three feet.

Parker watched the scene with feigned disinterest, but I choked back guffaws at the way his eyes trailed to the girls every thirty seconds, no matter how hard he tried not to watch them.

"Even with someone like Mel at home?" I asked. "Men really are all hopeless."

"Nothing personal," he said. "I think it might be biological. Survival of mankind, and all that."

I watched our server, who was on her third table since she'd taken our order and had a sea of them to cross between us and the bar. I stood.

"Enjoy the show. I'm going to get a glass of tea before my throat completely dries out."

If he answered, I didn't hear him.

Four whistles and a pinched ass later, I leaned on the polished walnut bar and waved to the pretty redhead who was mixing drinks faster than I could type. She nodded a hello at me and held up one finger before she drained the contents of a shaker into a glass of ice and added it to a tray.

A tall man in jeans and a red plaid button-down was next in line, and she leaned across the bar and asked for his order a second time when some of the guys started hooting. I looked to the stage and found a new dancer in a black bikini with silver sequins and a pair of precious open-toe silver stilettos with bows at the ankles. Maybe the dancers did have better shoes.

I turned back to find the bartender pulling a mason jar full of clear liquid from under the counter. She poured three fingers of it into a highball glass, screwed the lid back on, and stashed it back out of sight. Captain flannel tipped his white straw cowboy hat, dropped a few bills into her tip jar, and took his drink back to a table full of guys.

Hot damn. My eyes stayed fixed on the spot where the jar had been, Bobbi's comment about buying everything she possibly could from local folks running through my head on fast forward.

"Honey, what can I get you?" The bartender's pitch was high and irritated, like she'd asked the question more than once.

"Sorry." I smiled. "Just a glass of iced tea, please."

"At least you're easy," she smiled, filling a tall glass with ice and grabbing a pitcher.

"I know a couple guys who would disagree with that," I said.

She put the glass on the bar and I downed half of it in one gulp. Seriously. Like liquid crack. She refilled it. "It's all about finding the one who's worth it," she said. "Not easy to do when you work in a place like this."

"This place is fairly tame when you think about what it could be," I said.

"Bobbi runs a tight ship, no joke." She picked up an order chit and turned to grab a couple of bottles, pouring both liquors and some sour mix into a clean shaker. "But still. When this is what you see of men all day..."

"I hear you," I said over more hooting, thinking about the glassy look that had even come over Parker. I could imagine a girl would get jaded pretty quick. I scanned the crowd for our waitress, who was now across the fifty-yard line, but stopped at another table, and turned back to order Parker a Sam Adams.

Glasses in hand, I stepped away from the bar, the mason jar bouncing around my thoughts. I stole a look at the cowboy and his friends. They were all drinking beer, except him. He tossed his glass back as he watched the show, setting it on the table empty. I stared, halfway wanting him to slump over and solve the case for me, then feeling like I was going straight to Hell for having such a thought. He kept laughing and talking. I watched for so long one of his buddies noticed, and the guy turned and winked at me when his friend elbowed him and whispered something in his ear. I felt my cheeks heat and smiled, scurrying back to my table to gather Parker's jaw from the floor.

"What is it with y'all?" I asked as I sat down. "I know you've been to racier places than this, and you can look at a real live naked woman that you can touch anytime you damn well please."

He ran one hand through his perfectly-tousled blond hair. Every strand fell right back into place. "I think you need testosterone to understand, because I have no explanation for you." He sipped his beer and smiled. "Thanks."

"Our server is juggling seventy tables. I think Bobbi was understaffed for the crowd that turned out tonight."

"Your story was spot on." He caught my gaze with his green eyes. "I know you wondered after the old bat made a scene this afternoon, but this place is cool, on many levels. You did a good thing here. Stop worrying."

I smiled. "Thanks, Parker. You're a pretty good friend, you know it?"

"I'm good at everything. It's the price of being me."

"Modest, too."

"Honesty is much more endearing than modesty."

"You are too much." I drained my tea glass.

"That's what she said."

He caught me flat-footed with the last and I snorted iced tea when I laughed. Ouch. Tea trickled out my nose, my eyes watering because it burned. I ducked my head and groped for a napkin. "Jesus, Parker."

"I don't think I've made a girl snort anything since the sixth grade." He handed me a tissue. "I feel accomplished now."

"So glad I could be part of it."

He opened his mouth to say something else just as Bobbi fell into the booth beside me.

"Damn, I'm going to need to hire more servers if this keeps up," she huffed. "Running drinks is tiring."

"This is busier than you expected to be tonight, then?"

"Ohmigod, yes," she said. "We usually get about fifteen regulars in for dinner on Mondays, maybe two of whom could give a damn about the show. The girls have been after me to close on Monday nights for weeks, because they don't make much in tips. I was thinking about it, too, but I don't think I'll get any complaints tonight."

"No complaints from this corner." Parker smiled and offered a hand.

"I'm sorry, y'all—Grant Parker, Bobbi Jo, Bobbi Jo, this is Parker. He's a big fan of yours."

"Well, my grandaddy was a big fan of yours," she said. "I don't suppose you'd sign something for me? A napkin, or a menu? Made out to the club. I'll start a wall of fame."

"Anything you want." He smiled.

She trailed her eyes over him in a way that said Mel might not appreciate what she wanted, and I jumped back into the conversation.

"I'm glad the story helped," I said, trying to figure out how to ask about the moonshine without being too obvious and coming up with nothing. I took a deep breath and hoped my brownie points for pulling in so much business would stretch that far. "Hey, Bobbi, when you said the other day about buying local stuff," I toyed with the salt shaker, "does that extend to the liquor y'all serve?"

She stared for a minute. "I'm afraid I don't know if I follow you."

"I think you do," I said. "I think I saw a mason jar pop out from under the bar when I went to get my tea."

She sighed. "There are things that are different out here than they are in Richmond."

"And there are companies that produce moonshine that is regulated by the ABC," I said. "I have a hunch that's not the kind you're serving. I also have a suspicion that some backwoods shine might have been involved in the deaths of a couple of kids out here."

"TJ Okerson and his little girlfriend? Everyone says it was suicide," she said, her eyes widening.

"Listen, I don't want it getting around town that anyone thinks it might not be, and the sheriff decidedly disagrees with me," I said. "Until the tox screens come back, no one knows anything for sure, but there was moonshine—the local, unregulated kind—at both of the scenes, and I'm wondering if there was something wrong with it. A bad batch, maybe. Or a couple of spiked jars."

"Well, if the batch was bad, why isn't anyone else sick?" Bobbi asked.

"I don't know," I said, my eyes flitting to the big guy in the red shirt, who was still fine. "Maybe someone put something in it. But to find that out, I have to find out where it came from. I hear there are three stills that run on the island these days. Do you buy from all of them?"

"Just one. I've known the family forever. Went to school with the guys. They look a little scary, maybe, but they wouldn't hurt anybody."

"Do you mind if I have a look at the jar you have?"

"If I lose my ABC license, I'll have to close down," she said.

"I'm not looking to print where I got this particular information," I said. "I just want to see if it's the same kind."

She shrugged. "Sure."

The waitress set food in front of us just as Bobbi stood up.

"You two enjoy your dinner," Bobbi said. "I've got work to do, anyway. Just come over to the bar when you're through."

She excused herself. Parker bit into a rib and chewed thoughtfully, smiling at me as he swallowed.

"This is good barbecue. Hey, don't take this wrong, but are you sure the moonshine thing isn't just an interesting side story? I've met you. Poking into criminal crap that people don't want you nosing around in is kind of your schtick."

"I'm not sure about anything," I said. "The more I think about this, the more convoluted it gets. All the what ifs and possibilities are enough to give me a headache. I mean, start with the most obvious one: what if the sheriff is right?"

"I don't think so."

"But you're too close to the story to see that clearly."

"Are you? You told me you thought something was off from the get-go."

I chewed a mouthful of beans while I considered that.

"I did. I do." I sighed. "But, I have my own baggage with this story, Parker."

"I caught that when we talked to Bob this morning. You feel like sharing?"

I shook my head. "Way too long a story for a place this loud and crowded. But I've been playing devil's advocate with myself, trying to figure out if I'm projecting into this case, and I really don't think so. Trouble is, the puzzle is entirely too blurry for me to see what's going on if we're right and the sheriff's wrong. Some days, I miss good old-fashioned homicides. Smoking guns and open and shut cases are way less stressful."

He finished the ribs and moved on to his chicken. "Seriously, what is in this sauce?"

"Crack?" I grinned. "I think it's in the tea, too."

"Maybe. Anyway. I don't know how you do your job and stay off antidepressants. And I know you've caught shit from Bob before about some of your detective stories. But I'm with you on this one. Something's not right, and we seem to be the only people who give a damn about that. I'm really glad I have you in my corner."

"I'm not sure how much good I'm doing you. I can't figure which end is up, but something's definitely weird."

I wolfed down the rest of my food and another glass of tea and stood. "I'm going to go check out the local firewater. Be right back."

"Don't drink it," he called as I turned.

Check. I'd never tried anything stronger than a whiskey shot at a frat party once, and that made me sick.

I spotted Bobbi behind the bar, trying to help keep up with drink orders, and waited at one end until it looked like she had room to breathe. I waved, and she crooked one finger and raised the walk-through on the far end.

"I can trust you, right? You didn't make us look like smut peddlers in the paper, despite what Dorothy told you." She offered an uncertain smile that didn't quite reach her eyes. "This place is everything to me."

"I get it. I really do." I squeezed her hand. "These children were everything to their parents, too."

She nodded, pulling the jar from its hidey-hole and handing it over. "I've never heard of it making anyone sick," she said. "I mean, other than normal, hungover sick."

I turned the jar over in my hands. It didn't have a label.

"The one I saw at the bridge had a label on it," I said. "Does this ever have one?"

"The Sidell boys say that's stupid, because it makes it traceable," she said, shaking her head. "But I know some of them do. I've seen more moonshine than you can shake a tree limb at."

I looked sideways at her. "You grew up here," I said. "The sheriff said the kids have parties on the beach and at the bridge all the time."

Bobbi Jo laughed. "What else are they going to do?"

"Are there always a lot of kids?" I leveled a serious gaze at her. "Could you kill someone without being noticed?"

Her eyes widened. "I've never had occasion to wonder about that. I suppose it depends on how you went about it. Is it loud enough to mask gunfire? No. Someone would call the sheriff. But could you drown someone, or strangle them, maybe? If you were strong enough and got them away from everyone, sure."

I unscrewed the cap on the jar and smelled the contents, totally clearing what was still blocked of my sinuses. I shoved the jar and lid back toward Bobbi, my eyes watering again. "People drink this?"

"Never understood it myself, but it's a time-honored tradition. That's why I keep it. A lot of the guys who come in won't drink anything else."

"Maybe it burned off all their taste buds years ago." I swiped at my nose.

She laughed. "Could be. My granddaddy ran moonshine back in the day. Had the fastest car in ten counties. You know that's how NASCAR got started, right? Moonshine runners souping up their cars to outrun the law?" She screwed the lid back on the jar and stashed it.

"I heard that. This place is full of interesting history." I smiled. I liked Bobbi, but more than that, I respected what she was trying to do for her hometown, and the creativity with which she'd gone about it.

"My grandaddy used to tell a story about John Lennon coming into town once," she said. "He and Yoko wanted a retreat where no one would bother them, and they bought a place on the bay. A historical landmark with a mill that dates back to the revolution and was used to grind grain for Washington's troops."

"You're kidding. John Lennon lived in Mathews?"

"Well, no. He was killed before they got the house renovated. It sat empty for years, and the story goes that Yoko gave it to charity. The charity sold it to the current owners. But it's a fun bit of trivia."

I nodded, filing that away. I might be able to fit it into a story in passing, or maybe look it up and do a sidebar if I ever figured this mess out.

Bobbi stared at me for a long second. "Do you really think

someone murdered those kids? I can't remember the last time there was a murder in Mathews."

"That's because it was before you were born," I said. "I checked. I know it doesn't happen out here very often. And I'm not really sure what I think. All I know is my gut says there's something funky, and I seem to be the only one who thinks so. Funny, I usually hope I'm wrong when I'm doing stuff like this, but here, I'm not sure what to hope. The whole situation is just sad."

"That it is. TJ was a good kid."

"You knew him?" The way most folks seemed to feel about newcomers, I was a little surprised by that.

"My boyfriend is an assistant football coach at the high school. I wish I could've gone to the service today. I was going to, but then things went bonkers here and I couldn't get away."

I nodded. Everyone really did know everyone else. I kind of thought that was better in theory than in practice.

"Thanks for your help, Bobbi."

"It didn't look like it was much help," she laughed.

"Do you know who else makes moonshine? The jar I saw had three x's across the middle of it."

"That came from the Parsons place," she said. "They're on the island itself, and very—you ever see *Deliverance*?"

"I have." I raised my eyebrows. "I'm not sure I want to meet the living version."

"Probably best to stay clear unless you're packing," she advised.

Fabulous.

I dodged pinching fingers that had been through another round of drinks and found Parker downing the last of his beer, all the food baskets empty.

"You find what you were looking for?" he asked.

"Of course not. It couldn't be that easy. There's moonshine, but it's not the same kind Syd had. Moreover, Bobbi says the dudes who make the one Sydney drank are bad news."

"The kind of bad news that means you might get hurt messing with them?"

"But also the kind that means there might have been something wrong with the damned alcohol. So I really want to check that out. But I like breathing."

"What about your friend—the federal agent guy? Can he help?"

"I don't know. I'm working on that." Kyle would be a good person to have along. Except, of course, that he would never agree to let me tag along to a call like that. And what if he got shot chasing a lead I took him? I'd never get over that.

"You ready to get out of here?" I asked.

"Anytime you are," he said. "We're not telling Mel where we had dinner, right?"

"Mel will not give a rat's ass about you watching girls dance around in bikinis. But whatever you say."

He dug a few bills out of his pocket and dropped them in the pickle jar on the way out. "Just the same," he said.

My cell phone binged as we stepped outside and I pulled it out. I had seventeen texts from Bob.

"WHERE ARE YOU?" The most recent one read, all caps.

"Shit. That's never good." I flipped my scanner on when I got in the car, but it didn't pick up Richmond feed out there.

I dialed Bob's cell.

"What's wrong?" Parker started the engine.

"Don't know." I held up one finger.

"What the hell have you done?" Bob demanded when he picked up.

"I was covering the Okerson funeral all afternoon, just like you told me to," I said. "Didn't you get my email?"

"Of course I got your email," he barked. "And I don't appreciate you playing coy with me. Nichelle, this was supposed to be an exclusive. And you always play your investigative stuff close to the vest. So why the hell did the *Post* just tweet a teaser for a story questioning the suicide claim?"

I caught a breath and held it. "I have no idea."

"I'm supposed to believe that?" he asked. "How could they have gotten it? You, me, and Parker are the only people who know about it."

And Bobbi Jo. And the Okersons. And Sydney's mother. And Joey. And Kyle. But I didn't think it pertinent to mention that.

"The sheriff?" I asked. I couldn't imagine why he'd tell another reporter something he'd been vehemently denying to me all week.

I heard a female voice in the background. A distinctly whiny, high-pitched voice that hit my ears like railroad ties on a chalkboard. Shelby. I couldn't understand what she said, but Bob's voice tightened more, if that were even possible.

"They're running it tomorrow morning. I want something from you by nine. And I need the funeral write-up, too."

Crap. Since that was an exclusive, I'd planned to send it in after I got home.

I checked the clock. "Bob, it's seven-fifteen."

"And I am holding the front for copy I expect to have in my email by nine. Nichelle, I—" He stopped. "I don't want to believe you leaked this to the *Post* to try to impress them. I think I know you better than that. But you better hope you have more than they do, and that they have some other source. Because Andrews has gotten an earful of your D.C. ambitions this afternoon, and he's not happy."

Dammit. The publisher back on my case was not what I needed.

"Bob, I would never—"

"I told him that. Do not let me down."

"Yes, sir." I hung up, my mind frantically spinning through what I might be able to do with what I had in an hour. And what I should give up and what I should keep quiet.

"What gives?" Parker asked when I slung the phone into the dash.

"The *Post* has a story on possible foul play in TJ's death," I sighed, digging for my notebook. I paused. "Tony played in D.C. Do you think he might have talked to someone?"

Parker shook his head. "Not likely. I went through things with him. He promised he wouldn't talk to anyone but you. But I don't know that for a hundred percent."

I chewed my lip. "I don't want to intrude, but is there any chance we can go there and I can borrow a computer to write a story? Bob wants mine on the web tonight."

He laid on the gas and headed for the island. "They won't mind. And maybe someone else looking at it will wake the sheriff up?"

I nodded as the fields, nearly swallowed by the night, blurred past the windows. I wanted someone to take my theory seriously. But I also wanted the story to myself. Would it be good or bad if I beat the *Post* to this headline?

CHAPTER FOURTEEN

WE FOUGHT through the media circus at the gate and I huffed out another aggravated sigh.

"I should learn to keep my mouth shut, and maybe the universe will quit feeling it necessary to prove me wrong," I said. "I was just telling Bob they'd all take off after the funeral. I bet they got ten miles outside town before the tweet from the *Post* hit and they turned right the hell around."

"I wish they'd leave Tony and Ashton alone," Parker said, steering past the cameras and through the gate, watching the rearview for hitchhiking reporters.

"That, too."

Inside, Tony handed Parker a Corona and swore to us both they hadn't talked to a soul besides me and their families. He even called both sets of grandparents and quizzed them. No one admitted to having leaked their suspicions to the press. Since the story wasn't up yet, I couldn't see what the Post had, so I was writing blind when I sat down, trying to pick what to reveal and what to hold back. I wanted to beat them. But I didn't want to give away too much until I had the whole story.

. . .

Two-time Super Bowl MVP Tony Okerson and his wife, Ashton, buried their only son Monday, both unconvinced that local law enforcement in Mathews County are correct in their assertion that Tony Junior took his own life.

"I know my son," Ashton said in a tearful exclusive interview with the Richmond Telegraph. *"My baby did not do this."*

Ashton holds a degree in psychology from the University of Virginia and said her son had none of the signs of being suicidal.

"He was a happy kid," she said, her husband sitting beside her and nodding agreement. "I've been over every detail in my mind, looking for what I might have missed, and there wasn't anything. TJ was not depressed. He wasn't bullied. He was happy."

I quoted the sheriff last, purely so I could tell myself the story was balanced. No reason to believe it was anything but what it looked like, he insisted. I left out the moonshine, because I knew damned good and well no one but me knew about that. I wondered as I read back through the story if Lyle was the one who'd talked to the *Post*. He'd been around all week, and his stories were good, peppered with the kind of local flavor and insider comments that an out-of-town reporter would never know to look for. I'd seen him at the funeral that afternoon, too. But why would he talk to them? He didn't seem interested in notoriety. He'd said he wanted everyone to go away and leave the town alone.

I fired through my exclusive on the funeral next, my mind still half on the *Post*. What if they'd talked to someone I hadn't?

Sitting back in the chair, I sent both stories to Bob at five to nine, then clicked into Tony's web browser. I pulled up the *Post's* twitter feed and found the tweet that ruined my evening. *"Was it really suicide? Why some suspect foul play in the #TJOkerson case, only in tomorrow's edition."*

What. The. Everloving. Hell?

. . .

I dropped Parker at the office a little after midnight and grabbed my cell phone as soon as he shut the car door behind him.

"Miller," Kyle said sleepily.

"I'm sorry I woke you, but I need a favor," I said hurriedly, pointing the car toward my house.

"Nichelle? Hang on." The line was quiet for a second and then he came back on. "Sorry. I'm here. What's up?"

I wondered for a split second why he'd put me on hold, then told myself I had no reason to wonder about such things. And I didn't like the bite of jealousy that came with the thought, so I flipped my attention back to my story.

"I need tox results on TJ Okerson and Sydney Cobb. Like, now. And the sheriff in Mathews has less than no pull with anyone at the lab. I'm hoping you have a friend there you can light a fire under for me."

"I might." The hedging tone in his voice sent one of my eyebrows up.

"You don't sound sure about that," I said.

"I guess I'm not sure you want me to work the angle I have," he said. "There's a biologist there I've talked to about a couple of cases. She's cute. Seems to like me."

I didn't like the sound of that one little bit. And wanted to smack myself for feeling that way. Kyle was a good guy. He deserved to be happy.

"If she can process the samples they have faster, take her to lunch or something," I said, trying to unclench my teeth as the words slid through.

"I'm not interested—" he began.

"It's fine," I interrupted. "Really. Sorry. It's late, I'm beat. I could really use that report. Thanks."

"No problem."

"Kyle? One more thing?"

"Yeah?"

"If you're going to go charm her, ask for a full panel. I'd bet my shoe closet Sheriff Zeke asked them to screen for Vicodin and blood alcohol content. I'd like to know what else is there, if there's anything."

"You got it."

I went inside and fed Darcy, then tried to forget about Kyle's friend the biologist and focus on how the hell the *Post* was onto my story as I pulled the covers over me.

* * *

Tuesday was spent dodging media calls, appeasing my neglected Richmond sources, and avoiding pissy glares from Spence and Bob both. Thankfully, the *Post* hadn't printed anything about the moonshine, but they had so much of the rest of it dead to puzzling and unclear that I was afraid it was only a matter of time. They quoted the sheriff as having confirmed that Ashton and Tony suspected foul play, but who tipped them off in the first place was anyone's guess.

Aaron had an arrest in Monday's armed robbery, and my friend DonnaJo at the prosecutor's office had a seventeen-year-old going up on a capital murder charge over a drug deal gone bad. I sat through the opening arguments, fighting to keep my mind focused on the trial. Speeding back to the office, I didn't bother to work up a lead for the trial day one, instead running mentally through everyone I'd seen in Mathews in the past week.

By the time I'd filed both the trial and the robbery arrest stories, most of the other reporters were unplugging their computers and heading home, the section and copy editors talking about space and layouts. I clicked into my Internet browser, setting my scanner on my desk and turning up the volume. Being as I was in Richmond, I didn't want to miss anything else coming out of the PD. All I needed was to get on Aaron's shit list trying to help the Okersons.

I checked the clock. It was only a little after five, and Joey wasn't picking me up until seven-thirty.

Google, don't fail me now. I pored over public records for Mathews County, trying to figure out both what was going on, and how the *Post* knew there was anything going on.

I got nowhere on either front for a good while.

Pulling up the property tax records, I searched for the name Bobbi had mentioned as running triple-X moonshine. The family owned a house on the island that had passed through at least four generations. Cross-referencing the address in Google maps, I stared at the aerial satellite view. Trees obscured most of the property, save a little chunk of the roofline.

I slammed my hands down on my desk, wondering if it was possible for me to catch a teensy break on this one, and the silver frame that held a photo of my best friend Jenna's children clattered to the desktop. I stood it back up, staring at their adorable little smiles.

Family.

Everyone knew everyone.

Hot damn.

I pulled the marriage records for Mathews County and checked the last name from the property records, following the family tree all the way to sheriff Zeke. He was second cousin to the Parsons boys.

His whole "that's ABC police business" number made so much more sense as I stared at the trail on my screen. Sure, he was right about that, but at least now I knew why he was using it as an excuse to turn a blind eye to an illegal booze operation in his town.

Of course, it also meant I needed to tread carefully and make sure I had the story sewn up, because accusing the sheriff's cousin of murder could piss off said sheriff. Which I did not want to do.

Still mulling that, I noticed the clock and slapped the computer shut, shoving it into my bag and running for the elevator. I wanted to touch up my makeup and swap my white silk pants and coral top with matching strappy Manolos for a sexy dress and my newsprint Louboutins before Joey arrived..

Luckily, it was still too cool outside for me to have sweated off much of my makeup, so touching up only took a minute. I stepped into the last shoe as the doorbell rang.

Fixing a smile on my face and pulling in a deep breath I hoped would slow my pulse, I strode to the door. We'd never been on anything that seemed so much like a date. I might as well have been sixteen, waiting for a boy to come pin a corsage on me for the first time. Well. Except that boy had been Kyle.

But when I opened the door, I forgot all about Kyle. Joey leaned against the frame, looking downright dashing in a light gray suit, the emerald of his shirt perfect against his olive skin. There went my pulse again.

"You look beautiful," he said, his voice soft and low. He handed me a single, long-stemmed violet rose and laid a soft kiss on my cheek. Jesus, he smelled good.

I turned for the kitchen, looking for a vase for the rose, and he chuckled behind me. "I thought we were going out?"

"I have to put this in some water," I said.

"You like it? It's nearly the same color as your eyes."

I smiled, spinning back to him. "I love it. It's beautiful. Thank you."

Stretching up slightly, I only meant to brush my lips across his. He pulled me to him, slanting his mouth over mine in a much more serious kiss. I melted into his strong frame. The flower dropped to the floor, dead teenagers and moonshine falling away as I buried my fingers in his thick, dark hair.

One thing about Joey: he's a great kisser. Major league caliber. One arm cradled my shoulder, the other tightening around the small of my back as his lips parted. I returned the urgency, lightning flashing behind my eyelids as his tongue slid over mine. Sparks sped across my skin as his hand trailed up my spine, molding me to him. My toes scrunched inside my shoes, and I moved my hands to his chest, pushing the fabric of his jacket back over his shoulders.

He pulled back a millimeter, his eyes half-lidded and smoldering. "We are going out, aren't we?"

I swallowed the "we don't have to," before it popped through my lips, leaning back in his arms and trying to catch my breath. Dinner didn't sound nearly as appetizing as it had a few minutes earlier.

"We should." I trailed a row of tiny, soft kisses along his jaw and laid my head on his shoulder, taking long, deep breaths. His hands moved to stroke my hair.

"You sure? I still want to hear about those fantasies you were talking about the other night."

I let my breath out by degrees, reveling in the moment. I loved the way his voice rumbled in his chest when he talked, deep and strong and safe. It was an easy leap to wonder how it would sound if we were more horizontal.

I closed my eyes, letting the fantasy play for a few seconds.

Joey's lips. His hands. The things he could do with those lips and hands.

Moonshiners. Dead kids. Grieving parents.

Dammit, the things I sacrifice for my job.

I squeezed him for another second before I harnessed every ounce of willpower and stepped out of his arms.

"Where are we eating?" I asked, straightening my fitted forties-inspired black Calvin Klein dress. Hopefully nowhere I'd want to consume more than a few ounces of food, because the dress was already breathe-shallow snug.

"Well..." He let the word trail, his dark eyes flicking down the hallway toward my bedroom.

My heart jackhammered a few beats. I better get a Pulitzer for this.

I knelt and picked up the rose, laying it on the shelf of beach glass behind me. "I'll press this," I said, not trusting myself to stay in the house a millisecond longer. I stepped around him and walked down the steps. He pulled the door shut and locked it, following me to the car and opening my door.

"What are you hungry for?" He flashed a grin as he slid behind the wheel of his sleek black Lincoln.

"You cannot possibly understand how not hungry for food I am." I smiled as we started driving. "But I have to get this story. Not only do I have Tony and Ashton, grieving and wondering, now the *Post* has everybody and their dog out there looking for a killer."

"I saw that this morning. What happened?"

I sighed. "I got a big head? I had the exclusive with the parents and thought I had the story cornered. But, you know, I'm not the only nosy reporter around. Apparently, the *Post* has some folks who are better at being nosy."

"You're good at what you do. You'll get it."

"I hope so."

I wondered how, watching the familiar storefronts pass as he turned into Carytown. "Where are we going?"

He took a left into the parking lot at a chic French cafe. "This place good?"

"They have amazing bagel things they make fresh every day from French bread," I grinned. "I've only ever been here for breakfast."

"I have it on good authority that dinner is great, too." He shut off the engine and rounded the front of the car to open my door, pausing when he saw the lines creasing my forehead. "You're worried."

"Bob is annoyed with me. The publisher thinks I told the *Post* about TJ, thanks to our copy editor."

"You wouldn't do that." He dismissed the idea without a second thought, putting out a hand to help me out of the car. I grabbed it and hung on tighter than I should have, grateful tears pricking the backs of my eyes.

I blinked them away, clearing my throat. "Thank you."

"You have more integrity than anyone I've ever met," he said, holding my hand as we crossed the parking lot to the cafe door. He turned to me as he pulled it open. "It's one of the things I admire about you. Anyone who really knows you knows it. Your editor is nervous about losing the story, not about you being a mole for the *Post*. He'll come around."

I smiled a thank you at the hostess as we sat down, reaching across the table to squeeze Joey's fingers. "I needed to hear that today. Thanks."

"Glad to help." He returned the pressure, the look in his eyes making it very difficult to avoid crawling across the table and kissing him again. But the way my pulse and emotions were surging, that would lead to other things. Things that, there in the cushy booth, would lead to jail. So I kept my seat and smiled, instead.

He let go and tapped the menu, and I quickly settled on the rosemary chicken and turned my thoughts back to my story.

"The *Post* might have someone smarter than me, but they don't have you. Tell me about the guy we're talking to."

He sipped his water, and I found it easier to focus on his words if I skipped my eyes around the art on the walls or the pressed-plate ceiling, only stealing glances at him every few seconds.

"He does transportation and sales for a moonshining outfit out of Mathews," Joey said. "We have some mutual associates. There are several dry counties in Maryland and North Carolina, and a couple in Virginia, too. There are also a lot more places than I would have expected where you can't buy booze on Sundays."

"I saw that online. But why is it a big deal? That's what I don't understand. People can't stock up on Saturday?" I pulled a roll from a heavenly-smelling basket the server laid on the table and scooped butter onto my knife.

"I guess some people end up with hooch emergencies? Or don't live near enough to a liquor store, maybe?" Joey slid a knife into his roll. "I can't imagine. But I'm just the customer today. We're looking to buy a case from him. It was a good excuse for a meeting. Not exactly an interview, but I think you can get some useful information out of him."

"I can. And it's a good reason to spend the evening with you." I grinned, and his face lit up in response.

"There's that, too."

The waiter set our food down in front of us. When he left, I glanced at Joey.

"Maybe if you have time, we could pick up where we left off when we're done buying contraband alcohol." I twisted the napkin in my fingers, slightly amazed that I was brave enough to say that. And I hadn't even had any wine.

"Yeah? Well, let's go get it finished, then." The corners of his full lips edged up in a sexy smile, and my pulse took off at a gallop.

Lord, let's.

I picked at my chicken, and objected when Joey handed the server a credit card before the guy had even brought the check.

"You're doing me a favor," I said. "The least I can do is buy you dinner."

"On our first real date? I don't think so." He shook his head. "Next time, we'll talk about it."

My heart pounded. "Deal."

"Does that mean we're dating, now?" His dark eyes were serious.

I stared at him, my thoughts whirling. I wanted to squeal and say of course and wear his class ring (or whatever the grownup equivalent of that was). But...how would it ever work? And there was Kyle. I couldn't brush off the fact that I had feelings for him, too. I just didn't know how deep they went.

"We're trying things out," I said finally, choosing words carefully. "I like you. Probably more than I should. And not just because you can get me exclusives with shady characters. But it's been a pretty long time since I've done anything like this. I'm not sure how it works, period. Let alone how it works with so many complications."

He nodded. "I understand that. And I'll take it. I like you more than I should, too. I've tried to be your friend, but I want more. We'll see where it goes?"

"I'd like that." About as much as I like breathing.

"What about your," he paused, clearing his throat, "federal agent friend?"

"I don't see where it's any of his business. At least, not the particulars of it." I twisted the napkin some more. "Kyle is complicated."

"I don't give up easily." Joey took my hand, trailing the pad of his thumb over my knuckles. "And I'm used to getting what I want."

My breath caught when his eyes finished that sentence before he spoke the words. "As hard as I've tried not to, what I want is you."

Oh. My. God.

The waiter appeared with the credit card slip and Joey signed it, then stood and offered me a hand. "Ready to get this over with?"

I took his hand and returned his smile. "I haven't wanted to get through an interview more since the serial killer I saw on death row five years ago."

CHAPTER FIFTEEN

THE DRIVE TO MARYLAND FLEW, the woods lining I-95 blurring past the windows as we talked and laughed about everything from music and TV to politics. I knew Joey lived north of Richmond, but I'd never been sure how far north until he pulled into the parking lot of a fire-hollowed warehouse in a questionable part of Bethesda.

"This city is crazy," he said as he stopped the car. "Five blocks that way, there's a nice part of town."

"You're sure?" I looked around. "I'm skeptical, but I'll take your word for it."

"I live six blocks that way. It's nothing like this." He smiled. "But there are few places better to go when you don't want to be seen by anyone else."

I dug out a notebook and tried to concentrate on formulating casual questions for the moonshine salesman, but the smell of Joey's woodsy cologne mixed with whatever magical something made him so delicious kept my attention focused about a foot to my left.

I reached down and cracked my window, clicking out a pen. If we could buy Mathews-distilled moonshine here, it was going out of state. Which meant Kyle might be able to get a case opened at the ATF, and I might land the story of the year, and find a big chunk of my TJ Okerson puzzle, too. Assuming I was right about anything, anyway.

Priorities, Nichelle.

I repeated that on a loop in my head until an aging F-150 rolled into the parking lot. Joey moved to get out of the car, but paused when both doors on the truck opened.

Two large men, one in jeans and a Polo with a gleaming bald head and barber-close-shaven face, the other in overalls and a dingy wife beater with stringy hair and an untamed beard, met at the front of the pickup and nodded to us. Joey shot me a look, tense lines settling in his face, and pulled a small revolver from the low center console. He slipped it under his jacket without being seen through the windshield.

Shit.

"The driver is my guy. Bubba there, I'm not familiar with. You sit tight for a minute." He handed me the keys. "If anything goes wrong, lock the doors, crawl over here, and leave."

"I'm not leaving you," I said.

"I can take care of myself."

"So can I." I held his gaze, not blinking. "I'm not leaving here without you."

He sighed, turning his attention back to the surly redneck leaning on the hood of the pickup.

"Fine. I'm sure it's fine. Just sit here until I check it out."

He stepped out of the car and walked to the front bumper, talking to Mr. Clean before he turned to Bubba. If I hadn't been so worried, it would've been funny, watching Joey talk to this guy in one-strap overalls and flip flops who spit tobacco juice every other word.

Joey waved toward the car as he talked, and Mr. Clean nodded. Bubba scuffed a flip flop toe in the gravel and twisted his mouth to one side, staring at me through the windshield. I kept my expression neutral, difficult when I was pretty much scared to death.

Bubba nodded to Joey, and Joey backed toward my door, his hand hanging very near where I'd seen him stow the gun.

He pulled my door open and helped me out of the car. "Stay

behind me, and don't ask anyone's name," he said out of the corner of his mouth.

"I'm not stupid," I hissed back, nodding acknowledgement at the other two men.

"Evening, ma'am." Mr. Clean gave me a once-over when I stepped to the front of the car. "I understand you're interested in something a little stronger than a martini this evening."

I shook his hand, not breaking eye contact and standing up straight. I top six feet in my good shoes, and I wanted to look as invulnerable as I could, considering my cocktail dress. The gun under Joey's jacket was comforting.

I turned my head and smiled at Bubba. He spit on the ground.

"Martinis are last season," I said. "We heard y'all have something with a bit more kick to it."

"Don't know why you'd think such a thing," Bubba said. "Selling unregulated alcohol is against the law."

I looked between him, his friend, and Joey, not sure how I was supposed to answer that.

No one offered any assistance, Mr. Clean studying the shell of the nearby warehouse outlined in the night between us and the nice part of town, and Joey laying a casual arm across my torso, scooting me behind him a little more.

"Well, if we've come to the wrong place, I guess we should all just take our wallets and head home," I said, staring Bubba straight in the face. "Sorry to trouble you. You're sure you don't know where we might come by some genuine Virginia corn whiskey?"

"D'I look like I'd know anything about that?" He delivered the line with such a serious look I didn't dare give him a straight answer. Joey erupted into a coughing fit until he could stop laughing.

"We were told y'all might," I said. "I'm sorry for wasting your time." I took a step back.

"And what if I do? How d'I know you ain't wearing a wire or something? A fancy camera? You don't look like any kinda moonshine drinker I've ever seen."

He stepped forward and Joey slid in front of me.

"Where do you think you're going?" Joey looked down at Bubba. His steely voice and the tension in the part of his profile I could see were enough to send chills racing up my arms. Double shit. Thinking he might have hurt people and seeing him do it because I was stubborn were two entirely different things.

I laid a hand on his arm and leaned close to his ear. "Calm down."

"We ain't doing no business here if I can't check her for a wire," Bubba said.

"Over my dead body." Joey's voice was low and dangerous.

"We can arrange that, mister." Bubba glowered, rocking up on the balls of his feet so he was eye-to-eye with Joey.

I tugged Joey's elbow. I wanted the story. But not badly enough to let anyone get hurt.

"Look," I told Bubba hastily, scooting around the hood of the car and spinning before him. "Maybe you know something about the laws of physics that I don't, but I'd have to give up chocolate and bread for a month to fit a wire in this dress with me."

He eyed me shrewdly and motioned for me to turn again.

"I s'pose," he said when I obliged, a glimmer of respect in his dark eyes. He turned and walked to the back of the truck. I heard the hinges screech a protest when he let the tailgate down, and he returned with a plain cardboard box. "What is it I can help you with?"

"Can I see one of those?" I asked.

He opened the case and pulled out a jar, loosening the lid and passing it to me. "The first sample is free," he said, his eyes narrowing again.

"I trust your quality," I said.

"I insist."

I stared at him, and Joey laid two fingers on my elbow. "You don't have to drink it," he said.

Bubba's glare said refusing could be more headache than I might get from the moonshine. I looked at the jar. The triple-X insignia matched the one from the scene of Sydney's death.

Bubba nodded toward the jar.

Shit. What if it was a bad batch?

I shot Joey a glance from the corner of my eye, Bobbi's mention of *Deliverance* fitting with the moonshiner in front of me. I'd read enough to know a smidgen wouldn't hurt me, even if the stuff was spoiled. No one else was even sick, right?

Catching a breath and raising the jar to my lips, I took half a sip, heat spreading through me as I swallowed.

I blinked back tears. "Smooth," I choked out around a short cough. Kids were drinking this crap? My mouth and throat burned like I'd had a fire-eating lesson.

Bubba glanced at Joey. "I don't think it'll take much," he said in a voice so low I couldn't swear under oath I heard him right.

Joey produced a roll of twenties, peeled off ten, and picked up the box.

"Nice doing business with you," he said. "I'll be in touch."

Bubba's eyes raked over my dress again. "Will you?"

I wasn't sure how to answer that, so I ignored it and spun toward the car instead. Stopping halfway to the door, I turned back. Joey paused next to me.

"What kind of market do you y'all serve these days, anyway?" I asked Bubba. "I mean, you said we're not your typical customer."

"Lots of dry counties around here." Bubba shot a stream of tobacco juice from between his teeth that arced a good six feet. "I'd rather have more customers like you." He grinned, Copenhagen-stained drool dripping into his beard. Sexy.

I closed my eyes for a long blink. "People in dry counties have cars, right?" I asked.

"Say they go over to a store or across the state line and buy a bottle of whiskey," he said. "The government tracks everything with satellites and computers, you know. A body gets pulled over by the law on the way home, in a dry county, and possession will get them a night in jail, maybe longer, and a record. Moonshine is delivered. It's cheap. And it's off the books. Or the grid, like you city folks say. We live off the grid."

"Y'all do a lot of business with teenagers?" I asked.

Bubba shrugged. "Enough. Very carefully. I ain't got no objection to kids having a drink here and there. I got four boys, and kids'll do as they please. But that's trouble if the ABC catches you selling to minors. They get pissy about that faster than anything else. You seen all the stings they been running in stores on the TV?"

"I have." Damn. That didn't help me figure out where the kids got the moonshine. Or who took it to the party. And I was increasingly sure that was the key to this whole mess.

"Why d'you care?" Bubba asked.

"I'm curious. Occupational hazard. Thanks for indulging me."

"Much obliged for your business, ma'am." He climbed back into the truck.

Joey backed me into the passenger seat of his car, stowing the moonshine in the back floor board and shooting Mr. Clean an icy glare as he rounded the hood. The guy raised both hands and shook his head, calling something I couldn't make out. Joey didn't turn back, sliding back into the driver's seat and spinning the tires on his way out of the parking lot.

"I'm sorry," he said tightly, stopping at a light and tucking the gun back into the console. "I wouldn't have brought you out here if I'd known there was someone tagging along with him."

"I would have managed to convince you to bring me," I said, trying to keep my voice steady. It was shaking, as were my hands and knees. Hello, adrenaline rush.

Joey glanced at me as he laid on the accelerator on the onramp for I-95. "No, you really wouldn't have. I don't know who that guy was, but I know just enough about all this to know these are dangerous people. You handled yourself well. Nice, pointing out your dress. Though I didn't much care for the way he started looking at you when you did that."

"Everyone went home with the same number of holes they arrived with," I said. "That was my objective. I'm sure his wife thinks he's adorable, but he's not my type."

He glanced at me. "What is your type?"

"It seems tall, dark, and a little bit dangerous works nicely." When I thought really hard about that, it kind of fit him and Kyle both.

"Good to know." The corners of his lips tipped up a little.

I picked up my notebook and spent most of the drive home recording the details of our transaction. Moonshine being sold out of state. Check. But how to tell Kyle that without telling him how I knew it? I didn't have an answer. I noted the label on Bubba's brand, pulling out my cell phone and checking the photo of the one Sheriff Zeke had found near Sydney's body to make sure I remembered it right.

Wait.

I zoomed the photo in and stared, then reached behind my seat and pulled a jar from the box.

"One shot wasn't enough?" Joey asked.

"Hardy har har." I stuck my tongue out at him, holding the jar we'd bought up to the map light.

The one from the crime scene was faded across the middle. The one in my hand was not.

Which might just mean Bubba had refilled his ink cartridge since last week. But what if it was a coding system of some sort? I jotted that down and underlined it, returning the jar to the box.

"The labels are different," I said.

"Different how?"

"The one Sydney Cobb was drinking had this Triple-X label. But it was all faded across the middle. These aren't."

"What do you think that means?"

I sighed. "Hell if I know. Maybe nothing. Maybe everything. Any idea how I can find out which?"

"Not off the top of my head. But I'll let you know if I think of something." Joey grinned.

He turned onto my street, and I laid a hand on his arm. "I appreciate your help. I know you didn't want to do this. But these folks in Mathews deserve to know what happened to their children."

"That's the only reason I agreed to it." He parked the Lincoln in my driveway and turned to face me. "There's not much that scares me. But the idea of something happening to you...I can't stand it." He raised my hand to his lips, brushing them across the back.

A cavalcade of butterflies took flight in my middle as I stared into his dark eyes. Whatever he'd done or not done, he was telling me the truth. Better than half a decade of dealing with some of the best bull-shitters to walk the Earth had graced me with a good radar for lies, or even half-truths. Joey wasn't selling either.

He let his eyes fall shut and leaned to kiss me, and I put one finger across his lips. He flinched, confusion plain on his face.

"Come in," I said.

His eyes widened. "That the moonshine talking?"

"From half a sip two hours ago? Not even I'm that lightweight. I think I'll swear off the hard stuff, but I have a nice bottle of red in my wine rack." My voice shook again, with nerves instead of shock. "You feel like a nightcap?"

"I'd love one." He strode around the car and opened my door, pulling me close to him.

I felt my brow furrow at the bothered look on his face.

"What's wrong?" I asked. "You don't have to stay, if you don't want."

"Oh, I want." He flashed a tight smile before his face fell serious again. "What I don't want is for you to feel like you owe me anything. I took you to meet that guy because what you're doing is important. Not because I expect anything in return."

I laid my hands along both sides of his face, pulling it to mine. "Good. Because I wouldn't trade this for a news tip or interview if it meant a sure shot at the Pulitzer," I whispered, kissing him softly. "Let's go find that bottle of wine."

He turned for the door, one hand on the small of my back. By the time I got the lock opened, heat had spread from that spot through my entire core. I bent to scratch Darcy's ears, gathering minor control of my hormones.

Smiling, I directed Joey to the sofa and busied myself opening my splurge bottle of Chilean red. I gulped deep, calming breaths as I poured it into glasses, but sloshed a few drops onto the counter, anyway. What the hell was I doing? Joey was sexy, and gorgeous, and downright debonair. He struck me as the kind of man who did not lack experience in this area.

It'd been so long since I'd had a man in my bed that my side of the mattress sagged from disproportionate overuse. Aside from one short relationship in college, Kyle was the only guy I'd ever slept with. I'd spent years going on a lot of first dates, and I have a rule against sex on first dates. The resulting dry spell had turned into a drought. And I thought this was the way to end it? I hoped I remembered what to do well enough to avoid making a fool of myself.

Grabbing the glasses and feeding Darcy a biscuit to keep her quiet, I peeked into the living room. Joey was perched on the edge of my navy jacquard sofa, his fingers steepled under his chin and an unmistakably unnerved look on his face.

Thank you, God, for letting it not be just me.

"I had this at a party and bought a bottle the next day," I said as I walked into the room.

He jerked his head up and a slow grin spread across his face. I handed him his glass and pulled the clip out of my hair, letting it fall into its soft mahogany waves around my shoulders.

Sitting on the sofa next to him, I watched as he took a sip. "It's good," he said.

He reached across the cushion between us and laid a hand on my bare knee. I jumped and splattered wine onto the rug, but he didn't move. Neither did I, except to drain the rest of my glass in one gulp. I set it on the table and put my hand over his. Joey finished his glass just as quickly and put it next to mine.

"Really good." I wasn't even sure who said that. My eyes locked with his.

He wound his other arm around my waist and pulled me to him, his lips crushing mine for an instant before he parted them. He flicked the tip of his tongue into my mouth and I gasped, pulling him closer before he laid me back onto the cushions.

"Now can I hear about those fantasies?" he asked.

"They're sort of show more than tell."

"Show me."

I reached up and traced the line of his jaw with my fingertips, trailing them over his lips before I pulled his head down and kissed him. He moved his mouth to my throat, his tongue leaving a trail to the hollow, where my pulse threatened to pound right through my skin. He paused there, then planted a line of soft kisses along my collarbone to my shoulder, pushing the strap on my dress out of the way.

My fingers curled into his hair and I closed my eyes as everything but Joey disappeared from my radar.

He rested one hand alongside my head, pushing himself up easily and staring at me as though he wanted to memorize every freckle. I took a hitching breath. No one had ever looked at me quite that way.

"You know," he said, trailing the fingertips of his other hand in loose patterns on my shoulder, "you're not the only one with fantasies."

Holy Manolos.

"Good to know," I whispered, reaching up to flick open the buttons on his shirt. I worked the Windsor knot out of his tie and threw it, pushing the shirt open and running my fingers over the smooth skin underneath. I knew he was gorgeous, but the rock-hard lines under my fingers said he was in great shape, too.

"You want to know mine?" I pulled his shirt free of the waistband of his pants and pushed it back over his arms. He took it off and tossed it onto the chaise, and the way his muscles worked for the simple motions made my pulse pick up more steam.

"I'm waiting." He leaned over me. I propped myself up on my elbows and kissed him, sliding my tongue over his. He put one hand on the nape of my neck, then moved it down, unzipping my dress in a single motion. I wriggled my arms free and fell back into the pillows, but he stayed with me, never breaking the kiss.

"It sort of starts with you carrying me to bed," I whispered against his lips.

"I heard that part," he said, raising his head a touch and brushing one hand over the black satin of my bra. "But my fantasy starts with you asking me to."

"Consider yourself asked."

His chest jumped under my fingers with a sharp breath, and he lowered his lips back to mine. I lost myself in the kiss, sliding my hands to his bare shoulders. I moved my lips along the roughness of his jaw, pausing to swipe my tongue over his earlobe. The sound that came from his throat told me he liked that, so I did it again. He buried his hands in my hair, his breath speeding, then twisted and dropped to one knee next to the sofa.

He kissed me again before he stood and scooped me into his arms. My whole body shuddered.

A thousand breathless dreams.

And this was really happening.

We were halfway down the hall when the doorbell rang.

Joey froze. "You've got to be kidding."

I dropped my forehead to his shoulder, trying to catch my breath. Pressing my lips against his skin, I murmured a string of swearwords that would make Bubba the moonshiner blush. "Go away," I finished, bouncing my feet and turning Joey's face toward mine. "Where were we?"

"Wondering why someone's ringing your doorbell at twelve-thirty?" The soft look on his face dissolved into the tense lines I remembered from the parking lot.

I twisted my head toward the foyer. "Shit. You don't think Bubba followed us, do you?"

He sighed and set me on my feet. I grabbed for my dress and slipped my arms back into it, dropping another kiss at the nape of his neck as he turned back for the front of the house.

"If there's not a nuclear bomb in the house next door, I'm going to hate this person on principle for the rest of my days." I zipped my dress, moving toward the door.

Joey put a hand on my elbow. "Let me." He looked down. "I need a shirt."

Standing back, I admired the physique that had felt so nice under my fingers a few moments before. His shoulders were broad, the muscles rising into ridges where they met his neck. His biceps were defined and impressive without being veiny and scary. The twin divots at the base of his spine that just peeked over his belt hinted at a sculpted rear end and made my pulse race again.

"I'm not convinced you should ever wear a shirt again," I said, leaning against the wall.

He shot me a grin and ducked into the living room to retrieve his, pulling it on as he walked to the door. He peered out the trio of windows that lined the top and turned to me with a raised eyebrow. "It's a woman. Who looks nothing like Bubba."

What? My best friend, Jenna, was the only woman I could think of who would drop by unannounced, and if she was ringing my doorbell after midnight on a Tuesday, catastrophe was afoot. My stomach wrung as I crossed to the door.

I jerked it open to find a puffy-faced Ashton Okerson.

CHAPTER SIXTEEN

"Ashton?" I tossed a confused glance at Joey, who was leaning on the edge of the open door. He raised his eyebrows and I waved Ashton inside. "What can I do for you?" I asked.

"I," she choked on the syllable, dissolving into more tears.

I put an arm around her. "Come in," I said gently, ushering her to the sofa. I heard the latch click as Joey shut the door behind us.

I sat with Ashton, who buried her face in my shoulder and sobbed for a good five minutes. Joey stood in the doorway, a worried line running the length of his forehead. I thought about the questions I'd asked him about Tony and gambling, and felt a little sick when I considered that she might be about to tell me she did know why her son was dead.

When she finally sat up, I didn't think her own mother would recognize her swollen face.

"What on Earth?" I asked, locking my violet eyes with her blue ones.

"The sheriff," she spat, hauling in a deep breath and trying again. "He closed the case file. The coroner says TJ died of liver failure, and they've stopped looking. *If* they were looking in the first place. He's having a press conference in the morning, and I just...I got in my car and I drove and drove, and I finally asked Grant to send me your address. I hope I'm not intruding." Her eyes jumped to Joey and his half-buttoned shirt and she bit her lip. "I am. I'm so sorry." She moved to stand up, and I put a restraining hand on her arm.

"Not at all." I threw Joey an apologetic glance and he waved a hand, shaking his head in dismissal.

"I just didn't know where to go."

"Liver failure would track with a Vicodin overdose," I said gently, my brain switching gears. Did we have it all wrong? Had TJ killed himself?

"My son did not overdose on Vicodin," Ashton said, dropping her head into her hands and sobbing. "No one believes me. I know my baby. It's just not...there's no way."

I stared, my brain rewinding through years of repressed memories to my own mother crying almost the same thing.

"I believe you," I said.

Ashton sat up, sniffling, and I passed her a tissue box.

"Why?" she asked me.

I took a deep breath and closed my eyes.

"This happened to someone I loved once. Someone my mom loved," I began, glancing at Joey. Concern creased his brow and he crossed to the sofa, sitting on the arm and laying a hand on my shoulder.

"I guess it's always been part of the reason I do what I do." My voice cracked, and Joey's fingers sank into my shoulder, massaging the tightening muscles there. "No one believed her, either, and I saw so many things I thought I could help. Truth to find, injustices to expose. All the noble crap I tell myself when I'm chasing a story."

I took a shaky breath.

"Did you ever find out what happened to your friend?" Ashton asked.

"He was my mom's fiancee," I said. "And no. Nobody would listen. By the time my friend's dad did, it was too late."

"I'm so sorry. I know the feeling."

"I'm listening," I said, trying to smile. "Have you thought of anything else? Any other person who might have wanted something bad to happen to TJ?" I studied her carefully. Her swollen eyes told me nothing was off the table, and I was out of reasons not to ask.

"Is Tony into anything he shouldn't be? Or was he?" I asked, reaching involuntarily for Joey's hand and lacing my fingers in his. "Gambling? Drugs? Anything that could make TJ a target for someone who's trying to hurt y'all?"

She shook her head slowly, her face a blank mask of grief and confusion. "Tony was one of the cleanest guys in the league. His whole career, he never took anything he wasn't prescribed. He never cheated. He's a homebody."

"No steroids?" My grip on Joey's hand tightened. Forgive me. "Nothing organized crime would have a hand in?"

"Organized crime? Like *The Godfather*? Jesus, no. Tony would never." No doubt crept into her raw voice as she spoke.

I leaned my head back on Joey's chest. A soft chuckle rumbled under my ear.

"That puts us back to locals. Most likely local kids," I said. "What links TJ and Sydney? Anything besides their relationship?"

Ashton shook her head. "They had classes together. It's a small school, though. They all have the same teachers."

"How long have they known each other? Y'all only moved to the island a year or so ago, right?" I asked.

"Yeah." She nodded. "They grew up together in the summers, but they didn't start dating til after we moved out there."

Oh.

"Did Sydney date anyone before TJ?" I asked, a thousand Lifetime movies playing in my head.

"I'm sure she did, but I don't know who."

"Luke Bosley?" The creepy cold look in his eyes haunted my thoughts.

Ashton sucked on her lower lip. "Maybe? I don't know."

"Can you find out?" I asked.

"I can ask Tiffany."

I twisted my mouth to one side. "Any chance she's still awake?" I didn't want to be a pain, but I had no help coming from the cops and precious little to go on.

Ashton sat back. "You think someone might have killed TJ over who he was dating?"

I sighed. "If I'm being flat honest with you, Ashton, I haven't the first damned clue what I think. I'm doing a lot of flying blind and grasping at very thin threads. But I've covered a lot of murder cases in my years at the crime desk, and sex and money are always at the top of the motive list. Since TJ and Syd didn't have any money, I'm betting on the former."

"They weren't having sex. They were thinking about it. We'd just had that talk, because he said maybe this summer, when she came back from France, they might."

I smiled. "I didn't mean to imply anything. Just that unless there's an honest-to-God psychopath running around out there, we're dealing with an emotional crime. And they tend to be motivated by things like jealousy. Especially in a population where hormones are raging."

She tilted her head to one side and stared at me for a long moment. "You're talking like it was a murder."

"Isn't that what you think?"

She pulled her iPhone out of her bag, her children smiling at me from the back of her custom case. All three of them.

"I didn't think I'd convince anyone of that," she said. "Thank you. If you'll excuse me for two minutes, I'll get your answer from Tiff. She can sleep another time. If she sleeps at all."

I smiled a thank you and led Joey to the kitchen.

"Wow." He leaned on the edge of the yellow-tiled countertop and folded his arms across his chest.

"What do you think?"

"She's telling the truth about the dad," he said.

"I thought so, too."

"I asked around. Couldn't find a story anywhere about that guy so much as taking a leak in an alley. Found a couple people who tried to get him into something, but they said they never could."

"They wouldn't care enough about that now to hurt his kid?" I asked.

"Not likely." He shook his head. "I like your theory, if you want my honest opinion."

"Thanks."

"And I like the way you were with her. You're a good person, Nichelle. She needs help, and you'll help her, regardless of whether there's anything in it for you."

"I would. The story is a nice bonus, but this became about a lot more than the story the minute Sheriff Zeke made up his mind. I can't sit here and do nothing while this happens again."

"And that's what I don't like." Joey fixed me with a Baptist-preacher stare. "The cops are out. The sheriff's closing the case and he's not going to help you anymore. Once the press conference is over, the rest of the media will likely disperse. Which leaves you trying to pin a murder on someone who was crafty enough to get away with it. If they're that smart, they'll figure out you're looking. Maybe before you figure out who they are. Which means you could get hurt. That, I do not like."

I shivered under his gaze, though it wasn't cold in the room. "I can't walk away," I said. "They did that to my mom. It broke her. She's never been on another date, and Randy died when I was fourteen years old."

A tear escaped my eye before I could brush it away, and he pulled me into a hug. "I'm sorry," he whispered.

"Thanks." I swiped at my face. "Just don't give me a hard time about chasing this one, and we're good. I appreciate that you worry." I kissed his neck. "But I get a pass this time."

"Be careful, okay?"

"Will do."

"Nichelle?" Ashton called from the hallway.

I squeezed Joey and walked back to the foyer.

"Tiffany said Sydney's only ever had one other boyfriend, the year before she started going with TJ. But it wasn't Luke. It was Eli Morris."

"Any relation to Coach Morris?" I knew the answer before she opened her mouth.

"His only son."

* * *

Joey walked Ashton to her car while I wrote down everything she'd told me.

"I feel bad, letting her drive home," he said when he came back in, flopping down on the couch. I glanced at him from the corner of my eye, trying to focus on my notes and not how unbelievably sexy he looked. Stubble shaded his jaw, and his shirt was still untucked and half-unbuttoned. No tie. Yum.

Ashton had sort of mucked up our moment. Now I had a story to write, hopefully an exclusive until the sheriff's press conference. But since I wasn't any closer to figuring out how the *Post* had gotten the inside scoop, I wasn't sure of that, so time was not my friend.

"Yeah. I wish she'd stayed here. But she swears she'll be fine," I said. "I called Parker and he was going to call her husband and tell him she's on her way."

Joey nodded.

I put my notes down and reached for my computer.

"You have work to do?" he asked.

I scrunched my nose apologetically. "I really do. I want to get this up on the web early, so I need to get it ready and send it to Bob. He'll post it online at the crack of dawn. And maybe he'll be less annoyed with me as a bonus."

"He's not really mad at you," Joey said. "We covered this already."

"All the same, I'll feel better when he's fully back in my corner. I've been taking shit from the sports editor all week, and with Shelby filling in for Les, I can't handle anyone else gunning for me."

"What's wrong with the sports editor?"

"He's pissed because Parker asked me to take this story. Really has his panties in a bunch. It's creepy, because Spence has always been a super nice guy, and he's gone all stalker boy on me this week." I paused. "You don't think the *Post* got their story tip from him, do you?"

Joey frowned. "Couldn't he lose his job over that?"

"He could. At the very least, Bob would put him on leave. But someone who works for us had to have told them. I didn't run anything about it, and the families haven't talked to anyone but me."

"But to be fair, it's a small town," Joey said. "Everyone knows everyone's business out there. So someone else could have told the reporter from the *Post*."

"Maybe. But Bob and Rick thought it came from me, which means they have good enough reason to think it came from our newsroom."

"Why would the sports guy do that?"

"It gave away my exclusive before I was ready to run it, and got me in hot water with the bosses as a bonus. Anyone who's worked with me for ten minutes knows that's the surest way to get to me."

"I suppose it's possible." He shook his head. "I'm sorry."

I pondered it for another three seconds before I stood to walk him to the door.

"I don't have time to be worried about who Spence is talking to right now. Dead people first. Asshat sports guys later."

He stopped at the door and turned to face me, pulling me into his arms. "Where do I fit in?"

I kissed him, teasing the tip of his tongue with mine. "Wherever I can shoehorn in a stolen kiss or three," I said. "I'm sorry about tonight."

"Don't apologize. Your story is important right now. I'll wait. You still have plans for Friday?"

"Yes. I had to bail on Jenna, too. I'm going to a street dance in Mathews."

A dance I had a date for. Oy. Why couldn't things just be easy?

"I see."

"Enjoy your dance. Be careful." He smiled, opening the door before he put one finger under my chin and planted a soft kiss on my cheek. "I'll call you."

"You'd better." I closed the door behind him and watched him walk down the steps, wishing the evening had ended differently. Damn Zeke Waters and his craptastic timing.

"All right, Darcy. Let's catch us a murderer, shall we?" I asked the dog, going back to my computer.

I thought about trying Waters, but didn't want to piss him off. It was coming up on two.

TJ Okerson's death has officially been ruled a suicide by Mathews County Sheriff Zeke Waters, the boy's mother told the Richmond Telegraph *late Tuesday.*

"They're closing the case file," Ashton Okerson said, sobbing.

Ashton said the sheriff told her and her husband, three-time Super Bowl champion quarterback Tony Okerson, that the coroner said TJ died of liver failure.

That, along with the empty prescription bottle of Vicodin found at the scene with TJ and the evidence of alcohol consumption at the party he was attending, was apparently enough for Waters to rule out foul play and close his investigation. Waters wasn't immediately available for comment early Wednesday.

The Telegraph *reported yesterday that the Okerson family doesn't believe TJ took his own life, and Ashton said in this exclusive interview that the coroner's report doesn't change her feelings about that.*

I finished up with the sheriff's prior comments about the simplest explanation usually being the right one, and teased the press conference he was planning for the following day. I sent the story to Bob with an explanatory email and closed my computer at three-fifteen.

Darcy took longer than usual about doing her business when I let her outside, barking at the pitch-dark back corner of the yard until I stepped outside in my bare feet to carry her back in the house before she woke up the entire Fan.

"Spring. The rabbits come back. Yay."

Though most of Thumper's cousins that visited our yard were

twice as big as Darcy, she had no qualms about letting them know whose territory they were on. I locked the door and made a mental note to get a new bulb for the light.

She growled at the door while I set my coffee cup out for the morning, then gave up and followed me to bed.

I closed my eyes thinking of Joey's kisses, trying to keep my mom's anguished sobs and Randy's easy smile from haunting my dreams for another night. Ashton and Tony would end this with an answer if it was the last thing I ever did. I might not get the one they wanted, but I wasn't giving up.

CHAPTER SEVENTEEN

I SIDESTEPPED, punched, and *ap-chagi*'ed my way halfheartedly through body combat the next morning, what I knew about Mathews High occupying way more of my brain space than the workout.

TJ was a good kid by all accounts: happy, popular, and in love for the first time. No history of mental illness or depressive behavior. Not a damn thing there added up to suicide.

The sheriff was determined to rule it such and move on, but he also had a cousin who made black-market moonshine. And TJ might have been drinking it. Sydney had likely been drinking it. Except her jar had a faded label. I still had nothing for that.

I added Zeke's name to my growing mental suspect list. I didn't really think he'd hurt the kids, but I was surer by the minute that he was turning a blind eye to whoever had. I'd worked cops and courts long enough to know good ol' boys' networks run deep.

Then there was Evelyn. Instinct (and every true crime novel I'd ever read) said the M.O. in this case made it likely the killer was female. I could hardly wait for the dance Friday night. I just needed to corner her. If the tears I'd seen at the church Monday were guilty ones, it'd take about five minutes of grilling her to get a full confession and probably a blood sample.

Luke would be a tougher nut to crack. For me, anyway. He'd almost spilled something, I could swear, to Parker at the funeral reception. My plan was to have Kyle butter him up with compliments about his pitching. He definitely liked the limelight.

Ashton had added someone else to my list with her phone call the night before, too. Eli Morris was Sydney's ex. If the kids all moved in the same circles, chances were good he was at the party where TJ died. And jealousy is a powerful motive.

But no matter which way I turned the puzzle pieces, the liver failure was the stubborn one.

Boys have more of a tendency to be violent. Some kind of poisoning spoke of a woman's hand. But how did twiggy little Evelyn force-feed a boy TJ's size and strength enough pills to cause his young, healthy liver to shut down?

Oh, shit.

I ran out of my class with five minutes left, leaving messages for Tony, Ashton, and Parker before I got into the shower. I hadn't asked to see TJ's medical records before, but what if there was something else going on with the kid's liver? Something that would make it easier to kill than your average teenager's? I didn't know what that could be, exactly, but it was worth looking into. How many helmets to the torso had he taken in his lifetime?

Leapfrogging ahead and assuming that was the case, was I looking for someone who knew that? Or was it an accident?

So many questions.

And Bob's half-smile when I walked into his empty office for the morning news budget meeting with my hair still wet told me he wanted answers.

"That was a good piece this morning. It's already on the web and it's pinging around the Internet like a celebutante sex video."

I grinned. "Well, good. I think." I dropped into my customary high-backed orange velour wing chair. "Your face says I'm not totally off your shit list."

"There's a lot going on here this week." He sighed, slumping back in his chair. "Do I think you fed the *Post* a tip? No. I know you better than that. The story is everything to you. Just like it was to me. I also know this one has a personal tic for you, and you're not going to let it go. To be honest, I had my reservations when Parker told me he was asking you to take it. I gave him the green light because I knew you'd do a good job with the suicide story, show the family respect, and for his sake, I was hoping everyone else would follow your lead. It didn't ever occur to me that it would turn into a one-woman murder investigation."

I opened my mouth and then snapped it shut. "Bob, these people —" I began.

He raised one hand. "Deserve to know what happened to their kid? I know. I agree. Go get it. But for the love of God, watch yourself. Moonshiners and murderers and God knows what, and there are miles of woods and water out there that would be really good for hiding a nosy reporter."

"Point taken."

His eyes told me something was still bothering him, but the rest of the staff began to trickle in, and he shrugged helplessly and sat back.

Eunice came bearing a platter of something that smelled heavenly. I reached under the foil and came up with a square of cornbread speckled with cheese and sausage.

"You're like the evil diet fairy," I said, biting into the still-warm breakfast bread and grinning at Eunice. "I bet I'm putting back every calorie I burned at the gym this morning."

"You might be surprised," Eunice helped herself to one, and pushed the tray toward Bob. Since he'd had a heart attack not even twelve months before, and was on a strict low-fat, low-cholesterol diet, I frowned at her as I swallowed.

"My sister's been doctoring Grandmomma's recipes to make them more waistline-friendly, and I made this with fat free buttermilk, egg whites, turkey sausage, and low fat cheddar."

It tasted sinful. But it was healthy?

"I retract my previous statement." I grinned. "You are the best kind of diet fairy." I snagged another square and passed one to Bob before the rest of them disappeared.

"We do enough sitting in front of computers around here," Eunice said. "If I can trick folks into eating healthy, I'm doing a favor for my fellow man, right?"

"And a much appreciated good deed it is," Bob said around a mouthful of food.

Bob started the meeting and ran quickly through the copy highlights for the day. Halfway through sports, my cell phone buzzed a text from Tony: "Got your message. Call me."

Spence paused, turning slowly to me. "Do you need to take that? Don't let my little section rundown keep you from stealing a story from anyone else this morning."

"Spence, that's enough," Bob said.

The rest of the section editors squirmed in their seats and focused on the photos and front pages dotting Bob's walls. I met Spence's glare with one of my own, biting my tongue.

Bob switched to the business editor.

Studying my notes to avoid Spence's go-straight-to-Hell looks and everyone else's curiosity, I tapped the heel of my pearl-rimmed, black Nicholas Kirkwood sandals on the floor through the rest of the meeting. When Bob threw us out with his customary, "my office is not newsworthy, so get out and find me something to print," I popped to my feet.

"Nichelle," Bob said. "Hang out."

I twisted my mouth to one side. "I have a text that needs attention. Can I come back?"

He nodded. "Go on, but we need to talk."

Yes, we did.

I half-ran to my desk, grabbing the phone before I sat down to dial Tony's number. Please, Lord. A tiny break.

He picked up on the third ring, and I barely let him get the "hello," out before I blurted my question.

"Was there something wrong with TJ's liver?" I asked. "Something that might have made it fail easier than it should have?"

"I don't know," Tony sounded hesitant.

"You don't know? How can you not know if your kid had liver

problems that might have killed him?" I tried to rein in my frustration. "I'm sorry. I'm not—look, I can't imagine how hard this is for you, but you two seem to be pretty involved in what's going on with your kids. The coroner says liver failure. Ashton swears he didn't kill himself. If his liver was compromised, it might help me figure out what happened to him."

"I didn't push him," Tony said. "He played because he wanted to."

"Even though he was hurt?" I guessed.

"He took a nasty hit in football game his freshman year," Tony said. "Broke a rib. And it damaged his liver. The doctors said it was a miracle it still functioned. That's why I know he wasn't drinking too much, and why I'm sure he didn't OD on Vicodin."

"Why the hell did they prescribe him Vicodin if he had liver trouble?" I asked, scribbling down his comment, which made very little sense.

"They didn't, at first. But every other kind of pain medicine there is made him sick. He can't play baseball if he can't eat."

I nearly choked on the "so then don't play," offering a sympathetic silence instead. What makes sports the be all and end all of everything for some folks, anyway?

"TJ was careful about drinking. Never more than one or two, and not usually during a playing season at all. And he would never have taken Vicodin with booze. He knew better. He treated his body well. Taking good care of yourself is how you last through a long playing career."

Considering Tony's revelation, my brain careened off in another direction. As much as the memory of Ashton's swollen face haunted me, what if I was projecting?

"Tony," I began, clicking my pen in and out and searching for words that wouldn't sting. "If TJ knew that, about the booze and the painkillers, well..." I sighed. "Wouldn't that be a pretty effective way for him to commit suicide?"

Tony was quiet for so long I wondered if the call had dropped. "I suppose," he said finally. "But my son did not do this. I know it as sure as I know my passing record. Ashton said you believed her."

"I did. I do. I think. Every time I think I've made sense of part of this, the floor drops out from under me again."

"That, I really do understand," he said.

I tapped the pen on my notes, mulling my suspect list. "Would any of the other kids have known about this? The thing with TJ's liver?"

"I honestly have no idea," Tony said. "I don't know why they would, but maybe he might have told someone. Why?"

I jotted that down. Another blurry piece for my Mathews puzzle. "Just trying to find a thread to grasp today." I was quiet for a minute, Ashton's raw voice from the night before echoing in my ears. "Hey, Tony—did coach Morris know about TJ's liver?"

"It happened before we moved here. I don't remember ever mentioning it specifically, but the coaches look over the kids' medical records. So probably. But I'm not sure."

And if the coach knew, maybe his son did, too? I kept that to myself. It was thin, but maybe it would lead somewhere.

I thanked Tony for calling and disconnected the line before dialing my favorite coroner.

Ten minutes on the phone with Jacque Morgan, a senior medical examiner who shared my love of great shoes and claimed to be eternally grateful that I'd shared my eBay secrets with her, didn't get me much. Except that Vicodin overdose usually presents as suffocation.

"Everyone's different, though," she said. "People's bodies react differently to different substances. And I didn't work that case, so I can't tell you anything for sure."

"Who did work it?" I asked.

"Drake Carmichael. But the official statement is all he's cleared to release. They made that very clear at the staff meeting they called this morning."

"If the kid's liver was weak?" I asked, trying to sound hypothetical.

"It might fail before the lungs," she replied. "Again, not my case."

I thanked her and hung up, my watch telling me I needed to get on the road if I was going to make it to the press conference. I wasn't sure if I hoped Tony and Ashton would be there or not. I wanted to talk to Sydney's parents, too. Whatever had happened to the kids was linked, so digging around one was bound to help out with the other.

Throwing a glance at Bob's office, I pondered how mad he'd get at me for skipping out and decided he'd be a lot madder if I was late to the press conference and missed something. I'd catch up with him later.

I punched the button for the elevator, wondering if I was setting myself up to crash into a dead end.

* * *

Snagging the seat next to Lyle when I got into Mathews city hall, I pulled out a notebook and pen before turning to him.

"Have a nice weekend?" I asked.

"I've seen nicer. But at least no one else died." He shook his head. "I'm ready for all these TV cameras to disappear, I'll say that."

I glanced around. There were a dozen camera crews and a handful more reporters in the little council chambers. Charlie stood to my right, directing her cameraman to the extra footage she wanted. CNN was behind her, the Newport News stations scattered around the perimeter of the room. I scanned the faces of the seated reporters, but I couldn't tell the *Post* from *USA Today* based on sight.

Lyle cleared his throat. "In fairness, I have to tell you, you did a good thing with that story you ran on Bobbi's club. She's a great gal, and Dorothy Scott has been so ridiculous about this whole thing it's embarrassing. It needed to be printed. I know Zeke was glad to be rid of the conflict."

I nodded a thank you and considered asking him about the sheriff, but decided against it. Yet, anyway. I had some guys at the Richmond PD who skated the line between friend and source, and I knew working in a small town, Lyle was more likely to have a strong relationship with Waters. Since he used his first name and a fond tone when he spoke of him, I guessed it wasn't a strong hatred.

"Why didn't you run it?" I asked.

"My managing editor is Mr. Dorothy, Junior," he said, smirking.

"Damned if this isn't Mayberry come to life." I shook my head. "I grew up in Dallas and went from there to Syracuse to Richmond. But everyone really knows everyone out here."

He chuckled. "I don't think too hard about that. They all know each other's business, too. If I ruminate on that, I'll decide my life's work has no point."

"Local grapevine beats the paper?"

"More often than not."

I nodded understanding, and we both faced the front of the room when Waters stepped to the podium there.

He thanked everyone for coming and stood up straight, playing to the CNN camera behind Charlie.

"This has been a difficult week," he said. "For these two families, who could not be with us today, and for all of Mathews County. We are a big extended family, here, and tragedy hurts everyone. TJ and Sydney were bright young people with promising futures, and the entire community is poorer for their loss."

I scribbled, and Lyle held up a voice recorder.

"That said, I have the coroner's report here on TJ's cause of death." Waters waved a folder. "The autopsy revealed that he died of liver failure. That, coupled with evidence we found at the scene, has resulted in his death being officially ruled a suicide." He cut his dark eyes to me. "Despite what you might have read in the paper."

I rolled my eyes, but kept taking notes.

"This case is closed. And while we've enjoyed having you folks with us, we understand that you'll want to be on your way."

I looked up when he said the last, suddenly pondering Lyle's earlier comment.

Having the media underfoot wasn't fun for cops, or local reporters, certainly. But the "don't let the door hit you in the ass on your way out" didn't jive with the "we are family" crap they were throwing off, either. Bobbi had said her business had picked up some even before my story ran, with all the camera crews in town. Elmer said the same thing. And the cute little bakery where I'd stopped for coffee had a line of press people out the door and halfway down the block. Everyone was yakking about apricot scones, which I didn't get to try because they made them fresh every morning and were sold out before I made it to the front of the line.

The media was good for the local economy, which Bobbi said had been hurting.

So why did the sheriff and Lyle want everyone gone so badly?

And why hadn't Lyle ever done a story on the moonshiners? I mean, if I lived out here, it'd be the first thing on my must-get list.

I shot him a sideways glance. His eyes were trained on Waters, who'd just opened the floor to questions.

"Was there ever a reason to suspect foul play in this case, sheriff?" Charlie glanced at me as she asked that. So much for "let's go get the sports guys."

"We did our due diligence in the case, but our findings point to suicide," he said. "As I said earlier this week, the simplest answer is usually the right one."

I snorted softly, and the sheriff glared. I'd covered some pretty damned convoluted things in my time, and this was ranking up there with the best of them. I could not make myself buy his line.

Raising my hand, I returned his unblinking stare. He called on every other reporter in the room first, answering questions about the size of his department, the discovery of the body, and everything in between, before he nodded to me. "Miss Clarke?"

Slowly, I lowered my arm. "Do you have the tox screen back?"

I knew damn well he didn't. Aaron had cases in Richmond he'd been waiting on tox results for over two months on. And I'd heard nothing from Kyle about it.

"We do not."

I could have heard a Tic-Tac drop. I wondered if I was killing my exclusive, but I knew from the looks he was shooting my way that he was pissed and wouldn't talk to me outside a crowded room where it would be conspicuous for him to ignore me. "So, you don't know what caused the liver failure?" I asked.

"There was alcohol present, and an empty bottle of narcotics in the boy's pocket." Waters focused on CNN again. "As you well know."

I opened my mouth to say that wasn't exactly scientific evidence, but he picked up his folder and nodded to the crowd.

"If y'all will excuse me. Thank you for your time."

He disappeared out the side door while the gallery muttered, scribbled, and looked at me.

"You know he's probably right," Lyle said, looking around at the cameras.

"I know he thinks he is." I pinched my lips shut. I didn't trust Lyle anymore. Nodding a goodbye, I slipped out before Charlie could get her cameraman gathered up and follow.

* * *

Stepping into the *Star Wars* battle scene that is a high school passing period, I managed to navigate to the office unscathed, save for getting my toes crushed under a rolling backpack that was apparently carrying the entire library. I scurried under the sign marked "Administration," shutting the heavy door on the noise in the hallway.

The secretary I'd met the week before smiled when I looked up from examining my shoes. No damage, unbelievably. I didn't remember getting to class being so obstacle-ridden. I shook off the feeling of age that came with the thought and returned Norma's smile.

"How are you, honey? Those articles you did about TJ were nice," she said. "I can't believe his poor momma and daddy think somebody killed him. So sad. But I hear the sheriff has closed the case and ruled it a suicide. We half expected all the city reporters to be long gone by lunchtime. So what's on your mind today?"

I returned her bright smile. What was on my mind was that there was likely a murderer in the building. But I couldn't tell Norma that.

"I just feel so bad for the Okersons," I said, stalling. "I don't have any children, so I can't imagine what they're going through."

She fanned herself, dropping her hand over her heart. "I have two, and I don't want to think about it. I love those girls more than life itself."

"How old are they?" I asked, making small talk until I could find a way to ask her about Luke and Evelyn. And Eli, too.

"My oldest is twenty. She's a junior at RAU this year. And my baby is a sophomore here."

"You do not look old enough to have a daughter in college." I widened my eyes and waved a hand and she giggled.

"Why, thank you. Terry was just telling me last night how soft my skin is. Oil of Olay. My grandmomma was ninety-three when she passed and didn't look a minute over sixty in her casket. She swore by it."

"Terry? As in, Coach Morris?" I asked. She'd seemed sweet on him the first time we'd met. But didn't she say he was her sister's ex? Because...weird. Then again, how many single men in their early forties could there be in Mathews? Beggars and choosers, and all that.

"We've gotten closer here lately." Her Cover Girl True Red lips tipped up in a dreamy smile. "He's a wonderful man."

"He has a son, too, right?" I crossed to the counter and leaned casually against it.

"Eli." She nodded. "He's a talented boy. My favorite nephew."

Nephew. Stepson? A twinge shot through my head when I considered that for more than three and a half seconds, so I let it go.

"He goes to school here, too?"

"He's a junior. Straight A's. Drama club, baseball team. He's a good boy."

I smiled. "I'm sure y'all are very proud. Does he have a girlfriend?"

A dark look flashed across her face so quickly it could've been a trick of the light. "He's too busy for girls."

At sixteen. Uh huh.

I just nodded. "I know the feeling. Speaking of girls, do you know anything about Sydney Cobb?"

She shrugged. "Not really. She was popular with the kids. Like her mother. Tiff and I were friends once. Syd didn't ever really get into trouble, so I didn't see much of her up here."

I nodded. "There was a girl at the funeral service Monday," I said. "Tiny, blonde, pretty. She was really upset. But I haven't seen her

SMALL TOWN SPIN   627

anywhere since. I'm a little worried about her, with everything that's happened around here. I mean, I went to a five-A school in Texas, and we only lost two kids out of my class in four years. To a car accident. Y'all are way ahead of the national curve, and the police swear suicide spreads through teenagers faster than a bad case of mono in a game of spin the bottle."

She tipped her head to one side. "Blonde, you said? Oh. Evie? I wonder if that was Evelyn Miney?"

I fixed an interested, but noncommittal, expression on my face.

"I bet it was," she continued when I didn't say anything. "She had a thing for TJ. Everyone knew it. Kind of sad, really. I feel sorry for her. Lost her momma to cancer a few years back. And you know, I can't recall having seen her this week." She flipped a folder open and ran her finger about halfway down the paper inside before she turned a few pages and looked up at me. "She's been out of school all week. And her daddy goes away on business a fair amount." She pressed her fingers to her lips, reaching for the phone. "There's just been so much going on, no one bothered to ask why she wasn't here."

I watched, pinching my lips together, as she pulled off her clip-on earring and dialed the phone. Her expression went from worry to panic as she pressed the button in the cradle to disconnect. "She's not picking up."

She dialed again, only three keys this time, and I closed my eyes. Not another one. I felt a teeny bit bad for suspecting Evelyn. What if she'd just been sad about her friends? Just because they stopped talking to her didn't mean she wouldn't miss them.

I half-listened while Norma told the sheriff's dispatcher to send a deputy by to check on Evelyn, drumming my fingers on the desk and wondering about Luke. I had zero in the way of good excuses to ask Norma about him. Maybe I could get something from the coach, though.

"Does Coach Morris have a class right now?" I asked when she hung up. "I have just a few more things I'd like to talk to him about."

"No. He's at lunch. Probably in his office." She watched the phone like she could will it to ring.

"I hope she's all right," I said, turning back for the door. The hallway was silent, the kids all sorted into their classrooms.

"Me, too." Norma nodded.

I hurried down to the gym, hoping I wasn't about to have another dead kid to write about as much as I was hoping the coach would tell me something useful.

"Hello? Woman on deck," I called, poking my head into the boys' locker room. No answer.

I stepped inside, keeping my eyes level—just in case. "Coach Morris?"

I heard a clatter.

"Coach?" I walked toward the glass-walled office, but found it empty. Unease settled over me in a thick blanket as I walked the locker rows, looking for the source of the noise. "Hello?"

A metal-on-metal squeal sounded behind me and I nearly jumped out of my skin, grabbing the edge of a nearby bank of lockers to keep my balance as I whirled, images of ten zillion teen slasher flicks I'd watched with Kyle years before flashing through my head. There are few places creepier than an empty school.

I didn't see anyone behind me, but someone was in there. I put one hand on the locker and slipped my heels off, stowing one in my bag and turning the other stiletto-out in my hand. Creeping silently along the concrete floor in my bare feet, I peered around the edge of each locker bank before I scurried to the next, Kirkwood sandal raised and ready.

I was not getting chopped up and stuffed into lockers in a building full of people without a fight.

Soft footfalls sounded around the corner that led to the door. I held my breath, leaning back and locking my eyes on the doorway.

The door clicked shut.

I tiptoed to the little entry area, my hand on the cinderblock wall, steeling myself before I hopped around the corner, stiletto in the air.

The vestibule was empty, the door closed.

I sagged back against the wall and caught my breath. Something strange was going on in Mathews County.

I slid my shoes back onto my feet before I walked out into the gym. I found Morris crossing the basketball court.

"Hey there," he called, smiling. "Norma said you were looking for me. I must have passed you when I went to turn my attendance sheet in. She gets irritated with me for keeping it 'til the end of the day. I'm trying to do better." He grinned a goofy schoolboy-crush grin that matched her Coach-Morris-is-so-dreamy smile. It was like Peyton Place. With tractors.

"I just wanted to chat for a few minutes if you have time," I said, scanning the gym. "You didn't see anyone else in here on your way down, did you?"

He shook his head. "This is my free period. There shouldn't be anyone down here for another hour."

I nodded, keeping the fact that there had been to myself.

He waved me into the locker room, gesturing for me to have a seat in his office. I paused on my way, noticing the shiny locks hanging from the locker doors.

"Those weren't there last week," I said, turning a questioning look to Morris.

"One of the boys had some pills go missing out of his locker," he said. "I told them to bring locks in."

"What kind of pills?" My thoughts flashed to the empty bottle the cops found on TJ.

"Luke Bosley is diabetic," Morris said. "He takes pills to manage his blood sugar. His mother was ticked about having to pay full price for an early refill."

"Pills," I said, walking toward the office. "Not shots? I thought that was more common for adults."

Morris shrugged. "I don't know a whole lot about it. Luke's folks say it's genetic. Hit him during puberty. He handles it pretty well."

I sat down in a green plastic chair inside the office door, pondering that. Why would someone steal the kid's diabetes medication? Maybe teenagers knew something about getting high that I didn't. I smiled at Morris. His L-shaped metal desk rivaled mine in the piled-with-paper department.

Before either of us could speak, a gangly boy with dark hair and Morris's nose stuck his head around the corner. "Coach?" He turned warm brown eyes on me and smiled. "Oh, sorry. I'll come back."

Morris shook his head. "What do you need, Eli?" He took his seat and gestured to me. "This is Miss Clarke from the paper in Richmond. Miss Clarke, this is my son, Eli."

"I see the resemblance." I half-stood, holding a hand out to shake Eli's. "Nice to meet you." Resuming my seat, I crossed my legs and fished out a notebook and pen.

"I just wanted to ask you about tomorrow's lineup," Eli said to his dad. "It can wait."

"I haven't made it yet." Morris said, his tone holding an edge.

"What position do you play, Eli?" I asked before either of them could speak again.

"First base," he said. "Now, anyway."

I tried to be unobtrusive about writing that down, holding his gaze while my pen moved slowly over my notebook.

"That's an important position," I said.

"Better than left center field. I moved when Luke got pushed up to starting pitcher."

I held my eyebrows in place with effort, shooting a glance at Morris.

"Luke was a good first baseman," he said, defensiveness bleeding into his words. "He and TJ traded off the pitcher's mound and first. Eli's got good accuracy." He shot his son an affectionate grin, the tension in the room ebbing. "He's smart, too. Hasn't ever missed the honor roll."

"Syd helped me with math," Eli said, his voice cracking. "Even after we—well. Anyway. She was a good friend." He cast his eyes down, but not before I saw tears shining in them.

"I'm sorry for your loss," I said, unable to figure a way to shoehorn a question about his relationship with Sydney into the conversation without practically accusing him of murder. "Both of them."

His brow wrinkled briefly before he nodded. "Thank you."

I glanced between father and son, a nagging feeling I was missing something dancing through my thoughts. Staying quiet, I hoped one of them would fill in the blank. No one did.

"I hope y'all have a great season," I said finally, breaking an awkward, smiley silence.

"Thank you, ma'am." Eli nodded to his dad before he backed out of the office. "I better get to geometry. Nice to meet you, Miss Clarke."

I waved, then turned to Coach Morris. "Nice kid."

"Thank you. We're proud of him. What can I do for you today?"

"I just want to talk to you about the baseball team," I said. "Some of the other kids on it, how your season's looking without TJ pitching."

"Not as good as it was, that's for damned sure." He sat back in his chair. His face said there was something he wanted to add, but he didn't speak. I offered an encouraging smile, staying quiet.

"I saw your story this weekend, and the one in the *Washington Post*, too. Why do the Okersons think there's more to this than the sheriff does?" he asked finally. "Do you think they're right?"

Oh, boy. I twisted a lock of hair around my fingers, contemplating that. His face creased with worried lines.

"Why do you ask?" I countered, dropping my hair.

He sighed, running a hand over his face. "I've lived here all my life. Most people don't even lock their front doors at night. Jaywalking and public intoxication are about the most serious criminal offenses we see. A giant snapping turtle made the front page last week, for pity's sake. I don't want to think someone killed this boy."

"But you do, don't you?" I asked softly.

"I don't know. I'm not a hundred percent convinced of anything. But I think Zeke is making a mistake, writing it off so quick."

"Why?" I clicked out a pen and flipped to a clean piece of paper.

"After you came here last week, I cleaned out TJ's locker and took his bag by to his dad. I didn't want them to have to come here and do that, but Tony said Ashton wanted his stuff back before the service." His eyes flicked to the window that looked over the locker room. "His football cleats were in the back, forgotten after that last game."

I froze when Morris's eyes came back to mine.

"Tony told me they were worn out after that game," Morris said. "I flipped them over when I put them in his bag, and they weren't worn out. They were filed down. Sloppily, too. I guess his dad didn't look that close. Somebody caused the fall that wrecked his knee."

I didn't even need to write that down, watching as Morris shook his head. "But why?"

I studied him for a moment. Everyone following the story knew the Okersons thought TJ didn't commit suicide. Morris looked genuinely torn up over the idea, but he seemed to believe it, too. And he might know something that could help me—as long as his son wasn't the guilty one. I just had to step carefully with my questions.

"Talk to me about Luke Bosley, coach," I said.

"No." He pulled in a sharp breath and closed his eyes. "My God. Do you think?"

"I don't know," I said. "Something seems off to me, and you said his dad puts a lot of pressure on him, right?"

"What do you want to know?"

"Does he play football, too?" I asked.

"Backup quarterback," Morris said. The tension in his face said this wasn't the first time he'd had this thought.

"And if TJ hadn't had access to the best trainers and therapists because of his father—if he'd been a normal kid—that injury would have ended his playing career." I raised an eyebrow at him. "Luke's the new starting pitcher, just like his dad wanted, right?"

Morris pinched his lips into a tight line, emotions warring on his face for a good two minutes before he spoke again. "Son of a bitch. We have to call the sheriff." He reached for the phone and I raised a hand.

"Not so fast. He's convinced he's done, and I don't think he'll listen. There's a dance Friday night, though, and I have a plan. Sort of."

"Can I do anything to help you?" he asked, his eyes on something behind my head. I turned to find a photo of the baseball team taken after the regional championship win the previous spring. TJ grinned from the center.

I turned back to him, wincing at the anguish that was plain on his face.

"I'm bringing a friend with me, and I want Luke to talk to him," I said. "You think you could help with that?"

He nodded. "These boys—I have a son, too." He cleared his throat, but the catch in his voice didn't diminish. "I see my players almost as much as I see Eli this time of year. You can't not care about these kids when you do this job. At least, I can't. This week has been a nightmare. I keep looking for TJ at practice, expecting to see him warming up his arm or helping a freshman get more drop on his curve." A tear hovered on his lashes for a long second before it fell. He didn't bother to brush it away. "He was a great kid. I can't imagine what his folks are going through. And if someone did this to him—well, if I can help you, count me in. I'll be at the dance. Just point me to your friend and I'll introduce Luke."

I stood and offered my hand. "Thank you, coach. I appreciate it. And I'm very sorry for your loss."

"Thank you," he said. "I know we're not the big city, but some of us really appreciate your help with this." Sincerity rang in every word. Man, I hoped Eli didn't have anything to do with this.

I smiled. "Let's tell the sheriff that when we're done, shall we?"

"I've known Zeke since kindergarten, and I play poker with him twice a month. You bet I will, ma'am." He tipped his Mathews Eagles baseball cap.

Ma'am. I vowed to stop on the way home for new eye cream. Smiling a thank you, I left him to his lineup and hurried back to my car before the bell rang again, checking my text messages and wondering if I could find anything else about Luke before Friday night.

CHAPTER EIGHTEEN

THE REST of my week sped by in a blur of routine crime stories, a murder trial, and sleepless nights spent in equal parts thinking about Joey (who had disappeared, save for the occasional text) and trying to fit the pieces of the Mathews puzzle together.

Bob warned me to stay under everyone's radar and give Spence and Andrews time to cool off, which I didn't see happening soon with Shelby yapping at them. I smiled and nodded and shoved office politics aside, mostly because I'd learned that Shelby will be Shelby, and I had bigger fish to fry than Spencer Jacobs.

By Friday night, I was fairly convinced Luke was my guy, and excessively grateful Kyle was taking me to the dance. A seasoned, superstar ATF agent could surely pry a confession from a pissed-off teenage boy. And arrest his murderous little butt, too. Leaving me to hand Tony and Ashton their answer and go back to my regular life. If I played it right, I might not even have to tell my mom about this one. She'd been crazy busy. If I told her she was off the hook for reading the week's copy, she'd probably send me flowers.

I left work a little early and took Darcy out for a game of fetch. She took off for the back corner of the yard and dug furiously at something in the dirt. I picked up her stuffed squirrel and followed, squatting to examine her find when I saw it wasn't a dead animal.

Cigarette butts. Unfiltered ones. I counted seven.

I looked over the fence. My neighbor was as granola as a person could get this side of Berkeley, but maybe he had a friend who smoked. Darcy's barking and snarling at that part of the yard Tuesday night flashed through my thoughts, though, and I kept my ears open as we played, locking the door when I went back inside. Someone had been out there. The knowledge was slightly panic-inducing, and there was less than nothing I could do about it. I locked the doggie door for added measure and jumped when Darcy barked.

"Sorry. I'd rather keep you in one piece," I said.

Kyle appeared on my porch at five-thirty on the dot, and I caught a sharp breath when I opened the front door. The cotton of his red button-down molded to his muscular shoulders like hot fudge over ice cream, the short sleeves outlining his impressive biceps with heart-stopping precision. His fitted jeans sported creases that could cut glass over perfectly worn-in Justin ostrich dress boots. But it was the black felt Stetson on his head that stuck the "hey" in my throat. You can take the girl out of Texas, but a sexy cowboy is still sexy in Virginia.

"Evening." He tipped the hat and winked and my knees forgot how to work. Jesus. I hung onto the door and tried to look casual.

"Evening, yourself. You look nice, cowboy."

"You look beautiful." He offered a hand and I took it, my fingers tingling when he laced them with his. It still fit.

I smoothed my smocked, prairie-print dress as I climbed into a white pickup, side-eyeing him as he started the engine. "You sell your Explorer?"

"Borrowed this for tonight. Just thought it fit a little better. And you used to like my truck."

I shook my head, crossing my feet carefully so as not to scuff my chocolate-and-turquoise cowgirl boots. "I'm a little too old to be won over by a pickup and a nice hat." Or I should be, anyway.

"I know you're not convinced we belong together anymore," he said, keeping his eyes on the road. "I'm not even sure I'm the only guy in your life these days. But even if I'm not, I'm the one who knows you best."

I sighed, watching his profile and feeling a subject change coming on.

"So, I've had an interesting week." I filled him in on my chat with Coach Morris, and brought him up to speed on Luke and TJ and Sydney—she was my sticking point, because I couldn't nail down a motive for Luke killing her. Which brought me to Eli Morris. Who seemed like a nice enough kid. But Parker had told me baseball scouts would watch a first baseman more than they would an outfielder, and that plus Sydney equaled motive. I considered Coach Morris. He'd appeared genuinely torn up, and willing to help. But it had occurred to me that he might be trying to push my attention off his son. I wasn't sure that was likely, but it wasn't unlikely, given the tangled mess this story had been.

"What if the girl did kill herself? Assuming you're right and there was any foul play at work here, of course," Kyle said.

I pictured Tiffany's sure expression, the pain in her brown eyes.

"Anything is possible, but I'm not willing to start down that road yet," I said.

He nodded. "We'll just see what we can see. What about the girl you told me about? Are we looking for her?"

I twisted my mouth to one side. I knew from a (very) brief call with (an annoyed) Sheriff Zeke on Wednesday that Evelyn was alive and well, just cutting class because she said she couldn't take the stares and whispers. Which was either really sad, or damned suspicious, and I'd been unable to figure out which.

"I'm not sure she'll show, because she's been a hermit since TJ's funeral, from what I understand," I told Kyle. "But I can't tell if she's holed up because she's sad or because she feels guilty, and I hear this thing is a big freaking deal to the kids out here. They don't have too many places to hang out besides the beach and the 7-Eleven parking lot. So I'm hoping she won't be able to resist. I'd really like to have a chat with her."

"I'm not about to walk into an underage serving zone, am I?" Kyle asked, turning the truck onto 161 as the sun dropped out of the sky behind us.

"I can't imagine. I mean, it's in a public street. On the other hand, the sheriff's cousins are local moonshiners, so I'm not a hundred percent on that. But don't go busting out your badge unless someone cops to the murder, huh? Underage drinking is ABC police business, right?"

"Strictly speaking. Did my guy there ever call you back?"

"Nope. I didn't think anyone liked me less than the FBI until I ran across those guys. I guess it's a good thing I've never needed them for anything past a press-release follow-up before." I glanced at him. "And a good thing I have friends in the right places these days."

"You want me for more than my badge." He winked.

"You know, part of my reservation comes from my rule against dating cops."

"There's a rule? Why don't you tell a guy? I quit."

I snorted. "You may not do that," I said. "Someone I know tells me rules are made to be broken, anyhow."

"I'm a cop. I'm not sure I'm comfortable with that."

"Well, they can always be changed. I'll call a special session and rewrite the law. Maybe."

He reached over and squeezed my hand. More sparks. "You have my vote."

I flipped on the radio and watched the fields speed by as Kenny Chesney sang about kegs and closets. He had a point. Being a grownup isn't much fun sometimes.

"You know," Kyle said, "me being a cop comes in handy for you on occasion. I have a surprise for you."

I waited for him to go on, but he just sat there, a smile playing around his lips.

"Are you going to share?" I asked.

He glanced at me from the corner of his eye. "I suppose you need time to prepare."

"For what?"

"The ABC has a guy undercover out here, working a moonshining operation. We're supposed to meet him at ten. It's all strictly off the record, but you said that was okay."

I stared for a second, then leaned across the bench seat and planted a kiss on his cheek. Even if I couldn't quote the cop, maybe I could find out what was going on with the moonshine. If the ABC agent was in with the right crowd, I might even be able to figure out where TJ and Sydney had gotten it. I grabbed a pen and an old receipt out of the console in the truck and scribbled questions for the rest of the drive.

I directed Kyle into Elmer's antique store parking lot and he marveled at the old-time feel of the converted gas station, even using some of the same words I had as he took my hand and helped me hop down from the truck. It was effortless to fall back to a level of normal with Kyle. But did I want normal and comfortable, or did I want exciting and unknown?

A rainbow of lanterns zigzagged the width of Main Street, which was blocked off at both ends of the square. A table full of tween-aged girls supervised by Norma from the high school office sat across the head of the street. I handed the tallest kid a twenty. "Two, please."

"Cute bag!" Norma said, eyeing my little brown leather "necessary objects only" evening pouch. The front was decorated with hand-sewn turquoise beadwork.

"Thanks," I said. "I got it at a craft fair my mom dragged me to the last time I went home."

"It's nice of you to come," Norma said, handing me two printed cardstock tickets. I tucked them into my bag without looking at them.

"The Accidental Rednecks are playing," Norma said. "They're local, and they're real good. Don't leave without trying the barbecue. And the pie. My momma helps bake the pies."

I nodded, leading Kyle into the party. "Sounds great."

Food and beverage stations lined the sidewalks for half a block, hawking everything from fresh-caught seafood to funnel cakes and kettle corn.

We walked through picnic tables, complete with red-checkered tablecloths, toward the stage that spanned the far end of the street.

The band was cooking, playing covers of classic rock and modern country. The half-block in front of the stage was the dance floor, dotted with couples (age range: pre-adolescent to geriatric, which I found all kinds of charming) either dancing with each other or swaying to the beat as they watched the show. I turned toward the drink stand, remembering the last of my antibiotics was waiting in my bag, when the singer flipped his collar up and the band played the first strains of "Are You Lonesome Tonight?" Kyle caught my hand, taking the bag off my shoulder and dropping it to an empty tabletop.

"Dance with me," he said, his blue lasers locked on my eyes.

Speechless, I followed him to the dance floor.

Everyone else fell away, and if I didn't know better I'd swear Kyle had paid off the singer to write a set tailored for us: we swayed, two-stepped, and boogied through a dozen of my favorite songs before the band took a dinner break.

"I think that's our cue to go eat, too," I said, breathless. "And to get some investigating done." I looked around at the darkness that crowded in from all sides, held at bay by the pretty lanterns, and checked my watch. "Holy cow. We've been here for over an hour."

I grabbed my purse and joined a dozen people waiting in line for drinks. Smiling at the pretty bartender I recognized from Bobbi's club, I ordered an iced tea and shook the last tablet from my prescription bottle, swallowing it and tossing the bottle in the trash. I scanned the dancers for Luke, or Coach Morris, or Evelyn, but didn't see any of them.

"Maybe everyone's getting food," I said, pulling Kyle toward the barbecue table, my stomach reminding me that I had skipped lunch to get my juvenile murder trial wrap-up done and ready to go on the web before Charlie got it on the air. "You hungry?"

"I'm always hungry," he said, wriggling a suggestive eyebrow.

I rolled my eyes. "Chicken. Toast. Pickles."

It all smelled heavenly, and I was slightly surprised to find Bobbi serving it.

"You ladies doing all the food service for the party?" I asked. "How'd you swing that?"

She grinned. "Thanks to you, I'm not nearly the leper Dorothy made me out to be for the past year. The mayor came in for lunch—with his wife—and they asked me to come cater the party when they got a load of Grandmomma's sauce."

I ordered myself a C-cup and Kyle a rack of ribs, and dropped a twenty in her tip jar when she refused to take payment for the food.

I'd put exactly three bites in my mouth when I spotted Evelyn lurking near the ice cream stand.

"She's here." I dropped my fork and stood, straightening my dress. "The girl. I'll be back. Wish me luck."

"At least finish your dinner," Kyle said. "She's not going anywhere."

I stared at her pink-rimmed eyes—which I suspected were crimson under her concealer— and guarded expression. "I'm not so sure about that," I said. "Sit tight for a few. I won't be long."

I wandered toward the ice cream stand, skipping my eyes around the crowd and trying not to look too obvious. Turning to glance behind me at just the right moment, I practically tripped over Evelyn.

"I'm so sorry!" I said over the music, righting myself and putting a steadying hand on her arm. "Are you all right? I should look where I'm going."

She nodded, a smile teasing the corners of her lips. "You didn't hurt me, at any rate."

I tipped my head to one side and studied her. "Don't I know you?"

"This is Mathews. Everyone knows everyone."

I smiled. "It seems. But I'm from Richmond. Oh, I know!" I snapped my fingers. "I saw you at TJ's funeral. In the restroom. You were quite upset. Are you feeling a little better? Ice cream always helps me." I nodded to the cone in her hand.

"I'm all right. I guess. Better than TJ and Syd."

Sydney's funeral had been the day before, her parents waiting for out of town relatives to get flights arranged.

"It's such a sad situation," I said.

"Syd was my best friend." Her voice broke. "For my whole life. Until last year. Stupid boys. Stupid me." She ducked her head and covered her face with one hand, tears dripping from her face as fast as vanilla-chocolate swirl dripped from her fingers.

I passed her a napkin from the holder on the edge of a nearby table.

"Thanks." She looked up, sniffling, and tossed the cone into a trash can. "I just want to talk to her one more time. To tell her how sorry I am. How much I wish I could make it right. How stupid I was."

"I'm sure she knew," I said. "That you were sorry, I mean."

She shook her head, hard, her wispy blonde hair flying. "No, she didn't. TJ was so cute, and he was so good to her. I just wanted someone to treat me that way. Stupid TJ. Why did he have to be such a good guy?" Her eyes narrowed as she spoke, her tone changing from anguished to angry. Huh.

I shrugged. "It's just the way some people are," I said. "I'm sure he didn't mean to be offensive with it."

"Of course he didn't. Syd was an amazing person. She deserved TJ. I didn't wish anything bad for her. It's just not fair. I miss my momma. My dad is—" she paused, hauling in a steadying breath. "Well, anyway. Syd's folks loved her like my momma loved me. She was an only child, too."

"So I heard."

"I just wanted to tell her I was sorry. Then she ran off to France to get away from me. From TJ and me, maybe. And I tried to tell her at the party when she came home, but she threw her drink in my face and screamed that she hated me." She dissolved into a teary mess, mumbling what sounded like "hated me" over and over between hitching breaths.

Christ on a cracker. I leaned on the side of the ice cream trailer and patted Evelyn's heaving shoulder. Maybe I was wrong about Luke. What if this girl had blamed TJ for losing her BFF and then lost her shit when Sydney humiliated her after TJ was dead? I felt bad, trying to comfort her while wondering if she was a murderer, but I'd have felt worse if I walked off and left her sobbing like that.

I watched the crowd as I pondered, spotting Luke on the dance floor with a pretty redhead in a fabulous pink cotton dress. I kept my eyes on him as they moved, shimmying to "Little Sister" before she locked her hands behind his neck and he laid his on her hips when the keyboard player tapped out the opening notes of "The Dance."

Evelyn cried herself out and looked up, wiping the concealer off her eyes as she did so. She looked like an extra from *Night of the Demons*.

"Thanks. Everyone around here has treated me like a dog since TJ died. Worse, really. Most people like dogs."

I tried to smile. "It gets better."

"People keep telling me time will dull the pain. But does it get rid of the guilt?"

I'll take loaded questions for four hundred, Alex.

"I meant, just life in general. High school can kind of suck. But it gets better," I said. "Hang in there."

"I'm trying." She scrubbed at her face with the napkin, her eyes falling on a cluster of pretty girls who were actually pointing at her as they cackled and chatted. "It was a big mistake, me coming here tonight. I need to go home. But you were nice, and I needed that. I haven't seen or talked to much of anybody since the funeral."

"Don't mention it." I thought about what I'd managed to glean from the conversation. She was at the party where Sydney died. "Hey, Evelyn? What was Sydney drinking that last night?"

"Freaking moonshine." She wrinkled her nose. "I heard her tell someone it was a gift. Somebody told her it'd dull the pain. She'd had half the jar when she got pissed at me. She was having trouble walking, but she still managed to hit me with the stuff. It stings when it gets in your eyes."

I nodded. "Thanks."

I watched her go, noting the way she slumped her shoulders, trying to make herself as small as possible. I'd walked through most of high school like that in an effort to hide my height. It looked like Evelyn was just trying to hide.

I spun back to the dance floor, looking for Luke, and found Kyle blocking my view. "Well?" he asked.

"Still don't know. She's got some anger and guilt around all this.

And some daddy issues, too, I think, from the way she was talking." I
knew Em would say that could mess a teenage girl up. "It's hard to say
if she's upset for ruining her friendship with them and not having a
way to fix that or if she feels guilty for killing them. Sydney was definitely drinking moonshine, though. Evelyn said she had half a jar
before she flung the rest in Evelyn's face. Couldn't walk upright. And
someone gave it to her." That sentence stuck in my head. We were
dealing with something in the moonshine. I was as sure of it as I was
my shoe size. That stuff would mask just about any kind of nasty taste
I could imagine.

"That is a tough code to crack," Kyle said, turning and wrapping an
arm around my waist, pulling me to his side. "You see the other kid
you wanted to talk to?"

I looked up at him, liking my poisoned drink theory more as I
considered Luke. "He was on the dance floor thirty seconds ago," I
said. "He couldn't have gone far."

I searched the sidewalk on the opposite side of the street for
Luke's blond head, and saw Coach Morris first. He waved, crossing
quickly to shake Kyle's hand.

I introduced them, turning my most earnest smile on Morris. "Did
Eli come with you tonight, coach?" I asked. "I'm wondering if he was
at any of the parties last week. Maybe he saw something? Heard
something?"

Morris shook his head. "He said he didn't feel like it. Hasn't been
himself lately. He and TJ weren't exactly buddies, but he's torn up
over Sydney. She was a special girl."

Crap. But interesting, too. Torn up, sad? Or torn up, guilty?

"I just talked to Luke," Morris said, glancing around. "It's been hard
the past few days. I almost can't look at him. I can't believe he'd really
want to hurt his teammate."

"We are still in America," Kyle said. "There's the whole 'innocent
until proven guilty' thing."

"He tampered with TJ's cleats," the coach said.

"We think, anyway," I said, eyeing Morris. He was trying awfully
hard to hand Luke to us on a platter. Too hard?

"Not the same as murdering someone. I'm not saying he's not capable of it, because causing serious injury to a rival is a bad sign, but if he'd wanted TJ dead why not call him out to the beach or the baseball field alone and just shoot him?" Kyle asked.

The coach fell silent. "I don't know. Maybe he wasn't planning to kill him."

"That would be way more likely if there were signs of trauma to the body that indicated a spontaneous method." Kyle looked around. "Nicey, you said tall and blond." He pointed. "That kid?"

I followed his gaze and saw Luke making out with the redhead in the shadows next to the barbecue stand. "That's him."

Kyle turned to coach Morris. "How about an introduction?"

"Sure thing," Morris said, waving for Kyle to follow him across the street.

I started back for the table, hoping Bobbi's chicken was as good cold as it was warm, when a voice behind me stopped my foot in midair.

"Who is that, and what does he want with my son?"

I spun to find the woman who'd come looking for Luke at the funeral, dressed in a purple broomstick skirt and a floral-print top.

She nodded to me. "You were talking to Lucas at the funeral the other day. With a different fella. Who's that one?"

I smiled. "He's a baseball fan. Coach Morris was telling us about Luke's arm, and my friend wanted to meet him. I hear this is going to be a heck of a season for the Eagles."

Her shrewd expression softened slightly. "It will be now," she said, her eyes flicking from me to Kyle and the coach, then back again.

I blanched, staring at her for a second with a smile pasted across my face, my brain in hyperdrive, shifting puzzle pieces.

How many stories had I read about moms who were willing to kill for their children? Okay, most of them were defending their wee'uns' lives, shooting intruders or occasionally taking out child molesters. But hell—what if I suspected the wrong Bosley? I turned my eyes to the scene across the street.

Morris tapped Luke's shoulder and introduced Kyle. Luke broke into a big grin and offered a hand, dismissing the girl with a wave. She backed up a few steps, staring daggers at the coach.

"He's a good boy," Luke's mother said from my elbow. "He deserves a fair shot."

I tried to keep my trap shut and failed. "Did he not get a fair shot at some point? The coach said he's been on the team for three years running."

"He should have been the star. But TJ was there. Not even from here, with his famous daddy and all their money. My husband was the most winning pitcher in Mathews history until TJ came here. Lucas was destined to start for the Eagles from the cradle."

"He's been a starter since he was a sophomore," I said. "I found that impressive."

She cut her eyes to me. "He should be the star," she repeated. "People wanting to meet him, shake his hand. Give him scholarships that will get him the hell out of this town. He's got a fair shot now."

She walked toward Kyle and my jaw dropped, my mind racing.

What did I know about Mrs. Bosley?

She was the PTA President. Which meant she was at the school as much as the teachers. Evelyn said someone gave Sydney the moonshine she was drinking. Which Evelyn probably wouldn't mention if the someone had been her.

I froze, digging out my cell phone and opening the photos.

There was Syd's moonshine jar. And there was a piece of paper in the bag next to it.

Bright green, like the one I'd seen in TJ's locker. I closed my eyes and pictured the party flyer. Concave, and crinkled up along one edge.

Like it had been wrapped around a jar?

Hot damn.

I clicked back to the county marriage records and searched for Bosley. I found that Simon Bosley had married Lily Sidell the year before Luke was born.

Sidell. Elmer and Bobbi Jo said the Sidell family made moonshine.

Quickly, I tapped every word into a note before they faded. Then I texted my best friend. "I need to talk to you," I typed. "Sorry again for bailing on girls night, but can we get coffee in the morning? Need a mom's perspective."

She texted right back. "Sure, doll. You find your murderer yet?"

"Probably. If I could figure out which one of these Looney Tunes it is," I replied. "Lesson from this trip: there's no shortage of folks with motive out here."

"Fun. Thompson's @ 9:30. Can't wait to hear. Miss you. Xoxo"

"Thanks. Miss you. Xoxo"

I looked up as Coach Morris and Norma slow-danced into my sight line, her short frame fused to his tall one. Her eyes were closed, her head resting just below his shoulder. His arms cradled the small of her back, and his feet moved to the music—but Morris's eyes were on Luke Bosley, an unreadable expression on his face.

I knew the feeling.

Tucking the phone back in my bag, I smiled as Kyle crossed the street toward me. I collapsed into his chest when he offered me a hand, the crazy week finally biting me in the energy stores.

"Hello, there," he said, squeezing my shoulders.

"I am so. Tired." I said. "Can we go?"

"If you're ready," he said, glancing at his watch. "We should head out to the woods to meet my ABC guy. And wait 'til you hear what I got from the kid."

* * *

Kyle passed the turn off for the freeway and drove for about a mile with the guidance of the high beams, then hung a right onto a narrow dirt road that barely cut through the woods.

I glanced at him, then at the pitch-black surrounding the truck. "We're meeting someone here?" I asked.

"It's hard to find places no one can see out here," he said. "We have to protect his cover, or we'll put his life in very real danger."

I nodded.

He rolled to a stop in a teeny clearing, and I spotted the outline of a pickup with no headlights on coming the other way. Kyle turned the brights off, the sallow glow of the low beams not making much headway with the darkness. He stepped out of the truck without turning off the lights, walking around to open my door and help me down. I blinked away fatigue as I stood up, turning for the front of the car.

The undercover ABC agent stepped into the light and I froze for a split second, tightening my fingers on Kyle's arm as a stream of tobacco juice hit the dirt in front of Kyle's borrowed pickup.

Bubba—the same Bubba I'd met Tuesday night in Maryland—called a "Hello," and I swallowed a "Crap hell."

I pulled a dose of composure out of the chilly night air and strode past Kyle, putting out my hand. Bubba's eyes widened slightly when I stepped into the light, and I started talking before he could open his mouth.

"Thanks so much for coming to talk to me," I said. "Nichelle Clarke, *Richmond Telegraph*."

Kyle put a hand on my elbow and then shook Bubba's proffered one. "We're strictly off the record here," he said.

Bubba gave me a once-over. "We'd better be." He raised an eyebrow. "You sure you're not wearing a wire?"

I pinched my lips down on a smile. "Absolutely," I said. "I didn't even bring a notebook. But I sure could use some background on what's going on out here."

"I understand you think moonshine had something to do with TJ Okerson's death," Bubba said.

"At the risk of sounding paranoid, can I ask where you heard that?" The *Post*'s story whirled through my thoughts.

"From Agent Miller, there," Bubba said. "Who has a lot of respect at the ATF." He held my gaze as he spoke and I fidgeted, dropping my eyes to my boots. Kyle chuckled and thanked him.

"I don't know for sure what to think," I said. "But I know there was moonshine present at both scenes. And Sydney Cobb was definitely drinking it. Can you tell me where the triple-X label comes from?" My voice shook and I cleared my throat, praying Kyle would think I was just nervous. I'm a lousy liar.

Bubba smiled. "I believe I can. That's the Parsons family. I've been working a sting inside their operation for eighteen months," he said, leaning against the hood of the truck. "I understand you've called half the guys in my division looking for a comment this week, but they won't breathe a word about an investigation with an undercover officer in place."

So that's why they'd been so sweet. "That's common policy."

He spit again. "We've got three stills. Parsons has a business front at the auto body shop on Main, and there are a couple of places serving the stuff. I'm days away from a bust. And now you have dead kids? Part of the reason I came tonight was to find out what you know."

"Not a lot," I said, lighting on the "places serving" part of that and worrying about Bobbi. But I had zero ways to ask about that without implicating her, on the off chance she wasn't already on his list, so I moved on. "Moonshine was there at both parties, and like I said, Sydney was seen drinking it. Half a jar, I heard. I've seen two different labels on it, though. The one Sydney had was faded across the middle. A different one I saw was not."

"Faded how?" He looked interested.

"Like the ink went to gray and then back to black."

"I've never noticed that, and I've seen about every part of their operation."

I put a mental star by that.

"You said they sell it out of a body shop? Do a lot of kids come around to buy it?"

"I wouldn't say a lot of kids. Some, probably. I know we get more old guys than kids."

"Did you ever see TJ?"

"Not off the football field."

Damn.

"Does the sheriff know you're working out here?"

"It's agency policy to coordinate with local law enforcement."

"That's not an answer," I said.

"It's the best I can do."

I resisted the urge to lean back against Kyle, keeping everything as professional as I could considering the waves of exhaustion crashing over me.

"You know the sheriff has cousins in the moonshine trade, though?"

"He does. So does everybody else around here, to be fair."

"Have you heard anyone say anything about the dead kids? Any reason someone might want them dead?"

"Not a word."

"How about the moonshine? Any complaints of a bad batch lately?"

"Not that I've heard."

Double damn. I sighed, wading through thick thoughts in search of another question. The funky label. He'd never seen a faded one, so where had it come from?

"Do the Parsons sell unlabeled jars of triple-X to anyone?" I asked, bracing a hip against the truck's fender to stay on my feet.

"Not often. There are a few folks distributing across the state who prefer unlabeled jars. It's not as traceable that way."

"Why label them at all?"

"Vanity? Underground brand recognition? I have no idea."

So someone could be buying them unlabeled and putting the faded ones on themselves. Which meant knowing about the auto body front didn't help me. But it'd have to be someone the moonshiners trusted, from what he'd said. Someone like Lily Sidell Bosley?

"Do you know who takes the unlabeled ones?"

"Not by name. It's not a big group of people."

I nodded to myself, then smiled at Bubba. I was out of questions, which flipped my focus to getting Kyle the hell out of there before Bubba brought up our first meeting. "Thanks so much for talking to me," I said, offering my hand again. He shook it.

"If my name turns up in the newspaper—" he said.

"I don't have your name," I cut him off. "And I would never compromise a police officer's safety."

"I don't suppose I gave it to you, at that." He dropped my hand, holding my gaze with somber eyes. "Do yourself a favor and be careful. These guys aren't the type you screw around with, and they don't like the things they've been hearing about you. I wouldn't be surprised if they'd done a little research on you, too. Like, maybe on where you live."

I shivered in the breeze and nodded, the unfiltered cigarette butts in the corner of my yard flashing through my thoughts. "I appreciate the heads up." Not that I could keep the Mathews grapevine quiet.

He got back in his truck and started the engine after Kyle thanked him and told him to leave first.

"Thank you," I said, turning to Kyle.

"It didn't exactly solve your puzzle," he said, wrapping me in a tight hug after Bubba was out of sight. "And I'm more worried about you than I was before."

"There are unlabeled jars," I said, laying my head on his chest. "The faded ink is the key to something, here. I just have to find out who gets the unlabeled ones. And then who gave it to the kids."

"You will." He turned and opened the passenger door of the pickup. "You're pretty smart."

The heel of my boot caught on the edge of the door when I climbed back into the truck, tossing me forward into the floorboard. Graceful as a drunkard on stilts, party of one.

"Did you sneak some moonshine when I wasn't looking?" Kyle slid behind the wheel and offered me a hand as I clambered up into the seat. His fingers closed on the bare skin of my arm and I froze for a second at the warmth that radiated from his fingers, thinking about dancing close to him, feeling his breath on my cheek and his hands on my back.

I smiled as I smoothed my skirt. "Yeah, no. Once was all the exposure to that I'll ever need. I think I wear heels so much, other types of shoes throw me off."

"Too bad. The boots look good on you, Texas."

He turned his head to check the mirror as he started the truck and I studied his jawline, shaded auburn with stubble around his goatee. I sat on my fingers to keep from reaching out to see how it would feel under them. "The hat looks good on you, cowboy."

He turned back and flashed a grin. "You always have been a sucker for a Stetson and a pair of good boots."

"That was a long time ago." I gripped the door handle and averted my eyes, giving in to some very nice memories for a moment.

"But it was good. And it could be again."

I stared out the window, thinking about how natural his arms felt around me. It really could.

"You were amazing tonight," I said, my eyes on his sure hands, guiding the truck around dark curves.

"So were you. We still make a good team."

"I suppose we do. Thanks for believing me. And thanks for coming with me."

"Anytime, Lois. Your instincts are good."

"Thank you." That was high praise coming from Kyle. "So, what'd you find out from Luke?"

"He's capable of it, I think, but the way he seems so contemptuous of TJ and the temper he seems to barely conceal, I'm not sure the lack of trauma matches."

"Liver failure." I'd been mulling that since Tuesday, and had nothing to show for it. "I can't figure it."

"It would track with a Vicodin overdose," Kyle said gently.

"Don't go back there. My instincts are good, remember?" I said. "Besides, the coroner I talked to said the Vicodin should have caused suffocation first." Except TJ's liver was already damaged. But I wasn't offering up anything that might raise his doubts.

"I just feel like you need a voice of reason."

Subject change. "I talked to Luke's mother for about twelve seconds, but speaking of crazy." I shook my head. "I'm wondering if she might not fly to the top of the suspect list."

"Oh, yeah?"

"She went on about how TJ had an unfair advantage and Luke was the rightful star of the baseball team, and that's been rectified."

He whistled. "Like the cheerleader thing, you think?"

I grinned. "Very much." I'd gone through a true-crime phase, studying cases and the media reports on them for a chunk of my adolescence, and the Texas cheerleader murder was one of my favorites. A mom had killed the girl who was her daughter's big rival for a spot on the squad.

"Would she have had access to TJ's cleats?" Kyle asked. "I mean, do we still think Luke filed them down if we think mom might have killed TJ?"

"I cannot figure a way she'd be in the boys' locker room alone for good reason, but I'm sure she knows where it is and could come up with an excuse if she had to," I said. "Which is a long way around 'maybe.'"

"You're chasing vapor here, you know that, right? You have a boat-load of circumstantial evidence, but not a damned thing you can prove. Even if you are right. Which I'm not conceding just yet."

"Em agrees with me." I reminded him.

He was silent for a minute. "Yeah. And she's as good as it gets at criminal psychology. Every time I try to blow you off, I think about what you told me she said. But this is going to be tough to pin on anyone, honey."

"I like tough." I fell into silence as the dark fields outside gave way to freeway street lights. When he pulled off I-64 at the exit for my house, I sighed.

"Something about the moonshine could have caused liver failure, too," I said. "I know the jars I saw came from the Parsons family."

"I can't touch it if it's staying in the state. And the ABC is on it—you heard him, they've almost got enough for a bust."

"It's not. Staying in the state, I mean."

"How do you know that?" He pulled the truck into my driveway and turned to face me, his brow creasing. "I asked you about drinking it and you said 'once was enough,' too. What did you do?"

Dammit. Me and my big mouth. "I can't tell you." I fought to keep my voice even.

He held my gaze for a long moment. "I know this is important to you. But I can't look into it based on a lie, Nichelle. I'm walking a close line with getting in trouble as it is. I know a couple of guys who would say I've already put my nose too far in without an open investigation. If the wrong people decide that, I could lose my job."

"I'm not lying, and I certainly don't want you to lose your job." I fidgeted in the seat, groping for an answer. "People who wouldn't talk to you will talk to me. I promise you, I'm right. If that helps you with an excuse."

He studied every line of my face as I stared at him, trying to look earnest. I was telling the truth. Mostly, I just didn't want to tell him anything that would lead him back to Joey. I knew that was a bomb waiting for a trigger, but I wasn't looking to provide it.

"Did you go interview the moonshiners?" he exploded. "Do you have any idea how badly you could have gotten hurt?"

"But I didn't." I skirted the question, my breath coming faster. I tried to slow it. I didn't want Kyle to be mad at me.

He tipped his hat back. I turned toward him in the seat.

"I don't want you to get hurt." He reached for my hand.

"I don't, either." I squeezed his fingers. "I'm trying to be careful. Jeez, I've only been to Mathews by myself a couple of times."

He pressed his lips into a tight line, holding my gaze silently for a minute before he got out of the truck and came around to open my door.

My head swam when I stood up and I grabbed Kyle's arm to stay on my feet as the driveway wavered. He put one hand under my elbow and wound the other arm around my waist, concern furrowing his brow. "You okay?"

I blinked. "Wow. I guess my equilibrium is still off because of my cold."

He walked me to the door. I leaned back against the wall, ignoring the porch swing because of my unsteadiness.

"And here we are." Kyle's voice dropped. He rested one hand on the wall just above my head, facing me. I breathed the clean smell of his favorite cologne, his eyes holding mine.

My pulse quickened. "Who'd have thought you'd be walking me to the front door at the end of the night, like, ever again?"

"I could walk you inside, if you like." He tipped his hat back, leaning so close I could smell the cinnamon gum on his breath. He traced one finger along my cheekbone, and the light touch sent such a shockwave through me my knees buckled. Oh. My. God.

I closed my eyes and slid my hands up his chest to his shoulders, pulling him the rest of the way home. He brushed his lips lightly over mine, sending sparks skating across the back of my skull. My fingers dug in, pulling him closer, and I parted my lips and traced the line of his with the tip of my tongue. He wound one hand into my hair and deepened the kiss, his other arm sliding behind me and pulling me against him.

"Kyle," I whispered into his lips, trying to catch a steadying breath.

"Nicey," he murmured, kissing his way across my jaw to my neck. I shuddered at the electricity his goatee brushing my skin sent through me, knocking his hat to the floor as I clutched at the back of his head. His close-cropped hair was soft under my hands.

He trailed his mouth slowly up the side of my neck and returned to my lips, his tongue moving languidly over mine. The porch rocked under my feet.

"I need to go inside," I said, my breath coming so fast my vision blurred. When had Kyle gotten to be such a great kisser? Never mind. I probably didn't want to think about that. I was having trouble thinking about anything except wanting to lie down, and wanting to kiss Kyle some more. And how to reconcile those two things.

I fumbled a key out of my bag, handing it to him and leaning my head back against the wall, willing my pulse to slow.

It refused, a fine sheen of sweat frosting my skin in the cool night air. I gulped for breath as the lights in the house across the street wavered and then blinked out. From far away, I heard the door open. Darcy barked.

Then Kyle was saying my name with a don't-walk-out-in-front-of-that-bus urgency, and everything went dark.

CHAPTER NINETEEN

I OPENED my eyes to the brightest light this side of the pearly gates, groaning and waving it away as I clamped them shut again.

"Nicey?" Kyle still sounded far away, and it was so bright. What the hell?

"Where are we?" I asked, not opening my eyes. "And who turned on the high beams?"

"The ER," he said. "And the nurses did. While they were hooking you up to machines and trying to get your blood sugar back up."

"My blood sugar? Why would it need to go up?" Everything seemed sticky and hard to analyze.

"Because you haven't eaten all day and we danced for an hour and a half?" he asked. "You passed out and your skin was so clammy when I picked you up, it scared the shit out of me. I thought maybe you'd been faking your recovery and you had pneumonia or something. But I brought you here and they said your blood sugar crashed. It was forty-two when they checked it."

I shook my head, slitting my eyes open against the bright light. "I have never once in my life had a problem with my blood sugar. Am I getting diabetes or something?" That sounded scary.

The door opened on the end of my question and a balding man

with a lab coat, a kind smile and large, seventies-style bifocals answered. "You are not diabetic," he said. "But you do have to take better care of yourself. Agent Miller tells me you've been working even though you've been sick, and you don't eat properly. No case is that important." He checked an IV bag of yellowish fluid hanging over my cot, marked something in the chart, and had just turned back to me when the loudspeaker paged Dr. Gandy to the nurse's station. "Be right back," he said, darting out the door.

"Case?" I looked at Kyle, who was hunched over in a chair next to the cot, rubbing his temples.

He raised his head and grinned. "I might have flashed my badge and let them think you were my partner. They would've kicked me out to the waiting room, otherwise, and I didn't want to leave you back here alone."

I reached through the bedrail for his hand. "Thanks for looking out for me."

"Someone should."

"I do all right when I'm not unconscious."

He smiled. "Mostly."

"So. Blood sugar?"

"You said you were starving when we got food at the dance, but then you ran off to talk to the girl without eating, and I didn't see you go back to get your food. I assume from what the doctor said that you didn't eat it?"

I opened my mouth and then clamped it shut. "I got waylaid by Morris, and then talked to Luke's mother," I said. "And then I was so tired and we left."

"Another symptom of low blood sugar. So is being off balance and clammy skin."

"Well, hell. I didn't mean to."

"You need to stash a Powerbar in your purse," Kyle said.

The door opened again and a nurse came in. "There you are." She smiled. "Feeling a little better?"

"I think so." I glanced at Kyle, remembering suddenly what we'd been about to do when I'd passed out. "Compared to being uncon-scious, anyway."

"You need to remember to eat," she said, hanging a new IV bag and taking down the empty one.

"So I've heard. But this has never happened to me before. It's not like there haven't been plenty of days when I got busy and forgot to eat. So why now? Does this mean I'm going to get diabetes?" I had a hard time letting go of that worry. I hate needles.

"Not necessarily," she said. "Low blood sugar levels can be caused by a combination of things that have nothing to do with diabetes. Illness, poor sleeping habits, inadequate nutrition. Any of that sound familiar?"

I grimaced. "Maybe. But I'm a little freaked out because I've never had this problem before."

"Aging makes things in your body work less efficiently, as a general rule." She winked, noting the time on the chart and turning back for the door. "It only gets worse."

I rolled my eyes as the door closed behind her. "Aging. I'm not even thirty yet."

"I'm coming up on it quick," Kyle said. "I feel it some days, too. I can't lift as much at the gym as I could when I was twenty-four."

"I don't think I care for this getting older business." I plucked at the threads of the blanket across my lap.

"Beats the hell out of the alternative."

I sighed. "I always thought I'd be in a different place at thirty. Thirty was old. Dentures and walker old. Remember?"

"We were going to rule the world," Kyle said, squeezing my hand. "Have it all."

"Maybe we do." I said. "You're a bonafide hero—I mean, your career is shooting off into the stratosphere."

"I guess. I feel like it's been stalled lately. After my last big case, there's been a shortage of giant operations to run. I've been doing a lot of little one-off busts."

"You'll land another big fish soon. Aren't you, like, the youngest special agent big shot they've ever had, or something?"

"Haven't you, like, caught a couple of murderers and won some pretty impressive awards?" he countered.

"I guess."

"Thirty's not old. We'll pin that one on forty. 'Til we get there. We can move that line forever."

I smiled at the thought of turning forty with Kyle. Which gave me a warm-fuzzy and made me wonder again what the hell I was going to do about my love life. Such a massive mess required more brainpower than I had to spare.

"I know one thing: I wouldn't go back to being twenty-one for all the Manolos in the Saks warehouse. There's something to be said for that whole age and wisdom thing." I rolled my eyes up toward the bag of yellow fluid. "Is that the magic blood sugar juice?"

"I suppose." He sat back in the chair. "You seem to be feeling better."

"I'm sorry I ruined our evening."

"Eh. I'd be lying if I said I wasn't disappointed, but I'm more glad you're okay. Raincheck?"

"When the time is right." I closed my eyes. "I'm sleepy."

He kissed the back of my hand. "You rest."

I did.

The doctor pronounced me balanced and ready to go home at a few minutes after two, and Kyle delivered me there without further comment on our missed encounter. I knew him well enough to know that took immense self-control, and I kissed his cheek and thanked him for everything. I shut the door and fell into my bed, wanting nothing but to sleep off my crazy week.

CHAPTER TWENTY

PETER PAN FLITTING around the room wasn't usually part of the dream where I got offered a job covering the White House for the *Washington Post*—yet there he was, Tinkerbell hot on his heels.

Around the time the editor in my dream (who looked much more like Christian Bale than a newspaper editor ever actually would) began belting out *Second Star to the Right*, dream-me figured out my real-life phone must be ringing.

Groping for my cell phone, I cracked one eye enough to see that my bedroom was pitch-dark. Had I slept all day? I turned my head and groaned when I saw the clock. I hadn't even slept three hours.

"Money or shoes?" I mumbled into the phone, turning my head so I could hear. The only acceptable reason for this call was to tell me I'd won one of those things.

"Pardon?"

"Aaron?" I sat up and pushed my tangled hair out of my face. "It's four-forty-five. In the morning. On Saturday."

"You'll thank me when you've had some coffee," Aaron said. "I know you've been sick and I figured your scanner was off." Aaron hated working weekends and almost never called me at home. Which was the only reason I didn't hang up and dive back into my pillows.

"What's up?"

"I've got a hotel fire that will make a hell of a headline if you feel up to dragging yourself over here."

I shook the haze out of my head. A hotel fire? Andrews was still pissed at me, best I could tell. I needed all the brownie points I could get. "Thanks, Aaron. My scanner didn't even make it out of the car last night. I owe you one."

"Bring an extra cup of coffee. It's cold out here."

"Text me the address and give me twenty minutes." I clicked off the call and threw my sage duvet back. Darcy growled at me from her bed.

"I know. But what can I do?" I put my feet on the cold wood floor and wondered why I didn't have a rug for the bedroom.

Shuffling to the bathroom, I stretched out of sleep and pulled a pair of jeans and a heavy cable-knit sweater from the dryer that sat across from my bathtub. I scrubbed my face and brushed my teeth, yanking my hair back into a hasty ponytail since I didn't have time to wash it.

While Aaron's coffee brewed into a plastic Starbucks cup, I ran back to the bedroom and jammed my feet into a pair of lavender silk Manolo Blahnik sandals. An absolute eBay steal at less than two hundred dollars, because of a tiny pull in the fabric. A quick dot of clear nail polish, and it wasn't even visible.

Darcy raised her head, squinted at the overhead light, tucked her tiny face back under her paw, and resumed sleeping.

"Lucky dog," I mumbled, moving back toward the kitchen.

I put a lid on Aaron's coffee and punched the button to brew a cup for myself. The coffeemaker burbled, and I spooned half a can of Pro-Plan into Darcy's footed silver dish for when she got up.

I added a shot of sugar free white chocolate syrup and a little milk to my cup, then grabbed my bag and the coffee and headed for the car.

Flipping the scanner on, I listened for something about the fire, but it was eerily quiet. A hotel blaze should warrant a fair amount of beat cop and dispatch chatter, which meant someone had told them to shut up. Why? I checked my cell phone for a text with the address and my jaw dropped. Not just any hotel. The poshest hotel in town. I owed Aaron more than a coffee for the wake-up call.

Slamming the gas pedal to the floor accomplished two things: it got me to the grand whitewashed building with the knot of police cars and fire engines out front faster, and heated up the car a little quicker. By the time I got off the freeway, I was downright toasty, which was good since I was likely to spend the next couple of hours freezing my ass off. It would warm up quickly after sunrise, but early spring still carries winter's chill in the pre-dawn hours.

"Your coffee, detective." I presented the cup to Aaron with a flourish and he smiled.

"Thanks." He sipped it, staring at me. "You okay?"

"Do I look that bad?" I shook my head.

"You look a little peaked, as my momma would say."

"I managed to crash my blood sugar and earn myself a trip to the ER last night," I said. "I didn't get home 'til after two, and now here I am, awake and freezing with you." I looked around, spotting a gaggle of teenage girls in dreamy gowns and smeared makeup, huddled under a ratty wool blanket near the back of a fire truck. "What's going on, anyway?"

The front of the hotel didn't show signs of damage, and the fire-fighters milling about meant the blaze was under control. I hoped I wasn't about to get really irritated with Aaron for dragging me out of bed. But he knew what was news and what wasn't.

He grinned and shook his head. "Debutante ball meets Girls Gone Wild. The St. Mary's prom was here last night. Most of the kids got rooms, that being what kids like to do after the prom."

I nodded to the frocked group. "That them?"

"They've been begging us not to call their folks since I got here," he said. "Their boyfriends went on a drugstore run, and the girls had set up dozens of candles in the suite. Trying to set the mood, I guess."

"Wait." I tried not to laugh. "A bunch of teenagers trying to create a sex scene set fire to one of the most beautiful buildings on the eastern seaboard?"

Aaron nodded. "Told you."

"This will get blasted all over Facebook and Twitter," I said, a lead already whirling through my head. "And I need a few points with the big bosses right now. I could kiss you,"

"My wife probably wouldn't care after twenty-five years, but I'll take an owed favor." Aaron laughed. "I'm sure there'll be something I won't want to tell you sometime soon. You let it go when the time comes and we'll call it even."

I nodded. "Has Charlie been here?"

"Not yet, but she doesn't go on the air until six, and I'm pretty sure she sleeps with her scanner under her pillow," Aaron said. "She'll show."

As if on cue, the Channel Four van pulled up and parked right behind my car.

I watched as Charlie stepped from the passenger seat, her petite frame clad in a gorgeous camel wool peacoat and black pants, her makeup and blond bob flawless.

"Detective White." Charlie flashed a Colgate-commercial smile at Aaron. "Nichelle. You get bored out in the sticks?" Her tone was casual, but her eyes were way too curious. Scooping each other would always come first with Charlie and me. But I could live with that.

I grinned and shook my head. "No comment. Charlie, how is it that you don't ever have circles under your eyes? Are you a pod person, or something?"

"Just handy with a makeup brush, honey," Charlie smiled, arching an eyebrow at my ponytail and blotchy skin. "Lucky for you, you don't have to worry about the camera."

I rolled my eyes. "I got to sleep later than you did, I bet."

"Now, ladies." Aaron held up both hands in a peacemaker gesture. "Anyone want particulars on this incident?"

Charlie waved her cameraman over and handed Aaron a wireless mic. While he attached the unit to his belt and clipped the tiny microphone to his collar, I rummaged in my bag for a notebook and pen.

Charlie flashed Aaron a smile and he gave the camera a more official version of what he'd told me. "A group of teenagers started a small fire on the fifth floor with candles," he said. "The hotel's fire alarms alerted security, and the first crew from the Richmond Fire Department was on the scene in less than five minutes, containing the damage to three rooms."

"Was there any structural damage?" Charlie asked.

"The structural engineers haven't been here yet, but it doesn't look that way," Aaron said.

I jotted down his answer.

"Have any of the hotel guests been evacuated?" I asked. Charlie could dub the audio to put in her own transition and use Aaron's comment, anyway.

"Six other rooms on that side of the fifth floor were evacuated because of the smoke," Aaron said. "But the hotel had empty rooms to move those guests to."

"The Washington's historic decor dates back to the city's earliest days," Charlie said. "Was anything in the lobby damaged by smoke?"

"No," Aaron said. "And the hotel's management has assured us that at this time, there are no plans to close anything other than the affected rooms."

"Are the students being charged with anything?"

"I'm not taking them to jail, if that's what you're asking," Aaron said. "Whether or not they'll face charges will be up to the fire marshal and the CA." I jotted that down, the abbreviation for Commonwealth's Attorney still a teensy bit funny-looking after half a decade of writing about the Virginia prosecutor's office.

"Thanks, Detective," Charlie said, waving the cameraman toward the fire trucks that sat in the large circular drive in front of the hotel.

Aaron handed the microphone set back and nodded. "Of course."

She followed her cameraman to the fire trucks, grabbing a firefighter to interview.

"Why do I have a feeling there's something you're not saying?" I smiled at Aaron, glancing at the girls huddled under the blanket and wondering if they'd tell me anything.

"Because you know me too well?" He grinned. "Charlie didn't ask me what the kids were drinking. Or, planning to drink. But I have a feeling it might be of particular interest to you, since you were asking me about the ABC police and moonshine last week."

"No way." I stared at the debutantes. "These kids?"

"Teenagers are the perfect market for people making back-door booze. Everywhere, it seems."

"Did they say where they got it?"

"One of them has an older sister who bought it off someone in her dorm. They claim, anyway. But I ran the labels when the fire guys first handed it to me this morning. It's not a legal brand."

"It has a label?"

He nodded, turning around and opening the trunk of the cruiser. "Here."

We didn't need gloves because the kids had confessed to possession, making fingerprinting unnecessary. I took the full jar he handed me and turned it over. Triple X White Lightning.

"Son of a bitch." I tapped my foot, studying the label. It was faded across the middle, too.

"Look familiar?" Aaron asked.

"Indeed it does." I handed the jar back. "What are the chances you can have a lab analyze this stuff in some sort of timely fashion?"

"Why? They didn't drink it, and it didn't combust."

"Because the sheriff in Mathews has closed his investigation, which I know isn't your problem. This is what those kids were drinking, though. Someone poisoned them, I'm almost positive, but I don't know how. This label is weird, like the one on the jar the dead girl had. I want to know what's in it."

"Cause of death?"

I smiled. Aaron was a good detective. "Liver failure. The boy. The girl's isn't back yet."

"And you don't think the kid OD'd because why? That sounds like the most logical answer to me."

"I'm not even sure I have the words to tell you that," I said. "My gut says no. The parents say no. The coach says no. Good friend of mine who's a master shrink says not likely."

He nodded. "But the sheriff is done?"

"The sheriff has a cousin who's making moonshine." I shook the jar.

"A-ha." He chuckled. "Oh, the joys of small-town politics. They're not that different here, if you want to know the truth. People are just connected by friends and money instead of blood."

"Right? But I can't let someone get away with killing two kids because Sheriff Zeke wants to turn the other cheek to the criminal branch of his family tree, either."

"No. That doesn't seem right. But are you sure the moonshine had something to do with it?"

I snorted. "I'm not sure of a damned thing. There's more nebulous crap around this story than the big bang, Aaron. I'm just trying to cover all the bases. There was moonshine at both scenes. I heard last night that someone gave it to the girl as a gift, and for all I know, they spiked it with arsenic. I'm pretty sure TJ's invite to the party he died at was wrapped around a mason jar, too. TJ died of liver failure. I know too much rotgut could cause that eventually, but he was so young."

I stopped.

Except TJ's liver was already compromised.

"What if he didn't know he was drinking it?" I asked, talking more to myself than to Aaron. "Could you mix this shit with anything that would mask the God-awful taste?"

"I'm sure if you put enough syrup or sweet stuff with it. But would he have had enough of it to do anything if someone mixed it?"

"I remember once when I was in school, the guys mixed up a batch of Hawaiian Punch and Everclear in garbage can. One of the cheerleaders got so sick she had to have her stomach pumped because they kept telling her there was no alcohol in it and she drank a ton of it. You couldn't really taste it."

"I guess if there was enough sugar, you could pull that off. Maybe. I'm not a doctor, but I bet you know one you can run that by."

"The Vicodin." I nodded, thinking out loud some more. "Taking it with alcohol—this kind of alcohol—with a damaged liver. Could that do it?" I'd been trying for a week to figure out how someone could have given TJ an overdose of painkillers, but what if they didn't? What if he just took one, and thought he was drinking fruit punch?

It made at least as much sense than any of my other theories, anyhow.

"Good luck," Aaron said. "Can't wait to read all about it. Just don't go jumping ship for the big city if you scoop the *Post*'s guy out there."

"They've been quiet for a few days. But I'm sure if I can figure it out, they can, too. I have to be faster and make sure I'm right." I turned toward the fire truck. "Thanks, Aaron."

I took down the particulars of the hotel damage from the fire captain on the scene and managed to get a useable quote from the least-smeary-eyed of the girls just before a line of European cars arrived to collect them.

"We just wanted it to be a night to remember," she said. "That was the theme."

"Where did you get the booze?" I asked, trying not to sound urgent and looking around for Charlie.

"Candy's sister got it for us. From a friend in her dorm."

"Where does she go to school?"

"RAU."

I jotted that down. The last thing Richmond American University needed was more scandal. Three dead coeds in two years was quite enough. I contemplated calling the chancellor.

The girls were plucked up and ushered into cars, their parents cutting Charlie and me dirty looks. But she hadn't interviewed any of them on camera, and I wasn't using their names, so they'd get over it.

Back in the car, I cranked up my heater and headed for the office. It wasn't even six yet. I could get done, grab a nap, and still meet Jenna for coffee on time.

* * *

Young love gone awry led to thousands of dollars in damage when three rooms on the fifth floor of the historic Washington Hotel went up in flames in the wee hours of Saturday morning.

"We don't have an exact estimate on the damage yet, but there are a lot of antiques in this hotel," Richmond Fire Captain Keith Richeleaux said at the scene. "One of the rooms was mostly gutted, and two others sustained heavy damage."

Richmond Police Department Spokesman Aaron White said smoke damage forced the evacuation of four other rooms on the same floor.

"The structural engineers haven't been here yet, but it doesn't look [like there was structural damage]," White said.

I ended with the comment I'd gotten from the girl about wanting the night to be memorable. Once I'd read back through the story, I emailed it to Les, who had spent the day before acting shocked every time anyone commented on his full head of hair. I couldn't even make fun of him, I was so glad to have Shelby back at the copy desk and out from underfoot.

No one else was crazy enough to be in the newsroom at seven on a Saturday morning, though, so I got up and went to get more coffee from the breakroom. Walking back with a full cup, I nearly jumped out of my skin when Spencer Jacobs stepped off the elevator.

"Shit!" I gasped as the lava-hot liquid sloshed out onto my hand, switching the cup to my left and shaking the burned one.

"I'd say I was sorry, but I'd be lying," Spence said. "Karma's a bitch, ain't it?"

I rolled my eyes. "I think the most disappointing thing about this entire week, next to the tragedy of these children losing their lives, has been finding out that you are such a selfish prick. Have you stopped for three seconds to think beyond yourself and your ridiculous outrage about not being assigned this story? Which, by the way, you probably wouldn't write, anyway, because you don't write that much copy. So you've spent this whole time giving me shit because you didn't get to assign this story to one of your reporters? Really?"

I walked to the reception desk and set my coffee cup on the edge of it, grabbing a tissue from the box on the counter and wiping my hand.

"It should have been a sports story," he said. "You don't know that I wouldn't have written it. It's the kind of story that could make a career. Land me opportunities."

"You want to leave the *Telegraph*?" I blanched. "I had no idea."

"No one ever asks. Just because I'm a sports guy doesn't mean I'm not as smart as you are."

"I don't think anyone ever said that, either," I said. "I sure as hell couldn't keep up with all the numbers you guys have to."

"Why did you take this story?" His face looked pained. "It's the kind of break I've waited for for years. You have the spotlight around here all the time. Cops and courts are the meat and potatoes of news."

"Sports keeps the paper in business." I said. "I never knew you weren't happy writing sports. You seem to love it."

"I do love it. I want to do it for the AP. But I'm never going to get there with my ho-hum resume. Something like this Okerson thing could get me noticed."

I stared at him, my own goals of working for the *Washington Post* dancing around my head and melting at least part of my annoyance. "Why didn't you just come talk to me?" I asked. "If you hadn't been such a jerk, we could have found a way to work together on it."

"Because I'm capable of doing it myself," he snapped. "Why should I have to share a story that clearly falls under my beat with you? Wait. I know, because you're the editor's pet."

I bristled at that.

"If I'm the editor's anything, it's because I'm good at what I do. And the fact of the matter is that you have little or no experience dealing with cops, and this has become a sticky mess of a story. I appreciate that you have goals beyond this." I waved a hand around the newsroom. "But no one's goals are more important than the truth. Particularly when we're talking about a murder case the local cops are ignoring."

"Awfully convenient that the *Post* is the only other news outlet that knew about that." He smirked.

"You told them, didn't you?"

"I did not. I assume you did. As feet in the door go, a lead like that is great currency."

"I would never. This story is too important to me. For a number of reasons that have absolutely nothing to do with the *Post*."

"But scooping their reporter doesn't hurt anything. Which is why you're hanging onto the story."

"I'm hanging onto the story because I think I can help these people," I said, utter conviction in my voice. "I'm disappointed that the *Post* is poking around in it because I think it might be harder for me to do that with another reporter mucking things up." Every word true. I'd thought a lot about it, and the Okersons were more important than an "attagirl" from the *Post*. Which wouldn't turn into anything, anyway. Unless someone retired, no newspaper was hiring. "Thankfully, the TV folks seem to have dismissed it and gone on their way. Even Charlie hasn't been out there in a few days."

He shook his head. "No one is that noble. If you're right and this turns out to have been a murder, or two, even, you'll be the big superstar again. Keep it up, and the offer you want from the *Post* will come along sooner, rather than later."

"That's not what it's about," I said. "You ought to take a good look at what you want and why you want it, and turn that greedy self-involved speech right back around on yourself."

I picked up my coffee and turned back toward my little ivory cube as the elevator doors whispered open to reveal Shelby and Les, whose hair didn't look nearly as much like George Clooney's as he thought it did. He'd won the hair club equivalent of the booby prize on *Price Is Right*.

I scurried off before either of them could say a word, leaving Spence to bitch to them. They could have the "We Hate Nichelle Club" meeting out of my earshot, thank you very much.

They must've had quite a powwow, because it took Les an hour to kick back revisions on my fifteen-inch fire story. He wanted the room numbers that were affected and the number of kids involved. Picky Nitpickerson, but it was still better than answering to Shelby. She'd been a real pain in my ass for most of the week.

I dialed Aaron's cell and got the information I needed, wishing him a happy Saturday. I added two lines to my story and sent it back, clicking my computer off and closing it. I needed some better coffee and good sounding board. Between Thompson's and Jenna, I had them covered.

CHAPTER TWENTY-ONE

JENNA'S EYES popped wider by degrees as I talked for half an hour. When I finally sat back in the chair with my white mocha, she shook her head, bouncing her reddish-brown curls, and winced.

"The mom, huh?" she asked.

"I'm just wondering about the psyche here. I'm going to call my friend Emily in Dallas as soon as it's late enough there for me to call on Saturday without pissing her off. She's brilliant, but she doesn't have any kids, either. You do. Could you see killing for them?"

"If someone was trying to hurt them? Absolutely. For a better spot on the baseball roster? You have to be a special kind of bat-shit to rationalize that."

I nodded. "That's what I thought, too. But she's the president of the PTA. She has access to the kids and the school, right? Someone gave Syd that jar of moonshine, and I think TJ's party invite came wrapped around one. What if they were gifts from Luke's mom? She comes from a family that makes the stuff, too." It occurred to me that the funky label on Sydney's jar might've been a brilliant way to throw suspicion, since Lily's family didn't make Triple-X. Then again, it might just mean I was wrong.

"Well, there are people who are just crazy," Jenna said. "But just to argue the other side for a second: Does Luke have any brothers or sisters?"

"I don't know. Why?"

"Only children get doted on more," she said. "I don't have time to be invested enough in my kids' stuff to kill people. Not that I'm saying all people with one kid are loons. But it might explain some of the extreme stuff she said to you. I mean, if she didn't do it. She's so into his standing on the team because he's her only kid and that makes him her whole world. I get that. Doesn't mean she's crazy enough to murder someone."

"Hmmm. And my go-to mom of one source is unavailable for this story."

"You haven't told your mom about it yet, huh?" Jenna's tone turned gentle and she laid one hand over mine.

"I don't want to, if I can help it. Like, I don't even want to go 'look, mom, I saved the day!' if I can manage to figure this out."

"Surely she's seen the reports on TV. It's been all over everything for a week. Until the day before yesterday, anyway. Now they're talking about the middle east and celebrity baby names again."

"She's been so busy I wouldn't count on it, and even if she saw something in passing, that's different than her knowing what's really going on here."

"Then there's the part where she'll worry about you playing Nancy Drew again."

"Well. There's that." I chewed a bite of my muffin.

"That looks amazing," Jenna said.

"I'd offer you a bite, but I spent half the night in the ER getting my ass chewed for not eating."

"What?"

"Apparently one of the joys of getting old. My blood sugar crashed. Busy day, no food, dancing with Kyle, blah, blah, hospital."

"First, I take offense at that. If you're old, I'm decrepit, and I don't feel decrepit. Second, take better care of yourself. Third, what's the blah blah in the middle of the evening with Kyle?"

I tried to smother a grin, but it didn't work.

"Did you?" Jenna's eyes did the white-all-around thing again. "That guy is smoking hot. And there's something about a cop, too. I think it's the big strong protective thing. Maybe I'm not as liberal as I think."

"I thought you said I shouldn't rush back into anything with him?"

"That was before I met him." She sipped her coffee. "Because...damn."

I giggled. "You should have seen him last night. Full on cowboy gear right up to the hat. I thought I was going to fall down when I opened the door."

"So?"

I sighed. "We probably would have, if I hadn't passed out. He is a much better kisser than he was ten years ago."

"Aw, Nicey!" She shoved the muffin at me. "Eat something."

"It's so complicated." I bit into the muffin. "He is hot. And he's so sweet, and he's trying to help me with this case. But then there's Joey. When I'm with him, I think I could find a way to make it work. He's really a great guy."

"Except for the whole criminal overlord thing." Jenna rolled her eyes. "Haven't you ever seen that movie? You can't marry into the mob. It even ended badly for Michelle Pfeiffer."

"He's not asking me to marry him. But he did say he wanted me the other night."

"Holy crap."

"Yeah."

"Did you sleep with him?"

"Close only counts in horseshoes and hand grenades, right? That's what Papa Jim always says." The older couple who lived across the street from my mom had adopted me into their brood of grandchildren when I was little, and he was full of fun one-liners. Like Eunice.

"Close?"

"He was carrying me to bed when TJ's mom showed up and rang the doorbell."

Jenna covered her face with both hands. "What a mess. Poor guy. Poor you! Even if I'm not all that sweet on him, you seem to be."

"It'll work out." I finished the muffin and set the plate aside, picking up my latte. "So, we do or don't think Luke's mother is the killer?"

She puckered her lips. "I think maybe. But from what you told me, she could just be a serious helicopter mom, too. Just because she doesn't care that the other kid had to die to make a spot for hers, doesn't mean she killed him, you know?"

"I wonder if that kind of attitude and pressure could have pushed Luke over the edge and made him do it?" I mused.

"That is one I'm not sure I want to touch. How a kid could do something like that. It's why I like hearing about your job, but I don't think I could ever do it."

I nodded.

"Did you figure out how they died yet?" she asked.

"Cause of death is supposed to be back on Sydney Monday or Tuesday, according to the sheriff. I have new theory about TJ, though."

I filled her in on what I'd come up with that morning.

"Sounds logical. But damn. Diabolical. Using the kid's weak liver to kill him? Then pinning it on him as a suicide? What the hell is the matter with people?"

"I wish I could figure that out."

We talked for two more lattes, then hugged goodbye.

"Thanks for your insight," I said.

"Happy to help." She checked her watch. "But I really have to go. Gabby has a soccer game and Chad gets pissy when I'm late. He has to coach, and keeping up with the baby makes that a little difficult."

"Kiss her for me and tell her to go get 'em," I said, grabbing my little leather evening pouch, which I still hadn't had time to empty.

"You get some rest. And some food. No gym today," Jenna admonished in her best mom voice.

"Yes, ma'am."

I shuffled into my house ten minutes later, scratching Darcy behind the ears when she pawed at my ankle and seriously considering going back to bed. Just as I turned for the hallway, my cell phone buzzed. I reached into the pouch to grab it, but my fingers bounced off pens and change and my MasterCard without finding the phone. I dumped the bag out on the counter and retrieved it, punching the talk button when I recognized the Mathews area code on the screen.

"Nichelle Clarke."

"Nichelle, it's Lyle at the *Mathews Leader*," the deep voice on the other end of the line said. "Listen, I thought you ought to know, we've got another dead kid out here this morning. I figured Zeke wouldn't call you, and I know how pissed I'd be if that happened to me."

My breath stopped, Evelyn's crimson eyes flashing through my thoughts. "Shit. Who is it?"

"Luke Bosley."

"Good God." I snatched up my keys. "Thanks, Lyle. I owe you one."

"Maybe it'll be good karma, or something. Zeke's still at the Bosley house, but he'll be at the high school to take questions from the local press in the auditorium when they wrap up there." Lyle hung up.

I reached to sweep the scattered mess on the table back into my bag when something caught my eye. I picked up the tickets from the dance the night before. The center of the type was faded on the right end of one. And the left end of the other. Not straight across the middle, like the moonshine labels, but similar. I stared at the two tickets for a long moment, my brain shuffling through the images of the labels. I ran a finger along the edge of one ticket. They were card-stock, with perforated edges all around.

Laying them back on the table, I switched them, lining them up end-to-end with the faded type touching. I spread my thumb and finger over the span of the mistake and then held them up, picturing the jars. It was about the same.

The tickets had been printed on the same printer as the labels. As part of sheet that fed through, and then was torn apart. Who would've printed both things? Luke's mother was the PTA president, but the dance wasn't a school-sponsored event. Still, she might volunteer for other things.

I shook my head, stuffing the tickets back into my bag. Luke was dead. No way his mother was responsible.

"What the ever-loving hell is going on here, Darce?" I grumbled, shoving a cup under the coffee maker and adding white mocha syrup and milk before I twisted the top on, snatched a pack of Pop Tarts out of the pantry, and stomped to the car.

There was something there. But, I was too freaking exhausted to see it, very possibly.

I hopped on the freeway, trying Kyle's cell. Maybe he could talk me through it. Straight to voicemail. I checked the clock and saw that it was after noon. Sleeping in? I left a message telling him I was on my way to Mathews and asking him to call me as soon as he could.

I tried Joey. No answer. I left him an almost identical message, then dropped the phone into the cup holder as I pulled onto I-64, thinking about the tickets and wondering how I could match the fault with a printer. There must be a few hundred in the county. When I got tired of pondering that, I called Emily.

"What's up, girl?" She asked in place of "hello." "I never hear from you more than once every few months, and here you are twice in a few days."

"I just miss you. Homesick, and all," I said.

"You don't, either. You're working on something you want my help with. You find out more about that dead kid?"

"There are now three dead kids," I said. "And I'm pretty sure this is not the suicide epidemic the sheriff wants to make it out to be."

"Cops see things in very black and white terms," she said. "That makes it hard for them to get past an idea once they've settled on an explanation."

"I really wish this dude would get past this. I think it's going to take a warrant to figure it out." I explained the similarity between the tickets and the moonshine labels.

"Huh." She was quiet for a minute. "So, whoever printed the tickets for the street dance printed the labels on the moonshine jars. But only the ones the kids had."

"Even the kids in Richmond, though, which is the weirder part. That brand is sold out of the back of the auto body shop on the edge of Mathews. The ABC has an undercover guy out there working on a county-wide sting. So how did it end up being sold out of a dorm in Richmond?"

"Did someone fake the labels?"

"And put them on a bad batch of off-brand illegal moonshine?" I asked. "I didn't think about it that way. Maybe."

"Or they're printing labels on two printers and it's a coincidence," she said.

"I don't trust coincidences," I said. "I've covered crime for long enough to know that real ones are few and far between."

"Good luck," she said. "For what it's worth, I'm on your side. I've been reading the coverage of this all week, and it doesn't line up. But the sheriff probably won't listen to me, either. You have any suspects?"

"Only a half a dozen or so," I said. "I actually had you on my call list this morning to ask if you thought one of the other pitcher's mothers was capable of doing this. But then her son turned up dead this morning, so there goes that one. No way that woman killed her own kid."

"How about the other kids at the school?"

"Well, the dead boy was my chief suspect. But there are a couple of others. A girl who had a crush on TJ, and a boy who used to date Sydney have moved to the top of the list."

"Romantic entanglements can be good motivators for teenage murderers," she said. "Either of those kids have a history of violence?"

"Not that I've heard about, and everyone knows everything in this town. I can't figure how the kid who's dead today fits with the other two as far as motive goes, though."

"It's not impossible for a first violent act to be a murder at that age. They don't yet fully comprehend the permanence of death a lot of the time. And you watch yourself. If you get too close to what's going on, you might find yourself on the wrong end of an arsenic toddy, too."

I thanked her for her help, wondering how I might be able to get a little more face time with Eli.

CHAPTER TWENTY-TWO

I PULLED into the parking lot at the high school early, judging by the fact that there were only two other cars present, and neither of them belonged to the sheriff. No TV trucks, either. I smiled, thinking there was no way in hell Lyle had called Charlie. More brownie points for me, and not a one to spare with Spence hanging out with Les and Shelby for the day. Somehow the three of them conspiring to get me in trouble with Andrews seemed so much worse than Les and Shelby alone, even if I couldn't explain why.

I walked up the steps and found the front door unlocked. The sheriff must've had someone come open the school for the press conference.

Stepping into the foyer, my heels clicked on the tile floor eerily loud in the silence. I shook off the slasher-movie memories, the spring sunshine pouring through the doors helping.

I went to the auditorium, but it was locked, so I rounded the corner and peeked into the office. Norma sat in front of her computer, studying something on the screen through a pair of reading glasses perched on the end of her nose.

She looked up when I opened the door.

"Hey there! What brings you by here on a Saturday? I think I'm the only person in the building."

"Lyle called me," I said, furrowing my brow. "There's a press conference here today, right?"

"Oh, yes," she said. "Not for a while yet, though. They're still cleaning up at the Bosley place. I just don't know what's gotten into these children."

I shook my head. "You and me both."

"So sad. You're welcome to have a seat. I just have some data entry to catch up on. Everything's been so topsy-turvy here I haven't had time to do my job lately."

"Thanks." I sat down and pulled out my cell phone. I had a text from Kyle.

"Sorry I missed you. On with the lab. Your dead football player didn't take any Vicodin."

That's it? I stared at my screen.

"You're killing me! What happened?" I typed.

"Liver failure caused by massive Glucotrol overdose. There was a shit ton of it in his bloodstream."

Glucotrol. Luke was diabetic.

But Luke was also dead. And I didn't know how yet. What if someone had figured this out and killed him? But wait. Coach Morris said the lockers downstairs had shiny new locks because some of Luke's medicine was stolen. To poison TJ and make Luke look like the killer? Or did Luke say it was stolen because he lacked a better explanation for missing pills? Crap. More questions.

"You're sure?" I tapped back, my brain forging ahead a thousand miles a minute. If Kyle had the results, the sheriff would have them soon. Which meant so would everyone on their way in for the press conference, if he happened to run by his office first. And I still didn't know what the *Post* had or where their guy was getting his information.

Kyle's answer flashed on my screen. "They ran it twice. Elevated BAC and Glucotrol."

Ho. Ly. Crap. Somebody spiked the moonshine. With drugs, but not Vicodin. And if I hadn't asked Kyle to beg for a full screen, nobody would have known it, either. I tried to recall that conversation with Coach Morris word for word. Did he say what kind of medicine Luke took? Or anything else?

That Luke's diabetes was genetic. Did that mean his mother had it, too? But if it was her, why was her kid dead? I dismissed her from my list, focusing on who could have taken Luke's pills.

"Thank you! I'm in Mathews," I typed to Kyle. "Call you soon."

I took a deep breath and fixed a neutral expression on my face, looking up at Norma.

"I can't get over this thing with Luke Bosley. I was just talking to his momma last night."

She nodded, a sad look in her blue eyes. "Such a nice boy. He had problems, but you couldn't tell it. He was diabetic, you know."

"I heard that. Were there any other students here who had the same condition?"

Norma shook her head. "It's a small school."

I looked past her at the nurse's office, desperate to know what kind of medication Luke took. "Did Luke have to keep medicine here at school?"

"Sure he did. There's a bottle locked in the nurse's cabinet and probably some in his locker, too. Poor boy. He had to take pills, but then carry sugar in his pockets on the baseball field so if he got too low, he could get to it quickly."

Hot damn.

So the pills that had probably killed TJ were floating all over the school? But they belonged to Luke. I thought about Evelyn and Eli. It was a clever way to throw suspicion if the sheriff didn't go with the suicide story. But why hurt Luke? If the killer was setting him up, why kill him? To keep him from talking, maybe. What if Luke figured out they were taking his pills and confronted the killer? Or, what if he ran out of pills to take because they stole them?

I tapped "Glucotrol overdose" into my Google app and scanned the symptoms, trying not to picture TJ going through all the phases leading to death. Fatigue, dizziness, unsteadiness, clammy skin, fainting—I paused, reading them again.

All the things that had happened to me the night before.

Because my blood sugar had crashed.

I raced back through the events of the evening. I hadn't eaten or drunk anything that tasted off.

But I took a pill. Without really looking at it, I swallowed my last antibiotic.

About five hours before I passed out.

I scrolled down and checked the effective time.

"Someone poisoned me," I murmured.

"What was that, honey?" Norma asked.

"I—nothing, I'm sorry." I smiled. "Thinking out loud."

Who had I seen at the dance? Luke. His mother. Evelyn. Coach Morris. Most of the rest of the town. Even Dorothy had been there with her friends from the ladies' Bible group.

"I'm going to run to the little girls' room," Norma said, standing. "I'll be right back."

"Yes, ma'am."

She disappeared and I pulled a notebook from my bag, rummaging for a pen and coming up empty handed. Shit. I must have left it at home.

I got up and walked to Norma's desk to borrow one. Plucking a purple one from her Mathews Bait and Tackle coffee cup, I started to turn when my eyes fell on the corner of a paper sticking out of a manila folder.

No way.

I flipped the folder open.

The ticket paper.

She printed the tickets for the dance. Of course. She'd been sitting there selling them. I glanced at the nurse's dark doorway. She also worked in the school and had easy access to Luke's pills. And she'd told me her oldest daughter was a student at RAU. Puzzle pieces rained into horrifying order.

I glanced at the door, skirting the desk and wiggling the mouse. I sent the spreadsheet on the screen to the printer and held my breath.

It was slightly faded, right through the center of the page.

My heart pounding in my ears, I jumped to my feet and looked around for another exit, but didn't see one. I had a million questions about how and why, but right then the only thing I gave a damn about was getting out of that building.

I started for the door, but she came back in before I could go out.

"You need something, honey?" she asked, raising her eyebrows.

"Pen." I waved the purple one and smiled. "I borrowed one from you because I left mine at home."

"Help yourself," she said, resuming her seat. I watched her sit down and start typing again, at once terrified and fascinated. How could you murder a child--or maybe three--in a week's time, and just sit there and do spreadsheets?

I backed slowly toward the door, thinking if I could just get through it, I could run. I never took my eyes off Norma.

She stopped typing, her fingers hovering above the keys, but kept her eyes on the screen. Then she sighed.

"How long have you known?" she asked.

"Known what?" My voice broke between the words.

She turned slowly in her chair, a sweet smile on her face.

"Known it was me, honey." She opened a drawer and pulled out a black-handled revolver.

I dashed out the door before she squeezed the trigger, the explosion behind me making me run harder for the front door. The heel of one lavender Manolo sandal skidded on the tile as I rounded the corner into the main hallway. I caught my balance, sprinting over the inlay of the eagle just inside the foyer.

I fell against the front doors, but they didn't move. I jiggled the crash bar.

Locked.

"You don't think I'm that stupid, do you?" Norma called from the other end of the hallway.

I heard the gun cock. Figuring that was a rhetorical question, I dove for the nearest hallway, the shot zinging off the metal of the doors behind me.

My legs burned as I fled, not the first damned clue where I was going. Dark classrooms lined both sides of the hall, and it split into a T at the end, with lockers and more classrooms going one way, and a single door the other. Glancing behind me, I took door number two, saying a fast prayer and promising to give up chocolate for a year if the door opened. It did. I shut it softly behind me, looking for a lock, but not seeing one. A bank of high windows let in just enough sunlight to show me I was in the band hall.

I scanned the room for a hiding place, settling on a row of cubbyholes in the far corner that housed large drum sets and tubas. I pulled the tuba on the far end free, climbed in, and pulled the instrument in behind me.

Curled into a ball with my knees up my nose, I listened for Norma and hoped my breathing wasn't actually as loud as it sounded to me. How the bloody hell was I going to get out of this?

My phone! I wriggled an arm down my side into my pocket and got it free. It had full bars, but everyone I knew was two hours away.

Shit.

Wait. I'd called Tony on his cell phone to ask for a comment after the sheriff's press conference. When was that? Wednesday. I scrolled back through my recent calls until I found the one to a Mathews area code on Wednesday afternoon. "Thank you," I whispered. I punched talk as the door to the band hall opened. I dropped the phone into the curve of my lap, resting my forehead on my knees and trying to imitate a statue.

"Olly olly oxenfree." Norma's voice had taken on a manic edge. "Everyone out of hiding, now."

It sounded like she was walking through the room flipping over chairs and music stands. "I know you're in here, Nichelle," she called. "You can't hide forever. I managed to get TJ Okerson out of the way, for God's sake. I didn't spend a year planning all this so you could wreck it. Now just put on your big girl panties and come on out and face your fate."

A drum set crashed to the floor a few feet away and I flinched. Turning as far to the side as I could, I watched Norma's feet. When she got directly in front of my hiding place, I shoved the tuba with my right hand and foot, catching her off guard and knocking her over. She screamed—more indignation than pain, from the sound—and I heard the gun clatter against the cabinet across from us and fire. My cell phone bounced to the coffee-brown carpet as I scrambled to my feet.

Norma lay sprawled across the floor, but still had her grip on the gun. She swung it upward, and I dodged behind the end of the cabinet, snatching a trumpet off a shelf. She grunted, getting to her feet, and I called my biggest question.

"Why?"

"Why? You didn't get that with all the questions you asked me the other day?"

I replayed that conversation on fast forward.

"Eli."

"My Eli. He's such a good boy. So talented. He and Luke Bosley would have led the baseball team. But TJ came here and took everything he worked so hard for. Including his girlfriend. He's been so sad. Poor Terry couldn't figure out how to pull Eli out of his funk. A worried daddy is no good for romance."

"You killed TJ because you wanted to score with your ex-brother-in-law?" I couldn't stop the scorn pouring through my lips. "Jesus, lady. Have you talked to Jerry Springer's producers? You could have your own week."

"Keep talking. It just helps me aim better," she said. The gun hammer clicked back again and I tried to mentally count shots. One in the office. One in the hall, maybe two. And one into the cabinet. That left two or three bullets if she'd started with a fully-loaded gun.

She only needed one. She was six feet away.

I peeked out and she leveled the revolver and smiled. I reacted without thinking, hurling the trumpet at her head as hard as I could. It made a satisfying clang when it hit and she staggered backward and screamed, blood trickling over her left eye. Two points for the crime reporter.

The gun went flying, clattering into the dark reaches of the room behind her. She pressed a hand to her forehead and glared at me, turning for the gun. I stepped out and swung one foot up and around in a hooked side kick that caught her arm. She lurched away and squealed, a welp of blood appearing on her skin from my heel.

"Why Sydney?"

"She dumped my Eli for that boy," Norma spat. "She and that mother of hers. Always thinking they're too good for everyone else."

"I thought you said you were friends?"

"I said we were friends once. She married money. She's too good for me, now." The bitterness in her voice would've soured Eunice's creme brulee.

"And Luke was in Eli's way, too?" I guessed. "He was the easiest for you to get to with the Glucotrol, right?"

Norma shook her head. "I've known Luke since he was born. I would never hurt him. Annalynn over at the sheriff's office told her momma this morning that Luke shot himself in the head with one of his daddy's hunting rifles. God rest him. They put so much pressure on him. Word is, he left a note saying TJ and Sydney didn't have any worries anymore, and that sounded nice. Poor boy."

I didn't have time to fully process that before she stepped forward. I raised my hands, widening my feet into a punching stance. She paused by the desk, her fingers closing on the handle of a pair of scissors lying on the blotter. Damn.

"You can't make this look like a suicide," I said.

"Probably not, but I can make it look like someone else was responsible. Assuming anyone finds you. My cousin Sherman was none too happy about you asking questions about his moonshine, you know." She smiled. Just before she lunged. I dodged to one side, but she swung fast and winged my upper arm, hacking a jagged gash in my skin with the scissors. I yelped and grabbed for the wound.

"People will be here any minute," I panted, kicking a chair into her knees and smiling when she tripped over it.

"Why? It's Saturday." She jumped back to her feet.

"The press conference." I backed up another step.

"Is at the sheriff's office. I called Lyle and told him it was here. Right before I mentioned how sweet you were, and what a nice guy he is. I knew he'd call and tell you. If the Glucotrol I slipped into your purse last night worked, he wouldn't get you. If it didn't, you'd come running. I was right. I texted him that I was mistaken, and I'd sent you on your way. With Sherman to escort you." She grinned a too-wide-eyed grin that belonged in a horror movie. "You've been far too nosy. All the other reporters left town when Zeke closed the Okerson file. Not you. So many questions. I figure it's about time to make sure you never get this story to print."

She lunged forward again, swinging the scissors wildly, and I stepped back, stumbling over one of the music stands she'd knocked over. Hitting the floor, I shrank away from the crazed glassiness in her eyes as she hunched down in preparation to tackle me.

Every movement seemed to be through Jell-O, my eyes registered the action so slowly.

I bent one knee and whipped my lavender Manolo off, flipping it around so the heel pointed toward her and locking my elbows.

She couldn't stop herself.

I squinched my eyes shut.

She screamed, and something warm and wet trickled over my hand for an instant before she fell to the floor beside me, howling. I peeked through my lashes to find my stiletto buried up to the sole in the flesh between her chest and right shoulder. Ouch.

I scrambled to my feet, snatching the other shoe up as a weapon and kicking the scissors away from her hand. She stared at her wound, shock plain on her face.

"You stabbed me with a shoe."

"Technically, you impaled yourself on it trying to kill me."

Her eyes widened. "You bitch!" she screeched, pushing herself up with her left elbow. "I'll kill you!"

I backed toward my hiding cubby, spotting my phone on the floor and scooping it up just as I heard footfalls in the hallway.

"Nichelle!" Tony.

I cleared my throat, which didn't want to work. "In the band hall."

Turning my eyes back to Norma, who was frozen with terror, I smiled. "Fitting, I think. You go ahead and tell Mr. Okerson why his son deserved to die for being a good athlete. I'll wait."

Her face twisted into a mask of fury that didn't resemble anything human, and she grabbed a music stand and slung it in my direction just as the door opened, framing Tony and Coach Morris. I jumped backward, the stand thwacking into my ankle and sending a wave of pain up to my hip that I ignored.

"Are you all right?" Tony crossed the room in a half-dozen long strides, worry creasing his forehead as his eyes locked on my arm. I looked down to see that my sweater sleeve was a bloody mess, the gash deeper than I thought.

"Maybe I should sit," I said, slumping into a chair. "Somebody ought to tie Nutty McCrazy there up before she finds another weapon."

Tony stood over Norma, rage, sorrow, and pity warring over the planes of his famous face as she howled incoherently. He pulled one foot back, held it for a ten count, and then returned it to the floor.

"I've never hit a woman in my life."

"Start," the harsh word came from Morris, who was backing away from his new girlfriend with disgust plain in his eyes and tone.

Her eyes flew to him, her scream cutting off. "No. Terry, this was all for you. You and Eli. So we'd be together. Haven't I been good to you? Taken care of you? Helped you feel better? And Eli is so much happier."

"You," Morris floundered, his inability to process that flashing across his brow like a neon sign. "You murdered my favorite student so you could console your way into my bed? That's...There's not a word for what you are." He looked at Tony. "I. I can't. I'm so sorry, Mr. Okerson."

Tony nodded, a tear falling from the corner of one eye.

Morris shrugged helplessly, then turned on his heel and fled. "I'll get the sheriff," he called over his shoulder. "I can't sit here and look at her."

Norma burst into tears.

"There's a gun over there somewhere." I waved.

Tony collected it and sat down next to me, holding the gun on Norma with a clear give-me-a-reason set to his jaw. He winced at my arm. "You all right?"

"I've lost more blood. And I even had a tetanus shot last summer. So I'll live." I held pressure on the gash. "Plus, I've got one hell of a story to send in when I get patched up. Unless the *Post* has bugged the school, it's an exclusive, too."

He flashed a half-smile. "I think you earned it. Thank you."

"Happy to help."

CHAPTER TWENTY-THREE

ZEKE BROUGHT THE CAVALRY, offering me a grudging apology and refusing to look Tony in the eye as a team of paramedics extracted my sandal from Norma's shoulder.

The tall, silver haired medic bent over Norma grinned. "I thought I'd seen it all, but this is a new one on me." He offered my shoe to the sheriff. "You need this for evidence?"

"I don't believe I'll be prosecuting anyone over this," Zeke said.

The medic turned to me. "You want it back?"

I stared mournfully, trying not to look too closely at the globs of...I didn't want to know...that clung to the heel. "I love them, but I think they're done," I said. "Looks like I'll just have to shop for another pair."

Tony chuckled. "There's a way to look on the bright side."

A petite blonde medic examined my arm, asking me if I'd had a recent tetanus shot.

"I have," I said.

"You'll just need some stitches to close this up, then," she said. "We'll take you to the hospital in Gloucester."

"Oh, yay. Needles."

Tony grimaced. "I'm sorry you got hurt."

"I'm sorrier TJ did," I said.

He nodded. "I called Grant. He's on his way out here. I'll tell him to come to the hospital?"

"You didn't have to do that," I said. "I'm a big girl."

Parker was a good friend, but I wanted more than a friend right then. I couldn't commit to Kyle because I had feelings for Joey. I couldn't commit to Joey because he was a crime boss (well, that, and the fireworks that were Kyle's kisses). Emily would have a field day. I reached for my phone and texted them both. "So, I nabbed the killer. It's going to be a great story. Just a few stitches, and I'll call you later. Thanks for your help."

My cell phone pinged back with "What? How many stitches?" from Joey and "Where are you?" from Kyle, one on top of the other.

"Don't know yet. She got me with scissors," I tapped back to Joey.

"I'm in good hands. Call you soon," I told Kyle.

"Ready?" Tony asked, putting a hand under my elbow. "I told the medics I'd drive you. Didn't figure you wanted to share the ambulance with Norma."

"Thanks," I said. "You know, you're a nice guy. Why couldn't you have played for the Cowboys?"

He laughed. "It's all about money."

"Or sex." I cast a glance at Norma, strapped onto a stretcher and headed out the door with a silent stare on her face. "Almost always one of the two."

* * *

I sent Bob a short report for the web on Norma's arrest from the waiting room at the ER, where the triage nurse was less than impressed with my wound. Tony sat with me for half an hour, despite my objections. Parker ran in just before they called me back, and between his million-dollar grin and Tony's superstar status, the poor nurse trying to enforce the "family only" visitor policy didn't stand a chance.

"Just put him down as my brother," I told her as she blushed and stammered about the rules.

She smiled gratefully and nodded, leading me to a treatment room. Parker followed, and Tony hugged me gently before he left.

"Thank you. If there's ever anything I can do," he said.

"Do you know Troy Aikman?" I asked, only half-joking.

"As a matter of fact, I do."

"We'll talk," I said.

He waved as he walked out into the sunshine.

"So, can you write a story without sustaining mortal injuries?" Parker asked. "Bob is never going to let me hear the end of this."

"You? How many lectures do you think I'll get?" I pulled out my phone and checked my email. "See?" I asked, flipping the screen around to show off the "Excellent work. Now stop trying to get yourself killed," in my email.

Parker chuckled. "Thanks for helping them."

"Happy to." I took a deep breath, remembering Randy helping me learn to roller skate and smiling.

The stitches didn't even hurt as much, and the needles looked less scary. I wondered if I was becoming an old pro and didn't want to think about what that meant, so I dismissed it. Parker took me back to the school to get my car.

"I'm headed to Tony's," he said. "You want to come? Mel's already there. I left her with Ashton on my way to the hospital." His tight smile made me wonder what was going on there, but I didn't have the energy to ask right then. It couldn't be too serious if she'd tagged along to the Okerson's. I hoped.

"I'd love to, but I have work to do and sleep to catch up on," I said, ignoring the fifteenth text from either Joey or Kyle that had buzzed my cell phone in the past hour. I also had men to juggle. "Give them my best. Maybe next time. Especially if Troy can come hang out."

"He's a good guy," Parker said with a wink.

"Sure, rub it in, Mr. Celebrity." I grinned and waved as I climbed into the car.

* * *

I went back through my Mathews family tree file and found that Norma's uncle owned the auto body shop, and the triple-X white lightning still. A visit from Kyle, who showed up in the newsroom and refused to leave 'til he could escort me home, netted me the rest of the story.

"The ABC police have been working a sting on the three big stills in Mathews for over a year, like the agent said last night," he said, pulling Mel's chair into my cubicle. "I called him this morning to tell him what you're writing about, and the busts will all go down this weekend. They've got two sales fronts, three businesses that are serving it, plus manufacturing and interstate commerce cases. It's a huge bust."

I scribbled notes as he talked, already planning a sidebar story on the busts. And a call to Bobbi. It might not do any good, but it would probably help if she didn't get caught with it in the club. Joey hadn't known enough about it to be traceable, so I wasn't worried about him, for once.

I thanked Kyle and opened my laptop to start typing.

Mathews County Sheriff Zeke Waters arrested Norma Earlinger, 47, Saturday in connection with what the sheriff is now calling the double murder of Tony Okerson, Junior and his girlfriend Sydney Cobb, both juniors at Mathews High School.

"Obviously, the case has been reopened in light of recent developments," Waters said as he accompanied Earlinger to the emergency room after she was injured while trying to stab a Richmond Telegraph *reporter Saturday.*

Waters said the toxicity screen report on Okerson's blood came back from the state forensics lab Saturday, showing that the star quarterback for the Mathews Eagles died of liver failure caused by an overdose of Glucotrol, an insulin-stimulating medication used for management of type 2 diabetes. Earlinger, a secretary at the school, confessed to stealing the medication from a student's gym locker.

Lucas Bosley, a baseball teammate of Okerson's, was diabetic. He was found dead in his home Saturday morning, of an apparently self-inflicted gunshot wound. Waters said the death will be thoroughly investigated.

"There's nothing about this that doesn't suck," I told Kyle, sitting back in my chair as I finished the story with a plug for the suicide helpline. "Norma went off her rocker and killed TJ and Syd—and almost got away with it—using Luke's medicine. Which no one would have known if you hadn't pressed the lab to test his blood for something besides Vicodin and booze, so thanks."

"Anytime."

"But then Luke, who has parents who push him to the breaking point and a battle with depression he hides very well, buys the sheriff's suicide story. He figures if TJ and Syd did it, maybe it's not a bad idea. The medics said his mother told them he started a new antidepressant last week and was having wild mood swings. Crazy highs, like we saw at the dance last night, and lows...like this."

"Why didn't she tell anyone?"

"Afraid he'd get kicked off the baseball team. Which I don't doubt. Sad, sad situation."

"Amen." He brushed his fingers over the gauze dressing on my arm. "I'm glad you're all right."

"Me, too. Thanks for coming in. And for everything else."

"I'm always here," he said.

"That's good to know." I leaned the chair back and kissed him, then sent my story to Les and stood. "I think I've earned a day off."

"I'll drive you home."

* * *

Monday morning dawned bright and pollen-free. After a Sunday of sleeping in and letting Joey pamper me (his foot massages are as good as his kisses. Almost.), I felt nearly good as new.

And ready to have myself a little chat with my favorite copy editor.

I didn't find Shelby in her cube, or in Les's office. My head was on the verge of exploding when I walked past Bob's door and heard her shrill voice, patting herself on the back for doing such a stellar job filling in for Les while he was out. He chimed in to agree often.

I stopped outside the door and listened.

"And Nichelle wasn't even here most of the week, plus she leaked an important piece of information to the *Post*," Shelby said. "I think Les is right. She's overworked, Bob. Look how sick she got last week. It was a bad idea to give her the courthouse back last fall when we can afford another beat reporter's salary. Put me on the courthouse. You know I'm good enough to handle it, and we'll stand a better chance of staying on top of Charlie Lewis, too."

She had some nerve, that Shelby.

"Shelby, who takes care of your flying monkeys when you're here bothering me?" I asked, stepping through the door and smiling when she and Les both dropped their jaws on the tacky brown seventies carpet.

"I'd almost agree with you, myself," I continued, "except I had a very nice chat yesterday with Greg Lidner at the *Post*. Name ring a bell?"

Shelby's eyes widened for a split second before she arranged her face into a clueless expression. "Why would it?"

"Well, it seems he called here last week, looking for a comment about my story on TJ. Someone answered my phone. On Monday, at eleven. When I was on my way to TJ's funeral with Parker. A woman with a high-pitched voice who said she was me, and told him all about how I thought the sheriff was lying, reminding him three times to tell his editor where he got the information. Subtle, Shelby."

"I have no idea what you're talking about," she huffed, folding her arms across her chest.

"Sure you do. You hung around outside when Bob asked Parker and me to stay after the meeting." I didn't bother to inflect a question mark on the end of the sentence. "I'm just surprised you waited for him to call here instead of calling him. He got my cell number from Sheriff Waters and called me at home yesterday, quite surprised that I don't sound like a cartoon character on my cell phone. Nice guy."

"I would never—" Shelby turned an imploring look to Les, but the look on his face said he didn't believe her any more than Bob did.

"There's a line, Shelby," he said quietly, turning on his heel and walking out of the office. She tore after him and I dropped into a chair and grinned.

"I never believed it," Bob said. "But Andrews will be very interested to hear this."

"I'll let you tell him," I said. "He apologizes like a politician. It creeps me out."

"So, the *Post* called you?"

"For an interview. Not the job kind. Though the guy did say his editor was impressed."

"You can't leave. You love me."

"And I love Richmond. Right now, anyway." I smiled.

The rest of the section editors filed in and Spence stopped next to my chair, eyeballing the dressing on my bicep. "That looks nasty."

"I'm sure you could handle it, just like everything else about my job, right?" I said.

"I could have written the suicide coverage," he snapped.

"I think you ought to stick to your stat sheets and leave the criminals to the crime desk."

He opened his mouth to reply, but Bob's warning glare made him snap it shut.

He could stay mad 'til I left my house in garden clogs for all I cared. I sat back in my chair and pulled out a notebook as Bob started the rundown.

The meeting sped by in alternating throes of spirited discussion and laughter. Halfway through, my scanner squawked. I turned it down, pressing it to my ear. Hostage situation in a bank building.

"Holy Manolos." I jumped to my feet, waving the scanner when Bob gave me a raised eyebrow. "I have hostages today, chief. Save me some space."

"Have fun," he called as I ran for the elevator.

I got out of the garage and my phone binged a text. "Coming, Aaron," I said, stopping to glance at it.

Kyle: "Dinner tonight? I'm dying to know why the ABC's under-cover guy says he met with a pretty brunette last week. Who looks just like you. And came and went with a Mafia big shot he met through a transport contact the moonshiners use."

Holy. Crap.

* * *

Sign up for the Reader List and be the first to know about new releases and special offers from LynDee.

Join LynDee Walker's Reader List at LynDeeWalker.com

As a thank you for signing up, you'll receive a free copy of Fatal Features: A Nichelle Clarke Crime Thriller Novella.

DEVIL IN THE DEADLINE:
Nichelle Clarke #4

**A human sacrifice unlocks a chilling mystery, and leads Nichelle
Clarke into a world of unimaginable danger**.

When Richmond Police find a young woman's bloody remains spread
across a candle-lit altar in an abandoned power plant on the banks of
the James River, they give crime reporter Nichelle Clarke an all-access
pass in exchange for her help.

But the information Nichelle gets from the victim's friends only
draws her deeper into the mystery. Where did Jasmine come from?
How did she end up on the streets of Shockoe Bottom? And why
doesn't she have any dental records?

The answer trail stops at the front doors of a sprawling compound in
the foothills of the Blue Ridge, where Nichelle finds a secretive cult
leader and his devoted following. It is a world where lies become
truth, and money is the true idol. Money some people would do
anything to keep collecting...

Even if it means murdering a nosy reporter.

Get your copy today at LynDeeWalker.com

YOU MIGHT ALSO ENJOY...

The Nichelle Clarke Series

Front Page Fatality

Buried Leads

Small Town Spin

Devil in the Deadline

Cover Shot

Lethal Lifestyles

Deadly Politics

Hidden Victims

The Faith McClellan Series

Fear No Truth

Leave No Stone

Never miss a new release! Sign up to receive exclusive updates from author LynDee Walker.

LynDeeWalker.com/Newsletter

As a thank you for signing up, you'll receive a free copy of *Fatal Features: A Nichelle Clarke Crime Thriller Novella.*